FIVE CLASSIC
HORROR STORIES

Frankenstein,
The Strange Case of Dr. Jekyll & Mr. Hyde,
The Were-Wolf, Dracula, &
The Phantom of the Opera

Fantasy and Horror Classics

Read & Co.

Copyright © 2021 Fantasy and Horror Classics

This edition is published by Fantasy and Horror Classics,
an imprint of Read & Co.

This book is copyright and may not be reproduced or copied in any
way without the express permission of the publisher in writing.

British Library Cataloguing-in-Publication Data
A catalogue record for this book is available
from the British Library.

Read & Co. is part of Read Books Ltd.
For more information visit
www.readandcobooks.co.uk

CONTENTS

**FRANKENSTEIN;
OR, THE MODERN PROMETHEUS**
By Mary Wollstonecraft Shelley
First Published in 1818

THE STRANGE CASE
OF DR. JEKYLL & MR. HYDE
By Robert Louis Stevenson
First Published in 1886

THE WERE-WOLF
By Clemence Housman
First Published in 1896

DRACULA
By Bram Stoker
First Published in 1897

THE

PHANTOM OF THE OPERA

By Gaston Leroux

First Published in 1909

FRANKENSTEIN;

OR, THE MODERN PROMETHEUS

By Mary Wollstonecraft Shelley

First Published in 1818

MARY SHELLEY

Mary Shelley (née Mary Wollstonecraft Godwin) was born in Somers Town, London, in 1797. She came from rich literary heritage; her father was the political philosopher William Godwin, and her mother was the philosopher and feminist Mary Wollstonecraft. In 1812, when she was just fifteen, Mary met the poet Percy Bysshe Shelley. Shelley was married at the time, but the two spent the summer of 1814 travelling around Europe together. In 1815, Mary gave birth prematurely to a girl, and the infant died twelve days later. In her journal of March 19, 1815, Mary recorded a nightmare she'd had, now cited as a possible inspiration for her future masterwork, *Frankenstein*: "Dream that my little baby came to life again - that it had only been cold & that we rubbed it before the fire & it lived."

In the summer of 1816, the couple famously visited the poet Lord Byron at his villa beside Lake Geneva, in Switzerland. Storms and tumultuous weather (common in Shelley's future novel) confined them to the indoors, where they and Byron's assorted other guests took to reading to each other from a book of ghost stories. One evening, Byron challenged all his guests to write one themselves. The guests obliged, and Mary's story went on to become *Frankenstein*. Mary and Percy married later that year, and eighteen months later, in 1818 *Frankenstein* was published. Mary was only 21, and the novel was a huge success. The first edition of the book included a preface from Percy, and many, disbelieving that a young woman could have penned such a horror story, thought that the novel was his.

In 1819, following the death of another child, Mary suffered a nervous breakdown. This was compounded three years later when her husband drowned. Widowed at just 25, Mary returned to England, determined to continue profiting from her writing in order to support her one surviving son. Between 1827 and 1840, she was busy as an author and editor, penning three more novels and a number of short stories. However, she never experienced further success of the sort that *Frankenstein* had brought. Her final decade was blighted by illness, and throughout the 1840s she suffered from terrible headaches and bouts of paralysis in parts of her body. In 1851, at Chester Square, she died at the age of fifty-three from what her physician suspected was a brain tumour.

Shelley underwent a period of critical neglect after her death, due in part to the onset of the realist movement. For a long time she was chiefly remembered as the wife of Percy Bysshe Shelley, and it was not until 1989 that a full-length scholarly biography was published. In recent decades, the republication of almost all her writing, including her short fiction, has stimulated a new recognition of its value, and scholars now consider Mary Shelley to be a major figure in Romanticism.

LETTER 1

To Mrs. Saville, England.

St. Petersburgh, Dec. 11th, 17—.

You will rejoice to hear that no disaster has accompanied the commencement of an enterprise which you have regarded with such evil forebodings. I arrived here yesterday, and my first task is to assure my dear sister of my welfare and increasing confidence in the success of my undertaking.

I am already far north of London, and as I walk in the streets of Petersburgh, I feel a cold northern breeze play upon my cheeks, which braces my nerves and fills me with delight. Do you understand this feeling? This breeze, which has travelled from the regions towards which I am advancing, gives me a foretaste of those icy climes. Inspirited by this wind of promise, my daydreams become more fervent and vivid. I try in vain to be persuaded that the pole is the seat of frost and desolation; it ever presents itself to my imagination as the region of beauty and delight. There, Margaret, the sun is for ever visible, its broad disk just skirting the horizon and diffusing a perpetual splendour. There—for with your leave, my sister, I will put some trust in preceding navigators—there snow and frost are banished; and, sailing over a calm sea, we may be wafted to a land surpassing in wonders and in beauty every region hitherto discovered on the habitable globe. Its productions and features may be without example, as the phenomena of the heavenly bodies undoubtedly are in those undiscovered solitudes. What may not be expected in a country of eternal light? I may there discover the wondrous power which attracts the needle and may regulate a thousand celestial observations that require only this voyage to render their seeming eccentricities consistent for ever. I shall satiate my ardent curiosity with the sight of a part of the world never before visited, and may tread a land never before imprinted by the foot of man. These are my enticements, and they are sufficient to conquer all fear of danger or death and to induce me to commence this laborious voyage with the joy a child feels when he embarks in a little boat, with his holiday mates, on an expedition of discovery up his native river. But supposing all these conjectures to be false, you cannot contest the inestimable benefit which I shall confer on all mankind, to the last generation, by discovering a passage near the pole to those countries, to reach which at present so many months are requisite; or by ascertaining the secret of the magnet, which, if at all possible, can only be effected by an undertaking such as mine.

These reflections have dispelled the agitation with which I began my letter, and I feel my heart glow with an enthusiasm which elevates me to heaven, for nothing contributes so much to tranquillise the mind as a steady purpose—a point on which the soul may fix its intellectual eye. This expedition has been the favourite dream of my early years. I have read with ardour the accounts of the various voyages which have been made in the prospect of arriving at the North Pacific Ocean through the seas which surround the pole. You may remember that a history of all the voyages made for purposes of discovery composed the whole of our good Uncle Thomas' library. My education was neglected, yet I was passionately fond of reading. These volumes were my study day and night, and my familiarity with them increased that regret which I had felt, as a child, on learning that my father's dying injunction had forbidden my uncle to allow me to embark in a seafaring life.

These visions faded when I perused, for the first time, those poets whose effusions entranced my soul and lifted it to heaven. I also became a poet and for one year lived in a paradise of my own creation; I imagined that I also might obtain a niche in the temple where the names of Homer and Shakespeare are consecrated. You are well acquainted with my failure and how heavily I bore the disappointment. But just at that time I inherited the fortune of my cousin, and my thoughts were turned into the channel of their earlier bent.

Six years have passed since I resolved on my present undertaking. I can, even now, remember the hour from which I dedicated myself to this great enterprise. I commenced by inuring my body to hardship. I accompanied the whale-fishers on several expeditions to the North Sea; I voluntarily endured cold, famine, thirst, and want of sleep; I often worked harder than the common sailors during the day and devoted my nights to the study of mathematics, the theory of medicine, and those branches of physical science from which a naval adventurer might derive the greatest practical advantage. Twice I actually hired myself as an under-mate in a Greenland whaler, and acquitted myself to admiration.

I must own I felt a little proud when my captain offered me the second dignity in the vessel and entreated me to remain with the greatest earnestness, so valuable did he consider my services.

And now, dear Margaret, do I not deserve to accomplish some great purpose? My life might have been passed in ease and luxury, but I preferred glory to every enticement that wealth placed in my path. Oh, that some encouraging voice would answer in the affirmative! My courage and my resolution is firm; but my hopes fluctuate, and my spirits are often depressed. I am about to proceed on a long and difficult voyage, the emergencies of which will demand all my fortitude: I am required not only to raise the spirits of others, but sometimes to sustain my own, when theirs are failing.

This is the most favourable period for travelling in Russia. They fly quickly over the snow in their sledges; the motion is pleasant, and, in my opinion, far more agreeable than that of an English stagecoach. The cold is not excessive, if you are wrapped in furs—a dress which I have already adopted, for there is a great difference between walking the deck and remaining seated motionless for hours, when no exercise prevents the blood from actually freezing in your veins. I have no ambition to lose my life on the post-road between St. Petersburgh and Archangel.

I shall depart for the latter town in a fortnight or three weeks; and my intention is to hire a ship there, which can easily be done by paying the insurance for the owner, and to engage as many sailors as I think necessary among those who are accustomed to the whale-fishing. I do not intend to sail until the month of June; and when shall I return? Ah, dear sister, how can I answer this question? If I succeed, many, many months, perhaps years, will pass before you and I may meet. If I fail, you will see me again soon, or never.

Farewell, my dear, excellent Margaret. Heaven shower down blessings on you, and save me, that I may again and again testify my gratitude for all your love and kindness.

Your affectionate brother,
R. WALTON

LETTER 2

To Mrs. Saville, England.

Archangel, 28th March, 17—.

How slowly the time passes here, encompassed as I am by frost and snow! Yet a second step is taken towards my enterprise. I have hired a vessel and am occupied in collecting my sailors; those whom I have already engaged appear to be men on whom I can depend and are certainly possessed of dauntless courage.

But I have one want which I have never yet been able to satisfy, and the absence of the object of which I now feel as a most severe evil, I have no friend, Margaret: when I am glowing with the enthusiasm of success, there will be none to participate my joy; if I am assailed by disappointment, no one will endeavour to sustain me in dejection. I shall commit my thoughts to paper, it is true; but that is a poor medium for the communication of feeling. I desire the company of a man who could sympathise with me, whose eyes would reply to mine. You may deem me romantic, my dear sister, but I bitterly feel the want of a friend. I have no one near me, gentle yet courageous, possessed of a cultivated as well as of a capacious mind, whose tastes are like my own, to approve or amend my plans. How would such a friend repair the faults of your poor brother! I am too ardent in execution and too impatient of difficulties. But it is a still greater evil to me that I am self-educated: for the first fourteen years of my life I ran wild on a common and read nothing but our Uncle Thomas' books of voyages. At that age I became acquainted with the celebrated poets of our own country; but it was only when it had ceased to be in my power to derive its most important benefits from such a conviction that I perceived the necessity of becoming acquainted with more languages than that of my native country. Now I am twenty-eight and am in reality more illiterate than many schoolboys of fifteen. It is true that I have thought more and that my daydreams are more extended and magnificent, but they want (as the painters call it) *keeping;* and I greatly need a friend who would have sense enough not to despise me as romantic, and affection enough for me to endeavour to regulate my mind.

Well, these are useless complaints; I shall certainly find no friend on the wide ocean, nor even here in Archangel, among merchants and seamen. Yet some feelings, unallied to the dross of human nature, beat even in these rugged bosoms. My lieutenant, for instance, is a man of wonderful courage and enterprise; he is madly desirous of glory, or rather, to word my phrase more characteristically, of advancement in his profession. He is an Englishman, and in the midst of national and professional prejudices, unsoftened by cultivation, retains some of the noblest endowments of humanity. I first became acquainted with him on board a whale vessel; finding that he was unemployed in this city, I easily engaged him to assist in my enterprise.

The master is a person of an excellent disposition and is remarkable in the ship for his gentleness and the mildness of his discipline. This circumstance, added to his well-known integrity and dauntless courage, made me very desirous to engage him. A youth passed in solitude, my best years spent under your gentle and feminine fosterage, has so refined the groundwork of my character that I cannot overcome an intense distaste to the usual brutality exercised on board ship: I have never believed it to be necessary, and when I heard of a mariner equally noted for his kindliness of heart and the respect and obedience paid to him by his crew, I felt myself peculiarly fortunate in being able to secure his services. I heard of him first in rather a romantic manner, from a lady who owes to him the happiness of her life. This, briefly, is his story. Some years ago he loved a young Russian lady of moderate fortune, and having amassed a considerable sum in prize-money, the father of the girl consented to the match. He saw his mistress once before the destined ceremony; but she was bathed in tears, and throwing herself at his feet, entreated him to spare her, confessing at the same time that she loved another, but that he was poor, and that her father would never consent to the union. My generous friend reassured the suppliant, and on being informed of the name of her lover, instantly abandoned his pursuit. He had already bought a farm with his money, on which he had designed to pass the remainder of his life; but he bestowed the whole on his rival, together with the remains of his prize-money to purchase stock, and then himself solicited the young woman's father to consent to her marriage with her lover. But the old man decidedly refused, thinking himself bound in honour to my friend, who, when he found the father inexorable, quitted his country, nor returned until he heard that his former mistress was married according to her inclinations. "What a noble fellow!" you will exclaim. He is so; but then he is wholly uneducated: he is as silent as a Turk, and a kind of ignorant carelessness attends him, which, while it renders his conduct the more astonishing, detracts from the interest and sympathy which otherwise he would command.

Yet do not suppose, because I complain a little or because I can conceive a consolation for my toils which I may never know, that I am wavering in my resolutions. Those are as fixed as fate, and my voyage is only now delayed until the weather shall permit my embarkation. The winter has been dreadfully severe, but the spring promises well, and it is considered as a remarkably early season, so that perhaps I may sail sooner than I expected. I shall do nothing rashly: you know me sufficiently to confide in my prudence and considerateness whenever the safety of others is committed to my care.

I cannot describe to you my sensations on the near prospect of my undertaking. It is impossible to communicate to you a conception of the trembling sensation, half pleasurable and half fearful, with which I am preparing to depart. I am going to unexplored regions, to "the land of mist and snow," but I shall kill no albatross; therefore do not be alarmed for my safety or if I should come back to you as worn and woeful as the "Ancient Mariner." You will smile at my allusion, but I will disclose a secret. I have often attributed my attachment to, my passionate enthusiasm for, the dangerous mysteries of ocean to that production of the most imaginative of modern poets. There is something at work in my soul which I do not understand. I am practically industrious—painstaking, a workman to execute with perseverance and labour—but besides this there is a love for the marvellous, a belief in the marvellous, intertwined in all my projects, which hurries me out of the common pathways of men, even to the wild sea and unvisited regions I am about to explore.

But to return to dearer considerations. Shall I meet you again, after having traversed immense seas, and returned by the most southern cape of Africa or America? I dare not expect such success, yet I cannot bear to look on the reverse of the picture. Continue for the present to write to me by every opportunity: I may receive your letters on some occasions when I need them most to support my spirits. I love you very tenderly. Remember me with affection, should you never hear from me again.

Your affectionate brother,
ROBERT WALTON

LETTER 3

To Mrs. Saville, England.

July 7th, 17—.

My dear Sister,

I write a few lines in haste to say that I am safe—and well advanced on my voyage. This letter will reach England by a merchantman now on its homeward voyage from Archangel; more fortunate than I, who may not see my native land, perhaps, for many years. I am, however, in good spirits: my men are bold and apparently firm of purpose, nor do the floating sheets of ice that continually pass us, indicating the dangers of the region towards which we are advancing, appear to dismay them. We have already reached a very high latitude; but it is the height of summer, and although not so warm as in England, the southern gales, which blow us speedily towards those shores which I so ardently desire to attain, breathe a degree of renovating warmth which I had not expected. No incidents have hitherto befallen us that would make a figure in a letter. One or two stiff gales and the springing of a leak are accidents which experienced navigators scarcely remember to record, and I shall be well content if nothing worse happen to us during our voyage.

Adieu, my dear Margaret. Be assured that for my own sake, as well as yours, I will not rashly encounter danger. I will be cool, persevering, and prudent.

But success *shall* crown my endeavours. Wherefore not? Thus far I have gone, tracing a secure way over the pathless seas, the very stars themselves being witnesses and testimonies of my triumph. Why not still proceed over the untamed yet obedient element? What can stop the determined heart and resolved will of man?

My swelling heart involuntarily pours itself out thus. But I must finish. Heaven bless my beloved sister!

R. W.

LETTER 4

To Mrs. Saville, England.

August 5th, 17—.

So strange an accident has happened to us that I cannot forbear recording it, although it is very probable that you will see me before these papers can come into your possession.

Last Monday (July 31st) we were nearly surrounded by ice, which closed in the ship on all sides, scarcely leaving her the sea-room in which she floated. Our situation was somewhat dangerous, especially as we were compassed round by a very thick fog. We accordingly lay to, hoping that some change would take place in the atmosphere and weather.

About two o'clock the mist cleared away, and we beheld, stretched out in every direction, vast and irregular plains of ice, which seemed to have no end. Some of my comrades groaned, and my own mind began to grow watchful with anxious thoughts, when a strange sight suddenly attracted our attention and diverted our solicitude from our own situation. We perceived a low carriage, fixed on a sledge and drawn by dogs, pass on towards the north, at the distance of half a mile; a being which had the shape of a man, but apparently of gigantic stature, sat in the sledge and guided the dogs. We watched the rapid progress of the traveller with our telescopes until he was lost among the distant inequalities of the ice.

This appearance excited our unqualified wonder. We were, as we believed, many hundred miles from any land; but this apparition seemed to denote that it was not, in reality, so distant as we had supposed. Shut in, however, by ice, it was impossible to follow his track, which we had observed with the greatest attention.

About two hours after this occurrence we heard the ground sea, and before night the ice broke and freed our ship. We, however, lay to until the morning, fearing to encounter in the dark those large loose masses which float about after the breaking up of the ice.

I profited of this time to rest for a few hours.

In the morning, however, as soon as it was light, I went upon deck and found all the sailors busy on one side of the vessel, apparently talking to someone in the sea. It was, in fact, a sledge, like that we had seen before, which had drifted towards us in the night on a large fragment of ice. Only one dog remained alive; but there was a human being within it whom the sailors were persuading to enter the vessel. He was not, as the other traveller seemed to be, a savage inhabitant of some undiscovered island, but a European. When I appeared on deck the master said, "Here is our captain, and he will not allow you to perish on the open sea."

On perceiving me, the stranger addressed me in English, although with a foreign accent. "Before I come on board your vessel," said he, "will you have the kindness to inform me whither you are bound?"

You may conceive my astonishment on hearing such a question addressed to me from a man on the brink of destruction and to whom I should have supposed that my vessel would have been a resource which he would not have exchanged for the most precious wealth the earth can afford. I replied, however, that we were on a voyage of discovery towards the northern pole.

Upon hearing this he appeared satisfied and consented to come on board. Good God! Margaret, if you had seen the man who thus capitulated for his safety, your surprise would have been boundless. His limbs were nearly frozen, and his body dreadfully emaciated by fatigue and suffering. I never saw a man in so wretched a condition. We attempted to carry him into the cabin, but as soon as he had quitted the fresh air he fainted. We accordingly brought him back to the deck and restored him to animation by rubbing him with brandy and forcing him to swallow a small quantity. As soon as he showed signs of life we wrapped him up in blankets and placed him near the chimney of the kitchen stove. By slow degrees he recovered and ate a little soup, which restored him wonderfully.

Two days passed in this manner before he was able to speak, and I often feared that his sufferings had deprived him of understanding. When he had in some measure recovered, I removed him to my own cabin and attended on him as much as my duty would permit. I never saw a more interesting creature: his eyes have generally an expression of wildness, and even madness, but there are moments when, if anyone performs an act of kindness towards him or does him any the most trifling service, his whole countenance is lighted up, as it were, with a beam of benevolence and sweetness that I never saw equalled. But he is generally melancholy and despairing, and sometimes he gnashes his teeth, as if impatient of the weight of woes that oppresses him.

When my guest was a little recovered I had great trouble to keep off the men, who wished to ask him a thousand questions; but I would not allow him to be tormented by their idle curiosity, in a state of body and mind whose restoration evidently depended upon entire repose. Once, however, the lieutenant asked why he had come so far upon the ice in so strange a vehicle.

His countenance instantly assumed an aspect of the deepest gloom, and he replied, "To seek one who fled from me."

"And did the man whom you pursued travel in the same fashion?"

"Yes."

"Then I fancy we have seen him, for the day before we picked you up we saw some dogs drawing a sledge, with a man in it, across the ice."

This aroused the stranger's attention, and he asked a multitude of questions concerning the route which the dæmon, as he called him, had pursued. Soon after, when he was alone with me, he said, "I have, doubtless, excited your curiosity, as well as that of these good people; but you are too considerate to make inquiries."

"Certainly; it would indeed be very impertinent and inhuman in me to trouble you with any inquisitiveness of mine."

"And yet you rescued me from a strange and perilous situation; you have benevolently restored me to life."

Soon after this he inquired if I thought that the breaking up of the ice had destroyed the other sledge. I replied that I could not answer with any degree of certainty, for the ice had not broken until near midnight, and the traveller might have arrived at a place of safety before that time; but of this I could not judge.

From this time a new spirit of life animated the decaying frame of the stranger. He manifested the greatest eagerness to be upon deck to watch for the sledge which had before appeared; but I have persuaded him to remain in the cabin, for he is far too weak to sustain the rawness of the atmosphere. I have promised that someone should watch for him and give him instant notice if any new object should appear in sight.

Such is my journal of what relates to this strange occurrence up to the present day. The stranger has gradually improved in health but is very silent and appears uneasy when anyone except myself enters his cabin. Yet his manners are so conciliating and gentle that the sailors are all interested in him, although they have had very little communication with him. For my own part, I begin to love him as a brother, and his constant and deep grief fills me with sympathy and compassion. He must have been a noble creature in his better days, being even now in wreck so attractive and amiable.

I said in one of my letters, my dear Margaret, that I should find no friend on the wide ocean; yet I have found a man who, before his spirit had been broken by misery, I should have been happy to have possessed as the brother of my heart.

I shall continue my journal concerning the stranger at intervals, should I have any fresh incidents to record.

August 13th, 17—.

My affection for my guest increases every day. He excites at once my admiration and my pity to an astonishing degree. How can I see so noble a creature destroyed by misery without feeling the most poignant grief? He is so gentle, yet so wise; his mind is so cultivated, and when he speaks, although his words are culled with the choicest art, yet they flow with rapidity and unparalleled eloquence.

He is now much recovered from his illness and is continually on the deck, apparently watching for the sledge that preceded his own. Yet, although unhappy, he is not so utterly occupied by his own misery but that he interests himself deeply in the projects of others. He has frequently conversed with me on mine, which I have communicated to him without disguise. He entered attentively into all my arguments in favour of my eventual success and into every minute detail of the measures I had taken to secure it. I was easily led by the sympathy which he evinced to use the language of my heart, to give utterance to the burning ardour of my soul and to say, with all the fervour that warmed me, how gladly I would sacrifice my fortune, my existence, my every hope, to the furtherance of my enterprise. One man's life or death were but a small price to pay for the acquirement of the knowledge which I sought, for the dominion I should acquire and transmit over the elemental foes of our race. As I spoke, a dark gloom spread over my listener's countenance. At first I perceived that he tried to suppress his emotion; he placed his hands before his eyes, and my voice quivered and failed me as I beheld tears trickle fast from between his fingers; a groan burst from his heaving breast. I paused; at length he spoke, in broken accents: "Unhappy man! Do you share my madness? Have you drunk also of the intoxicating draught? Hear me; let me reveal my tale, and you will dash the cup from your lips!"

Such words, you may imagine, strongly excited my curiosity; but the paroxysm of grief that had seized the stranger overcame his weakened powers, and many hours of repose and tranquil conversation were necessary to restore his composure.

Having conquered the violence of his feelings, he appeared to despise himself for being the slave of passion; and quelling the dark tyranny of despair, he led me again to converse concerning myself personally. He asked me the history of my earlier years. The tale was quickly told, but it awakened various trains of reflection. I spoke of my desire of finding a friend, of my thirst for a more intimate sympathy with a fellow mind than had ever fallen to my lot, and expressed my conviction that a man could boast of little happiness who did not enjoy this blessing.

"I agree with you," replied the stranger; "we are unfashioned creatures, but half made up, if one wiser, better, dearer than ourselves—such a friend ought to be—do not lend his aid to perfectionate our weak and faulty natures. I once had a friend, the most noble of human creatures, and am entitled, therefore, to judge respecting friendship. You have hope, and the world before you, and have no cause for despair. But I—I have lost everything and cannot begin life anew."

As he said this his countenance became expressive of a calm, settled grief that touched me to the heart. But he was silent and presently retired to his cabin.

Even broken in spirit as he is, no one can feel more deeply than he does the beauties of nature. The starry sky, the sea, and every sight afforded by these wonderful regions seem still to have the power of elevating his soul from earth. Such a man has a double existence: he may suffer misery and be overwhelmed by disappointments, yet when he has retired into himself, he will be like a celestial spirit that has a halo around him, within whose circle no grief or folly ventures.

Will you smile at the enthusiasm I express concerning this divine wanderer? You would not if you saw him. You have been tutored and refined by books and retirement from the world, and you are therefore somewhat fastidious; but this only renders you the more fit to appreciate the extraordinary merits of this wonderful man. Sometimes I have endeavoured to discover what quality it is which he possesses that elevates him so immeasurably above any other person I ever knew. I believe it to be an intuitive discernment, a quick but never-failing power of judgment, a penetration into the causes of things, unequalled for clearness and precision; add to this a facility of expression and a voice whose varied intonations are soul-subduing music.

August 19th, 17—.

Yesterday the stranger said to me, "You may easily perceive, Captain Walton, that I have suffered great and unparalleled misfortunes. I had determined at one time that the memory of these evils should die with me, but you have won me to alter my determination. You seek for knowledge and wisdom, as I once did; and I ardently hope that the gratification of your wishes may not be a serpent to sting you, as mine has been. I do not know that the relation of my disasters will be useful to you; yet, when I reflect that you are pursuing the same course, exposing yourself to the same dangers which have rendered me what I am, I imagine that you may deduce an apt moral from my tale, one that may direct you if you succeed in your undertaking and console you in case of failure. Prepare to hear of occurrences which are usually deemed marvellous. Were we among the tamer scenes of nature I might fear to encounter your unbelief, perhaps your ridicule; but many things will appear possible in these wild and mysterious regions which would provoke the laughter of those unacquainted with the ever-varied powers of nature; nor can I doubt but that my tale conveys in its series internal evidence of the truth of the events of which it is composed."

You may easily imagine that I was much gratified by the offered communication, yet I could not endure that he should renew his grief by a recital of his misfortunes. I felt the greatest eagerness to hear the promised narrative, partly from curiosity and partly from a strong desire to ameliorate his fate if it were in my power. I expressed these feelings in my answer.

"I thank you," he replied, "for your sympathy, but it is useless; my fate is nearly fulfilled. I wait but for one event, and then I shall repose in peace. I understand your feeling," continued he, perceiving that I wished to interrupt him; "but you are mistaken, my friend, if thus you will allow me to name you; nothing can alter my destiny; listen to my history, and you will perceive how irrevocably it is determined."

He then told me that he would commence his narrative the next day when I should be at leisure. This promise drew from me the warmest thanks. I have resolved every night, when I am not imperatively occupied by my duties, to record, as nearly as possible in his own words, what he has related during the day. If I should be engaged, I will at least make notes. This manuscript will doubtless afford you the greatest pleasure; but to me, who know him, and who hear it from his own lips—with what interest and sympathy shall I read it in some future day! Even now, as I commence my task, his full-toned voice swells in my ears; his lustrous eyes dwell on me with all their melancholy sweetness; I see his thin hand raised in animation, while the lineaments of his face are irradiated by the soul within. Strange and harrowing must be his story, frightful the storm which embraced the gallant vessel on its course and wrecked it—thus!

CHAPTER I

I am by birth a Genevese, and my family is one of the most distinguished of that republic. My ancestors had been for many years counsellors and syndics, and my father had filled several public situations with honour and reputation. He was respected by all who knew him for his integrity and indefatigable attention to public business. He passed his younger days perpetually occupied by the affairs of his country; a variety of circumstances had prevented his marrying early, nor was it until the decline of life that he became a husband and the father of a family.

As the circumstances of his marriage illustrate his character, I cannot refrain from relating them. One of his most intimate friends was a merchant who, from a flourishing state, fell, through numerous mischances, into poverty. This man, whose name was Beaufort, was of a proud and unbending disposition and could not bear to live in poverty and oblivion in the same country where he had formerly been distinguished for his rank and magnificence. Having paid his debts, therefore, in the most honourable manner, he retreated with his daughter to the town of Lucerne, where he lived unknown and in wretchedness. My father loved Beaufort with the truest friendship and was deeply grieved by his retreat in these unfortunate circumstances. He bitterly deplored the false pride which led his friend to a conduct so little worthy of the affection that united them. He lost no time in endeavouring to seek him out, with the hope of persuading him to begin the world again through his credit and assistance.

Beaufort had taken effectual measures to conceal himself, and it was ten months before my father discovered his abode. Overjoyed at this discovery, he hastened to the house, which was situated in a mean street near the Reuss. But when he entered, misery and despair alone welcomed him. Beaufort had saved but a very small sum of money from the wreck of his fortunes, but it was sufficient to provide him with sustenance for some months, and in the meantime he hoped to procure some respectable employment in a merchant's house. The interval was, consequently, spent in inaction; his grief only became more deep and rankling when he had leisure for reflection, and at length it took so fast hold of his mind that at the end of three months he lay on a bed of sickness, incapable of any exertion.

His daughter attended him with the greatest tenderness, but she saw with despair that their little fund was rapidly decreasing and that there was no other prospect of support. But Caroline Beaufort possessed a mind of an uncommon mould, and her courage rose to support her in her adversity. She procured plain work; she plaited straw and by various means contrived to earn a pittance scarcely sufficient to support life.

Several months passed in this manner. Her father grew worse; her time was more entirely occupied in attending him; her means of subsistence decreased; and in the tenth month her father died in her arms, leaving her an orphan and a beggar. This last blow overcame her, and she knelt by Beaufort's coffin weeping bitterly, when my father entered the chamber. He came like a protecting spirit to the poor girl, who committed herself to his care; and after the interment of his friend he conducted her to Geneva and placed her under the protection of a relation. Two years after this event Caroline became his wife.

There was a considerable difference between the ages of my parents, but this circumstance seemed to unite them only closer in bonds of devoted affection. There was a sense of justice in my father's upright mind which rendered it necessary that he should approve highly to love strongly. Perhaps during former years he had suffered from the late-discovered unworthiness of one beloved and so was disposed to set a greater value on tried worth. There was a show of gratitude and worship in his attachment to my mother, differing wholly from the doting fondness of age, for it was inspired by reverence for her virtues and a desire to be the means of, in some degree, recompensing her for the sorrows she had endured, but which gave inexpressible grace to his behaviour to her. Everything was made to yield to her wishes and her convenience. He strove to shelter her, as a fair exotic is sheltered by the gardener, from every rougher wind and to surround her with all that could tend to excite pleasurable emotion in her soft and benevolent mind. Her health, and even the tranquillity of her hitherto constant spirit, had been shaken by what she had gone through. During the two years that had elapsed previous to their marriage my father had gradually relinquished all his public functions; and immediately after their union they sought the pleasant climate of Italy, and the change of scene and interest attendant on a tour through that land of wonders, as a restorative for her weakened frame.

From Italy they visited Germany and France. I, their eldest child, was born at Naples, and as an infant accompanied them in their rambles. I remained for several years their only child. Much as they were attached to each other, they seemed to draw inexhaustible stores of affection from a very mine of love to bestow them upon me. My mother's tender caresses and my father's smile of benevolent pleasure while regarding me are my first recollections. I was their plaything and their idol, and something better—their child, the innocent and helpless creature bestowed on them by Heaven, whom to bring up to good, and whose future lot it was in their hands to direct to happiness or misery, according as they fulfilled their duties towards me. With this deep consciousness of what they owed towards the being to which they had given life, added to the active spirit of tenderness that animated both, it may be imagined that while during every hour of my infant life I received a lesson of patience, of charity, and of self-control, I was so guided by a silken cord that all seemed but one train of enjoyment to me.

For a long time I was their only care. My mother had much desired to have a daughter, but I continued their single offspring. When I was about five years old, while making an excursion beyond the frontiers of Italy, they passed a week on the shores of the Lake of Como. Their benevolent disposition often made them enter the cottages of the poor. This, to my mother, was more than a duty; it was a necessity, a passion—remembering what she had suffered, and how she had been relieved—for her to act in her turn the guardian angel to the afflicted. During one of their walks a poor cot in the foldings of a vale attracted their notice as being singularly disconsolate, while the number of half-clothed children gathered about it spoke of penury in its worst shape. One day, when my father had gone by himself to Milan, my mother, accompanied by me, visited this abode. She found a peasant and his wife, hard working, bent down by care and labour, distributing a scanty meal to five hungry babes. Among these there was one which attracted my mother far above all the rest. She appeared of a different stock. The four others were dark-eyed, hardy little vagrants; this child was thin and very fair. Her hair was the brightest living gold, and despite the poverty of her clothing, seemed to set a crown of distinction on her head. Her brow was clear and ample, her blue eyes cloudless, and her lips and the moulding of her face so expressive of sensibility and sweetness that none could behold her without looking on her as of a distinct species, a being heaven-sent, and bearing a celestial stamp in all her features.

The peasant woman, perceiving that my mother fixed eyes of wonder and admiration on this lovely girl, eagerly communicated her history. She was not her child, but the daughter of a Milanese nobleman. Her mother was a German and had died on giving her birth. The infant had been placed with these good people to nurse: they were better off then. They had not been long married, and their eldest child was but just born. The father of their charge was one of those Italians nursed in the memory of the antique glory of Italy—one among the *schiavi ognor frementi,* who exerted himself to obtain the liberty of his country. He became the victim of its weakness. Whether he had died or still lingered in the dungeons of Austria was not known. His property was confiscated; his child became an orphan and a beggar. She continued with her foster parents and bloomed in their rude abode, fairer than a garden rose among dark-leaved brambles.

When my father returned from Milan, he found playing with me in the hall of our villa a child fairer than pictured cherub—a creature who seemed to shed radiance from her looks and whose form and motions were lighter than the chamois of the hills. The apparition was soon explained. With his permission my mother prevailed on her rustic guardians to yield their charge to her. They were fond of the sweet orphan. Her presence had seemed a blessing to them, but it would be unfair to her to keep her in poverty and want when Providence afforded her such powerful protection. They consulted their village priest, and the result was that Elizabeth Lavenza became the inmate of my parents' house—my more than sister—the beautiful and adored companion of all my occupations and my pleasures.

Everyone loved Elizabeth. The passionate and almost reverential attachment with which all regarded her became, while I shared it, my pride and my delight. On the evening previous to her being brought to my home, my mother had said playfully, "I have a pretty present for my Victor—tomorrow he shall have it." And when, on the morrow, she presented Elizabeth to me as her promised gift, I, with childish seriousness, interpreted her words literally and looked upon Elizabeth as mine—mine to protect, love, and cherish. All praises bestowed on her I received as made to a possession of my own. We called each other familiarly by the name of cousin. No word, no expression could body forth the kind of relation in which she stood to me—my more than sister, since till death she was to be mine only.

CHAPTER II

We were brought up together; there was not quite a year difference in our ages. I need not say that we were strangers to any species of disunion or dispute. Harmony was the soul of our companionship, and the diversity and contrast that subsisted in our characters drew us nearer together. Elizabeth was of a calmer and more concentrated disposition; but, with all my ardour, I was capable of a more intense application and was more deeply smitten with the thirst for knowledge. She busied herself with following the aerial creations of the poets; and in the majestic and wondrous scenes which surrounded our Swiss home —the sublime shapes of the mountains, the changes of the seasons, tempest and calm, the silence of winter, and the life and turbulence of our Alpine summers—she found ample scope for admiration and delight. While my companion contemplated with a serious and satisfied spirit the magnificent appearances of things, I delighted in investigating their causes. The world was to me a secret which I desired to divine. Curiosity, earnest research to learn the hidden laws of nature, gladness akin to rapture, as they were unfolded to me, are among the earliest sensations I can remember.

On the birth of a second son, my junior by seven years, my parents gave up entirely their wandering life and fixed themselves in their native country. We possessed a house in Geneva, and a *campagne* on Belrive, the eastern shore of the lake, at the distance of rather more than a league from the city. We resided principally in the latter, and the lives of my parents were passed in considerable seclusion. It was my temper to avoid a crowd and to attach myself fervently to a few. I was indifferent, therefore, to my school-fellows in general; but I united myself in the bonds of the closest friendship to one among them. Henry Clerval was the son of a merchant of Geneva. He was a boy of singular talent and fancy. He loved enterprise, hardship, and even danger for its own sake. He was deeply read in books of chivalry and romance. He composed heroic songs and began to write many a tale of enchantment and knightly adventure. He tried to make us act plays and to enter into masquerades, in which the characters were drawn from the heroes of Roncesvalles, of the Round Table of King Arthur, and the chivalrous train who shed their blood to redeem the holy sepulchre from the hands of the infidels.

No human being could have passed a happier childhood than myself. My parents were possessed by the very spirit of kindness and indulgence. We felt that they were not the tyrants to rule our lot according to their caprice, but the agents and creators of all the many delights which we enjoyed. When I mingled with other families I distinctly discerned how peculiarly fortunate my lot was, and gratitude assisted the development of filial love.

My temper was sometimes violent, and my passions vehement; but by some law in my temperature they were turned not towards childish pursuits but to an eager desire to learn, and not to learn all things indiscriminately. I confess that neither the structure of languages, nor the code of governments, nor the politics of various states possessed attractions for me. It was the secrets of heaven and earth that I desired to learn; and whether it was the outward substance of things or the inner spirit of nature and the mysterious soul of man that occupied me, still my inquiries were directed to the metaphysical, or in its highest sense, the physical secrets of the world.

Meanwhile Clerval occupied himself, so to speak, with the moral relations of things. The busy stage of life, the virtues of heroes, and the actions of men were his theme; and his hope and his dream was to become one among those whose names are recorded in story as the gallant and adventurous benefactors of our species. The saintly soul of Elizabeth shone like a shrine-dedicated lamp in our peaceful home. Her sympathy was ours; her smile, her soft voice, the sweet glance of her celestial eyes, were ever there to bless and animate us. She was the living spirit of love to soften and attract; I might have become sullen in my study, rough through the ardour of my nature, but that she was there to subdue me to a semblance of her own gentleness. And Clerval—could aught ill entrench on the noble spirit of Clerval? Yet he might not have been so perfectly humane, so thoughtful in his generosity, so full of kindness and tenderness amidst his passion for adventurous exploit, had she not unfolded to him the real loveliness of beneficence and made the doing good the end and aim of his soaring ambition.

I feel exquisite pleasure in dwelling on the recollections of childhood, before misfortune had tainted my mind and changed its bright visions of extensive usefulness into gloomy and narrow reflections upon self. Besides, in drawing the picture of my early days, I also record those events which led, by insensible steps, to my after tale of misery, for when I would account to myself for the birth of that passion which afterwards ruled my destiny I find it arise, like a mountain river, from ignoble and almost forgotten sources; but, swelling as it proceeded, it became the torrent which, in its course, has swept away all my hopes and joys.

Natural philosophy is the genius that has regulated my fate; I desire, therefore, in this narration, to state those facts which led to my predilection for that science. When I was thirteen years of age we all went on a party of pleasure to the baths near Thonon; the inclemency of the weather obliged us to remain a day confined to the inn. In this house I chanced to find a volume of the works of Cornelius Agrippa. I opened it with apathy; the theory which he attempts to demonstrate and the wonderful facts which he relates soon changed this feeling into enthusiasm. A new light seemed to dawn upon my mind, and bounding with joy, I communicated my discovery to my father. My father looked carelessly at the title page of my book and said, "Ah! Cornelius Agrippa! My dear Victor, do not waste your time upon this; it is sad trash."

If, instead of this remark, my father had taken the pains to explain to me that the principles of Agrippa had been entirely exploded and that a modern system of science had been introduced which possessed much greater powers than the ancient, because the powers of the latter were chimerical, while those of the former were real and practical, under such circumstances I should certainly have thrown Agrippa aside and have contented my imagination, warmed as it was, by returning with greater ardour to my former studies. It is even possible that the train of my ideas would never have received the fatal impulse that led to my ruin. But the cursory glance my father had taken of my volume by no means assured me that he was acquainted with its contents, and I continued to read with the greatest avidity.

When I returned home my first care was to procure the whole works of this author, and afterwards of Paracelsus and Albertus Magnus. I read and studied the wild fancies of these writers with delight; they appeared to me treasures known to few besides myself. I have described myself as always having been imbued with a fervent longing to penetrate the secrets of nature. In spite of the intense labour and wonderful discoveries of modern philosophers, I always came from my studies discontented and unsatisfied. Sir Isaac Newton is said to have avowed that he felt like a child picking up shells beside the great and unexplored ocean of truth. Those of his successors in each branch of natural philosophy with whom I was acquainted appeared even to my boy's apprehensions as tyros engaged in the same pursuit.

The untaught peasant beheld the elements around him and was acquainted with their practical uses. The most learned philosopher knew little more. He had partially unveiled the face of Nature, but her immortal lineaments were still a wonder and a mystery. He might dissect, anatomise, and give names; but, not to speak of a final cause, causes in their secondary and tertiary grades were utterly unknown to him. I had gazed upon the fortifications and impediments that seemed to keep human beings from entering the citadel of nature, and rashly and ignorantly I had repined.

But here were books, and here were men who had penetrated deeper and knew more. I took their word for all that they averred, and I became their disciple. It may appear strange that such should arise in the eighteenth century; but while I followed the routine of education in the schools of Geneva, I was, to a great degree, self-taught with regard to my favourite studies. My father was not scientific, and I was left to struggle with a child's blindness, added to a student's thirst for knowledge. Under the guidance of my new preceptors I entered with the greatest diligence into the search of the philosopher's stone and the elixir of life; but the latter soon obtained my undivided attention. Wealth was an inferior object, but what glory would attend the discovery if I could banish disease from the human frame and render man invulnerable to any but a violent death!

Nor were these my only visions. The raising of ghosts or devils was a promise liberally accorded by my favourite authors, the fulfilment of which I most eagerly sought; and if my incantations were always unsuccessful, I attributed the failure rather to my own inexperience and mistake than to a want of skill or fidelity in my instructors. And thus for a time I was occupied by exploded systems, mingling, like an unadept, a thousand contradictory theories and floundering desperately in a very slough of multifarious knowledge, guided by an ardent imagination and childish reasoning, till an accident again changed the current of my ideas.

When I was about fifteen years old we had retired to our house near Belrive, when we witnessed a most violent and terrible thunderstorm. It advanced from behind the mountains of Jura, and the thunder burst at once with frightful loudness from various quarters of the heavens. I remained, while the storm lasted, watching its progress with curiosity and delight. As I stood at the door, on a sudden I beheld a stream of fire issue from an old and beautiful oak which stood about twenty yards from our house; and so soon as the dazzling light vanished, the oak had disappeared, and nothing remained but a blasted stump. When we visited it the next morning, we found the tree shattered in a singular manner. It was not splintered by the shock, but entirely reduced to thin ribbons of wood. I never beheld anything so utterly destroyed.

Before this I was not unacquainted with the more obvious laws of electricity. On this occasion a man of great research in natural philosophy was with us, and excited by this catastrophe, he entered on the explanation of a theory which he had formed on the subject of electricity and galvanism, which was at once new and astonishing to me. All that he said threw greatly into the shade Cornelius Agrippa, Albertus Magnus, and Paracelsus, the lords of my imagination; but by some fatality the overthrow of these men disinclined me to pursue my accustomed studies. It seemed to me as if nothing would or could ever be known. All that had so long engaged my attention suddenly grew despicable. By one of those caprices of the mind which we are perhaps most subject to in early youth, I at once gave up my former occupations, set down natural history and all its progeny as a deformed and abortive creation, and entertained the greatest disdain for a would-be science which could never even step within the threshold of real knowledge. In this mood of mind I betook myself to the mathematics and the branches of study appertaining to that science as being built upon secure foundations, and so worthy of my consideration.

Thus strangely are our souls constructed, and by such slight ligaments are we bound to prosperity or ruin. When I look back, it seems to me as if this almost miraculous change of inclination and will was the immediate suggestion of the guardian angel of my life—the last effort made by the spirit of preservation to avert the storm that was even then hanging in the stars and ready to envelop me. Her victory was announced by an unusual tranquillity and gladness of soul which followed the relinquishing of my ancient and latterly tormenting studies. It was thus that I was to be taught to associate evil with their prosecution, happiness with their disregard.

It was a strong effort of the spirit of good, but it was ineffectual. Destiny was too potent, and her immutable laws had decreed my utter and terrible destruction.

CHAPTER III

When I had attained the age of seventeen my parents resolved that I should become a student at the university of Ingolstadt. I had hitherto attended the schools of Geneva, but my father thought it necessary for the completion of my education that I should be made acquainted with other customs than those of my native country. My departure was therefore fixed at an early date, but before the day resolved upon could arrive, the first misfortune of my life occurred—an omen, as it were, of my future misery.

Elizabeth had caught the scarlet fever; her illness was severe, and she was in the greatest danger. During her illness many arguments had been urged to persuade my mother to refrain from attending upon her. She had at first yielded to our entreaties, but when she heard that the life of her favourite was menaced, she could no longer control her anxiety. She attended her sickbed; her watchful attentions triumphed over the malignity of the distemper—Elizabeth was saved, but the consequences of this imprudence were fatal to her preserver. On the third day my mother sickened; her fever was accompanied by the most alarming symptoms, and the looks of her medical attendants prognosticated the worst event. On her deathbed the fortitude and benignity of this best of women did not desert her. She joined the hands of Elizabeth and myself. "My children," she said, "my firmest hopes of future happiness were placed on the prospect of your union. This expectation will now be the consolation of your father. Elizabeth, my love, you must supply my place to my younger children. Alas! I regret that I am taken from you; and, happy and beloved as I have been, is it not hard to quit you all? But these are not thoughts befitting me; I will endeavour to resign myself cheerfully to death and will indulge a hope of meeting you in another world."

She died calmly, and her countenance expressed affection even in death. I need not describe the feelings of those whose dearest ties are rent by that most irreparable evil, the void that presents itself to the soul, and the despair that is exhibited on the countenance. It is so long before the mind can persuade itself that she whom we saw every day and whose very existence appeared a part of our own can have departed for ever—that the brightness of a beloved eye can have been extinguished and the sound of a voice so familiar and dear to the ear can be hushed, never more to be heard. These are the reflections of the first days; but when the lapse of time proves the reality of the evil, then the actual bitterness of grief commences. Yet from whom has not that rude hand rent away some dear connection? And why should I describe a sorrow which all have felt, and must feel? The time at length arrives when grief is rather an indulgence than a necessity; and the smile that plays upon the lips, although it may be deemed a sacrilege, is not banished. My mother was dead, but we had still duties which we ought to perform; we must continue our course with the rest and learn to think ourselves fortunate whilst one remains whom the spoiler has not seized.

My departure for Ingolstadt, which had been deferred by these events, was now again determined upon. I obtained from my father a respite of some weeks. It appeared to me sacrilege so soon to leave the repose, akin to death, of the house of mourning and to rush into the thick of life. I was new to sorrow, but it did not the less alarm me. I was unwilling to quit the sight of those that remained to me, and above all, I desired to see my sweet Elizabeth in some degree consoled.

She indeed veiled her grief and strove to act the comforter to us all. She looked steadily on life and assumed its duties with courage and zeal. She devoted herself to those whom she had been taught to call her uncle and cousins. Never was she so enchanting as at this time, when she recalled the sunshine of her smiles and spent them upon us. She forgot even her own regret in her endeavours to make us forget.

The day of my departure at length arrived. Clerval spent the last evening with us. He had endeavoured to persuade his father to permit him to accompany me and to become my fellow student, but in vain. His father was a narrow-minded trader and saw idleness and ruin in the aspirations and ambition of his son. Henry deeply felt the misfortune of being debarred from a liberal education. He said little, but when he spoke I read in his kindling eye and in his animated glance a restrained but firm resolve not to be chained to the miserable details of commerce.

We sat late. We could not tear ourselves away from each other nor persuade ourselves to say the word "Farewell!" It was said, and we retired under the pretence of seeking repose, each fancying that the other was deceived; but when at morning's dawn I descended to the carriage which was to convey me away, they were all there—my father again to bless me, Clerval to press my hand once more, my Elizabeth to renew her entreaties that I would write often and to bestow the last feminine attentions on her playmate and friend.

I threw myself into the chaise that was to convey me away and indulged in the most melancholy reflections. I, who had ever been surrounded by amiable companions, continually engaged in endeavouring to bestow mutual pleasure—I was now alone. In the university whither I was going I must form my own friends and be my own protector. My life had hitherto been remarkably secluded and domestic, and this had given me invincible repugnance to new countenances. I loved my brothers, Elizabeth, and Clerval; these were "old familiar faces," but I believed myself totally unfitted for the company of strangers. Such were my reflections as I commenced my journey; but as I proceeded, my spirits and hopes rose. I ardently desired the acquisition of knowledge. I had often, when at home, thought it hard to remain during my youth cooped up in one place and had longed to enter the world and take my station among other human beings. Now my desires were complied with, and it would, indeed, have been folly to repent.

I had sufficient leisure for these and many other reflections during my journey to Ingolstadt, which was long and fatiguing. At length the high white steeple of the town met my eyes. I alighted and was conducted to my solitary apartment to spend the evening as I pleased.

The next morning I delivered my letters of introduction and paid a visit to some of the principal professors. Chance—or rather the evil influence, the Angel of Destruction, which asserted omnipotent sway over me from the moment I turned my reluctant steps from my father's door—led me first to M. Krempe, professor of natural philosophy. He was an uncouth man, but deeply imbued in the secrets of his science. He asked me several questions concerning my progress in the different branches of science appertaining to natural philosophy. I replied carelessly, and partly in contempt, mentioned the names of my alchemists as the principal authors I had studied. The professor stared. "Have you," he said, "really spent your time in studying such nonsense?"

I replied in the affirmative. "Every minute," continued M. Krempe with warmth, "every instant that you have wasted on those books is utterly and entirely lost. You have burdened your memory with exploded systems and useless names. Good God! In what desert land have you lived, where no one was kind enough to inform you that these fancies which you have so greedily imbibed are a thousand years old and as musty as they are ancient? I little expected, in this enlightened and scientific age, to find a disciple of Albertus Magnus and Paracelsus. My dear sir, you must begin your studies entirely anew."

So saying, he stepped aside and wrote down a list of several books treating of natural philosophy which he desired me to procure, and dismissed me after mentioning that in the beginning of the following week he intended to commence a course of lectures upon natural philosophy in its general relations, and that M. Waldman, a fellow professor, would lecture upon chemistry the alternate days that he omitted.

I returned home not disappointed, for I have said that I had long considered those authors useless whom the professor reprobated; but I returned not at all the more inclined to recur to these studies in any shape. M. Krempe was a little squat man with a gruff voice and a repulsive countenance; the teacher, therefore, did not prepossess me in favour of his pursuits. In rather a too philosophical and connected a strain, perhaps, I have given an account of the conclusions I had come to concerning them in my early years. As a child I had not been content with the results promised by the modern professors of natural science. With a confusion of ideas only to be accounted for by my extreme youth and my want of a guide on such matters, I had retrod the steps of knowledge along the paths of time and exchanged the discoveries of recent inquirers for the dreams of forgotten alchemists. Besides, I had a contempt for the uses of modern natural philosophy. It was very different when the masters of the science sought immortality and power; such views, although futile, were grand; but now the scene was changed. The ambition of the inquirer seemed to limit itself to the annihilation of those visions on which my interest in science was chiefly founded. I was required to exchange chimeras of boundless grandeur for realities of little worth.

Such were my reflections during the first two or three days of my residence at Ingolstadt, which were chiefly spent in becoming acquainted with the localities and the principal residents in my new abode. But as the ensuing week commenced, I thought of the information which M. Krempe had given me concerning the lectures. And although I could not consent to go and hear that little conceited fellow deliver sentences out of a pulpit, I recollected what he had said of M. Waldman, whom I had never seen, as he had hitherto been out of town.

Partly from curiosity and partly from idleness, I went into the lecturing room, which M. Waldman entered shortly after. This professor was very unlike his colleague. He appeared about fifty years of age, but with an aspect expressive of the greatest benevolence; a few grey hairs covered his temples, but those at the back of his head were nearly black. His person was short but remarkably erect and his voice the sweetest I had ever heard. He began his lecture by a recapitulation of the history of chemistry and the various improvements made by different men of learning, pronouncing with fervour the names of the most distinguished discoverers. He then took a cursory view of the present state of the science and explained many of its elementary terms. After having made a few preparatory experiments, he concluded with a panegyric upon modern chemistry, the terms of which I shall never forget:

"The ancient teachers of this science," said he, "promised impossibilities and performed nothing. The modern masters promise very little; they know that metals cannot be transmuted and that the elixir of life is a chimera but these philosophers, whose hands seem only made to dabble in dirt, and their eyes to pore over the microscope or crucible, have indeed performed miracles. They penetrate into the recesses of nature and show how she works in her hiding-places. They ascend into the heavens; they have discovered how the blood circulates, and the nature of the air we breathe. They have acquired new and almost unlimited powers; they can command the thunders of heaven, mimic the earthquake, and even mock the invisible world with its own shadows."

Such were the professor's words—rather let me say such the words of the fate—enounced to destroy me. As he went on I felt as if my soul were grappling with a palpable enemy; one by one the various keys were touched which formed the mechanism of my being; chord after chord was sounded, and soon my mind was filled with one thought, one conception, one purpose. So much has been done, exclaimed the soul of Frankenstein—more, far more, will I achieve; treading in the steps already marked, I will pioneer a new way, explore unknown powers, and unfold to the world the deepest mysteries of creation.

I closed not my eyes that night. My internal being was in a state of insurrection and turmoil; I felt that order would thence arise, but I had no power to produce it. By degrees, after the morning's dawn, sleep came. I awoke, and my yesternight's thoughts were as a dream. There only remained a resolution to return to my ancient studies and to devote myself to a science for which I believed myself to possess a natural talent. On the same day I paid M. Waldman a visit. His manners in private were even more mild and attractive than in public, for there was a certain dignity in his mien during his lecture which in his own house was replaced by the greatest affability and kindness. I gave him pretty nearly the same account of my former pursuits as I had given to his fellow professor. He heard with attention the little narration concerning my studies and smiled at the names of Cornelius Agrippa and Paracelsus, but without the contempt that M. Krempe had exhibited. He said that "These were men to whose indefatigable zeal modern philosophers were indebted for most of the foundations of their knowledge. They had left to us, as an easier task, to give new names and arrange in connected classifications the facts which they in a great degree had been the instruments of bringing to light. The labours of men of genius, however erroneously directed, scarcely ever fail in ultimately turning to the solid advantage of mankind." I listened to his statement, which was delivered without any presumption or affectation, and then added that his lecture had removed my prejudices against modern chemists; I expressed myself in measured terms, with the modesty and deference due from a youth to his instructor, without letting escape (inexperience in life would have made me ashamed) any of the enthusiasm which stimulated my intended labours. I requested his advice concerning the books I ought to procure.

"I am happy," said M. Waldman, "to have gained a disciple; and if your application equals your ability, I have no doubt of your success. Chemistry is that branch of natural philosophy in which the greatest improvements have been and may be made; it is on that account that I have made it my peculiar study; but at the same time, I have not neglected the other branches of science. A man would make but a very sorry chemist if he attended to that department of human knowledge alone. If your wish is to become really a man of science and not merely a petty experimentalist, I should advise you to apply to every branch of natural philosophy, including mathematics."

He then took me into his laboratory and explained to me the uses of his various machines, instructing me as to what I ought to procure and promising me the use of his own when I should have advanced far enough in the science not to derange their mechanism. He also gave me the list of books which I had requested, and I took my leave.

Thus ended a day memorable to me; it decided my future destiny.

CHAPTER IV

From this day natural philosophy, and particularly chemistry, in the most comprehensive sense of the term, became nearly my sole occupation. I read with ardour those works, so full of genius and discrimination, which modern inquirers have written on these subjects. I attended the lectures and cultivated the acquaintance of the men of science of the university, and I found even in M. Krempe a great deal of sound sense and real information, combined, it is true, with a repulsive physiognomy and manners, but not on that account the less valuable. In M. Waldman I found a true friend. His gentleness was never tinged by dogmatism, and his instructions were given with an air of frankness and good nature that banished every idea of pedantry. In a thousand ways he smoothed for me the path of knowledge and made the most abstruse inquiries clear and facile to my apprehension. My application was at first fluctuating and uncertain; it gained strength as I proceeded and soon became so ardent and eager that the stars often disappeared in the light of morning whilst I was yet engaged in my laboratory.

As I applied so closely, it may be easily conceived that my progress was rapid. My ardour was indeed the astonishment of the students, and my proficiency that of the masters. Professor Krempe often asked me, with a sly smile, how Cornelius Agrippa went on, whilst M. Waldman expressed the most heartfelt exultation in my progress. Two years passed in this manner, during which I paid no visit to Geneva, but was engaged, heart and soul, in the pursuit of some discoveries which I hoped to make. None but those who have experienced them can conceive of the enticements of science. In other studies you go as far as others have gone before you, and there is nothing more to know; but in a scientific pursuit there is continual food for discovery and wonder. A mind of moderate capacity which closely pursues one study must infallibly arrive at great proficiency in that study; and I, who continually sought the attainment of one object of pursuit and was solely wrapped up in this, improved so rapidly that at the end of two years I made some discoveries in the improvement of some chemical instruments, which procured me great esteem and admiration at the university. When I had arrived at this point and had become as well acquainted with the theory and practice of natural philosophy as depended on the lessons of any of the professors at Ingolstadt, my residence there being no longer conducive to my improvements, I thought of returning to my friends and my native town, when an incident happened that protracted my stay.

One of the phenomena which had peculiarly attracted my attention was the structure of the human frame, and, indeed, any animal endued with life. Whence, I often asked myself, did the principle of life proceed? It was a bold question, and one which has ever been considered as a mystery; yet with how many things are we upon the brink of becoming acquainted, if cowardice or carelessness did not restrain our inquiries. I revolved these circumstances in my mind and determined thenceforth to apply myself more particularly to those branches of natural philosophy which relate to physiology. Unless I had been animated by an almost supernatural enthusiasm, my application to this study would have been irksome and almost intolerable. To examine the causes of life, we must first have recourse to death. I became acquainted with the science of anatomy, but this was not sufficient; I must also observe the natural decay and corruption of the human body. In my education my father had taken the greatest precautions that my mind should be impressed with no supernatural horrors. I do not ever remember to have trembled at a tale of superstition or to have feared the apparition of a spirit. Darkness had no effect upon my fancy, and a churchyard was to me merely the receptacle of bodies deprived of life, which, from being the seat of beauty and strength, had become food for the worm. Now I was led to examine the cause and progress of this decay and forced to spend days and nights in vaults and charnel-houses. My attention was fixed upon every object the most insupportable to the delicacy of the human feelings. I saw how the fine form of man was degraded and wasted; I beheld the corruption of death succeed to the blooming cheek of life; I saw how the worm inherited the wonders of the eye and brain. I paused, examining and analysing all the minutiae of causation, as exemplified in the change from life to death, and death to life, until from the midst of this darkness a sudden light broke in upon me—a light so brilliant and wondrous, yet so simple, that while I became dizzy with the immensity of the prospect which it illustrated, I was surprised that among so many men of genius who had directed their inquiries towards the same science, that I alone should be reserved to discover so astonishing a secret.

Remember, I am not recording the vision of a madman. The sun does not more certainly shine in the heavens than that which I now affirm is true. Some miracle might have produced it, yet the stages of the discovery were distinct and probable. After days and nights of incredible labour and fatigue, I succeeded in discovering the cause of generation and life; nay, more, I became myself capable of bestowing animation upon lifeless matter.

The astonishment which I had at first experienced on this discovery soon gave place to delight and rapture. After so much time spent in painful labour, to arrive at once at the summit of my desires was the most gratifying consummation of my toils. But this discovery was so great and overwhelming that all the steps by which I had been progressively led to it were obliterated, and I beheld only the result. What had been the study and desire of the wisest men since the creation of the world was now within my grasp. Not that, like a magic scene, it all opened upon me at once: the information I had obtained was of a nature rather to direct my endeavours so soon as I should point them towards the object of my search than to exhibit that object already accomplished. I was like the Arabian who had been buried with the dead and found a passage to life, aided only by one glimmering and seemingly ineffectual light.

I see by your eagerness and the wonder and hope which your eyes express, my friend, that you expect to be informed of the secret with which I am acquainted; that cannot be; listen patiently until the end of my story, and you will easily perceive why I am reserved upon that subject. I will not lead you on, unguarded and ardent as I then was, to your destruction and infallible misery. Learn from me, if not by my precepts, at least by my example, how dangerous is the acquirement of knowledge and how much happier that man is who believes his native town to be the world, than he who aspires to become greater than his nature will allow.

When I found so astonishing a power placed within my hands, I hesitated a long time concerning the manner in which I should employ it. Although I possessed the capacity of bestowing animation, yet to prepare a frame for the reception of it, with all its intricacies of fibres, muscles, and veins, still remained a work of inconceivable difficulty and labour. I doubted at first whether I should attempt the creation of a being like myself, or one of simpler organization; but my imagination was too much exalted by my first success to permit me to doubt of my ability to give life to an animal as complex and wonderful as man. The materials at present within my command hardly appeared adequate to so arduous an undertaking, but I doubted not that I should ultimately succeed. I prepared myself for a multitude of reverses; my operations might be incessantly baffled, and at last my work be imperfect, yet when I considered the improvement which every day takes place in science and mechanics, I was encouraged to hope my present attempts would at least lay the foundations of future success. Nor could I consider the magnitude and complexity of my plan as any argument of its impracticability. It was with these feelings that I began the creation of a human being. As the minuteness of the parts formed a great hindrance to my speed, I resolved, contrary to my first intention, to make the being of a gigantic stature, that is to say, about eight feet in height, and proportionably large. After having formed this determination and having spent some months in successfully collecting and arranging my materials, I began.

No one can conceive the variety of feelings which bore me onwards, like a hurricane, in the first enthusiasm of success. Life and death appeared to me ideal bounds, which I should first break through, and pour a torrent of light into our dark world. A new species would bless me as its creator and source; many happy and excellent natures would owe their being to me. No father could claim the gratitude of his child so completely as I should deserve theirs. Pursuing these reflections, I thought that if I could bestow animation upon lifeless matter, I might in process of time (although I now found it impossible) renew life where death had apparently devoted the body to corruption.

These thoughts supported my spirits, while I pursued my undertaking with unremitting ardour. My cheek had grown pale with study, and my person had become emaciated with confinement. Sometimes, on the very brink of certainty, I failed; yet still I clung to the hope which the next day or the next hour might realise. One secret which I alone possessed was the hope to which I had dedicated myself; and the moon gazed on my midnight labours, while, with unrelaxed and breathless eagerness, I pursued nature to her hiding-places. Who shall conceive the horrors of my secret toil as I dabbled among the unhallowed damps of the grave or tortured the living animal to animate the lifeless clay? My limbs now tremble, and my eyes swim with the remembrance; but then a resistless and almost frantic impulse urged me forward; I seemed to have lost all soul or sensation but for this one pursuit. It was indeed but a passing trance, that only made me feel with renewed acuteness so soon as, the unnatural stimulus ceasing to operate, I had returned to my old habits. I collected bones from charnel-houses and disturbed, with profane fingers, the tremendous secrets of the human frame. In a solitary chamber, or rather cell, at the top of the house, and separated from all the other apartments by a gallery and staircase, I kept my workshop of filthy creation; my eyeballs were starting from their sockets in attending to the details of my employment. The dissecting room and the slaughter-house furnished many of my materials; and often did my human nature turn with loathing from my occupation, whilst, still urged on by an eagerness which perpetually increased, I brought my work near to a conclusion.

The summer months passed while I was thus engaged, heart and soul, in one pursuit. It was a most beautiful season; never did the fields bestow a more plentiful harvest or the vines yield a more luxuriant vintage, but my eyes were insensible to the charms of nature. And the same feelings which made me neglect the scenes around me caused me also to forget those friends who were so many miles absent, and whom I had not seen for so long a time. I knew my silence disquieted them, and I well remembered the words of my father: "I know that while you are pleased with yourself you will think of us with affection, and we shall hear regularly from you. You must pardon me if I regard any interruption in your correspondence as a proof that your other duties are equally neglected."

I knew well therefore what would be my father's feelings, but I could not tear my thoughts from my employment, loathsome in itself, but which had taken an irresistible hold of my imagination. I wished, as it were, to procrastinate all that related to my feelings of affection until the great object, which swallowed up every habit of my nature, should be completed.

I then thought that my father would be unjust if he ascribed my neglect to vice or faultiness on my part, but I am now convinced that he was justified in conceiving that I should not be altogether free from blame. A human being in perfection ought always to preserve a calm and peaceful mind and never to allow passion or a transitory desire to disturb his tranquillity. I do not think that the pursuit of knowledge is an exception to this rule. If the study to which you apply yourself has a tendency to weaken your affections and to destroy your taste for those simple pleasures in which no alloy can possibly mix, then that study is certainly unlawful, that is to say, not befitting the human mind. If this rule were always observed; if no man allowed any pursuit whatsoever to interfere with the tranquillity of his domestic affections, Greece had not been enslaved, Cæsar would have spared his country, America would have been discovered more gradually, and the empires of Mexico and Peru had not been destroyed.

But I forget that I am moralizing in the most interesting part of my tale, and your looks remind me to proceed.

My father made no reproach in his letters and only took notice of my silence by inquiring into my occupations more particularly than before. Winter, spring, and summer passed away during my labours; but I did not watch the blossom or the expanding leaves—sights which before always yielded me supreme delight—so deeply was I engrossed in my occupation. The leaves of that year had withered before my work drew near to a close, and now every day showed me more plainly how well I had succeeded. But my enthusiasm was checked by my anxiety, and I appeared rather like one doomed by slavery to toil in the mines, or any other unwholesome trade than an artist occupied by his favourite employment. Every night I was oppressed by a slow fever, and I became nervous to a most painful degree; the fall of a leaf startled me, and I shunned my fellow creatures as if I had been guilty of a crime. Sometimes I grew alarmed at the wreck I perceived that I had become; the energy of my purpose alone sustained me: my labours would soon end, and I believed that exercise and amusement would then drive away incipient disease; and I promised myself both of these when my creation should be complete.

CHAPTER V

It was on a dreary night of November that I beheld the accomplishment of my toils. With an anxiety that almost amounted to agony, I collected the instruments of life around me, that I might infuse a spark of being into the lifeless thing that lay at my feet. It was already one in the morning; the rain pattered dismally against the panes, and my candle was nearly burnt out, when, by the glimmer of the half-extinguished light, I saw the dull yellow eye of the creature open; it breathed hard, and a convulsive motion agitated its limbs.

How can I describe my emotions at this catastrophe, or how delineate the wretch whom with such infinite pains and care I had endeavoured to form? His limbs were in proportion, and I had selected his features as beautiful. Beautiful! Great God! His yellow skin scarcely covered the work of muscles and arteries beneath; his hair was of a lustrous black, and flowing; his teeth of a pearly whiteness; but these luxuriances only formed a more horrid contrast with his watery eyes, that seemed almost of the same colour as the dun-white sockets in which they were set, his shrivelled complexion and straight black lips.

The different accidents of life are not so changeable as the feelings of human nature. I had worked hard for nearly two years, for the sole purpose of infusing life into an inanimate body. For this I had deprived myself of rest and health. I had desired it with an ardour that far exceeded moderation; but now that I had finished, the beauty of the dream vanished, and breathless horror and disgust filled my heart. Unable to endure the aspect of the being I had created, I rushed out of the room and continued a long time traversing my bed-chamber, unable to compose my mind to sleep. At length lassitude succeeded to the tumult I had before endured, and I threw myself on the bed in my clothes, endeavouring to seek a few moments of forgetfulness. But it was in vain; I slept, indeed, but I was disturbed by the wildest dreams. I thought I saw Elizabeth, in the bloom of health, walking in the streets of Ingolstadt. Delighted and surprised, I embraced her, but as I imprinted the first kiss on her lips, they became livid with the hue of death; her features appeared to change, and I thought that I held the corpse of my dead mother in my arms; a shroud enveloped her form, and I saw the grave-worms crawling in the folds of the flannel. I started from my sleep with horror; a cold dew covered my forehead, my teeth chattered, and every limb became convulsed; when, by the dim and yellow light of the moon, as it forced its way through the window shutters, I beheld the wretch—the miserable monster whom I had created. He held up the curtain of the bed; and his eyes, if eyes they may be called, were fixed on me. His jaws opened, and he muttered some inarticulate sounds, while a grin wrinkled his cheeks. He might have spoken, but I did not hear; one hand was stretched out, seemingly to detain me, but I escaped and rushed downstairs. I took refuge in the courtyard belonging to the house which I inhabited, where I remained during the rest of the night, walking up and down in the greatest agitation, listening attentively, catching and fearing each sound as if it were to announce the approach of the demoniacal corpse to which I had so miserably given life.

Oh! No mortal could support the horror of that countenance. A mummy again endued with animation could not be so hideous as that wretch. I had gazed on him while unfinished; he was ugly then, but when those muscles and joints were rendered capable of motion, it became a thing such as even Dante could not have conceived.

I passed the night wretchedly. Sometimes my pulse beat so quickly and hardly that I felt the palpitation of every artery; at others, I nearly sank to the ground through languor and extreme weakness. Mingled with this horror, I felt the bitterness of disappointment; dreams that had been my food and pleasant rest for so long a space were now become a hell to me; and the change was so rapid, the overthrow so complete!

Morning, dismal and wet, at length dawned and discovered to my sleepless and aching eyes the church of Ingolstadt, its white steeple and clock, which indicated the sixth hour. The porter opened the gates of the court, which had that night been my asylum, and I issued into the streets, pacing them with quick steps, as if I sought to avoid the wretch whom I feared every turning of the street would present to my view. I did not dare return to the apartment which I inhabited, but felt impelled to hurry on, although drenched by the rain which poured from a black and comfortless sky.

I continued walking in this manner for some time, endeavouring by bodily exercise to ease the load that weighed upon my mind. I traversed the streets without any clear conception of where I was or what I was doing. My heart palpitated in the sickness of fear, and I hurried on with irregular steps, not daring to look about me:

Like one who, on a lonely road,
Doth walk in fear and dread,
And, having once turned round, walks on,
And turns no more his head;
Because he knows a frightful fiend
Doth close behind him tread.

—Coleridge's *"Ancient Mariner."*

Continuing thus, I came at length opposite to the inn at which the various diligences and carriages usually stopped. Here I paused, I knew not why; but I remained some minutes with my eyes fixed on a coach that was coming towards me from the other end of the street. As it drew nearer I observed that it was the Swiss diligence; it stopped just where I was standing, and on the door being opened, I perceived Henry Clerval, who, on seeing me, instantly sprung out. "My dear Frankenstein," exclaimed he, "how glad I am to see you! How fortunate that you should be here at the very moment of my alighting!"

Nothing could equal my delight on seeing Clerval; his presence brought back to my thoughts my father, Elizabeth, and all those scenes of home so dear to my recollection. I grasped his hand, and in a moment forgot my horror and misfortune; I felt suddenly, and for the first time during many months, calm and serene joy. I welcomed my friend, therefore, in the most cordial manner, and we walked towards my college. Clerval continued talking for some time about our mutual friends and his own good fortune in being permitted to come to Ingolstadt. "You may easily believe," said he, "how great was the difficulty to persuade my father that all necessary knowledge was not comprised in the noble art of book-keeping; and, indeed, I believe I left him incredulous to the last, for his constant answer to my unwearied entreaties was the same as that of the Dutch schoolmaster in The Vicar of Wakefield: 'I have ten thousand florins a year without Greek, I eat heartily without Greek.' But his affection for me at length overcame his dislike of learning, and he has permitted me to undertake a voyage of discovery to the land of knowledge."

"It gives me the greatest delight to see you; but tell me how you left my father, brothers, and Elizabeth."

"Very well, and very happy, only a little uneasy that they hear from you so seldom. By the by, I mean to lecture you a little upon their account myself. But, my dear Frankenstein," continued he, stopping short and gazing full in my face, "I did not before remark how very ill you appear;

so thin and pale; you look as if you had been watching for several nights."

"You have guessed right; I have lately been so deeply engaged in one occupation that I have not allowed myself sufficient rest, as you see; but I hope, I sincerely hope, that all these employments are now at an end and that I am at length free."

I trembled excessively; I could not endure to think of, and far less to allude to, the occurrences of the preceding night. I walked with a quick pace, and we soon arrived at my college. I then reflected, and the thought made me shiver, that the creature whom I had left in my apartment might still be there, alive and walking about. I dreaded to behold this monster, but I feared still more that Henry should see him. Entreating him, therefore, to remain a few minutes at the bottom of the stairs, I darted up towards my own room. My hand was already on the lock of the door before I recollected myself. I then paused, and a cold shivering came over me. I threw the door forcibly open, as children are accustomed to do when they expect a spectre to stand in waiting for them on the other side; but nothing appeared. I stepped fearfully in: the apartment was empty, and my bedroom was also freed from its hideous guest. I could hardly believe that so great a good fortune could have befallen me, but when I became assured that my enemy had indeed fled, I clapped my hands for joy and ran down to Clerval.

We ascended into my room, and the servant presently brought breakfast; but I was unable to contain myself. It was not joy only that possessed me; I felt my flesh tingle with excess of sensitiveness, and my pulse beat rapidly. I was unable to remain for a single instant in the same place; I jumped over the chairs, clapped my hands, and laughed aloud. Clerval at first attributed my unusual spirits to joy on his arrival, but when he observed me more attentively, he saw a wildness in my eyes for which he could not account, and my loud, unrestrained, heartless laughter frightened and astonished him.

"My dear Victor," cried he, "what, for God's sake, is the matter? Do not laugh in that manner. How ill you are! What is the cause of all this?"

"Do not ask me," cried I, putting my hands before my eyes, for I thought I saw the dreaded spectre glide into the room; "*he* can tell. Oh, save me! Save me!" I imagined that the monster seized me; I struggled furiously and fell down in a fit.

Poor Clerval! What must have been his feelings? A meeting, which he anticipated with such joy, so strangely turned to bitterness. But I was not the witness of his grief, for I was lifeless and did not recover my senses for a long, long time.

This was the commencement of a nervous fever which confined me for several months. During all that time Henry was my only nurse. I afterwards learned that, knowing my father's advanced age and unfitness for so long a journey, and how wretched my sickness would make Elizabeth, he spared them this grief by concealing the extent of my disorder. He knew that I could not have a more kind and attentive nurse than himself; and, firm in the hope he felt of my recovery, he did not doubt that, instead of doing harm, he performed the kindest action that he could towards them.

But I was in reality very ill, and surely nothing but the unbounded and unremitting attentions of my friend could have restored me to life. The form of the monster on whom I had bestowed existence was for ever before my eyes, and I raved incessantly concerning him. Doubtless my words surprised Henry; he at first believed them to be the wanderings of my disturbed imagination, but the pertinacity with which I continually recurred to the same subject persuaded him that my disorder indeed owed its origin to some uncommon and terrible event.

By very slow degrees, and with frequent relapses that alarmed and grieved my friend, I recovered. I remember the first time I became capable of observing outward objects with any kind of pleasure, I perceived that the fallen leaves had disappeared and that the young buds were shooting forth from the trees that shaded my window. It was a divine spring, and the season contributed greatly to my convalescence. I felt also sentiments of joy and affection revive in my bosom; my gloom disappeared, and in a short time I became as cheerful as before I was attacked by the fatal passion.

"Dearest Clerval," exclaimed I, "how kind, how very good you are to me. This whole winter, instead of being spent in study, as you promised yourself, has been consumed in my sick room. How shall I ever repay you? I feel the greatest remorse for the disappointment of which I have been the occasion, but you will forgive me."

"You will repay me entirely if you do not discompose yourself, but get well as fast as you can; and since you appear in such good spirits, I may speak to you on one subject, may I not?"

I trembled. One subject! What could it be? Could he allude to an object on whom I dared not even think?

"Compose yourself," said Clerval, who observed my change of colour, "I will not mention it if it agitates you; but your father and cousin would be very happy if they received a letter from you in your own handwriting. They hardly know how ill you have been and are uneasy at your long silence."

"Is that all, my dear Henry? How could you suppose that my first thought would not fly towards those dear, dear friends whom I love and who are so deserving of my love?"

"If this is your present temper, my friend, you will perhaps be glad to see

a letter that has been lying here some days for you; it is from your cousin,
I believe."

CHAPTER VI

Clerval then put the following letter into my hands. It was from my own Elizabeth:

"My dearest Cousin,

"You have been ill, very ill, and even the constant letters of dear kind Henry are not sufficient to reassure me on your account. You are forbidden to write—to hold a pen; yet one word from you, dear Victor, is necessary to calm our apprehensions. For a long time I have thought that each post would bring this line, and my persuasions have restrained my uncle from undertaking a journey to Ingolstadt. I have prevented his encountering the inconveniences and perhaps dangers of so long a journey, yet how often have I regretted not being able to perform it myself! I figure to myself that the task of attending on your sickbed has devolved on some mercenary old nurse, who could never guess your wishes nor minister to them with the care and affection of your poor cousin. Yet that is over now: Clerval writes that indeed you are getting better. I eagerly hope that you will confirm this intelligence soon in your own handwriting.

"Get well—and return to us. You will find a happy, cheerful home and friends who love you dearly. Your father's health is vigorous, and he asks but to see you, but to be assured that you are well; and not a care will ever cloud his benevolent countenance. How pleased you would be to remark the improvement of our Ernest! He is now sixteen and full of activity and spirit. He is desirous to be a true Swiss and to enter into foreign service, but we cannot part with him, at least until his elder brother returns to us. My uncle is not pleased with the idea of a military career in a distant country, but Ernest never had your powers of application. He looks upon study as an odious fetter; his time is spent in the open air, climbing the hills or rowing on the lake. I fear that he will become an idler unless we yield the point and permit him to enter on the profession which he has selected.

"Little alteration, except the growth of our dear children, has taken place since you left us. The blue lake and snow-clad mountains—they never change; and I think our placid home and our contented hearts are regulated by the same immutable laws. My trifling occupations take up my time and amuse me, and I am rewarded for any exertions by seeing none but happy, kind faces around me. Since you left us, but one change has taken place in our little household. Do you remember on what occasion Justine Moritz entered our family? Probably you do not; I will relate her history, therefore in a few words. Madame Moritz, her mother, was a widow with four children, of whom Justine was the third. This girl had always been the favourite of her father, but through a strange perversity, her mother could not endure her, and after the death of M. Moritz, treated her very ill. My aunt observed this, and when Justine was twelve years of age, prevailed on her mother to allow her to live at our house. The republican institutions of our country have produced simpler and happier manners than those which prevail in the great monarchies that surround it. Hence there is less distinction between the several classes of its inhabitants; and the lower orders, being neither so poor nor so despised, their manners are more refined and moral. A servant in Geneva does not mean the same thing as a servant in France and England. Justine, thus received in our family, learned the duties of a servant, a condition which, in our fortunate country, does not include the idea of ignorance and a sacrifice of the dignity of a human being.

"Justine, you may remember, was a great favourite of yours; and I recollect you once remarked that if you were in an ill humour, one glance from Justine could dissipate it, for the same reason that Ariosto gives concerning the beauty of Angelica—she looked so frank-hearted and happy. My aunt conceived a great attachment for her, by which she was induced to give her an education superior to that which she had at first intended. This benefit was fully repaid; Justine was the most grateful little creature in the world: I do not mean that she made any professions I never heard one pass her lips, but you could see by her eyes that she almost adored her protectress. Although her disposition was gay and in many respects inconsiderate, yet she paid the greatest attention to every gesture of my aunt. She thought her the model of all excellence and endeavoured to imitate her phraseology and manners, so that even now she often reminds me of her.

"When my dearest aunt died every one was too much occupied in their own grief to notice poor Justine, who had attended her during her illness with the most anxious affection. Poor Justine was very ill; but other trials were reserved for her.

"One by one, her brothers and sister died; and her mother, with the exception of her neglected daughter, was left childless. The conscience of the woman was troubled; she began to think that the deaths of her favourites was a judgement from heaven to chastise her partiality. She was a Roman

Catholic; and I believe her confessor confirmed the idea which she had conceived. Accordingly, a few months after your departure for Ingolstadt, Justine was called home by her repentant mother. Poor girl! She wept when she quitted our house; she was much altered since the death of my aunt; grief had given softness and a winning mildness to her manners, which had before been remarkable for vivacity. Nor was her residence at her mother's house of a nature to restore her gaiety. The poor woman was very vacillating in her repentance. She sometimes begged Justine to forgive her unkindness, but much oftener accused her of having caused the deaths of her brothers and sister. Perpetual fretting at length threw Madame Moritz into a decline, which at first increased her irritability, but she is now at peace for ever. She died on the first approach of cold weather, at the beginning of this last winter. Justine has just returned to us; and I assure you I love her tenderly. She is very clever and gentle, and extremely pretty; as I mentioned before, her mien and her expression continually remind me of my dear aunt.

"I must say also a few words to you, my dear cousin, of little darling William. I wish you could see him; he is very tall of his age, with sweet laughing blue eyes, dark eyelashes, and curling hair. When he smiles, two little dimples appear on each cheek, which are rosy with health. He has already had one or two little *wives*, but Louisa Biron is his favourite, a pretty little girl of five years of age.

"Now, dear Victor, I dare say you wish to be indulged in a little gossip concerning the good people of Geneva. The pretty Miss Mansfield has already received the congratulatory visits on her approaching marriage with a young Englishman, John Melbourne, Esq. Her ugly sister, Manon, married M. Duvillard, the rich banker, last autumn. Your favourite schoolfellow, Louis Manoir, has suffered several misfortunes since the departure of Clerval from Geneva. But he has already recovered his spirits, and is reported to be on the point of marrying a lively pretty Frenchwoman, Madame Tavernier. She is a widow, and much older than Manoir; but she is very much admired, and a favourite with everybody.

"I have written myself into better spirits, dear cousin; but my anxiety returns upon me as I conclude. Write, dearest Victor,—one line—one word will be a blessing to us. Ten thousand thanks to Henry for his kindness, his affection, and his many letters; we are sincerely grateful. Adieu! my cousin; take care of yourself; and, I entreat you, write!

"Elizabeth Lavenza.

"Geneva, March 18th, 17—."

"Dear, dear Elizabeth!" I exclaimed, when I had read her letter: "I will write instantly and relieve them from the anxiety they must feel." I wrote, and this exertion greatly fatigued me; but my convalescence had commenced, and proceeded regularly. In another fortnight I was able to leave my chamber.

One of my first duties on my recovery was to introduce Clerval to the several professors of the university. In doing this, I underwent a kind of rough usage, ill befitting the wounds that my mind had sustained. Ever since the fatal night, the end of my labours, and the beginning of my misfortunes, I had conceived a violent antipathy even to the name of natural philosophy. When I was otherwise quite restored to health, the sight of a chemical instrument would renew all the agony of my nervous symptoms. Henry saw this, and had removed all my apparatus from my view. He had also changed my apartment; for he perceived that I had acquired a dislike for the room which had previously been my laboratory. But these cares of Clerval were made of no avail when I visited the professors. M. Waldman inflicted torture when he praised, with kindness and warmth, the astonishing progress I had made in the sciences. He soon perceived that I disliked the subject; but not guessing the real cause, he attributed my feelings to modesty, and changed the subject from my improvement, to the science itself, with a desire, as I evidently saw, of drawing me out. What could I do? He meant to please, and he tormented me. I felt as if he had placed carefully, one by one, in my view those instruments which were to be afterwards used in putting me to a slow and cruel death. I writhed under his words, yet dared not exhibit the pain I felt. Clerval, whose eyes and feelings were always quick in discerning the sensations of others, declined the subject, alleging, in excuse, his total ignorance; and the conversation took a more general turn. I thanked my friend from my heart, but I did not speak. I saw plainly that he was surprised, but he never attempted to draw my secret from me; and although I loved him with a mixture of affection and reverence that knew no bounds, yet I could never persuade myself to confide in him that event which was so often present to my recollection, but which I feared the detail to another would only impress more deeply.

M. Krempe was not equally docile; and in my condition at that time, of almost insupportable sensitiveness, his harsh blunt encomiums gave me even more pain than the benevolent approbation of M. Waldman. "D—n the fellow!" cried he; "why, M. Clerval, I assure you he has outstript us all. Ay, stare if you please; but it is nevertheless true. A youngster who, but a few years ago, believed in Cornelius Agrippa as firmly as in the gospel, has now set himself at the head of the university; and if he is not soon pulled down, we shall all be out of countenance.—Ay, ay," continued he, observing my face expressive of suffering, "M. Frankenstein is modest; an excellent quality in a young man. Young men should be diffident of themselves, you know, M. Clerval: I was myself when young; but that wears out in a very short time."

M. Krempe had now commenced an eulogy on himself, which happily turned the conversation from a subject that was so annoying to me.

Clerval had never sympathised in my tastes for natural science; and his literary pursuits differed wholly from those which had occupied me. He came to the university with the design of making himself complete master of the oriental languages, and thus he should open a field for the plan of life he had marked out for himself. Resolved to pursue no inglorious career, he turned his eyes toward the East, as affording scope for his spirit of enterprise. The Persian, Arabic, and Sanskrit languages engaged his attention, and I was easily induced to enter on the same studies. Idleness had ever been irksome to me, and now that I wished to fly from reflection, and hated my former studies, I felt great relief in being the fellow-pupil with my friend, and found not only instruction but consolation in the works of the orientalists. I did not, like him, attempt a critical knowledge of their dialects, for I did not contemplate making any other use of them than temporary amusement. I read merely to understand their meaning, and they well repaid my labours. Their melancholy is soothing, and their joy elevating, to a degree I never experienced in studying the authors of any other country. When you read their writings, life appears to consist in a warm sun and a garden of roses,—in the smiles and frowns of a fair enemy, and the fire that consumes your own heart. How different from the manly and heroical poetry of Greece and Rome!

Summer passed away in these occupations, and my return to Geneva was fixed for the latter end of autumn; but being delayed by several accidents, winter and snow arrived, the roads were deemed impassable, and my journey was retarded until the ensuing spring. I felt this delay very bitterly; for I longed to see my native town and my beloved friends. My return had only been delayed so long, from an unwillingness to leave Clerval in a strange place, before he had become acquainted with any of its inhabitants. The winter, however, was spent cheerfully; and although the spring was uncommonly late, when it came its beauty compensated for its dilatoriness.

The month of May had already commenced, and I expected the letter daily which was to fix the date of my departure, when Henry proposed a pedestrian tour in the environs of Ingolstadt, that I might bid a personal farewell to the country I had so long inhabited. I acceded with pleasure to this proposition: I was fond of exercise, and Clerval had always been my favourite companion in the ramble of this nature that I had taken among the scenes of my native country.

We passed a fortnight in these perambulations: my health and spirits had long been restored, and they gained additional strength from the salubrious air I breathed, the natural incidents of our progress, and the conversation of my friend. Study had before secluded me from the intercourse of my fellow-creatures, and rendered me unsocial; but Clerval called forth the better feelings of my heart; he again taught me to love the aspect of nature, and the cheerful faces of children. Excellent friend! how sincerely you did love me, and endeavour to elevate my mind until it was on a level with your own. A selfish pursuit had cramped and narrowed me, until your gentleness and affection warmed and opened my senses; I became the same happy creature who, a few years ago, loved and beloved by all, had no sorrow or care. When happy, inanimate nature had the power of bestowing on me the most delightful sensations. A serene sky and verdant fields filled me with ecstasy. The present season was indeed divine; the flowers of spring bloomed in the hedges, while those of summer were already in bud. I was undisturbed by thoughts which during the preceding year had pressed upon me, notwithstanding my endeavours to throw them off, with an invincible burden.

Henry rejoiced in my gaiety, and sincerely sympathised in my feelings: he exerted himself to amuse me, while he expressed the sensations that filled his soul. The resources of his mind on this occasion were truly astonishing: his conversation was full of imagination; and very often, in imitation of the Persian and Arabic writers, he invented tales of wonderful fancy and passion. At other times he repeated my favourite poems, or drew me out into arguments, which he supported with great ingenuity.

We returned to our college on a Sunday afternoon: the peasants were dancing, and every one we met appeared gay and happy. My own spirits were high, and I bounded along with feelings of unbridled joy and hilarity.

CHAPTER VII

On my return, I found the following letter from my father:—

"MY DEAR VICTOR,

"You have probably waited impatiently for a letter to fix the date of your return to us; and I was at first tempted to write only a few lines, merely mentioning the day on which I should expect you. But that would be a cruel kindness, and I dare not do it. What would be your surprise, my son, when you expected a happy and glad welcome, to behold, on the contrary, tears and wretchedness? And how, Victor, can I relate our misfortune? Absence cannot have rendered you callous to our joys and griefs; and how shall I inflict pain on my long absent son? I wish to prepare you for the woeful news, but I know it is impossible; even now your eye skims over the page to seek the words which are to convey to you the horrible tidings.

"William is dead!—that sweet child, whose smiles delighted and warmed my heart, who was so gentle, yet so gay! Victor, he is murdered!

"I will not attempt to console you; but will simply relate the circumstances of the transaction.

"Last Thursday (May 7th), I, my niece, and your two brothers, went to walk in Plainpalais. The evening was warm and serene, and we prolonged our walk farther than usual. It was already dusk before we thought of returning; and then we discovered that William and Ernest, who had gone on before, were not to be found. We accordingly rested on a seat until they should return. Presently Ernest came, and enquired if we had seen his brother; he said, that he had been playing with him, that William had run away to hide himself, and that he vainly sought for him, and afterwards waited for a long time, but that he did not return.

"This account rather alarmed us, and we continued to search for him until night fell, when Elizabeth conjectured that he might have returned to the house. He was not there. We returned again, with torches; for I could not rest, when I thought that my sweet boy had lost himself, and was exposed to all the damps and dews of night; Elizabeth also suffered extreme anguish. About five in the morning I discovered my lovely boy, whom the night before I had seen blooming and active in health, stretched on the grass livid and motionless; the print of the murder's finger was on his neck.

"He was conveyed home, and the anguish that was visible in my countenance betrayed the secret to Elizabeth. She was very earnest to see the corpse. At first I attempted to prevent her but she persisted, and entering the room where it lay, hastily examined the neck of the victim, and clasping her hands exclaimed, 'O God! I have murdered my darling child!'

"She fainted, and was restored with extreme difficulty. When she again lived, it was only to weep and sigh. She told me, that that same evening William had teased her to let him wear a very valuable miniature that she possessed of your mother. This picture is gone, and was doubtless the temptation which urged the murderer to the deed. We have no trace of him at present, although our exertions to discover him are unremitted; but they will not restore my beloved William!

"Come, dearest Victor; you alone can console Elizabeth. She weeps continually, and accuses herself unjustly as the cause of his death; her words pierce my heart. We are all unhappy; but will not that be an additional motive for you, my son, to return and be our comforter? Your dear mother! Alas, Victor! I now say, Thank God she did not live to witness the cruel, miserable death of her youngest darling!

"Come, Victor; not brooding thoughts of vengeance against the assassin, but with feelings of peace and gentleness, that will heal, instead of festering, the wounds of our minds. Enter the house of mourning, my friend, but with kindness and affection for those who love you, and not with hatred for your enemies.

"Your affectionate and afflicted father,
"ALPHONSE FRANKENSTEIN.

"Geneva, May 12th, 17—."

Clerval, who had watched my countenance as I read this letter, was surprised to observe the despair that succeeded the joy I at first expressed on receiving new from my friends. I threw the letter on the table, and covered my face with my hands.

"My dear Frankenstein," exclaimed Henry, when he perceived me weep with bitterness, "are you always to be unhappy? My dear friend, what has happened?"

I motioned him to take up the letter, while I walked up and down the room in the extremest agitation. Tears also gushed from the eyes of Clerval, as he read the account of my misfortune.

"I can offer you no consolation, my friend," said he; "your disaster is irreparable. What do you intend to do?"

"To go instantly to Geneva: come with me, Henry, to order the horses."

During our walk, Clerval endeavoured to say a few words of consolation; he could only express his heartfelt sympathy. "Poor William!" said he, "dear lovely child, he now sleeps with his angel mother! Who that had seen him bright and joyous in his young beauty, but must weep over his untimely loss! To die so miserably; to feel the murderer's grasp! How much more a murdered that could destroy radiant innocence! Poor little fellow! one only consolation have we; his friends mourn and weep, but he is at rest. The pang is over, his sufferings are at an end for ever. A sod covers his gentle form, and he knows no pain. He can no longer be a subject for pity; we must reserve that for his miserable survivors."

Clerval spoke thus as we hurried through the streets; the words impressed themselves on my mind and I remembered them afterwards in solitude. But now, as soon as the horses arrived, I hurried into a cabriolet, and bade farewell to my friend.

My journey was very melancholy. At first I wished to hurry on, for I longed to console and sympathise with my loved and sorrowing friends; but when I drew near my native town, I slackened my progress. I could hardly sustain the multitude of feelings that crowded into my mind. I passed through scenes familiar to my youth, but which I had not seen for nearly six years. How altered every thing might be during that time! One sudden and desolating change had taken place; but a thousand little circumstances might have by degrees worked other alterations, which, although they were done more tranquilly, might not be the less decisive. Fear overcame me; I dared no advance, dreading a thousand nameless evils that made me tremble, although I was unable to define them.

I remained two days at Lausanne, in this painful state of mind. I contemplated the lake: the waters were placid; all around was calm; and the snowy mountains, "the palaces of nature," were not changed. By degrees the calm and heavenly scene restored me, and I continued my journey towards Geneva.

The road ran by the side of the lake, which became narrower as I approached my native town. I discovered more distinctly the black sides of Jura, and the bright summit of Mont Blanc. I wept like a child. "Dear mountains! my own beautiful lake! how do you welcome your wanderer? Your summits are clear; the sky and lake are blue and placid. Is this to prognosticate peace, or to mock at my unhappiness?"

I fear, my friend, that I shall render myself tedious by dwelling on these preliminary circumstances; but they were days of comparative happiness, and I think of them with pleasure. My country, my beloved country! who but a native can tell the delight I took in again beholding thy streams, thy mountains, and, more than all, thy lovely lake!

Yet, as I drew nearer home, grief and fear again overcame me. Night also closed around; and when I could hardly see the dark mountains, I felt still more gloomily. The picture appeared a vast and dim scene of evil, and I foresaw obscurely that I was destined to become the most wretched of human beings. Alas! I prophesied truly, and failed only in one single circumstance, that in all the misery I imagined and dreaded, I did not conceive the hundredth part of the anguish I was destined to endure.

It was completely dark when I arrived in the environs of Geneva; the gates of the town were already shut; and I was obliged to pass the night at Secheron, a village at the distance of half a league from the city. The sky was serene; and, as I was unable to rest, I resolved to visit the spot where my poor William had been murdered. As I could not pass through the town, I was obliged to cross the lake in a boat to arrive at Plainpalais. During this short voyage I saw the lightning playing on the summit of Mont Blanc in the most beautiful figures. The storm appeared to approach rapidly, and, on landing, I ascended a low hill, that I might observe its progress. It advanced; the heavens were clouded, and I soon felt the rain coming slowly in large drops, but its violence quickly increased.

I quitted my seat, and walked on, although the darkness and storm increased every minute, and the thunder burst with a terrific crash over my head. It was echoed from Salêve, the Juras, and the Alps of Savoy; vivid flashes of lightning dazzled my eyes, illuminating the lake, making it appear like a vast sheet of fire; then for an instant every thing seemed of a pitchy darkness, until the eye recovered itself from the preceding flash. The storm, as is often the case in Switzerland, appeared at once in various parts of the heavens. The most violent storm hung exactly north of the town, over the part of the lake which lies between the promontory of Belrive and the village of Copêt. Another storm enlightened Jura with faint flashes; and another darkened and sometimes disclosed the Môle, a peaked mountain to the east of the lake.

While I watched the tempest, so beautiful yet terrific, I wandered on with a hasty step. This noble war in the sky elevated my spirits; I clasped my hands, and exclaimed aloud, "William, dear angel! this is thy funeral, this thy dirge!" As I said these words, I perceived in the gloom a figure which stole from behind a clump of trees near me; I stood fixed, gazing intently: I could not be mistaken. A flash of lightning illuminated the object, and discovered its shape plainly to me; its gigantic stature, and the deformity of its aspect more hideous than belongs to humanity, instantly informed me that it was the wretch, the filthy dæmon, to whom I had given life. What did he there? Could he be (I shuddered at the conception) the murderer of my brother? No sooner did that idea cross my imagination, than I became convinced of its truth; my teeth chattered, and I was forced to lean against a tree for support. The figure passed me quickly, and I lost it in the gloom. Nothing in human shape could have destroyed the fair child. *He* was the murderer! I could not doubt it. The mere presence of the idea was an irresistible proof of the fact. I thought of pursuing the devil; but it would have been in vain, for another flash discovered him to me hanging among the rocks of the nearly perpendicular ascent of Mont Salêve, a hill that bounds Plainpalais on the south. He soon reached the summit, and disappeared.

I remained motionless. The thunder ceased; but the rain still continued, and the scene was enveloped in an impenetrable darkness. I revolved in my mind the events which I had until now sought to forget: the whole train of my progress toward the creation; the appearance of the works of my own hands at my bedside; its departure. Two years had now nearly elapsed since the night on which he first received life; and was this his first crime? Alas! I had turned loose into the world a depraved wretch, whose delight was in carnage and misery; had he not murdered my brother?

No one can conceive the anguish I suffered during the remainder of the night, which I spent, cold and wet, in the open air. But I did not feel the inconvenience of the weather; my imagination was busy in scenes of evil and despair. I considered the being whom I had cast among mankind, and endowed with the will and power to effect purposes of horror, such as the deed which he had now done, nearly in the light of my own vampire, my own spirit let loose from the grave, and forced to destroy all that was dear to me.

Day dawned; and I directed my steps towards the town. The gates were open, and I hastened to my father's house. My first thought was to discover what I knew of the murderer, and cause instant pursuit to be made. But I paused when I reflected on the story that I had to tell. A being whom I myself had formed, and endued with life, had met me at midnight among the precipices of an inaccessible mountain. I remembered also the nervous fever with which I had been seized just at the time that I dated my creation, and which would give an air of delirium to a tale otherwise so utterly improbable. I well knew that if any other had communicated such a relation to me, I should have looked upon it as the ravings of insanity. Besides, the strange nature of the animal would elude all pursuit, even if I were so far credited as to persuade my relatives to commence it. And then of what use would be pursuit? Who could arrest a creature capable of scaling the overhanging sides of Mont Salêve? These reflections determined me, and I resolved to remain silent.

It was about five in the morning when I entered my father's house. I told the servants not to disturb the family, and went into the library to attend their usual hour of rising.

Six years had elapsed, passed in a dream but for one indelible trace, and I stood in the same place where I had last embraced my father before my departure for Ingolstadt. Beloved and venerable parent! He still remained to me. I gazed on the picture of my mother, which stood over the mantel-piece. It was an historical subject, painted at my father's desire, and represented Caroline Beaufort in an agony of despair, kneeling by the coffin of her dead father. Her garb was rustic, and her cheek pale; but there was an air of dignity and beauty, that hardly permitted the sentiment of pity. Below this picture was a miniature of William; and my tears flowed when I looked upon it. While I was thus engaged, Ernest entered: he had heard me arrive, and hastened to welcome me: "Welcome, my dearest Victor," said he. "Ah! I wish you had come three months ago, and then you would have found us all joyous and delighted. You come to us now to share a misery which nothing can alleviate; yet your presence will, I hope, revive our father, who seems sinking under his misfortune; and your persuasions will induce poor Elizabeth to cease her vain and tormenting self-accusations.—Poor William! he was our darling and our pride!"

Tears, unrestrained, fell from my brother's eyes; a sense of mortal agony crept over my frame. Before, I had only imagined the wretchedness of my desolated home; the reality came on me as a new, and a not less terrible, disaster. I tried to calm Ernest; I enquired more minutely concerning my father, and here I named my cousin.

"She most of all," said Ernest, "requires consolation; she accused herself of having caused the death of my brother, and that made her very wretched. But since the murderer has been discovered—"

"The murderer discovered! Good God! how can that be? who could attempt to pursue him? It is impossible; one might as well try to overtake the winds, or confine a mountain-stream with a straw. I saw him too; he was free last night!"

"I do not know what you mean," replied my brother, in accents of wonder, "but to us the discovery we have made completes our misery. No one would believe it at first; and even now Elizabeth will not be convinced, notwithstanding all the evidence. Indeed, who would credit that Justine Moritz, who was so amiable, and fond of all the family, could suddenly become so capable of so frightful, so appalling a crime?"

"Justine Moritz! Poor, poor girl, is she the accused? But it is wrongfully; every one knows that; no one believes it, surely, Ernest?"

"No one did at first; but several circumstances came out, that have almost forced conviction upon us; and her own behaviour has been so confused, as to add to the evidence of facts a weight that, I fear, leaves no hope for doubt. But she will be tried today, and you will then hear all."

He then related that, the morning on which the murder of poor William had been discovered, Justine had been taken ill, and confined to her bed for several days. During this interval, one of the servants, happening to examine the apparel she had worn on the night of the murder, had discovered in her pocket the picture of my mother, which had been judged to be the temptation of the murderer. The servant instantly showed it to one of the others, who, without saying a word to any of the family, went to a magistrate; and, upon their deposition, Justine was apprehended. On being charged with the fact, the poor girl confirmed the suspicion in a great measure by her extreme confusion of manner.

This was a strange tale, but it did not shake my faith; and I replied earnestly, "You are all mistaken; I know the murderer. Justine, poor, good Justine, is innocent."

At that instant my father entered. I saw unhappiness deeply impressed on his countenance, but he endeavoured to welcome me cheerfully; and, after we had exchanged our mournful greeting, would have introduced some other topic than that of our disaster, had not Ernest exclaimed, "Good God, papa! Victor says that he knows who was the murderer of poor William."

"We do also, unfortunately," replied my father, "for indeed I had rather have been for ever ignorant than have discovered so much depravity and ungratitude in one I valued so highly."

"My dear father, you are mistaken; Justine is innocent."

"If she is, God forbid that she should suffer as guilty. She is to be tried today, and I hope, I sincerely hope, that she will be acquitted."

This speech calmed me. I was firmly convinced in my own mind that Justine, and indeed every human being, was guiltless of this murder. I had no fear, therefore, that any circumstantial evidence could be brought forward strong enough to convict her. My tale was not one to announce publicly; its astounding horror would be looked upon as madness by the vulgar. Did any one indeed exist, except I, the creator, who would believe, unless his senses convinced him, in the existence of the living monument of presumption and rash ignorance which I had let loose upon the world?

We were soon joined by Elizabeth. Time had altered her since I last beheld her; it had endowed her with loveliness surpassing the beauty of her childish years. There was the same candour, the same vivacity, but it was allied to an expression more full of sensibility and intellect. She welcomed me with the greatest affection. "Your arrival, my dear cousin," said she, "fills me with hope. You perhaps will find some means to justify my poor guiltless Justine. Alas! who is safe, if she be convicted of crime? I rely on her innocence as certainly as I do upon my own. Our misfortune is doubly hard to us; we have not only lost that lovely darling boy, but this poor girl, whom I sincerely love, is to be torn away by even a worse fate. If she is condemned, I never shall know joy more. But she will not, I am sure she will not; and then I shall be happy again, even after the sad death of my little William."

"She is innocent, my Elizabeth," said I, "and that shall be proved; fear nothing, but let your spirits be cheered by the assurance of her acquittal."

"How kind and generous you are! every one else believes in her guilt, and that made me wretched, for I knew that it was impossible: and to see every one else prejudiced in so deadly a manner rendered me hopeless and despairing." She wept.

"Dearest niece," said my father, "dry your tears. If she is, as you believe, innocent, rely on the justice of our laws, and the activity with which I shall prevent the slightest shadow of partiality."

CHAPTER VIII

We passed a few sad hours until eleven o'clock, when the trial was to commence. My father and the rest of the family being obliged to attend as witnesses, I accompanied them to the court. During the whole of this wretched mockery of justice I suffered living torture. It was to be decided whether the result of my curiosity and lawless devices would cause the death of two of my fellow beings: one a smiling babe full of innocence and joy, the other far more dreadfully murdered, with every aggravation of infamy that could make the murder memorable in horror. Justine also was a girl of merit and possessed qualities which promised to render her life happy; now all was to be obliterated in an ignominious grave, and I the cause! A thousand times rather would I have confessed myself guilty of the crime ascribed to Justine, but I was absent when it was committed, and such a declaration would have been considered as the ravings of a madman and would not have exculpated her who suffered through me.

The appearance of Justine was calm. She was dressed in mourning, and her countenance, always engaging, was rendered, by the solemnity of her feelings, exquisitely beautiful. Yet she appeared confident in innocence and did not tremble, although gazed on and execrated by thousands, for all the kindness which her beauty might otherwise have excited was obliterated in the minds of the spectators by the imagination of the enormity she was supposed to have committed. She was tranquil, yet her tranquillity was evidently constrained; and as her confusion had before been adduced as a proof of her guilt, she worked up her mind to an appearance of courage. When she entered the court she threw her eyes round it and quickly discovered where we were seated. A tear seemed to dim her eye when she saw us, but she quickly recovered herself, and a look of sorrowful affection seemed to attest her utter guiltlessness.

The trial began, and after the advocate against her had stated the charge, several witnesses were called. Several strange facts combined against her, which might have staggered anyone who had not such proof of her innocence as I had. She had been out the whole of the night on which the murder had been committed and towards morning had been perceived by a market-woman not far from the spot where the body of the murdered child had been afterwards found. The woman asked her what she did there, but she looked very strangely and only returned a confused and unintelligible answer. She returned to the house about eight o'clock, and when one inquired where she had passed the night, she replied that she had been looking for the child and demanded earnestly if anything had been heard concerning him. When shown the body, she fell into violent hysterics and kept her bed for several days. The picture was then produced which the servant had found in her pocket; and when Elizabeth, in a faltering voice, proved that it was the same which, an hour before the child had been missed, she had placed round his neck, a murmur of horror and indignation filled the court.

Justine was called on for her defence. As the trial had proceeded, her countenance had altered. Surprise, horror, and misery were strongly expressed. Sometimes she struggled with her tears, but when she was desired to plead, she collected her powers and spoke in an audible although variable voice.

"God knows," she said, "how entirely I am innocent. But I do not pretend that my protestations should acquit me; I rest my innocence on a plain and simple explanation of the facts which have been adduced against me, and I hope the character I have always borne will incline my judges to a favourable interpretation where any circumstance appears doubtful or suspicious."

She then related that, by the permission of Elizabeth, she had passed the evening of the night on which the murder had been committed at the house of an aunt at Chêne, a village situated at about a league from Geneva. On her return, at about nine o'clock, she met a man who asked her if she had seen anything of the child who was lost. She was alarmed by this account and passed several hours in looking for him, when the gates of Geneva were shut, and she was forced to remain several hours of the night in a barn belonging to a cottage, being unwilling to call up the inhabitants, to whom she was well known. Most of the night she spent here watching; towards morning she believed that she slept for a few minutes; some steps disturbed her, and she awoke. It was dawn, and she quitted her asylum, that she might again endeavour to find my brother. If she had gone near the spot where his body lay, it was without her knowledge. That she had been bewildered when questioned by the market-woman was not surprising, since she had passed a sleepless night and the fate of poor William was yet uncertain. Concerning the picture she could give no account.

"I know," continued the unhappy victim, "how heavily and fatally this one circumstance weighs against me, but I have no power of explaining it; and when I have expressed my utter ignorance, I am only left to conjecture concerning the probabilities by which it might have been placed in my pocket. But here also I am checked. I believe that I have no enemy on earth, and none surely would have been so wicked as to destroy me wantonly. Did the murderer place it there? I know of no opportunity afforded him for so doing; or, if I had, why should he have stolen the jewel, to part with it again so soon?

"I commit my cause to the justice of my judges, yet I see no room for hope. I beg permission to have a few witnesses examined concerning my character, and if their testimony shall not overweigh my supposed guilt, I must be condemned, although I would pledge my salvation on my innocence."

Several witnesses were called who had known her for many years, and they spoke well of her; but fear and hatred of the crime of which they supposed her guilty rendered them timorous and unwilling to come forward. Elizabeth saw even this last resource, her excellent dispositions and irreproachable conduct, about to fail the accused, when, although violently agitated, she desired permission to address the court.

"I am," said she, "the cousin of the unhappy child who was murdered, or rather his sister, for I was educated by and have lived with his parents ever since and even long before his birth. It may therefore be judged indecent in me to come forward on this occasion, but when I see a fellow creature about to perish through the cowardice of her pretended friends, I wish to be allowed to speak, that I may say what I know of her character. I am well acquainted with the accused. I have lived in the same house with her, at one time for five and at another for nearly two years. During all that period she appeared to me the most amiable and benevolent of human creatures. She nursed Madame Frankenstein, my aunt, in her last illness, with the greatest affection and care and afterwards attended her own mother during a tedious illness, in a manner that excited the admiration of all who knew her, after which she again lived in my uncle's house, where she was beloved by all the family. She was warmly attached to the child who is now dead and acted towards him like a most affectionate mother. For my own part, I do not hesitate to say that, notwithstanding all the evidence produced against her, I believe and rely on her perfect innocence. She had no temptation for such an action; as to the bauble on which the chief proof rests, if she had earnestly desired it, I should have willingly given it to her, so much do I esteem and value her."

A murmur of approbation followed Elizabeth's simple and powerful appeal, but it was excited by her generous interference, and not in favour of poor Justine, on whom the public indignation was turned with renewed violence, charging her with the blackest ingratitude. She herself wept as Elizabeth spoke, but she did not answer. My own agitation and anguish was extreme during the whole trial. I believed in her innocence; I knew it. Could the dæmon who had (I did not for a minute doubt) murdered my brother also in his hellish sport have betrayed the innocent to death and ignominy? I could not sustain the horror of my situation, and when I perceived that the popular voice and the countenances of the judges had already condemned my unhappy victim, I rushed out of the court in agony. The tortures of the accused did not equal mine; she was sustained by innocence, but the fangs of remorse tore my bosom and would not forgo their hold.

I passed a night of unmingled wretchedness. In the morning I went to the court; my lips and throat were parched. I dared not ask the fatal question, but I was known, and the officer guessed the cause of my visit. The ballots had been thrown; they were all black, and Justine was condemned.

I cannot pretend to describe what I then felt. I had before experienced sensations of horror, and I have endeavoured to bestow upon them adequate expressions, but words cannot convey an idea of the heart-sickening despair that I then endured. The person to whom I addressed myself added that Justine had already confessed her guilt. "That evidence," he observed, "was hardly required in so glaring a case, but I am glad of it, and, indeed, none of our judges like to condemn a criminal upon circumstantial evidence, be it ever so decisive."

This was strange and unexpected intelligence; what could it mean? Had my eyes deceived me? And was I really as mad as the whole world would believe me to be if I disclosed the object of my suspicions? I hastened to return home, and Elizabeth eagerly demanded the result.

"My cousin," replied I, "it is decided as you may have expected; all judges had rather that ten innocent should suffer than that one guilty should escape. But she has confessed."

This was a dire blow to poor Elizabeth, who had relied with firmness upon Justine's innocence. "Alas!" said she. "How shall I ever again believe in human goodness? Justine, whom I loved and esteemed as my sister, how could she put on those smiles of innocence only to betray? Her mild eyes seemed incapable of any severity or guile, and yet she has committed a murder."

Soon after we heard that the poor victim had expressed a desire to see my cousin. My father wished her not to go but said that he left it to her own judgment and feelings to decide. "Yes," said Elizabeth, "I will go, although she is guilty; and you, Victor, shall accompany me; I cannot go alone." The idea of this visit was torture to me, yet I could not refuse.

We entered the gloomy prison chamber and beheld Justine sitting on some straw at the farther end; her hands were manacled, and her head rested on her knees. She rose on seeing us enter, and when we were left alone with her, she threw herself at the feet of Elizabeth, weeping bitterly. My cousin wept also.

"Oh, Justine!" said she. "Why did you rob me of my last consolation? I relied on your innocence, and although I was then very wretched, I was not so miserable as I am now."

"And do you also believe that I am so very, very wicked? Do you also join with my enemies to crush me, to condemn me as a murderer?" Her voice was suffocated with sobs.

"Rise, my poor girl," said Elizabeth; "why do you kneel, if you are innocent? I am not one of your enemies, I believed you guiltless, notwithstanding every evidence, until I heard that you had yourself declared your guilt. That report, you say, is false; and be assured, dear Justine, that nothing can shake my confidence in you for a moment, but your own confession."

"I did confess, but I confessed a lie. I confessed, that I might obtain absolution; but now that falsehood lies heavier at my heart than all my other sins. The God of heaven forgive me! Ever since I was condemned, my confessor has besieged me; he threatened and menaced, until I almost began to think that I was the monster that he said I was. He threatened excommunication and hell fire in my last moments if I continued obdurate. Dear lady, I had none to support me; all looked on me as a wretch doomed to ignominy and perdition. What could I do? In an evil hour I subscribed to a lie; and now only am I truly miserable."

She paused, weeping, and then continued, "I thought with horror, my sweet lady, that you should believe your Justine, whom your blessed aunt had so highly honoured, and whom you loved, was a creature capable of a crime which none but the devil himself could have perpetrated. Dear William! dearest blessed child! I soon shall see you again in heaven, where we shall all be happy; and that consoles me, going as I am to suffer ignominy and death."

"Oh, Justine! Forgive me for having for one moment distrusted you. Why did you confess? But do not mourn, dear girl. Do not fear. I will proclaim, I will prove your innocence. I will melt the stony hearts of your enemies by my tears and prayers. You shall not die! You, my playfellow, my companion, my sister, perish on the scaffold! No! No! I never could survive so horrible a misfortune."

Justine shook her head mournfully. "I do not fear to die," she said; "that pang is past. God raises my weakness and gives me courage to endure the worst. I leave a sad and bitter world; and if you remember me and think of me as of one unjustly condemned, I am resigned to the fate awaiting me.

Learn from me, dear lady, to submit in patience to the will of heaven!"

During this conversation I had retired to a corner of the prison room, where I could conceal the horrid anguish that possessed me. Despair! Who dared talk of that? The poor victim, who on the morrow was to pass the awful boundary between life and death, felt not, as I did, such deep and bitter agony. I gnashed my teeth and ground them together, uttering a groan that came from my inmost soul. Justine started. When she saw who it was, she approached me and said, "Dear sir, you are very kind to visit me; you, I hope, do not believe that I am guilty?"

I could not answer. "No, Justine," said Elizabeth; "he is more convinced of your innocence than I was, for even when he heard that you had confessed, he did not credit it."

"I truly thank him. In these last moments I feel the sincerest gratitude towards those who think of me with kindness. How sweet is the affection of others to such a wretch as I am! It removes more than half my misfortune, and I feel as if I could die in peace now that my innocence is acknowledged by you, dear lady, and your cousin."

Thus the poor sufferer tried to comfort others and herself. She indeed gained the resignation she desired. But I, the true murderer, felt the never-dying worm alive in my bosom, which allowed of no hope or consolation. Elizabeth also wept and was unhappy, but hers also was the misery of innocence, which, like a cloud that passes over the fair moon, for a while hides but cannot tarnish its brightness. Anguish and despair had penetrated into the core of my heart; I bore a hell within me which nothing could extinguish. We stayed several hours with Justine, and it was with great difficulty that Elizabeth could tear herself away. "I wish," cried she, "that I were to die with you; I cannot live in this world of misery."

Justine assumed an air of cheerfulness, while she with difficulty repressed her bitter tears. She embraced Elizabeth and said in a voice of half-suppressed emotion, "Farewell, sweet lady, dearest Elizabeth, my beloved and only friend; may heaven, in its bounty, bless and preserve you; may this be the last misfortune that you will ever suffer! Live, and be happy, and make others so."

And on the morrow Justine died. Elizabeth's heart-rending eloquence failed to move the judges from their settled conviction in the criminality of the saintly sufferer. My passionate and indignant appeals were lost upon them. And when I received their cold answers and heard the harsh, unfeeling reasoning of these men, my purposed avowal died away on my lips. Thus I might proclaim myself a madman, but not revoke the sentence passed upon my wretched victim. She perished on the scaffold as a murderess!

From the tortures of my own heart, I turned to contemplate the deep and voiceless grief of my Elizabeth. This also was my doing! And my father's woe, and the desolation of that late so smiling home all was the work of my thrice-accursed hands! Ye weep, unhappy ones, but these are not your last tears! Again shall you raise the funeral wail, and the sound of your lamentations shall again and again be heard! Frankenstein, your son, your kinsman, your early, much-loved friend; he who would spend each vital drop of blood for your sakes, who has no thought nor sense of joy except as it is mirrored also in your dear countenances, who would fill the air with blessings and spend his life in serving you—he bids you weep, to shed countless tears; happy beyond his hopes, if thus inexorable fate be satisfied, and if the destruction pause before the peace of the grave have succeeded to your sad torments!

Thus spoke my prophetic soul, as, torn by remorse, horror, and despair, I beheld those I loved spend vain sorrow upon the graves of William and Justine, the first hapless victims to my unhallowed arts.

CHAPTER IX

Nothing is more painful to the human mind than, after the feelings have been worked up by a quick succession of events, the dead calmness of inaction and certainty which follows and deprives the soul both of hope and fear. Justine died, she rested, and I was alive. The blood flowed freely in my veins, but a weight of despair and remorse pressed on my heart which nothing could remove. Sleep fled from my eyes; I wandered like an evil spirit, for I had committed deeds of mischief beyond description horrible, and more, much more (I persuaded myself) was yet behind. Yet my heart overflowed with kindness and the love of virtue. I had begun life with benevolent intentions and thirsted for the moment when I should put them in practice and make myself useful to my fellow beings. Now all was blasted; instead of that serenity of conscience which allowed me to look back upon the past with self-satisfaction, and from thence to gather promise of new hopes, I was seized by remorse and the sense of guilt, which hurried me away to a hell of intense tortures such as no language can describe.

This state of mind preyed upon my health, which had perhaps never entirely recovered from the first shock it had sustained. I shunned the face of man; all sound of joy or complacency was torture to me; solitude was my only consolation—deep, dark, deathlike solitude.

My father observed with pain the alteration perceptible in my disposition and habits and endeavoured by arguments deduced from the feelings of his serene conscience and guiltless life to inspire me with fortitude and awaken in me the courage to dispel the dark cloud which brooded over me. "Do you think, Victor," said he, "that I do not suffer also? No one could love a child more than I loved your brother"—tears came into his eyes as he spoke—"but is it not a duty to the survivors that we should refrain from augmenting their unhappiness by an appearance of immoderate grief? It is also a duty owed to yourself, for excessive sorrow prevents improvement or enjoyment, or even the discharge of daily usefulness, without which no man is fit for society."

This advice, although good, was totally inapplicable to my case; I should have been the first to hide my grief and console my friends if remorse had not mingled its bitterness, and terror its alarm, with my other sensations. Now I could only answer my father with a look of despair and endeavour to hide myself from his view.

About this time we retired to our house at Belrive. This change was particularly agreeable to me. The shutting of the gates regularly at ten o'clock and the impossibility of remaining on the lake after that hour had rendered our residence within the walls of Geneva very irksome to me. I was now free. Often, after the rest of the family had retired for the night, I took the boat and passed many hours upon the water. Sometimes, with my sails set, I was carried by the wind; and sometimes, after rowing into the middle of the lake, I left the boat to pursue its own course and gave way to my own miserable reflections. I was often tempted, when all was at peace around me, and I the only unquiet thing that wandered restless in a scene so beautiful and heavenly—if I except some bat, or the frogs, whose harsh and interrupted croaking was heard only when I approached the shore—often, I say, I was tempted to plunge into the silent lake, that the waters might close over me and my calamities for ever. But I was restrained, when I thought of the heroic and suffering Elizabeth, whom I tenderly loved, and whose existence was bound up in mine. I thought also of my father and surviving brother; should I by my base desertion leave them exposed and unprotected to the malice of the fiend whom I had let loose among them?

At these moments I wept bitterly and wished that peace would revisit my mind only that I might afford them consolation and happiness. But that could not be. Remorse extinguished every hope. I had been the author of unalterable evils, and I lived in daily fear lest the monster whom I had created should perpetrate some new wickedness. I had an obscure feeling that all was not over and that he would still commit some signal crime, which by its enormity should almost efface the recollection of the past. There was always scope for fear so long as anything I loved remained behind. My abhorrence of this fiend cannot be conceived. When I thought of him I gnashed my teeth, my eyes became inflamed, and I ardently wished to extinguish that life which I had so thoughtlessly bestowed. When I reflected on his crimes and malice, my hatred and revenge burst all bounds of moderation. I would have made a pilgrimage to the highest peak of the Andes, could I, when there, have precipitated him to their base. I wished to see him again, that I might wreak the utmost extent of abhorrence on his head and avenge the deaths of William and Justine.

Our house was the house of mourning. My father's health was deeply shaken by the horror of the recent events. Elizabeth was sad and desponding; she no longer took delight in her ordinary occupations; all pleasure seemed to her sacrilege toward the dead; eternal woe and tears she then thought was the just tribute she should pay to innocence so blasted and destroyed. She was no longer that happy creature who in earlier youth wandered with me on the banks of the lake and talked with ecstasy of our future prospects. The first of those sorrows which are sent to wean us from the earth had visited her, and its dimming influence quenched her dearest smiles.

"When I reflect, my dear cousin," said she, "on the miserable death of Justine Moritz, I no longer see the world and its works as they before appeared to me. Before, I looked upon the accounts of vice and injustice that I read in books or heard from others as tales of ancient days or imaginary evils; at least they were remote and more familiar to reason than to the imagination; but now misery has come home, and men appear to me as monsters thirsting for each other's blood. Yet I am certainly unjust. Everybody believed that poor girl to be guilty; and if she could have committed the crime for which she suffered, assuredly she would have been the most depraved of human creatures. For the sake of a few jewels, to have murdered the son of her benefactor and friend, a child whom she had nursed from its birth, and appeared to love as if it had been her own! I could not consent to the death of any human being, but certainly I should have thought such a creature unfit to remain in the society of men. But she was innocent. I know, I feel she was innocent; you are of the same opinion, and that confirms me. Alas! Victor, when falsehood can look so like the truth, who can assure themselves of certain happiness? I feel as if I were walking on the edge of a precipice, towards which thousands are crowding and endeavouring to plunge me into the abyss. William and Justine were assassinated, and the murderer escapes; he walks about the world free, and perhaps respected. But even if I were condemned to suffer on the scaffold for the same crimes, I would not change places with such a wretch."

I listened to this discourse with the extremest agony. I, not in deed, but in effect, was the true murderer. Elizabeth read my anguish in my countenance, and kindly taking my hand, said, "My dearest friend, you must calm yourself. These events have affected me, God knows how deeply; but I am not so wretched as you are. There is an expression of despair, and sometimes of revenge, in your countenance that makes me tremble. Dear Victor, banish these dark passions. Remember the friends around you, who centre all their hopes in you. Have we lost the power of rendering you happy? Ah! While we love, while we are true to each other, here in this land of peace and beauty, your native country, we may reap every tranquil blessing—what can disturb our peace?"

And could not such words from her whom I fondly prized before every other gift of fortune suffice to chase away the fiend that lurked in my heart? Even as she spoke I drew near to her, as if in terror, lest at that very moment the destroyer had been near to rob me of her.

Thus not the tenderness of friendship, nor the beauty of earth, nor of heaven, could redeem my soul from woe; the very accents of love were ineffectual. I was encompassed by a cloud which no beneficial influence could penetrate. The wounded deer dragging its fainting limbs to some untrodden brake, there to gaze upon the arrow which had pierced it, and to die, was but a type of me.

Sometimes I could cope with the sullen despair that overwhelmed me, but sometimes the whirlwind passions of my soul drove me to seek, by bodily exercise and by change of place, some relief from my intolerable sensations. It was during an access of this kind that I suddenly left my home, and bending my steps towards the near Alpine valleys, sought in the magnificence, the eternity of such scenes, to forget myself and my ephemeral, because human, sorrows. My wanderings were directed towards the valley of Chamounix. I had visited it frequently during my boyhood. Six years had passed since then: *I* was a wreck, but nought had changed in those savage and enduring scenes.

I performed the first part of my journey on horseback. I afterwards hired a mule, as the more sure-footed and least liable to receive injury on these rugged roads. The weather was fine; it was about the middle of the month of August, nearly two months after the death of Justine, that miserable epoch from which I dated all my woe. The weight upon my spirit was sensibly lightened as I plunged yet deeper in the ravine of Arve. The immense mountains and precipices that overhung me on every side, the sound of the river raging among the rocks, and the dashing of the waterfalls around spoke of a power mighty as Omnipotence—and I ceased to fear or to bend before any being less almighty than that which had created and ruled the elements, here displayed in their most terrific guise. Still, as I ascended higher, the valley assumed a more magnificent and astonishing character. Ruined castles hanging on the precipices of piny mountains, the impetuous Arve, and cottages every here and there peeping forth from among the trees formed a scene of singular beauty. But it was augmented and rendered sublime by the mighty Alps, whose white and shining pyramids and domes towered above all, as belonging to another earth, the habitations of another race of beings.

I passed the bridge of Pélissier, where the ravine, which the river forms, opened before me, and I began to ascend the mountain that overhangs it. Soon after, I entered the valley of Chamounix. This valley is more wonderful and sublime, but not so beautiful and picturesque as that of Servox, through which I had just passed. The high and snowy mountains were its immediate boundaries, but I saw no more ruined castles and fertile fields. Immense glaciers approached the road; I heard the rumbling thunder of the falling avalanche and marked the smoke of its passage. Mont Blanc, the supreme and magnificent Mont Blanc, raised itself from the surrounding *aiguilles*, and its tremendous *dôme* overlooked the valley.

A tingling long-lost sense of pleasure often came across me during this journey. Some turn in the road, some new object suddenly perceived and recognised, reminded me of days gone by, and were associated with the lighthearted gaiety of boyhood. The very winds whispered in soothing accents, and maternal Nature bade me weep no more. Then again the kindly influence ceased to act—I found myself fettered again to grief and indulging in all the misery of reflection. Then I spurred on my animal, striving so to forget the world, my fears, and more than all, myself—or, in a more desperate fashion, I alighted and threw myself on the grass, weighed down by horror and despair.

At length I arrived at the village of Chamounix. Exhaustion succeeded to the extreme fatigue both of body and of mind which I had endured. For a short space of time I remained at the window watching the pallid lightnings that played above Mont Blanc and listening to the rushing of the Arve, which pursued its noisy way beneath. The same lulling sounds acted as a lullaby to my too keen sensations; when I placed my head upon my pillow, sleep crept over me; I felt it as it came and blessed the giver of oblivion.

CHAPTER X

I spent the following day roaming through the valley. I stood beside the sources of the Arveiron, which take their rise in a glacier, that with slow pace is advancing down from the summit of the hills to barricade the valley. The abrupt sides of vast mountains were before me; the icy wall of the glacier overhung me; a few shattered pines were scattered around; and the solemn silence of this glorious presence-chamber of imperial Nature was broken only by the brawling waves or the fall of some vast fragment, the thunder sound of the avalanche or the cracking, reverberated along the mountains, of the accumulated ice, which, through the silent working of immutable laws, was ever and anon rent and torn, as if it had been but a plaything in their hands. These sublime and magnificent scenes afforded me the greatest consolation that I was capable of receiving. They elevated me from all littleness of feeling, and although they did not remove my grief, they subdued and tranquillised it. In some degree, also, they diverted my mind from the thoughts over which it had brooded for the last month. I retired to rest at night; my slumbers, as it were, waited on and ministered to by the assemblance of grand shapes which I had contemplated during the day. They congregated round me; the unstained snowy mountain-top, the glittering pinnacle, the pine woods, and ragged bare ravine, the eagle, soaring amidst the clouds—they all gathered round me and bade me be at peace.

Where had they fled when the next morning I awoke? All of soul-inspiriting fled with sleep, and dark melancholy clouded every thought. The rain was pouring in torrents, and thick mists hid the summits of the mountains, so that I even saw not the faces of those mighty friends. Still I would penetrate their misty veil and seek them in their cloudy retreats. What were rain and storm to me? My mule was brought to the door, and I resolved to ascend to the summit of Montanvert. I remembered the effect that the view of the tremendous and ever-moving glacier had produced upon my mind when I first saw it. It had then filled me with a sublime ecstasy that gave wings to the soul and allowed it to soar from the obscure world to light and joy. The sight of the awful and majestic in nature had indeed always the effect of solemnising my mind and causing me to forget the passing cares of life. I determined to go without a guide, for I was well acquainted with the path, and the presence of another would destroy the solitary grandeur of the scene.

The ascent is precipitous, but the path is cut into continual and short windings, which enable you to surmount the perpendicularity of the mountain. It is a scene terrifically desolate. In a thousand spots the traces of the winter avalanche may be perceived, where trees lie broken and strewed on the ground, some entirely destroyed, others bent, leaning upon the jutting rocks of the mountain or transversely upon other trees. The path, as you ascend higher, is intersected by ravines of snow, down which stones continually roll from above; one of them is particularly dangerous, as the slightest sound, such as even speaking in a loud voice, produces a concussion of air sufficient to draw destruction upon the head of the speaker. The pines are not tall or luxuriant, but they are sombre and add an air of severity to the scene. I looked on the valley beneath; vast mists were rising from the rivers which ran through it and curling in thick wreaths around the opposite mountains, whose summits were hid in the uniform clouds, while rain poured from the dark sky and added to the melancholy impression I received from the objects around me. Alas! Why does man boast of sensibilities superior to those apparent in the brute; it only renders them more necessary beings. If our impulses were confined to hunger, thirst, and desire, we might be nearly free; but now we are moved by every wind that blows and a chance word or scene that that word may convey to us.

> We rest; a dream has power to poison sleep.
>   We rise; one wand'ring thought pollutes the day.
> We feel, conceive, or reason; laugh or weep,
>   Embrace fond woe, or cast our cares away;
> It is the same: for, be it joy or sorrow,
>   The path of its departure still is free.
> Man's yesterday may ne'er be like his morrow;
>   Nought may endure but mutability!

It was nearly noon when I arrived at the top of the ascent. For some time I sat upon the rock that overlooks the sea of ice. A mist covered both that and the surrounding mountains. Presently a breeze dissipated the cloud, and I descended upon the glacier. The surface is very uneven, rising like the waves of a troubled sea, descending low, and interspersed by rifts that sink deep. The field of ice is almost a league in width, but I spent nearly two hours in crossing it. The opposite mountain is a bare perpendicular rock. From the side where I now stood Montanvert was exactly opposite, at the distance of a league; and above it rose Mont Blanc, in awful majesty. I remained in a recess of the rock, gazing on this wonderful and stupendous scene. The sea, or rather the vast river of ice, wound among its dependent mountains, whose aerial summits hung over its recesses. Their icy and glittering peaks shone in the sunlight over the clouds. My heart, which was before sorrowful, now swelled with something like joy; I exclaimed, "Wandering spirits, if indeed ye wander, and do not rest in your narrow beds, allow me this faint happiness, or take me, as your companion, away from the joys of life."

As I said this I suddenly beheld the figure of a man, at some distance, advancing towards me with superhuman speed. He bounded over the crevices in the ice, among which I had walked with caution; his stature, also, as he approached, seemed to exceed that of man. I was troubled; a mist came over my eyes, and I felt a faintness seize me, but I was quickly restored by the cold gale of the mountains. I perceived, as the shape came nearer (sight tremendous and abhorred!) that it was the wretch whom I had created. I trembled with rage and horror, resolving to wait his approach and then close with him in mortal combat. He approached; his countenance bespoke bitter anguish, combined with disdain and malignity, while its unearthly ugliness rendered it almost too horrible for human eyes. But I scarcely observed this; rage and hatred had at first deprived me of utterance, and I recovered only to overwhelm him with words expressive of furious detestation and contempt.

"Devil," I exclaimed, "do you dare approach me? And do not you fear the fierce vengeance of my arm wreaked on your miserable head? Begone, vile insect! Or rather, stay, that I may trample you to dust! And, oh! That I could, with the extinction of your miserable existence, restore those victims whom you have so diabolically murdered!"

"I expected this reception," said the dæmon. "All men hate the wretched; how, then, must I be hated, who am miserable beyond all living things! Yet you, my creator, detest and spurn me, thy creature, to whom thou art bound by ties only dissoluble by the annihilation of one of us. You purpose to kill me. How dare you sport thus with life? Do your duty towards me, and I will do mine towards you and the rest of mankind. If you will comply with my conditions, I will leave them and you at peace; but if you refuse, I will glut the maw of death, until it be satiated with the blood of your remaining friends."

"Abhorred monster! Fiend that thou art! The tortures of hell are too mild a vengeance for thy crimes. Wretched devil! You reproach me with your creation, come on, then, that I may extinguish the spark which I so negligently bestowed."

My rage was without bounds; I sprang on him, impelled by all the feelings which can arm one being against the existence of another.

He easily eluded me and said,

"Be calm! I entreat you to hear me before you give vent to your hatred on my devoted head. Have I not suffered enough, that you seek to increase my misery? Life, although it may only be an accumulation of anguish, is dear to me, and I will defend it. Remember, thou hast made me more powerful than thyself; my height is superior to thine, my joints more supple. But I will not be tempted to set myself in opposition to thee. I am thy creature, and I will be even mild and docile to my natural lord and king if thou wilt also perform thy part, the which thou owest me. Oh, Frankenstein, be not equitable to every other and trample upon me alone, to whom thy justice, and even thy clemency and affection, is most due. Remember that I am thy creature; I ought to be thy Adam, but I am rather the fallen angel, whom thou drivest from joy for no misdeed. Everywhere I see bliss, from which I alone am irrevocably excluded. I was benevolent and good; misery made me a fiend. Make me happy, and I shall again be virtuous."

"Begone! I will not hear you. There can be no community between you and me; we are enemies. Begone, or let us try our strength in a fight, in which one must fall."

"How can I move thee? Will no entreaties cause thee to turn a favourable eye upon thy creature, who implores thy goodness and compassion? Believe me, Frankenstein, I was benevolent; my soul glowed with love and humanity; but am I not alone, miserably alone? You, my creator, abhor me; what hope can I gather from your fellow creatures, who owe me nothing? They spurn and hate me. The desert mountains and dreary glaciers are my refuge. I have wandered here many days; the caves of ice, which I only do not fear, are a dwelling to me, and the only one which man does not grudge. These bleak skies I hail, for they are kinder to me than your fellow beings. If the multitude of mankind knew of my existence, they would do as you do, and arm themselves for my destruction. Shall I not then hate them who abhor me? I will keep no terms with my enemies. I am miserable, and they shall share my wretchedness. Yet it is in your power to recompense me, and deliver them from an evil which it only remains for you to make so great, that not only you and your family, but thousands of others, shall be swallowed up in the whirlwinds of its rage. Let your compassion be moved, and do not disdain me. Listen to my tale; when you have heard that, abandon or commiserate me, as you shall judge that I deserve. But hear me. The guilty are allowed, by human laws, bloody as they are, to speak in their own defence before they are condemned. Listen to me, Frankenstein. You accuse me of murder, and yet you would, with a satisfied conscience, destroy your own creature. Oh, praise the eternal justice of man! Yet I ask you not to spare me; listen to me, and then, if you can, and if you will, destroy the work of your hands."

"Why do you call to my remembrance," I rejoined, "circumstances of which I shudder to reflect, that I have been the miserable origin and author? Cursed be the day, abhorred devil, in which you first saw light! Cursed (although I curse myself) be the hands that formed you! You have made me wretched beyond expression. You have left me no power to consider whether I am just to you or not. Begone! Relieve me from the sight of your detested form."

"Thus I relieve thee, my creator," he said, and placed his hated hands before my eyes, which I flung from me with violence; "thus I take from thee a sight which you abhor. Still thou canst listen to me and grant me thy compassion. By the virtues that I once possessed, I demand this from you. Hear my tale; it is long and strange, and the temperature of this place is not fitting to your fine sensations; come to the hut upon the mountain. The sun is yet high in the heavens; before it descends to hide itself behind your snowy precipices and illuminate another world, you will have heard my story and can decide. On you it rests, whether I quit for ever the neighbourhood of man and lead a harmless life, or become the scourge of your fellow creatures and the author of your own speedy ruin."

As he said this he led the way across the ice; I followed. My heart was full, and I did not answer him, but as I proceeded, I weighed the various arguments that he had used and determined at least to listen to his tale. I was partly urged by curiosity, and compassion confirmed my resolution. I had hitherto supposed him to be the murderer of my brother, and I eagerly sought a confirmation or denial of this opinion. For the first time, also, I felt what the duties of a creator towards his creature were, and that I ought to render him happy before I complained of his wickedness. These motives urged me to comply with his demand. We crossed the ice, therefore, and ascended the opposite rock. The air was cold, and the rain again began to descend; we entered the hut, the fiend with an air of exultation, I with a heavy heart and depressed spirits. But I consented to listen, and seating myself by the fire which my odious companion had lighted, he thus began his tale.

CHAPTER XI

"It is with considerable difficulty that I remember the original era of my being; all the events of that period appear confused and indistinct. A strange multiplicity of sensations seized me, and I saw, felt, heard, and smelt at the same time; and it was, indeed, a long time before I learned to distinguish between the operations of my various senses. By degrees, I remember, a stronger light pressed upon my nerves, so that I was obliged to shut my eyes. Darkness then came over me and troubled me, but hardly had I felt this when, by opening my eyes, as I now suppose, the light poured in upon me again. I walked and, I believe, descended, but I presently found a great alteration in my sensations. Before, dark and opaque bodies had surrounded me, impervious to my touch or sight; but I now found that I could wander on at liberty, with no obstacles which I could not either surmount or avoid. The light became more and more oppressive to me, and the heat wearying me as I walked, I sought a place where I could receive shade. This was the forest near Ingolstadt; and here I lay by the side of a brook resting from my fatigue, until I felt tormented by hunger and thirst. This roused me from my nearly dormant state, and I ate some berries which I found hanging on the trees or lying on the ground. I slaked my thirst at the brook, and then lying down, was overcome by sleep.

"It was dark when I awoke; I felt cold also, and half frightened, as it were, instinctively, finding myself so desolate. Before I had quitted your apartment, on a sensation of cold, I had covered myself with some clothes, but these were insufficient to secure me from the dews of night. I was a poor, helpless, miserable wretch; I knew, and could distinguish, nothing; but feeling pain invade me on all sides, I sat down and wept.

"Soon a gentle light stole over the heavens and gave me a sensation of pleasure. I started up and beheld a radiant form rise from among the trees. [The moon] I gazed with a kind of wonder. It moved slowly, but it enlightened my path, and I again went out in search of berries. I was still cold when under one of the trees I found a huge cloak, with which I covered myself, and sat down upon the ground. No distinct ideas occupied my mind; all was confused. I felt light, and hunger, and thirst, and darkness; innumerable sounds rang in my ears, and on all sides various scents saluted me; the only object that I could distinguish was the bright moon, and I fixed my eyes on that with pleasure.

"Several changes of day and night passed, and the orb of night had greatly lessened, when I began to distinguish my sensations from each other. I gradually saw plainly the clear stream that supplied me with drink and the trees that shaded me with their foliage. I was delighted when I first discovered that a pleasant sound, which often saluted my ears, proceeded from the throats of the little winged animals who had often intercepted the light from my eyes. I began also to observe, with greater accuracy, the forms that surrounded me and to perceive the boundaries of the radiant roof of light which canopied me. Sometimes I tried to imitate the pleasant songs of the birds but was unable. Sometimes I wished to express my sensations in my own mode, but the uncouth and inarticulate sounds which broke from me frightened me into silence again.

"The moon had disappeared from the night, and again, with a lessened form, showed itself, while I still remained in the forest. My sensations had by this time become distinct, and my mind received every day additional ideas. My eyes became accustomed to the light and to perceive objects in their right forms; I distinguished the insect from the herb, and by degrees, one herb from another. I found that the sparrow uttered none but harsh notes, whilst those of the blackbird and thrush were sweet and enticing.

"One day, when I was oppressed by cold, I found a fire which had been left by some wandering beggars, and was overcome with delight at the warmth I experienced from it. In my joy I thrust my hand into the live embers, but quickly drew it out again with a cry of pain. How strange, I thought, that the same cause should produce such opposite effects! I examined the materials of the fire, and to my joy found it to be composed of wood. I quickly collected some branches, but they were wet and would not burn. I was pained at this and sat still watching the operation of the fire. The wet wood which I had placed near the heat dried and itself became inflamed. I reflected on this, and by touching the various branches, I discovered the cause and busied myself in collecting a great quantity of wood, that I might dry it and have a plentiful supply of fire. When night came on and brought sleep with it, I was in the greatest fear lest my fire should be extinguished. I covered it carefully with dry wood and leaves and placed wet branches upon it; and then, spreading my cloak, I lay on the ground and sank into sleep.

"It was morning when I awoke, and my first care was to visit the fire. I uncovered it, and a gentle breeze quickly fanned it into a flame. I observed this also and contrived a fan of branches, which roused the embers when they were nearly extinguished. When night came again I found, with pleasure, that the fire gave light as well as heat and that the discovery of this element was useful to me in my food, for I found some of the offals that the travellers had left had been roasted, and tasted much more savoury than the berries I gathered from the trees. I tried, therefore, to dress my food in the same manner, placing it on the live embers. I found that the berries were spoiled by this operation, and the nuts and roots much improved.

"Food, however, became scarce, and I often spent the whole day searching in vain for a few acorns to assuage the pangs of hunger. When I found this, I resolved to quit the place that I had hitherto inhabited, to seek for one where the few wants I experienced would be more easily satisfied. In this emigration I exceedingly lamented the loss of the fire which I had obtained through accident and knew not how to reproduce it. I gave several hours to the serious consideration of this difficulty, but I was obliged to relinquish all attempt to supply it, and wrapping myself up in my cloak, I struck across the wood towards the setting sun. I passed three days in these rambles and at length discovered the open country. A great fall of snow had taken place the night before, and the fields were of one uniform white; the appearance was disconsolate, and I found my feet chilled by the cold damp substance that covered the ground.

"It was about seven in the morning, and I longed to obtain food and shelter; at length I perceived a small hut, on a rising ground, which had doubtless been built for the convenience of some shepherd. This was a new sight to me, and I examined the structure with great curiosity. Finding the door open, I entered. An old man sat in it, near a fire, over which he was preparing his breakfast. He turned on hearing a noise, and perceiving me, shrieked loudly, and quitting the hut, ran across the fields with a speed of which his debilitated form hardly appeared capable. His appearance, different from any I had ever before seen, and his flight somewhat surprised me. But I was enchanted by the appearance of the hut; here the snow and rain could not penetrate; the ground was dry; and it presented to me then as exquisite and divine a retreat as Pandæmonium appeared to the dæmons of hell after their sufferings in the lake of fire. I greedily devoured the remnants of the shepherd's breakfast, which consisted of bread, cheese, milk, and wine; the latter, however, I did not like. Then, overcome by fatigue, I lay down among some straw and fell asleep.

"It was noon when I awoke, and allured by the warmth of the sun, which shone brightly on the white ground, I determined to recommence my travels; and, depositing the remains of the peasant's breakfast in a wallet I found, I proceeded across the fields for several hours, until at sunset I arrived at a village. How miraculous did this appear! The huts, the neater cottages, and stately houses engaged my admiration by turns. The vegetables in the gardens, the milk and cheese that I saw placed at the windows of some of the cottages, allured my appetite. One of the best of these I entered, but I had hardly placed my foot within the door before the children shrieked, and one of the women fainted. The whole village was roused; some fled, some attacked me, until, grievously bruised by stones and many other kinds of missile weapons, I escaped to the open country and fearfully took refuge in a low hovel, quite bare, and making a wretched appearance after the palaces I had beheld in the village. This hovel however, joined a cottage of a neat and pleasant appearance, but after my late dearly bought experience, I dared not enter it. My place of refuge was constructed of wood, but so low that I could with difficulty sit upright in it. No wood, however, was placed on the earth, which formed the floor, but it was dry; and although the wind entered it by innumerable chinks, I found it an agreeable asylum from the snow and rain.

"Here, then, I retreated and lay down happy to have found a shelter, however miserable, from the inclemency of the season, and still more from the barbarity of man. As soon as morning dawned I crept from my kennel, that I might view the adjacent cottage and discover if I could remain in the habitation I had found. It was situated against the back of the cottage and surrounded on the sides which were exposed by a pig sty and a clear pool of water. One part was open, and by that I had crept in; but now I covered every crevice by which I might be perceived with stones and wood, yet in such a manner that I might move them on occasion to pass out; all the light I enjoyed came through the sty, and that was sufficient for me.

"Having thus arranged my dwelling and carpeted it with clean straw, I retired, for I saw the figure of a man at a distance, and I remembered too well my treatment the night before to trust myself in his power. I had first, however, provided for my sustenance for that day by a loaf of coarse bread, which I purloined, and a cup with which I could drink more conveniently than from my hand of the pure water which flowed by my retreat. The floor was a little raised, so that it was kept perfectly dry, and by its vicinity to the chimney of the cottage it was tolerably warm.

"Being thus provided, I resolved to reside in this hovel until something should occur which might alter my determination. It was indeed a paradise compared to the bleak forest, my former residence, the rain-dropping branches, and dank earth. I ate my breakfast with pleasure and was about to remove a plank to procure myself a little water when I heard a step, and looking through a small chink, I beheld a young creature, with a pail on her head, passing before my hovel. The girl was young and of gentle demeanour, unlike what I have since found cottagers and farmhouse servants to be. Yet she was meanly dressed, a coarse blue petticoat and a linen jacket being her only garb; her fair hair was plaited but not adorned: she looked patient yet sad. I lost sight of her, and in about a quarter of an hour she returned bearing the pail, which was now partly filled with milk. As she walked along, seemingly incommoded by the burden, a young man met her, whose countenance expressed a deeper despondence. Uttering a few sounds with an air of melancholy, he took the pail from her head and bore it to the cottage himself. She followed, and they disappeared. Presently I saw the young man again, with some tools in his hand, cross the field behind the cottage; and the girl was also busied, sometimes in the house and sometimes in the yard.

"On examining my dwelling, I found that one of the windows of the cottage had formerly occupied a part of it, but the panes had been filled up with wood. In one of these was a small and almost imperceptible chink through which the eye could just penetrate. Through this crevice a small room was visible, whitewashed and clean but very bare of furniture. In one corner, near a small fire, sat an old man, leaning his head on his hands in a disconsolate attitude. The young girl was occupied in arranging the cottage; but presently she took something out of a drawer, which employed her hands, and she sat down beside the old man, who, taking up an instrument, began to play and to produce sounds sweeter than the voice of the thrush or the nightingale. It was a lovely sight, even to me, poor wretch who had never beheld aught beautiful before. The silver hair and benevolent countenance of the aged cottager won my reverence, while the gentle manners of the girl enticed my love. He played a sweet mournful air which I perceived drew tears from the eyes of his amiable companion, of which the old man took no notice, until she sobbed audibly; he then pronounced a few sounds, and the fair creature, leaving her work, knelt at his feet. He raised her and smiled with such kindness and affection that I felt sensations of a peculiar and overpowering nature; they were a mixture of pain and pleasure, such as I had never before experienced, either from hunger or cold, warmth or food; and I withdrew from the window, unable to bear these emotions.

"Soon after this the young man returned, bearing on his shoulders a load of wood. The girl met him at the door, helped to relieve him of his burden, and taking some of the fuel into the cottage, placed it on the fire; then she and the youth went apart into a nook of the cottage, and he showed her a large loaf and a piece of cheese. She seemed pleased and went into the garden for some roots and plants, which she placed in water, and then upon the fire. She afterwards continued her work, whilst the young man went into the garden and appeared busily employed in digging and pulling up roots. After he had been employed thus about an hour, the young woman joined him and they entered the cottage together.

"The old man had, in the meantime, been pensive, but on the appearance of his companions he assumed a more cheerful air, and they sat down to eat. The meal was quickly dispatched. The young woman was again occupied in arranging the cottage, the old man walked before the cottage in the sun for a few minutes, leaning on the arm of the youth. Nothing could exceed in beauty the contrast between these two excellent creatures. One was old, with silver hairs and a countenance beaming with benevolence and love; the younger was slight and graceful in his figure, and his features were moulded with the finest symmetry, yet his eyes and attitude expressed the utmost sadness and despondency. The old man returned to the cottage, and the youth, with tools different from those he had used in the morning, directed his steps across the fields.

"Night quickly shut in, but to my extreme wonder, I found that the cottagers had a means of prolonging light by the use of tapers, and was delighted to find that the setting of the sun did not put an end to the pleasure I experienced in watching my human neighbours. In the evening the young girl and her companion were employed in various occupations which I did not understand; and the old man again took up the instrument which produced the divine sounds that had enchanted me in the morning. So soon as he had finished, the youth began, not to play, but to utter sounds that were monotonous, and neither resembling the harmony of the old man's instrument nor the songs of the birds; I since found that he read aloud, but at that time I knew nothing of the science of words or letters.

"The family, after having been thus occupied for a short time, extinguished their lights and retired, as I conjectured, to rest."

CHAPTER XII

"I lay on my straw, but I could not sleep. I thought of the occurrences of the day. What chiefly struck me was the gentle manners of these people, and I longed to join them, but dared not. I remembered too well the treatment I had suffered the night before from the barbarous villagers, and resolved, whatever course of conduct I might hereafter think it right to pursue, that for the present I would remain quietly in my hovel, watching and endeavouring to discover the motives which influenced their actions.

"The cottagers arose the next morning before the sun. The young woman arranged the cottage and prepared the food, and the youth departed after the first meal.

"This day was passed in the same routine as that which preceded it. The young man was constantly employed out of doors, and the girl in various laborious occupations within. The old man, whom I soon perceived to be blind, employed his leisure hours on his instrument or in contemplation. Nothing could exceed the love and respect which the younger cottagers exhibited towards their venerable companion. They performed towards him every little office of affection and duty with gentleness, and he rewarded them by his benevolent smiles.

"They were not entirely happy. The young man and his companion often went apart and appeared to weep. I saw no cause for their unhappiness, but I was deeply affected by it. If such lovely creatures were miserable, it was less strange that I, an imperfect and solitary being, should be wretched. Yet why were these gentle beings unhappy? They possessed a delightful house (for such it was in my eyes) and every luxury; they had a fire to warm them when chill and delicious viands when hungry; they were dressed in excellent clothes; and, still more, they enjoyed one another's company and speech, interchanging each day looks of affection and kindness. What did their tears imply? Did they really express pain? I was at first unable to solve these questions, but perpetual attention and time explained to me many appearances which were at first enigmatic.

"A considerable period elapsed before I discovered one of the causes of the uneasiness of this amiable family: it was poverty, and they suffered that evil in a very distressing degree. Their nourishment consisted entirely of the vegetables of their garden and the milk of one cow, which gave very little during the winter, when its masters could scarcely procure food to support it. They often, I believe, suffered the pangs of hunger very poignantly, especially the two younger cottagers, for several times they placed food before the old man when they reserved none for themselves.

"This trait of kindness moved me sensibly. I had been accustomed, during the night, to steal a part of their store for my own consumption, but when I found that in doing this I inflicted pain on the cottagers, I abstained and satisfied myself with berries, nuts, and roots which I gathered from a neighbouring wood.

"I discovered also another means through which I was enabled to assist their labours. I found that the youth spent a great part of each day in collecting wood for the family fire, and during the night I often took his tools, the use of which I quickly discovered, and brought home firing sufficient for the consumption of several days.

"I remember, the first time that I did this, the young woman, when she opened the door in the morning, appeared greatly astonished on seeing a great pile of wood on the outside. She uttered some words in a loud voice, and the youth joined her, who also expressed surprise. I observed, with pleasure, that he did not go to the forest that day, but spent it in repairing the cottage and cultivating the garden.

"By degrees I made a discovery of still greater moment. I found that these people possessed a method of communicating their experience and feelings to one another by articulate sounds. I perceived that the words they spoke sometimes produced pleasure or pain, smiles or sadness, in the minds and countenances of the hearers. This was indeed a godlike science, and I ardently desired to become acquainted with it. But I was baffled in every attempt I made for this purpose. Their pronunciation was quick, and the words they uttered, not having any apparent connection with visible objects, I was unable to discover any clue by which I could unravel the mystery of their reference. By great application, however, and after having remained during the space of several revolutions of the moon in my hovel, I discovered the names that were given to some of the most familiar objects of discourse; I learned and applied the words, *fire, milk, bread,* and *wood.* I learned also the names of the cottagers themselves. The youth and his companion had each of them several names, but the old man had only one, which was *father.* The girl was called *sister* or *Agatha,* and the youth *Felix, brother,* or *son.* I cannot describe the delight I felt when I learned the ideas appropriated to each of these sounds and was able to pronounce them. I distinguished several other words without being able as yet to understand or apply them, such as *good, dearest, unhappy.*

"I spent the winter in this manner. The gentle manners and beauty of the cottagers greatly endeared them to me; when they were unhappy, I felt depressed; when they rejoiced, I sympathised in their joys. I saw few human beings besides them, and if any other happened to enter the cottage, their harsh manners and rude gait only enhanced to me the superior accomplishments of my friends. The old man, I could perceive, often endeavoured to encourage his children, as sometimes I found that he called them, to cast off their melancholy. He would talk in a cheerful accent, with an expression of goodness that bestowed pleasure even upon me. Agatha listened with respect, her eyes sometimes filled with tears, which she endeavoured to wipe away unperceived; but I generally found that her countenance and tone were more cheerful after having listened to the exhortations of her father. It was not thus with Felix. He was always the saddest of the group, and even to my unpractised senses, he appeared to have suffered more deeply than his friends. But if his countenance was more sorrowful, his voice was more cheerful than that of his sister, especially when he addressed the old man.

"I could mention innumerable instances which, although slight, marked the dispositions of these amiable cottagers. In the midst of poverty and want, Felix carried with pleasure to his sister the first little white flower that peeped out from beneath the snowy ground. Early in the morning, before she had risen, he cleared away the snow that obstructed her path to the milk-house, drew water from the well, and brought the wood from the outhouse, where, to his perpetual astonishment, he found his store always replenished by an invisible hand. In the day, I believe, he worked sometimes for a neighbouring farmer, because he often went forth and did not return until dinner, yet brought no wood with him. At other times he worked in the garden, but as there was little to do in the frosty season, he read to the old man and Agatha.

"This reading had puzzled me extremely at first, but by degrees I discovered that he uttered many of the same sounds when he read as when he talked. I conjectured, therefore, that he found on the paper signs for speech which he understood, and I ardently longed to comprehend these also; but how was that possible when I did not even understand the sounds for which they stood as signs? I improved, however, sensibly in this science, but not sufficiently to follow up any kind of conversation, although I applied my whole mind to the endeavour, for I easily perceived that, although I eagerly longed to discover myself to the cottagers, I ought not to make the attempt until I had first become master of their language, which knowledge might enable me to make them overlook the deformity of my figure, for with this also the contrast perpetually presented to my eyes had made me acquainted.

"I had admired the perfect forms of my cottagers—their grace, beauty, and delicate complexions; but how was I terrified when I viewed myself in a transparent pool! At first I started back, unable to believe that it was indeed I who was reflected in the mirror; and when I became fully convinced that I was in reality the monster that I am, I was filled with the bitterest sensations of despondence and mortification. Alas! I did not yet entirely know the fatal effects of this miserable deformity.

"As the sun became warmer and the light of day longer, the snow vanished, and I beheld the bare trees and the black earth. From this time Felix was more employed, and the heart-moving indications of impending famine disappeared. Their food, as I afterwards found, was coarse, but it was wholesome; and they procured a sufficiency of it. Several new kinds of plants sprang up in the garden, which they dressed; and these signs of comfort increased daily as the season advanced.

"The old man, leaning on his son, walked each day at noon, when it did not rain, as I found it was called when the heavens poured forth its waters. This frequently took place, but a high wind quickly dried the earth, and the season became far more pleasant than it had been.

"My mode of life in my hovel was uniform. During the morning I attended the motions of the cottagers, and when they were dispersed in various occupations, I slept; the remainder of the day was spent in observing my friends. When they had retired to rest, if there was any moon or the night was star-light, I went into the woods and collected my own food and fuel for the cottage. When I returned, as often as it was necessary, I cleared their path from the snow and performed those offices that I had seen done by Felix. I afterwards found that these labours, performed by an invisible hand, greatly astonished them; and once or twice I heard them, on these occasions, utter the words *good spirit, wonderful*; but I did not then understand the signification of these terms.

"My thoughts now became more active, and I longed to discover the motives and feelings of these lovely creatures; I was inquisitive to know why Felix appeared so miserable and Agatha so sad. I thought (foolish wretch!) that it might be in my power to restore happiness to these deserving people. When I slept or was absent, the forms of the venerable blind father, the gentle Agatha, and the excellent Felix flitted before me. I looked upon them as superior beings who would be the arbiters of my future destiny. I formed in my imagination a thousand pictures of presenting myself to them, and their reception of me. I imagined that they would be disgusted, until, by my gentle demeanour and conciliating words, I should first win their favour and afterwards their love.

"These thoughts exhilarated me and led me to apply with fresh ardour to the acquiring the art of language. My organs were indeed harsh, but supple; and although my voice was very unlike the soft music of their tones, yet I pronounced such words as I understood with tolerable ease. It was as the ass and the lap-dog; yet surely the gentle ass whose intentions were affectionate, although his manners were rude, deserved better treatment than blows and execration.

"The pleasant showers and genial warmth of spring greatly altered the aspect of the earth. Men who before this change seemed to have been hid in caves dispersed themselves and were employed in various arts of cultivation. The birds sang in more cheerful notes, and the leaves began to bud forth on the trees. Happy, happy earth! Fit habitation for gods, which, so short a time before, was bleak, damp, and unwholesome. My spirits were elevated by the enchanting appearance of nature; the past was blotted from my memory, the present was tranquil, and the future gilded by bright rays of hope and anticipations of joy."

CHAPTER XIII

"I now hasten to the more moving part of my story. I shall relate events that impressed me with feelings which, from what I had been, have made me what I am.

"Spring advanced rapidly; the weather became fine and the skies cloudless. It surprised me that what before was desert and gloomy should now bloom with the most beautiful flowers and verdure. My senses were gratified and refreshed by a thousand scents of delight and a thousand sights of beauty.

"It was on one of these days, when my cottagers periodically rested from labour—the old man played on his guitar, and the children listened to him—that I observed the countenance of Felix was melancholy beyond expression; he sighed frequently, and once his father paused in his music, and I conjectured by his manner that he inquired the cause of his son's sorrow. Felix replied in a cheerful accent, and the old man was recommencing his music when someone tapped at the door.

"It was a lady on horseback, accompanied by a country-man as a guide. The lady was dressed in a dark suit and covered with a thick black veil. Agatha asked a question, to which the stranger only replied by pronouncing, in a sweet accent, the name of Felix. Her voice was musical but unlike that of either of my friends. On hearing this word, Felix came up hastily to the lady, who, when she saw him, threw up her veil, and I beheld a countenance of angelic beauty and expression. Her hair of a shining raven black, and curiously braided; her eyes were dark, but gentle, although animated; her features of a regular proportion, and her complexion wondrously fair, each cheek tinged with a lovely pink.

"Felix seemed ravished with delight when he saw her, every trait of sorrow vanished from his face, and it instantly expressed a degree of ecstatic joy, of which I could hardly have believed it capable; his eyes sparkled, as his cheek flushed with pleasure; and at that moment I thought him as beautiful as the stranger. She appeared affected by different feelings; wiping a few tears from her lovely eyes, she held out her hand to Felix, who kissed it rapturously and called her, as well as I could distinguish, his sweet Arabian. She did not appear to understand him, but smiled. He assisted her to dismount, and dismissing her guide, conducted her into the cottage. Some conversation took place between him and his father, and the young stranger knelt at the old man's feet and would have kissed his hand, but he raised her and embraced her affectionately.

"I soon perceived that although the stranger uttered articulate sounds and appeared to have a language of her own, she was neither understood by nor herself understood the cottagers. They made many signs which I did not comprehend, but I saw that her presence diffused gladness through the cottage, dispelling their sorrow as the sun dissipates the morning mists. Felix seemed peculiarly happy and with smiles of delight welcomed his Arabian. Agatha, the ever-gentle Agatha, kissed the hands of the lovely stranger, and pointing to her brother, made signs which appeared to me to mean that he had been sorrowful until she came. Some hours passed thus, while they, by their countenances, expressed joy, the cause of which I did not comprehend. Presently I found, by the frequent recurrence of some sound which the stranger repeated after them, that she was endeavouring to learn their language; and the idea instantly occurred to me that I should make use of the same instructions to the same end. The stranger learned about twenty words at the first lesson; most of them, indeed, were those which I had before understood, but I profited by the others.

"As night came on, Agatha and the Arabian retired early. When they separated Felix kissed the hand of the stranger and said, 'Good night sweet Safie.' He sat up much longer, conversing with his father, and by the frequent repetition of her name I conjectured that their lovely guest was the subject of their conversation. I ardently desired to understand them, and bent every faculty towards that purpose, but found it utterly impossible.

"The next morning Felix went out to his work, and after the usual occupations of Agatha were finished, the Arabian sat at the feet of the old man, and taking his guitar, played some airs so entrancingly beautiful that they at once drew tears of sorrow and delight from my eyes. She sang, and her voice flowed in a rich cadence, swelling or dying away like a nightingale of the woods.

"When she had finished, she gave the guitar to Agatha, who at first declined it. She played a simple air, and her voice accompanied it in sweet accents, but unlike the wondrous strain of the stranger. The old man appeared enraptured and said some words which Agatha endeavoured to explain to Safie, and by which he appeared to wish to express that she bestowed on him the greatest delight by her music.

"The days now passed as peaceably as before, with the sole alteration that joy had taken place of sadness in the countenances of my friends. Safie was always gay and happy; she and I improved rapidly in the knowledge of language, so that in two months I began to comprehend most of the words uttered by my protectors.

"In the meanwhile also the black ground was covered with herbage, and the green banks interspersed with innumerable flowers, sweet to the scent and the eyes, stars of pale radiance among the moonlight woods; the sun became warmer, the nights clear and balmy; and my nocturnal rambles were an extreme pleasure to me, although they were considerably shortened by the late setting and early rising of the sun, for I never ventured abroad during daylight, fearful of meeting with the same treatment I had formerly endured in the first village which I entered.

"My days were spent in close attention, that I might more speedily master the language; and I may boast that I improved more rapidly than the Arabian, who understood very little and conversed in broken accents, whilst I comprehended and could imitate almost every word that was spoken.

"While I improved in speech, I also learned the science of letters as it was taught to the stranger, and this opened before me a wide field for wonder and delight.

"The book from which Felix instructed Safie was Volney's *Ruins of Empires*. I should not have understood the purport of this book had not Felix, in reading it, given very minute explanations. He had chosen this work, he said, because the declamatory style was framed in imitation of the Eastern authors. Through this work I obtained a cursory knowledge of history and a view of the several empires at present existing in the world; it gave me an insight into the manners, governments, and religions of the different nations of the earth. I heard of the slothful Asiatics, of the stupendous genius and mental activity of the Grecians, of the wars and wonderful virtue of the early Romans—of their subsequent degenerating— of the decline of that mighty empire, of chivalry, Christianity, and kings. I heard of the discovery of the American hemisphere and wept with Safie over the hapless fate of its original inhabitants.

"These wonderful narrations inspired me with strange feelings. Was man, indeed, at once so powerful, so virtuous and magnificent, yet so vicious and base? He appeared at one time a mere scion of the evil principle and at another as all that can be conceived of noble and godlike. To be a great and virtuous man appeared the highest honour that can befall a sensitive being; to be base and vicious, as many on record have been, appeared the lowest degradation, a condition more abject than that of the blind mole or harmless worm. For a long time I could not conceive how one man could go forth to murder his fellow, or even why there were laws and governments;

but when I heard details of vice and bloodshed, my wonder ceased and I turned away with disgust and loathing.

"Every conversation of the cottagers now opened new wonders to me. While I listened to the instructions which Felix bestowed upon the Arabian, the strange system of human society was explained to me. I heard of the division of property, of immense wealth and squalid poverty, of rank, descent, and noble blood.

"The words induced me to turn towards myself. I learned that the possessions most esteemed by your fellow creatures were high and unsullied descent united with riches. A man might be respected with only one of these advantages, but without either he was considered, except in very rare instances, as a vagabond and a slave, doomed to waste his powers for the profits of the chosen few! And what was I? Of my creation and creator I was absolutely ignorant, but I knew that I possessed no money, no friends, no kind of property. I was, besides, endued with a figure hideously deformed and loathsome; I was not even of the same nature as man. I was more agile than they and could subsist upon coarser diet; I bore the extremes of heat and cold with less injury to my frame; my stature far exceeded theirs. When I looked around I saw and heard of none like me. Was I, then, a monster, a blot upon the earth, from which all men fled and whom all men disowned?

"I cannot describe to you the agony that these reflections inflicted upon me; I tried to dispel them, but sorrow only increased with knowledge. Oh, that I had for ever remained in my native wood, nor known nor felt beyond the sensations of hunger, thirst, and heat!

"Of what a strange nature is knowledge! It clings to the mind when it has once seized on it like a lichen on the rock. I wished sometimes to shake off all thought and feeling, but I learned that there was but one means to overcome the sensation of pain, and that was death—a state which I feared yet did not understand. I admired virtue and good feelings and loved the gentle manners and amiable qualities of my cottagers, but I was shut out from intercourse with them, except through means which I obtained by stealth, when I was unseen and unknown, and which rather increased than satisfied the desire I had of becoming one among my fellows. The gentle words of Agatha and the animated smiles of the charming Arabian were not for me. The mild exhortations of the old man and the lively conversation of the loved Felix were not for me. Miserable, unhappy wretch!

"Other lessons were impressed upon me even more deeply. I heard of the difference of sexes, and the birth and growth of children, how the father doted on the smiles of the infant, and the lively sallies of the older child, how all the life and cares of the mother were wrapped up in the precious charge, how the mind of youth expanded and gained knowledge, of brother, sister, and all the various relationships which bind one human being to another in mutual bonds.

"But where were my friends and relations? No father had watched my infant days, no mother had blessed me with smiles and caresses; or if they had, all my past life was now a blot, a blind vacancy in which I distinguished nothing. From my earliest remembrance I had been as I then was in height and proportion. I had never yet seen a being resembling me or who claimed any intercourse with me. What was I? The question again recurred, to be answered only with groans.

"I will soon explain to what these feelings tended, but allow me now to return to the cottagers, whose story excited in me such various feelings of indignation, delight, and wonder, but which all terminated in additional love and reverence for my protectors (for so I loved, in an innocent, half-painful self-deceit, to call them)."

CHAPTER XIV

"Some time elapsed before I learned the history of my friends. It was one which could not fail to impress itself deeply on my mind, unfolding as it did a number of circumstances, each interesting and wonderful to one so utterly inexperienced as I was.

"The name of the old man was De Lacey. He was descended from a good family in France, where he had lived for many years in affluence, respected by his superiors and beloved by his equals. His son was bred in the service of his country, and Agatha had ranked with ladies of the highest distinction. A few months before my arrival they had lived in a large and luxurious city called Paris, surrounded by friends and possessed of every enjoyment which virtue, refinement of intellect, or taste, accompanied by a moderate fortune, could afford.

"The father of Safie had been the cause of their ruin. He was a Turkish merchant and had inhabited Paris for many years, when, for some reason which I could not learn, he became obnoxious to the government. He was seized and cast into prison the very day that Safie arrived from Constantinople to join him. He was tried and condemned to death. The injustice of his sentence was very flagrant; all Paris was indignant; and it was judged that his religion and wealth rather than the crime alleged against him had been the cause of his condemnation.

"Felix had accidentally been present at the trial; his horror and indignation were uncontrollable when he heard the decision of the court. He made, at that moment, a solemn vow to deliver him and then looked around for the means. After many fruitless attempts to gain admittance to the prison, he found a strongly grated window in an unguarded part of the building, which lighted the dungeon of the unfortunate Muhammadan, who, loaded with chains, waited in despair the execution of the barbarous sentence. Felix visited the grate at night and made known to the prisoner his intentions in his favour. The Turk, amazed and delighted, endeavoured to kindle the zeal of his deliverer by promises of reward and wealth. Felix rejected his offers with contempt, yet when he saw the lovely Safie, who was allowed to visit her father and who by her gestures expressed her lively gratitude, the youth could not help owning to his own mind that the captive possessed a treasure which would fully reward his toil and hazard.

"The Turk quickly perceived the impression that his daughter had made on the heart of Felix and endeavoured to secure him more entirely in his interests by the promise of her hand in marriage so soon as he should be conveyed to a place of safety. Felix was too delicate to accept this offer, yet he looked forward to the probability of the event as to the consummation of his happiness.

"During the ensuing days, while the preparations were going forward for the escape of the merchant, the zeal of Felix was warmed by several letters that he received from this lovely girl, who found means to express her thoughts in the language of her lover by the aid of an old man, a servant of her father who understood French. She thanked him in the most ardent terms for his intended services towards her parent, and at the same time she gently deplored her own fate.

"I have copies of these letters, for I found means, during my residence in the hovel, to procure the implements of writing; and the letters were often in the hands of Felix or Agatha. Before I depart I will give them to you; they will prove the truth of my tale; but at present, as the sun is already far declined, I shall only have time to repeat the substance of them to you.

"Safie related that her mother was a Christian Arab, seized and made a slave by the Turks; recommended by her beauty, she had won the heart of the father of Safie, who married her. The young girl spoke in high and enthusiastic terms of her mother, who, born in freedom, spurned the bondage to which she was now reduced. She instructed her daughter in the tenets of her religion and taught her to aspire to higher powers of intellect and an independence of spirit forbidden to the female followers of Muhammad. This lady died, but her lessons were indelibly impressed on the mind of Safie, who sickened at the prospect of again returning to Asia and being immured within the walls of a harem, allowed only to occupy herself with infantile amusements, ill-suited to the temper of her soul, now accustomed to grand ideas and a noble emulation for virtue. The prospect of marrying a Christian and remaining in a country where women were allowed to take a rank in society was enchanting to her.

"The day for the execution of the Turk was fixed, but on the night previous to it he quitted his prison and before morning was distant many leagues from Paris. Felix had procured passports in the name of his father, sister, and himself. He had previously communicated his plan to the former, who aided the deceit by quitting his house, under the pretence of a journey and concealed himself, with his daughter, in an obscure part of Paris.

"Felix conducted the fugitives through France to Lyons and across Mont

Cenis to Leghorn, where the merchant had decided to wait a favourable opportunity of passing into some part of the Turkish dominions.

"Safie resolved to remain with her father until the moment of his departure, before which time the Turk renewed his promise that she should be united to his deliverer; and Felix remained with them in expectation of that event; and in the meantime he enjoyed the society of the Arabian, who exhibited towards him the simplest and tenderest affection. They conversed with one another through the means of an interpreter, and sometimes with the interpretation of looks; and Safie sang to him the divine airs of her native country.

"The Turk allowed this intimacy to take place and encouraged the hopes of the youthful lovers, while in his heart he had formed far other plans. He loathed the idea that his daughter should be united to a Christian, but he feared the resentment of Felix if he should appear lukewarm, for he knew that he was still in the power of his deliverer if he should choose to betray him to the Italian state which they inhabited. He revolved a thousand plans by which he should be enabled to prolong the deceit until it might be no longer necessary, and secretly to take his daughter with him when he departed. His plans were facilitated by the news which arrived from Paris.

"The government of France were greatly enraged at the escape of their victim and spared no pains to detect and punish his deliverer. The plot of Felix was quickly discovered, and De Lacey and Agatha were thrown into prison. The news reached Felix and roused him from his dream of pleasure. His blind and aged father and his gentle sister lay in a noisome dungeon while he enjoyed the free air and the society of her whom he loved. This idea was torture to him. He quickly arranged with the Turk that if the latter should find a favourable opportunity for escape before Felix could return to Italy, Safie should remain as a boarder at a convent at Leghorn; and then, quitting the lovely Arabian, he hastened to Paris and delivered himself up to the vengeance of the law, hoping to free De Lacey and Agatha by this proceeding.

"He did not succeed. They remained confined for five months before the trial took place, the result of which deprived them of their fortune and condemned them to a perpetual exile from their native country.

"They found a miserable asylum in the cottage in Germany, where I discovered them. Felix soon learned that the treacherous Turk, for whom he and his family endured such unheard-of oppression, on discovering that his deliverer was thus reduced to poverty and ruin, became a traitor to good feeling and honour and had quitted Italy with his daughter, insultingly sending Felix a pittance of money to aid him, as he said, in some plan of future maintenance.

"Such were the events that preyed on the heart of Felix and rendered him, when I first saw him, the most miserable of his family. He could have endured poverty, and while this distress had been the meed of his virtue, he gloried in it; but the ingratitude of the Turk and the loss of his beloved Safie were misfortunes more bitter and irreparable. The arrival of the Arabian now infused new life into his soul.

"When the news reached Leghorn that Felix was deprived of his wealth and rank, the merchant commanded his daughter to think no more of her lover, but to prepare to return to her native country. The generous nature of Safie was outraged by this command; she attempted to expostulate with her father, but he left her angrily, reiterating his tyrannical mandate.

"A few days after, the Turk entered his daughter's apartment and told her hastily that he had reason to believe that his residence at Leghorn had been divulged and that he should speedily be delivered up to the French government; he had consequently hired a vessel to convey him to Constantinople, for which city he should sail in a few hours. He intended to leave his daughter under the care of a confidential servant, to follow at her leisure with the greater part of his property, which had not yet arrived at Leghorn.

"When alone, Safie resolved in her own mind the plan of conduct that it would become her to pursue in this emergency. A residence in Turkey was abhorrent to her; her religion and her feelings were alike averse to it. By some papers of her father which fell into her hands she heard of the exile of her lover and learnt the name of the spot where he then resided. She hesitated some time, but at length she formed her determination. Taking with her some jewels that belonged to her and a sum of money, she quitted Italy with an attendant, a native of Leghorn, but who understood the common language of Turkey, and departed for Germany.

"She arrived in safety at a town about twenty leagues from the cottage of De Lacey, when her attendant fell dangerously ill. Safie nursed her with the most devoted affection, but the poor girl died, and the Arabian was left alone, unacquainted with the language of the country and utterly ignorant of the customs of the world. She fell, however, into good hands. The Italian had mentioned the name of the spot for which they were bound, and after her death the woman of the house in which they had lived took care that Safie should arrive in safety at the cottage of her lover."

CHAPTER XV

"Such was the history of my beloved cottagers. It impressed me deeply. I learned, from the views of social life which it developed, to admire their virtues and to deprecate the vices of mankind.

"As yet I looked upon crime as a distant evil, benevolence and generosity were ever present before me, inciting within me a desire to become an actor in the busy scene where so many admirable qualities were called forth and displayed. But in giving an account of the progress of my intellect, I must not omit a circumstance which occurred in the beginning of the month of August of the same year.

"One night during my accustomed visit to the neighbouring wood where I collected my own food and brought home firing for my protectors, I found on the ground a leathern portmanteau containing several articles of dress and some books. I eagerly seized the prize and returned with it to my hovel. Fortunately the books were written in the language, the elements of which I had acquired at the cottage; they consisted of *Paradise Lost*, a volume of *Plutarch's Lives*, and the *Sorrows of Werter*. The possession of these treasures gave me extreme delight; I now continually studied and exercised my mind upon these histories, whilst my friends were employed in their ordinary occupations.

"I can hardly describe to you the effect of these books. They produced in me an infinity of new images and feelings, that sometimes raised me to ecstasy, but more frequently sunk me into the lowest dejection. In the *Sorrows of Werter*, besides the interest of its simple and affecting story, so many opinions are canvassed and so many lights thrown upon what had hitherto been to me obscure subjects that I found in it a never-ending source of speculation and astonishment. The gentle and domestic manners it described, combined with lofty sentiments and feelings, which had for their object something out of self, accorded well with my experience among my protectors and with the wants which were for ever alive in my own bosom. But I thought Werter himself a more divine being than I had ever beheld or imagined; his character contained no pretension, but it sank deep. The disquisitions upon death and suicide were calculated to fill me with wonder. I did not pretend to enter into the merits of the case, yet I inclined towards the opinions of the hero, whose extinction I wept, without precisely understanding it.

"As I read, however, I applied much personally to my own feelings and condition. I found myself similar yet at the same time strangely unlike to the beings concerning whom I read and to whose conversation I was a listener. I sympathised with and partly understood them, but I was unformed in mind; I was dependent on none and related to none. 'The path of my departure was free,' and there was none to lament my annihilation. My person was hideous and my stature gigantic. What did this mean? Who was I? What was I? Whence did I come? What was my destination? These questions continually recurred, but I was unable to solve them.

"The volume of *Plutarch's Lives* which I possessed contained the histories of the first founders of the ancient republics. This book had a far different effect upon me from the *Sorrows of Werter*. I learned from Werter's imaginations despondency and gloom, but Plutarch taught me high thoughts; he elevated me above the wretched sphere of my own reflections, to admire and love the heroes of past ages. Many things I read surpassed my understanding and experience. I had a very confused knowledge of kingdoms, wide extents of country, mighty rivers, and boundless seas. But I was perfectly unacquainted with towns and large assemblages of men. The cottage of my protectors had been the only school in which I had studied human nature, but this book developed new and mightier scenes of action. I read of men concerned in public affairs, governing or massacring their species. I felt the greatest ardour for virtue rise within me, and abhorrence for vice, as far as I understood the signification of those terms, relative as they were, as I applied them, to pleasure and pain alone. Induced by these feelings, I was of course led to admire peaceable lawgivers, Numa, Solon, and Lycurgus, in preference to Romulus and Theseus. The patriarchal lives of my protectors caused these impressions to take a firm hold on my mind; perhaps, if my first introduction to humanity had been made by a young soldier, burning for glory and slaughter, I should have been imbued with different sensations.

"But *Paradise Lost* excited different and far deeper emotions. I read it, as I had read the other volumes which had fallen into my hands, as a true history. It moved every feeling of wonder and awe that the picture of an omnipotent God warring with his creatures was capable of exciting. I often referred the several situations, as their similarity struck me, to my own. Like Adam, I was apparently united by no link to any other being in existence; but his state was far different from mine in every other respect. He had come forth from the hands of God a perfect creature, happy and prosperous, guarded by the especial care of his Creator; he was allowed to converse with and acquire knowledge from beings of a superior nature, but I was wretched, helpless, and alone. Many times I considered Satan as the fitter emblem of my condition, for often, like him, when I viewed the bliss of my protectors, the bitter gall of envy rose within me.

"Another circumstance strengthened and confirmed these feelings. Soon after my arrival in the hovel I discovered some papers in the pocket of the dress which I had taken from your laboratory. At first I had neglected them, but now that I was able to decipher the characters in which they were written, I began to study them with diligence. It was your journal of the four months that preceded my creation. You minutely described in these papers every step you took in the progress of your work; this history was mingled with accounts of domestic occurrences. You doubtless recollect these papers. Here they are. Everything is related in them which bears reference to my accursed origin; the whole detail of that series of disgusting circumstances which produced it is set in view; the minutest description of my odious and loathsome person is given, in language which painted your own horrors and rendered mine indelible. I sickened as I read. 'Hateful day when I received life!' I exclaimed in agony. 'Accursed creator! Why did you form a monster so hideous that even *you* turned from me in disgust? God, in pity, made man beautiful and alluring, after his own image; but my form is a filthy type of yours, more horrid even from the very resemblance. Satan had his companions, fellow devils, to admire and encourage him, but I am solitary and abhorred.'

"These were the reflections of my hours of despondency and solitude; but when I contemplated the virtues of the cottagers, their amiable and benevolent dispositions, I persuaded myself that when they should become acquainted with my admiration of their virtues they would compassionate me and overlook my personal deformity. Could they turn from their door one, however monstrous, who solicited their compassion and friendship? I resolved, at least, not to despair, but in every way to fit myself for an interview with them which would decide my fate. I postponed this attempt for some months longer, for the importance attached to its success inspired me with a dread lest I should fail. Besides, I found that my understanding improved so much with every day's experience that I was unwilling to commence this undertaking until a few more months should have added to my sagacity.

"Several changes, in the meantime, took place in the cottage. The presence of Safie diffused happiness among its inhabitants, and I also found that a greater degree of plenty reigned there. Felix and Agatha spent more time in amusement and conversation, and were assisted in their labours by servants. They did not appear rich, but they were contented and happy; their feelings were serene and peaceful, while mine became every day more tumultuous. Increase of knowledge only discovered to me more clearly what a wretched outcast I was. I cherished hope, it is true, but it vanished when I beheld my person reflected in water or my shadow in the moonshine, even as that frail image and that inconstant shade.

"I endeavoured to crush these fears and to fortify myself for the trial which in a few months I resolved to undergo; and sometimes I allowed my thoughts, unchecked by reason, to ramble in the fields of Paradise, and dared to fancy amiable and lovely creatures sympathising with my feelings and cheering my gloom; their angelic countenances breathed smiles of consolation. But it was all a dream; no Eve soothed my sorrows nor shared my thoughts; I was alone. I remembered Adam's supplication to his Creator. But where was mine? He had abandoned me, and in the bitterness of my heart I cursed him.

"Autumn passed thus. I saw, with surprise and grief, the leaves decay and fall, and nature again assume the barren and bleak appearance it had worn when I first beheld the woods and the lovely moon. Yet I did not heed the bleakness of the weather; I was better fitted by my conformation for the endurance of cold than heat. But my chief delights were the sight of the flowers, the birds, and all the gay apparel of summer; when those deserted me, I turned with more attention towards the cottagers. Their happiness was not decreased by the absence of summer. They loved and sympathised with one another; and their joys, depending on each other, were not interrupted by the casualties that took place around them. The more I saw of them, the greater became my desire to claim their protection and kindness; my heart yearned to be known and loved by these amiable creatures; to see their sweet looks directed towards me with affection was the utmost limit of my ambition. I dared not think that they would turn them from me with disdain and horror. The poor that stopped at their door were never driven away. I asked, it is true, for greater treasures than a little food or rest: I required kindness and sympathy; but I did not believe myself utterly unworthy of it.

"The winter advanced, and an entire revolution of the seasons had taken place since I awoke into life. My attention at this time was solely directed towards my plan of introducing myself into the cottage of my protectors. I revolved many projects, but that on which I finally fixed was to enter the dwelling when the blind old man should be alone. I had sagacity enough to discover that the unnatural hideousness of my person was the chief object of horror with those who had formerly beheld me. My voice, although harsh, had nothing terrible in it; I thought, therefore, that if in the absence of his children I could gain the good will and mediation of the old De Lacey, I might by his means be tolerated by my younger protectors.

"One day, when the sun shone on the red leaves that strewed the ground and diffused cheerfulness, although it denied warmth, Safie, Agatha, and Felix departed on a long country walk, and the old man, at his own desire, was left alone in the cottage. When his children had departed, he took up his guitar and played several mournful but sweet airs, more sweet and mournful than I had ever heard him play before. At first his countenance was illuminated with pleasure, but as he continued, thoughtfulness and sadness succeeded; at length, laying aside the instrument, he sat absorbed in reflection.

"My heart beat quick; this was the hour and moment of trial, which would decide my hopes or realise my fears. The servants were gone to a neighbouring fair. All was silent in and around the cottage; it was an excellent opportunity; yet, when I proceeded to execute my plan, my limbs failed me and I sank to the ground. Again I rose, and exerting all the firmness of which I was master, removed the planks which I had placed before my hovel to conceal my retreat. The fresh air revived me, and with renewed determination I approached the door of their cottage.

"I knocked. 'Who is there?' said the old man. 'Come in.'

"I entered. 'Pardon this intrusion,' said I; 'I am a traveller in want of a little rest; you would greatly oblige me if you would allow me to remain a few minutes before the fire.'

"'Enter,' said De Lacey, 'and I will try in what manner I can to relieve your wants; but, unfortunately, my children are from home, and as I am blind, I am afraid I shall find it difficult to procure food for you.'

"'Do not trouble yourself, my kind host; I have food; it is warmth and rest only that I need.'

"I sat down, and a silence ensued. I knew that every minute was precious to me, yet I remained irresolute in what manner to commence the interview, when the old man addressed me.

'By your language, stranger, I suppose you are my countryman; are you French?'

"'No; but I was educated by a French family and understand that language only. I am now going to claim the protection of some friends, whom I sincerely love, and of whose favour I have some hopes.'

"'Are they Germans?'

"'No, they are French. But let us change the subject. I am an unfortunate and deserted creature, I look around and I have no relation or friend upon earth. These amiable people to whom I go have never seen me and know little of me. I am full of fears, for if I fail there, I am an outcast in the world for ever.'

"'Do not despair. To be friendless is indeed to be unfortunate, but the hearts of men, when unprejudiced by any obvious self-interest, are full of brotherly love and charity. Rely, therefore, on your hopes; and if these friends are good and amiable, do not despair.'

"'They are kind—they are the most excellent creatures in the world; but, unfortunately, they are prejudiced against me. I have good dispositions; my life has been hitherto harmless and in some degree beneficial; but a fatal prejudice clouds their eyes, and where they ought to see a feeling and kind friend, they behold only a detestable monster.'

"'That is indeed unfortunate; but if you are really blameless, cannot you undeceive them?'

"'I am about to undertake that task; and it is on that account that I feel so many overwhelming terrors. I tenderly love these friends; I have, unknown to them, been for many months in the habits of daily kindness towards them; but they believe that I wish to injure them, and it is that prejudice which I wish to overcome.'

"'Where do these friends reside?'

"'Near this spot.'

"The old man paused and then continued, 'If you will unreservedly confide to me the particulars of your tale, I perhaps may be of use in undeceiving them. I am blind and cannot judge of your countenance, but there is something in your words which persuades me that you are sincere. I am poor and an exile, but it will afford me true pleasure to be in any way serviceable to a human creature.'

"'Excellent man! I thank you and accept your generous offer. You raise me from the dust by this kindness; and I trust that, by your aid, I shall not be driven from the society and sympathy of your fellow creatures.'

"'Heaven forbid! Even if you were really criminal, for that can only drive you to desperation, and not instigate you to virtue. I also am unfortunate; I and my family have been condemned, although innocent; judge, therefore, if I do not feel for your misfortunes.'

"'How can I thank you, my best and only benefactor? From your lips first have I heard the voice of kindness directed towards me; I shall be for ever grateful; and your present humanity assures me of success with those friends whom I am on the point of meeting.'

"'May I know the names and residence of those friends?'

"I paused. This, I thought, was the moment of decision, which was to rob me of or bestow happiness on me for ever. I struggled vainly for firmness sufficient to answer him, but the effort destroyed all my remaining strength; I sank on the chair and sobbed aloud. At that moment I heard the steps of my younger protectors. I had not a moment to lose, but seizing the hand of the old man, I cried, 'Now is the time! Save and protect me! You and your family are the friends whom I seek. Do not you desert me in the hour of trial!'

"'Great God!' exclaimed the old man. 'Who are you?'

"At that instant the cottage door was opened, and Felix, Safie, and Agatha entered. Who can describe their horror and consternation on beholding me? Agatha fainted, and Safie, unable to attend to her friend, rushed out of the cottage. Felix darted forward, and with supernatural force tore me from his father, to whose knees I clung, in a transport of fury, he dashed me to the ground and struck me violently with a stick. I could have torn him limb from limb, as the lion rends the antelope. But my heart sank within me as with bitter sickness, and I refrained. I saw him on the point of repeating his blow, when, overcome by pain and anguish, I quitted the cottage, and in the general tumult escaped unperceived to my hovel."

CHAPTER XVI

"Cursed, cursed creator! Why did I live? Why, in that instant, did I not extinguish the spark of existence which you had so wantonly bestowed? I know not; despair had not yet taken possession of me; my feelings were those of rage and revenge. I could with pleasure have destroyed the cottage and its inhabitants and have glutted myself with their shrieks and misery.

"When night came I quitted my retreat and wandered in the wood; and now, no longer restrained by the fear of discovery, I gave vent to my anguish in fearful howlings. I was like a wild beast that had broken the toils, destroying the objects that obstructed me and ranging through the wood with a stag-like swiftness. Oh! What a miserable night I passed! The cold stars shone in mockery, and the bare trees waved their branches above me; now and then the sweet voice of a bird burst forth amidst the universal stillness. All, save I, were at rest or in enjoyment; I, like the arch-fiend, bore a hell within me, and finding myself unsympathised with, wished to tear up the trees, spread havoc and destruction around me, and then to have sat down and enjoyed the ruin.

"But this was a luxury of sensation that could not endure; I became fatigued with excess of bodily exertion and sank on the damp grass in the sick impotence of despair. There was none among the myriads of men that existed who would pity or assist me; and should I feel kindness towards my enemies? No; from that moment I declared everlasting war against the species, and more than all, against him who had formed me and sent me forth to this insupportable misery.

"The sun rose; I heard the voices of men and knew that it was impossible to return to my retreat during that day. Accordingly I hid myself in some thick underwood, determining to devote the ensuing hours to reflection on my situation.

"The pleasant sunshine and the pure air of day restored me to some degree of tranquillity; and when I considered what had passed at the cottage, I could not help believing that I had been too hasty in my conclusions. I had certainly acted imprudently. It was apparent that my conversation had interested the father in my behalf, and I was a fool in having exposed my person to the horror of his children. I ought to have familiarised the old

De Lacey to me, and by degrees to have discovered myself to the rest of his family, when they should have been prepared for my approach. But I did not believe my errors to be irretrievable, and after much consideration I resolved to return to the cottage, seek the old man, and by my representations win him to my party.

"These thoughts calmed me, and in the afternoon I sank into a profound sleep; but the fever of my blood did not allow me to be visited by peaceful dreams. The horrible scene of the preceding day was for ever acting before my eyes; the females were flying and the enraged Felix tearing me from his father's feet. I awoke exhausted, and finding that it was already night, I crept forth from my hiding-place, and went in search of food.

"When my hunger was appeased, I directed my steps towards the well-known path that conducted to the cottage. All there was at peace. I crept into my hovel and remained in silent expectation of the accustomed hour when the family arose. That hour passed, the sun mounted high in the heavens, but the cottagers did not appear. I trembled violently, apprehending some dreadful misfortune. The inside of the cottage was dark, and I heard no motion; I cannot describe the agony of this suspense.

"Presently two countrymen passed by, but pausing near the cottage, they entered into conversation, using violent gesticulations; but I did not understand what they said, as they spoke the language of the country, which differed from that of my protectors. Soon after, however, Felix approached with another man; I was surprised, as I knew that he had not quitted the cottage that morning, and waited anxiously to discover from his discourse the meaning of these unusual appearances.

"'Do you consider,' said his companion to him, 'that you will be obliged to pay three months' rent and to lose the produce of your garden? I do not wish to take any unfair advantage, and I beg therefore that you will take some days to consider of your determination.'

"'It is utterly useless,' replied Felix; 'we can never again inhabit your cottage. The life of my father is in the greatest danger, owing to the dreadful circumstance that I have related. My wife and my sister will never recover from their horror. I entreat you not to reason with me any more. Take possession of your tenement and let me fly from this place.'

"Felix trembled violently as he said this. He and his companion entered the cottage, in which they remained for a few minutes, and then departed. I never saw any of the family of De Lacey more.

"I continued for the remainder of the day in my hovel in a state of utter and stupid despair. My protectors had departed and had broken the only link that held me to the world. For the first time the feelings of revenge and hatred filled my bosom, and I did not strive to control them, but allowing myself to be borne away by the stream, I bent my mind towards injury and death. When I thought of my friends, of the mild voice of De Lacey, the gentle eyes of Agatha, and the exquisite beauty of the Arabian, these thoughts vanished and a gush of tears somewhat soothed me. But again when I reflected that they had spurned and deserted me, anger returned, a rage of anger, and unable to injure anything human, I turned my fury towards inanimate objects. As night advanced, I placed a variety of combustibles around the cottage, and after having destroyed every vestige of cultivation in the garden, I waited with forced impatience until the moon had sunk to commence my operations.

"As the night advanced, a fierce wind arose from the woods and quickly dispersed the clouds that had loitered in the heavens; the blast tore along like a mighty avalanche and produced a kind of insanity in my spirits that burst all bounds of reason and reflection. I lighted the dry branch of a tree and danced with fury around the devoted cottage, my eyes still fixed on the western horizon, the edge of which the moon nearly touched. A part of its orb was at length hid, and I waved my brand; it sank, and with a loud scream I fired the straw, and heath, and bushes, which I had collected. The wind fanned the fire, and the cottage was quickly enveloped by the flames, which clung to it and licked it with their forked and destroying tongues.

"As soon as I was convinced that no assistance could save any part of the habitation, I quitted the scene and sought for refuge in the woods.

"And now, with the world before me, whither should I bend my steps? I resolved to fly far from the scene of my misfortunes; but to me, hated and despised, every country must be equally horrible. At length the thought of you crossed my mind. I learned from your papers that you were my father, my creator; and to whom could I apply with more fitness than to him who had given me life? Among the lessons that Felix had bestowed upon Safie, geography had not been omitted; I had learned from these the relative situations of the different countries of the earth. You had mentioned Geneva as the name of your native town, and towards this place I resolved to proceed.

"But how was I to direct myself? I knew that I must travel in a southwesterly direction to reach my destination, but the sun was my only guide. I did not know the names of the towns that I was to pass through, nor could I ask information from a single human being; but I did not despair. From you only could I hope for succour, although towards you I felt no sentiment but that of hatred. Unfeeling, heartless creator! You had endowed me with perceptions and passions and then cast me abroad an object for the scorn and horror of mankind. But on you only had I any claim for pity and redress, and from you I determined to seek that justice which I vainly attempted to gain from any other being that wore the human form.

"My travels were long and the sufferings I endured intense. It was late in autumn when I quitted the district where I had so long resided. I travelled only at night, fearful of encountering the visage of a human being. Nature decayed around me, and the sun became heatless; rain and snow poured around me; mighty rivers were frozen; the surface of the earth was hard and chill, and bare, and I found no shelter. Oh, earth! How often did I imprecate curses on the cause of my being! The mildness of my nature had fled, and all within me was turned to gall and bitterness. The nearer I approached to your habitation, the more deeply did I feel the spirit of revenge enkindled in my heart. Snow fell, and the waters were hardened, but I rested not. A few incidents now and then directed me, and I possessed a map of the country; but I often wandered wide from my path. The agony of my feelings allowed me no respite; no incident occurred from which my rage and misery could not extract its food; but a circumstance that happened when I arrived on the confines of Switzerland, when the sun had recovered its warmth and the earth again began to look green, confirmed in an especial manner the bitterness and horror of my feelings.

"I generally rested during the day and travelled only when I was secured by night from the view of man. One morning, however, finding that my path lay through a deep wood, I ventured to continue my journey after the sun had risen; the day, which was one of the first of spring, cheered even me by the loveliness of its sunshine and the balminess of the air. I felt emotions of gentleness and pleasure, that had long appeared dead, revive within me. Half surprised by the novelty of these sensations, I allowed myself to be borne away by them, and forgetting my solitude and deformity, dared to be happy. Soft tears again bedewed my cheeks, and I even raised my humid eyes with thankfulness towards the blessed sun, which bestowed such joy upon me.

"I continued to wind among the paths of the wood, until I came to its boundary, which was skirted by a deep and rapid river, into which many of the trees bent their branches, now budding with the fresh spring. Here I paused, not exactly knowing what path to pursue, when I heard the sound of voices, that induced me to conceal myself under the shade of a cypress. I was scarcely hid when a young girl came running towards the spot where I was concealed, laughing, as if she ran from someone in sport. She continued her course along the precipitous sides of the river, when suddenly her foot slipped, and she fell into the rapid stream. I rushed from my hiding-place and with extreme labour, from the force of the current, saved her and dragged her to shore. She was senseless, and I endeavoured by every means in my power to restore animation, when I was suddenly interrupted by the approach of a rustic, who was probably the person from whom she had playfully fled. On seeing me, he darted towards me, and tearing the girl from my arms, hastened towards the deeper parts of the wood. I followed speedily, I hardly knew why; but when the man saw me draw near, he aimed a gun, which he carried, at my body and fired. I sank to the ground, and my injurer, with increased swiftness, escaped into the wood.

"This was then the reward of my benevolence! I had saved a human being from destruction, and as a recompense I now writhed under the miserable pain of a wound which shattered the flesh and bone. The feelings of kindness and gentleness which I had entertained but a few moments before gave place to hellish rage and gnashing of teeth. Inflamed by pain, I vowed eternal hatred and vengeance to all mankind. But the agony of my wound overcame me; my pulses paused, and I fainted.

"For some weeks I led a miserable life in the woods, endeavouring to cure the wound which I had received. The ball had entered my shoulder, and I knew not whether it had remained there or passed through; at any rate I had no means of extracting it. My sufferings were augmented also by the oppressive sense of the injustice and ingratitude of their infliction. My daily vows rose for revenge—a deep and deadly revenge, such as would alone compensate for the outrages and anguish I had endured.

"After some weeks my wound healed, and I continued my journey. The labours I endured were no longer to be alleviated by the bright sun or gentle breezes of spring; all joy was but a mockery which insulted my desolate state and made me feel more painfully that I was not made for the enjoyment of pleasure.

"But my toils now drew near a close, and in two months from this time I reached the environs of Geneva.

"It was evening when I arrived, and I retired to a hiding-place among the fields that surround it to meditate in what manner I should apply to you. I was oppressed by fatigue and hunger and far too unhappy to enjoy the gentle breezes of evening or the prospect of the sun setting behind the stupendous mountains of Jura.

"At this time a slight sleep relieved me from the pain of reflection, which was disturbed by the approach of a beautiful child, who came running into the recess I had chosen, with all the sportiveness of infancy. Suddenly, as I gazed on him, an idea seized me that this little creature was unprejudiced and had lived too short a time to have imbibed a horror of deformity. If, therefore, I could seize him and educate him as my companion and friend,

I should not be so desolate in this peopled earth.

"Urged by this impulse, I seized on the boy as he passed and drew him towards me. As soon as he beheld my form, he placed his hands before his eyes and uttered a shrill scream; I drew his hand forcibly from his face and said, 'Child, what is the meaning of this? I do not intend to hurt you; listen to me.'

"He struggled violently. 'Let me go,' he cried; 'monster! Ugly wretch! You wish to eat me and tear me to pieces. You are an ogre. Let me go, or I will tell my papa.'

"'Boy, you will never see your father again; you must come with me.'

"'Hideous monster! Let me go. My papa is a syndic—he is M. Frankenstein—he will punish you. You dare not keep me.'

"'Frankenstein! you belong then to my enemy—to him towards whom I have sworn eternal revenge; you shall be my first victim.'

"The child still struggled and loaded me with epithets which carried despair to my heart; I grasped his throat to silence him, and in a moment he lay dead at my feet.

"I gazed on my victim, and my heart swelled with exultation and hellish triumph; clapping my hands, I exclaimed, 'I too can create desolation; my enemy is not invulnerable; this death will carry despair to him, and a thousand other miseries shall torment and destroy him.'

"As I fixed my eyes on the child, I saw something glittering on his breast. I took it; it was a portrait of a most lovely woman. In spite of my malignity, it softened and attracted me. For a few moments I gazed with delight on her dark eyes, fringed by deep lashes, and her lovely lips; but presently my rage returned; I remembered that I was for ever deprived of the delights that such beautiful creatures could bestow and that she whose resemblance I contemplated would, in regarding me, have changed that air of divine benignity to one expressive of disgust and affright.

"Can you wonder that such thoughts transported me with rage? I only wonder that at that moment, instead of venting my sensations in exclamations and agony, I did not rush among mankind and perish in the attempt to destroy them.

"While I was overcome by these feelings, I left the spot where I had committed the murder, and seeking a more secluded hiding-place, I entered a barn which had appeared to me to be empty. A woman was sleeping on some straw; she was young, not indeed so beautiful as her whose portrait I held, but of an agreeable aspect and blooming in the loveliness of youth and health. Here, I thought, is one of those whose joy-imparting smiles are bestowed on all but me. And then I bent over her and whispered, 'Awake, fairest, thy lover is near—he who would give his life but to obtain one look of affection from thine eyes; my beloved, awake!'

"The sleeper stirred; a thrill of terror ran through me. Should she indeed awake, and see me, and curse me, and denounce the murderer? Thus would she assuredly act if her darkened eyes opened and she beheld me. The thought was madness; it stirred the fiend within me—not I, but she, shall suffer; the murder I have committed because I am for ever robbed of all that she could give me, she shall atone. The crime had its source in her; be hers the punishment! Thanks to the lessons of Felix and the sanguinary laws of man, I had learned now to work mischief. I bent over her and placed the portrait securely in one of the folds of her dress. She moved again, and I fled.

"For some days I haunted the spot where these scenes had taken place, sometimes wishing to see you, sometimes resolved to quit the world and its miseries for ever. At length I wandered towards these mountains, and have ranged through their immense recesses, consumed by a burning passion which you alone can gratify. We may not part until you have promised to comply with my requisition. I am alone and miserable; man will not associate with me; but one as deformed and horrible as myself would not deny herself to me. My companion must be of the same species and have the same defects. This being you must create."

CHAPTER XVII

The being finished speaking and fixed his looks upon me in the expectation of a reply. But I was bewildered, perplexed, and unable to arrange my ideas sufficiently to understand the full extent of his proposition. He continued,

"You must create a female for me with whom I can live in the interchange of those sympathies necessary for my being. This you alone can do, and I demand it of you as a right which you must not refuse to concede."

The latter part of his tale had kindled anew in me the anger that had died away while he narrated his peaceful life among the cottagers, and as he said this I could no longer suppress the rage that burned within me.

"I do refuse it," I replied; "and no torture shall ever extort a consent from me. You may render me the most miserable of men, but you shall never make me base in my own eyes. Shall I create another like yourself, whose joint wickedness might desolate the world. Begone! I have answered you; you may torture me, but I will never consent."

"You are in the wrong," replied the fiend; "and instead of threatening, I am content to reason with you. I am malicious because I am miserable. Am I not shunned and hated by all mankind? You, my creator, would tear me to pieces and triumph; remember that, and tell me why I should pity man more than he pities me? You would not call it murder if you could precipitate me into one of those ice-rifts and destroy my frame, the work of your own hands. Shall I respect man when he condemns me? Let him live with me in the interchange of kindness, and instead of injury I would bestow every benefit upon him with tears of gratitude at his acceptance. But that cannot be; the human senses are insurmountable barriers to our union. Yet mine shall not be the submission of abject slavery. I will revenge my injuries; if I cannot inspire love, I will cause fear, and chiefly towards you my arch-enemy, because my creator, do I swear inextinguishable hatred. Have a care; I will work at your destruction, nor finish until I desolate your heart, so that you shall curse the hour of your birth."

A fiendish rage animated him as he said this; his face was wrinkled into contortions too horrible for human eyes to behold; but presently he calmed himself and proceeded—

"I intended to reason. This passion is detrimental to me, for you do not reflect that *you* are the cause of its excess. If any being felt emotions of benevolence towards me, I should return them a hundred and a hundredfold; for that one creature's sake I would make peace with the whole kind! But I now indulge in dreams of bliss that cannot be realised. What I ask of you is reasonable and moderate; I demand a creature of another sex, but as hideous as myself; the gratification is small, but it is all that I can receive, and it shall content me. It is true, we shall be monsters, cut off from all the world; but on that account we shall be more attached to one another. Our lives will not be happy, but they will be harmless and free from the misery I now feel. Oh! My creator, make me happy; let me feel gratitude towards you for one benefit! Let me see that I excite the sympathy of some existing thing; do not deny me my request!"

I was moved. I shuddered when I thought of the possible consequences of my consent, but I felt that there was some justice in his argument. His tale and the feelings he now expressed proved him to be a creature of fine sensations, and did I not as his maker owe him all the portion of happiness that it was in my power to bestow? He saw my change of feeling and continued,

"If you consent, neither you nor any other human being shall ever see us again; I will go to the vast wilds of South America. My food is not that of man; I do not destroy the lamb and the kid to glut my appetite; acorns and berries afford me sufficient nourishment. My companion will be of the same nature as myself and will be content with the same fare. We shall make our bed of dried leaves; the sun will shine on us as on man and will ripen our food. The picture I present to you is peaceful and human, and you must feel that you could deny it only in the wantonness of power and cruelty. Pitiless as you have been towards me, I now see compassion in your eyes; let me seize the favourable moment and persuade you to promise what I so ardently desire."

"You propose," replied I, "to fly from the habitations of man, to dwell in those wilds where the beasts of the field will be your only companions. How can you, who long for the love and sympathy of man, persevere in this exile? You will return and again seek their kindness, and you will meet with their detestation; your evil passions will be renewed, and you will then have a companion to aid you in the task of destruction. This may not be; cease to argue the point, for I cannot consent."

"How inconstant are your feelings! But a moment ago you were moved by my representations, and why do you again harden yourself to my complaints? I swear to you, by the earth which I inhabit, and by you that made me, that with the companion you bestow, I will quit the neighbourhood of man and dwell, as it may chance, in the most savage of places. My evil passions will have fled, for I shall meet with sympathy! My life will flow quietly away, and in my dying moments I shall not curse my maker."

His words had a strange effect upon me. I compassionated him and sometimes felt a wish to console him, but when I looked upon him, when I saw the filthy mass that moved and talked, my heart sickened and my feelings were altered to those of horror and hatred. I tried to stifle these sensations; I thought that as I could not sympathise with him, I had no right to withhold from him the small portion of happiness which was yet in my power to bestow.

"You swear," I said, "to be harmless; but have you not already shown a degree of malice that should reasonably make me distrust you? May not even this be a feint that will increase your triumph by affording a wider scope for your revenge?"

"How is this? I must not be trifled with, and I demand an answer. If I have no ties and no affections, hatred and vice must be my portion; the love of another will destroy the cause of my crimes, and I shall become a thing of whose existence everyone will be ignorant. My vices are the children of a forced solitude that I abhor, and my virtues will necessarily arise when I live in communion with an equal. I shall feel the affections of a sensitive being and become linked to the chain of existence and events from which I am now excluded."

I paused some time to reflect on all he had related and the various arguments which he had employed. I thought of the promise of virtues which he had displayed on the opening of his existence and the subsequent blight of all kindly feeling by the loathing and scorn which his protectors had manifested towards him. His power and threats were not omitted in my calculations; a creature who could exist in the ice-caves of the glaciers and hide himself from pursuit among the ridges of inaccessible precipices was a being possessing faculties it would be vain to cope with. After a long pause of reflection I concluded that the justice due both to him and my fellow creatures demanded of me that I should comply with his request. Turning to him, therefore, I said,

"I consent to your demand, on your solemn oath to quit Europe for ever, and every other place in the neighbourhood of man, as soon as I shall deliver into your hands a female who will accompany you in your exile."

"I swear," he cried, "by the sun, and by the blue sky of heaven, and by the fire of love that burns my heart, that if you grant my prayer, while they exist you shall never behold me again. Depart to your home and commence your labours; I shall watch their progress with unutterable anxiety; and fear not but that when you are ready I shall appear."

Saying this, he suddenly quitted me, fearful, perhaps, of any change in my sentiments. I saw him descend the mountain with greater speed than the flight of an eagle, and quickly lost among the undulations of the sea of ice.

His tale had occupied the whole day, and the sun was upon the verge of the horizon when he departed. I knew that I ought to hasten my descent towards the valley, as I should soon be encompassed in darkness; but my heart was heavy, and my steps slow. The labour of winding among the little paths of the mountain and fixing my feet firmly as I advanced perplexed me, occupied as I was by the emotions which the occurrences of the day had produced. Night was far advanced when I came to the halfway resting-place and seated myself beside the fountain. The stars shone at intervals as the clouds passed from over them; the dark pines rose before me, and every here and there a broken tree lay on the ground; it was a scene of wonderful solemnity and stirred strange thoughts within me. I wept bitterly, and clasping my hands in agony, I exclaimed, "Oh! stars and clouds and winds, ye are all about to mock me; if ye really pity me, crush sensation and memory; let me become as nought; but if not, depart, depart, and leave me in darkness."

These were wild and miserable thoughts, but I cannot describe to you how the eternal twinkling of the stars weighed upon me and how I listened to every blast of wind as if it were a dull ugly siroc on its way to consume me.

Morning dawned before I arrived at the village of Chamounix; I took no rest, but returned immediately to Geneva. Even in my own heart I could give no expression to my sensations—they weighed on me with a mountain's weight and their excess destroyed my agony beneath them. Thus I returned home, and entering the house, presented myself to the family. My haggard and wild appearance awoke intense alarm, but I answered no question, scarcely did I speak. I felt as if I were placed under a ban—as if I had no right to claim their sympathies—as if never more might I enjoy companionship with them. Yet even thus I loved them to adoration; and to save them, I resolved to dedicate myself to my most abhorred task. The prospect of such an occupation made every other circumstance of existence pass before me like a dream, and that thought only had to me the reality of life.

CHAPTER XVIII

Day after day, week after week, passed away on my return to Geneva; and I could not collect the courage to recommence my work. I feared the vengeance of the disappointed fiend, yet I was unable to overcome my repugnance to the task which was enjoined me. I found that I could not compose a female without again devoting several months to profound study and laborious disquisition. I had heard of some discoveries having been made by an English philosopher, the knowledge of which was material to my success, and I sometimes thought of obtaining my father's consent to visit England for this purpose; but I clung to every pretence of delay and shrank from taking the first step in an undertaking whose immediate necessity began to appear less absolute to me. A change indeed had taken place in me; my health, which had hitherto declined, was now much restored; and my spirits, when unchecked by the memory of my unhappy promise, rose proportionably. My father saw this change with pleasure, and he turned his thoughts towards the best method of eradicating the remains of my melancholy, which every now and then would return by fits, and with a devouring blackness overcast the approaching sunshine. At these moments I took refuge in the most perfect solitude. I passed whole days on the lake alone in a little boat, watching the clouds and listening to the rippling of the waves, silent and listless. But the fresh air and bright sun seldom failed to restore me to some degree of composure, and on my return I met the salutations of my friends with a readier smile and a more cheerful heart.

It was after my return from one of these rambles that my father, calling me aside, thus addressed me,

"I am happy to remark, my dear son, that you have resumed your former pleasures and seem to be returning to yourself. And yet you are still unhappy and still avoid our society. For some time I was lost in conjecture as to the cause of this, but yesterday an idea struck me, and if it is well founded, I conjure you to avow it. Reserve on such a point would be not only useless, but draw down treble misery on us all."

I trembled violently at his exordium, and my father continued—

"I confess, my son, that I have always looked forward to your marriage with our dear Elizabeth as the tie of our domestic comfort and the stay of my declining years. You were attached to each other from your earliest infancy; you studied together, and appeared, in dispositions and tastes, entirely suited to one another. But so blind is the experience of man that what I conceived to be the best assistants to my plan may have entirely destroyed it. You, perhaps, regard her as your sister, without any wish that she might become your wife. Nay, you may have met with another whom you may love; and considering yourself as bound in honour to Elizabeth, this struggle may occasion the poignant misery which you appear to feel."

"My dear father, reassure yourself. I love my cousin tenderly and sincerely. I never saw any woman who excited, as Elizabeth does, my warmest admiration and affection. My future hopes and prospects are entirely bound up in the expectation of our union."

"The expression of your sentiments of this subject, my dear Victor, gives me more pleasure than I have for some time experienced. If you feel thus, we shall assuredly be happy, however present events may cast a gloom over us. But it is this gloom which appears to have taken so strong a hold of your mind that I wish to dissipate. Tell me, therefore, whether you object to an immediate solemnisation of the marriage. We have been unfortunate, and recent events have drawn us from that everyday tranquillity befitting my years and infirmities. You are younger; yet I do not suppose, possessed as you are of a competent fortune, that an early marriage would at all interfere with any future plans of honour and utility that you may have formed. Do not suppose, however, that I wish to dictate happiness to you or that a delay on your part would cause me any serious uneasiness. Interpret my words with candour and answer me, I conjure you, with confidence and sincerity."

I listened to my father in silence and remained for some time incapable of offering any reply. I revolved rapidly in my mind a multitude of thoughts and endeavoured to arrive at some conclusion. Alas! To me the idea of an immediate union with my Elizabeth was one of horror and dismay. I was bound by a solemn promise which I had not yet fulfilled and dared not break, or if I did, what manifold miseries might not impend over me and my devoted family! Could I enter into a festival with this deadly weight yet hanging round my neck and bowing me to the ground? I must perform my engagement and let the monster depart with his mate before I allowed myself to enjoy the delight of a union from which I expected peace.

I remembered also the necessity imposed upon me of either journeying to England or entering into a long correspondence with those philosophers of that country whose knowledge and discoveries were of indispensable use to me in my present undertaking. The latter method of obtaining the desired intelligence was dilatory and unsatisfactory; besides, I had an insurmountable aversion to the idea of engaging myself in my loathsome task in my father's house while in habits of familiar intercourse with those I loved. I knew that a thousand fearful accidents might occur, the slightest of which would disclose a tale to thrill all connected with me with horror. I was aware also that I should often lose all self-command, all capacity of hiding the harrowing sensations that would possess me during the progress of my unearthly occupation. I must absent myself from all I loved while thus employed. Once commenced, it would quickly be achieved, and I might be restored to my family in peace and happiness. My promise fulfilled, the monster would depart for ever. Or (so my fond fancy imaged) some accident might meanwhile occur to destroy him and put an end to my slavery for ever.

These feelings dictated my answer to my father. I expressed a wish to visit England, but concealing the true reasons of this request, I clothed my desires under a guise which excited no suspicion, while I urged my desire with an earnestness that easily induced my father to comply. After so long a period of an absorbing melancholy that resembled madness in its intensity and effects, he was glad to find that I was capable of taking pleasure in the idea of such a journey, and he hoped that change of scene and varied amusement would, before my return, have restored me entirely to myself.

The duration of my absence was left to my own choice; a few months, or at most a year, was the period contemplated. One paternal kind precaution he had taken to ensure my having a companion. Without previously communicating with me, he had, in concert with Elizabeth, arranged that Clerval should join me at Strasburgh. This interfered with the solitude I coveted for the prosecution of my task; yet at the commencement of my journey the presence of my friend could in no way be an impediment, and truly I rejoiced that thus I should be saved many hours of lonely, maddening reflection. Nay, Henry might stand between me and the intrusion of my foe. If I were alone, would he not at times force his abhorred presence on me to remind me of my task or to contemplate its progress?

To England, therefore, I was bound, and it was understood that my union with Elizabeth should take place immediately on my return. My father's age rendered him extremely averse to delay. For myself, there was one reward I promised myself from my detested toils—one consolation for my unparalleled sufferings; it was the prospect of that day when, enfranchised from my miserable slavery, I might claim Elizabeth and forget the past in my union with her.

I now made arrangements for my journey, but one feeling haunted me which filled me with fear and agitation. During my absence I should leave my friends unconscious of the existence of their enemy and unprotected from his attacks, exasperated as he might be by my departure. But he had promised to follow me wherever I might go, and would he not accompany me to England? This imagination was dreadful in itself, but soothing inasmuch as it supposed the safety of my friends. I was agonised with the idea of the possibility that the reverse of this might happen. But through the whole period during which I was the slave of my creature I allowed myself to be governed by the impulses of the moment; and my present sensations strongly intimated that the fiend would follow me and exempt my family from the danger of his machinations.

It was in the latter end of September that I again quitted my native country. My journey had been my own suggestion, and Elizabeth therefore acquiesced, but she was filled with disquiet at the idea of my suffering, away from her, the inroads of misery and grief. It had been her care which provided me a companion in Clerval—and yet a man is blind to a thousand minute circumstances which call forth a woman's sedulous attention. She longed to bid me hasten my return; a thousand conflicting emotions rendered her mute as she bade me a tearful, silent farewell.

I threw myself into the carriage that was to convey me away, hardly knowing whither I was going, and careless of what was passing around. I remembered only, and it was with a bitter anguish that I reflected on it, to order that my chemical instruments should be packed to go with me. Filled with dreary imaginations, I passed through many beautiful and majestic scenes, but my eyes were fixed and unobserving. I could only think of the bourne of my travels and the work which was to occupy me whilst they endured.

After some days spent in listless indolence, during which I traversed many leagues, I arrived at Strasburgh, where I waited two days for Clerval. He came. Alas, how great was the contrast between us! He was alive to every new scene, joyful when he saw the beauties of the setting sun, and more happy when he beheld it rise and recommence a new day. He pointed out to me the shifting colours of the landscape and the appearances of the sky. "This is what it is to live," he cried; "now I enjoy existence! But you, my dear Frankenstein, wherefore are you desponding and sorrowful!" In truth, I was occupied by gloomy thoughts and neither saw the descent of the evening star nor the golden sunrise reflected in the Rhine. And you, my friend, would be far more amused with the journal of Clerval, who observed the scenery with an eye of feeling and delight, than in listening to my reflections. I, a miserable wretch, haunted by a curse that shut up every avenue to enjoyment.

We had agreed to descend the Rhine in a boat from Strasburgh to

Rotterdam, whence we might take shipping for London. During this voyage we passed many willowy islands and saw several beautiful towns. We stayed a day at Mannheim, and on the fifth from our departure from Strasburgh, arrived at Mainz. The course of the Rhine below Mainz becomes much more picturesque. The river descends rapidly and winds between hills, not high, but steep, and of beautiful forms. We saw many ruined castles standing on the edges of precipices, surrounded by black woods, high and inaccessible. This part of the Rhine, indeed, presents a singularly variegated landscape. In one spot you view rugged hills, ruined castles overlooking tremendous precipices, with the dark Rhine rushing beneath; and on the sudden turn of a promontory, flourishing vineyards with green sloping banks and a meandering river and populous towns occupy the scene.

We travelled at the time of the vintage and heard the song of the labourers as we glided down the stream. Even I, depressed in mind, and my spirits continually agitated by gloomy feelings, even I was pleased. I lay at the bottom of the boat, and as I gazed on the cloudless blue sky, I seemed to drink in a tranquillity to which I had long been a stranger. And if these were my sensations, who can describe those of Henry? He felt as if he had been transported to Fairy-land and enjoyed a happiness seldom tasted by man. "I have seen," he said, "the most beautiful scenes of my own country; I have visited the lakes of Lucerne and Uri, where the snowy mountains descend almost perpendicularly to the water, casting black and impenetrable shades, which would cause a gloomy and mournful appearance were it not for the most verdant islands that relieve the eye by their gay appearance; I have seen this lake agitated by a tempest, when the wind tore up whirlwinds of water and gave you an idea of what the water-spout must be on the great ocean; and the waves dash with fury the base of the mountain, where the priest and his mistress were overwhelmed by an avalanche and where their dying voices are still said to be heard amid the pauses of the nightly wind; I have seen the mountains of La Valais, and the Pays de Vaud; but this country, Victor, pleases me more than all those wonders. The mountains of Switzerland are more majestic and strange, but there is a charm in the banks of this divine river that I never before saw equalled. Look at that castle which overhangs yon precipice; and that also on the island, almost concealed amongst the foliage of those lovely trees; and now that group of labourers coming from among their vines; and that village half hid in the recess of the mountain. Oh, surely the spirit that inhabits and guards this place has a soul more in harmony with man than those who pile the glacier or retire to the inaccessible peaks of the mountains of our own country."

Clerval! Beloved friend! Even now it delights me to record your words and to dwell on the praise of which you are so eminently deserving. He was a being formed in the "very poetry of nature." His wild and enthusiastic imagination was chastened by the sensibility of his heart. His soul overflowed with ardent affections, and his friendship was of that devoted and wondrous nature that the worldly-minded teach us to look for only in the imagination. But even human sympathies were not sufficient to satisfy his eager mind. The scenery of external nature, which others regard only with admiration, he loved with ardour:—

> ——The sounding cataract
> Haunted him like a passion: the tall rock,
> The mountain, and the deep and gloomy wood,
> Their colours and their forms, were then to him
> An appetite; a feeling, and a love,
> That had no need of a remoter charm,
> By thought supplied, or any interest
> Unborrow'd from the eye.

—Wordsworth's "Tintern Abbey".

And where does he now exist? Is this gentle and lovely being lost for ever? Has this mind, so replete with ideas, imaginations fanciful and magnificent, which formed a world, whose existence depended on the life of its creator;—has this mind perished? Does it now only exist in my memory? No, it is not thus; your form so divinely wrought, and beaming with beauty, has decayed, but your spirit still visits and consoles your unhappy friend.

Pardon this gush of sorrow; these ineffectual words are but a slight tribute to the unexampled worth of Henry, but they soothe my heart, overflowing with the anguish which his remembrance creates. I will proceed with my tale.

Beyond Cologne we descended to the plains of Holland; and we resolved to post the remainder of our way, for the wind was contrary and the stream of the river was too gentle to aid us.

Our journey here lost the interest arising from beautiful scenery, but we arrived in a few days at Rotterdam, whence we proceeded by sea to England. It was on a clear morning, in the latter days of December, that I first saw the white cliffs of Britain. The banks of the Thames presented a new scene; they were flat but fertile, and almost every town was marked by the remembrance of some story. We saw Tilbury Fort and remembered the Spanish Armada, Gravesend, Woolwich, and Greenwich—places which I had heard of even in my country.

At length we saw the numerous steeples of London, St. Paul's towering above all, and the Tower famed in English history.

CHAPTER XIX

London was our present point of rest; we determined to remain several months in this wonderful and celebrated city. Clerval desired the intercourse of the men of genius and talent who flourished at this time, but this was with me a secondary object; I was principally occupied with the means of obtaining the information necessary for the completion of my promise and quickly availed myself of the letters of introduction that I had brought with me, addressed to the most distinguished natural philosophers.

If this journey had taken place during my days of study and happiness, it would have afforded me inexpressible pleasure. But a blight had come over my existence, and I only visited these people for the sake of the information they might give me on the subject in which my interest was so terribly profound. Company was irksome to me; when alone, I could fill my mind with the sights of heaven and earth; the voice of Henry soothed me, and I could thus cheat myself into a transitory peace. But busy, uninteresting, joyous faces brought back despair to my heart. I saw an insurmountable barrier placed between me and my fellow men; this barrier was sealed with the blood of William and Justine, and to reflect on the events connected with those names filled my soul with anguish.

But in Clerval I saw the image of my former self; he was inquisitive and anxious to gain experience and instruction. The difference of manners which he observed was to him an inexhaustible source of instruction and amusement. He was also pursuing an object he had long had in view. His design was to visit India, in the belief that he had in his knowledge of its various languages, and in the views he had taken of its society, the means of materially assisting the progress of European colonization and trade. In Britain only could he further the execution of his plan. He was for ever busy, and the only check to his enjoyments was my sorrowful and dejected mind. I tried to conceal this as much as possible, that I might not debar him from the pleasures natural to one who was entering on a new scene of life, undisturbed by any care or bitter recollection. I often refused to accompany him, alleging another engagement, that I might remain alone. I now also began to collect the materials necessary for my new creation, and this was to me like the torture of single drops of water continually falling on the head.

Every thought that was devoted to it was an extreme anguish, and every word that I spoke in allusion to it caused my lips to quiver, and my heart to palpitate.

After passing some months in London, we received a letter from a person in Scotland who had formerly been our visitor at Geneva. He mentioned the beauties of his native country and asked us if those were not sufficient allurements to induce us to prolong our journey as far north as Perth, where he resided. Clerval eagerly desired to accept this invitation, and I, although I abhorred society, wished to view again mountains and streams and all the wondrous works with which Nature adorns her chosen dwelling-places.

We had arrived in England at the beginning of October, and it was now February. We accordingly determined to commence our journey towards the north at the expiration of another month. In this expedition we did not intend to follow the great road to Edinburgh, but to visit Windsor, Oxford, Matlock, and the Cumberland lakes, resolving to arrive at the completion of this tour about the end of July. I packed up my chemical instruments and the materials I had collected, resolving to finish my labours in some obscure nook in the northern highlands of Scotland.

We quitted London on the 27th of March and remained a few days at Windsor, rambling in its beautiful forest. This was a new scene to us mountaineers; the majestic oaks, the quantity of game, and the herds of stately deer were all novelties to us.

From thence we proceeded to Oxford. As we entered this city, our minds were filled with the remembrance of the events that had been transacted there more than a century and a half before. It was here that Charles I. had collected his forces. This city had remained faithful to him, after the whole nation had forsaken his cause to join the standard of Parliament and liberty. The memory of that unfortunate king and his companions, the amiable Falkland, the insolent Goring, his queen, and son, gave a peculiar interest to every part of the city which they might be supposed to have inhabited. The spirit of elder days found a dwelling here, and we delighted to trace its footsteps. If these feelings had not found an imaginary gratification, the appearance of the city had yet in itself sufficient beauty to obtain our admiration. The colleges are ancient and picturesque; the streets are almost magnificent; and the lovely Isis, which flows beside it through meadows of exquisite verdure, is spread forth into a placid expanse of waters, which reflects its majestic assemblage of towers, and spires, and domes, embosomed among aged trees.

I enjoyed this scene, and yet my enjoyment was embittered both by the memory of the past and the anticipation of the future. I was formed for peaceful happiness. During my youthful days discontent never visited my mind, and if I was ever overcome by *ennui*, the sight of what is beautiful in nature or the study of what is excellent and sublime in the productions of man could always interest my heart and communicate elasticity to my spirits. But I am a blasted tree; the bolt has entered my soul; and I felt then that I should survive to exhibit what I shall soon cease to be—a miserable spectacle of wrecked humanity, pitiable to others and intolerable to myself.

We passed a considerable period at Oxford, rambling among its environs and endeavouring to identify every spot which might relate to the most animating epoch of English history. Our little voyages of discovery were often prolonged by the successive objects that presented themselves. We visited the tomb of the illustrious Hampden and the field on which that patriot fell. For a moment my soul was elevated from its debasing and miserable fears to contemplate the divine ideas of liberty and self-sacrifice of which these sights were the monuments and the remembrancers. For an instant I dared to shake off my chains and look around me with a free and lofty spirit, but the iron had eaten into my flesh, and I sank again, trembling and hopeless, into my miserable self.

We left Oxford with regret and proceeded to Matlock, which was our next place of rest. The country in the neighbourhood of this village resembled, to a greater degree, the scenery of Switzerland; but everything is on a lower scale, and the green hills want the crown of distant white Alps which always attend on the piny mountains of my native country. We visited the wondrous cave and the little cabinets of natural history, where the curiosities are disposed in the same manner as in the collections at Servox and Chamounix. The latter name made me tremble when pronounced by Henry, and I hastened to quit Matlock, with which that terrible scene was thus associated.

From Derby, still journeying northwards, we passed two months in Cumberland and Westmorland. I could now almost fancy myself among the Swiss mountains. The little patches of snow which yet lingered on the northern sides of the mountains, the lakes, and the dashing of the rocky streams were all familiar and dear sights to me. Here also we made some acquaintances, who almost contrived to cheat me into happiness. The delight of Clerval was proportionably greater than mine; his mind expanded in the company of men of talent, and he found in his own nature greater capacities and resources than he could have imagined himself to have possessed while he associated with his inferiors. "I could pass my life here," said he to me; "and among these mountains I should scarcely regret Switzerland and the Rhine."

But he found that a traveller's life is one that includes much pain amidst its enjoyments. His feelings are for ever on the stretch; and when he begins to sink into repose, he finds himself obliged to quit that on which he rests in pleasure for something new, which again engages his attention, and which also he forsakes for other novelties.

We had scarcely visited the various lakes of Cumberland and Westmorland and conceived an affection for some of the inhabitants when the period of our appointment with our Scotch friend approached, and we left them to travel on. For my own part I was not sorry. I had now neglected my promise for some time, and I feared the effects of the dæmon's disappointment. He might remain in Switzerland and wreak his vengeance on my relatives. This idea pursued me and tormented me at every moment from which I might otherwise have snatched repose and peace. I waited for my letters with feverish impatience; if they were delayed I was miserable and overcome by a thousand fears; and when they arrived and I saw the superscription of Elizabeth or my father, I hardly dared to read and ascertain my fate. Sometimes I thought that the fiend followed me and might expedite my remissness by murdering my companion. When these thoughts possessed me, I would not quit Henry for a moment, but followed him as his shadow, to protect him from the fancied rage of his destroyer. I felt as if I had committed some great crime, the consciousness of which haunted me. I was guiltless, but I had indeed drawn down a horrible curse upon my head, as mortal as that of crime.

I visited Edinburgh with languid eyes and mind; and yet that city might have interested the most unfortunate being. Clerval did not like it so well as Oxford, for the antiquity of the latter city was more pleasing to him. But the beauty and regularity of the new town of Edinburgh, its romantic castle and its environs, the most delightful in the world, Arthur's Seat, St. Bernard's Well, and the Pentland Hills, compensated him for the change and filled him with cheerfulness and admiration. But I was impatient to arrive at the termination of my journey.

We left Edinburgh in a week, passing through Coupar, St. Andrew's, and along the banks of the Tay, to Perth, where our friend expected us. But I was in no mood to laugh and talk with strangers or enter into their feelings or plans with the good humour expected from a guest; and accordingly I told Clerval that I wished to make the tour of Scotland alone. "Do you," said I, "enjoy yourself, and let this be our rendezvous. I may be absent a month or two; but do not interfere with my motions, I entreat you; leave me to peace and solitude for a short time; and when I return, I hope it will be with a lighter heart, more congenial to your own temper."

Henry wished to dissuade me, but seeing me bent on this plan, ceased to remonstrate. He entreated me to write often. "I had rather be with you," he said, "in your solitary rambles, than with these Scotch people, whom I do not know; hasten, then, my dear friend, to return, that I may again feel myself somewhat at home, which I cannot do in your absence."

Having parted from my friend, I determined to visit some remote spot of Scotland and finish my work in solitude. I did not doubt but that the monster followed me and would discover himself to me when I should have finished, that he might receive his companion.

With this resolution I traversed the northern highlands and fixed on one of the remotest of the Orkneys as the scene of my labours. It was a place fitted for such a work, being hardly more than a rock whose high sides were continually beaten upon by the waves. The soil was barren, scarcely affording pasture for a few miserable cows, and oatmeal for its inhabitants, which consisted of five persons, whose gaunt and scraggy limbs gave tokens of their miserable fare. Vegetables and bread, when they indulged in such luxuries, and even fresh water, was to be procured from the mainland, which was about five miles distant.

On the whole island there were but three miserable huts, and one of these was vacant when I arrived. This I hired. It contained but two rooms, and these exhibited all the squalidness of the most miserable penury. The thatch had fallen in, the walls were unplastered, and the door was off its hinges. I ordered it to be repaired, bought some furniture, and took possession, an incident which would doubtless have occasioned some surprise had not all the senses of the cottagers been benumbed by want and squalid poverty. As it was, I lived ungazed at and unmolested, hardly thanked for the pittance of food and clothes which I gave, so much does suffering blunt even the coarsest sensations of men.

In this retreat I devoted the morning to labour; but in the evening, when the weather permitted, I walked on the stony beach of the sea to listen to the waves as they roared and dashed at my feet. It was a monotonous yet ever-changing scene. I thought of Switzerland; it was far different from this desolate and appalling landscape. Its hills are covered with vines, and its cottages are scattered thickly in the plains. Its fair lakes reflect a blue and gentle sky, and when troubled by the winds, their tumult is but as the play of a lively infant when compared to the roarings of the giant ocean.

In this manner I distributed my occupations when I first arrived, but as I proceeded in my labour, it became every day more horrible and irksome to me. Sometimes I could not prevail on myself to enter my laboratory for several days, and at other times I toiled day and night in order to complete my work. It was, indeed, a filthy process in which I was engaged. During my first experiment, a kind of enthusiastic frenzy had blinded me to the horror of my employment; my mind was intently fixed on the consummation of my labour, and my eyes were shut to the horror of my proceedings. But now I went to it in cold blood, and my heart often sickened at the work of my hands.

Thus situated, employed in the most detestable occupation, immersed in a solitude where nothing could for an instant call my attention from the actual scene in which I was engaged, my spirits became unequal; I grew restless and nervous. Every moment I feared to meet my persecutor. Sometimes I sat with my eyes fixed on the ground, fearing to raise them lest they should encounter the object which I so much dreaded to behold. I feared to wander from the sight of my fellow creatures lest when alone he should come to claim his companion.

In the mean time I worked on, and my labour was already considerably advanced. I looked towards its completion with a tremulous and eager hope, which I dared not trust myself to question but which was intermixed with obscure forebodings of evil that made my heart sicken in my bosom.

CHAPTER XX

I sat one evening in my laboratory; the sun had set, and the moon was just rising from the sea; I had not sufficient light for my employment, and I remained idle, in a pause of consideration of whether I should leave my labour for the night or hasten its conclusion by an unremitting attention to it. As I sat, a train of reflection occurred to me which led me to consider the effects of what I was now doing. Three years before, I was engaged in the same manner and had created a fiend whose unparalleled barbarity had desolated my heart and filled it for ever with the bitterest remorse. I was now about to form another being of whose dispositions I was alike ignorant; she might become ten thousand times more malignant than her mate and delight, for its own sake, in murder and wretchedness. He had sworn to quit the neighbourhood of man and hide himself in deserts, but she had not; and she, who in all probability was to become a thinking and reasoning animal, might refuse to comply with a compact made before her creation. They might even hate each other; the creature who already lived loathed his own deformity, and might he not conceive a greater abhorrence for it when it came before his eyes in the female form? She also might turn with disgust from him to the superior beauty of man; she might quit him, and he be again alone, exasperated by the fresh provocation of being deserted by one of his own species.

Even if they were to leave Europe and inhabit the deserts of the new world, yet one of the first results of those sympathies for which the dæmon thirsted would be children, and a race of devils would be propagated upon the earth who might make the very existence of the species of man a condition precarious and full of terror. Had I right, for my own benefit, to inflict this curse upon everlasting generations? I had before been moved by the sophisms of the being I had created; I had been struck senseless by his fiendish threats; but now, for the first time, the wickedness of my promise burst upon me; I shuddered to think that future ages might curse me as their pest, whose selfishness had not hesitated to buy its own peace at the price, perhaps, of the existence of the whole human race.

I trembled and my heart failed within me, when, on looking up, I saw by the light of the moon the dæmon at the casement. A ghastly grin wrinkled his lips as he gazed on me, where I sat fulfilling the task which he had allotted to me. Yes, he had followed me in my travels; he had loitered in forests, hid himself in caves, or taken refuge in wide and desert heaths; and he now came to mark my progress and claim the fulfilment of my promise.

As I looked on him, his countenance expressed the utmost extent of malice and treachery. I thought with a sensation of madness on my promise of creating another like to him, and trembling with passion, tore to pieces the thing on which I was engaged. The wretch saw me destroy the creature on whose future existence he depended for happiness, and with a howl of devilish despair and revenge, withdrew.

I left the room, and locking the door, made a solemn vow in my own heart never to resume my labours; and then, with trembling steps, I sought my own apartment. I was alone; none were near me to dissipate the gloom and relieve me from the sickening oppression of the most terrible reveries.

Several hours passed, and I remained near my window gazing on the sea; it was almost motionless, for the winds were hushed, and all nature reposed under the eye of the quiet moon. A few fishing vessels alone specked the water, and now and then the gentle breeze wafted the sound of voices as the fishermen called to one another. I felt the silence, although I was hardly conscious of its extreme profundity, until my ear was suddenly arrested by the paddling of oars near the shore, and a person landed close to my house.

In a few minutes after, I heard the creaking of my door, as if some one endeavoured to open it softly. I trembled from head to foot; I felt a presentiment of who it was and wished to rouse one of the peasants who dwelt in a cottage not far from mine; but I was overcome by the sensation of helplessness, so often felt in frightful dreams, when you in vain endeavour to fly from an impending danger, and was rooted to the spot.

Presently I heard the sound of footsteps along the passage; the door opened, and the wretch whom I dreaded appeared. Shutting the door, he approached me and said in a smothered voice,

"You have destroyed the work which you began; what is it that you intend? Do you dare to break your promise? I have endured toil and misery; I left Switzerland with you; I crept along the shores of the Rhine, among its willow islands and over the summits of its hills. I have dwelt many months in the heaths of England and among the deserts of Scotland. I have endured incalculable fatigue, and cold, and hunger; do you dare destroy my hopes?"

"Begone! I do break my promise; never will I create another like yourself, equal in deformity and wickedness."

"Slave, I before reasoned with you, but you have proved yourself unworthy of my condescension. Remember that I have power; you believe yourself miserable, but I can make you so wretched that the light of day will be hateful to you. You are my creator, but I am your master; obey!"

"The hour of my irresolution is past, and the period of your power is arrived. Your threats cannot move me to do an act of wickedness; but they confirm me in a determination of not creating you a companion in vice. Shall I, in cool blood, set loose upon the earth a dæmon whose delight is in death and wretchedness? Begone! I am firm, and your words will only exasperate my rage."

The monster saw my determination in my face and gnashed his teeth in the impotence of anger. "Shall each man," cried he, "find a wife for his bosom, and each beast have his mate, and I be alone? I had feelings of affection, and they were requited by detestation and scorn. Man! You may hate, but beware! Your hours will pass in dread and misery, and soon the bolt will fall which must ravish from you your happiness for ever. Are you to be happy while I grovel in the intensity of my wretchedness? You can blast my other passions, but revenge remains—revenge, henceforth dearer than light or food! I may die, but first you, my tyrant and tormentor, shall curse the sun that gazes on your misery. Beware, for I am fearless and therefore powerful. I will watch with the wiliness of a snake, that I may sting with its venom. Man, you shall repent of the injuries you inflict."

"Devil, cease; and do not poison the air with these sounds of malice. I have declared my resolution to you, and I am no coward to bend beneath words. Leave me; I am inexorable."

"It is well. I go; but remember, I shall be with you on your wedding-night."

I started forward and exclaimed, "Villain! Before you sign my death-warrant, be sure that you are yourself safe."

I would have seized him, but he eluded me and quitted the house with precipitation. In a few moments I saw him in his boat, which shot across the waters with an arrowy swiftness and was soon lost amidst the waves.

All was again silent, but his words rang in my ears. I burned with rage to pursue the murderer of my peace and precipitate him into the ocean. I walked up and down my room hastily and perturbed, while my imagination conjured up a thousand images to torment and sting me. Why had I not followed him and closed with him in mortal strife? But I had suffered him to depart, and he had directed his course towards the mainland. I shuddered to think who might be the next victim sacrificed to his insatiate revenge. And then I thought again of his words—*I will be with you on your wedding-night.* That, then, was the period fixed for the fulfilment of my destiny. In that hour I should die and at once satisfy and extinguish his malice. The prospect did not move me to fear; yet when I thought of my beloved

Elizabeth, of her tears and endless sorrow, when she should find her lover so barbarously snatched from her, tears, the first I had shed for many months, streamed from my eyes, and I resolved not to fall before my enemy without a bitter struggle.

The night passed away, and the sun rose from the ocean; my feelings became calmer, if it may be called calmness when the violence of rage sinks into the depths of despair. I left the house, the horrid scene of the last night's contention, and walked on the beach of the sea, which I almost regarded as an insuperable barrier between me and my fellow creatures; nay, a wish that such should prove the fact stole across me. I desired that I might pass my life on that barren rock, wearily, it is true, but uninterrupted by any sudden shock of misery. If I returned, it was to be sacrificed or to see those whom I most loved die under the grasp of a dæmon whom I had myself created.

I walked about the isle like a restless spectre, separated from all it loved and miserable in the separation. When it became noon, and the sun rose higher, I lay down on the grass and was overpowered by a deep sleep. I had been awake the whole of the preceding night, my nerves were agitated, and my eyes inflamed by watching and misery. The sleep into which I now sank refreshed me; and when I awoke, I again felt as if I belonged to a race of human beings like myself, and I began to reflect upon what had passed with greater composure; yet still the words of the fiend rang in my ears like a death-knell; they appeared like a dream, yet distinct and oppressive as a reality.

The sun had far descended, and I still sat on the shore, satisfying my appetite, which had become ravenous, with an oaten cake, when I saw a fishing-boat land close to me, and one of the men brought me a packet; it contained letters from Geneva, and one from Clerval entreating me to join him. He said that he was wearing away his time fruitlessly where he was, that letters from the friends he had formed in London desired his return to complete the negotiation they had entered into for his Indian enterprise. He could not any longer delay his departure; but as his journey to London might be followed, even sooner than he now conjectured, by his longer voyage, he entreated me to bestow as much of my society on him as I could spare. He besought me, therefore, to leave my solitary isle and to meet him at Perth, that we might proceed southwards together. This letter in a degree recalled me to life, and I determined to quit my island at the expiration of two days.

Yet, before I departed, there was a task to perform, on which I shuddered to reflect; I must pack up my chemical instruments, and for that purpose I must enter the room which had been the scene of my odious work, and I must handle those utensils the sight of which was sickening to me. The next morning, at daybreak, I summoned sufficient courage and unlocked the door of my laboratory. The remains of the half-finished creature, whom I had destroyed, lay scattered on the floor, and I almost felt as if I had mangled the living flesh of a human being. I paused to collect myself and then entered the chamber. With trembling hand I conveyed the instruments out of the room, but I reflected that I ought not to leave the relics of my work to excite the horror and suspicion of the peasants; and I accordingly put them into a basket, with a great quantity of stones, and laying them up, determined to throw them into the sea that very night; and in the meantime I sat upon the beach, employed in cleaning and arranging my chemical apparatus.

Nothing could be more complete than the alteration that had taken place in my feelings since the night of the appearance of the dæmon. I had before regarded my promise with a gloomy despair as a thing that, with whatever consequences, must be fulfilled; but I now felt as if a film had been taken from before my eyes and that I for the first time saw clearly. The idea of renewing my labours did not for one instant occur to me; the threat I had heard weighed on my thoughts, but I did not reflect that a voluntary act of mine could avert it. I had resolved in my own mind that to create another like the fiend I had first made would be an act of the basest and most atrocious selfishness, and I banished from my mind every thought that could lead to a different conclusion.

Between two and three in the morning the moon rose; and I then, putting my basket aboard a little skiff, sailed out about four miles from the shore. The scene was perfectly solitary; a few boats were returning towards land, but I sailed away from them. I felt as if I was about the commission of a dreadful crime and avoided with shuddering anxiety any encounter with my fellow creatures. At one time the moon, which had before been clear, was suddenly overspread by a thick cloud, and I took advantage of the moment of darkness and cast my basket into the sea; I listened to the gurgling sound as it sank and then sailed away from the spot. The sky became clouded, but the air was pure, although chilled by the northeast breeze that was then rising. But it refreshed me and filled me with such agreeable sensations that I resolved to prolong my stay on the water, and fixing the rudder in a direct position, stretched myself at the bottom of the boat. Clouds hid the moon, everything was obscure, and I heard only the sound of the boat as its keel cut through the waves; the murmur lulled me, and in a short time I slept soundly.

I do not know how long I remained in this situation, but when I awoke I found that the sun had already mounted considerably. The wind was high, and the waves continually threatened the safety of my little skiff. I found that the wind was northeast and must have driven me far from the coast from which I had embarked. I endeavoured to change my course but quickly found that if I again made the attempt the boat would be instantly filled with water. Thus situated, my only resource was to drive before the wind. I confess that I felt a few sensations of terror. I had no compass with me and was so slenderly acquainted with the geography of this part of the world that the sun was of little benefit to me. I might be driven into the wide Atlantic and feel all the tortures of starvation or be swallowed up in the immeasurable waters that roared and buffeted around me. I had already been out many hours and felt the torment of a burning thirst, a prelude to my other sufferings. I looked on the heavens, which were covered by clouds that flew before the wind, only to be replaced by others; I looked upon the sea; it was to be my grave. "Fiend," I exclaimed, "your task is already fulfilled!" I thought of Elizabeth, of my father, and of Clerval—all left behind, on whom the monster might satisfy his sanguinary and merciless passions. This idea plunged me into a reverie so despairing and frightful that even now, when the scene is on the point of closing before me for ever, I shudder to reflect on it.

Some hours passed thus; but by degrees, as the sun declined towards the horizon, the wind died away into a gentle breeze and the sea became free from breakers. But these gave place to a heavy swell; I felt sick and hardly able to hold the rudder, when suddenly I saw a line of high land towards the south.

Almost spent, as I was, by fatigue and the dreadful suspense I endured for several hours, this sudden certainty of life rushed like a flood of warm joy to my heart, and tears gushed from my eyes.

How mutable are our feelings, and how strange is that clinging love we have of life even in the excess of misery! I constructed another sail with a part of my dress and eagerly steered my course towards the land. It had a wild and rocky appearance, but as I approached nearer I easily perceived the traces of cultivation. I saw vessels near the shore and found myself suddenly transported back to the neighbourhood of civilised man. I carefully traced the windings of the land and hailed a steeple which I at length saw issuing from behind a small promontory. As I was in a state of extreme debility, I resolved to sail directly towards the town, as a place where I could most easily procure nourishment. Fortunately I had money with me. As I turned the promontory I perceived a small neat town and a good harbour, which I entered, my heart bounding with joy at my unexpected escape.

As I was occupied in fixing the boat and arranging the sails, several people crowded towards the spot. They seemed much surprised at my appearance, but instead of offering me any assistance, whispered together with gestures that at any other time might have produced in me a slight sensation of alarm. As it was, I merely remarked that they spoke English, and I therefore addressed them in that language. "My good friends," said I, "will you be so kind as to tell me the name of this town and inform me where I am?"

"You will know that soon enough," replied a man with a hoarse voice. "Maybe you are come to a place that will not prove much to your taste, but you will not be consulted as to your quarters, I promise you."

I was exceedingly surprised on receiving so rude an answer from a stranger, and I was also disconcerted on perceiving the frowning and angry countenances of his companions. "Why do you answer me so roughly?" I replied. "Surely it is not the custom of Englishmen to receive strangers so inhospitably."

"I do not know," said the man, "what the custom of the English may be, but it is the custom of the Irish to hate villains."

While this strange dialogue continued, I perceived the crowd rapidly increase. Their faces expressed a mixture of curiosity and anger, which annoyed and in some degree alarmed me. I inquired the way to the inn, but no one replied. I then moved forward, and a murmuring sound arose from the crowd as they followed and surrounded me, when an ill-looking man approaching tapped me on the shoulder and said, "Come, sir, you must follow me to Mr. Kirwin's to give an account of yourself."

"Who is Mr. Kirwin? Why am I to give an account of myself? Is not this a free country?"

"Ay, sir, free enough for honest folks. Mr. Kirwin is a magistrate, and you are to give an account of the death of a gentleman who was found murdered here last night."

This answer startled me, but I presently recovered myself. I was innocent; that could easily be proved; accordingly I followed my conductor in silence and was led to one of the best houses in the town. I was ready to sink from fatigue and hunger, but being surrounded by a crowd, I thought it politic to rouse all my strength, that no physical debility might be construed into apprehension or conscious guilt. Little did I then expect the calamity that was in a few moments to overwhelm me and extinguish in horror and despair all fear of ignominy or death.

I must pause here, for it requires all my fortitude to recall the memory of the frightful events which I am about to relate, in proper detail, to my recollection.

CHAPTER XXI

I was soon introduced into the presence of the magistrate, an old benevolent man with calm and mild manners. He looked upon me, however, with some degree of severity, and then, turning towards my conductors, he asked who appeared as witnesses on this occasion.

About half a dozen men came forward; and, one being selected by the magistrate, he deposed that he had been out fishing the night before with his son and brother-in-law, Daniel Nugent, when, about ten o'clock, they observed a strong northerly blast rising, and they accordingly put in for port. It was a very dark night, as the moon had not yet risen; they did not land at the harbour, but, as they had been accustomed, at a creek about two miles below. He walked on first, carrying a part of the fishing tackle, and his companions followed him at some distance. As he was proceeding along the sands, he struck his foot against something and fell at his length on the ground. His companions came up to assist him, and by the light of their lantern they found that he had fallen on the body of a man, who was to all appearance dead. Their first supposition was that it was the corpse of some person who had been drowned and was thrown on shore by the waves, but on examination they found that the clothes were not wet and even that the body was not then cold. They instantly carried it to the cottage of an old woman near the spot and endeavoured, but in vain, to restore it to life. It appeared to be a handsome young man, about five and twenty years of age. He had apparently been strangled, for there was no sign of any violence except the black mark of fingers on his neck.

The first part of this deposition did not in the least interest me, but when the mark of the fingers was mentioned I remembered the murder of my brother and felt myself extremely agitated; my limbs trembled, and a mist came over my eyes, which obliged me to lean on a chair for support. The magistrate observed me with a keen eye and of course drew an unfavourable augury from my manner.

The son confirmed his father's account, but when Daniel Nugent was called he swore positively that just before the fall of his companion, he saw a boat, with a single man in it, at a short distance from the shore; and as far as he could judge by the light of a few stars, it was the same boat in which I had just landed.

A woman deposed that she lived near the beach and was standing at the door of her cottage, waiting for the return of the fishermen, about an hour before she heard of the discovery of the body, when she saw a boat with only one man in it push off from that part of the shore where the corpse was afterwards found.

Another woman confirmed the account of the fishermen having brought the body into her house; it was not cold. They put it into a bed and rubbed it, and Daniel went to the town for an apothecary, but life was quite gone.

Several other men were examined concerning my landing, and they agreed that, with the strong north wind that had arisen during the night, it was very probable that I had beaten about for many hours and had been obliged to return nearly to the same spot from which I had departed. Besides, they observed that it appeared that I had brought the body from another place, and it was likely that as I did not appear to know the shore, I might have put into the harbour ignorant of the distance of the town of —— from the place where I had deposited the corpse.

Mr. Kirwin, on hearing this evidence, desired that I should be taken into the room where the body lay for interment, that it might be observed what effect the sight of it would produce upon me. This idea was probably suggested by the extreme agitation I had exhibited when the mode of the murder had been described. I was accordingly conducted, by the magistrate and several other persons, to the inn. I could not help being struck by the strange coincidences that had taken place during this eventful night; but, knowing that I had been conversing with several persons in the island I had inhabited about the time that the body had been found, I was perfectly tranquil as to the consequences of the affair.

I entered the room where the corpse lay and was led up to the coffin. How can I describe my sensations on beholding it? I feel yet parched with horror, nor can I reflect on that terrible moment without shuddering and agony. The examination, the presence of the magistrate and witnesses, passed like a dream from my memory when I saw the lifeless form of Henry Clerval stretched before me. I gasped for breath, and throwing myself on the body, I exclaimed, "Have my murderous machinations deprived you also, my dearest Henry, of life? Two I have already destroyed; other victims await their destiny; but you, Clerval, my friend, my benefactor—"

The human frame could no longer support the agonies that I endured, and I was carried out of the room in strong convulsions.

A fever succeeded to this. I lay for two months on the point of death; my ravings, as I afterwards heard, were frightful; I called myself the murderer of William, of Justine, and of Clerval. Sometimes I entreated my attendants to assist me in the destruction of the fiend by whom I was tormented; and at others I felt the fingers of the monster already grasping my neck, and screamed aloud with agony and terror. Fortunately, as I spoke my native language, Mr. Kirwin alone understood me; but my gestures and bitter cries were sufficient to affright the other witnesses.

Why did I not die? More miserable than man ever was before, why did I not sink into forgetfulness and rest? Death snatches away many blooming children, the only hopes of their doting parents; how many brides and youthful lovers have been one day in the bloom of health and hope, and the next a prey for worms and the decay of the tomb! Of what materials was I made that I could thus resist so many shocks, which, like the turning of the wheel, continually renewed the torture?

But I was doomed to live and in two months found myself as awaking from a dream, in a prison, stretched on a wretched bed, surrounded by gaolers, turnkeys, bolts, and all the miserable apparatus of a dungeon. It was morning, I remember, when I thus awoke to understanding; I had forgotten the particulars of what had happened and only felt as if some great misfortune had suddenly overwhelmed me; but when I looked around and saw the barred windows and the squalidness of the room in which I was, all flashed across my memory and I groaned bitterly.

This sound disturbed an old woman who was sleeping in a chair beside me. She was a hired nurse, the wife of one of the turnkeys, and her countenance expressed all those bad qualities which often characterise that class. The lines of her face were hard and rude, like that of persons accustomed to see without sympathising in sights of misery. Her tone expressed her entire indifference; she addressed me in English, and the voice struck me as one that I had heard during my sufferings.

"Are you better now, sir?" said she.

I replied in the same language, with a feeble voice, "I believe I am; but if it be all true, if indeed I did not dream, I am sorry that I am still alive to feel this misery and horror."

"For that matter," replied the old woman, "if you mean about the gentleman you murdered, I believe that it were better for you if you were dead, for I fancy it will go hard with you! However, that's none of my business; I am sent to nurse you and get you well; I do my duty with a safe conscience; it were well if everybody did the same."

I turned with loathing from the woman who could utter so unfeeling a speech to a person just saved, on the very edge of death; but I felt languid and unable to reflect on all that had passed. The whole series of my life appeared to me as a dream; I sometimes doubted if indeed it were all true, for it never presented itself to my mind with the force of reality.

As the images that floated before me became more distinct, I grew feverish; a darkness pressed around me; no one was near me who soothed me with the gentle voice of love; no dear hand supported me. The physician came and prescribed medicines, and the old woman prepared them for me; but utter carelessness was visible in the first, and the expression of brutality was strongly marked in the visage of the second. Who could be interested in the fate of a murderer but the hangman who would gain his fee?

These were my first reflections, but I soon learned that Mr. Kirwin had shown me extreme kindness. He had caused the best room in the prison to be prepared for me (wretched indeed was the best); and it was he who had provided a physician and a nurse. It is true, he seldom came to see me, for although he ardently desired to relieve the sufferings of every human creature, he did not wish to be present at the agonies and miserable ravings of a murderer. He came, therefore, sometimes to see that I was not neglected, but his visits were short and with long intervals.

One day, while I was gradually recovering, I was seated in a chair, my eyes half open and my cheeks livid like those in death. I was overcome by gloom and misery and often reflected I had better seek death than desire to remain in a world which to me was replete with wretchedness. At one time I considered whether I should not declare myself guilty and suffer the penalty of the law, less innocent than poor Justine had been. Such were my thoughts when the door of my apartment was opened and Mr. Kirwin entered. His countenance expressed sympathy and compassion; he drew a chair close to mine and addressed me in French,

"I fear that this place is very shocking to you; can I do anything to make you more comfortable?"

"I thank you, but all that you mention is nothing to me; on the whole earth there is no comfort which I am capable of receiving."

"I know that the sympathy of a stranger can be but of little relief to one borne down as you are by so strange a misfortune. But you will, I hope, soon quit this melancholy abode, for doubtless evidence can easily be brought to free you from the criminal charge."

"That is my least concern; I am, by a course of strange events, become the most miserable of mortals. Persecuted and tortured as I am and have been, can death be any evil to me?"

"Nothing indeed could be more unfortunate and agonising than the strange chances that have lately occurred. You were thrown, by some surprising accident, on this shore, renowned for its hospitality, seized immediately, and charged with murder. The first sight that was presented to your eyes was the body of your friend, murdered in so unaccountable a manner and placed, as it were, by some fiend across your path."

As Mr. Kirwin said this, notwithstanding the agitation I endured on this retrospect of my sufferings, I also felt considerable surprise at the knowledge he seemed to possess concerning me. I suppose some astonishment was exhibited in my countenance, for Mr. Kirwin hastened to say,

"Immediately upon your being taken ill, all the papers that were on your person were brought me, and I examined them that I might discover some trace by which I could send to your relations an account of your misfortune and illness. I found several letters, and, among others, one which I discovered from its commencement to be from your father. I instantly wrote to Geneva; nearly two months have elapsed since the departure of my letter. But you are ill; even now you tremble; you are unfit for agitation of any kind."

"This suspense is a thousand times worse than the most horrible event; tell me what new scene of death has been acted, and whose murder I am now to lament?"

"Your family is perfectly well," said Mr. Kirwin with gentleness; "and someone, a friend, is come to visit you."

I know not by what chain of thought the idea presented itself, but it instantly darted into my mind that the murderer had come to mock at my misery and taunt me with the death of Clerval, as a new incitement for me to comply with his hellish desires. I put my hand before my eyes, and cried out in agony,

"Oh! Take him away! I cannot see him; for God's sake, do not let him enter!"

Mr. Kirwin regarded me with a troubled countenance. He could not help regarding my exclamation as a presumption of my guilt and said in rather a severe tone,

"I should have thought, young man, that the presence of your father would have been welcome instead of inspiring such violent repugnance."

"My father!" cried I, while every feature and every muscle was relaxed from anguish to pleasure. "Is my father indeed come? How kind, how very kind! But where is he, why does he not hasten to me?"

My change of manner surprised and pleased the magistrate; perhaps he thought that my former exclamation was a momentary return of delirium, and now he instantly resumed his former benevolence. He rose and quitted the room with my nurse, and in a moment my father entered it.

Nothing, at this moment, could have given me greater pleasure than the arrival of my father. I stretched out my hand to him and cried,

"Are you then safe—and Elizabeth—and Ernest?"

My father calmed me with assurances of their welfare and endeavoured, by dwelling on these subjects so interesting to my heart, to raise my desponding spirits; but he soon felt that a prison cannot be the abode of cheerfulness. "What a place is this that you inhabit, my son!" said he, looking mournfully at the barred windows and wretched appearance of the room. "You travelled to seek happiness, but a fatality seems to pursue you. And poor Clerval—"

The name of my unfortunate and murdered friend was an agitation too great to be endured in my weak state; I shed tears.

"Alas! Yes, my father," replied I; "some destiny of the most horrible kind hangs over me, and I must live to fulfil it, or surely I should have died on the coffin of Henry."

We were not allowed to converse for any length of time, for the precarious state of my health rendered every precaution necessary that could ensure tranquillity. Mr. Kirwin came in and insisted that my strength should not be exhausted by too much exertion. But the appearance of my father was to me like that of my good angel, and I gradually recovered my health.

As my sickness quitted me, I was absorbed by a gloomy and black melancholy that nothing could dissipate. The image of Clerval was for ever before me, ghastly and murdered. More than once the agitation into which these reflections threw me made my friends dread a dangerous relapse. Alas! Why did they preserve so miserable and detested a life? It was surely that I might fulfil my destiny, which is now drawing to a close. Soon, oh, very soon, will death extinguish these throbbings and relieve me from the mighty weight of anguish that bears me to the dust; and, in executing the award of justice, I shall also sink to rest. Then the appearance of death was distant, although the wish was ever present to my thoughts; and I often sat for hours motionless and speechless, wishing for some mighty revolution that might bury me and my destroyer in its ruins.

The season of the assizes approached. I had already been three months in prison, and although I was still weak and in continual danger of a relapse, I was obliged to travel nearly a hundred miles to the country town where the court was held. Mr. Kirwin charged himself with every care of collecting witnesses and arranging my defence. I was spared the disgrace of appearing publicly as a criminal, as the case was not brought before the court that decides on life and death. The grand jury rejected the bill, on its being proved that I was on the Orkney Islands at the hour the body of my friend was found; and a fortnight after my removal I was liberated from prison.

My father was enraptured on finding me freed from the vexations of a criminal charge, that I was again allowed to breathe the fresh atmosphere and permitted to return to my native country. I did not participate in these feelings, for to me the walls of a dungeon or a palace were alike hateful. The cup of life was poisoned for ever, and although the sun shone upon me, as upon the happy and gay of heart, I saw around me nothing but a dense and frightful darkness, penetrated by no light but the glimmer of two eyes that glared upon me. Sometimes they were the expressive eyes of Henry, languishing in death, the dark orbs nearly covered by the lids and the long black lashes that fringed them; sometimes it was the watery, clouded eyes of the monster, as I first saw them in my chamber at Ingolstadt.

My father tried to awaken in me the feelings of affection. He talked of Geneva, which I should soon visit, of Elizabeth and Ernest; but these words only drew deep groans from me. Sometimes, indeed, I felt a wish for happiness and thought with melancholy delight of my beloved cousin or longed, with a devouring *maladie du pays*, to see once more the blue lake and rapid Rhone, that had been so dear to me in early childhood; but my general state of feeling was a torpor in which a prison was as welcome a residence as the divinest scene in nature; and these fits were seldom interrupted but by paroxysms of anguish and despair. At these moments I often endeavoured to put an end to the existence I loathed, and it required unceasing attendance and vigilance to restrain me from committing some dreadful act of violence.

Yet one duty remained to me, the recollection of which finally triumphed over my selfish despair. It was necessary that I should return without delay to Geneva, there to watch over the lives of those I so fondly loved and to lie in wait for the murderer, that if any chance led me to the place of his concealment, or if he dared again to blast me by his presence, I might, with unfailing aim, put an end to the existence of the monstrous image which I had endued with the mockery of a soul still more monstrous. My father still desired to delay our departure, fearful that I could not sustain the fatigues of a journey, for I was a shattered wreck—the shadow of a human being. My strength was gone. I was a mere skeleton, and fever night and day preyed upon my wasted frame.

Still, as I urged our leaving Ireland with such inquietude and impatience, my father thought it best to yield. We took our passage on board a vessel bound for Havre-de-Grace and sailed with a fair wind from the Irish shores. It was midnight. I lay on the deck looking at the stars and listening to the dashing of the waves. I hailed the darkness that shut Ireland from my sight, and my pulse beat with a feverish joy when I reflected that I should soon see Geneva. The past appeared to me in the light of a frightful dream; yet the vessel in which I was, the wind that blew me from the detested shore of Ireland, and the sea which surrounded me, told me too forcibly that I was deceived by no vision and that Clerval, my friend and dearest companion, had fallen a victim to me and the monster of my creation. I repassed, in my memory, my whole life; my quiet happiness while residing with my family in Geneva, the death of my mother, and my departure for Ingolstadt. I remembered, shuddering, the mad enthusiasm that hurried me on to the creation of my hideous enemy, and I called to mind the night in which he first lived. I was unable to pursue the train of thought; a thousand feelings pressed upon me, and I wept bitterly.

Ever since my recovery from the fever, I had been in the custom of taking every night a small quantity of laudanum, for it was by means of this drug only that I was enabled to gain the rest necessary for the preservation of life. Oppressed by the recollection of my various misfortunes, I now swallowed double my usual quantity and soon slept profoundly. But sleep did not afford me respite from thought and misery; my dreams presented a thousand objects that scared me. Towards morning I was possessed by a kind of nightmare; I felt the fiend's grasp in my neck and could not free myself from it; groans and cries rang in my ears. My father, who was watching over me, perceiving my restlessness, awoke me; the dashing waves were around, the cloudy sky above, the fiend was not here: a sense of security, a feeling that a truce was established between the present hour and the irresistible, disastrous future imparted to me a kind of calm forgetfulness, of which the human mind is by its structure peculiarly susceptible.

CHAPTER XXII

The voyage came to an end. We landed, and proceeded to Paris. I soon found that I had overtaxed my strength and that I must repose before I could continue my journey. My father's care and attentions were indefatigable, but he did not know the origin of my sufferings and sought erroneous methods to remedy the incurable ill. He wished me to seek amusement in society. I abhorred the face of man. Oh, not abhorred! They were my brethren, my fellow beings, and I felt attracted even to the most repulsive among them, as to creatures of an angelic nature and celestial mechanism. But I felt that I had no right to share their intercourse. I had unchained an enemy among them whose joy it was to shed their blood and to revel in their groans. How they would, each and all, abhor me and hunt me from the world, did they know my unhallowed acts and the crimes which had their source in me!

My father yielded at length to my desire to avoid society and strove by various arguments to banish my despair. Sometimes he thought that I felt deeply the degradation of being obliged to answer a charge of murder, and he endeavoured to prove to me the futility of pride.

"Alas! My father," said I, "how little do you know me. Human beings, their feelings and passions, would indeed be degraded if such a wretch as I felt pride. Justine, poor unhappy Justine, was as innocent as I, and she suffered the same charge; she died for it; and I am the cause of this—I murdered her. William, Justine, and Henry—they all died by my hands."

My father had often, during my imprisonment, heard me make the same assertion; when I thus accused myself, he sometimes seemed to desire an explanation, and at others he appeared to consider it as the offspring of delirium, and that, during my illness, some idea of this kind had presented itself to my imagination, the remembrance of which I preserved in my convalescence. I avoided explanation and maintained a continual silence concerning the wretch I had created. I had a persuasion that I should be supposed mad, and this in itself would for ever have chained my tongue. But, besides, I could not bring myself to disclose a secret which would fill my hearer with consternation and make fear and unnatural horror the inmates of his breast. I checked, therefore, my impatient thirst for sympathy and was silent when I would have given the world to have confided the fatal secret.

Yet, still, words like those I have recorded would burst uncontrollably from me. I could offer no explanation of them, but their truth in part relieved the burden of my mysterious woe.

Upon this occasion my father said, with an expression of unbounded wonder, "My dearest Victor, what infatuation is this? My dear son, I entreat you never to make such an assertion again."

"I am not mad," I cried energetically; "the sun and the heavens, who have viewed my operations, can bear witness of my truth. I am the assassin of those most innocent victims; they died by my machinations. A thousand times would I have shed my own blood, drop by drop, to have saved their lives; but I could not, my father, indeed I could not sacrifice the whole human race."

The conclusion of this speech convinced my father that my ideas were deranged, and he instantly changed the subject of our conversation and endeavoured to alter the course of my thoughts. He wished as much as possible to obliterate the memory of the scenes that had taken place in Ireland and never alluded to them or suffered me to speak of my misfortunes.

As time passed away I became more calm; misery had her dwelling in my heart, but I no longer talked in the same incoherent manner of my own crimes; sufficient for me was the consciousness of them. By the utmost self-violence I curbed the imperious voice of wretchedness, which sometimes desired to declare itself to the whole world, and my manners were calmer and more composed than they had ever been since my journey to the sea of ice.

A few days before we left Paris on our way to Switzerland, I received the following letter from Elizabeth:

"My dear Friend,

"It gave me the greatest pleasure to receive a letter from my uncle dated at Paris; you are no longer at a formidable distance, and I may hope to see you in less than a fortnight. My poor cousin, how much you must have suffered! I expect to see you looking even more ill than when you quitted Geneva. This winter has been passed most miserably, tortured as I have been by anxious suspense; yet I hope to see peace in your countenance and to find that your heart is not totally void of comfort and tranquillity.

"Yet I fear that the same feelings now exist that made you so miserable a year ago, even perhaps augmented by time. I would not disturb you at this period, when so many misfortunes weigh upon you, but a conversation that I had with my uncle previous to his departure renders some explanation necessary before we meet.

Explanation! You may possibly say, What can Elizabeth have to explain? If you really say this, my questions are answered and all my doubts satisfied. But you are distant from me, and it is possible that you may dread and yet be pleased with this explanation; and in a probability of this being the case, I dare not any longer postpone writing what, during your absence, I have often wished to express to you but have never had the courage to begin.

"You well know, Victor, that our union had been the favourite plan of your parents ever since our infancy. We were told this when young, and taught to look forward to it as an event that would certainly take place. We were affectionate playfellows during childhood, and, I believe, dear and valued friends to one another as we grew older. But as brother and sister often entertain a lively affection towards each other without desiring a more intimate union, may not such also be our case? Tell me, dearest Victor. Answer me, I conjure you by our mutual happiness, with simple truth—Do you not love another?

"You have travelled; you have spent several years of your life at Ingolstadt; and I confess to you, my friend, that when I saw you last autumn so unhappy, flying to solitude from the society of every creature, I could not help supposing that you might regret our connection and believe yourself bound in honour to fulfil the wishes of your parents, although they opposed themselves to your inclinations. But this is false reasoning. I confess to you, my friend, that I love you and that in my airy dreams of futurity you have been my constant friend and companion. But it is your happiness I desire as well as my own when I declare to you that our marriage would render me eternally miserable unless it were the dictate of your own free choice. Even now I weep to think that, borne down as you are by the cruellest misfortunes, you may stifle, by the word *honour*, all hope of that love and happiness which would alone restore you to yourself. I, who have so disinterested an affection for you, may increase your miseries tenfold by being an obstacle to your wishes. Ah! Victor, be assured that your cousin and playmate has too sincere a love for you not to be made miserable by this supposition. Be happy, my friend; and if you obey me in this one request, remain satisfied that nothing on earth will have the power to interrupt my tranquillity.

"Do not let this letter disturb you; do not answer tomorrow, or the next day, or even until you come, if it will give you pain. My uncle will send me news of your health, and if I see but one smile on your lips when we meet, occasioned by this or any other exertion of mine, I shall need no other happiness.

"Elizabeth Lavenza.
"Geneva, May 18th, 17—"

This letter revived in my memory what I had before forgotten, the threat of the fiend—"*I will be with you on your wedding-night!*" Such was my sentence, and on that night would the dæmon employ every art to destroy me and tear me from the glimpse of happiness which promised partly to console my sufferings. On that night he had determined to consummate his crimes by my death. Well, be it so; a deadly struggle would then assuredly take place, in which if he were victorious I should be at peace and his power over me be at an end. If he were vanquished, I should be a free man. Alas! What freedom? Such as the peasant enjoys when his family have been massacred before his eyes, his cottage burnt, his lands laid waste, and he is turned adrift, homeless, penniless, and alone, but free. Such would be my liberty except that in my Elizabeth I possessed a treasure, alas, balanced by those horrors of remorse and guilt which would pursue me until death.

Sweet and beloved Elizabeth! I read and reread her letter, and some softened feelings stole into my heart and dared to whisper paradisiacal dreams of love and joy; but the apple was already eaten, and the angel's arm bared to drive me from all hope. Yet I would die to make her happy. If the monster executed his threat, death was inevitable; yet, again, I considered whether my marriage would hasten my fate. My destruction might indeed arrive a few months sooner, but if my torturer should suspect that I postponed it, influenced by his menaces, he would surely find other and perhaps more dreadful means of revenge. He had vowed *to be with me on my wedding-night*, yet he did not consider that threat as binding him to peace in the meantime, for as if to show me that he was not yet satiated with blood, he had murdered Clerval immediately after the enunciation of his threats. I resolved, therefore, that if my immediate union with my cousin would conduce either to hers or my father's happiness, my adversary's designs against my life should not retard it a single hour.

In this state of mind I wrote to Elizabeth. My letter was calm and affectionate. "I fear, my beloved girl," I said, "little happiness remains for us on earth; yet all that I may one day enjoy is centred in you. Chase away your idle fears; to you alone do I consecrate my life and my endeavours for contentment. I have one secret, Elizabeth, a dreadful one; when revealed to you, it will chill your frame with horror, and then, far from being surprised at my misery, you will only wonder that I survive what I have endured. I will confide this tale of misery and terror to you the day after our marriage shall take place, for, my sweet cousin, there must be perfect confidence between us. But until then, I conjure you, do not mention or allude to it. This I most earnestly entreat, and I know you will comply."

In about a week after the arrival of Elizabeth's letter we returned to Geneva. The sweet girl welcomed me with warm affection, yet tears were in her eyes as she beheld my emaciated frame and feverish cheeks. I saw a change in her also. She was thinner and had lost much of that heavenly vivacity that had before charmed me; but her gentleness and soft looks of compassion made her a more fit companion for one blasted and miserable as I was.

The tranquillity which I now enjoyed did not endure. Memory brought madness with it, and when I thought of what had passed, a real insanity possessed me; sometimes I was furious and burnt with rage, sometimes low and despondent. I neither spoke nor looked at anyone, but sat motionless, bewildered by the multitude of miseries that overcame me.

Elizabeth alone had the power to draw me from these fits; her gentle voice would soothe me when transported by passion and inspire me with human feelings when sunk in torpor. She wept with me and for me. When reason returned, she would remonstrate and endeavour to inspire me with resignation. Ah! It is well for the unfortunate to be resigned, but for the guilty there is no peace. The agonies of remorse poison the luxury there is otherwise sometimes found in indulging the excess of grief.

Soon after my arrival my father spoke of my immediate marriage with Elizabeth. I remained silent.

"Have you, then, some other attachment?"

"None on earth. I love Elizabeth and look forward to our union with delight. Let the day therefore be fixed; and on it I will consecrate myself, in life or death, to the happiness of my cousin."

"My dear Victor, do not speak thus. Heavy misfortunes have befallen us, but let us only cling closer to what remains and transfer our love for those whom we have lost to those who yet live. Our circle will be small but bound close by the ties of affection and mutual misfortune. And when time shall have softened your despair, new and dear objects of care will be born to replace those of whom we have been so cruelly deprived."

Such were the lessons of my father. But to me the remembrance of the threat returned; nor can you wonder that, omnipotent as the fiend had yet been in his deeds of blood, I should almost regard him as invincible, and that when he had pronounced the words "*I shall be with you on your wedding-night,*" I should regard the threatened fate as unavoidable. But death was no evil to me if the loss of Elizabeth were balanced with it, and I therefore, with a contented and even cheerful countenance, agreed with my father that if my cousin would consent, the ceremony should take place in ten days, and thus put, as I imagined, the seal to my fate.

Great God! If for one instant I had thought what might be the hellish intention of my fiendish adversary, I would rather have banished myself for ever from my native country and wandered a friendless outcast over the earth than have consented to this miserable marriage. But, as if possessed of magic powers, the monster had blinded me to his real intentions; and when I thought that I had prepared only my own death, I hastened that of a far dearer victim.

As the period fixed for our marriage drew nearer, whether from cowardice or a prophetic feeling, I felt my heart sink within me. But I concealed my feelings by an appearance of hilarity that brought smiles and joy to the countenance of my father, but hardly deceived the ever-watchful and nicer eye of Elizabeth. She looked forward to our union with placid contentment, not unmingled with a little fear, which past misfortunes had impressed, that what now appeared certain and tangible happiness might soon dissipate into an airy dream and leave no trace but deep and everlasting regret.

Preparations were made for the event, congratulatory visits were received, and all wore a smiling appearance. I shut up, as well as I could, in my own heart the anxiety that preyed there and entered with seeming earnestness into the plans of my father, although they might only serve as the decorations of my tragedy. Through my father's exertions a part of the inheritance of Elizabeth had been restored to her by the Austrian government. A small possession on the shores of Como belonged to her. It was agreed that, immediately after our union, we should proceed to Villa Lavenza and spend our first days of happiness beside the beautiful lake near which it stood.

In the meantime I took every precaution to defend my person in case the fiend should openly attack me. I carried pistols and a dagger constantly about me and was ever on the watch to prevent artifice, and by these means gained a greater degree of tranquillity. Indeed, as the period approached, the threat appeared more as a delusion, not to be regarded as worthy to disturb my peace, while the happiness I hoped for in my marriage wore a greater appearance of certainty as the day fixed for its solemnisation drew nearer and I heard it continually spoken of as an occurrence which no accident could possibly prevent.

Elizabeth seemed happy; my tranquil demeanour contributed greatly to calm her mind. But on the day that was to fulfil my wishes and my destiny, she was melancholy, and a presentiment of evil pervaded her; and perhaps also she thought of the dreadful secret which I had promised to reveal to her on the following day. My father was in the meantime overjoyed, and, in the bustle of preparation, only recognised in the melancholy of his niece the diffidence of a bride.

After the ceremony was performed a large party assembled at my father's, but it was agreed that Elizabeth and I should commence our journey by water, sleeping that night at Evian and continuing our voyage on the following day. The day was fair, the wind favourable; all smiled on our nuptial embarkation.

Those were the last moments of my life during which I enjoyed the feeling of happiness. We passed rapidly along; the sun was hot, but we were sheltered from its rays by a kind of canopy while we enjoyed the beauty of the scene, sometimes on one side of the lake, where we saw Mont Salêve, the pleasant banks of Montalègre, and at a distance, surmounting all, the beautiful Mont Blanc, and the assemblage of snowy mountains that in vain endeavour to emulate her; sometimes coasting the opposite banks, we saw the mighty Jura opposing its dark side to the ambition that would quit its native country, and an almost insurmountable barrier to the invader who should wish to enslave it.

I took the hand of Elizabeth. "You are sorrowful, my love. Ah! If you knew what I have suffered and what I may yet endure, you would endeavour to let me taste the quiet and freedom from despair that this one day at least permits me to enjoy."

"Be happy, my dear Victor," replied Elizabeth; "there is, I hope, nothing to distress you; and be assured that if a lively joy is not painted in my face, my heart is contented. Something whispers to me not to depend too much on the prospect that is opened before us, but I will not listen to such a sinister voice. Observe how fast we move along and how the clouds, which sometimes obscure and sometimes rise above the dome of Mont Blanc, render this scene of beauty still more interesting. Look also at the innumerable fish that are swimming in the clear waters, where we can distinguish every pebble that lies at the bottom. What a divine day! How happy and serene all nature appears!"

Thus Elizabeth endeavoured to divert her thoughts and mine from all reflection upon melancholy subjects. But her temper was fluctuating; joy for a few instants shone in her eyes, but it continually gave place to distraction and reverie.

The sun sank lower in the heavens; we passed the river Drance and observed its path through the chasms of the higher and the glens of the lower hills. The Alps here come closer to the lake, and we approached the amphitheatre of mountains which forms its eastern boundary. The spire of Evian shone under the woods that surrounded it and the range of mountain above mountain by which it was overhung.

The wind, which had hitherto carried us along with amazing rapidity, sank at sunset to a light breeze; the soft air just ruffled the water and caused a pleasant motion among the trees as we approached the shore, from which it wafted the most delightful scent of flowers and hay. The sun sank beneath the horizon as we landed, and as I touched the shore I felt those cares and fears revive which soon were to clasp me and cling to me for ever.

CHAPTER XXIII

It was eight o'clock when we landed; we walked for a short time on the shore, enjoying the transitory light, and then retired to the inn and contemplated the lovely scene of waters, woods, and mountains, obscured in darkness, yet still displaying their black outlines.

The wind, which had fallen in the south, now rose with great violence in the west. The moon had reached her summit in the heavens and was beginning to descend; the clouds swept across it swifter than the flight of the vulture and dimmed her rays, while the lake reflected the scene of the busy heavens, rendered still busier by the restless waves that were beginning to rise. Suddenly a heavy storm of rain descended.

I had been calm during the day, but so soon as night obscured the shapes of objects, a thousand fears arose in my mind. I was anxious and watchful, while my right hand grasped a pistol which was hidden in my bosom; every sound terrified me, but I resolved that I would sell my life dearly and not shrink from the conflict until my own life or that of my adversary was extinguished.

Elizabeth observed my agitation for some time in timid and fearful silence, but there was something in my glance which communicated terror to her, and trembling, she asked, "What is it that agitates you, my dear Victor? What is it you fear?"

"Oh! Peace, peace, my love," replied I; "this night, and all will be safe; but this night is dreadful, very dreadful."

I passed an hour in this state of mind, when suddenly I reflected how fearful the combat which I momentarily expected would be to my wife, and I earnestly entreated her to retire, resolving not to join her until I had obtained some knowledge as to the situation of my enemy.

She left me, and I continued some time walking up and down the passages of the house and inspecting every corner that might afford a retreat to my adversary. But I discovered no trace of him and was beginning to conjecture that some fortunate chance had intervened to prevent the execution of his menaces when suddenly I heard a shrill and dreadful scream. It came from the room into which Elizabeth had retired. As I heard it, the whole truth rushed into my mind, my arms dropped, the motion of every muscle and fibre was suspended; I could feel the blood trickling in my veins and tingling in the extremities of my limbs. This state lasted but for an instant; the scream was repeated, and I rushed into the room.

Great God! Why did I not then expire! Why am I here to relate the destruction of the best hope and the purest creature on earth? She was there, lifeless and inanimate, thrown across the bed, her head hanging down and her pale and distorted features half covered by her hair. Everywhere I turn I see the same figure—her bloodless arms and relaxed form flung by the murderer on its bridal bier. Could I behold this and live? Alas! Life is obstinate and clings closest where it is most hated. For a moment only did I lose recollection; I fell senseless on the ground.

When I recovered I found myself surrounded by the people of the inn; their countenances expressed a breathless terror, but the horror of others appeared only as a mockery, a shadow of the feelings that oppressed me. I escaped from them to the room where lay the body of Elizabeth, my love, my wife, so lately living, so dear, so worthy. She had been moved from the posture in which I had first beheld her, and now, as she lay, her head upon her arm and a handkerchief thrown across her face and neck, I might have supposed her asleep. I rushed towards her and embraced her with ardour, but the deadly languor and coldness of the limbs told me that what I now held in my arms had ceased to be the Elizabeth whom I had loved and cherished. The murderous mark of the fiend's grasp was on her neck, and the breath had ceased to issue from her lips.

While I still hung over her in the agony of despair, I happened to look up. The windows of the room had before been darkened, and I felt a kind of panic on seeing the pale yellow light of the moon illuminate the chamber. The shutters had been thrown back, and with a sensation of horror not to be described, I saw at the open window a figure the most hideous and abhorred. A grin was on the face of the monster; he seemed to jeer, as with his fiendish finger he pointed towards the corpse of my wife. I rushed towards the window, and drawing a pistol from my bosom, fired; but he eluded me, leaped from his station, and running with the swiftness of lightning, plunged into the lake.

The report of the pistol brought a crowd into the room. I pointed to the spot where he had disappeared, and we followed the track with boats; nets were cast, but in vain. After passing several hours, we returned hopeless, most of my companions believing it to have been a form conjured up by my fancy. After having landed, they proceeded to search the country, parties going in different directions among the woods and vines.

I attempted to accompany them and proceeded a short distance from the house, but my head whirled round, my steps were like those of a drunken man, I fell at last in a state of utter exhaustion; a film covered my eyes, and my skin was parched with the heat of fever. In this state I was carried back and placed on a bed, hardly conscious of what had happened; my eyes wandered round the room as if to seek something that I had lost.

After an interval I arose, and as if by instinct, crawled into the room where the corpse of my beloved lay. There were women weeping around; I hung over it and joined my sad tears to theirs; all this time no distinct idea presented itself to my mind, but my thoughts rambled to various subjects, reflecting confusedly on my misfortunes and their cause. I was bewildered, in a cloud of wonder and horror. The death of William, the execution of Justine, the murder of Clerval, and lastly of my wife; even at that moment I knew not that my only remaining friends were safe from the malignity of the fiend; my father even now might be writhing under his grasp, and Ernest might be dead at his feet. This idea made me shudder and recalled me to action. I started up and resolved to return to Geneva with all possible speed.

There were no horses to be procured, and I must return by the lake; but the wind was unfavourable, and the rain fell in torrents. However, it was hardly morning, and I might reasonably hope to arrive by night. I hired men to row and took an oar myself, for I had always experienced relief from mental torment in bodily exercise. But the overflowing misery I now felt, and the excess of agitation that I endured rendered me incapable of any exertion. I threw down the oar, and leaning my head upon my hands, gave way to every gloomy idea that arose. If I looked up, I saw scenes which were familiar to me in my happier time and which I had contemplated but the day before in the company of her who was now but a shadow and a recollection. Tears streamed from my eyes. The rain had ceased for a moment, and I saw the fish play in the waters as they had done a few hours before; they had then been observed by Elizabeth. Nothing is so painful to the human mind as a great and sudden change. The sun might shine or the clouds might lower, but nothing could appear to me as it had done the day before. A fiend had snatched from me every hope of future happiness; no creature had ever been so miserable as I was; so frightful an event is single in the history of man.

But why should I dwell upon the incidents that followed this last overwhelming event? Mine has been a tale of horrors; I have reached their *acme*, and what I must now relate can but be tedious to you. Know that, one by one, my friends were snatched away; I was left desolate. My own strength is exhausted, and I must tell, in a few words, what remains of my hideous narration.

I arrived at Geneva. My father and Ernest yet lived, but the former sunk under the tidings that I bore. I see him now, excellent and venerable old man! His eyes wandered in vacancy, for they had lost their charm and their delight—his Elizabeth, his more than daughter, whom he doted on with all that affection which a man feels, who in the decline of life, having few affections, clings more earnestly to those that remain. Cursed, cursed be the fiend that brought misery on his grey hairs and doomed him to waste in wretchedness! He could not live under the horrors that were accumulated around him; the springs of existence suddenly gave way; he was unable to rise from his bed, and in a few days he died in my arms.

What then became of me? I know not; I lost sensation, and chains and darkness were the only objects that pressed upon me. Sometimes, indeed, I dreamt that I wandered in flowery meadows and pleasant vales with the friends of my youth, but I awoke and found myself in a dungeon. Melancholy followed, but by degrees I gained a clear conception of my miseries and situation and was then released from my prison. For they had called me mad, and during many months, as I understood, a solitary cell had been my habitation.

Liberty, however, had been a useless gift to me, had I not, as I awakened to reason, at the same time awakened to revenge. As the memory of past misfortunes pressed upon me, I began to reflect on their cause—the monster whom I had created, the miserable dæmon whom I had sent abroad into the world for my destruction. I was possessed by a maddening rage when I thought of him, and desired and ardently prayed that I might have him within my grasp to wreak a great and signal revenge on his cursed head.

Nor did my hate long confine itself to useless wishes; I began to reflect on the best means of securing him; and for this purpose, about a month after my release, I repaired to a criminal judge in the town and told him that I had an accusation to make, that I knew the destroyer of my family, and that I required him to exert his whole authority for the apprehension of the murderer.

The magistrate listened to me with attention and kindness. "Be assured, sir," said he, "no pains or exertions on my part shall be spared to discover the villain."

"I thank you," replied I; "listen, therefore, to the deposition that I have to make. It is indeed a tale so strange that I should fear you would not credit it were there not something in truth which, however wonderful, forces conviction. The story is too connected to be mistaken for a dream, and I have no motive for falsehood." My manner as I thus addressed him was impressive but calm; I had formed in my own heart a resolution to pursue my destroyer to death, and this purpose quieted my agony and for an interval reconciled me to life. I now related my history briefly but with firmness and precision, marking the dates with accuracy and never deviating into invective or exclamation.

The magistrate appeared at first perfectly incredulous, but as I continued he became more attentive and interested; I saw him sometimes shudder with horror; at others a lively surprise, unmingled with disbelief, was painted on his countenance.

When I had concluded my narration, I said, "This is the being whom I accuse and for whose seizure and punishment I call upon you to exert your whole power. It is your duty as a magistrate, and I believe and hope that your feelings as a man will not revolt from the execution of those functions on this occasion."

This address caused a considerable change in the physiognomy of my own auditor. He had heard my story with that half kind of belief that is given to a tale of spirits and supernatural events; but when he was called upon to act officially in consequence, the whole tide of his incredulity returned. He, however, answered mildly, "I would willingly afford you every aid in your pursuit, but the creature of whom you speak appears to have powers which would put all my exertions to defiance. Who can follow an animal which can traverse the sea of ice and inhabit caves and dens where no man would venture to intrude? Besides, some months have elapsed since the commission of his crimes, and no one can conjecture to what place he has wandered or what region he may now inhabit."

"I do not doubt that he hovers near the spot which I inhabit, and if he has indeed taken refuge in the Alps, he may be hunted like the chamois and destroyed as a beast of prey. But I perceive your thoughts; you do not credit my narrative and do not intend to pursue my enemy with the punishment which is his desert."

As I spoke, rage sparkled in my eyes; the magistrate was intimidated. "You are mistaken," said he. "I will exert myself, and if it is in my power to seize the monster, be assured that he shall suffer punishment proportionate to his crimes. But I fear, from what you have yourself described to be his properties, that this will prove impracticable; and thus, while every proper measure is pursued, you should make up your mind to disappointment."

"That cannot be; but all that I can say will be of little avail. My revenge is of no moment to you; yet, while I allow it to be a vice, I confess that it is the devouring and only passion of my soul. My rage is unspeakable when I reflect that the murderer, whom I have turned loose upon society, still exists. You refuse my just demand; I have but one resource, and I devote myself, either in my life or death, to his destruction."

I trembled with excess of agitation as I said this; there was a frenzy in my manner, and something, I doubt not, of that haughty fierceness which the martyrs of old are said to have possessed. But to a Genevan magistrate, whose mind was occupied by far other ideas than those of devotion and heroism, this elevation of mind had much the appearance of madness. He endeavoured to soothe me as a nurse does a child and reverted to my tale as the effects of delirium.

"Man," I cried, "how ignorant art thou in thy pride of wisdom! Cease; you know not what it is you say."

I broke from the house angry and disturbed and retired to meditate on some other mode of action.

CHAPTER XXIV

My present situation was one in which all voluntary thought was swallowed up and lost. I was hurried away by fury; revenge alone endowed me with strength and composure; it moulded my feelings and allowed me to be calculating and calm at periods when otherwise delirium or death would have been my portion.

My first resolution was to quit Geneva for ever; my country, which, when I was happy and beloved, was dear to me, now, in my adversity, became hateful. I provided myself with a sum of money, together with a few jewels which had belonged to my mother, and departed.

And now my wanderings began which are to cease but with life. I have traversed a vast portion of the earth and have endured all the hardships which travellers in deserts and barbarous countries are wont to meet. How I have lived I hardly know; many times have I stretched my failing limbs upon the sandy plain and prayed for death. But revenge kept me alive; I dared not die and leave my adversary in being.

When I quitted Geneva my first labour was to gain some clue by which I might trace the steps of my fiendish enemy. But my plan was unsettled, and I wandered many hours round the confines of the town, uncertain what path I should pursue. As night approached I found myself at the entrance of the cemetery where William, Elizabeth, and my father reposed. I entered it and approached the tomb which marked their graves. Everything was silent except the leaves of the trees, which were gently agitated by the wind; the night was nearly dark, and the scene would have been solemn and affecting even to an uninterested observer. The spirits of the departed seemed to flit around and to cast a shadow, which was felt but not seen, around the head of the mourner.

The deep grief which this scene had at first excited quickly gave way to rage and despair. They were dead, and I lived; their murderer also lived, and to destroy him I must drag out my weary existence. I knelt on the grass and kissed the earth and with quivering lips exclaimed, "By the sacred earth on which I kneel, by the shades that wander near me, by the deep and eternal grief that I feel, I swear; and by thee, O Night, and the spirits that preside over thee, to pursue the dæmon who caused this misery, until he or I shall perish in mortal conflict. For this purpose I will preserve my life; to execute this dear revenge will I again behold the sun and tread the green herbage of earth, which otherwise should vanish from my eyes for ever. And I call on you, spirits of the dead, and on you, wandering ministers of vengeance, to aid and conduct me in my work. Let the cursed and hellish monster drink deep of agony; let him feel the despair that now torments me."

I had begun my adjuration with solemnity and an awe which almost assured me that the shades of my murdered friends heard and approved my devotion, but the furies possessed me as I concluded, and rage choked my utterance.

I was answered through the stillness of night by a loud and fiendish laugh. It rang on my ears long and heavily; the mountains re-echoed it, and I felt as if all hell surrounded me with mockery and laughter. Surely in that moment I should have been possessed by frenzy and have destroyed my miserable existence but that my vow was heard and that I was reserved for vengeance. The laughter died away, when a well-known and abhorred voice, apparently close to my ear, addressed me in an audible whisper, "I am satisfied, miserable wretch! You have determined to live, and I am satisfied."

I darted towards the spot from which the sound proceeded, but the devil eluded my grasp. Suddenly the broad disk of the moon arose and shone full upon his ghastly and distorted shape as he fled with more than mortal speed.

I pursued him, and for many months this has been my task. Guided by a slight clue, I followed the windings of the Rhone, but vainly. The blue Mediterranean appeared, and by a strange chance, I saw the fiend enter by night and hide himself in a vessel bound for the Black Sea. I took my passage in the same ship, but he escaped, I know not how.

Amidst the wilds of Tartary and Russia, although he still evaded me, I have ever followed in his track. Sometimes the peasants, scared by this horrid apparition, informed me of his path; sometimes he himself, who feared that if I lost all trace of him I should despair and die, left some mark to guide me. The snows descended on my head, and I saw the print of his huge step on the white plain. To you first entering on life, to whom care is new and agony unknown, how can you understand what I have felt and still feel? Cold, want, and fatigue were the least pains which I was destined to endure; I was cursed by some devil and carried about with me my eternal hell; yet still a spirit of good followed and directed my steps and when I most murmured would suddenly extricate me from seemingly insurmountable difficulties. Sometimes, when nature, overcome by hunger, sank under the exhaustion, a repast was prepared for me in the desert that restored and inspirited me. The fare was, indeed, coarse, such as the peasants of the country ate, but I will not doubt that it was set there by the spirits that I had invoked to aid me. Often, when all was dry, the heavens cloudless, and I was parched by thirst, a slight cloud would bedim the sky, shed the few drops that revived me, and vanish.

I followed, when I could, the courses of the rivers; but the dæmon generally avoided these, as it was here that the population of the country chiefly collected. In other places human beings were seldom seen, and I generally subsisted on the wild animals that crossed my path. I had money with me and gained the friendship of the villagers by distributing it; or I brought with me some food that I had killed, which, after taking a small part, I always presented to those who had provided me with fire and utensils for cooking.

My life, as it passed thus, was indeed hateful to me, and it was during sleep alone that I could taste joy. O blessed sleep! Often, when most miserable, I sank to repose, and my dreams lulled me even to rapture. The spirits that guarded me had provided these moments, or rather hours, of happiness that I might retain strength to fulfil my pilgrimage. Deprived of this respite, I should have sunk under my hardships. During the day I was sustained and inspirited by the hope of night, for in sleep I saw my friends, my wife, and my beloved country; again I saw the benevolent countenance of my father, heard the silver tones of my Elizabeth's voice, and beheld Clerval enjoying health and youth. Often, when wearied by a toilsome march, I persuaded myself that I was dreaming until night should come and that I should then enjoy reality in the arms of my dearest friends. What agonising fondness did I feel for them! How did I cling to their dear forms, as sometimes they haunted even my waking hours, and persuade myself that they still lived! At such moments vengeance, that burned within me, died in my heart, and I pursued my path towards the destruction of the dæmon more as a task enjoined by heaven, as the mechanical impulse of some power of which I was unconscious, than as the ardent desire of my soul.

What his feelings were whom I pursued I cannot know. Sometimes, indeed, he left marks in writing on the barks of the trees or cut in stone that guided me and instigated my fury. "My reign is not yet over"—these words were legible in one of these inscriptions—"you live, and my power is complete. Follow me; I seek the everlasting ices of the north, where you will feel the misery of cold and frost, to which I am impassive. You will find near this place, if you follow not too tardily, a dead hare; eat and be refreshed. Come on, my enemy; we have yet to wrestle for our lives, but many hard and miserable hours must you endure until that period shall arrive."

Scoffing devil! Again do I vow vengeance; again do I devote thee, miserable fiend, to torture and death. Never will I give up my search until he or I perish; and then with what ecstasy shall I join my Elizabeth and my departed friends, who even now prepare for me the reward of my tedious toil and horrible pilgrimage!

As I still pursued my journey to the northward, the snows thickened and the cold increased in a degree almost too severe to support. The peasants were shut up in their hovels, and only a few of the most hardy ventured forth to seize the animals whom starvation had forced from their hiding-places to seek for prey. The rivers were covered with ice, and no fish could be procured; and thus I was cut off from my chief article of maintenance.

The triumph of my enemy increased with the difficulty of my labours. One inscription that he left was in these words: "Prepare! Your toils only begin; wrap yourself in furs and provide food, for we shall soon enter upon a journey where your sufferings will satisfy my everlasting hatred."

My courage and perseverance were invigorated by these scoffing words; I resolved not to fail in my purpose, and calling on Heaven to support me, I continued with unabated fervour to traverse immense deserts, until the ocean appeared at a distance and formed the utmost boundary of the horizon. Oh! How unlike it was to the blue seasons of the south! Covered with ice, it was only to be distinguished from land by its superior wildness and ruggedness. The Greeks wept for joy when they beheld the Mediterranean from the hills of Asia, and hailed with rapture the boundary of their toils. I did not weep, but I knelt down and with a full heart thanked my guiding spirit for conducting me in safety to the place where I hoped, notwithstanding my adversary's gibe, to meet and grapple with him.

Some weeks before this period I had procured a sledge and dogs and thus traversed the snows with inconceivable speed. I know not whether the fiend possessed the same advantages, but I found that, as before I had daily lost ground in the pursuit, I now gained on him, so much so that when I first saw the ocean he was but one day's journey in advance, and I hoped to intercept him before he should reach the beach. With new courage, therefore, I pressed on, and in two days arrived at a wretched hamlet on the seashore. I inquired of the inhabitants concerning the fiend and gained accurate information. A gigantic monster, they said, had arrived the night before, armed with a gun and many pistols, putting to flight the inhabitants of a solitary cottage through fear of his terrific appearance. He had carried off their store of winter food, and placing it in a sledge, to draw which he had seized on a numerous drove of trained dogs, he had harnessed them, and the same night, to the joy of the horror-struck villagers, had pursued his journey across the sea in a direction that led to no land; and they conjectured that he must speedily be destroyed by the breaking of the ice or frozen by the eternal frosts.

On hearing this information I suffered a temporary access of despair. He had escaped me, and I must commence a destructive and almost endless journey across the mountainous ices of the ocean, amidst cold that few of the inhabitants could long endure and which I, the native of a genial and sunny climate, could not hope to survive. Yet at the idea that the fiend should live and be triumphant, my rage and vengeance returned, and like a mighty tide, overwhelmed every other feeling. After a slight repose, during which the spirits of the dead hovered round and instigated me to toil and revenge, I prepared for my journey.

I exchanged my land-sledge for one fashioned for the inequalities of the Frozen Ocean, and purchasing a plentiful stock of provisions, I departed from land.

I cannot guess how many days have passed since then, but I have endured misery which nothing but the eternal sentiment of a just retribution burning within my heart could have enabled me to support. Immense and rugged mountains of ice often barred up my passage, and I often heard the thunder of the ground sea, which threatened my destruction. But again the frost came and made the paths of the sea secure.

By the quantity of provision which I had consumed, I should guess that I had passed three weeks in this journey; and the continual protraction of hope, returning back upon the heart, often wrung bitter drops of despondency and grief from my eyes. Despair had indeed almost secured her prey, and I should soon have sunk beneath this misery. Once, after the poor animals that conveyed me had with incredible toil gained the summit of a sloping ice mountain, and one, sinking under his fatigue, died, I viewed the expanse before me with anguish, when suddenly my eye caught a dark speck upon the dusky plain. I strained my sight to discover what it could be and uttered a wild cry of ecstasy when I distinguished a sledge and the distorted proportions of a well-known form within. Oh! With what a burning gush did hope revisit my heart! Warm tears filled my eyes, which I hastily wiped away, that they might not intercept the view I had of the dæmon; but still my sight was dimmed by the burning drops, until, giving way to the emotions that oppressed me, I wept aloud.

But this was not the time for delay; I disencumbered the dogs of their dead companion, gave them a plentiful portion of food, and after an hour's rest, which was absolutely necessary, and yet which was bitterly irksome to me, I continued my route. The sledge was still visible, nor did I again lose sight of it except at the moments when for a short time some ice-rock concealed it with its intervening crags. I indeed perceptibly gained on it, and when, after nearly two days' journey, I beheld my enemy at no more than a mile distant, my heart bounded within me.

But now, when I appeared almost within grasp of my foe, my hopes were suddenly extinguished, and I lost all trace of him more utterly than I had ever done before. A ground sea was heard; the thunder of its progress, as the waters rolled and swelled beneath me, became every moment more ominous and terrific. I pressed on, but in vain. The wind arose; the sea roared; and, as with the mighty shock of an earthquake, it split and cracked with a tremendous and overwhelming sound. The work was soon finished; in a few minutes a tumultuous sea rolled between me and my enemy, and I was left drifting on a scattered piece of ice that was continually lessening and thus preparing for me a hideous death.

In this manner many appalling hours passed; several of my dogs died, and I myself was about to sink under the accumulation of distress when I saw your vessel riding at anchor and holding forth to me hopes of succour and life. I had no conception that vessels ever came so far north and was astounded at the sight. I quickly destroyed part of my sledge to construct oars, and by these means was enabled, with infinite fatigue, to move my ice raft in the direction of your ship. I had determined, if you were going southwards, still to trust myself to the mercy of the seas rather than abandon my purpose. I hoped to induce you to grant me a boat with which I could pursue my enemy. But your direction was northwards. You took me on board when my vigour was exhausted, and I should soon have sunk under my multiplied hardships into a death which I still dread, for my task is unfulfilled.

Oh! When will my guiding spirit, in conducting me to the dæmon, allow me the rest I so much desire; or must I die, and he yet live? If I do, swear to me, Walton, that he shall not escape, that you will seek him and satisfy my vengeance in his death. And do I dare to ask of you to undertake my pilgrimage, to endure the hardships that I have undergone? No; I am not so selfish. Yet, when I am dead, if he should appear, if the ministers of vengeance should conduct him to you, swear that he shall not live—swear that he shall not triumph over my accumulated woes and survive to add to the list of his dark crimes. He is eloquent and persuasive, and once his words had even power over my heart; but trust him not. His soul is as hellish as his form, full of treachery and fiend-like malice. Hear him not; call on the names of William, Justine, Clerval, Elizabeth, my father, and of the wretched Victor, and thrust your sword into his heart. I will hover near and direct the steel aright.

WALTON, *in continuation.*

August 26th, 17—.

You have read this strange and terrific story, Margaret; and do you not feel your blood congeal with horror, like that which even now curdles mine? Sometimes, seized with sudden agony, he could not continue his tale; at others, his voice broken, yet piercing, uttered with difficulty the words so replete with anguish. His fine and lovely eyes were now lighted up with indignation, now subdued to downcast sorrow and quenched in infinite wretchedness. Sometimes he commanded his countenance and tones and related the most horrible incidents with a tranquil voice, suppressing every mark of agitation; then, like a volcano bursting forth, his face would suddenly change to an expression of the wildest rage as he shrieked out imprecations on his persecutor.

His tale is connected and told with an appearance of the simplest truth, yet I own to you that the letters of Felix and Safie, which he showed me, and the apparition of the monster seen from our ship, brought to me a greater conviction of the truth of his narrative than his asseverations, however earnest and connected. Such a monster has, then, really existence! I cannot doubt it, yet I am lost in surprise and admiration. Sometimes I endeavoured to gain from Frankenstein the particulars of his creature's formation, but on this point he was impenetrable.

"Are you mad, my friend?" said he. "Or whither does your senseless curiosity lead you? Would you also create for yourself and the world a demoniacal enemy? Peace, peace! Learn my miseries and do not seek to increase your own."

Frankenstein discovered that I made notes concerning his history; he asked to see them and then himself corrected and augmented them in many places, but principally in giving the life and spirit to the conversations he held with his enemy. "Since you have preserved my narration," said he, "I would not that a mutilated one should go down to posterity."

Thus has a week passed away, while I have listened to the strangest tale that ever imagination formed. My thoughts and every feeling of my soul have been drunk up by the interest for my guest which this tale and his own elevated and gentle manners have created. I wish to soothe him, yet can I counsel one so infinitely miserable, so destitute of every hope of consolation, to live? Oh, no! The only joy that he can now know will be when he composes his shattered spirit to peace and death. Yet he enjoys one comfort, the offspring of solitude and delirium; he believes that when in dreams he holds converse with his friends and derives from that communion consolation for his miseries or excitements to his vengeance, that they are not the creations of his fancy, but the beings themselves who visit him from the regions of a remote world. This faith gives a solemnity to his reveries that render them to me almost as imposing and interesting as truth.

Our conversations are not always confined to his own history and misfortunes. On every point of general literature he displays unbounded knowledge and a quick and piercing apprehension. His eloquence is forcible and touching; nor can I hear him, when he relates a pathetic incident or endeavours to move the passions of pity or love, without tears. What a glorious creature must he have been in the days of his prosperity, when he is thus noble and godlike in ruin! He seems to feel his own worth and the greatness of his fall.

"When younger," said he, "I believed myself destined for some great enterprise. My feelings are profound, but I possessed a coolness of judgment that fitted me for illustrious achievements. This sentiment of the worth of my nature supported me when others would have been oppressed, for I deemed it criminal to throw away in useless grief those talents that might be useful to my fellow creatures. When I reflected on the work I had completed, no less a one than the creation of a sensitive and rational animal, I could not rank myself with the herd of common projectors. But this thought, which supported me in the commencement of my career, now serves only to plunge me lower in the dust. All my speculations and hopes are as nothing, and like the archangel who aspired to omnipotence, I am chained in an eternal hell. My imagination was vivid, yet my powers of analysis and application were intense; by the union of these qualities I conceived the idea and executed the creation of a man. Even now I cannot recollect without passion my reveries while the work was incomplete. I trod heaven in my thoughts, now exulting in my powers, now burning with the idea of their effects. From my infancy I was imbued with high hopes and a lofty ambition; but how am I sunk! Oh! My friend, if you had known me as I once was, you would not recognise me in this state of degradation. Despondency rarely visited my heart; a high destiny seemed to bear me on, until I fell, never, never again to rise."

Must I then lose this admirable being? I have longed for a friend; I have sought one who would sympathise with and love me. Behold, on these desert seas I have found such a one, but I fear I have gained him only to know his value and lose him. I would reconcile him to life, but he repulses the idea.

"I thank you, Walton," he said, "for your kind intentions towards so miserable a wretch; but when you speak of new ties and fresh affections, think you that any can replace those who are gone? Can any man be to me as Clerval was, or any woman another Elizabeth? Even where the affections are not strongly moved by any superior excellence, the companions of our childhood always possess a certain power over our minds which hardly any later friend can obtain. They know our infantine dispositions, which, however they may be afterwards modified, are never eradicated; and they can judge of our actions with more certain conclusions as to the integrity of our motives. A sister or a brother can never, unless indeed such symptoms have been shown early, suspect the other of fraud or false dealing, when another friend, however strongly he may be attached, may, in spite of himself, be contemplated with suspicion. But I enjoyed friends, dear not only through habit and association, but from their own merits; and wherever I am, the soothing voice of my Elizabeth and the conversation of Clerval will be ever whispered in my ear. They are dead, and but one feeling in such a solitude can persuade me to preserve my life. If I were engaged in any high undertaking or design, fraught with extensive utility to my fellow creatures, then could I live to fulfil it. But such is not my destiny; I must pursue and destroy the being to whom I gave existence; then my lot on earth will be fulfilled and I may die."

MY BELOVED SISTER,

September 2d.

I write to you, encompassed by peril and ignorant whether I am ever doomed to see again dear England and the dearer friends that inhabit it. I am surrounded by mountains of ice which admit of no escape and threaten every moment to crush my vessel. The brave fellows whom I have persuaded to be my companions look towards me for aid, but I have none to bestow. There is something terribly appalling in our situation, yet my courage and hopes do not desert me. Yet it is terrible to reflect that the lives of all these men are endangered through me. If we are lost, my mad schemes are the cause.

And what, Margaret, will be the state of your mind? You will not hear of my destruction, and you will anxiously await my return. Years will pass, and you will have visitings of despair and yet be tortured by hope. Oh! My beloved sister, the sickening failing of your heart-felt expectations is, in prospect, more terrible to me than my own death. But you have a husband and lovely children; you may be happy. Heaven bless you and make you so!

My unfortunate guest regards me with the tenderest compassion. He endeavours to fill me with hope and talks as if life were a possession which he valued. He reminds me how often the same accidents have happened to other navigators who have attempted this sea, and in spite of myself, he fills me with cheerful auguries. Even the sailors feel the power of his eloquence; when he speaks, they no longer despair; he rouses their energies, and while they hear his voice they believe these vast mountains of ice are mole-hills which will vanish before the resolutions of man. These feelings are transitory; each day of expectation delayed fills them with fear, and I almost dread a mutiny caused by this despair.

September 5th.

A scene has just passed of such uncommon interest that, although it is highly probable that these papers may never reach you, yet I cannot forbear recording it.

We are still surrounded by mountains of ice, still in imminent danger of being crushed in their conflict. The cold is excessive, and many of my unfortunate comrades have already found a grave amidst this scene of desolation. Frankenstein has daily declined in health; a feverish fire still glimmers in his eyes, but he is exhausted, and when suddenly roused to any exertion, he speedily sinks again into apparent lifelessness.

I mentioned in my last letter the fears I entertained of a mutiny. This morning, as I sat watching the wan countenance of my friend—his eyes half closed and his limbs hanging listlessly—I was roused by half a dozen of the sailors, who demanded admission into the cabin. They entered, and their leader addressed me. He told me that he and his companions had been chosen by the other sailors to come in deputation to me to make me a requisition which, in justice, I could not refuse. We were immured in ice and should probably never escape, but they feared that if, as was possible, the ice should dissipate and a free passage be opened, I should be rash enough to continue my voyage and lead them into fresh dangers, after they might happily have surmounted this. They insisted, therefore, that I should engage with a solemn promise that if the vessel should be freed I would instantly direct my course southwards.

This speech troubled me. I had not despaired, nor had I yet conceived the idea of returning if set free. Yet could I, in justice, or even in possibility, refuse this demand? I hesitated before I answered, when Frankenstein, who had at first been silent, and indeed appeared hardly to have force enough to attend, now roused himself; his eyes sparkled, and his cheeks flushed with momentary vigour. Turning towards the men, he said,

"What do you mean? What do you demand of your captain? Are you, then, so easily turned from your design? Did you not call this a glorious expedition? "And wherefore was it glorious? Not because the way was smooth and placid as a southern sea, but because it was full of dangers and terror, because at every new incident your fortitude was to be called forth and your courage exhibited, because danger and death surrounded it, and these you were to brave and overcome. For this was it a glorious, for this was it an honourable undertaking. You were hereafter to be hailed as the benefactors of your species, your names adored as belonging to brave men who encountered death for honour and the benefit of mankind. And now, behold, with the first imagination of danger, or, if you will, the first mighty and terrific trial of your courage, you shrink away and are content to be handed down as men who had not strength enough to endure cold and peril; and so, poor souls, they were chilly and returned to their warm firesides. Why, that requires not this preparation; ye need not have come thus far and dragged your captain to the shame of a defeat merely to prove yourselves cowards. Oh! Be men, or be more than men. Be steady to your purposes and firm as a rock. This ice is not made of such stuff as your hearts may be; it is mutable and cannot withstand you if you say that it shall not. Do not return to your families with the stigma of disgrace marked on your brows. Return as heroes who have fought and conquered and who know not what it is to turn their backs on the foe."

He spoke this with a voice so modulated to the different feelings expressed in his speech, with an eye so full of lofty design and heroism, that can you wonder that these men were moved? They looked at one another and were unable to reply. I spoke; I told them to retire and consider of what had been said, that I would not lead them farther north if they strenuously desired the contrary, but that I hoped that, with reflection, their courage would return.

They retired and I turned towards my friend, but he was sunk in languor and almost deprived of life.

How all this will terminate, I know not, but I had rather die than return shamefully, my purpose unfulfilled. Yet I fear such will be my fate; the men, unsupported by ideas of glory and honour, can never willingly continue to endure their present hardships.

September 7th.

The die is cast; I have consented to return if we are not destroyed. Thus are my hopes blasted by cowardice and indecision; I come back ignorant and disappointed. It requires more philosophy than I possess to bear this injustice with patience.

September 12th.

It is past; I am returning to England. I have lost my hopes of utility and glory; I have lost my friend. But I will endeavour to detail these bitter circumstances to you, my dear sister; and while I am wafted towards England and towards you, I will not despond.

September 9th, the ice began to move, and roarings like thunder were heard at a distance as the islands split and cracked in every direction. We were in the most imminent peril, but as we could only remain passive, my chief attention was occupied by my unfortunate guest whose illness increased in such a degree that he was entirely confined to his bed. The ice cracked behind us and was driven with force towards the north; a breeze sprang from the west, and on the 11th the passage towards the south became perfectly free. When the sailors saw this and that their return to their native country was apparently assured, a shout of tumultuous joy broke from them, loud and long-continued. Frankenstein, who was dozing, awoke and asked the cause of the tumult. "They shout," I said, "because they will soon return to England."

"Do you, then, really return?"

"Alas! Yes; I cannot withstand their demands. I cannot lead them unwillingly to danger, and I must return."

"Do so, if you will; but I will not. You may give up your purpose, but mine is assigned to me by Heaven, and I dare not. I am weak, but surely the spirits who assist my vengeance will endow me with sufficient strength." Saying this, he endeavoured to spring from the bed, but the exertion was too great for him; he fell back and fainted.

It was long before he was restored, and I often thought that life was entirely extinct. At length he opened his eyes; he breathed with difficulty and was unable to speak. The surgeon gave him a composing draught and ordered us to leave him undisturbed. In the meantime he told me that my friend had certainly not many hours to live.

His sentence was pronounced, and I could only grieve and be patient. I sat by his bed, watching him; his eyes were closed, and I thought he slept; but presently he called to me in a feeble voice, and bidding me come near, said, "Alas! The strength I relied on is gone; I feel that I shall soon die, and he, my enemy and persecutor, may still be in being. Think not, Walton, that in the last moments of my existence I feel that burning hatred and ardent desire of revenge I once expressed; but I feel myself justified in desiring the death of my adversary. During these last days I have been occupied in examining my past conduct; nor do I find it blamable. In a fit of enthusiastic madness I created a rational creature and was bound towards him to assure, as far as was in my power, his happiness and well-being. This was my duty, but there was another still paramount to that. My duties towards the beings of my own species had greater claims to my attention because they included a greater proportion of happiness or misery. Urged by this view, I refused, and I did right in refusing, to create a companion for the first creature. He showed unparalleled malignity and selfishness in evil; he destroyed my friends; he devoted to destruction beings who possessed exquisite sensations, happiness, and wisdom; nor do I know where this thirst for vengeance may end. Miserable himself that he may render no other wretched, he ought to die. The task of his destruction was mine, but I have failed. When actuated by selfish and vicious motives, I asked you to undertake my unfinished work, and I renew this request now, when I am only induced by reason and virtue.

"Yet I cannot ask you to renounce your country and friends to fulfil this task; and now that you are returning to England, you will have little chance of meeting with him. But the consideration of these points, and the well balancing of what you may esteem your duties, I leave to you; my judgment and ideas are already disturbed by the near approach of death. I dare not ask you to do what I think right, for I may still be misled by passion.

"That he should live to be an instrument of mischief disturbs me; in other respects, this hour, when I momentarily expect my release, is the only happy one which I have enjoyed for several years. The forms of the beloved dead flit before me, and I hasten to their arms. Farewell, Walton! Seek happiness in tranquillity and avoid ambition, even if it be only the apparently innocent one of distinguishing yourself in science and discoveries. Yet why do I say this? I have myself been blasted in these hopes, yet another may succeed."

His voice became fainter as he spoke, and at length, exhausted by his effort, he sank into silence. About half an hour afterwards he attempted again to speak but was unable; he pressed my hand feebly, and his eyes closed for ever, while the irradiation of a gentle smile passed away from his lips.

Margaret, what comment can I make on the untimely extinction of this glorious spirit? What can I say that will enable you to understand the depth of my sorrow? All that I should express would be inadequate and feeble. My tears flow; my mind is overshadowed by a cloud of disappointment. But I journey towards England, and I may there find consolation.

I am interrupted. What do these sounds portend? It is midnight; the breeze blows fairly, and the watch on deck scarcely stir.

Again there is a sound as of a human voice, but hoarser; it comes from the cabin where the remains of Frankenstein still lie. I must arise and examine.

Good night, my sister.

Great God! what a scene has just taken place! I am yet dizzy with the remembrance of it. I hardly know whether I shall have the power to detail it; yet the tale which I have recorded would be incomplete without this final and wonderful catastrophe.

I entered the cabin where lay the remains of my ill-fated and admirable friend. Over him hung a form which I cannot find words to describe— gigantic in stature, yet uncouth and distorted in its proportions. As he hung over the coffin, his face was concealed by long locks of ragged hair; but one vast hand was extended, in colour and apparent texture like that of a mummy. When he heard the sound of my approach, he ceased to utter exclamations of grief and horror and sprung towards the window. Never did I behold a vision so horrible as his face, of such loathsome yet appalling hideousness. I shut my eyes involuntarily and endeavoured to recollect what were my duties with regard to this destroyer. I called on him to stay.

He paused, looking on me with wonder, and again turning towards the lifeless form of his creator, he seemed to forget my presence, and every feature and gesture seemed instigated by the wildest rage of some uncontrollable passion.

"That is also my victim!" he exclaimed. "In his murder my crimes are consummated; the miserable series of my being is wound to its close! Oh, Frankenstein! Generous and self-devoted being! What does it avail that I now ask thee to pardon me? I, who irretrievably destroyed thee by destroying all thou lovedst. Alas! He is cold, he cannot answer me."

His voice seemed suffocated, and my first impulses, which had suggested to me the duty of obeying the dying request of my friend in destroying his enemy, were now suspended by a mixture of curiosity and compassion. I approached this tremendous being; I dared not again raise my eyes to his face, there was something so scaring and unearthly in his ugliness. I attempted to speak, but the words died away on my lips. The monster continued to utter wild and incoherent self-reproaches. At length I gathered resolution to address him in a pause of the tempest of his passion.

"Your repentance," I said, "is now superfluous. If you had listened to the voice of conscience and heeded the stings of remorse before you had urged your diabolical vengeance to this extremity, Frankenstein would yet have lived."

"And do you dream?" said the dæmon. "Do you think that I was then dead to agony and remorse? He," he continued, pointing to the corpse, "he suffered not in the consummation of the deed. Oh! Not the ten-thousandth portion of the anguish that was mine during the lingering detail of its execution. A frightful selfishness hurried me on, while my heart was poisoned with remorse. Think you that the groans of Clerval were music to my ears? My heart was fashioned to be susceptible of love and sympathy, and when wrenched by misery to vice and hatred, it did not endure the violence of the change without torture such as you cannot even imagine.

"After the murder of Clerval I returned to Switzerland, heart-broken and overcome. I pitied Frankenstein; my pity amounted to horror; I abhorred myself. But when I discovered that he, the author at once of my existence and of its unspeakable torments, dared to hope for happiness, that while he accumulated wretchedness and despair upon me he sought his own enjoyment in feelings and passions from the indulgence of which I was for ever barred, then impotent envy and bitter indignation filled me with an insatiable thirst for vengeance. I recollected my threat and resolved that it should be accomplished. I knew that I was preparing for myself a deadly torture, but I was the slave, not the master, of an impulse which I detested yet could not disobey. Yet when she died! Nay, then I was not miserable. I had cast off all feeling, subdued all anguish, to riot in the excess of my despair. Evil thenceforth became my good. Urged thus far, I had no choice but to adapt my nature to an element which I had willingly chosen. The completion of my demoniacal design became an insatiable passion. And now it is ended; there is my last victim!"

I was at first touched by the expressions of his misery; yet, when I called to mind what Frankenstein had said of his powers of eloquence and persuasion, and when I again cast my eyes on the lifeless form of my friend, indignation was rekindled within me. "Wretch!" I said. "It is well that you come here to whine over the desolation that you have made. You throw a torch into a pile of buildings, and when they are consumed, you sit among the ruins and lament the fall. Hypocritical fiend! If he whom you mourn still lived, still would he be the object, again would he become the prey, of your accursed vengeance. It is not pity that you feel; you lament only because the victim of your malignity is withdrawn from your power."

"Oh, it is not thus—not thus," interrupted the being. "Yet such must be the impression conveyed to you by what appears to be the purport of my actions. Yet I seek not a fellow feeling in my misery. No sympathy may I ever find. When I first sought it, it was the love of virtue, the feelings of happiness and affection with which my whole being overflowed, that I wished to be participated. But now that virtue has become to me a shadow, and that happiness and affection are turned into bitter and loathing despair, in what should I seek for sympathy? I am content to suffer alone while my sufferings shall endure; when I die, I am well satisfied that abhorrence and opprobrium should load my memory. Once my fancy was soothed with dreams of virtue, of fame, and of enjoyment. Once I falsely hoped to meet with beings who, pardoning my outward form, would love me for the excellent qualities which I was capable of unfolding. I was nourished with high thoughts of honour and devotion. But now crime has degraded me beneath the meanest animal. No guilt, no mischief, no malignity, no misery, can be found comparable to mine. When I run over the frightful catalogue of my sins, I cannot believe that I am the same creature whose thoughts were once filled with sublime and transcendent visions of the beauty and the majesty of goodness. But it is even so; the fallen angel becomes a malignant devil. Yet even that enemy of God and man had friends and associates in his desolation; I am alone.

"You, who call Frankenstein your friend, seem to have a knowledge of my crimes and his misfortunes. But in the detail which he gave you of them he could not sum up the hours and months of misery which I endured wasting in impotent passions. For while I destroyed his hopes, I did not satisfy my own desires. They were for ever ardent and craving; still I desired love and fellowship, and I was still spurned. Was there no injustice in this? Am I to be thought the only criminal, when all humankind sinned against me? Why do you not hate Felix, who drove his friend from his door with contumely? Why do you not execrate the rustic who sought to destroy the saviour of his child? Nay, these are virtuous and immaculate beings! I, the miserable and the abandoned, am an abortion, to be spurned at, and kicked, and trampled on. Even now my blood boils at the recollection of this injustice.

"But it is true that I am a wretch. I have murdered the lovely and the helpless; I have strangled the innocent as they slept and grasped to death his throat who never injured me or any other living thing. I have devoted my creator, the select specimen of all that is worthy of love and admiration among men, to misery; I have pursued him even to that irremediable ruin. There he lies, white and cold in death. You hate me, but your abhorrence cannot equal that with which I regard myself. I look on the hands which executed the deed; I think on the heart in which the imagination of it was conceived and long for the moment when these hands will meet my eyes, when that imagination will haunt my thoughts no more.

"Fear not that I shall be the instrument of future mischief. My work is nearly complete. Neither yours nor any man's death is needed to consummate the series of my being and accomplish that which must be done, but it requires my own. Do not think that I shall be slow to perform this sacrifice. I shall quit your vessel on the ice raft which brought me thither and shall seek the most northern extremity of the globe; I shall collect my funeral pile and consume to ashes this miserable frame, that its remains may afford no light to any curious and unhallowed wretch who would create such another as I have been. I shall die. I shall no longer feel the agonies which now consume me or be the prey of feelings unsatisfied, yet unquenched. He is dead who called me into being; and when I shall be no more, the very remembrance of us both will speedily vanish. I shall no longer see the sun or stars or feel the winds play on my cheeks. Light, feeling, and sense will pass away; and in this condition must I find my happiness. Some years ago, when the images which this world affords first opened upon me, when I felt the cheering warmth of summer and heard the rustling of the leaves and the warbling of the birds, and these were all to me, I should have wept to die; now it is my only consolation. Polluted by crimes and torn by the bitterest remorse, where can I find rest but in death?

"Farewell! I leave you, and in you the last of humankind whom these eyes will ever behold. Farewell, Frankenstein! If thou wert yet alive and yet cherished a desire of revenge against me, it would be better satiated in my life than in my destruction. But it was not so; thou didst seek my extinction, that I might not cause greater wretchedness; and if yet, in some mode unknown to me, thou hadst not ceased to think and feel, thou wouldst not desire against me a vengeance greater than that which I feel. Blasted as thou wert, my agony was still superior to thine, for the bitter sting of remorse will not cease to rankle in my wounds until death shall close them for ever.

"But soon," he cried with sad and solemn enthusiasm, "I shall die, and what I now feel be no longer felt. Soon these burning miseries will be extinct. I shall ascend my funeral pile triumphantly and exult in the agony of the torturing flames. The light of that conflagration will fade away; my ashes will be swept into the sea by the winds. My spirit will sleep in peace, or if it thinks, it will not surely think thus. Farewell."

He sprang from the cabin-window as he said this, upon the ice raft which lay close to the vessel. He was soon borne away by the waves and lost in darkness and distance.

THE
STRANGE CASE
of
DR. JEKYLL & MR. HYDE

By Robert Louis Stevenson

First Published in 1886

Robert Louis Stevenson

Robert Lewis Balfour Stevenson was born in Edinburgh, Scotland in 1850. Aged seventeen, he enrolled at the University of Edinburgh, but he was a disinterested student whose bohemian lifestyle detracted from his studies, and four years later, in April of 1971, he declared his decision to pursue a life of letters. A keen traveller, Stevenson became involved with a number of European literary circles, and had his first paid piece, an essay entitled 'Roads', published in 1873.

Stevenson suffered from various ailments and a "weak chest" for the whole of his life, and spent much of his adult years searching for a place of residence suitable to his state of ill health. In 1880, he married Fanny Van de Grift, and they moved between France, Britain and California together. It was during these years that Stevenson produced much of his best-known work – *Treasure Island,* in 1883, *The Strange Case of Dr Jekyll and Mr Hyde,* in 1886, and *Black Arrow,* in 1888.

Following the death of his father in 1887, Stevenson devoted his later years to travels in the Pacific. During the late 1880s, he spent extended periods of time in both the Hawaiian and Samoan Islands, befriending many native and colonial leaders of the day and writing a number of accounts of his travels. In 1890 he purchased a 400-acre tract of land in Samoa, where he would remain for the rest of his life.

By 1894, still suffering from various ailments, he fell into a state of depression, and in December of that year, while straining to open a bottle of wine, he collapsed, most likely from a cerebral haemorrhage. A few hours later he was dead, aged just 44. Stevenson remains highly popular to this day, and is ranked the 26th most translated author in the world.

STORY OF THE DOOR

Mr. Utterson the lawyer was a man of a rugged countenance that was never lighted by a smile; cold, scanty and embarrassed in discourse; backward in sentiment; lean, long, dusty, dreary and yet somehow lovable. At friendly meetings, and when the wine was to his taste, something eminently human beaconed from his eye; something indeed which never found its way into his talk, but which spoke not only in these silent symbols of the after-dinner face, but more often and loudly in the acts of his life. He was austere with himself; drank gin when he was alone, to mortify a taste for vintages; and though he enjoyed the theatre, had not crossed the doors of one for twenty years. But he had an approved tolerance for others; sometimes wondering, almost with envy, at the high pressure of spirits involved in their misdeeds; and in any extremity inclined to help rather than to reprove. "I incline to Cain's heresy," he used to say quaintly: "I let my brother go to the devil in his own way." In this character, it was frequently his fortune to be the last reputable acquaintance and the last good influence in the lives of downgoing men. And to such as these, so long as they came about his chambers, he never marked a shade of change in his demeanour.

No doubt the feat was easy to Mr. Utterson; for he was undemonstrative at the best, and even his friendship seemed to be founded in a similar catholicity of good-nature. It is the mark of a modest man to accept his friendly circle ready-made from the hands of opportunity; and that was the lawyer's way. His friends were those of his own blood or those whom he had known the longest; his affections, like ivy, were the growth of time, they implied no aptness in the object. Hence, no doubt the bond that united him to Mr. Richard Enfield, his distant kinsman, the well-known man about town. It was a nut to crack for many, what these two could see in each other, or what subject they could find in common. It was reported by those who encountered them in their Sunday walks, that they said nothing, looked singularly dull and would hail with obvious relief the appearance of a friend. For all that, the two men put the greatest store by these excursions, counted them the chief jewel of each week, and not only set aside occasions of pleasure, but even resisted the calls of business, that they might enjoy them uninterrupted.

It chanced on one of these rambles that their way led them down a by-street in a busy quarter of London. The street was small and what is called quiet, but it drove a thriving trade on the weekdays. The inhabitants were all doing well, it seemed and all emulously hoping to do better still, and laying out the surplus of their grains in coquetry; so that the shop fronts stood along that thoroughfare with an air of invitation, like rows of smiling saleswomen. Even on Sunday, when it veiled its more florid charms and lay comparatively empty of passage, the street shone out in contrast to its dingy neighbourhood, like a fire in a forest; and with its freshly painted shutters, well-polished brasses, and general cleanliness and gaiety of note, instantly caught and pleased the eye of the passenger.

Two doors from one corner, on the left hand going east the line was broken by the entry of a court; and just at that point a certain sinister block of building thrust forward its gable on the street. It was two storeys high; showed no window, nothing but a door on the lower storey and a blind forehead of discoloured wall on the upper; and bore in every feature, the marks of prolonged and sordid negligence. The door, which was equipped with neither bell nor knocker, was blistered and distained. Tramps slouched into the recess and struck matches on the panels; children kept shop upon the steps; the schoolboy had tried his knife on the mouldings; and for close on a generation, no one had appeared to drive away these random visitors or to repair their ravages.

Mr. Enfield and the lawyer were on the other side of the by-street; but when they came abreast of the entry, the former lifted up his cane and pointed.

"Did you ever remark that door?" he asked; and when his companion had replied in the affirmative, "It is connected in my mind," added he, "with a very odd story."

"Indeed?" said Mr. Utterson, with a slight change of voice, "and what was that?"

"Well, it was this way," returned Mr. Enfield: "I was coming home from some place at the end of the world, about three o'clock of a black winter morning, and my way lay through a part of town where there was literally nothing to be seen but lamps. Street after street and all the folks asleep—street after street, all lighted up as if for a procession and all as empty as a church—till at last I got into that state of mind when a man listens and listens and begins to long for the sight of a policeman. All at once, I saw two figures: one a little man who was stumping along eastward at a good walk, and the other a girl of maybe eight or ten who was running as hard as she was able down a cross street. Well, sir, the two ran into one another naturally enough at the corner; and then came the horrible part of the thing;

for the man trampled calmly over the child's body and left her screaming on the ground. It sounds nothing to hear, but it was hellish to see. It wasn't like a man; it was like some damned Juggernaut. I gave a few halloa, took to my heels, collared my gentleman, and brought him back to where there was already quite a group about the screaming child. He was perfectly cool and made no resistance, but gave me one look, so ugly that it brought out the sweat on me like running. The people who had turned out were the girl's own family; and pretty soon, the doctor, for whom she had been sent put in his appearance. Well, the child was not much the worse, more frightened, according to the sawbones; and there you might have supposed would be an end to it. But there was one curious circumstance. I had taken a loathing to my gentleman at first sight. So had the child's family, which was only natural. But the doctor's case was what struck me. He was the usual cut and dry apothecary, of no particular age and colour, with a strong Edinburgh accent and about as emotional as a bagpipe. Well, sir, he was like the rest of us; every time he looked at my prisoner, I saw that sawbones turn sick and white with the desire to kill him. I knew what was in his mind, just as he knew what was in mine; and killing being out of the question, we did the next best. We told the man we could and would make such a scandal out of this as should make his name stink from one end of London to the other. If he had any friends or any credit, we undertook that he should lose them. And all the time, as we were pitching it in red hot, we were keeping the women off him as best we could for they were as wild as harpies. I never saw a circle of such hateful faces; and there was the man in the middle, with a kind of black sneering coolness—frightened too, I could see that— but carrying it off, sir, really like Satan. 'If you choose to make capital out of this accident,' said he, 'I am naturally helpless. No gentleman but wishes to avoid a scene,' says he. 'Name your figure.' Well, we screwed him up to a hundred pounds for the child's family; he would have clearly liked to stick out; but there was something about the lot of us that meant mischief, and at last he struck. The next thing was to get the money; and where do you think he carried us but to that place with the door?—whipped out a key, went in, and presently came back with the matter of ten pounds in gold and a cheque for the balance on Coutts's, drawn payable to bearer and signed with a name that I can't mention, though it's one of the points of my story, but it was a name at least very well known and often printed. The figure was stiff; but the signature was good for more than that if it was only genuine. I took the liberty of pointing out to my gentleman that the whole business looked apocryphal, and that a man does not, in real life, walk into a cellar door at four in the morning and come out with another man's cheque for close upon a hundred pounds. But he was quite easy and sneering. 'Set your mind at rest,' says he, 'I will stay with you till the banks open and cash the cheque myself.' So we all set off, the doctor, and the child's father, and our friend and myself, and passed the rest of the night in my chambers; and next day, when we had breakfasted, went in a body to the bank. I gave in the cheque myself, and said I had every reason to believe it was a forgery. Not a bit of it. The cheque was genuine."

"Tut-tut!" said Mr. Utterson.

"I see you feel as I do," said Mr. Enfield. "Yes, it's a bad story. For my man was a fellow that nobody could have to do with, a really damnable man; and the person that drew the cheque is the very pink of the proprieties, celebrated too, and (what makes it worse) one of your fellows who do what they call good. Blackmail, I suppose; an honest man paying through the nose for some of the capers of his youth. Black Mail House is what I call the place with the door, in consequence. Though even that, you know, is far from explaining all," he added, and with the words fell into a vein of musing.

From this he was recalled by Mr. Utterson asking rather suddenly: "And you don't know if the drawer of the cheque lives there?"

"A likely place, isn't it?" returned Mr. Enfield. "But I happen to have noticed his address; he lives in some square or other."

"And you never asked about the—place with the door?" said Mr. Utterson.

"No, sir; I had a delicacy," was the reply. "I feel very strongly about putting questions; it partakes too much of the style of the day of judgment. You start a question, and it's like starting a stone. You sit quietly on the top of a hill; and away the stone goes, starting others; and presently some bland old bird (the last you would have thought of) is knocked on the head in his own back garden and the family have to change their name. No sir, I make it a rule of mine: the more it looks like Queer Street, the less I ask."

"A very good rule, too," said the lawyer.

"But I have studied the place for myself," continued Mr. Enfield. "It seems scarcely a house. There is no other door, and nobody goes in or out of that one but, once in a great while, the gentleman of my adventure. There are three windows looking on the court on the first floor; none below; the windows are always shut but they're clean. And then there is a chimney which is generally smoking; so somebody must live there. And yet it's not so sure; for the buildings are so packed together about the court, that it's hard to say where one ends and another begins."

The pair walked on again for a while in silence; and then "Enfield," said Mr. Utterson, "that's a good rule of yours."

"Yes, I think it is," returned Enfield.

"But for all that," continued the lawyer, "there's one point I want to ask. I want to ask the name of that man who walked over the child."

"Well," said Mr. Enfield, "I can't see what harm it would do. It was a man of the name of Hyde."

"Hm," said Mr. Utterson. "What sort of a man is he to see?"

"He is not easy to describe. There is something wrong with his appearance; something displeasing, something down-right detestable. I never saw a man I so disliked, and yet I scarce know why. He must be deformed somewhere; he gives a strong feeling of deformity, although I couldn't specify the point. He's an extraordinary looking man, and yet I really can name nothing out of the way. No, sir; I can make no hand of it; I can't describe him. And it's not want of memory; for I declare I can see him this moment."

Mr. Utterson again walked some way in silence and obviously under a weight of consideration. "You are sure he used a key?" he inquired at last.

"My dear sir . . . " began Enfield, surprised out of himself.

"Yes, I know," said Utterson; "I know it must seem strange. The fact is, if I do not ask you the name of the other party, it is because I know it already. You see, Richard, your tale has gone home. If you have been inexact in any point you had better correct it."

"I think you might have warned me," returned the other with a touch of sullenness. "But I have been pedantically exact, as you call it. The fellow had a key; and what's more, he has it still. I saw him use it not a week ago."

Mr. Utterson sighed deeply but said never a word; and the young man presently resumed. "Here is another lesson to say nothing," said he. "I am ashamed of my long tongue. Let us make a bargain never to refer to this again."

"With all my heart," said the lawyer. "I shake hands on that, Richard."

SEARCH FOR MR. HYDE

That evening Mr. Utterson came home to his bachelor house in sombre spirits and sat down to dinner without relish. It was his custom of a Sunday, when this meal was over, to sit close by the fire, a volume of some dry divinity on his reading desk, until the clock of the neighbouring church rang out the hour of twelve, when he would go soberly and gratefully to bed. On this night however, as soon as the cloth was taken away, he took up a candle and went into his business room. There he opened his safe, took from the most private part of it a document endorsed on the envelope as Dr. Jekyll's Will and sat down with a clouded brow to study its contents. The will was holograph, for Mr. Utterson though he took charge of it now that it was made, had refused to lend the least assistance in the making of it; it provided not only that, in case of the decease of Henry Jekyll, M.D., D.C.L., L.L.D., F.R.S., etc., all his possessions were to pass into the hands of his "friend and benefactor Edward Hyde," but that in case of Dr. Jekyll's "disappearance or unexplained absence for any period exceeding three calendar months," the said Edward Hyde should step into the said Henry Jekyll's shoes without further delay and free from any burthen or obligation beyond the payment of a few small sums to the members of the doctor's household. This document had long been the lawyer's eyesore. It offended him both as a lawyer and as a lover of the sane and customary sides of life, to whom the fanciful was the immodest. And hitherto it was his ignorance of Mr. Hyde that had swelled his indignation; now, by a sudden turn, it was his knowledge. It was already bad enough when the name was but a name of which he could learn no more. It was worse when it began to be clothed upon with detestable attributes; and out of the shifting, insubstantial mists that had so long baffled his eye, there leaped up the sudden, definite presentment of a fiend.

"I thought it was madness," he said, as he replaced the obnoxious paper in the safe, "and now I begin to fear it is disgrace."

With that he blew out his candle, put on a greatcoat, and set forth in the direction of Cavendish Square, that citadel of medicine, where his friend, the great Dr. Lanyon, had his house and received his crowding patients. "If anyone knows, it will be Lanyon," he had thought.

The solemn butler knew and welcomed him; he was subjected to no stage of delay, but ushered direct from the door to the dining-room where Dr. Lanyon sat alone over his wine. This was a hearty, healthy, dapper, red-faced gentleman, with a shock of hair prematurely white, and a boisterous and decided manner. At sight of Mr. Utterson, he sprang up from his chair and welcomed him with both hands. The geniality, as was the way of the man, was somewhat theatrical to the eye; but it reposed on genuine feeling. For these two were old friends, old mates both at school and college, both thorough respectors of themselves and of each other, and what does not always follow, men who thoroughly enjoyed each other's company.

After a little rambling talk, the lawyer led up to the subject which so disagreeably preoccupied his mind.

"I suppose, Lanyon," said he, "you and I must be the two oldest friends that Henry Jekyll has?"

"I wish the friends were younger," chuckled Dr. Lanyon. "But I suppose we are. And what of that? I see little of him now."

"Indeed?" said Utterson. "I thought you had a bond of common interest."

"We had," was the reply. "But it is more than ten years since Henry Jekyll became too fanciful for me. He began to go wrong, wrong in mind; and though of course I continue to take an interest in him for old sake's sake, as they say, I see and I have seen devilish little of the man. Such unscientific balderdash," added the doctor, flushing suddenly purple, "would have estranged Damon and Pythias."

This little spirit of temper was somewhat of a relief to Mr. Utterson. "They have only differed on some point of science," he thought; and being a man of no scientific passions (except in the matter of conveyancing), he even added: "It is nothing worse than that!" He gave his friend a few seconds to recover his composure, and then approached the question he had come to put. "Did you ever come across a *protégé* of his—one Hyde?" he asked.

"Hyde?" repeated Lanyon. "No. Never heard of him. Since my time."

That was the amount of information that the lawyer carried back with him to the great, dark bed on which he tossed to and fro, until the small hours of the morning began to grow large. It was a night of little ease to his toiling mind, toiling in mere darkness and besieged by questions.

Six o'clock struck on the bells of the church that was so conveniently near to Mr. Utterson's dwelling, and still he was digging at the problem. Hitherto it had touched him on the intellectual side alone; but now his imagination also was engaged, or rather enslaved; and as he lay and tossed in the gross darkness of the night and the curtained room, Mr. Enfield's tale went by before his mind in a scroll of lighted pictures. He would be aware of the great field of lamps of a nocturnal city; then of the figure of a man walking swiftly; then of a child running from the doctor's; and then these met, and that human Juggernaut trod the child down and passed on regardless of her screams. Or else he would see a room in a rich house, where his friend lay asleep, dreaming and smiling at his dreams; and then the door of that room would be opened, the curtains of the bed plucked apart, the sleeper recalled, and lo! there would stand by his side a figure to whom power was given, and even at that dead hour, he must rise and do its bidding. The figure in these two phases haunted the lawyer all night; and if at any time he dozed over, it was but to see it glide more stealthily through sleeping houses, or move the more swiftly and still the more swiftly, even to dizziness, through wider labyrinths of lamplighted city, and at every street corner crush a child and leave her screaming. And still the figure had no face by which he might know it; even in his dreams, it had no face, or one that baffled him and melted before his eyes; and thus it was that there sprang up and grew apace in the lawyer's mind a singularly strong, almost an inordinate, curiosity to behold the features of the real Mr. Hyde. If he could but once set eyes on him, he thought the mystery would lighten and perhaps roll altogether away, as was the habit of mysterious things when well examined. He might see a reason for his friend's strange preference or bondage (call it which you please) and even for the startling clause of the will. At least it would be a face worth seeing: the face of a man who was without bowels of mercy: a face which had but to show itself to raise up, in the mind of the unimpressionable Enfield, a spirit of enduring hatred.

From that time forward, Mr. Utterson began to haunt the door in the by-street of shops. In the morning before office hours, at noon when business was plenty and time scarce, at night under the face of the fogged city moon, by all lights and at all hours of solitude or concourse, the lawyer was to be found on his chosen post.

"If he be Mr. Hyde," he had thought, "I shall be Mr. Seek."

And at last his patience was rewarded. It was a fine dry night; frost in the air; the streets as clean as a ballroom floor; the lamps, unshaken by any wind, drawing a regular pattern of light and shadow. By ten o'clock, when the shops were closed, the by-street was very solitary and, in spite of the low growl of London from all round, very silent. Small sounds carried far; domestic sounds out of the houses were clearly audible on either side of the roadway; and the rumour of the approach of any passenger preceded him by a long time. Mr. Utterson had been some minutes at his post, when he was aware of an odd light footstep drawing near. In the course of his nightly patrols, he had long grown accustomed to the quaint effect with which the footfalls of a single person, while he is still a great way off, suddenly spring out distinct from the vast hum and clatter of the city. Yet his attention had never before been so sharply and decisively arrested; and it was with a strong, superstitious prevision of success that he withdrew into the entry of the court.

The steps drew swiftly nearer, and swelled out suddenly louder as they turned the end of the street. The lawyer, looking forth from the entry, could soon see what manner of man he had to deal with. He was small and very plainly dressed and the look of him, even at that distance, went somehow strongly against the watcher's inclination. But he made straight for the door, crossing the roadway to save time; and as he came, he drew a key from his pocket like one approaching home.

Mr. Utterson stepped out and touched him on the shoulder as he passed. "Mr. Hyde, I think?"

Mr. Hyde shrank back with a hissing intake of the breath. But his fear was only momentary; and though he did not look the lawyer in the face, he answered coolly enough: "That is my name. What do you want?"

"I see you are going in," returned the lawyer. "I am an old friend of Dr. Jekyll's—Mr. Utterson of Gaunt Street—you must have heard of my name; and meeting you so conveniently, I thought you might admit me."

"You will not find Dr. Jekyll; he is from home," replied Mr. Hyde, blowing in the key. And then suddenly, but still without looking up, "How did you know me?" he asked.

"On your side," said Mr. Utterson "will you do me a favour?"

"With pleasure," replied the other. "What shall it be?"

"Will you let me see your face?" asked the lawyer.

Mr. Hyde appeared to hesitate, and then, as if upon some sudden reflection, fronted about with an air of defiance; and the pair stared at each other pretty fixedly for a few seconds. "Now I shall know you again," said Mr. Utterson. "It may be useful."

"Yes," returned Mr. Hyde, "It is as well we have met; and *à propos*, you should have my address." And he gave a number of a street in Soho.

"Good God!" thought Mr. Utterson, "can he, too, have been thinking of the will?" But he kept his feelings to himself and only grunted in acknowledgment of the address.

"And now," said the other, "how did you know me?"

"By description," was the reply.

"Whose description?"

"We have common friends," said Mr. Utterson.

"Common friends," echoed Mr. Hyde, a little hoarsely. "Who are they?"

"Jekyll, for instance," said the lawyer.

"He never told you," cried Mr. Hyde, with a flush of anger. "I did not think you would have lied."

"Come," said Mr. Utterson, "that is not fitting language."

The other snarled aloud into a savage laugh; and the next moment, with extraordinary quickness, he had unlocked the door and disappeared into the house.

The lawyer stood awhile when Mr. Hyde had left him, the picture of disquietude. Then he began slowly to mount the street, pausing every step or two and putting his hand to his brow like a man in mental perplexity. The problem he was thus debating as he walked, was one of a class that is rarely solved. Mr. Hyde was pale and dwarfish, he gave an impression of deformity without any nameable malformation, he had a displeasing smile, he had borne himself to the lawyer with a sort of murderous mixture of timidity and boldness, and he spoke with a husky, whispering and somewhat broken voice; all these were points against him, but not all of these together could explain the hitherto unknown disgust, loathing and fear with which Mr. Utterson regarded him. "There must be something else," said the perplexed gentleman. "There *is* something more, if I could find a name for it. God bless me, the man seems hardly human! Something troglodytic, shall we say? or can it be the old story of Dr. Fell? or is it the mere radiance of a foul soul that thus transpires through, and transfigures, its clay continent? The last, I think; for, O my poor old Harry Jekyll, if ever I read Satan's signature upon a face, it is on that of your new friend."

Round the corner from the by-street, there was a square of ancient, handsome houses, now for the most part decayed from their high estate and let in flats and chambers to all sorts and conditions of men; map-engravers, architects, shady lawyers and the agents of obscure enterprises. One house, however, second from the corner, was still occupied entire; and at the door of this, which wore a great air of wealth and comfort, though it was now plunged in darkness except for the fanlight, Mr. Utterson stopped and knocked. A well-dressed, elderly servant opened the door.

"Is Dr. Jekyll at home, Poole?" asked the lawyer.

"I will see, Mr. Utterson," said Poole, admitting the visitor, as he spoke, into a large, low-roofed, comfortable hall paved with flags, warmed (after the fashion of a country house) by a bright, open fire, and furnished with costly cabinets of oak. "Will you wait here by the fire, sir? or shall I give you a light in the dining-room?"

"Here, thank you," said the lawyer, and he drew near and leaned on the tall fender. This hall, in which he was now left alone, was a pet fancy of his friend the doctor's; and Utterson himself was wont to speak of it as the pleasantest room in London. But tonight there was a shudder in his blood; the face of Hyde sat heavy on his memory; he felt (what was rare with him) a nausea and distaste of life; and in the gloom of his spirits, he seemed to read a menace in the flickering of the firelight on the polished cabinets and the uneasy starting of the shadow on the roof. He was ashamed of his relief, when Poole presently returned to announce that Dr. Jekyll was gone out.

"I saw Mr. Hyde go in by the old dissecting room, Poole," he said. "Is that right, when Dr. Jekyll is from home?"

"Quite right, Mr. Utterson, sir," replied the servant. "Mr. Hyde has a key."

"Your master seems to repose a great deal of trust in that young man, Poole," resumed the other musingly.

"Yes, sir, he does indeed," said Poole. "We have all orders to obey him."

"I do not think I ever met Mr. Hyde?" asked Utterson.

"O, dear no, sir. He never *dines* here," replied the butler. "Indeed we see very little of him on this side of the house; he mostly comes and goes by the laboratory."

"Well, good-night, Poole."

"Good-night, Mr. Utterson."

And the lawyer set out homeward with a very heavy heart. "Poor Harry Jekyll," he thought, "my mind misgives me he is in deep waters! He was wild when he was young; a long while ago to be sure; but in the law of God, there is no statute of limitations. Ay, it must be that; the ghost of some old sin, the cancer of some concealed disgrace: punishment coming, *pede claudo*, years after memory has forgotten and self-love condoned the fault." And the lawyer, scared by the thought, brooded awhile on his own past, groping in all the corners of memory, least by chance some Jack-in-the-Box of an old iniquity should leap to light there. His past was fairly blameless; few men could read the rolls of their life with less apprehension; yet he was humbled to the dust by the many ill things he had done, and raised up again into a sober and fearful gratitude by the many he had come so near to doing yet avoided. And then by a return on his former subject, he conceived a spark of hope. "This Master Hyde, if he were studied," thought he, "must have secrets of his own; black secrets, by the look of him; secrets compared to which poor Jekyll's worst would be like sunshine. Things cannot continue as they are. It turns me cold to think of this creature stealing like a thief to Harry's bedside; poor Harry, what a wakening! And the danger of it; for if this Hyde suspects the existence of the will, he may grow impatient to inherit. Ay, I must put my shoulders to the wheel—if Jekyll will but let me," he added, "if Jekyll will only let me." For once more he saw before his mind's eye, as clear as transparency, the strange clauses of the will.

DR. JEKYLL WAS QUITE AT EASE

A fortnight later, by excellent good fortune, the doctor gave one of his pleasant dinners to some five or six old cronies, all intelligent, reputable men and all judges of good wine; and Mr. Utterson so contrived that he remained behind after the others had departed. This was no new arrangement, but a thing that had befallen many scores of times. Where Utterson was liked, he was liked well. Hosts loved to detain the dry lawyer, when the light-hearted and loose-tongued had already their foot on the threshold; they liked to sit a while in his unobtrusive company, practising for solitude, sobering their minds in the man's rich silence after the expense and strain of gaiety. To this rule, Dr. Jekyll was no exception; and as he now sat on the opposite side of the fire—a large, well-made, smooth-faced man of fifty, with something of a slyish cast perhaps, but every mark of capacity and kindness—you could see by his looks that he cherished for Mr. Utterson a sincere and warm affection.

"I have been wanting to speak to you, Jekyll," began the latter. "You know that will of yours?"

A close observer might have gathered that the topic was distasteful; but the doctor carried it off gaily. "My poor Utterson," said he, "you are unfortunate in such a client. I never saw a man so distressed as you were by my will; unless it were that hide-bound pedant, Lanyon, at what he called my scientific heresies. O, I know he's a good fellow—you needn't frown—an excellent fellow, and I always mean to see more of him; but a hide-bound pedant for all that; an ignorant, blatant pedant. I was never more disappointed in any man than Lanyon."

"You know I never approved of it," pursued Utterson, ruthlessly disregarding the fresh topic.

"My will? Yes, certainly, I know that," said the doctor, a trifle sharply. "You have told me so."

"Well, I tell you so again," continued the lawyer. "I have been learning something of young Hyde."

The large handsome face of Dr. Jekyll grew pale to the very lips, and there came a blackness about his eyes. "I do not care to hear more," said he. "This is a matter I thought we had agreed to drop."

"What I heard was abominable," said Utterson.

"It can make no change. You do not understand my position," returned the doctor, with a certain incoherency of manner. "I am painfully situated, Utterson; my position is a very strange—a very strange one. It is one of those affairs that cannot be mended by talking."

"Jekyll," said Utterson, "you know me: I am a man to be trusted. Make a clean breast of this in confidence; and I make no doubt I can get you out of it."

"My good Utterson," said the doctor, "this is very good of you, this is downright good of you, and I cannot find words to thank you in. I believe you fully; I would trust you before any man alive, ay, before myself, if I could make the choice; but indeed it isn't what you fancy; it is not as bad as that; and just to put your good heart at rest, I will tell you one thing: the moment I choose, I can be rid of Mr. Hyde. I give you my hand upon that; and I thank you again and again; and I will just add one little word, Utterson, that I'm sure you'll take in good part: this is a private matter, and I beg of you to let it sleep."

Utterson reflected a little, looking in the fire.

"I have no doubt you are perfectly right," he said at last, getting to his feet.

"Well, but since we have touched upon this business, and for the last time I hope," continued the doctor, "there is one point I should like you to understand. I have really a very great interest in poor Hyde. I know you have seen him; he told me so; and I fear he was rude. But I do sincerely take a great, a very great interest in that young man; and if I am taken away, Utterson, I wish you to promise me that you will bear with him and get his rights for him. I think you would, if you knew all; and it would be a weight off my mind if you would promise."

"I can't pretend that I shall ever like him," said the lawyer.

"I don't ask that," pleaded Jekyll, laying his hand upon the other's arm; "I only ask for justice; I only ask you to help him for my sake, when I am no longer here."

Utterson heaved an irrepressible sigh. "Well," said he, "I promise."

THE CAREW MURDER CASE

Nearly a year later, in the month of October, 18—, London was startled by a crime of singular ferocity and rendered all the more notable by the high position of the victim. The details were few and startling. A maid servant living alone in a house not far from the river, had gone upstairs to bed about eleven. Although a fog rolled over the city in the small hours, the early part of the night was cloudless, and the lane, which the maid's window overlooked, was brilliantly lit by the full moon. It seems she was romantically given, for she sat down upon her box, which stood immediately under the window, and fell into a dream of musing. Never (she used to say, with streaming tears, when she narrated that experience), never had she felt more at peace with all men or thought more kindly of the world. And as she so sat she became aware of an aged beautiful gentleman with white hair, drawing near along the lane; and advancing to meet him, another and very small gentleman, to whom at first she paid less attention. When they had come within speech (which was just under the maid's eyes) the older man bowed and accosted the other with a very pretty manner of politeness. It did not seem as if the subject of his address were of great importance; indeed, from his pointing, it sometimes appeared as if he were only inquiring his way; but the moon shone on his face as he spoke, and the girl was pleased to watch it, it seemed to breathe such an innocent and old-world kindness of disposition, yet with something high too, as of a well-founded self-content. Presently her eye wandered to the other, and she was surprised to recognise in him a certain Mr. Hyde, who had once visited her master and for whom she had conceived a dislike. He had in his hand a heavy cane, with which he was trifling; but he answered never a word, and seemed to listen with an ill-contained impatience. And then all of a sudden he broke out in a great flame of anger, stamping with his foot, brandishing the cane, and carrying on (as the maid described it) like a madman. The old gentleman took a step back, with the air of one very much surprised and a trifle hurt; and at that Mr. Hyde broke out of all bounds and clubbed him to the earth. And next moment, with ape-like fury, he was trampling his victim under foot and hailing down a storm of blows, under which the bones were audibly shattered and the body jumped upon the roadway. At the horror of these sights and sounds, the maid fainted.

It was two o'clock when she came to herself and called for the police. The murderer was gone long ago; but there lay his victim in the middle of the lane, incredibly mangled. The stick with which the deed had been done, although it was of some rare and very tough and heavy wood, had broken in the middle under the stress of this insensate cruelty; and one splintered half had rolled in the neighbouring gutter—the other, without doubt, had been carried away by the murderer. A purse and gold watch were found upon the victim: but no cards or papers, except a sealed and stamped envelope, which he had been probably carrying to the post, and which bore the name and address of Mr. Utterson.

This was brought to the lawyer the next morning, before he was out of bed; and he had no sooner seen it and been told the circumstances, than he shot out a solemn lip. "I shall say nothing till I have seen the body," said he; "this may be very serious. Have the kindness to wait while I dress." And with the same grave countenance he hurried through his breakfast and drove to the police station, whither the body had been carried. As soon as he came into the cell, he nodded.

"Yes," said he, "I recognise him. I am sorry to say that this is Sir Danvers Carew."

"Good God, sir," exclaimed the officer, "is it possible?" And the next moment his eye lighted up with professional ambition. "This will make a deal of noise," he said. "And perhaps you can help us to the man." And he briefly narrated what the maid had seen, and showed the broken stick.

Mr. Utterson had already quailed at the name of Hyde; but when the stick was laid before him, he could doubt no longer; broken and battered as it was, he recognised it for one that he had himself presented many years before to Henry Jekyll.

"Is this Mr. Hyde a person of small stature?" he inquired.

"Particularly small and particularly wicked-looking, is what the maid calls him," said the officer.

Mr. Utterson reflected; and then, raising his head, "If you will come with me in my cab," he said, "I think I can take you to his house."

It was by this time about nine in the morning, and the first fog of the season. A great chocolate-coloured pall lowered over heaven, but the wind was continually charging and routing these embattled vapours; so that as the cab crawled from street to street, Mr. Utterson beheld a marvelous number of degrees and hues of twilight; for here it would be dark like the back-end of evening; and there would be a glow of a rich, lurid brown, like the light of some strange conflagration; and here, for a moment, the fog would be quite broken up, and a haggard shaft of daylight would glance in between the swirling wreaths. The dismal quarter of Soho seen under these changing glimpses, with its muddy ways, and slatternly passengers, and its lamps, which had never been extinguished or had been kindled afresh to combat this mournful reinvasion of darkness, seemed, in the lawyer's eyes, like a district of some city in a nightmare. The thoughts of his mind, besides, were of the gloomiest dye; and when he glanced at the companion of his drive, he was conscious of some touch of that terror of the law and the law's officers, which may at times assail the most honest.

As the cab drew up before the address indicated, the fog lifted a little and showed him a dingy street, a gin palace, a low French eating house, a shop for the retail of penny numbers and twopenny salads, many ragged children huddled in the doorways, and many women of many different nationalities passing out, key in hand, to have a morning glass; and the next moment the fog settled down again upon that part, as brown as umber, and cut him off from his blackguardly surroundings. This was the home of Henry Jekyll's favourite; of a man who was heir to a quarter of a million sterling.

An ivory-faced and silvery-haired old woman opened the door. She had an evil face, smoothed by hypocrisy: but her manners were excellent. Yes, she said, this was Mr. Hyde's, but he was not at home; he had been in that night very late, but he had gone away again in less than an hour; there was nothing strange in that; his habits were very irregular, and he was often absent; for instance, it was nearly two months since she had seen him till yesterday.

"Very well, then, we wish to see his rooms," said the lawyer; and when the woman began to declare it was impossible, "I had better tell you who this person is," he added. "This is Inspector Newcomen of Scotland Yard."

A flash of odious joy appeared upon the woman's face. "Ah!" said she, "he is in trouble! What has he done?"

Mr. Utterson and the inspector exchanged glances. "He don't seem a very popular character," observed the latter. "And now, my good woman, just let me and this gentleman have a look about us."

In the whole extent of the house, which but for the old woman remained otherwise empty, Mr. Hyde had only used a couple of rooms; but these were furnished with luxury and good taste. A closet was filled with wine; the plate was of silver, the napery elegant; a good picture hung upon the walls, a gift (as Utterson supposed) from Henry Jekyll, who was much of a connoisseur; and the carpets were of many plies and agreeable in colour. At this moment, however, the rooms bore every mark of having been recently and hurriedly ransacked; clothes lay about the floor, with their pockets inside out; lockfast drawers stood open; and on the hearth there lay a pile of grey ashes, as though many papers had been burned. From these embers the inspector disinterred the butt end of a green cheque book, which had resisted the action of the fire; the other half of the stick was found behind the door; and as this clinched his suspicions, the officer declared himself delighted. A visit to the bank, where several thousand pounds were found to be lying to the murderer's credit, completed his gratification.

"You may depend upon it, sir," he told Mr. Utterson: "I have him in my hand. He must have lost his head, or he never would have left the stick or, above all, burned the cheque book. Why, money's life to the man. We have nothing to do but wait for him at the bank, and get out the handbills."

This last, however, was not so easy of accomplishment; for Mr. Hyde had numbered few familiars—even the master of the servant maid had only seen him twice; his family could nowhere be traced; he had never been photographed; and the few who could describe him differed widely, as common observers will. Only on one point were they agreed; and that was the haunting sense of unexpressed deformity with which the fugitive impressed his beholders.

INCIDENT OF THE LETTER

It was late in the afternoon, when Mr. Utterson found his way to Dr. Jekyll's door, where he was at once admitted by Poole, and carried down by the kitchen offices and across a yard which had once been a garden, to the building which was indifferently known as the laboratory or dissecting rooms. The doctor had bought the house from the heirs of a celebrated surgeon; and his own tastes being rather chemical than anatomical, had changed the destination of the block at the bottom of the garden. It was the first time that the lawyer had been received in that part of his friend's quarters; and he eyed the dingy, windowless structure with curiosity, and gazed round with a distasteful sense of strangeness as he crossed the theatre, once crowded with eager students and now lying gaunt and silent, the tables laden with chemical apparatus, the floor strewn with crates and littered with packing straw, and the light falling dimly through the foggy cupola. At the further end, a flight of stairs mounted to a door covered with red baize; and through this, Mr. Utterson was at last received into the doctor's cabinet. It was a large room fitted round with glass presses, furnished, among other things, with a cheval-glass and a business table, and looking out upon the court by three dusty windows barred with iron. The fire burned in the grate; a lamp was set lighted on the chimney shelf, for even in the houses the fog began to lie thickly; and there, close up to the warmth, sat Dr. Jekyll, looking deathly sick. He did not rise to meet his visitor, but held out a cold hand and bade him welcome in a changed voice.

"And now," said Mr. Utterson, as soon as Poole had left them, "you have heard the news?"

The doctor shuddered. "They were crying it in the square," he said. "I heard them in my dining-room."

"One word," said the lawyer. "Carew was my client, but so are you, and I want to know what I am doing. You have not been mad enough to hide this fellow?"

"Utterson, I swear to God," cried the doctor, "I swear to God I will never set eyes on him again. I bind my honour to you that I am done with him in this world. It is all at an end. And indeed he does not want my help; you do not know him as I do; he is safe, he is quite safe; mark my words, he will never more be heard of."

The lawyer listened gloomily; he did not like his friend's feverish manner. "You seem pretty sure of him," said he; "and for your sake, I hope you may be right. If it came to a trial, your name might appear."

"I am quite sure of him," replied Jekyll; "I have grounds for certainty that I cannot share with any one. But there is one thing on which you may advise me. I have—I have received a letter; and I am at a loss whether I should show it to the police. I should like to leave it in your hands, Utterson; you would judge wisely, I am sure; I have so great a trust in you."

"You fear, I suppose, that it might lead to his detection?" asked the lawyer.

"No," said the other. "I cannot say that I care what becomes of Hyde; I am quite done with him. I was thinking of my own character, which this hateful business has rather exposed."

Utterson ruminated awhile; he was surprised at his friend's selfishness, and yet relieved by it. "Well," said he, at last, "let me see the letter."

The letter was written in an odd, upright hand and signed "Edward Hyde": and it signified, briefly enough, that the writer's benefactor, Dr. Jekyll, whom he had long so unworthily repaid for a thousand generosities, need labour under no alarm for his safety, as he had means of escape on which he placed a sure dependence. The lawyer liked this letter well enough; it put a better colour on the intimacy than he had looked for; and he blamed himself for some of his past suspicions.

"Have you the envelope?" he asked.

"I burned it," replied Jekyll, "before I thought what I was about. But it bore no postmark. The note was handed in."

"Shall I keep this and sleep upon it?" asked Utterson.

"I wish you to judge for me entirely," was the reply. "I have lost confidence in myself."

"Well, I shall consider," returned the lawyer. "And now one word more: it was Hyde who dictated the terms in your will about that disappearance?"

The doctor seemed seized with a qualm of faintness; he shut his mouth tight and nodded.

"I knew it," said Utterson. "He meant to murder you. You had a fine escape."

"I have had what is far more to the purpose," returned the doctor solemnly: "I have had a lesson—O God, Utterson, what a lesson I have had!" And he covered his face for a moment with his hands.

On his way out, the lawyer stopped and had a word or two with Poole. "By the bye," said he, "there was a letter handed in to-day: what was the messenger like?" But Poole was positive nothing had come except by post;

"and only circulars by that," he added.

This news sent off the visitor with his fears renewed. Plainly the letter had come by the laboratory door; possibly, indeed, it had been written in the cabinet; and if that were so, it must be differently judged, and handled with the more caution. The newsboys, as he went, were crying themselves hoarse along the footways: "Special edition. Shocking murder of an M.P." That was the funeral oration of one friend and client; and he could not help a certain apprehension lest the good name of another should be sucked down in the eddy of the scandal. It was, at least, a ticklish decision that he had to make; and self-reliant as he was by habit, he began to cherish a longing for advice. It was not to be had directly; but perhaps, he thought, it might be fished for.

Presently after, he sat on one side of his own hearth, with Mr. Guest, his head clerk, upon the other, and midway between, at a nicely calculated distance from the fire, a bottle of a particular old wine that had long dwelt unsunned in the foundations of his house. The fog still slept on the wing above the drowned city, where the lamps glimmered like carbuncles; and through the muffle and smother of these fallen clouds, the procession of the town's life was still rolling in through the great arteries with a sound as of a mighty wind. But the room was gay with firelight. In the bottle the acids were long ago resolved; the imperial dye had softened with time, as the colour grows richer in stained windows; and the glow of hot autumn afternoons on hillside vineyards, was ready to be set free and to disperse the fogs of London. Insensibly the lawyer melted. There was no man from whom he kept fewer secrets than Mr. Guest; and he was not always sure that he kept as many as he meant. Guest had often been on business to the doctor's; he knew Poole; he could scarce have failed to hear of Mr. Hyde's familiarity about the house; he might draw conclusions: was it not as well, then, that he should see a letter which put that mystery to right? and above all since Guest, being a great student and critic of handwriting, would consider the step natural and obliging? The clerk, besides, was a man of counsel; he could scarce read so strange a document without dropping a remark; and by that remark Mr. Utterson might shape his future course.

"This is a sad business about Sir Danvers," he said.

"Yes, sir, indeed. It has elicited a great deal of public feeling," returned Guest. "The man, of course, was mad."

"I should like to hear your views on that," replied Utterson. "I have a document here in his handwriting; it is between ourselves, for I scarce know what to do about it; it is an ugly business at the best. But there it is; quite in your way: a murderer's autograph."

Guest's eyes brightened, and he sat down at once and studied it with passion. "No sir," he said: "not mad; but it is an odd hand."

"And by all accounts a very odd writer," added the lawyer.

Just then the servant entered with a note.

"Is that from Dr. Jekyll, sir?" inquired the clerk. "I thought I knew the writing. Anything private, Mr. Utterson?"

"Only an invitation to dinner. Why? Do you want to see it?"

"One moment. I thank you, sir;" and the clerk laid the two sheets of paper alongside and sedulously compared their contents. "Thank you, sir," he said at last, returning both; "it's a very interesting autograph."

There was a pause, during which Mr. Utterson struggled with himself. "Why did you compare them, Guest?" he inquired suddenly.

"Well, sir," returned the clerk, "there's a rather singular resemblance; the two hands are in many points identical: only differently sloped."

"Rather quaint," said Utterson.

"It is, as you say, rather quaint," returned Guest.

"I wouldn't speak of this note, you know," said the master.

"No, sir," said the clerk. "I understand."

But no sooner was Mr. Utterson alone that night, than he locked the note into his safe, where it reposed from that time forward. "What!" he thought. "Henry Jekyll forge for a murderer!" And his blood ran cold in his veins.

INCIDENT OF DR. LANYON

Time ran on; thousands of pounds were offered in reward, for the death of Sir Danvers was resented as a public injury; but Mr. Hyde had disappeared out of the ken of the police as though he had never existed. Much of his past was unearthed, indeed, and all disreputable: tales came out of the man's cruelty, at once so callous and violent; of his vile life, of his strange associates, of the hatred that seemed to have surrounded his career; but of his present whereabouts, not a whisper. From the time he had left the house in Soho on the morning of the murder, he was simply blotted out; and gradually, as time drew on, Mr. Utterson began to recover from the hotness of his alarm, and to grow more at quiet with himself. The death of Sir Danvers was, to his way of thinking, more than paid for by the disappearance of Mr. Hyde. Now that that evil influence had been withdrawn, a new life began for Dr. Jekyll. He came out of his seclusion, renewed relations with his friends, became once more their familiar guest and entertainer; and whilst he had always been known for charities, he was now no less distinguished for religion. He was busy, he was much in the open air, he did good; his face seemed to open and brighten, as if with an inward consciousness of service; and for more than two months, the doctor was at peace.

On the 8th of January Utterson had dined at the doctor's with a small party; Lanyon had been there; and the face of the host had looked from one to the other as in the old days when the trio were inseparable friends. On the 12th, and again on the 14th, the door was shut against the lawyer. "The doctor was confined to the house," Poole said, "and saw no one." On the 15th, he tried again, and was again refused; and having now been used for the last two months to see his friend almost daily, he found this return of solitude to weigh upon his spirits. The fifth night he had in Guest to dine with him; and the sixth he betook himself to Dr. Lanyon's.

There at least he was not denied admittance; but when he came in, he was shocked at the change which had taken place in the doctor's appearance. He had his death-warrant written legibly upon his face. The rosy man had grown pale; his flesh had fallen away; he was visibly balder and older; and yet it was not so much these tokens of a swift physical decay that arrested the lawyer's notice, as a look in the eye and quality of manner that seemed to testify to some deep-seated terror of the mind. It was unlikely that the doctor should fear death; and yet that was what Utterson was tempted to suspect. "Yes," he thought; "he is a doctor, he must know his own state and that his days are counted; and the knowledge is more than he can bear." And yet when Utterson remarked on his ill looks, it was with an air of great firmness that Lanyon declared himself a doomed man.

"I have had a shock," he said, "and I shall never recover. It is a question of weeks. Well, life has been pleasant; I liked it; yes, sir, I used to like it. I sometimes think if we knew all, we should be more glad to get away."

"Jekyll is ill, too," observed Utterson. "Have you seen him?"

But Lanyon's face changed, and he held up a trembling hand. "I wish to see or hear no more of Dr. Jekyll," he said in a loud, unsteady voice. "I am quite done with that person; and I beg that you will spare me any allusion to one whom I regard as dead."

"Tut, tut!" said Mr. Utterson; and then after a considerable pause, "Can't I do anything?" he inquired. "We are three very old friends, Lanyon; we shall not live to make others."

"Nothing can be done," returned Lanyon; "ask himself."

"He will not see me," said the lawyer.

"I am not surprised at that," was the reply. "Some day, Utterson, after I am dead, you may perhaps come to learn the right and wrong of this. I cannot tell you. And in the meantime, if you can sit and talk with me of other things, for God's sake, stay and do so; but if you cannot keep clear of this accursed topic, then in God's name, go, for I cannot bear it."

As soon as he got home, Utterson sat down and wrote to Jekyll, complaining of his exclusion from the house, and asking the cause of this unhappy break with Lanyon; and the next day brought him a long answer, often very pathetically worded, and sometimes darkly mysterious in drift. The quarrel with Lanyon was incurable. "I do not blame our old friend," Jekyll wrote, "but I share his view that we must never meet. I mean from henceforth to lead a life of extreme seclusion; you must not be surprised, nor must you doubt my friendship, if my door is often shut even to you. You must suffer me to go my own dark way. I have brought on myself a punishment and a danger that I cannot name. If I am the chief of sinners, I am the chief of sufferers also. I could not think that this earth contained a place for sufferings and terrors so unmanning; and you can do but one thing, Utterson, to lighten this destiny, and that is to respect my silence." Utterson was amazed; the dark influence of Hyde had been withdrawn, the doctor had returned to his old tasks and amities; a week ago, the prospect had smiled with every promise of a cheerful and an honoured age; and now in a moment, friendship, and peace of mind, and the whole tenor of his life were wrecked. So great and unprepared a change pointed to madness; but in view of Lanyon's manner and words, there must lie for it some deeper ground.

A week afterwards Dr. Lanyon took to his bed, and in something less than a fortnight he was dead. The night after the funeral, at which he had been sadly affected, Utterson locked the door of his business room, and sitting there by the light of a melancholy candle, drew out and set before him an envelope addressed by the hand and sealed with the seal of his dead friend. "PRIVATE: for the hands of G. J. Utterson ALONE, and in case of his predecease *to be destroyed unread*," so it was emphatically superscribed; and the lawyer dreaded to behold the contents. "I have buried one friend to-day," he thought: "what if this should cost me another?" And then he condemned the fear as a disloyalty, and broke the seal. Within there was another enclosure, likewise sealed, and marked upon the cover as "not to be opened till the death or disappearance of Dr. Henry Jekyll." Utterson could not trust his eyes. Yes, it was disappearance; here again, as in the mad will which he had long ago restored to its author, here again were the idea of a disappearance and the name of Henry Jekyll bracketted. But in the will, that idea had sprung from the sinister suggestion of the man Hyde; it was set there with a purpose all too plain and horrible. Written by the hand of Lanyon, what should it mean? A great curiosity came on the trustee, to disregard the prohibition and dive at once to the bottom of these mysteries; but professional honour and faith to his dead friend were stringent obligations; and the packet slept in the inmost corner of his private safe.

It is one thing to mortify curiosity, another to conquer it; and it may be doubted if, from that day forth, Utterson desired the society of his surviving friend with the same eagerness. He thought of him kindly; but his thoughts were disquieted and fearful. He went to call indeed; but he was perhaps relieved to be denied admittance; perhaps, in his heart, he preferred to speak with Poole upon the doorstep and surrounded by the air and sounds of the open city, rather than to be admitted into that house of voluntary bondage, and to sit and speak with its inscrutable recluse. Poole had, indeed, no very pleasant news to communicate. The doctor, it appeared, now more than ever confined himself to the cabinet over the laboratory, where he would sometimes even sleep; he was out of spirits, he had grown very silent, he did not read; it seemed as if he had something on his mind. Utterson became so used to the unvarying character of these reports, that he fell off little by little in the frequency of his visits.

INCIDENT AT THE WINDOW

It chanced on Sunday, when Mr. Utterson was on his usual walk with Mr. Enfield, that their way lay once again through the by-street; and that when they came in front of the door, both stopped to gaze on it.

"Well," said Enfield, "that story's at an end at least. We shall never see more of Mr. Hyde."

"I hope not," said Utterson. "Did I ever tell you that I once saw him, and shared your feeling of repulsion?"

"It was impossible to do the one without the other," returned Enfield. "And by the way, what an ass you must have thought me, not to know that this was a back way to Dr. Jekyll's! It was partly your own fault that I found it out, even when I did."

"So you found it out, did you?" said Utterson. "But if that be so, we may step into the court and take a look at the windows. To tell you the truth, I am uneasy about poor Jekyll; and even outside, I feel as if the presence of a friend might do him good."

The court was very cool and a little damp, and full of premature twilight, although the sky, high up overhead, was still bright with sunset. The middle one of the three windows was half-way open; and sitting close beside it, taking the air with an infinite sadness of mien, like some disconsolate prisoner, Utterson saw Dr. Jekyll.

"What! Jekyll!" he cried. "I trust you are better."

"I am very low, Utterson," replied the doctor drearily, "very low. It will not last long, thank God."

"You stay too much indoors," said the lawyer. "You should be out, whipping up the circulation like Mr. Enfield and me. (This is my cousin—Mr. Enfield—Dr. Jekyll.) Come now; get your hat and take a quick turn with us."

"You are very good," sighed the other. "I should like to very much; but no, no, no, it is quite impossible; I dare not. But indeed, Utterson, I am very glad to see you; this is really a great pleasure; I would ask you and Mr. Enfield up, but the place is really not fit."

"Why, then," said the lawyer, good-naturedly, "the best thing we can do is to stay down here and speak with you from where we are."

"That is just what I was about to venture to propose," returned the doctor with a smile. But the words were hardly uttered, before the smile was struck out of his face and succeeded by an expression of such abject terror and despair, as froze the very blood of the two gentlemen below. They saw it but for a glimpse for the window was instantly thrust down; but that glimpse had been sufficient, and they turned and left the court without a word. In silence, too, they traversed the by-street; and it was not until they had come into a neighbouring thoroughfare, where even upon a Sunday there were still some stirrings of life, that Mr. Utterson at last turned and looked at his companion. They were both pale; and there was an answering horror in their eyes.

"God forgive us, God forgive us," said Mr. Utterson.

But Mr. Enfield only nodded his head very seriously, and walked on once more in silence.

THE LAST NIGHT

Mr. Utterson was sitting by his fireside one evening after dinner, when he was surprised to receive a visit from Poole.

"Bless me, Poole, what brings you here?" he cried; and then taking a second look at him, "What ails you?" he added; "is the doctor ill?"

"Mr. Utterson," said the man, "there is something wrong."

"Take a seat, and here is a glass of wine for you," said the lawyer. "Now, take your time, and tell me plainly what you want."

"You know the doctor's ways, sir," replied Poole, "and how he shuts himself up. Well, he's shut up again in the cabinet; and I don't like it, sir—I wish I may die if I like it. Mr. Utterson, sir, I'm afraid."

"Now, my good man," said the lawyer, "be explicit. What are you afraid of?"

"I've been afraid for about a week," returned Poole, doggedly disregarding the question, "and I can bear it no more."

The man's appearance amply bore out his words; his manner was altered for the worse; and except for the moment when he had first announced his terror, he had not once looked the lawyer in the face. Even now, he sat with the glass of wine untasted on his knee, and his eyes directed to a corner of the floor. "I can bear it no more," he repeated.

"Come," said the lawyer, "I see you have some good reason, Poole; I see there is something seriously amiss. Try to tell me what it is."

"I think there's been foul play," said Poole, hoarsely.

"Foul play!" cried the lawyer, a good deal frightened and rather inclined to be irritated in consequence. "What foul play! What does the man mean?"

"I daren't say, sir," was the answer; "but will you come along with me and see for yourself?"

Mr. Utterson's only answer was to rise and get his hat and greatcoat; but he observed with wonder the greatness of the relief that appeared upon the butler's face, and perhaps with no less, that the wine was still untasted when he set it down to follow.

It was a wild, cold, seasonable night of March, with a pale moon, lying on her back as though the wind had tilted her, and flying wrack of the most diaphanous and lawny texture. The wind made talking difficult, and flecked the blood into the face. It seemed to have swept the streets unusually bare of passengers, besides; for Mr. Utterson thought he had never seen that part of London so deserted. He could have wished it otherwise; never in his life had he been conscious of so sharp a wish to see and touch his fellow-creatures; for struggle as he might, there was borne in upon his mind a crushing anticipation of calamity. The square, when they got there, was full of wind and dust, and the thin trees in the garden were lashing themselves along the railing. Poole, who had kept all the way a pace or two ahead, now pulled up in the middle of the pavement, and in spite of the biting weather, took off his hat and mopped his brow with a red pocket-handkerchief. But for all the hurry of his coming, these were not the dews of exertion that he wiped away, but the moisture of some strangling anguish; for his face was white and his voice, when he spoke, harsh and broken.

"Well, sir," he said, "here we are, and God grant there be nothing wrong."

"Amen, Poole," said the lawyer.

Thereupon the servant knocked in a very guarded manner; the door was opened on the chain; and a voice asked from within, "Is that you, Poole?"

"It's all right," said Poole. "Open the door."

The hall, when they entered it, was brightly lighted up; the fire was built high; and about the hearth the whole of the servants, men and women, stood huddled together like a flock of sheep. At the sight of Mr. Utterson, the housemaid broke into hysterical whimpering; and the cook, crying out "Bless God! it's Mr. Utterson," ran forward as if to take him in her arms.

"What, what? Are you all here?" said the lawyer peevishly. "Very irregular, very unseemly; your master would be far from pleased."

"They're all afraid," said Poole.

Blank silence followed, no one protesting; only the maid lifted her voice and now wept loudly.

"Hold your tongue!" Poole said to her, with a ferocity of accent that testified to his own jangled nerves; and indeed, when the girl had so suddenly raised the note of her lamentation, they had all started and turned towards the inner door with faces of dreadful expectation. "And now," continued the butler, addressing the knife-boy, "reach me a candle, and we'll get this through hands at once." And then he begged Mr. Utterson to follow him, and led the way to the back garden.

"Now, sir," said he, "you come as gently as you can. I want you to hear, and I don't want you to be heard. And see here, sir, if by any chance he was to ask you in, don't go."

Mr. Utterson's nerves, at this unlooked-for termination, gave a jerk that nearly threw him from his balance; but he recollected his courage and followed the butler into the laboratory building through the surgical theatre, with its lumber of crates and bottles, to the foot of the stair. Here Poole motioned him to stand on one side and listen; while he himself, setting down the candle and making a great and obvious call on his resolution, mounted the steps and knocked with a somewhat uncertain hand on the red baize of the cabinet door.

"Mr. Utterson, sir, asking to see you," he called; and even as he did so, once more violently signed to the lawyer to give ear.

A voice answered from within: "Tell him I cannot see anyone," it said complainingly.

"Thank you, sir," said Poole, with a note of something like triumph in his voice; and taking up his candle, he led Mr. Utterson back across the yard and into the great kitchen, where the fire was out and the beetles were leaping on the floor.

"Sir," he said, looking Mr. Utterson in the eyes, "Was that my master's voice?"

"It seems much changed," replied the lawyer, very pale, but giving look for look.

"Changed? Well, yes, I think so," said the butler. "Have I been twenty years in this man's house, to be deceived about his voice? No, sir; master's made away with; he was made away with eight days ago, when we heard him cry out upon the name of God; and *who's* in there instead of him, and *why* it stays there, is a thing that cries to Heaven, Mr. Utterson!"

"This is a very strange tale, Poole; this is rather a wild tale my man," said Mr. Utterson, biting his finger. "Suppose it were as you suppose, supposing Dr. Jekyll to have been—well, murdered, what could induce the murderer to stay? That won't hold water; it doesn't commend itself to reason."

"Well, Mr. Utterson, you are a hard man to satisfy, but I'll do it yet," said Poole. "All this last week (you must know) him, or it, whatever it is that lives in that cabinet, has been crying night and day for some sort of medicine and cannot get it to his mind. It was sometimes his way—the master's, that is— to write his orders on a sheet of paper and throw it on the stair. We've had nothing else this week back; nothing but papers, and a closed door, and the very meals left there to be smuggled in when nobody was looking. Well, sir, every day, ay, and twice and thrice in the same day, there have been orders and complaints, and I have been sent flying to all the wholesale chemists in town. Every time I brought the stuff back, there would be another paper telling me to return it, because it was not pure, and another order to a different firm. This drug is wanted bitter bad, sir, whatever for."

"Have you any of these papers?" asked Mr. Utterson.

Poole felt in his pocket and handed out a crumpled note, which the lawyer, bending nearer to the candle, carefully examined. Its contents ran thus: "Dr. Jekyll presents his compliments to Messrs. Maw. He assures them that their last sample is impure and quite useless for his present purpose. In the year 18—, Dr. J. purchased a somewhat large quantity from Messrs. M. He now begs them to search with most sedulous care, and should any of the same quality be left, forward it to him at once. Expense is no consideration. The importance of this to Dr. J. can hardly be exaggerated." So far the letter had run composedly enough, but here with a sudden splutter of the pen, the writer's emotion had broken loose. "For God's sake," he added, "find me some of the old."

"This is a strange note," said Mr. Utterson; and then sharply, "How do you come to have it open?"

"The man at Maw's was main angry, sir, and he threw it back to me like so much dirt," returned Poole.

"This is unquestionably the doctor's hand, do you know?" resumed the lawyer.

"I thought it looked like it," said the servant rather sulkily; and then, with another voice, "But what matters hand of write?" he said. "I've seen him!"

"Seen him?" repeated Mr. Utterson. "Well?"

"That's it!" said Poole. "It was this way. I came suddenly into the theatre from the garden. It seems he had slipped out to look for this drug or whatever it is; for the cabinet door was open, and there he was at the far end of the room digging among the crates. He looked up when I came in, gave a kind of cry, and whipped upstairs into the cabinet. It was but for one minute that I saw him, but the hair stood upon my head like quills. Sir, if that was my master, why had he a mask upon his face? If it was my master, why did he cry out like a rat, and run from me? I have served him long enough. And then . . . " The man paused and passed his hand over his face.

"These are all very strange circumstances," said Mr. Utterson, "but I think I begin to see daylight. Your master, Poole, is plainly seized with one of those maladies that both torture and deform the sufferer; hence, for aught I know, the alteration of his voice; hence the mask and the avoidance of his friends; hence his eagerness to find this drug, by means of which the poor soul retains some hope of ultimate recovery—God grant that he be not deceived! There is my explanation; it is sad enough, Poole, ay, and appalling to consider; but it is plain and natural, hangs well together, and delivers us from all exorbitant alarms."

"Sir," said the butler, turning to a sort of mottled pallor, "that thing was not my master, and there's the truth. My master"—here he looked round him and began to whisper—"is a tall, fine build of a man, and this was more of a dwarf." Utterson attempted to protest. "O, sir," cried Poole, "do you think I do not know my master after twenty years? Do you think I do not know where his head comes to in the cabinet door, where I saw him every morning of my life? No, sir, that thing in the mask was never Dr. Jekyll— God knows what it was, but it was never Dr. Jekyll; and it is the belief of my heart that there was murder done."

"Poole," replied the lawyer, "if you say that, it will become my duty to make certain. Much as I desire to spare your master's feelings, much as I am puzzled by this note which seems to prove him to be still alive, I shall consider it my duty to break in that door."

"Ah, Mr. Utterson, that's talking!" cried the butler.

"And now comes the second question," resumed Utterson: "Who is going to do it?"

"Why, you and me, sir," was the undaunted reply.

"That's very well said," returned the lawyer; "and whatever comes of it, I shall make it my business to see you are no loser."

"There is an axe in the theatre," continued Poole; "and you might take the kitchen poker for yourself."

The lawyer took that rude but weighty instrument into his hand, and balanced it. "Do you know, Poole," he said, looking up, "that you and I are about to place ourselves in a position of some peril?"

"You may say so, sir, indeed," returned the butler.

"It is well, then that we should be frank," said the other. "We both think more than we have said; let us make a clean breast. This masked figure that you saw, did you recognise it?"

"Well, sir, it went so quick, and the creature was so doubled up, that I could hardly swear to that," was the answer. "But if you mean, was it Mr. Hyde?—why, yes, I think it was! You see, it was much of the same bigness; and it had the same quick, light way with it; and then who else could have got in by the laboratory door? You have not forgot, sir, that at the time of the murder he had still the key with him? But that's not all. I don't know, Mr. Utterson, if you ever met this Mr. Hyde?"

"Yes," said the lawyer, "I once spoke with him."

"Then you must know as well as the rest of us that there was something queer about that gentleman—something that gave a man a turn—I don't know rightly how to say it, sir, beyond this: that you felt in your marrow kind of cold and thin."

"I own I felt something of what you describe," said Mr. Utterson.

"Quite so, sir," returned Poole. "Well, when that masked thing like a monkey jumped from among the chemicals and whipped into the cabinet, it went down my spine like ice. O, I know it's not evidence, Mr. Utterson; I'm book-learned enough for that; but a man has his feelings, and I give you my bible-word it was Mr. Hyde!"

"Ay, ay," said the lawyer. "My fears incline to the same point. Evil, I fear, founded—evil was sure to come—of that connection. Ay truly, I believe you; I believe poor Harry is killed; and I believe his murderer (for what purpose, God alone can tell) is still lurking in his victim's room. Well, let our name be vengeance. Call Bradshaw."

The footman came at the summons, very white and nervous.

"Pull yourself together, Bradshaw," said the lawyer. "This suspense, I know, is telling upon all of you; but it is now our intention to make an end of it. Poole, here, and I are going to force our way into the cabinet. If all is well, my shoulders are broad enough to bear the blame. Meanwhile, lest anything should really be amiss, or any malefactor seek to escape by the back, you and the boy must go round the corner with a pair of good sticks and take your post at the laboratory door. We give you ten minutes to get to your stations."

As Bradshaw left, the lawyer looked at his watch. "And now, Poole, let us get to ours," he said; and taking the poker under his arm, led the way into the yard. The scud had banked over the moon, and it was now quite dark. The wind, which only broke in puffs and draughts into that deep well of building, tossed the light of the candle to and fro about their steps, until they came into the shelter of the theatre, where they sat down silently to wait. London hummed solemnly all around; but nearer at hand, the stillness was only broken by the sounds of a footfall moving to and fro along the cabinet floor.

"So it will walk all day, sir," whispered Poole; "ay, and the better part of the night. Only when a new sample comes from the chemist, there's a bit of a break. Ah, it's an ill conscience that's such an enemy to rest! Ah, sir, there's blood foully shed in every step of it! But hark again, a little closer—put your heart in your ears, Mr. Utterson, and tell me, is that the doctor's foot?"

The steps fell lightly and oddly, with a certain swing, for all they went so slowly; it was different indeed from the heavy creaking tread of Henry Jekyll. Utterson sighed. "Is there never anything else?" he asked.

Poole nodded. "Once," he said. "Once I heard it weeping!"

"Weeping? how that?" said the lawyer, conscious of a sudden chill of horror.

"Weeping like a woman or a lost soul," said the butler. "I came away with that upon my heart, that I could have wept too."

But now the ten minutes drew to an end. Poole disinterred the axe from under a stack of packing straw; the candle was set upon the nearest table to light them to the attack; and they drew near with bated breath to where that patient foot was still going up and down, up and down, in the quiet of the night.

"Jekyll," cried Utterson, with a loud voice, "I demand to see you." He paused a moment, but there came no reply. "I give you fair warning, our suspicions are aroused, and I must and shall see you," he resumed; "if not by fair means, then by foul—if not of your consent, then by brute force!"

"Utterson," said the voice, "for God's sake, have mercy!"

"Ah, that's not Jekyll's voice—it's Hyde's!" cried Utterson. "Down with the door, Poole!"

Poole swung the axe over his shoulder; the blow shook the building, and the red baize door leaped against the lock and hinges. A dismal screech, as of mere animal terror, rang from the cabinet. Up went the axe again, and again the panels crashed and the frame bounded; four times the blow fell; but the wood was tough and the fittings were of excellent workmanship; and it was not until the fifth, that the lock burst and the wreck of the door fell inwards on the carpet.

The besiegers, appalled by their own riot and the stillness that had succeeded, stood back a little and peered in. There lay the cabinet before their eyes in the quiet lamplight, a good fire glowing and chattering on the hearth, the kettle singing its thin strain, a drawer or two open, papers neatly set forth on the business table, and nearer the fire, the things laid out for tea; the quietest room, you would have said, and, but for the glazed presses full of chemicals, the most commonplace that night in London.

Right in the middle there lay the body of a man sorely contorted and still twitching. They drew near on tiptoe, turned it on its back and beheld the face of Edward Hyde. He was dressed in clothes far too large for him, clothes of the doctor's bigness; the cords of his face still moved with a semblance of life, but life was quite gone; and by the crushed phial in the hand and the strong smell of kernels that hung upon the air, Utterson knew that he was looking on the body of a self-destroyer.

"We have come too late," he said sternly, "whether to save or punish. Hyde is gone to his account; and it only remains for us to find the body of your master."

The far greater proportion of the building was occupied by the theatre, which filled almost the whole ground storey and was lighted from above, and by the cabinet, which formed an upper storey at one end and looked upon the court. A corridor joined the theatre to the door on the by-street; and with this the cabinet communicated separately by a second flight of stairs. There were besides a few dark closets and a spacious cellar. All these they now thoroughly examined. Each closet needed but a glance, for all were empty, and all, by the dust that fell from their doors, had stood long unopened. The cellar, indeed, was filled with crazy lumber, mostly dating from the times of the surgeon who was Jekyll's predecessor; but even as they opened the door they were advertised of the uselessness of further search, by the fall of a perfect mat of cobweb which had for years sealed up the entrance. Nowhere was there any trace of Henry Jekyll, dead or alive.

Poole stamped on the flags of the corridor. "He must be buried here," he said, hearkening to the sound.

"Or he may have fled," said Utterson, and he turned to examine the door in the by-street. It was locked; and lying near by on the flags, they found the key, already stained with rust.

"This does not look like use," observed the lawyer.

"Use!" echoed Poole. "Do you not see, sir, it is broken? much as if a man had stamped on it."

"Ay," continued Utterson, "and the fractures, too, are rusty." The two men looked at each other with a scare. "This is beyond me, Poole," said the lawyer. "Let us go back to the cabinet."

They mounted the stair in silence, and still with an occasional awestruck glance at the dead body, proceeded more thoroughly to examine the contents of the cabinet. At one table, there were traces of chemical work, various measured heaps of some white salt being laid on glass saucers, as though for an experiment in which the unhappy man had been prevented.

"That is the same drug that I was always bringing him," said Poole; and even as he spoke, the kettle with a startling noise boiled over.

This brought them to the fireside, where the easy-chair was drawn cosily up, and the tea things stood ready to the sitter's elbow, the very sugar in the cup. There were several books on a shelf; one lay beside the tea things open, and Utterson was amazed to find it a copy of a pious work, for which Jekyll had several times expressed a great esteem, annotated, in his own hand with startling blasphemies.

Next, in the course of their review of the chamber, the searchers came to the cheval-glass, into whose depths they looked with an involuntary horror. But it was so turned as to show them nothing but the rosy glow playing on the roof, the fire sparkling in a hundred repetitions along the glazed front of the presses, and their own pale and fearful countenances stooping to look in.

"This glass has seen some strange things, sir," whispered Poole.

"And surely none stranger than itself," echoed the lawyer in the same tones. "For what did Jekyll"—he caught himself up at the word with a start, and then conquering the weakness—"what could Jekyll want with it?" he said.

"You may say that!" said Poole.

Next they turned to the business table. On the desk, among the neat array of papers, a large envelope was uppermost, and bore, in the doctor's hand, the name of Mr. Utterson. The lawyer unsealed it, and several enclosures fell to the floor. The first was a will, drawn in the same eccentric terms as the one which he had returned six months before, to serve as a testament in case of death and as a deed of gift in case of disappearance; but in place of the name of Edward Hyde, the lawyer, with indescribable amazement read the name of Gabriel John Utterson. He looked at Poole, and then back at the paper, and last of all at the dead malefactor stretched upon the carpet.

"My head goes round," he said. "He has been all these days in possession; he had no cause to like me; he must have raged to see himself displaced; and he has not destroyed this document."

He caught up the next paper; it was a brief note in the doctor's hand and dated at the top. "O Poole!" the lawyer cried, "he was alive and here this day. He cannot have been disposed of in so short a space; he must be still alive, he must have fled! And then, why fled? and how? and in that case, can we venture to declare this suicide? O, we must be careful. I foresee that we may yet involve your master in some dire catastrophe."

"Why don't you read it, sir?" asked Poole.

"Because I fear," replied the lawyer solemnly. "God grant I have no cause for it!" And with that he brought the paper to his eyes and read as follows:

> "MY DEAR UTTERSON,—When this shall fall into your hands, I shall have disappeared, under what circumstances I have not the penetration to foresee, but my instinct and all the circumstances of my nameless situation tell me that the end is sure and must be early. Go then, and first read the narrative which Lanyon warned me he was to place in your hands; and if you care to hear more, turn to the confession of
>
> "Your unworthy and unhappy friend,
> "HENRY JEKYLL."

"There was a third enclosure?" asked Utterson.

"Here, sir," said Poole, and gave into his hands a considerable packet sealed in several places.

The lawyer put it in his pocket. "I would say nothing of this paper. If your master has fled or is dead, we may at least save his credit. It is now ten; I must go home and read these documents in quiet; but I shall be back before midnight, when we shall send for the police."

They went out, locking the door of the theatre behind them; and Utterson, once more leaving the servants gathered about the fire in the hall, trudged back to his office to read the two narratives in which this mystery was now to be explained.

DR. LANYON'S NARRATIVE

On the ninth of January, now four days ago, I received by the evening delivery a registered envelope, addressed in the hand of my colleague and old school companion, Henry Jekyll. I was a good deal surprised by this; for we were by no means in the habit of correspondence; I had seen the man, dined with him, indeed, the night before; and I could imagine nothing in our intercourse that should justify formality of registration. The contents increased my wonder; for this is how the letter ran:

"10*th December*, 18—.

"DEAR LANYON,—You are one of my oldest friends; and although we may have differed at times on scientific questions, I cannot remember, at least on my side, any break in our affection. There was never a day when, if you had said to me, 'Jekyll, my life, my honour, my reason, depend upon you,' I would not have sacrificed my left hand to help you. Lanyon, my life, my honour, my reason, are all at your mercy; if you fail me to-night, I am lost. You might suppose, after this preface, that I am going to ask you for something dishonourable to grant. Judge for yourself.

"I want you to postpone all other engagements for to-night—ay, even if you were summoned to the bedside of an emperor; to take a cab, unless your carriage should be actually at the door; and with this letter in your hand for consultation, to drive straight to my house. Poole, my butler, has his orders; you will find him waiting your arrival with a locksmith. The door of my cabinet is then to be forced; and you are to go in alone; to open the glazed press (letter E) on the left hand, breaking the lock if it be shut; and to draw out, *with all its contents as they stand*, the fourth drawer from the top or (which is the same thing) the third from the bottom. In my extreme distress of mind, I have a morbid fear of misdirecting you; but even if I am in error, you may know the right drawer by its contents: some powders, a phial and a paper book. This drawer I beg of you to carry back with you to Cavendish Square exactly as it stands.

"That is the first part of the service: now for the second. You should be back, if you set out at once on the receipt of this, long before midnight; but

I will leave you that amount of margin, not only in the fear of one of those obstacles that can neither be prevented nor foreseen, but because an hour when your servants are in bed is to be preferred for what will then remain to do. At midnight, then, I have to ask you to be alone in your consulting room, to admit with your own hand into the house a man who will present himself in my name, and to place in his hands the drawer that you will have brought with you from my cabinet. Then you will have played your part and earned my gratitude completely. Five minutes afterwards, if you insist upon an explanation, you will have understood that these arrangements are of capital importance; and that by the neglect of one of them, fantastic as they must appear, you might have charged your conscience with my death or the shipwreck of my reason.

"Confident as I am that you will not trifle with this appeal, my heart sinks and my hand trembles at the bare thought of such a possibility. Think of me at this hour, in a strange place, labouring under a blackness of distress that no fancy can exaggerate, and yet well aware that, if you will but punctually serve me, my troubles will roll away like a story that is told. Serve me, my dear Lanyon and save

"Your friend,
"H. J.

"P.S.—I had already sealed this up when a fresh terror struck upon my soul. It is possible that the post-office may fail me, and this letter not come into your hands until to-morrow morning. In that case, dear Lanyon, do my errand when it shall be most convenient for you in the course of the day; and once more expect my messenger at midnight. It may then already be too late; and if that night passes without event, you will know that you have seen the last of Henry Jekyll."

Upon the reading of this letter, I made sure my colleague was insane; but till that was proved beyond the possibility of doubt, I felt bound to do as he requested. The less I understood of this farrago, the less I was in a position to judge of its importance; and an appeal so worded could not be set aside without a grave responsibility. I rose accordingly from table, got into a hansom, and drove straight to Jekyll's house. The butler was awaiting my arrival; he had received by the same post as mine a registered letter of instruction, and had sent at once for a locksmith and a carpenter. The tradesmen came while we were yet speaking; and we moved in a body to old Dr. Denman's surgical theatre, from which (as you are doubtless aware) Jekyll's private cabinet is most conveniently entered. The door was very strong, the lock excellent; the carpenter avowed he would have great trouble and have to do much damage, if force were to be used; and the locksmith was near despair. But this last was a handy fellow, and after two hour's work, the door stood open. The press marked E was unlocked; and I took out the drawer, had it filled up with straw and tied in a sheet, and returned with it to Cavendish Square.

Here I proceeded to examine its contents. The powders were neatly enough made up, but not with the nicety of the dispensing chemist; so that it was plain they were of Jekyll's private manufacture; and when I opened one of the wrappers I found what seemed to me a simple crystalline salt of a white colour. The phial, to which I next turned my attention, might have been about half full of a blood-red liquor, which was highly pungent to the sense of smell and seemed to me to contain phosphorus and some volatile ether. At the other ingredients I could make no guess. The book was an ordinary version book and contained little but a series of dates. These covered a period of many years, but I observed that the entries ceased nearly a year ago and quite abruptly. Here and there a brief remark was appended to a date, usually no more than a single word: "double" occurring perhaps six times in a total of several hundred entries; and once very early in the list and followed by several marks of exclamation, "total failure!!!" All this, though it whetted my curiosity, told me little that was definite. Here were a phial of some salt, and the record of a series of experiments that had led (like too many of Jekyll's investigations) to no end of practical usefulness. How could the presence of these articles in my house affect either the honour, the sanity, or the life of my flighty colleague? If his messenger could go to one place, why could he not go to another? And even granting some impediment, why was this gentleman to be received by me in secret? The more I reflected the more convinced I grew that I was dealing with a case of cerebral disease; and though I dismissed my servants to bed, I loaded an old revolver, that I might be found in some posture of self-defence.

Twelve o'clock had scarce rung out over London, ere the knocker sounded very gently on the door. I went myself at the summons, and found a small man crouching against the pillars of the portico.

"Are you come from Dr. Jekyll?" I asked.

He told me "yes" by a constrained gesture; and when I had bidden him enter, he did not obey me without a searching backward glance into the darkness of the square. There was a policeman not far off, advancing with his bull's eye open; and at the sight, I thought my visitor started and made greater haste.

These particulars struck me, I confess, disagreeably; and as I followed him into the bright light of the consulting room, I kept my hand ready on my weapon. Here, at last, I had a chance of clearly seeing him. I had never set eyes on him before, so much was certain. He was small, as I have said; I was struck besides with the shocking expression of his face, with his remarkable combination of great muscular activity and great apparent debility of constitution, and—last but not least—with the odd, subjective disturbance caused by his neighbourhood. This bore some resemblance to incipient rigour, and was accompanied by a marked sinking of the pulse. At the time, I set it down to some idiosyncratic, personal distaste, and merely wondered at the acuteness of the symptoms; but I have since had reason to believe the cause to lie much deeper in the nature of man, and to turn on some nobler hinge than the principle of hatred.

This person (who had thus, from the first moment of his entrance, struck in me what I can only describe as a disgustful curiosity) was dressed in a fashion that would have made an ordinary person laughable; his clothes, that is to say, although they were of rich and sober fabric, were enormously too large for him in every measurement—the trousers hanging on his legs and rolled up to keep them from the ground, the waist of the coat below his haunches, and the collar sprawling wide upon his shoulders. Strange to relate, this ludicrous accoutrement was far from moving me to laughter. Rather, as there was something abnormal and misbegotten in the very essence of the creature that now faced me—something seizing, surprising and revolting—this fresh disparity seemed but to fit in with and to reinforce it; so that to my interest in the man's nature and character, there was added a curiosity as to his origin, his life, his fortune and status in the world.

These observations, though they have taken so great a space to be set down in, were yet the work of a few seconds. My visitor was, indeed, on fire with sombre excitement.

"Have you got it?" he cried. "Have you got it?" And so lively was his impatience that he even laid his hand upon my arm and sought to shake me.

I put him back, conscious at his touch of a certain icy pang along my blood. "Come, sir," said I. "You forget that I have not yet the pleasure of your acquaintance. Be seated, if you please." And I showed him an example, and sat down myself in my customary seat and with as fair an imitation of my ordinary manner to a patient, as the lateness of the hour, the nature of my preoccupations, and the horror I had of my visitor, would suffer me to muster.

"I beg your pardon, Dr. Lanyon," he replied civilly enough. "What you say is very well founded; and my impatience has shown its heels to my politeness. I come here at the instance of your colleague, Dr. Henry Jekyll, on a piece of business of some moment; and I understood . . . " He paused and put his hand to his throat, and I could see, in spite of his collected manner, that he was wrestling against the approaches of the hysteria—"I understood, a drawer . . . "

But here I took pity on my visitor's suspense, and some perhaps on my own growing curiosity.

"There it is, sir," said I, pointing to the drawer, where it lay on the floor behind a table and still covered with the sheet.

He sprang to it, and then paused, and laid his hand upon his heart; I could hear his teeth grate with the convulsive action of his jaws; and his face was so ghastly to see that I grew alarmed both for his life and reason.

"Compose yourself," said I.

He turned a dreadful smile to me, and as if with the decision of despair, plucked away the sheet. At sight of the contents, he uttered one loud sob of such immense relief that I sat petrified. And the next moment, in a voice that was already fairly well under control, "Have you a graduated glass?" he asked.

I rose from my place with something of an effort and gave him what he asked.

He thanked me with a smiling nod, measured out a few minims of the red tincture and added one of the powders. The mixture, which was at first of a reddish hue, began, in proportion as the crystals melted, to brighten in colour, to effervesce audibly, and to throw off small fumes of vapour. Suddenly and at the same moment, the ebullition ceased and the compound changed to a dark purple, which faded again more slowly to a watery green. My visitor, who had watched these metamorphoses with a keen eye, smiled, set down the glass upon the table, and then turned and looked upon me with an air of scrutiny.

"And now," said he, "to settle what remains. Will you be wise? will you be guided? will you suffer me to take this glass in my hand and to go forth from your house without further parley? or has the greed of curiosity too much command of you? Think before you answer, for it shall be done as you decide. As you decide, you shall be left as you were before, and neither richer nor wiser, unless the sense of service rendered to a man in mortal distress may be counted as a kind of riches of the soul. Or, if you shall so prefer to choose, a new province of knowledge and new avenues to fame and power shall be laid open to you, here, in this room, upon the instant; and your sight shall be blasted by a prodigy to stagger the unbelief of Satan."

"Sir," said I, affecting a coolness that I was far from truly possessing, "you speak enigmas, and you will perhaps not wonder that I hear you with no very strong impression of belief. But I have gone too far in the way of inexplicable services to pause before I see the end."

"It is well," replied my visitor. "Lanyon, you remember your vows: what follows is under the seal of our profession. And now, you who have so long been bound to the most narrow and material views, you who have denied the virtue of transcendental medicine, you who have derided your superiors—behold!"

He put the glass to his lips and drank at one gulp. A cry followed; he reeled, staggered, clutched at the table and held on, staring with injected eyes, gasping with open mouth; and as I looked there came, I thought, a change—he seemed to swell—his face became suddenly black and the features seemed to melt and alter—and the next moment, I had sprung to my feet and leaped back against the wall, my arms raised to shield me from that prodigy, my mind submerged in terror.

"O God!" I screamed, and "O God!" again and again; for there before my eyes—pale and shaken, and half fainting, and groping before him with his hands, like a man restored from death—there stood Henry Jekyll!

What he told me in the next hour, I cannot bring my mind to set on paper. I saw what I saw, I heard what I heard, and my soul sickened at it; and yet now when that sight has faded from my eyes, I ask myself if I believe it, and I cannot answer. My life is shaken to its roots; sleep has left me; the deadliest terror sits by me at all hours of the day and night; and I feel that my days are numbered, and that I must die; and yet I shall die incredulous. As for the moral turpitude that man unveiled to me, even with tears of penitence, I cannot, even in memory, dwell on it without a start of horror. I will say but one thing, Utterson, and that (if you can bring your mind to credit it) will be more than enough. The creature who crept into my house that night was, on Jekyll's own confession, known by the name of Hyde and hunted for in every corner of the land as the murderer of Carew.

HASTIE LANYON.

HENRY JEKYLL'S
FULL STATEMENT OF THE CASE

I was born in the year 18— to a large fortune, endowed besides with excellent parts, inclined by nature to industry, fond of the respect of the wise and good among my fellowmen, and thus, as might have been supposed, with every guarantee of an honourable and distinguished future. And indeed the worst of my faults was a certain impatient gaiety of disposition, such as has made the happiness of many, but such as I found it hard to reconcile with my imperious desire to carry my head high, and wear a more than commonly grave countenance before the public. Hence it came about that I concealed my pleasures; and that when I reached years of reflection, and began to look round me and take stock of my progress and position in the world, I stood already committed to a profound duplicity of life. Many a man would have even blazoned such irregularities as I was guilty of; but from the high views that I had set before me, I regarded and hid them with an almost morbid sense of shame. It was thus rather the exacting nature of my aspirations than any particular degradation in my faults, that made me what I was, and, with even a deeper trench than in the majority of men, severed in me those provinces of good and ill which divide and compound man's dual nature. In this case, I was driven to reflect deeply and inveterately on that hard law of life, which lies at the root of religion and is one of the most plentiful springs of distress. Though so profound a double-dealer, I was in no sense a hypocrite; both sides of me were in dead earnest; I was no more myself when I laid aside restraint and plunged in shame, than when I laboured, in the eye of day, at the furtherance of knowledge or the relief of sorrow and suffering. And it chanced that the direction of my scientific studies, which led wholly towards the mystic and the transcendental, reacted and shed a strong light on this consciousness of the perennial war among my members. With every day, and from both sides of my intelligence, the moral and the intellectual, I thus drew steadily nearer to that truth, by whose partial discovery I have been doomed to such a dreadful shipwreck: that man is not truly one, but truly two. I say two, because the state of my own knowledge does not pass beyond that point. Others will follow, others will outstrip me on the same lines; and I hazard the guess that man will be ultimately known for a mere polity of multifarious, incongruous and independent denizens. I, for my part, from the nature of my life, advanced infallibly in one direction and in one direction only. It was on the moral side, and in my own person, that I learned to recognise the thorough and primitive duality of man; I saw that, of the two natures that contended in the field of my consciousness, even if I could rightly be said to be either, it was only because I was radically both; and from an early date, even before the course of my scientific discoveries had begun to suggest the most naked possibility of such a miracle, I had learned to dwell with pleasure, as a beloved daydream, on the thought of the separation of these elements. If each, I told myself, could be housed in separate identities, life would be relieved of all that was unbearable; the unjust might go his way, delivered from the aspirations and remorse of his more upright twin; and the just could walk steadfastly and securely on his upward path, doing the good things in which he found his pleasure, and no longer exposed to disgrace and penitence by the hands of this extraneous evil. It was the curse of mankind that these incongruous faggots were thus bound together—that in the agonised womb of consciousness, these polar twins should be continuously struggling. How, then were they dissociated?

I was so far in my reflections when, as I have said, a side light began to shine upon the subject from the laboratory table. I began to perceive more deeply than it has ever yet been stated, the trembling immateriality, the mistlike transience, of this seemingly so solid body in which we walk attired. Certain agents I found to have the power to shake and pluck back that fleshly vestment, even as a wind might toss the curtains of a pavilion. For two good reasons, I will not enter deeply into this scientific branch of my confession. First, because I have been made to learn that the doom and burthen of our life is bound for ever on man's shoulders, and when the attempt is made to cast it off, it but returns upon us with more unfamiliar and more awful pressure. Second, because, as my narrative will make, alas! too evident, my discoveries were incomplete. Enough then, that I not only recognised my natural body from the mere aura and effulgence of certain of the powers that made up my spirit, but managed to compound a drug by which these powers should be dethroned from their supremacy, and a second form and countenance substituted, none the less natural to me because they were the expression, and bore the stamp of lower elements in my soul.

I hesitated long before I put this theory to the test of practice. I knew well that I risked death; for any drug that so potently controlled and shook the very fortress of identity, might, by the least scruple of an overdose or at the least inopportunity in the moment of exhibition, utterly blot out that immaterial tabernacle which I looked to it to change. But the temptation of a discovery so singular and profound at last overcame the suggestions of alarm. I had long since prepared my tincture; I purchased at once, from a firm of wholesale chemists, a large quantity of a particular salt which I knew, from my experiments, to be the last ingredient required; and late one accursed night, I compounded the elements, watched them boil and smoke together in the glass, and when the ebullition had subsided, with a strong glow of courage, drank off the potion.

The most racking pangs succeeded: a grinding in the bones, deadly nausea, and a horror of the spirit that cannot be exceeded at the hour of birth or death. Then these agonies began swiftly to subside, and I came to myself as if out of a great sickness. There was something strange in my sensations, something indescribably new and, from its very novelty, incredibly sweet. I felt younger, lighter, happier in body; within I was conscious of a heady recklessness, a current of disordered sensual images running like a millrace in my fancy, a solution of the bonds of obligation, an unknown but not an innocent freedom of the soul. I knew myself, at the first breath of this new life, to be more wicked, tenfold more wicked, sold a slave to my original evil; and the thought, in that moment, braced and delighted me like wine. I stretched out my hands, exulting in the freshness of these sensations; and in the act, I was suddenly aware that I had lost in stature.

There was no mirror, at that date, in my room; that which stands beside me as I write, was brought there later on and for the very purpose of these transformations. The night however, was far gone into the morning—the morning, black as it was, was nearly ripe for the conception of the day—the inmates of my house were locked in the most rigorous hours of slumber; and I determined, flushed as I was with hope and triumph, to venture in my new shape as far as to my bedroom. I crossed the yard, wherein the constellations looked down upon me, I could have thought, with wonder, the first creature of that sort that their unsleeping vigilance had yet disclosed to them; I stole through the corridors, a stranger in my own house; and coming to my room, I saw for the first time the appearance of Edward Hyde.

I must here speak by theory alone, saying not that which I know, but that which I suppose to be most probable. The evil side of my nature, to which I had now transferred the stamping efficacy, was less robust and less developed than the good which I had just deposed. Again, in the course of my life, which had been, after all, nine tenths a life of effort, virtue and control, it had been much less exercised and much less exhausted. And hence, as I think, it came about that Edward Hyde was so much smaller, slighter and younger than Henry Jekyll. Even as good shone upon the countenance of the one, evil was written broadly and plainly on the face of the other. Evil besides (which I must still believe to be the lethal side of man) had left on that body an imprint of deformity and decay. And yet when I looked upon that ugly idol in the glass, I was conscious of no repugnance, rather of a leap of welcome. This, too, was myself. It seemed natural and human. In my eyes it bore a livelier image of the spirit, it seemed more express and single, than the imperfect and divided countenance I had been hitherto accustomed to call mine. And in so far I was doubtless right. I have observed that when I wore the semblance of Edward Hyde, none could come near to me at first without a visible misgiving of the flesh. This, as I take it, was because all human beings, as we meet them, are commingled out of good and evil: and Edward Hyde, alone in the ranks of mankind, was pure evil.

I lingered but a moment at the mirror: the second and conclusive experiment had yet to be attempted; it yet remained to be seen if I had lost my identity beyond redemption and must flee before daylight from a house that was no longer mine; and hurrying back to my cabinet, I once more prepared and drank the cup, once more suffered the pangs of dissolution, and came to myself once more with the character, the stature and the face of Henry Jekyll.

That night I had come to the fatal cross-roads. Had I approached my discovery in a more noble spirit, had I risked the experiment while under the empire of generous or pious aspirations, all must have been otherwise, and from these agonies of death and birth, I had come forth an angel instead of a fiend. The drug had no discriminating action; it was neither diabolical nor divine; it but shook the doors of the prisonhouse of my disposition; and like the captives of Philippi, that which stood within ran forth. At that time my virtue slumbered; my evil, kept awake by ambition, was alert and swift to seize the occasion; and the thing that was projected was Edward Hyde. Hence, although I had now two characters as well as two appearances, one was wholly evil, and the other was still the old Henry Jekyll, that incongruous compound of whose reformation and improvement I had already learned to despair. The movement was thus wholly toward the worse.

Even at that time, I had not conquered my aversions to the dryness of a life of study. I would still be merrily disposed at times; and as my pleasures were (to say the least) undignified, and I was not only well known and highly considered, but growing towards the elderly man, this incoherency of my life was daily growing more unwelcome. It was on this side that my new power tempted me until I fell in slavery. I had but to drink the cup, to doff at once the body of the noted professor, and to assume, like a thick cloak, that of Edward Hyde. I smiled at the notion; it seemed to me at the time to be humourous; and I made my preparations with the most studious care. I took and furnished that house in Soho, to which Hyde was tracked by the police; and engaged as a housekeeper a creature whom I knew well to be silent and unscrupulous. On the other side, I announced to my servants that a Mr. Hyde (whom I described) was to have full liberty and power about my house in the square; and to parry mishaps, I even called and made myself a familiar object, in my second character. I next drew up that will to which you so much objected; so that if anything befell me in the person of Dr. Jekyll, I could enter on that of Edward Hyde without pecuniary loss. And thus fortified, as I supposed, on every side, I began to profit by the strange immunities of my position.

Men have before hired bravos to transact their crimes, while their own person and reputation sat under shelter. I was the first that ever did so for his pleasures. I was the first that could plod in the public eye with a load of genial respectability, and in a moment, like a schoolboy, strip off these lendings and spring headlong into the sea of liberty. But for me, in my impenetrable mantle, the safety was complete. Think of it—I did not even exist! Let me but escape into my laboratory door, give me but a second or two to mix and swallow the draught that I had always standing ready; and whatever he had done, Edward Hyde would pass away like the stain of breath upon a mirror; and there in his stead, quietly at home, trimming the midnight lamp in his study, a man who could afford to laugh at suspicion, would be Henry Jekyll.

The pleasures which I made haste to seek in my disguise were, as I have said, undignified; I would scarce use a harder term. But in the hands of Edward Hyde, they soon began to turn toward the monstrous. When I would come back from these excursions, I was often plunged into a kind of wonder at my vicarious depravity. This familiar that I called out of my own soul, and sent forth alone to do his good pleasure, was a being inherently malign and villainous; his every act and thought centered on self; drinking pleasure with bestial avidity from any degree of torture to another; relentless like a man of stone. Henry Jekyll stood at times aghast before the acts of Edward Hyde; but the situation was apart from ordinary laws, and insidiously relaxed the grasp of conscience. It was Hyde, after all, and Hyde alone, that was guilty. Jekyll was no worse; he woke again to his good qualities seemingly unimpaired; he would even make haste, where it was possible, to undo the evil done by Hyde. And thus his conscience slumbered.

Into the details of the infamy at which I thus connived (for even now I can scarce grant that I committed it) I have no design of entering; I mean but to point out the warnings and the successive steps with which my chastisement approached. I met with one accident which, as it brought on no consequence, I shall no more than mention. An act of cruelty to a child aroused against me the anger of a passer-by, whom I recognised the other day in the person of your kinsman; the doctor and the child's family joined him; there were moments when I feared for my life; and at last, in order to pacify their too just resentment, Edward Hyde had to bring them to the door, and pay them in a cheque drawn in the name of Henry Jekyll. But this danger was easily eliminated from the future, by opening an account at another bank in the name of Edward Hyde himself; and when, by sloping my own hand backward, I had supplied my double with a signature, I thought I sat beyond the reach of fate.

Some two months before the murder of Sir Danvers, I had been out for one of my adventures, had returned at a late hour, and woke the next day in bed with somewhat odd sensations. It was in vain I looked about me; in vain I saw the decent furniture and tall proportions of my room in the square; in vain that I recognised the pattern of the bed curtains and the design of the mahogany frame; something still kept insisting that I was not where I was, that I had not wakened where I seemed to be, but in the little room in Soho where I was accustomed to sleep in the body of Edward Hyde. I smiled to myself, and in my psychological way, began lazily to inquire into the elements of this illusion, occasionally, even as I did so, dropping back into a comfortable morning doze. I was still so engaged when, in one of my more wakeful moments, my eyes fell upon my hand. Now the hand of Henry Jekyll (as you have often remarked) was professional in shape and size; it was large, firm, white and comely. But the hand which I now saw, clearly enough, in the yellow light of a mid-London morning, lying half shut on the bedclothes, was lean, corded, knuckly, of a dusky pallor and thickly shaded with a swart growth of hair. It was the hand of Edward Hyde.

I must have stared upon it for near half a minute, sunk as I was in the mere stupidity of wonder, before terror woke up in my breast as sudden and startling as the crash of cymbals; and bounding from my bed I rushed to the mirror. At the sight that met my eyes, my blood was changed into something exquisitely thin and icy. Yes, I had gone to bed Henry Jekyll, I had awakened Edward Hyde. How was this to be explained? I asked myself; and then, with another bound of terror—how was it to be remedied? It was well on in the morning; the servants were up; all my drugs were in the cabinet—a long journey down two pairs of stairs, through the back passage, across the open court and through the anatomical theatre, from where I was then standing horror-struck. It might indeed be possible to cover my face; but of what use was that, when I was unable to conceal the alteration in my stature? And then with an overpowering sweetness of relief, it came back upon my mind that the servants were already used to the coming and going of my second self. I had soon dressed, as well as I was able, in clothes of my own size: had soon passed through the house, where Bradshaw stared and drew back at seeing Mr. Hyde at such an hour and in such a strange array; and ten minutes later, Dr. Jekyll had returned to his own shape and was sitting down, with a darkened brow, to make a feint of breakfasting.

Small indeed was my appetite. This inexplicable incident, this reversal of my previous experience, seemed, like the Babylonian finger on the wall, to be spelling out the letters of my judgment; and I began to reflect more seriously than ever before on the issues and possibilities of my double existence. That part of me which I had the power of projecting, had lately been much exercised and nourished; it had seemed to me of late as though the body of Edward Hyde had grown in stature, as though (when I wore that form) I were conscious of a more generous tide of blood; and I began to spy a danger that, if this were much prolonged, the balance of my nature might be permanently overthrown, the power of voluntary change be forfeited, and the character of Edward Hyde become irrevocably mine. The power of the drug had not been always equally displayed. Once, very early in my career, it had totally failed me; since then I had been obliged on more than one occasion to double, and once, with infinite risk of death, to treble the amount; and these rare uncertainties had cast hitherto the sole shadow on my contentment. Now, however, and in the light of that morning's accident, I was led to remark that whereas, in the beginning, the difficulty had been to throw off the body of Jekyll, it had of late gradually but decidedly transferred itself to the other side. All things therefore seemed to point to this; that I was slowly losing hold of my original and better self, and becoming slowly incorporated with my second and worse.

Between these two, I now felt I had to choose. My two natures had memory in common, but all other faculties were most unequally shared between them. Jekyll (who was composite) now with the most sensitive apprehensions, now with a greedy gusto, projected and shared in the pleasures and adventures of Hyde; but Hyde was indifferent to Jekyll, or but remembered him as the mountain bandit remembers the cavern in which he conceals himself from pursuit. Jekyll had more than a father's interest; Hyde had more than a son's indifference. To cast in my lot with Jekyll, was to die to those appetites which I had long secretly indulged and had of late begun to pamper. To cast it in with Hyde, was to die to a thousand interests and aspirations, and to become, at a blow and forever, despised and friendless. The bargain might appear unequal; but there was still another consideration in the scales; for while Jekyll would suffer smartingly in the fires of abstinence, Hyde would be not even conscious of all that he had lost.

Strange as my circumstances were, the terms of this debate are as old and commonplace as man; much the same inducements and alarms cast the die for any tempted and trembling sinner; and it fell out with me, as it falls with so vast a majority of my fellows, that I chose the better part and was found wanting in the strength to keep to it.

Yes, I preferred the elderly and discontented doctor, surrounded by friends and cherishing honest hopes; and bade a resolute farewell to the liberty, the comparative youth, the light step, leaping impulses and secret pleasures, that I had enjoyed in the disguise of Hyde. I made this choice perhaps with some unconscious reservation, for I neither gave up the house in Soho, nor destroyed the clothes of Edward Hyde, which still lay ready in my cabinet. For two months, however, I was true to my determination; for two months, I led a life of such severity as I had never before attained to, and enjoyed the compensations of an approving conscience. But time began at last to obliterate the freshness of my alarm; the praises of conscience began to grow into a thing of course; I began to be tortured with throes and longings, as of Hyde struggling after freedom; and at last, in an hour of moral weakness, I once again compounded and swallowed the transforming draught.

I do not suppose that, when a drunkard reasons with himself upon his vice, he is once out of five hundred times affected by the dangers that he runs through his brutish, physical insensibility; neither had I, long as I had considered my position, made enough allowance for the complete moral insensibility and insensate readiness to evil, which were the leading characters of Edward Hyde. Yet it was by these that I was punished. My devil had been long caged, he came out roaring. I was conscious, even when I took the draught, of a more unbridled, a more furious propensity to ill. It must have been this, I suppose, that stirred in my soul that tempest of impatience with which I listened to the civilities of my unhappy victim; I declare, at least, before God, no man morally sane could have been guilty of that crime upon so pitiful a provocation; and that I struck in no more reasonable spirit than that in which a sick child may break a plaything. But I had voluntarily stripped myself of all those balancing instincts by which even the worst of us continues to walk with some degree of steadiness among temptations; and in my case, to be tempted, however slightly, was to fall.

Instantly the spirit of hell awoke in me and raged. With a transport of glee, I mauled the unresisting body, tasting delight from every blow; and it was not till weariness had begun to succeed, that I was suddenly, in the top fit of my delirium, struck through the heart by a cold thrill of terror. A mist dispersed; I saw my life to be forfeit; and fled from the scene of these excesses, at once glorying and trembling, my lust of evil gratified and stimulated, my love of life screwed to the topmost peg. I ran to the house in Soho, and (to make assurance doubly sure) destroyed my papers; thence I set out through the lamplit streets, in the same divided ecstasy of mind, gloating on my crime, light-headedly devising others in the future, and yet still hastening and still hearkening in my wake for the steps of the avenger. Hyde had a song upon his lips as he compounded the draught, and as he drank it, pledged the dead man. The pangs of transformation had not done tearing him, before Henry Jekyll, with streaming tears of gratitude and remorse, had fallen upon his knees and lifted his clasped hands to God. The veil of self-indulgence was rent from head to foot. I saw my life as a whole: I followed it up from the days of childhood, when I had walked with my father's hand, and through the self-denying toils of my professional life, to arrive again and again, with the same sense of unreality, at the damned horrors of the evening. I could have screamed aloud; I sought with tears and prayers to smother down the crowd of hideous images and sounds with which my memory swarmed against me; and still, between the petitions, the ugly face of my iniquity stared into my soul. As the acuteness of this remorse began to die away, it was succeeded by a sense of joy. The problem of my conduct was solved. Hyde was thenceforth impossible; whether I would or not, I was now confined to the better part of my existence; and O, how I rejoiced to think of it! with what willing humility I embraced anew the restrictions of natural life! with what sincere renunciation I locked the door by which I had so often gone and come, and ground the key under my heel!

The next day, came the news that the murder had been overlooked, that the guilt of Hyde was patent to the world, and that the victim was a man high in public estimation. It was not only a crime, it had been a tragic folly. I think I was glad to know it; I think I was glad to have my better impulses thus buttressed and guarded by the terrors of the scaffold. Jekyll was now my city of refuge; let but Hyde peep out an instant, and the hands of all men would be raised to take and slay him.

I resolved in my future conduct to redeem the past; and I can say with honesty that my resolve was fruitful of some good. You know yourself how earnestly, in the last months of the last year, I laboured to relieve suffering; you know that much was done for others, and that the days passed quietly, almost happily for myself. Nor can I truly say that I wearied of this beneficent and innocent life; I think instead that I daily enjoyed it more completely; but I was still cursed with my duality of purpose; and as the first edge of my penitence wore off, the lower side of me, so long indulged, so recently chained down, began to growl for licence. Not that I dreamed of resuscitating Hyde; the bare idea of that would startle me to frenzy: no, it was in my own person that I was once more tempted to trifle with my conscience; and it was as an ordinary secret sinner that I at last fell before the assaults of temptation.

There comes an end to all things; the most capacious measure is filled at last; and this brief condescension to my evil finally destroyed the balance of my soul. And yet I was not alarmed; the fall seemed natural, like a return to the old days before I had made my discovery. It was a fine, clear, January day, wet under foot where the frost had melted, but cloudless overhead; and the Regent's Park was full of winter chirrupings and sweet with spring odours. I sat in the sun on a bench; the animal within me licking the chops of memory; the spiritual side a little drowsed, promising subsequent penitence, but not yet moved to begin. After all, I reflected, I was like my neighbours; and then I smiled, comparing myself with other men, comparing my active good-will with the lazy cruelty of their neglect. And at the very moment of that vainglorious thought, a qualm came over me, a horrid nausea and the most deadly shuddering. These passed away, and left me faint; and then as in its turn faintness subsided, I began to be aware of a change in the temper of my thoughts, a greater boldness, a contempt of danger, a solution of the bonds of obligation. I looked down; my clothes hung formlessly on my shrunken limbs; the hand that lay on my knee was corded and hairy. I was once more Edward Hyde. A moment before I had been safe of all men's respect, wealthy, beloved—the cloth laying for me in the dining-room at home; and now I was the common quarry of mankind, hunted, houseless, a known murderer, thrall to the gallows.

My reason wavered, but it did not fail me utterly. I have more than once observed that in my second character, my faculties seemed sharpened to a point and my spirits more tensely elastic; thus it came about that, where Jekyll perhaps might have succumbed, Hyde rose to the importance of the moment. My drugs were in one of the presses of my cabinet; how was I to reach them? That was the problem that (crushing my temples in my hands) I set myself to solve. The laboratory door I had closed. If I sought to enter by the house, my own servants would consign me to the gallows. I saw I must employ another hand, and thought of Lanyon. How was he to be reached? how persuaded? Supposing that I escaped capture in the streets, how was I to make my way into his presence? and how should I, an unknown and displeasing visitor, prevail on the famous physician to rifle the study of his colleague, Dr. Jekyll? Then I remembered that of my original character, one part remained to me: I could write my own hand; and once I had conceived that kindling spark, the way that I must follow became lighted up from end to end.

Thereupon, I arranged my clothes as best I could, and summoning a passing hansom, drove to an hotel in Portland Street, the name of which I chanced to remember. At my appearance (which was indeed comical enough, however tragic a fate these garments covered) the driver could not conceal his mirth. I gnashed my teeth upon him with a gust of devilish fury; and the smile withered from his face—happily for him—yet more happily for myself, for in another instant I had certainly dragged him from his perch. At the inn, as I entered, I looked about me with so black a countenance as made the attendants tremble; not a look did they exchange in my presence; but obsequiously took my orders, led me to a private room, and brought me wherewithal to write. Hyde in danger of his life was a creature new to me; shaken with inordinate anger, strung to the pitch of murder, lusting to inflict pain. Yet the creature was astute; mastered his fury with a great effort of the will; composed his two important letters, one to Lanyon and one to Poole; and that he might receive actual evidence of their being posted, sent them out with directions that they should be registered. Thenceforward, he sat all day over the fire in the private room, gnawing his nails; there he dined, sitting alone with his fears, the waiter visibly quailing before his eye; and thence, when the night was fully come, he set forth in the corner of a closed cab, and was driven to and fro about the streets of the city. He, I say—I cannot say, I. That child of Hell had nothing human; nothing lived in him but fear and hatred. And when at last, thinking the driver had begun to grow suspicious, he discharged the cab and ventured on foot, attired in his misfitting clothes, an object marked out for observation, into the midst of the nocturnal passengers, these two base passions raged within him like a tempest. He walked fast, hunted by his fears, chattering to himself, skulking through the less frequented thoroughfares, counting the minutes that still divided him from midnight. Once a woman spoke to him, offering, I think, a box of lights. He smote her in the face, and she fled.

When I came to myself at Lanyon's, the horror of my old friend perhaps affected me somewhat: I do not know; it was at least but a drop in the sea to the abhorrence with which I looked back upon these hours. A change had come over me. It was no longer the fear of the gallows, it was the horror of being Hyde that racked me. I received Lanyon's condemnation partly in a dream; it was partly in a dream that I came home to my own house and got into bed. I slept after the prostration of the day, with a stringent and profound slumber which not even the nightmares that wrung me could avail to break. I awoke in the morning shaken, weakened, but refreshed. I still hated and feared the thought of the brute that slept within me, and I had not of course forgotten the appalling dangers of the day before; but

I was once more at home, in my own house and close to my drugs; and gratitude for my escape shone so strong in my soul that it almost rivalled the brightness of hope.

I was stepping leisurely across the court after breakfast, drinking the chill of the air with pleasure, when I was seized again with those indescribable sensations that heralded the change; and I had but the time to gain the shelter of my cabinet, before I was once again raging and freezing with the passions of Hyde. It took on this occasion a double dose to recall me to myself; and alas! six hours after, as I sat looking sadly in the fire, the pangs returned, and the drug had to be re-administered. In short, from that day forth it seemed only by a great effort as of gymnastics, and only under the immediate stimulation of the drug, that I was able to wear the countenance of Jekyll. At all hours of the day and night, I would be taken with the premonitory shudder; above all, if I slept, or even dozed for a moment in my chair, it was always as Hyde that I awakened. Under the strain of this continually impending doom and by the sleeplessness to which I now condemned myself, ay, even beyond what I had thought possible to man, I became, in my own person, a creature eaten up and emptied by fever, languidly weak both in body and mind, and solely occupied by one thought: the horror of my other self. But when I slept, or when the virtue of the medicine wore off, I would leap almost without transition (for the pangs of transformation grew daily less marked) into the possession of a fancy brimming with images of terror, a soul boiling with causeless hatreds, and a body that seemed not strong enough to contain the raging energies of life. The powers of Hyde seemed to have grown with the sickliness of Jekyll. And certainly the hate that now divided them was equal on each side. With Jekyll, it was a thing of vital instinct. He had now seen the full deformity of that creature that shared with him some of the phenomena of consciousness, and was co-heir with him to death: and beyond these links of community, which in themselves made the most poignant part of his distress, he thought of Hyde, for all his energy of life, as of something not only hellish but inorganic. This was the shocking thing; that the slime of the pit seemed to utter cries and voices; that the amorphous dust gesticulated and sinned; that what was dead, and had no shape, should usurp the offices of life. And this again, that that insurgent horror was knit to him closer than a wife, closer than an eye; lay caged in his flesh, where he heard it mutter and felt it struggle to be born; and at every hour of weakness, and in the confidence of slumber, prevailed against him, and deposed him out of life. The hatred of Hyde for Jekyll was of a different order. His terror of the gallows drove him continually to commit temporary suicide, and return to his subordinate station of a part instead of a person; but he loathed the necessity, he loathed the despondency into which Jekyll was now fallen, and he resented the dislike with which he was himself regarded. Hence the ape-like tricks that he would play me, scrawling in my own hand blasphemies on the pages of my books, burning the letters and destroying the portrait of my father; and indeed, had it not been for his fear of death, he would long ago have ruined himself in order to involve me in the ruin. But his love of life is wonderful; I go further: I, who sicken and freeze at the mere thought of him, when I recall the abjection and passion of this attachment, and when I know how he fears my power to cut him off by suicide, I find it in my heart to pity him.

It is useless, and the time awfully fails me, to prolong this description; no one has ever suffered such torments, let that suffice; and yet even to these, habit brought—no, not alleviation—but a certain callousness of soul, a certain acquiescence of despair; and my punishment might have gone on for years, but for the last calamity which has now fallen, and which has finally severed me from my own face and nature. My provision of the salt, which had never been renewed since the date of the first experiment, began to run low. I sent out for a fresh supply and mixed the draught; the ebullition followed, and the first change of colour, not the second; I drank it and it was without efficiency. You will learn from Poole how I have had London ransacked; it was in vain; and I am now persuaded that my first supply was impure, and that it was that unknown impurity which lent efficacy to the draught.

About a week has passed, and I am now finishing this statement under the influence of the last of the old powders. This, then, is the last time, short of a miracle, that Henry Jekyll can think his own thoughts or see his own face (now how sadly altered!) in the glass. Nor must I delay too long to bring my writing to an end; for if my narrative has hitherto escaped destruction, it has been by a combination of great prudence and great good luck. Should the throes of change take me in the act of writing it, Hyde will tear it in pieces; but if some time shall have elapsed after I have laid it by, his wonderful selfishness and circumscription to the moment will probably save it once again from the action of his ape-like spite. And indeed the doom that is closing on us both has already changed and crushed him. Half an hour from now, when I shall again and forever reindue that hated personality, I know how I shall sit shuddering and weeping in my chair, or continue, with the most strained and fearstruck ecstasy of listening, to pace up and down this room (my last earthly refuge) and give ear to every sound of menace. Will Hyde die upon the scaffold? or will he find courage to release himself at the last moment? God knows; I am careless; this is my true hour of death, and what is to follow concerns another than myself. Here then, as I lay down the pen and proceed to seal up my confession, I bring the life of that unhappy Henry Jekyll to an end.

THE WERE-WOLF

By Clemence Housman

First Published in 1896

CLEMENCE HOUSMAN

Clemence Housman was born in Bromsgrove, England in 1861. Her brother was the renowned A. E. Housman, the pre-eminent classicist of his age and arguably one of the greatest scholars of all time. In 1883 Housman enrolled at art college in London, where she learnt the art of wood-engraving. It was while here that she first began to write short works of speculative fiction.

Housman split her time between the Suffragette movement – in which she was a leading figure – and novel-writing. She wasn't prolific, producing only three novels – *The Were-Wolf*, *Unknown Sea* and *The Life Of Sir Aglovale De Galis* – between 1896 and 1905. Of these, *The Were-Wolf*, published in 1896 is her most well-known. H. P. Lovecraft said of the novel that it "attains a high degree of gruesome tension and achieves to some extent the atmosphere of authentic folklore."

Housman was almost a hundred years old when she died at her home in Bromsgrove.

THE WERE-WOLF

The great farm hall was ablaze with the fire-light, and noisy with laughter and talk and many-sounding work. None could be idle but the very young and the very old: little Rol, who was hugging a puppy, and old Trella, whose palsied hand fumbled over her knitting. The early evening had closed in, and the farm-servants, come from their outdoor work, had assembled in the ample hall, which gave space for a score or more of workers. Several of the men were engaged in carving, and to these were yielded the best place and light; others made or repaired fishing-tackle and harness, and a great seine net occupied three pairs of hands. Of the women most were sorting and mixing eider feather and chopping straw to add to it. Looms were there, though not in present use, but three wheels whirred emulously, and the finest and swiftest thread of the three ran between the fingers of the house-mistress. Near her were some children, busy too, plaiting wicks for candles and lamps. Each group of workers had a lamp in its centre, and those farthest from the fire had live heat from two braziers filled with glowing wood embers, replenished now and again from the generous hearth. But the flicker of the great fire was manifest to remotest corners, and prevailed beyond the limits of the weaker lights.

Little Rol grew tired of his puppy, dropped it incontinently, and made an onslaught on Tyr, the old wolf-hound, who basked dozing, whimpering and twitching in his hunting dreams. Prone went Rol beside Tyr, his young arms round the shaggy neck, his curls against the black jowl. Tyr gave a perfunctory lick, and stretched with a sleepy sigh. Rol growled and rolled and shoved invitingly, but could only gain from the old dog placid toleration and a half-observant blink. "Take that then!" said Rol, indignant at this ignoring of his advances, and sent the puppy sprawling against the dignity that disdained him as playmate. The dog took no notice, and the child wandered off to find amusement elsewhere.

The baskets of white eider feathers caught his eye far off in a distant corner. He slipped under the table, and crept along on all-fours, the ordinary common-place custom of walking down a room upright not being to his fancy. When close to the women he lay still for a moment watching, with his elbows on the floor and his chin in his palms. One of the women seeing him nodded and smiled, and presently he crept out behind her skirts and passed, hardly noticed, from one to another, till he found opportunity to possess himself of a large handful of feathers. With these he traversed the length of the room, under the table again, and emerged near the spinners. At the feet of the youngest he curled himself round, sheltered by her knees from the observation of the others, and disarmed her of interference by secretly displaying his handful with a confiding smile. A dubious nod satisfied him, and presently he started on the play he had devised. He took a tuft of the white down, and gently shook it free of his fingers close to the whirl of the wheel. The wind of the swift motion took it, spun it round and round in widening circles, till it floated above like a slow white moth. Little Rol's eyes danced, and the row of his small teeth shone in a silent laugh of delight. Another and another of the white tufts was sent whirling round like a winged thing in a spider's web, and floating clear at last. Presently the handful failed.

Rol sprawled forward to survey the room, and contemplate another journey under the table. His shoulder, thrusting forward, checked the wheel for an instant; he shifted hastily. The wheel flew on with a jerk, and the thread snapped. "Naughty Rol!" said the girl. The swiftest wheel stopped also, and the house-mistress, Rol's aunt, leaned forward, and sighting the low curly head, gave a warning against mischief, and sent him off to old Trella's corner.

Rol obeyed, and after a discreet period of obedience, sidled out again down the length of the room farthest from his aunt's eye. As he slipped in among the men, they looked up to see that their tools might be, as far as possible, out of reach of Rol's hands, and close to their own. Nevertheless, before long he managed to secure a fine chisel and take off its point on the leg of the table. The carver's strong objections to this disconcerted Rol, who for five minutes thereafter effaced himself under the table.

During this seclusion he contemplated the many pairs of legs that surrounded him, and almost shut out the light of the fire. How very odd some of the legs were: some were curved where they should be straight, some were straight where they should be curved, and, as Rol said to himself, "they all seemed screwed on differently." Some were tucked away modestly under the benches, others were thrust far out under the table, encroaching on Rol's own particular domain. He stretched out his own short legs and regarded them critically, and, after comparison, favourably. Why were not all legs made like his, or like *his*?

These legs approved by Rol were a little apart from the rest. He crawled opposite and again made comparison. His face grew quite solemn as he thought of the innumerable days to come before his legs could be as long and strong. He hoped they would be just like those, his models, as straight as to bone, as curved as to muscle.

A few moments later Sweyn of the long legs felt a small hand caressing his foot, and looking down, met the upturned eyes of his little cousin Rol. Lying on his back, still softly patting and stroking the young man's foot, the child was quiet and happy for a good while. He watched the movement of the strong deft hands, and the shifting of the bright tools. Now and then, minute chips of wood, puffed off by Sweyn, fell down upon his face. At last he raised himself, very gently, lest a jog should wake impatience in the carver, and crossing his own legs round Sweyn's ankle, clasping with his arms too, laid his head against the knee. Such act is evidence of a child's most wonderful hero-worship. Quite content was Rol, and more than content when Sweyn paused a minute to joke, and pat his head and pull his curls. Quiet he remained, as long as quiescence is possible to limbs young as his. Sweyn forgot he was near, hardly noticed when his leg was gently released, and never saw the stealthy abstraction of one of his tools.

Ten minutes thereafter was a lamentable wail from low on the floor, rising to the full pitch of Rol's healthy lungs; for his hand was gashed across, and the copious bleeding terrified him. Then was there soothing and comforting, washing and binding, and a modicum of scolding, till the loud outcry sank into occasional sobs, and the child, tear-stained and subdued, was returned to the chimney-corner settle, where Trella nodded.

In the reaction after pain and fright, Rol found that the quiet of that fire-lit corner was to his mind. Tyr, too, disdained him no longer, but, roused by his sobs, showed all the concern and sympathy that a dog can by licking and wistful watching. A little shame weighed also upon his spirits. He wished he had not cried quite so much. He remembered how once Sweyn had come home with his arm torn down from the shoulder, and a dead bear; and how he had never winced nor said a word, though his lips turned white with pain. Poor little Rol gave another sighing sob over his own faint-hearted shortcomings.

The light and motion of the great fire began to tell strange stories to the child, and the wind in the chimney roared a corroborative note now and then. The great black mouth of the chimney, impending high over the hearth, received as into a mysterious gulf murky coils of smoke and brightness of aspiring sparks; and beyond, in the high darkness, were muttering and wailing and strange doings, so that sometimes the smoke rushed back in panic, and curled out and up to the roof, and condensed itself to invisibility among the rafters. And then the wind would rage after its lost prey, and rush round the house, rattling and shrieking at window and door.

In a lull, after one such loud gust, Rol lifted his head in surprise and listened. A lull had also come on the babel of talk, and thus could be heard with strange distinctness a sound outside the door—the sound of a child's voice, a child's hands. "Open, open; let me in!" piped the little voice from low down, lower than the handle, and the latch rattled as though a tiptoe child reached up to it, and soft small knocks were struck. One near the door sprang up and opened it. "No one is here," he said. Tyr lifted his head and gave utterance to a howl, loud, prolonged, most dismal.

Sweyn, not able to believe that his ears had deceived him, got up and went to the door. It was a dark night; the clouds were heavy with snow, that had fallen fitfully when the wind lulled. Untrodden snow lay up to the porch; there was no sight nor sound of any human being. Sweyn strained his eyes far and near, only to see dark sky, pure snow, and a line of black fir trees on a hill brow, bowing down before the wind. "It must have been the wind," he said, and closed the door.

Many faces looked scared. The sound of a child's voice had been so distinct—and the words "Open, open; let me in!" The wind might creak the wood, or rattle the latch, but could not speak with a child's voice, nor knock with the soft plain blows that a plump fist gives. And the strange unusual howl of the wolf-hound was an omen to be feared, be the rest what it might. Strange things were said by one and another, till the rebuke of the house-mistress quelled them into far-off whispers. For a time after there was uneasiness, constraint, and silence; then the chill fear thawed by degrees, and the babble of talk flowed on again.

Yet half-an-hour later a very slight noise outside the door sufficed to arrest every hand, every tongue. Every head was raised, every eye fixed in one direction. "It is Christian; he is late," said Sweyn.

No, no; this is a feeble shuffle, not a young man's tread. With the sound of uncertain feet came the hard tap-tap of a stick against the door, and the high-pitched voice of eld, "Open, open; let me in!" Again Tyr flung up his head in a long doleful howl.

Before the echo of the tapping stick and the high voice had fairly died away, Sweyn had sprung across to the door and flung it wide. "No one again," he said in a steady voice, though his eyes looked startled as he stared out. He saw the lonely expanse of snow, the clouds swagging low, and between the two the line of dark fir-trees bowing in the wind. He closed the door without a word of comment, and re-crossed the room.

A score of blanched faces were turned to him as though he must be solver of the enigma. He could not be unconscious of this mute eye-questioning, and it disturbed his resolute air of composure. He hesitated, glanced towards his mother, the house-mistress, then back at the frightened folk, and gravely, before them all, made the sign of the cross. There was a flutter of hands as the sign was repeated by all, and the dead silence was stirred as by a huge sigh, for the held breath of many was freed as though the sign gave magic relief.

Even the house-mistress was perturbed. She left her wheel and crossed the room to her son, and spoke with him for a moment in a low tone that none could overhear. But a moment later her voice was high-pitched and loud, so that all might benefit by her rebuke of the "heathen chatter" of one of the girls. Perhaps she essayed to silence thus her own misgivings and forebodings.

No other voice dared speak now with its natural fulness. Low tones made intermittent murmurs, and now and then silence drifted over the whole room. The handling of tools was as noiseless as might be, and suspended on the instant if the door rattled in a gust of wind. After a time Sweyn left his work, joined the group nearest the door, and loitered there on the pretence of giving advice and help to the unskilful.

A man's tread was heard outside in the porch. "Christian!" said Sweyn and his mother simultaneously, he confidently, she authoritatively, to set the checked wheels going again. But Tyr flung up his head with an appalling howl.

"Open, open; let me in!"

It was a man's voice, and the door shook and rattled as a man's strength beat against it. Sweyn could feel the planks quivering, as on the instant his hand was upon the door, flinging it open, to face the blank porch, and beyond only snow and sky, and firs aslant in the wind.

He stood for a long minute with the open door in his hand. The bitter wind swept in with its icy chill, but a deadlier chill of fear came swifter, and seemed to freeze the beating of hearts. Sweyn stepped back to snatch up a great bearskin cloak.

"Sweyn, where are you going?"

"No farther than the porch, mother," and he stepped out and closed the door.

He wrapped himself in the heavy fur, and leaning against the most sheltered wall of the porch, steeled his nerves to face the devil and all his works. No sound of voices came from within; the most distinct sound was the crackle and roar of the fire.

It was bitterly cold. His feet grew numb, but he forbore stamping them into warmth lest the sound should strike panic within; nor would he leave the porch, nor print a foot-mark on the untrodden white that declared so absolutely how no human voices and hands could have approached the door since snow fell two hours or more ago. "When the wind drops there will be more snow," thought Sweyn.

For the best part of an hour he kept his watch, and saw no living thing—heard no unwonted sound. "I will freeze here no longer," he muttered, and re-entered.

One woman gave a half-suppressed scream as his hand was laid on the latch, and then a gasp of relief as he came in. No one questioned him, only his mother said, in a tone of forced unconcern, "Could you not see Christian coming?" as though she were made anxious only by the absence of her younger son. Hardly had Sweyn stamped near to the fire than clear knocking was heard at the door. Tyr leapt from the hearth, his eyes red as the fire, his fangs showing white in the black jowl, his neck ridged and bristling; and overleaping Rol, ramped at the door, barking furiously.

Outside the door a clear mellow voice was calling. Tyr's bark made the words undistinguishable. No one offered to stir towards the door before Sweyn.

He stalked down the room resolutely, lifted the latch, and swung back the door.

A white-robed woman glided in.

No wraith! Living—beautiful—young.

Tyr leapt upon her.

Lithely she baulked the sharp fangs with folds of her long fur robe, and snatching from her girdle a small two-edged axe, whirled it up for a blow of defence.

Sweyn caught the dog by the collar, and dragged him off yelling and struggling.

The stranger stood in the doorway motionless, one foot set forward, one arm flung up, till the house-mistress hurried down the room; and Sweyn, relinquishing to others the furious Tyr, turned again to close the door, and offer excuse for so fierce a greeting. Then she lowered her arm, slung the axe in its place at her waist, loosened the furs about her face, and shook over her shoulders the long white robe—all as it were with the sway of one movement.

She was a maiden, tall and very fair. The fashion of her dress was strange, half masculine, yet not unwomanly. A fine fur tunic, reaching but little below the knee, was all the skirt she wore; below were the cross-bound shoes and leggings that a hunter wears. A white fur cap was set low upon the brows, and from its edge strips of fur fell lappet-wise about her shoulders; two of these at her entrance had been drawn forward and crossed about her throat, but now, loosened and thrust back, left unhidden long plaits of fair hair that lay forward on shoulder and breast, down to the ivory-studded girdle where the axe gleamed.

Sweyn and his mother led the stranger to the hearth without question or sign of curiosity, till she voluntarily told her tale of a long journey to distant kindred, a promised guide unmet, and signals and landmarks mistaken.

"Alone!" exclaimed Sweyn in astonishment. "Have you journeyed thus far, a hundred leagues, alone?"

She answered "Yes" with a little smile.

"Over the hills and the wastes! Why, the folk there are savage and wild as beasts."

She dropped her hand upon her axe with a laugh of some scorn.

"I fear neither man nor beast; some few fear me." And then she told strange tales of fierce attack and defence, and of the bold free huntress life she had led.

Her words came a little slowly and deliberately, as though she spoke in a scarce familiar tongue; now and then she hesitated, and stopped in a phrase, as though for lack of some word.

She became the centre of a group of listeners. The interest she excited dissipated, in some degree, the dread inspired by the mysterious voices. There was nothing ominous about this young, bright, fair reality, though her aspect was strange.

Little Rol crept near, staring at the stranger with all his might. Unnoticed, he softly stroked and patted a corner of her soft white robe that reached to the floor in ample folds. He laid his cheek against it caressingly, and then edged up close to her knees.

"What is your name?" he asked.

The stranger's smile and ready answer, as she looked down, saved Rol from the rebuke merited by his unmannerly question.

"My real name," she said, "would be uncouth to your ears and tongue. The folk of this country have given me another name, and from this" (she laid her hand on the fur robe) "they call me 'White Fell.'"

Little Rol repeated it to himself, stroking and patting as before. "White Fell, White Fell."

The fair face, and soft, beautiful dress pleased Rol. He knelt up, with his eyes on her face and an air of uncertain determination, like a robin's on a doorstep, and plumped his elbows into her lap with a little gasp at his own audacity.

"Rol!" exclaimed his aunt; but, "Oh, let him!" said White Fell, smiling and stroking his head; and Rol stayed.

He advanced farther, and panting at his own adventurousness in the face of his aunt's authority, climbed up on to her knees. Her welcoming arms hindered any protest. He nestled happily, fingering the axe head, the ivory studs in her girdle, the ivory clasp at her throat, the plaits of fair hair; rubbing his head against the softness of her fur-clad shoulder, with a child's full confidence in the kindness of beauty.

White Fell had not uncovered her head, only knotted the pendant fur loosely behind her neck. Rol reached up his hand towards it, whispering her name to himself, "White Fell, White Fell," then slid his arms round her neck, and kissed her—once—twice. She laughed delightedly, and kissed him again.

"The child plagues you?" said Sweyn.

"No, indeed," she answered, with an earnestness so intense as to seem disproportionate to the occasion.

Rol settled himself again on her lap, and began to unwind the bandage bound round his hand. He paused a little when he saw where the blood had soaked through; then went on till his hand was bare and the cut displayed, gaping and long, though only skin deep. He held it up towards White Fell, desirous of her pity and sympathy.

At sight of it, and the blood-stained linen, she drew in her breath suddenly, clasped Rol to her—hard, hard—till he began to struggle. Her face was hidden behind the boy, so that none could see its expression. It had lighted up with a most awful glee.

Afar, beyond the fir-grove, beyond the low hill behind, the absent Christian was hastening his return. From daybreak he had been afoot, carrying notice of a bear hunt to all the best hunters of the farms and hamlets that lay within a radius of twelve miles. Nevertheless, having been detained till a late hour, he now broke into a run, going with a long smooth stride of apparent ease that fast made the miles diminish.

He entered the midnight blackness of the fir-grove with scarcely slackened pace, though the path was invisible; and passing through into the open again, sighted the farm lying a furlong off down the slope. Then he sprang out freely, and almost on the instant gave one great sideways leap, and stood still. There in the snow was the track of a great wolf.

His hand went to his knife, his only weapon. He stooped, knelt down, to bring his eyes to the level of a beast, and peered about; his teeth set, his heart beat a little harder than the pace of his running insisted on. A solitary wolf, nearly always savage and of large size, is a formidable beast that will not hesitate to attack a single man. This wolf-track was the largest Christian had ever seen, and, so far as he could judge, recently made. It led from under the fir-trees down the slope. Well for him, he thought, was the delay that had so vexed him before: well for him that he had not passed through the dark fir-grove when that danger of jaws lurked there. Going warily, he followed the track.

It led down the slope, across a broad ice-bound stream, along the level beyond, making towards the farm. A less precise knowledge had doubted, and guessed that here might have come straying big Tyr or his like; but Christian was sure, knowing better than to mistake between footmark of dog and wolf.

Straight on—straight on towards the farm.

Surprised and anxious grew Christian, that a prowling wolf should dare so near. He drew his knife and pressed on, more hastily, more keen-eyed. Oh that Tyr were with him!

Straight on, straight on, even to the very door, where the snow failed. His heart seemed to give a great leap and then stop. There the track *ended*.

Nothing lurked in the porch, and there was no sign of return. The firs stood straight against the sky, the clouds lay low; for the wind had fallen and a few snowflakes came drifting down. In a horror of surprise, Christian stood dazed a moment: then he lifted the latch and went in. His glance took in all the old familiar forms and faces, and with them that of the stranger, fur-clad and beautiful. The awful truth flashed upon him: he knew what she was.

Only a few were startled by the rattle of the latch as he entered. The room was filled with bustle and movement, for it was the supper hour, when all tools were laid aside, and trestles and tables shifted. Christian had no knowledge of what he said and did; he moved and spoke mechanically, half thinking that soon he must wake from this horrible dream. Sweyn and his mother supposed him to be cold and dead-tired, and spared all unnecessary questions. And he found himself seated beside the hearth, opposite that dreadful Thing that looked like a beautiful girl; watching her every movement, curdling with horror to see her fondle the child Rol.

Sweyn stood near them both, intent upon White Fell also; but how differently! She seemed unconscious of the gaze of both—neither aware of the chill dread in the eyes of Christian, nor of Sweyn's warm admiration.

These two brothers, who were twins, contrasted greatly, despite their striking likeness. They were alike in regular profile, fair brown hair, and deep blue eyes; but Sweyn's features were perfect as a young god's, while Christian's showed faulty details. Thus, the line of his mouth was set too straight, the eyes shelved too deeply back, and the contour of the face flowed in less generous curves than Sweyn's. Their height was the same, but Christian was too slender for perfect proportion, while Sweyn's well-knit frame, broad shoulders, and muscular arms, made him pre-eminent for manly beauty as well as for strength. As a hunter Sweyn was without rival; as a fisher without rival. All the countryside acknowledged him to be the best wrestler, rider, dancer, singer. Only in speed could he be surpassed, and in that only by his younger brother. All others Sweyn could distance fairly; but Christian could outrun him easily. Ay, he could keep pace with Sweyn's most breathless burst, and laugh and talk the while. Christian took little pride in his fleetness of foot, counting a man's legs to be the least worthy of his members. He had no envy of his brother's athletic superiority, though to several feats he had made a moderate second. He loved as only a twin can love—proud of all that Sweyn did, content with all that Sweyn was; humbly content also that his own great love should not be so exceedingly returned, since he knew himself to be so far less love-worthy.

Christian dared not, in the midst of women and children, launch the horror that he knew into words. He waited to consult his brother; but Sweyn did not, or would not, notice the signal he made, and kept his face always turned towards White Fell. Christian drew away from the hearth, unable to remain passive with that dread upon him.

"Where is Tyr?" he said suddenly. Then, catching sight of the dog in a distant corner, "Why is he chained there?"

"He flew at the stranger," one answered.

Christian's eyes glowed. "Yes?" he said, interrogatively.

"He was within an ace of having his brain knocked out."

"Tyr?"

"Yes; she was nimbly up with that little axe she has at her waist. It was well for old Tyr that his master throttled him off."

Christian went without a word to the corner where Tyr was chained. The dog rose up to meet him, as piteous and indignant as a dumb beast can be. He stroked the black head. "Good Tyr! brave dog!"

They knew, they only; and the man and the dumb dog had comfort of each other.

Christian's eyes turned again towards White Fell: Tyr's also, and he strained against the length of the chain. Christian's hand lay on the dog's neck, and he felt it ridge and bristle with the quivering of impotent fury. Then he began to quiver in like manner, with a fury born of reason, not instinct; as impotent morally as was Tyr physically. Oh! the woman's form that he dare not touch! Anything but that, and he with Tyr would be free to kill or be killed.

Then he returned to ask fresh questions.

"How long has the stranger been here?"

"She came about half-an-hour before you."

"Who opened the door to her?"

"Sweyn: no one else dared."

The tone of the answer was mysterious.

"Why?" queried Christian. "Has anything strange happened? Tell me."

For answer he was told in a low undertone of the summons at the door thrice repeated without human agency; and of Tyr's ominous howls; and of Sweyn's fruitless watch outside.

Christian turned towards his brother in a torment of impatience for a word apart. The board was spread, and Sweyn was leading White Fell to the guest's place. This was more awful: she would break bread with them under the roof-tree!

He started forward, and touching Sweyn's arm, whispered an urgent entreaty. Sweyn stared, and shook his head in angry impatience.

Thereupon Christian would take no morsel of food.

His opportunity came at last. White Fell questioned of the landmarks of the country, and of one Cairn Hill, which was an appointed meeting-place at which she was due that night. The house-mistress and Sweyn both exclaimed.

"It is three long miles away," said Sweyn; "with no place for shelter but a wretched hut. Stay with us this night, and I will show you the way to-morrow."

White Fell seemed to hesitate. "Three miles," she said; "then I should be able to see or hear a signal."

"I will look out," said Sweyn; "then, if there be no signal, you must not leave us."

He went to the door. Christian rose silently, and followed him out.

"Sweyn, do you know what she is?"

Sweyn, surprised at the vehement grasp, and low hoarse voice, made answer:

"She? Who? White Fell?"

"Yes."

"She is the most beautiful girl I have ever seen."

"She is a Were-Wolf."

Sweyn burst out laughing. "Are you mad?" he asked.

"No; here, see for yourself."

Christian drew him out of the porch, pointing to the snow where the footmarks had been. Had been, for now they were not. Snow was falling fast, and every dint was blotted out.

"Well?" asked Sweyn.

"Had you come when I signed to you, you would have seen for yourself."

"Seen what?"

"The footprints of a wolf leading up to the door; none leading away."

It was impossible not to be startled by the tone alone, though it was hardly above a whisper. Sweyn eyed his brother anxiously, but in the darkness could make nothing of his face. Then he laid his hands kindly and re-assuringly on Christian's shoulders and felt how he was quivering with excitement and horror.

"One sees strange things," he said, "when the cold has got into the brain behind the eyes; you came in cold and worn out."

"No," interrupted Christian. "I saw the track first on the brow of the slope, and followed it down right here to the door. This is no delusion."

Sweyn in his heart felt positive that it was. Christian was given to day-dreams and strange fancies, though never had he been possessed with so mad a notion before.

"Don't you believe me?" said Christian desperately. "You must. I swear it is sane truth. Are you blind? Why, even Tyr knows."

"You will be clearer headed to-morrow after a night's rest. Then come too, if you will, with White Fell, to the Hill Cairn; and if you have doubts still, watch and follow, and see what footprints she leaves."

Galled by Sweyn's evident contempt Christian turned abruptly to the door. Sweyn caught him back.

"What now, Christian? What are you going to do?"

"You do not believe me; my mother shall."

Sweyn's grasp tightened. "You shall not tell her," he said authoritatively.

Customarily Christian was so docile to his brother's mastery that it was now a surprising thing when he wrenched himself free vigorously, and said as determinedly as Sweyn, "She shall know!" but Sweyn was nearer the door and would not let him pass.

"There has been scare enough for one night already. If this notion of yours will keep, broach it to-morrow." Christian would not yield.

"Women are so easily scared," pursued Sweyn, "and are ready to believe any folly without shadow of proof. Be a man, Christian, and fight this notion of a Were-Wolf by yourself."

"If you would believe me," began Christian.

"I believe you to be a fool," said Sweyn, losing patience. "Another, who was not your brother, might believe you to be a knave, and guess that you had transformed White Fell into a Were-Wolf because she smiled more readily on me than on you."

The jest was not without foundation, for the grace of White Fell's bright looks had been bestowed on him, on Christian never a whit. Sweyn's coxcombery was always frank, and most forgiveable, and not without fair colour.

"If you want an ally," continued Sweyn, "confide in old Trella. Out of her stores of wisdom, if her memory holds good, she can instruct you in the orthodox manner of tackling a Were-Wolf. If I remember aright, you should watch the suspected person till midnight, when the beast's form must be resumed, and retained ever after if a human eye sees the change; or, better still, sprinkle hands and feet with holy water, which is certain death. Oh! never fear, but old Trella will be equal to the occasion."

Sweyn's contempt was no longer good-humoured; some touch of irritation or resentment rose at this monstrous doubt of White Fell. But Christian was too deeply distressed to take offence.

"You speak of them as old wives' tales; but if you had seen the proof I have seen, you would be ready at least to wish them true, if not also to put them to the test."

"Well," said Sweyn, with a laugh that had a little sneer in it, "put them to the test! I will not object to that, if you will only keep your notions to yourself. Now, Christian, give me your word for silence, and we will freeze here no longer."

Christian remained silent.

Sweyn put his hands on his shoulders again and vainly tried to see his face in the darkness.

"We have never quarrelled yet, Christian?"

"I have never quarrelled," returned the other, aware for the first time that his dictatorial brother had sometimes offered occasion for quarrel, had he been ready to take it.

"Well," said Sweyn emphatically, "if you speak against White Fell to any other, as to-night you have spoken to me—we shall."

He delivered the words like an ultimatum, turned sharp round, and re-entered the house. Christian, more fearful and wretched than before, followed.

"Snow is falling fast: not a single light is to be seen."

White Fell's eyes passed over Christian without apparent notice, and turned bright and shining upon Sweyn.

"Nor any signal to be heard?" she queried. "Did you not hear the sound of a sea-horn?"

"I saw nothing, and heard nothing; and signal or no signal, the heavy snow would keep you here perforce."

She smiled her thanks beautifully. And Christian's heart sank like lead with a deadly foreboding, as he noted what a light was kindled in Sweyn's eyes by her smile.

That night, when all others slept, Christian, the weariest of all, watched outside the guest-chamber till midnight was past. No sound, not the faintest, could be heard. Could the old tale be true of the midnight change? What was on the other side of the door, a woman or a beast? he would have given his right hand to know. Instinctively he laid his hand on the latch, and drew it softly, though believing that bolts fastened the inner side. The door yielded to his hand; he stood on the threshold; a keen gust of air cut at him; the window stood open; the room was empty.

So Christian could sleep with a somewhat lightened heart.

In the morning there was surprise and conjecture when White Fell's absence was discovered. Christian held his peace. Not even to his brother did he say how he knew that she had fled before midnight; and Sweyn, though evidently greatly chagrined, seemed to disdain reference to the subject of Christian's fears.

The elder brother alone joined the bear hunt; Christian found pretext to stay behind. Sweyn, being out of humour, manifested his contempt by uttering not a single expostulation.

All that day, and for many a day after, Christian would never go out of sight of his home. Sweyn alone noticed how he manœuvred for this, and was clearly annoyed by it. White Fell's name was never mentioned between them, though not seldom was it heard in general talk. Hardly a day passed but little Rol asked when White Fell would come again: pretty White Fell, who kissed like a snowflake. And if Sweyn answered, Christian would be quite sure that the light in his eyes, kindled by White Fell's smile, had not yet died out.

Little Rol! Naughty, merry, fairhaired little Rol. A day came when his feet raced over the threshold never to return; when his chatter and laugh were heard no more; when tears of anguish were wept by eyes that never would see his bright head again: never again, living or dead.

He was seen at dusk for the last time, escaping from the house with his puppy, in freakish rebellion against old Trella. Later, when his absence had begun to cause anxiety, his puppy crept back to the farm, cowed, whimpering and yelping, a pitiful, dumb lump of terror, without intelligence or courage to guide the frightened search.

Rol was never found, nor any trace of him. Where he had perished was never known; how he had perished was known only by an awful guess—a wild beast had devoured him.

Christian heard the conjecture "a wolf"; and a horrible certainty flashed upon him that he knew what wolf it was. He tried to declare what he knew, but Sweyn saw him start at the words with white face and struggling lips; and, guessing his purpose, pulled him back, and kept him silent, hardly, by his imperious grip and wrathful eyes, and one low whisper.

That Christian should retain his most irrational suspicion against beautiful White Fell was, to Sweyn, evidence of a weak obstinacy of mind that would but thrive upon expostulation and argument. But this evident intention to direct the passions of grief and anguish to a hatred and fear of the fair stranger, such as his own, was intolerable, and Sweyn set his will against it. Again Christian yielded to his brother's stronger words and will, and against his own judgment consented to silence.

Repentance came before the new moon, the first of the year, was old. White Fell came again, smiling as she entered, as though assured of a glad and kindly welcome; and, in truth, there was only one who saw again her fair face and strange white garb without pleasure. Sweyn's face glowed with delight, while Christian's grew pale and rigid as death. He had given his word to keep silence; but he had not thought that she would dare to come again. Silence was impossible, face to face with that Thing, impossible. Irrepressibly he cried out:

"Where is Rol?"

Not a quiver disturbed White Fell's face. She heard, yet remained bright and tranquil. Sweyn's eyes flashed round at his brother dangerously. Among the women some tears fell at the poor child's name; but none caught alarm from its sudden utterance, for the thought of Rol rose naturally. Where was little Rol, who had nestled in the stranger's arms, kissing her; and watched for her since; and prattled of her daily?

Christian went out silently. One only thing there was that he could do, and he must not delay. His horror overmastered any curiosity to hear White Fell's smooth excuses and smiling apologies for her strange and uncourteous departure; or her easy tale of the circumstances of her return; or to watch her bearing as she heard the sad tale of little Rol.

The swiftest runner of the country-side had started on his hardest race: little less than three leagues and back, which he reckoned to accomplish in two hours, though the night was moonless and the way rugged. He rushed against the still cold air till it felt like a wind upon his face. The dim homestead sank below the ridges at his back, and fresh ridges of snowlands rose out of the obscure horizon-level to drive past him as the stirless air drove, and sink away behind into obscure level again. He took no conscious heed of landmarks, not even when all sign of a path was gone under depths of snow. His will was set to reach his goal with unexampled speed; and thither by instinct his physical forces bore him, without one definite thought to guide.

And the idle brain lay passive, inert, receiving into its vacancy restless siftings of past sights and sounds: Rol, weeping, laughing, playing, coiled in the arms of that dreadful Thing: Tyr—O Tyr!—white fangs in the black jowl: the women who wept on The foolish puppy, precious for the child's last touch: footprints from pine wood to door: the smiling face among furs, of such womanly beauty—smiling—smiling: and Sweyn's face.

"Sweyn, Sweyn, O Sweyn, my brother!"

Sweyn's angry laugh possessed his ear within the sound of the wind of his speed; Sweyn's scorn assailed more quick and keen than the biting cold at his throat. And yet he was unimpressed by any thought of how Sweyn's anger and scorn would rise, if this errand were known.

Sweyn was a sceptic. His utter disbelief in Christian's testimony regarding the footprints was based upon positive scepticism. His reason refused to bend in accepting the possibility of the supernatural materialised. That a living beast could ever be other than palpably bestial—pawed, toothed, shagged, and eared as such, was to him incredible; far more that a human presence could be transformed from its god-like aspect, upright, free-handed, with brows, and speech, and laughter. The wild and fearful legends that he had known from childhood and then believed, he regarded now as built upon facts distorted, overlaid by imagination, and quickened by superstition. Even the strange summons at the threshold, that he himself had vainly answered, was, after the first shock of surprise, rationally explained by him as malicious foolery on the part of some clever trickster, who withheld the key to the enigma.

To the younger brother all life was a spiritual mystery, veiled from his clear knowledge by the density of flesh. Since he knew his own body to be linked to the complex and antagonistic forces that constitute one soul, it seemed to him not impossibly strange that one spiritual force should possess divers forms for widely various manifestation. Nor, to him, was it great effort to believe that as pure water washes away all natural foulness, so water, holy by consecration, must needs cleanse God's world from that supernatural evil Thing. Therefore, faster than ever man's foot had covered those leagues, he sped under the dark, still night, over the waste, trackless snow-ridges to the far-away church, where salvation lay in the holy-water stoup at the door. His faith was as firm as any that wrought miracles in days past, simple as a child's wish, strong as a man's will.

He was hardly missed during these hours, every second of which was by him fulfilled to its utmost extent by extremest effort that sinews and nerves could attain. Within the homestead the while, the easy moments went bright with words and looks of unwonted animation, for the kindly, hospitable instincts of the inmates were roused into cordial expression of welcome and interest by the grace and beauty of the returned stranger.

But Sweyn was eager and earnest, with more than a host's courteous warmth. The impression that at her first coming had charmed him, that had lived since through memory, deepened now in her actual presence. Sweyn, the matchless among men, acknowledged in this fair White Fell a spirit high and bold as his own, and a frame so firm and capable that only bulk was lacking for equal strength. Yet the white skin was moulded most smoothly, without such muscular swelling as made his might evident. Such love as his frank self-love could concede was called forth by an ardent admiration for this supreme stranger. More admiration than love was in his passion, and therefore he was free from a lover's hesitancy and delicate reserve and doubts. Frankly and boldly he courted her favour by looks and tones, and an address that came of natural ease, needless of skill by practice.

Nor was she a woman to be wooed otherwise. Tender whispers and sighs would never gain her ear; but her eyes would brighten and shine if she heard of a brave feat, and her prompt hand in sympathy fall swiftly on the axe-haft and clasp it hard. That movement ever fired Sweyn's admiration anew; he watched for it, strove to elicit it, and glowed when it came. Wonderful and beautiful was that wrist, slender and steel-strong; also the smooth shapely hand, that curved so fast and firm, ready to deal instant death.

Desiring to feel the pressure of these hands, this bold lover schemed with palpable directness, proposing that she should hear how their hunting songs were sung, with a chorus that signalled hands to be clasped. So his splendid voice gave the verses, and, as the chorus was taken up, he claimed her hands, and, even through the easy grip, felt, as he desired, the strength that was latent, and the vigour that quickened the very fingertips, as the song fired her, and her voice was caught out of her by the rhythmic swell, and rang clear on the top of the closing surge.

Afterwards she sang alone. For contrast, or in the pride of swaying moods by her voice, she chose a mournful song that drifted along in a minor chant, sad as a wind that dirges:

> "Oh, let me go!
> Around spin wreaths of snow;
> The dark earth sleeps below.

"Far up the plain
Moans on a voice of pain:
'Where shall my babe be lain?'

"In my white breast
Lay the sweet life to rest!
Lay, where it can lie best!

"'Hush! hush its cries!
Dense night is on the skies:
Two stars are in thine eyes.'

"Come, babe, away!
But lie thou till dawn be grey,
Who must be dead by day.

"This cannot last;
But, ere the sickening blast,
All sorrow shall be past;

"And kings shall be
Low bending at thy knee,
Worshipping life from thee.

"For men long sore
To hope of what's before,—
To leave the things of yore.

"Mine, and not thine,
How deep their jewels shine!
Peace laps thy head, not mine."

Old Trella came tottering from her corner, shaken to additional palsy by
an aroused memory. She strained her dim eyes towards the singer, and then
bent her head, that the one ear yet sensible to sound might avail of every
note. At the close, groping forward, she murmured with the high-pitched
quaver of old age:

"So she sang, my Thora; my last and brightest. What is she like, she whose
voice is like my dead Thora's? Are her eyes blue?"

"Blue as the sky."

"So were my Thora's! Is her hair fair, and in plaits to the waist?" "Even so," answered White Fell herself, and met the advancing hands with her own, and guided them to corroborate her words by touch.

"Like my dead Thora's," repeated the old woman; and then her trembling hands rested on the fur-clad shoulders, and she bent forward and kissed the smooth fair face that White Fell upturned, nothing loth, to receive and return the caress.

So Christian saw them as he entered.

He stood a moment. After the starless darkness and the icy night air, and the fierce silent two hours' race, his senses reeled on sudden entrance into warmth, and light, and the cheery hum of voices. A sudden unforeseen anguish assailed him, as now first he entertained the possibility of being overmatched by her wiles and her daring, if at the approach of pure death she should start up at bay transformed to a terrible beast, and achieve a savage glut at the last. He looked with horror and pity on the harmless, helpless folk, so unwitting of outrage to their comfort and security. The dreadful Thing in their midst, that was veiled from their knowledge by womanly beauty, was a centre of pleasant interest. There, before him, signally impressive, was poor old Trella, weakest and feeblest of all, in fond nearness. And a moment might bring about the revelation of a monstrous horror—a ghastly, deadly danger, set loose and at bay, in a circle of girls and women and careless defenceless men: so hideous and terrible a thing as might crack the brain, or curdle the heart stone dead.

And he alone of the throng prepared!

For one breathing space he faltered, no longer than that, while over him swept the agony of compunction that yet could not make him surrender his purpose.

He alone? Nay, but Tyr also; and he crossed to the dumb sole sharer of his knowledge.

So timeless is thought that a few seconds only lay between his lifting of the latch and his loosening of Tyr's collar; but in those few seconds succeeding his first glance, as lightning-swift had been the impulses of others, their motion as quick and sure. Sweyn's vigilant eye had darted upon him, and instantly his every fibre was alert with hostile instinct; and, half divining, half incredulous, of Christian's object in stooping to Tyr, he came hastily, wary, wrathful, resolute to oppose the malice of his wild-eyed brother.

But beyond Sweyn rose White Fell, blanching white as her furs, and with eyes grown fierce and wild. She leapt down the room to the door, whirling her long robe closely to her. "Hark!" she panted. "The signal horn! Hark, I must go!" as she snatched at the latch to be out and away.

For one precious moment Christian had hesitated on the half-loosened collar; for, except the womanly form were exchanged for the bestial, Tyr's jaws would gnash to rags his honour of manhood. Then he heard her voice, and turned—too late.

As she tugged at the door, he sprang across grasping his flask, but Sweyn dashed between, and caught him back irresistibly, so that a most frantic effort only availed to wrench one arm free. With that, on the impulse of sheer despair, he cast at her with all his force. The door swung behind her, and the flask flew into fragments against it. Then, as Sweyn's grasp slackened, and he met the questioning astonishment of surrounding faces, with a hoarse inarticulate cry: "God help us all!" he said. "She is a Were-Wolf."

Sweyn turned upon him, "Liar, coward!" and his hands gripped his brother's throat with deadly force, as though the spoken word could be killed so; and as Christian struggled, lifted him clear off his feet and flung him crashing backward. So furious was he, that, as his brother lay motionless, he stirred him roughly with his foot, till their mother came between, crying shame; and yet then he stood by, his teeth set, his brows knit, his hands clenched, ready to enforce silence again violently, as Christian rose staggering and bewildered.

But utter silence and submission were more than he expected, and turned his anger into contempt for one so easily cowed and held in subjection by mere force. "He is mad!" he said, turning on his heel as he spoke, so that he lost his mother's look of pained reproach at this sudden free utterance of what was a lurking dread within her.

Christian was too spent for the effort of speech. His hard-drawn breath laboured in great sobs; his limbs were powerless and unstrung in utter relax after hard service. Failure in his endeavour induced a stupor of misery and despair. In addition was the wretched humiliation of open violence and strife with his brother, and the distress of hearing misjudging contempt expressed without reserve; for he was aware that Sweyn had turned to allay the scared excitement half by imperious mastery, half by explanation and argument, that showed painful disregard of brotherly consideration. All this unkindness of his twin he charged upon the fell Thing who had wrought this their first dissension, and, ah! most terrible thought, interposed between them so effectually, that Sweyn was wilfully blind and deaf on her account, resentful of interference, arbitrary beyond reason.

Dread and perplexity unfathomable darkened upon him; unshared, the burden was overwhelming: a foreboding of unspeakable calamity, based upon his ghastly discovery, bore down upon him, crushing out hope of power to withstand impending fate.

Sweyn the while was observant of his brother, despite the continual check of finding, turn and glance when he would, Christian's eyes always upon him, with a strange look of helpless distress, discomposing enough to the angry aggressor. "Like a beaten dog!" he said to himself, rallying contempt to withstand compunction. Observation set him wondering on Christian's exhausted condition. The heavy labouring breath and the slack inert fall of the limbs told surely of unusual and prolonged exertion. And then why had close upon two hours' absence been followed by open hostility against White Fell?

Suddenly, the fragments of the flask giving a clue, he guessed all, and faced about to stare at his brother in amaze. He forgot that the motive scheme was against White Fell, demanding derision and resentment from him; that was swept out of remembrance by astonishment and admiration for the feat of speed and endurance. In eagerness to question he inclined to attempt a generous part and frankly offer to heal the breach; but Christian's depression and sad following gaze provoked him to self-justification by recalling the offence of that outrageous utterance against White Fell; and the impulse passed. Then other considerations counselled silence; and afterwards a humour possessed him to wait and see how Christian would find opportunity to proclaim his performance and establish the fact, without exciting ridicule on account of the absurdity of the errand.

This expectation remained unfulfilled. Christian never attempted the proud avowal that would have placed his feat on record to be told to the next generation.

That night Sweyn and his mother talked long and late together, shaping into certainty the suspicion that Christian's mind had lost its balance, and discussing the evident cause. For Sweyn, declaring his own love for White Fell, suggested that his unfortunate brother, with a like passion, they being twins in loves as in birth, had through jealousy and despair turned from love to hate, until reason failed at the strain, and a craze developed, which the malice and treachery of madness made a serious and dangerous force.

So Sweyn theorised, convincing himself as he spoke; convincing afterwards others who advanced doubts against White Fell; fettering his judgment by his advocacy, and by his staunch defence of her hurried flight silencing his own inner consciousness of the unaccountability of her action.

But a little time and Sweyn lost his vantage in the shock of a fresh horror at the homestead. Trella was no more, and her end a mystery. The poor old woman crawled out in a bright gleam to visit a bed-ridden gossip living beyond the fir-grove. Under the trees she was last seen, halting for her companion, sent back for a forgotten present. Quick alarm sprang, calling every man to the search. Her stick was found among the brushwood only a few paces from the path, but no track or stain, for a gusty wind was sifting the snow from the branches, and hid all sign of how she came by her death.

So panic-stricken were the farm folk that none dared go singly on the search. Known danger could be braced, but not this stealthy Death that walked by day invisible, that cut off alike the child in his play and the aged woman so near to her quiet grave.

"Rol she kissed; Trella she kissed!" So rang Christian's frantic cry again and again, till Sweyn dragged him away and strove to keep him apart, albeit in his agony of grief and remorse he accused himself wildly as answerable for the tragedy, and gave clear proof that the charge of madness was well founded, if strange looks and desperate, incoherent words were evidence enough.

But thenceforward all Sweyn's reasoning and mastery could not uphold White Fell above suspicion. He was not called upon to defend her from accusation when Christian had been brought to silence again; but he well knew the significance of this fact, that her name, formerly uttered freely and often, he never heard now: it was huddled away into whispers that he could not catch.

The passing of time did not sweep away the superstitious fears that Sweyn despised. He was angry and anxious; eager that White Fell should return, and, merely by her bright gracious presence, reinstate herself in favour; but doubtful if all his authority and example could keep from her notice an altered aspect of welcome; and he foresaw clearly that Christian would prove unmanageable, and might be capable of some dangerous outbreak.

For a time the twins' variance was marked, on Sweyn's part by an air of rigid indifference, on Christian's by heavy downcast silence, and a nervous apprehensive observation of his brother. Superadded to his remorse and foreboding, Sweyn's displeasure weighed upon him intolerably, and the remembrance of their violent rupture was a ceaseless misery. The elder brother, self-sufficient and insensitive, could little know how deeply his unkindness stabbed. A depth and force of affection such as Christian's was unknown to him. The loyal subservience that he could not appreciate had encouraged him to domineer; this strenuous opposition to his reason and will was accounted as furious malice, if not sheer insanity.

Christian's surveillance galled him incessantly, and embarrassment and danger he foresaw as the outcome. Therefore, that suspicion might be lulled, he judged it wise to make overtures for peace. Most easily done. A little kindliness, a few evidences of consideration, a slight return of the old brotherly imperiousness, and Christian replied by a gratefulness and relief that might have touched him had he understood all, but instead, increased his secret contempt.

So successful was this finesse, that when, late on a day, a message summoning Christian to a distance was transmitted by Sweyn, no doubt of its genuineness occurred. When, his errand proved useless, he set out to return, mistake or misapprehension was all that he surmised. Not till he sighted the homestead, lying low between the night-grey snow ridges, did vivid recollection of the time when he had tracked that horror to the door rouse an intense dread, and with it a hardly-defined suspicion.

His grasp tightened on the bear-spear that he carried as a staff; every sense was alert, every muscle strung; excitement urged him on, caution checked him, and the two governed his long stride, swiftly, noiselessly, to the climax he felt was at hand.

As he drew near to the outer gates, a light shadow stirred and went, as though the grey of the snow had taken detached motion. A darker shadow stayed and faced Christian, striking his life-blood chill with utmost despair.

Sweyn stood before him, and surely, the shadow that went was White Fell.

They had been together—close. Had she not been in his arms, near enough for lips to meet?

There was no moon, but the stars gave light enough to show that Sweyn's face was flushed and elate. The flush remained, though the expression changed quickly at sight of his brother. How, if Christian had seen all, should one of his frenzied outbursts be met and managed: by resolution? by indifference? He halted between the two, and as a result, he swaggered.

"White Fell?" questioned Christian, hoarse and breathless.

"Yes?"

Sweyn's answer was a query, with an intonation that implied he was clearing the ground for action.

From Christian came: "Have you kissed her?" like a bolt direct, staggering Sweyn by its sheer prompt temerity.

He flushed yet darker, and yet half-smiled over this earnest of success he had won. Had there been really between himself and Christian the rivalry that he imagined, his face had enough of the insolence of triumph to exasperate jealous rage.

"You dare ask this!"

"Sweyn, O Sweyn, I must know! You have!"

The ring of despair and anguish in his tone angered Sweyn, misconstruing it. Jealousy urging to such presumption was intolerable.

"Mad fool!" he said, constraining himself no longer. "Win for yourself a woman to kiss. Leave mine without question. Such an one as I should desire to kiss is such an one as shall never allow a kiss to you."

Then Christian fully understood his supposition.

"I—I!" he cried. "White Fell—that deadly Thing! Sweyn, are you blind, mad? I would save you from her: a Were-Wolf!"

Sweyn maddened again at the accusation—a dastardly way of revenge, as he conceived; and instantly, for the second time, the brothers were at strife violently.

But Christian was now too desperate to be scrupulous; for a dim glimpse had shot a possibility into his mind, and to be free to follow it the striking of his brother was a necessity. Thank God! he was armed, and so Sweyn's equal.

Facing his assailant with the bear-spear, he struck up his arms, and with the butt end hit hard so that he fell. The matchless runner leapt away on the instant, to follow a forlorn hope. Sweyn, on regaining his feet, was as amazed as angry at this unaccountable flight. He knew in his heart that his brother was no coward, and that it was unlike him to shrink from an encounter because defeat was certain, and cruel humiliation from a vindictive victor probable. Of the uselessness of pursuit he was well aware: he must abide his chagrin, content to know that his time for advantage would come. Since White Fell had parted to the right, Christian to the left, the event of a sequent encounter did not occur to him. And now Christian, acting on the dim glimpse he had had, just as Sweyn turned upon him, of something that moved against the sky along the ridge behind the homestead, was staking his only hope on a chance, and his own superlative speed. If what he saw was really White Fell, he guessed she was bending her steps towards the open wastes; and there was just a possibility that, by a straight dash, and a desperate perilous leap over a sheer bluff, he might yet meet her or head her. And then: he had no further thought.

It was past, the quick, fierce race, and the chance of death at the leap; and he halted in a hollow to fetch his breath and to look: did she come? had she gone?

She came.

She came with a smooth, gliding, noiseless speed, that was neither walking nor running; her arms were folded in her furs that were drawn tight about her body; the white lappets from her head were wrapped and knotted closely beneath her face; her eyes were set on a far distance. So she went till the even sway of her going was startled to a pause by Christian.

"Fell!"

She drew a quick, sharp breath at the sound of her name thus mutilated, and faced Sweyn's brother. Her eyes glittered; her upper lip was lifted, and shewed the teeth. The half of her name, impressed with an ominous sense as uttered by him, warned her of the aspect of a deadly foe. Yet she cast loose her robes till they trailed ample, and spoke as a mild woman.

"What would you?"

Then Christian answered with his solemn dreadful accusation:

"You kissed Rol—and Rol is dead! You kissed Trella: she is dead! You have kissed Sweyn, my brother; but he shall not die!"

He added: "You may live till midnight."

The edge of the teeth and the glitter of the eyes stayed a moment, and her right hand also slid down to the axe haft. Then, without a word, she swerved from him, and sprang out and away swiftly over the snow.

And Christian sprang out and away, and followed her swiftly over the snow, keeping behind, but half-a-stride's length from her side.

So they went running together, silent, towards the vast wastes of snow, where no living thing but they two moved under the stars of night.

Never before had Christian so rejoiced in his powers. The gift of speed, and the training of use and endurance were priceless to him now. Though midnight was hours away, he was confident that, go where that Fell Thing would, hasten as she would, she could not outstrip him nor escape from him. Then, when came the time for transformation, when the woman's form made no longer a shield against a man's hand, he could slay or be slain to save Sweyn. He had struck his dear brother in dire extremity, but he could not, though reason urged, strike a woman.

For one mile, for two miles they ran: White Fell ever foremost, Christian ever at equal distance from her side, so near that, now and again, her out-flying furs touched him. She spoke no word; nor he. She never turned her head to look at him, nor swerved to evade him; but, with set face looking forward, sped straight on, over rough, over smooth, aware of his nearness by the regular beat of his feet, and the sound of his breath behind.

In a while she quickened her pace. From the first, Christian had judged of her speed as admirable, yet with exulting security in his own excelling and enduring whatever her efforts. But, when the pace increased, he found himself put to the test as never had he been before in any race. Her feet, indeed, flew faster than his; it was only by his length of stride that he kept his place at her side. But his heart was high and resolute, and he did not fear failure yet.

So the desperate race flew on. Their feet struck up the powdery snow, their breath smoked into the sharp clear air, and they were gone before the air was cleared of snow and vapour. Now and then Christian glanced up to judge, by the rising of the stars, of the coming of midnight. So long—so long!

White Fell held on without slack. She, it was evident, with confidence in her speed proving matchless, as resolute to outrun her pursuer as he to endure till midnight and fulfil his purpose. And Christian held on, still self-assured. He could not fail; he would not fail. To avenge Rol and Trella was motive enough for him to do what man could do; but for Sweyn more. She had kissed Sweyn, but he should not die too: with Sweyn to save he could not fail.

Never before was such a race as this; no, not when in old Greece man and maid raced together with two fates at stake; for the hard running was sustained unabated, while star after star rose and went wheeling up towards midnight, for one hour, for two hours.

Then Christian saw and heard what shot him through with fear. Where a fringe of trees hung round a slope he saw something dark moving, and heard a yelp, followed by a full horrid cry, and the dark spread out upon the snow, a pack of wolves in pursuit.

Of the beasts alone he had little cause for fear; at the pace he held he could distance them, four-footed though they were. But of White Fell's wiles he had infinite apprehension, for how might she not avail herself of the savage jaws of these wolves, akin as they were to half her nature. She vouchsafed to them nor look nor sign; but Christian, on an impulse to assure himself that she should not escape him, caught and held the back-flung edge of her furs, running still.

She turned like a flash with a beastly snarl, teeth and eyes gleaming again. Her axe shone, on the upstroke, on the downstroke, as she hacked at his hand. She had lopped it off at the wrist, but that he parried with the bear-spear. Even then, she shore through the shaft and shattered the bones of the hand at the same blow, so that he loosed perforce.

Then again they raced on as before, Christian not losing a pace, though his left hand swung useless, bleeding and broken.

The snarl, indubitable, though modified from a woman's organs, the vicious fury revealed in teeth and eyes, the sharp arrogant pain of her maiming blow, caught away Christian's heed of the beasts behind, by striking into him close vivid realisation of the infinitely greater danger that ran before him in that deadly Thing.

When he bethought him to look behind, lo! the pack had but reached their tracks, and instantly slunk aside, cowed; the yell of pursuit changing to yelps and whines. So abhorrent was that fell creature to beast as to man.

She had drawn her furs more closely to her, disposing them so that, instead of flying loose to her heels, no drapery hung lower than her knees, and this without a check to her wonderful speed, nor embarrassment by the cumbering of the folds. She held her head as before; her lips were firmly set, only the tense nostrils gave her breath; not a sign of distress witnessed to the long sustaining of that terrible speed.

But on Christian by now the strain was telling palpably. His head weighed heavy, and his breath came labouring in great sobs; the bear spear would have been a burden now. His heart was beating like a hammer, but such a dulness oppressed his brain, that it was only by degrees he could realise his helpless state; wounded and weaponless, chasing that terrible Thing, that was a fierce, desperate, axe-armed woman, except she should assume the beast with fangs yet more formidable.

And still the far slow stars went lingering nearly an hour from midnight.

So far was his brain astray that an impression took him that she was fleeing from the midnight stars, whose gain was by such slow degrees that a time equalling days and days had gone in the race round the northern circle of the world, and days and days as long might last before the end—except she slackened, or except he failed.

But he would not fail yet.

How long had he been praying so? He had started with a self-confidence and reliance that had felt no need for that aid; and now it seemed the only means by which to restrain his heart from swelling beyond the compass of his body, by which to cherish his brain from dwindling and shrivelling quite away. Some sharp-toothed creature kept tearing and dragging on his maimed left hand; he never could see it, he could not shake it off; but he prayed it off at times.

The clear stars before him took to shuddering, and he knew why: they shuddered at sight of what was behind him. He had never divined before that strange things hid themselves from men under pretence of being snow-clad mounds or swaying trees; but now they came slipping out from their harmless covers to follow him, and mock at his impotence to make a kindred Thing resolve to truer form. He knew the air behind him was thronged; he heard the hum of innumerable murmurings together; but his eyes could never catch them, they were too swift and nimble. Yet he knew they were there, because, on a backward glance, he saw the snow mounds surge as they grovelled flatlings out of sight; he saw the trees reel as they screwed themselves rigid past recognition among the boughs.

And after such glance the stars for awhile returned to steadfastness, and an infinite stretch of silence froze upon the chill grey world, only deranged by the swift even beat of the flying feet, and his own—slower from the longer stride, and the sound of his breath. And for some clear moments he knew that his only concern was, to sustain his speed regardless of pain and distress, to deny with every nerve he had her power to outstrip him or to widen the space between them, till the stars crept up to midnight. Then out again would come that crowd invisible, humming and hustling behind, dense and dark enough, he knew, to blot out the stars at his back, yet ever skipping and jerking from his sight.

A hideous check came to the race. White Fell swirled about and leapt to the right, and Christian, unprepared for so prompt a lurch, found close at his feet a deep pit yawning, and his own impetus past control. But he snatched at her as he bore past, clasping her right arm with his one whole hand, and the two swung together upon the brink.

And her straining away in self preservation was vigorous enough to counter-balance his headlong impulse, and brought them reeling together to safety.

Then, before he was verily sure that they were not to perish so, crashing down, he saw her gnashing in wild pale fury as she wrenched to be free; and since her right hand was in his grasp, used her axe left-handed, striking back at him.

The blow was effectual enough even so; his right arm dropped powerless, gashed, and with the lesser bone broken, that jarred with horrid pain when he let it swing as he leaped out again, and ran to recover the few feet she had gained from his pause at the shock.

The near escape and this new quick pain made again every faculty alive and intense. He knew that what he followed was most surely Death animate: wounded and helpless, he was utterly at her mercy if so she should realise and take action. Hopeless to avenge, hopeless to save, his very despair for Sweyn swept him on to follow, and follow, and precede the kiss-doomed to death. Could he yet fail to hunt that Thing past midnight, out of the womanly form alluring and treacherous, into lasting restraint of the bestial, which was the last shred of hope left from the confident purpose of the outset?

"Sweyn, Sweyn, O Sweyn!" He thought he was praying, though his heart wrung out nothing but this: "Sweyn, Sweyn, O Sweyn!"

The last hour from midnight had lost half its quarters, and the stars went lifting up the great minutes; and again his greatening heart, and his shrinking brain, and the sickening agony that swung at either side, conspired to appal the will that had only seeming empire over his feet.

Now White Fell's body was so closely enveloped that not a lap nor an edge flew free. She stretched forward strangely aslant, leaning from the upright poise of a runner. She cleared the ground at times by long bounds, gaining an increase of speed that Christian agonised to equal.

Because the stars pointed that the end was nearing, the black brood came behind again, and followed, noising. Ah! if they could but be kept quiet and still, nor slip their usual harmless masks to encourage with their interest the last speed of their most deadly congener. What shape had they? Should he ever know? If it were not that he was bound to compel the fell Thing that ran before him into her truer form, he might face about and follow them. No—no—not so; if he might do anything but what he did—race, race, and racing bear this agony, he would just stand still and die, to be quit of the pain of breathing.

He grew bewildered, uncertain of his own identity, doubting of his own true form. He could not be really a man, no more than that running Thing was really a woman; his real form was only hidden under embodiment of a man, but what it was he did not know. And Sweyn's real form he did not know. Sweyn lay fallen at his feet, where he had struck him down—his own brother—he: he stumbled over him, and had to overleap him and race harder because she who had kissed Sweyn leapt so fast. "Sweyn, Sweyn, O Sweyn!"

Why did the stars stop to shudder? Midnight else had surely come!

The leaning, leaping Thing looked back at him with a wild, fierce look, and laughed in savage scorn and triumph. He saw in a flash why, for within a time measurable by seconds she would have escaped him utterly. As the land lay, a slope of ice sunk on the one hand; on the other hand a steep rose, shouldering forwards; between the two was space for a foot to be planted, but none for a body to stand; yet a juniper bough, thrusting out, gave a handhold secure enough for one with a resolute grasp to swing past the perilous place, and pass on safe.

Though the first seconds of the last moment were going, she dared to flash back a wicked look, and laugh at the pursuer who was impotent to grasp.

The crisis struck convulsive life into his last supreme effort; his will surged up indomitable, his speed proved matchless yet. He leapt with a rush, passed her before her laugh had time to go out, and turned short, barring the way, and braced to withstand her.

She came hurling desperate, with a feint to the right hand, and then launched herself upon him with a spring like a wild beast when it leaps to kill. And he, with one strong arm and a hand that could not hold, with one strong hand and an arm that could not guide and sustain, he caught and held her even so. And they fell together. And because he felt his whole arm slipping, and his whole hand loosing, to slack the dreadful agony of the wrenched bone above, he caught and held with his teeth the tunic at her knee, as she struggled up and wrung off his hands to overleap him victorious.

Like lightning she snatched her axe, and struck him on the neck, deep—once, twice—his life-blood gushed out, staining her feet.

The stars touched midnight.

The death scream he heard was not his, for his set teeth had hardly yet relaxed when it rang out; and the dreadful cry began with a woman's shriek, and changed and ended as the yell of a beast. And before the final blank overtook his dying eyes, he saw that She gave place to It; he saw more, that Life gave place to Death—causelessly, incomprehensibly.

For he did not presume that no holy water could be more holy, more potent to destroy an evil thing than the life-blood of a pure heart poured out for another in free willing devotion.

His own true hidden reality that he had desired to know grew palpable, recognisable. It seemed to him just this: a great glad abounding hope that he had saved his brother; too expansive to be contained by the limited form of a sole man, it yearned for a new embodiment infinite as the stars.

What did it matter to that true reality that the man's brain shrank, shrank, till it was nothing; that the man's body could not retain the huge pain of his heart, and heaved it out through the red exit riven at the neck; that the black noise came again hurtling from behind, reinforced by that dissolved shape, and blotted out for ever the man's sight, hearing, sense.

* * * * *

In the early grey of day Sweyn chanced upon the footprints of a man—of a runner, as he saw by the shifted snow; and the direction they had taken aroused curiosity, since a little farther their line must be crossed by the edge of a sheer height. He turned to trace them. And so doing, the length of the stride struck his attention—a stride long as his own if he ran. He knew he was following Christian.

In his anger he had hardened himself to be indifferent to the night-long absence of his brother; but now, seeing where the footsteps went, he was seized with compunction and dread. He had failed to give thought and care to his poor frantic twin, who might—was it possible?—have rushed to a frantic death.

His heart stood still when he came to the place where the leap had been taken. A piled edge of snow had fallen too, and nothing but snow lay below when he peered. Along the upper edge he ran for a furlong, till he came to a dip where he could slip and climb down, and then back again on the lower level to the pile of fallen snow. There he saw that the vigorous running had started afresh.

He stood pondering; vexed that any man should have taken that leap where he had not ventured to follow; vexed that he had been beguiled to such painful emotions; guessing vainly at Christian's object in this mad freak. He began sauntering along, half unconsciously following his brother's track; and so in a while he came to the place where the footprints were doubled.

Small prints were these others, small as a woman's, though the pace from one to another was longer than that which the skirts of women allow.

Did not White Fell tread so?

A dreadful guess appalled him, so dreadful that he recoiled from belief. Yet his face grew ashy white, and he gasped to fetch back motion to his checked heart. Unbelievable? Closer attention showed how the smaller footfall had altered for greater speed, striking into the snow with a deeper onset and a lighter pressure on the heels. Unbelievable? Could any woman but White Fell run so? Could any man but Christian run so? The guess became a certainty. He was following where alone in the dark night White Fell had fled from Christian pursuing.

Such villainy set heart and brain on fire with rage and indignation: such villainy in his own brother, till lately love-worthy, praiseworthy, though a fool for meekness. He would kill Christian; had he lives many as the footprints he had trodden, vengeance should demand them all. In a tempest of murderous hate he followed on in haste, for the track was plain enough, starting with such a burst of speed as could not be maintained, but brought him back soon to a plod for the spent, sobbing breath to be regulated. He cursed Christian aloud and called White Fell's name on high in a frenzied expense of passion. His grief itself was a rage, being such an intolerable anguish of pity and shame at the thought of his love, White Fell, who had parted from his kiss free and radiant, to be hounded straightway by his brother mad with jealousy, fleeing for more than life while her lover was housed at his ease. If he had but known, he raved, in impotent rebellion at the cruelty of events, if he had but known that his strength and love might have availed in her defence; now the only service to her that he could render was to kill Christian.

As a woman he knew she was matchless in speed, matchless in strength; but Christian was matchless in speed among men, nor easily to be matched in strength. Brave and swift and strong though she were, what chance had she against a man of his strength and inches, frantic, too, and intent on horrid revenge against his brother, his successful rival?

Mile after mile he followed with a bursting heart; more piteous, more tragic, seemed the case at this evidence of White Fell's splendid supremacy, holding her own so long against Christian's famous speed. So long, so long that his love and admiration grew more and more boundless, and his grief and indignation therewith also. Whenever the track lay clear he ran, with such reckless prodigality of strength, that it soon was spent, and he dragged on heavily, till, sometimes on the ice of a mere, sometimes on a wind-swept place, all signs were lost; but, so undeviating had been their line that a course straight on, and then short questing to either hand, recovered them again.

Hour after hour had gone by through more than half that winter day, before ever he came to the place where the trampled snow showed that a scurry of feet had come—and gone! Wolves' feet—and gone most amazingly! Only a little beyond he came to the lopped point of Christian's bear-spear; farther on he would see where the remnant of the useless shaft had been dropped. The snow here was dashed with blood, and the footsteps of the two had fallen closer together. Some hoarse sound of exultation came from him that might have been a laugh had breath sufficed. "O White Fell, my poor, brave love! Well struck!" he groaned, torn by his pity and great admiration, as he guessed surely how she had turned and dealt a blow.

The sight of the blood inflamed him as it might a beast that ravens. He grew mad with a desire to have Christian by the throat once again, not to loose this time till he had crushed out his life, or beat out his life, or stabbed out his life; or all these, and torn him piecemeal likewise: and ah! then, not till then, bleed his heart with weeping, like a child, like a girl, over the piteous fate of his poor lost love.

On—on—on—through the aching time, toiling and straining in the track of those two superb runners, aware of the marvel of their endurance, but unaware of the marvel of their speed, that, in the three hours before midnight had overpassed all that vast distance that he could only traverse from twilight to twilight. For clear daylight was passing when he came to the edge of an old marl-pit, and saw how the two who had gone before had stamped and trampled together in desperate peril on the verge. And here fresh blood stains spoke to him of a valiant defence against his infamous brother; and he followed where the blood had dripped till the cold had staunched its flow, taking a savage gratification from this evidence that Christian had been gashed deeply, maddening afresh with desire to do likewise more excellently, and so slake his murderous hate. And he began to know that through all his despair he had entertained a germ of hope, that grew apace, rained upon by his brother's blood.

He strove on as best he might, wrung now by an access of hope, now of despair, in agony to reach the end, however terrible, sick with the aching of the toiled miles that deferred it.

And the light went lingering out of the sky, giving place to uncertain stars.

He came to the finish.

Two bodies lay in a narrow place. Christian's was one, but the other beyond not White Fell's.

There where the footsteps ended lay a great white wolf.

At the sight Sweyn's strength was blasted; body and soul he was struck down grovelling.

The stars had grown sure and intense before he stirred from where he had dropped prone. Very feebly he crawled to his dead brother, and laid his hands upon him, and crouched so, afraid to look or stir farther.

Cold, stiff, hours dead. Yet the dead body was his only shelter and stay in that most dreadful hour. His soul, stripped bare of all sceptic comfort, cowered, shivering, naked, abject; and the living clung to the dead out of piteous need for grace from the soul that had passed away.

He rose to his knees, lifting the body. Christian had fallen face forward in the snow, with his arms flung up and wide, and so had the frost made him rigid: strange, ghastly, unyielding to Sweyn's lifting, so that he laid him down again and crouched above, with his arms fast round him, and a low heart-wrung groan.

When at last he found force to raise his brother's body and gather it in his arms, tight clasped to his breast, he tried to face the Thing that lay beyond. The sight set his limbs in a palsy with horror and dread. His senses had failed and fainted in utter cowardice, but for the strength that came from holding dead Christian in his arms, enabling him to compel his eyes to endure the sight, and take into the brain the complete aspect of the Thing. No wound, only blood stains on the feet. The great grim jaws had a savage grin, though dead-stiff. And his kiss: he could bear it no longer, and turned away, nor ever looked again.

And the dead man in his arms, knowing the full horror, had followed and faced it for his sake; had suffered agony and death for his sake; in the neck was the deep death gash, one arm and both hands were dark with frozen blood, for his sake! Dead he knew him, as in life he had not known him, to give the right meed of love and worship. Because the outward man lacked perfection and strength equal to his, he had taken the love and worship of that great pure heart as his due; he, so unworthy in the inner reality, so mean, so despicable, callous, and contemptuous towards the brother who had laid down his life to save him. He longed for utter annihilation, that so he might lose the agony of knowing himself so unworthy such perfect love. The frozen calm of death on the face appalled him. He dared not touch it with lips that had cursed so lately, with lips fouled by kiss of the horror that had been death.

He struggled to his feet, still clasping Christian. The dead man stood upright within his arm, frozen rigid. The eyes were not quite closed; the head had stiffened, bowed slightly to one side; the arms stayed straight and wide.

It was the figure of one crucified, the blood-stained hands also conforming.

So living and dead went back along the track that one had passed in the deepest passion of love, and one in the deepest passion of hate. All that night Sweyn toiled through the snow, bearing the weight of dead Christian, treading back along the steps he before had trodden, when he was wronging with vilest thoughts, and cursing with murderous hatred, the brother who all the while lay dead for his sake.

Cold, silence, darkness encompassed the strong man bowed with the dolorous burden; and yet he knew surely that that night he entered hell, and trod hell-fire along the homeward road, and endured through it only because Christian was with him. And he knew surely that to him Christian had been as Christ, and had suffered and died to save him from his sins.

DRACULA

By Bram Stoker

First Published in 1897

BRAM STOKER

Abraham 'Bram' Stoker was born in Dublin, Ireland in 1847. Stoker was a semi-invalid as a child, and was bedridden until he started school at the age of seven. However, he made a full recovery and went on to excel as an athlete at Trinity College, which he enrolled at in 1864. Stoker graduated with honours in mathematics in 1870, and was also president of the university's philosophical society.

Stoker developed an interest in theatre, and became theatre critic for the *Dublin Evening Mail* in his early twenties. It was following a favourable review he gave of an 1876 Henry Irving production of *Hamlet* that Stoker and Irving struck up a friendship. Three years later, in the same year that Stoker married Florence Balcombe (whose former suitor was Oscar Wilde), he became acting-manager and then business manager of Irving's Lyceum Theatre – a post he went on to hold for 27 years. As a result of his close friendship with Irving (the most famous actor of his day), Stoker became something of a socialite. He mingled with London's high society, meeting writers such as Sir Arthur Conan Doyle, and travelled extensively in the United States, where he spent time with both Theodore Roosevelt and Walt Whitman.

While working for Irving, Stoker began to write novels, eventually producing a total of fifteen works of fiction. Although most met with at least mild success, Stoker is best known for his 1897 publication, *Dracula*. This work – an epistolary novel weaving hypnotism, magic, the supernatural, and other elements of Gothic fiction – went on to sell over one million copies, and has never been out of print. Today, the novel and its eponymous protagonist remain so well-known that one can actually visit the castle of Count Dracula in the Transylvanian region of Romania – despite the fact that Stoker never even went there himself.

After a series of strokes, Stoker died in London in 1912, aged 64.

CHAPTER I

JONATHAN HARKER'S JOURNAL

(Kept in shorthand.)

3 May. Bistritz.—Left Munich at 8:35 P. M., on 1st May, arriving at Vienna early next morning; should have arrived at 6:46, but train was an hour late. Buda-Pesth seems a wonderful place, from the glimpse which I got of it from the train and the little I could walk through the streets. I feared to go very far from the station, as we had arrived late and would start as near the correct time as possible. The impression I had was that we were leaving the West and entering the East; the most western of splendid bridges over the Danube, which is here of noble width and depth, took us among the traditions of Turkish rule.

We left in pretty good time, and came after nightfall to Klausenburgh. Here I stopped for the night at the Hotel Royale. I had for dinner, or rather supper, a chicken done up some way with red pepper, which was very good but thirsty. (*Mem.*, get recipe for Mina.) I asked the waiter, and he said it was called "paprika hendl," and that, as it was a national dish, I should be able to get it anywhere along the Carpathians. I found my smattering of German very useful here; indeed, I don't know how I should be able to get on without it.

Having had some time at my disposal when in London, I had visited the British Museum, and made search among the books and maps in the library regarding Transylvania; it had struck me that some foreknowledge of the country could hardly fail to have some importance in dealing with a nobleman of that country. I find that the district he named is in the extreme east of the country, just on the borders of three states, Transylvania, Moldavia and Bukovina, in the midst of the Carpathian mountains; one of the wildest and least known portions of Europe. I was not able to light on any map or work giving the exact locality of the Castle Dracula, as there are no maps of this country as yet to compare with our own Ordnance Survey maps; but I found that Bistritz, the post town named by Count Dracula, is a fairly well-known place. I shall enter here some of my notes, as they may refresh my memory when I talk over my travels with Mina.

In the population of Transylvania there are four distinct nationalities: Saxons in the South, and mixed with them the Wallachs, who are the descendants of the Dacians; Magyars in the West, and Szekelys in the East and North. I am going among the latter, who claim to be descended from Attila and the Huns. This may be so, for when the Magyars conquered the country in the eleventh century they found the Huns settled in it. I read that every known superstition in the world is gathered into the horseshoe of the Carpathians, as if it were the centre of some sort of imaginative whirlpool; if so my stay may be very interesting. (*Mem.*, I must ask the Count all about them.)

I did not sleep well, though my bed was comfortable enough, for I had all sorts of queer dreams. There was a dog howling all night under my window, which may have had something to do with it; or it may have been the paprika, for I had to drink up all the water in my carafe, and was still thirsty. Towards morning I slept and was wakened by the continuous knocking at my door, so I guess I must have been sleeping soundly then. I had for breakfast more paprika, and a sort of porridge of maize flour which they said was "mamaliga," and egg-plant stuffed with forcemeat, a very excellent dish, which they call "impletata." (*Mem.*, get recipe for this also.) I had to hurry breakfast, for the train started a little before eight, or rather it ought to have done so, for after rushing to the station at 7:30 I had to sit in the carriage for more than an hour before we began to move. It seems to me that the further east you go the more unpunctual are the trains. What ought they to be in China?

All day long we seemed to dawdle through a country which was full of beauty of every kind. Sometimes we saw little towns or castles on the top of steep hills such as we see in old missals; sometimes we ran by rivers and streams which seemed from the wide stony margin on each side of them to be subject to great floods. It takes a lot of water, and running strong, to sweep the outside edge of a river clear. At every station there were groups of people, sometimes crowds, and in all sorts of attire. Some of them were just like the peasants at home or those I saw coming through France and Germany, with short jackets and round hats and home-made trousers; but others were very picturesque. The women looked pretty, except when you got near them, but they were very clumsy about the waist. They had all full white sleeves of some kind or other, and most of them had big belts with a lot of strips of something fluttering from them like the dresses in a ballet, but of course there were petticoats under them. The strangest figures we saw were the Slovaks, who were more barbarian than the rest, with their big cow-boy hats, great baggy dirty-white trousers, white linen shirts, and enormous heavy leather belts, nearly a foot wide, all studded over with brass nails. They wore high boots, with their trousers tucked into them, and had long black hair and heavy black moustaches. They are very picturesque, but do not look prepossessing. On the stage they would be set down at once as some old Oriental band of brigands. They are, however, I am told, very harmless and rather wanting in natural self-assertion.

It was on the dark side of twilight when we got to Bistritz, which is a very interesting old place. Being practically on the frontier—for the Borgo Pass leads from it into Bukovina—it has had a very stormy existence, and it certainly shows marks of it. Fifty years ago a series of great fires took place, which made terrible havoc on five separate occasions. At the very beginning of the seventeenth century it underwent a siege of three weeks and lost 13,000 people, the casualties of war proper being assisted by famine and disease.

Count Dracula had directed me to go to the Golden Krone Hotel, which I found, to my great delight, to be thoroughly old-fashioned, for of course I wanted to see all I could of the ways of the country. I was evidently expected, for when I got near the door I faced a cheery-looking elderly woman in the usual peasant dress—white undergarment with long double apron, front, and back, of coloured stuff fitting almost too tight for modesty. When I came close she bowed and said, "The Herr Englishman?" "Yes," I said, "Jonathan Harker." She smiled, and gave some message to an elderly man in white shirt-sleeves, who had followed her to the door. He went, but immediately returned with a letter:—

"My Friend.—Welcome to the Carpathians. I am anxiously expecting you. Sleep well to-night. At three to-morrow the diligence will start for Bukovina; a place on it is kept for you. At the Borgo Pass my carriage will await you and will bring you to me. I trust that your journey from London has been a happy one, and that you will enjoy your stay in my beautiful land.

"Your friend,
"Dracula."

4 May.—I found that my landlord had got a letter from the Count, directing him to secure the best place on the coach for me; but on making

inquiries as to details he seemed somewhat reticent, and pretended that he could not understand my German. This could not be true, because up to then he had understood it perfectly; at least, he answered my questions exactly as if he did. He and his wife, the old lady who had received me, looked at each other in a frightened sort of way. He mumbled out that the money had been sent in a letter, and that was all he knew. When I asked him if he knew Count Dracula, and could tell me anything of his castle, both he and his wife crossed themselves, and, saying that they knew nothing at all, simply refused to speak further. It was so near the time of starting that I had no time to ask any one else, for it was all very mysterious and not by any means comforting.

Just before I was leaving, the old lady came up to my room and said in a very hysterical way:

"Must you go? Oh! young Herr, must you go?" She was in such an excited state that she seemed to have lost her grip of what German she knew, and mixed it all up with some other language which I did not know at all. I was just able to follow her by asking many questions. When I told her that I must go at once, and that I was engaged on important business, she asked again:

"Do you know what day it is?" I answered that it was the fourth of May. She shook her head as she said again:

"Oh, yes! I know that! I know that, but do you know what day it is?" On my saying that I did not understand, she went on:

"It is the eve of St. George's Day. Do you not know that to-night, when the clock strikes midnight, all the evil things in the world will have full sway? Do you know where you are going, and what you are going to?" She was in such evident distress that I tried to comfort her, but without effect. Finally she went down on her knees and implored me not to go; at least to wait a day or two before starting. It was all very ridiculous but I did not feel comfortable. However, there was business to be done, and I could allow nothing to interfere with it. I therefore tried to raise her up, and said, as gravely as I could, that I thanked her, but my duty was imperative, and that I must go. She then rose and dried her eyes, and taking a crucifix from her neck offered it to me. I did not know what to do, for, as an English Churchman, I have been taught to regard such things as in some measure idolatrous, and yet it seemed so ungracious to refuse an old lady meaning so well and in such a state of mind. She saw, I suppose, the doubt in my face, for she put the rosary round my neck, and said, "For your mother's sake," and went out of the room. I am writing up this part of the diary whilst I am waiting for the coach, which is, of course, late; and the crucifix is still round my neck. Whether it is the old lady's fear, or the many ghostly traditions of this place, or the crucifix itself, I do not know, but I am not feeling nearly as easy in my mind as usual. If this book should ever reach Mina before I do, let it bring my good-bye. Here comes the coach!

5 May. The Castle.—The grey of the morning has passed, and the sun is high over the distant horizon, which seems jagged, whether with trees or hills I know not, for it is so far off that big things and little are mixed. I am not sleepy, and, as I am not to be called till I awake, naturally I write till sleep comes. There are many odd things to put down, and, lest who reads them may fancy that I dined too well before I left Bistritz, let me put down my dinner exactly. I dined on what they called "robber steak"—bits of bacon, onion, and beef, seasoned with red pepper, and strung on sticks and roasted over the fire, in the simple style of the London cat's meat! The wine was Golden Mediasch, which produces a queer sting on the tongue, which is, however, not disagreeable. I had only a couple of glasses of this, and nothing else.

When I got on the coach the driver had not taken his seat, and I saw him talking with the landlady. They were evidently talking of me, for every now and then they looked at me, and some of the people who were sitting on the bench outside the door—which they call by a name meaning "word-bearer"—came and listened, and then looked at me, most of them pityingly. I could hear a lot of words often repeated, queer words, for there were many nationalities in the crowd; so I quietly got my polyglot dictionary from my bag and looked them out. I must say they were not cheering to me, for amongst them were "Ordog"—Satan, "pokol"—hell, "stregoica"—witch, "vrolok" and "vlkoslak"—both of which mean the same thing, one being Slovak and the other Servian for something that is either were-wolf or vampire. (*Mem.,* I must ask the Count about these superstitions)

When we started, the crowd round the inn door, which had by this time swelled to a considerable size, all made the sign of the cross and pointed two fingers towards me. With some difficulty I got a fellow-passenger to tell me what they meant; he would not answer at first, but on learning that I was English, he explained that it was a charm or guard against the evil eye. This was not very pleasant for me, just starting for an unknown place to meet an unknown man; but every one seemed so kind-hearted, and so sorrowful, and so sympathetic that I could not but be touched. I shall never forget the last glimpse which I had of the inn-yard and its crowd of picturesque figures, all crossing themselves, as they stood round the wide archway, with its background of rich foliage of oleander and orange trees in green tubs clustered in the centre of the yard. Then our driver, whose wide linen drawers covered the whole front of the box-seat—"gotza" they call them—

cracked his big whip over his four small horses, which ran abreast, and we set off on our journey.

I soon lost sight and recollection of ghostly fears in the beauty of the scene as we drove along, although had I known the language, or rather languages, which my fellow-passengers were speaking, I might not have been able to throw them off so easily. Before us lay a green sloping land full of forests and woods, with here and there steep hills, crowned with clumps of trees or with farmhouses, the blank gable end to the road. There was everywhere a bewildering mass of fruit blossom—apple, plum, pear, cherry; and as we drove by I could see the green grass under the trees spangled with the fallen petals. In and out amongst these green hills of what they call here the "Mittel Land" ran the road, losing itself as it swept round the grassy curve, or was shut out by the straggling ends of pine woods, which here and there ran down the hillsides like tongues of flame. The road was rugged, but still we seemed to fly over it with a feverish haste. I could not understand then what the haste meant, but the driver was evidently bent on losing no time in reaching Borgo Prund. I was told that this road is in summertime excellent, but that it had not yet been put in order after the winter snows. In this respect it is different from the general run of roads in the Carpathians, for it is an old tradition that they are not to be kept in too good order. Of old the Hospadars would not repair them, lest the Turk should think that they were preparing to bring in foreign troops, and so hasten the war which was always really at loading point.

Beyond the green swelling hills of the Mittel Land rose mighty slopes of forest up to the lofty steeps of the Carpathians themselves. Right and left of us they towered, with the afternoon sun falling full upon them and bringing out all the glorious colours of this beautiful range, deep blue and purple in the shadows of the peaks, green and brown where grass and rock mingled, and an endless perspective of jagged rock and pointed crags, till these were themselves lost in the distance, where the snowy peaks rose grandly. Here and there seemed mighty rifts in the mountains, through which, as the sun began to sink, we saw now and again the white gleam of falling water. One of my companions touched my arm as we swept round the base of a hill and opened up the lofty, snow-covered peak of a mountain, which seemed, as we wound on our serpentine way, to be right before us:—

"Look! Isten szek!"—"God's seat!"—and he crossed himself reverently.

As we wound on our endless way, and the sun sank lower and lower behind us, the shadows of the evening began to creep round us. This was emphasised by the fact that the snowy mountain-top still held the sunset, and seemed to glow out with a delicate cool pink. Here and there we passed

Cszeks and Slovaks, all in picturesque attire, but I noticed that goitre was painfully prevalent. By the roadside were many crosses, and as we swept by, my companions all crossed themselves. Here and there was a peasant man or woman kneeling before a shrine, who did not even turn round as we approached, but seemed in the self-surrender of devotion to have neither eyes nor ears for the outer world. There were many things new to me: for instance, hay-ricks in the trees, and here and there very beautiful masses of weeping birch, their white stems shining like silver through the delicate green of the leaves. Now and again we passed a leiter-wagon—the ordinary peasant's cart—with its long, snake-like vertebra, calculated to suit the inequalities of the road. On this were sure to be seated quite a group of home-coming peasants, the Cszeks with their white, and the Slovaks with their coloured, sheepskins, the latter carrying lance-fashion their long staves, with axe at end. As the evening fell it began to get very cold, and the growing twilight seemed to merge into one dark mistiness the gloom of the trees, oak, beech, and pine, though in the valleys which ran deep between the spurs of the hills, as we ascended through the Pass, the dark firs stood out here and there against the background of late-lying snow. Sometimes, as the road was cut through the pine woods that seemed in the darkness to be closing down upon us, great masses of greyness, which here and there bestrewed the trees, produced a peculiarly weird and solemn effect, which carried on the thoughts and grim fancies engendered earlier in the evening, when the falling sunset threw into strange relief the ghost-like clouds which amongst the Carpathians seem to wind ceaselessly through the valleys. Sometimes the hills were so steep that, despite our driver's haste, the horses could only go slowly. I wished to get down and walk up them, as we do at home, but the driver would not hear of it. "No, no," he said; "you must not walk here; the dogs are too fierce"; and then he added, with what he evidently meant for grim pleasantry—for he looked round to catch the approving smile of the rest—"and you may have enough of such matters before you go to sleep." The only stop he would make was a moment's pause to light his lamps.

When it grew dark there seemed to be some excitement amongst the passengers, and they kept speaking to him, one after the other, as though urging him to further speed. He lashed the horses unmercifully with his long whip, and with wild cries of encouragement urged them on to further exertions. Then through the darkness I could see a sort of patch of grey light ahead of us, as though there were a cleft in the hills. The excitement of the passengers grew greater; the crazy coach rocked on its great leather springs, and swayed like a boat tossed on a stormy sea. I had to hold on. The road grew more level, and we appeared to fly along. Then the mountains seemed to come nearer to us on each side and to frown down upon us; we were entering on the Borgo Pass. One by one several of the passengers offered me gifts, which they pressed upon me with an earnestness which would take no denial; these were certainly of an odd and varied kind, but each was given in simple good faith, with a kindly word, and a blessing, and that strange mixture of fear-meaning movements which I had seen outside the hotel at Bistritz—the sign of the cross and the guard against the evil eye. Then, as we flew along, the driver leaned forward, and on each side the passengers, craning over the edge of the coach, peered eagerly into the darkness. It was evident that something very exciting was either happening or expected, but though I asked each passenger, no one would give me the slightest explanation. This state of excitement kept on for some little time; and at last we saw before us the Pass opening out on the eastern side. There were dark, rolling clouds overhead, and in the air the heavy, oppressive sense of thunder. It seemed as though the mountain range had separated two atmospheres, and that now we had got into the thunderous one. I was now myself looking out for the conveyance which was to take me to the Count. Each moment I expected to see the glare of lamps through the blackness; but all was dark. The only light was the flickering rays of our own lamps, in which the steam from our hard-driven horses rose in a white cloud. We could see now the sandy road lying white before us, but there was on it no sign of a vehicle. The passengers drew back with a sigh of gladness, which seemed to mock my own disappointment. I was already thinking what I had best do, when the driver, looking at his watch, said to the others something which I could hardly hear, it was spoken so quietly and in so low a tone; I thought it was "An hour less than the time." Then turning to me, he said in German worse than my own:—

"There is no carriage here. The Herr is not expected after all. He will now come on to Bukovina, and return to-morrow or the next day; better the next day." Whilst he was speaking the horses began to neigh and snort and plunge wildly, so that the driver had to hold them up. Then, amongst a chorus of screams from the peasants and a universal crossing of themselves, a calèche, with four horses, drove up behind us, overtook us, and drew up beside the coach. I could see from the flash of our lamps, as the rays fell on them, that the horses were coal-black and splendid animals. They were driven by a tall man, with a long brown beard and a great black hat, which seemed to hide his face from us. I could only see the gleam of a pair of very bright eyes, which seemed red in the lamplight, as he turned to us. He said to the driver:—

"You are early to-night, my friend." The man stammered in reply:—
"The English Herr was in a hurry," to which the stranger replied:—
"That is why, I suppose, you wished him to go on to Bukovina. You cannot deceive me, my friend; I know too much, and my horses are swift." As he spoke he smiled, and the lamplight fell on a hard-looking mouth, with very red lips and sharp-looking teeth, as white as ivory. One of my companions whispered to another the line from Burger's "Lenore":—

"Denn die Todten reiten schnell"—
("*For the dead travel fast.*")

The strange driver evidently heard the words, for he looked up with a gleaming smile. The passenger turned his face away, at the same time putting out his two fingers and crossing himself. "Give me the Herr's luggage," said the driver; and with exceeding alacrity my bags were handed out and put in the calèche. Then I descended from the side of the coach, as the calèche was close alongside, the driver helping me with a hand which caught my arm in a grip of steel; his strength must have been prodigious. Without a word he shook his reins, the horses turned, and we swept into the darkness of the Pass. As I looked back I saw the steam from the horses of the coach by the light of the lamps, and projected against it the figures of my late companions crossing themselves. Then the driver cracked his whip and called to his horses, and off they swept on their way to Bukovina. As they sank into the darkness I felt a strange chill, and a lonely feeling came over me; but a cloak was thrown over my shoulders, and a rug across my knees, and the driver said in excellent German:—

"The night is chill, mein Herr, and my master the Count bade me take all care of you. There is a flask of slivovitz (the plum brandy of the country) underneath the seat, if you should require it." I did not take any, but it was a comfort to know it was there all the same. I felt a little strangely, and not a little frightened. I think had there been any alternative I should have taken it, instead of prosecuting that unknown night journey. The carriage went at a hard pace straight along, then we made a complete turn and went along another straight road. It seemed to me that we were simply going over and over the same ground again; and so I took note of some salient point, and found that this was so. I would have liked to have asked the driver what this all meant, but I really feared to do so, for I thought that, placed as I was, any protest would have had no effect in case there had been an intention to delay. By-and-by, however, as I was curious to know how time was passing, I struck a match, and by its flame looked at my watch; it was within a few minutes of midnight. This gave me a sort of shock, for I suppose the general superstition about midnight was increased by my recent experiences. I waited with a sick feeling of suspense.

Then a dog began to howl somewhere in a farmhouse far down the road—a long, agonised wailing, as if from fear. The sound was taken up by another dog, and then another and another, till, borne on the wind which now sighed softly through the Pass, a wild howling began, which seemed to come from all over the country, as far as the imagination could grasp it through the gloom of the night. At the first howl the horses began to strain and rear, but the driver spoke to them soothingly, and they quieted down, but shivered and sweated as though after a runaway from sudden fright. Then, far off in the distance, from the mountains on each side of us began a louder and a sharper howling—that of wolves—which affected both the horses and myself in the same way—for I was minded to jump from the calèche and run, whilst they reared again and plunged madly, so that the driver had to use all his great strength to keep them from bolting. In a few minutes, however, my own ears got accustomed to the sound, and the horses so far became quiet that the driver was able to descend and to stand before them. He petted and soothed them, and whispered something in their ears, as I have heard of horse-tamers doing, and with extraordinary effect, for under his caresses they became quite manageable again, though they still trembled. The driver again took his seat, and shaking his reins, started off at a great pace. This time, after going to the far side of the Pass, he suddenly turned down a narrow roadway which ran sharply to the right.

Soon we were hemmed in with trees, which in places arched right over the roadway till we passed as through a tunnel; and again great frowning rocks guarded us boldly on either side. Though we were in shelter, we could hear the rising wind, for it moaned and whistled through the rocks, and the branches of the trees crashed together as we swept along. It grew colder and colder still, and fine, powdery snow began to fall, so that soon we and all around us were covered with a white blanket. The keen wind still carried the howling of the dogs, though this grew fainter as we went on our way. The baying of the wolves sounded nearer and nearer, as though they were closing round on us from every side. I grew dreadfully afraid, and the horses shared my fear. The driver, however, was not in the least disturbed; he kept turning his head to left and right, but I could not see anything through the darkness.

Suddenly, away on our left, I saw a faint flickering blue flame. The driver saw it at the same moment; he at once checked the horses, and, jumping to the ground, disappeared into the darkness. I did not know what to do, the less as the howling of the wolves grew closer; but while I wondered the driver suddenly appeared again, and without a word took his seat, and we resumed our journey. I think I must have fallen asleep and kept dreaming of the incident, for it seemed to be repeated endlessly, and now looking back, it is like a sort of awful nightmare. Once the flame appeared so near the road, that even in the darkness around us I could watch the driver's motions. He went rapidly to where the blue flame arose—it must have been very faint, for it did not seem to illumine the place around it at all—and gathering a few stones, formed them into some device. Once there appeared a strange optical effect: when he stood between me and the flame he did not obstruct it, for I could see its ghostly flicker all the same. This startled me, but as the effect was only momentary, I took it that my eyes deceived me straining through the darkness. Then for a time there were no blue flames, and we sped onwards through the gloom, with the howling of the wolves around us, as though they were following in a moving circle.

At last there came a time when the driver went further afield than he had yet gone, and during his absence, the horses began to tremble worse than ever and to snort and scream with fright. I could not see any cause for it, for the howling of the wolves had ceased altogether; but just then the moon, sailing through the black clouds, appeared behind the jagged crest of a beetling, pine-clad rock, and by its light I saw around us a ring of wolves, with white teeth and lolling red tongues, with long, sinewy limbs and shaggy hair. They were a hundred times more terrible in the grim silence which held them than even when they howled. For myself, I felt a sort of paralysis of fear. It is only when a man feels himself face to face with such horrors that he can understand their true import.

All at once the wolves began to howl as though the moonlight had had some peculiar effect on them. The horses jumped about and reared, and looked helplessly round with eyes that rolled in a way painful to see; but the living ring of terror encompassed them on every side; and they had perforce to remain within it. I called to the coachman to come, for it seemed to me that our only chance was to try to break out through the ring and to aid his approach. I shouted and beat the side of the calèche, hoping by the noise to scare the wolves from that side, so as to give him a chance of reaching the trap. How he came there, I know not, but I heard his voice raised in a tone of imperious command, and looking towards the sound, saw him stand in the roadway. As he swept his long arms, as though brushing aside some impalpable obstacle, the wolves fell back and back further still. Just then a heavy cloud passed across the face of the moon, so that we were again in darkness.

When I could see again the driver was climbing into the calèche, and the wolves had disappeared. This was all so strange and uncanny that a dreadful fear came upon me, and I was afraid to speak or move. The time seemed interminable as we swept on our way, now in almost complete darkness, for the rolling clouds obscured the moon. We kept on ascending, with occasional periods of quick descent, but in the main always ascending. Suddenly, I became conscious of the fact that the driver was in the act of pulling up the horses in the courtyard of a vast ruined castle, from whose tall black windows came no ray of light, and whose broken battlements showed a jagged line against the moonlit sky.

CHAPTER II

JONATHAN HARKER'S JOURNAL—*continued*

5 May.—I must have been asleep, for certainly if I had been fully awake I must have noticed the approach of such a remarkable place. In the gloom the courtyard looked of considerable size, and as several dark ways led from it under great round arches, it perhaps seemed bigger than it really is. I have not yet been able to see it by daylight.

When the calèche stopped, the driver jumped down and held out his hand to assist me to alight. Again I could not but notice his prodigious strength. His hand actually seemed like a steel vice that could have crushed mine if he had chosen. Then he took out my traps, and placed them on the ground beside me as I stood close to a great door, old and studded with large iron nails, and set in a projecting doorway of massive stone. I could see even in the dim light that the stone was massively carved, but that the carving had been much worn by time and weather. As I stood, the driver jumped again into his seat and shook the reins; the horses started forward, and trap and all disappeared down one of the dark openings.

I stood in silence where I was, for I did not know what to do. Of bell or knocker there was no sign; through these frowning walls and dark window openings it was not likely that my voice could penetrate. The time I waited seemed endless, and I felt doubts and fears crowding upon me. What sort of place had I come to, and among what kind of people? What sort of grim adventure was it on which I had embarked? Was this a customary incident in the life of a solicitor's clerk sent out to explain the purchase of a London estate to a foreigner? Solicitor's clerk! Mina would not like that. Solicitor—for just before leaving London I got word that my examination was successful; and I am now a full-blown solicitor! I began to rub my eyes and pinch myself to see if I were awake. It all seemed like a horrible nightmare to me, and I expected that I should suddenly awake, and find myself at home, with the dawn struggling in through the windows, as I had now and again felt in the morning after a day of overwork. But my flesh answered the pinching test, and my eyes were not to be deceived.

I was indeed awake and among the Carpathians. All I could do now was to be patient, and to wait the coming of the morning.

Just as I had come to this conclusion I heard a heavy step approaching behind the great door, and saw through the chinks the gleam of a coming light. Then there was the sound of rattling chains and the clanking of massive bolts drawn back. A key was turned with the loud grating noise of long disuse, and the great door swung back.

Within, stood a tall old man, clean shaven save for a long white moustache, and clad in black from head to foot, without a single speck of colour about him anywhere. He held in his hand an antique silver lamp, in which the flame burned without chimney or globe of any kind, throwing long quivering shadows as it flickered in the draught of the open door. The old man motioned me in with his right hand with a courtly gesture, saying in excellent English, but with a strange intonation:—

"Welcome to my house! Enter freely and of your own will!" He made no motion of stepping to meet me, but stood like a statue, as though his gesture of welcome had fixed him into stone. The instant, however, that I had stepped over the threshold, he moved impulsively forward, and holding out his hand grasped mine with a strength which made me wince, an effect which was not lessened by the fact that it seemed as cold as ice—more like the hand of a dead than a living man. Again he said:—

"Welcome to my house. Come freely. Go safely; and leave something of the happiness you bring!" The strength of the handshake was so much akin to that which I had noticed in the driver, whose face I had not seen, that for a moment I doubted if it were not the same person to whom I was speaking; so to make sure, I said interrogatively:—

"Count Dracula?" He bowed in a courtly way as he replied:—

"I am Dracula; and I bid you welcome, Mr. Harker, to my house. Come in; the night air is chill, and you must need to eat and rest." As he was speaking, he put the lamp on a bracket on the wall, and stepping out, took my luggage; he had carried it in before I could forestall him. I protested but he insisted:—

"Nay, sir, you are my guest. It is late, and my people are not available. Let me see to your comfort myself." He insisted on carrying my traps along the passage, and then up a great winding stair, and along another great passage, on whose stone floor our steps rang heavily. At the end of this he threw open a heavy door, and I rejoiced to see within a well-lit room in which a table was spread for supper, and on whose mighty hearth a great fire of logs, freshly replenished, flamed and flared.

The Count halted, putting down my bags, closed the door, and crossing the room, opened another door, which led into a small octagonal room lit by a single lamp, and seemingly without a window of any sort. Passing through this, he opened another door, and motioned me to enter. It was a welcome sight; for here was a great bedroom well lighted and warmed with another log fire,—also added to but lately, for the top logs were fresh—which sent a hollow roar up the wide chimney. The Count himself left my luggage inside and withdrew, saying, before he closed the door:—

"You will need, after your journey, to refresh yourself by making your toilet. I trust you will find all you wish. When you are ready, come into the other room, where you will find your supper prepared."

The light and warmth and the Count's courteous welcome seemed to have dissipated all my doubts and fears. Having then reached my normal state, I discovered that I was half famished with hunger; so making a hasty toilet, I went into the other room.

I found supper already laid out. My host, who stood on one side of the great fireplace, leaning against the stonework, made a graceful wave of his hand to the table, and said:—

"I pray you, be seated and sup how you please. You will, I trust, excuse me that I do not join you; but I have dined already, and I do not sup."

I handed to him the sealed letter which Mr. Hawkins had entrusted to me. He opened it and read it gravely; then, with a charming smile, he handed it to me to read. One passage of it, at least, gave me a thrill of pleasure.

"I must regret that an attack of gout, from which malady I am a constant sufferer, forbids absolutely any travelling on my part for some time to come; but I am happy to say I can send a sufficient substitute, one in whom I have every possible confidence. He is a young man, full of energy and talent in his own way, and of a very faithful disposition. He is discreet and silent, and has grown into manhood in my service. He shall be ready to attend on you when you will during his stay, and shall take your instructions in all matters."

The Count himself came forward and took off the cover of a dish, and I fell to at once on an excellent roast chicken. This, with some cheese and a salad and a bottle of old Tokay, of which I had two glasses, was my supper. During the time I was eating it the Count asked me many questions as to my journey, and I told him by degrees all I had experienced.

By this time I had finished my supper, and by my host's desire had drawn up a chair by the fire and begun to smoke a cigar which he offered me, at the same time excusing himself that he did not smoke. I had now an opportunity of observing him, and found him of a very marked physiognomy.

His face was a strong—a very strong—aquiline, with high bridge of the thin nose and peculiarly arched nostrils; with lofty domed forehead, and hair growing scantily round the temples but profusely elsewhere. His eyebrows were very massive, almost meeting over the nose, and with bushy hair that seemed to curl in its own profusion. The mouth, so far as I could see it under the heavy moustache, was fixed and rather cruel-looking, with peculiarly sharp white teeth; these protruded over the lips, whose remarkable ruddiness showed astonishing vitality in a man of his years. For the rest, his ears were pale, and at the tops extremely pointed; the chin was broad and strong, and the cheeks firm though thin. The general effect was one of extraordinary pallor.

Hitherto I had noticed the backs of his hands as they lay on his knees in the firelight, and they had seemed rather white and fine; but seeing them now close to me, I could not but notice that they were rather coarse—broad, with squat fingers. Strange to say, there were hairs in the centre of the palm. The nails were long and fine, and cut to a sharp point. As the Count leaned over me and his hands touched me, I could not repress a shudder. It may have been that his breath was rank, but a horrible feeling of nausea came over me, which, do what I would, I could not conceal. The Count, evidently noticing it, drew back; and with a grim sort of smile, which showed more than he had yet done his protuberant teeth, sat himself down again on his own side of the fireplace. We were both silent for a while; and as I looked towards the window I saw the first dim streak of the coming dawn. There seemed a strange stillness over everything; but as I listened I heard as if from down below in the valley the howling of many wolves. The Count's eyes gleamed, and he said:—

"Listen to them—the children of the night. What music they make!" Seeing, I suppose, some expression in my face strange to him, he added:—

"Ah, sir, you dwellers in the city cannot enter into the feelings of the hunter." Then he rose and said:—

"But you must be tired. Your bedroom is all ready, and to-morrow you shall sleep as late as you will. I have to be away till the afternoon; so sleep well and dream well!" With a courteous bow, he opened for me himself the door to the octagonal room, and I entered my bedroom . . . .

I am all in a sea of wonders. I doubt; I fear; I think strange things, which I dare not confess to my own soul. God keep me, if only for the sake of those dear to me!

7 May.—It is again early morning, but I have rested and enjoyed the last twenty-four hours. I slept till late in the day, and awoke of my own accord. When I had dressed myself I went into the room where we had supped, and found a cold breakfast laid out, with coffee kept hot by the pot being placed on the hearth. There was a card on the table, on which was written:—

"I have to be absent for a while. Do not wait for me.—D." I set to and enjoyed a hearty meal. When I had done, I looked for a bell, so that I might

let the servants know I had finished; but I could not find one. There are
certainly odd deficiencies in the house, considering the extraordinary
evidences of wealth which are round me. The table service is of gold, and
so beautifully wrought that it must be of immense value. The curtains and
upholstery of the chairs and sofas and the hangings of my bed are of the
costliest and most beautiful fabrics, and must have been of fabulous value
when they were made, for they are centuries old, though in excellent order.
I saw something like them in Hampton Court, but there they were worn
and frayed and moth-eaten. But still in none of the rooms is there a mirror.
There is not even a toilet glass on my table, and I had to get the little shaving
glass from my bag before I could either shave or brush my hair. I have not
yet seen a servant anywhere, or heard a sound near the castle except the
howling of wolves. Some time after I had finished my meal—I do not know
whether to call it breakfast or dinner, for it was between five and six o'clock
when I had it—I looked about for something to read, for I did not like to
go about the castle until I had asked the Count's permission. There was
absolutely nothing in the room, book, newspaper, or even writing materials;
so I opened another door in the room and found a sort of library. The door
opposite mine I tried, but found it locked.

In the library I found, to my great delight, a vast number of English
books, whole shelves full of them, and bound volumes of magazines and
newspapers. A table in the centre was littered with English magazines and
newspapers, though none of them were of very recent date. The books were
of the most varied kind—history, geography, politics, political economy,
botany, geology, law—all relating to England and English life and customs
and manners. There were even such books of reference as the London
Directory, the "Red" and "Blue" books, Whitaker's Almanac, the Army and
Navy Lists, and—it somehow gladdened my heart to see it—the Law List.

Whilst I was looking at the books, the door opened, and the Count
entered. He saluted me in a hearty way, and hoped that I had had a good
night's rest. Then he went on:—

"I am glad you found your way in here, for I am sure there is much that
will interest you. These companions"—and he laid his hand on some of
the books—"have been good friends to me, and for some years past, ever
since I had the idea of going to London, have given me many, many hours
of pleasure. Through them I have come to know your great England; and
to know her is to love her. I long to go through the crowded streets of your
mighty London, to be in the midst of the whirl and rush of humanity, to
share its life, its change, its death, and all that makes it what it is. But alas! as
yet I only know your tongue through books. To you, my friend, I look that

I know it to speak."

"But, Count," I said, "you know and speak English thoroughly!" He bowed gravely.

"I thank you, my friend, for your all too-flattering estimate, but yet I fear that I am but a little way on the road I would travel. True, I know the grammar and the words, but yet I know not how to speak them."

"Indeed," I said, "you speak excellently."

"Not so," he answered. "Well, I know that, did I move and speak in your London, none there are who would not know me for a stranger. That is not enough for me. Here I am noble; I am *boyar*; the common people know me, and I am master. But a stranger in a strange land, he is no one; men know him not—and to know not is to care not for. I am content if I am like the rest, so that no man stops if he see me, or pause in his speaking if he hear my words, 'Ha, ha! a stranger!' I have been so long master that I would be master still—or at least that none other should be master of me. You come to me not alone as agent of my friend Peter Hawkins, of Exeter, to tell me all about my new estate in London. You shall, I trust, rest here with me awhile, so that by our talking I may learn the English intonation; and I would that you tell me when I make error, even of the smallest, in my speaking. I am sorry that I had to be away so long to-day; but you will, I know, forgive one who has so many important affairs in hand."

Of course I said all I could about being willing, and asked if I might come into that room when I chose. He answered: "Yes, certainly," and added:—

"You may go anywhere you wish in the castle, except where the doors are locked, where of course you will not wish to go. There is reason that all things are as they are, and did you see with my eyes and know with my knowledge, you would perhaps better understand." I said I was sure of this, and then he went on:—

"We are in Transylvania; and Transylvania is not England. Our ways are not your ways, and there shall be to you many strange things. Nay, from what you have told me of your experiences already, you know something of what strange things there may be."

This led to much conversation; and as it was evident that he wanted to talk, if only for talking's sake, I asked him many questions regarding things that had already happened to me or come within my notice. Sometimes he sheered off the subject, or turned the conversation by pretending not to understand; but generally he answered all I asked most frankly. Then as time went on, and I had got somewhat bolder, I asked him of some of the strange things of the preceding night, as, for instance, why the coachman went to the places where he had seen the blue flames. He then explained to me that it was commonly believed that on a certain night of the year—last night, in fact, when all evil spirits are supposed to have unchecked sway—a blue flame is seen over any place where treasure has been concealed. "That treasure has been hidden," he went on, "in the region through which you came last night, there can be but little doubt; for it was the ground fought over for centuries by the Wallachian, the Saxon, and the Turk. Why, there is hardly a foot of soil in all this region that has not been enriched by the blood of men, patriots or invaders. In old days there were stirring times, when the Austrian and the Hungarian came up in hordes, and the patriots went out to meet them—men and women, the aged and the children too—and waited their coming on the rocks above the passes, that they might sweep destruction on them with their artificial avalanches. When the invader was triumphant he found but little, for whatever there was had been sheltered in the friendly soil."

"But how," said I, "can it have remained so long undiscovered, when there is a sure index to it if men will but take the trouble to look?" The Count smiled, and as his lips ran back over his gums, the long, sharp, canine teeth showed out strangely; he answered:—

"Because your peasant is at heart a coward and a fool! Those flames only appear on one night; and on that night no man of this land will, if he can help it, stir without his doors. And, dear sir, even if he did he would not know what to do. Why, even the peasant that you tell me of who marked the place of the flame would not know where to look in daylight even for his own work. Even you would not, I dare be sworn, be able to find these places again?"

"There you are right," I said. "I know no more than the dead where even to look for them." Then we drifted into other matters.

"Come," he said at last, "tell me of London and of the house which you have procured for me." With an apology for my remissness, I went into my own room to get the papers from my bag. Whilst I was placing them in order I heard a rattling of china and silver in the next room, and as I passed through, noticed that the table had been cleared and the lamp lit, for it was by this time deep into the dark. The lamps were also lit in the study or library, and I found the Count lying on the sofa, reading, of all things in the world, an English Bradshaw's Guide. When I came in he cleared the books and papers from the table; and with him I went into plans and deeds and figures of all sorts. He was interested in everything, and asked me a myriad questions about the place and its surroundings. He clearly had studied beforehand all he could get on the subject of the neighbourhood, for he evidently at the end knew very much more than I did. When I remarked this, he answered:—

"Well, but, my friend, is it not needful that I should? When I go there I shall be all alone, and my friend Harker Jonathan—nay, pardon me, I fall into my country's habit of putting your patronymic first—my friend Jonathan Harker will not be by my side to correct and aid me. He will be in Exeter, miles away, probably working at papers of the law with my other friend, Peter Hawkins. So!"

We went thoroughly into the business of the purchase of the estate at Purfleet. When I had told him the facts and got his signature to the necessary papers, and had written a letter with them ready to post to Mr. Hawkins, he began to ask me how I had come across so suitable a place. I read to him the notes which I had made at the time, and which I inscribe here:—

"At Purfleet, on a by-road, I came across just such a place as seemed to be required, and where was displayed a dilapidated notice that the place was for sale. It is surrounded by a high wall, of ancient structure, built of heavy stones, and has not been repaired for a large number of years. The closed gates are of heavy old oak and iron, all eaten with rust.

"The estate is called Carfax, no doubt a corruption of the old *Quatre Face*, as the house is four-sided, agreeing with the cardinal points of the compass. It contains in all some twenty acres, quite surrounded by the solid stone wall above mentioned. There are many trees on it, which make it in places gloomy, and there is a deep, dark-looking pond or small lake, evidently fed by some springs, as the water is clear and flows away in a fair-sized stream. The house is very large and of all periods back, I should say, to mediæval times, for one part is of stone immensely thick, with only a few windows high up and heavily barred with iron. It looks like part of a keep, and is close to an old chapel or church. I could not enter it, as I had not the key of the door leading to it from the house, but I have taken with my kodak views of it from various points. The house has been added to, but in a very straggling way, and I can only guess at the amount of ground it covers, which must be very great. There are but few houses close at hand, one being a very large house only recently added to and formed into a private lunatic asylum. It is not, however, visible from the grounds."

When I had finished, he said:—

"I am glad that it is old and big. I myself am of an old family, and to live in a new house would kill me. A house cannot be made habitable in a day; and, after all, how few days go to make up a century. I rejoice also that there is a chapel of old times. We Transylvanian nobles love not to think that our bones may lie amongst the common dead. I seek not gaiety nor mirth, not the bright voluptuousness of much sunshine and sparkling waters which please the young and gay. I am no longer young; and my heart, through weary years of mourning over the dead, is not attuned to mirth. Moreover, the walls of my castle are broken; the shadows are many, and the wind breathes cold through the broken battlements and casements. I love the shade and the shadow, and would be alone with my thoughts when I may." Somehow his words and his look did not seem to accord, or else it was that his cast of face made his smile look malignant and saturnine.

Presently, with an excuse, he left me, asking me to put all my papers together. He was some little time away, and I began to look at some of the books around me. One was an atlas, which I found opened naturally at England, as if that map had been much used. On looking at it I found in certain places little rings marked, and on examining these I noticed that one was near London on the east side, manifestly where his new estate was situated; the other two were Exeter, and Whitby on the Yorkshire coast.

It was the better part of an hour when the Count returned. "Aha!" he said; "still at your books? Good! But you must not work always. Come; I am informed that your supper is ready." He took my arm, and we went into the next room, where I found an excellent supper ready on the table. The Count again excused himself, as he had dined out on his being away from home. But he sat as on the previous night, and chatted whilst I ate. After supper I smoked, as on the last evening, and the Count stayed with me, chatting and asking questions on every conceivable subject, hour after hour. I felt that it was getting very late indeed, but I did not say anything, for I felt under obligation to meet my host's wishes in every way. I was not sleepy, as the long sleep yesterday had fortified me; but I could not help experiencing that chill which comes over one at the coming of the dawn, which is like, in its way, the turn of the tide. They say that people who are near death die generally at the change to the dawn or at the turn of the tide; any one who has when tired, and tied as it were to his post, experienced this change in the atmosphere can well believe it. All at once we heard the crow of a cock coming up with preternatural shrillness through the clear morning air; Count Dracula, jumping to his feet, said:—

"Why, there is the morning again! How remiss I am to let you stay up so long. You must make your conversation regarding my dear new country of England less interesting, so that I may not forget how time flies by us," and, with a courtly bow, he quickly left me.

I went into my own room and drew the curtains, but there was little to notice; my window opened into the courtyard, all I could see was the warm grey of quickening sky. So I pulled the curtains again, and have written of this day.

8 May.—I began to fear as I wrote in this book that I was getting too diffuse; but now I am glad that I went into detail from the first, for there is something so strange about this place and all in it that I cannot but feel uneasy. I wish I were safe out of it, or that I had never come. It may be that this strange night-existence is telling on me; but would that that were all! If there were any one to talk to I could bear it, but there is no one. I have only the Count to speak with, and he!—I fear I am myself the only living soul within the place. Let me be prosaic so far as facts can be; it will help me to bear up, and imagination must not run riot with me. If it does I am lost. Let me say at once how I stand—or seem to.

I only slept a few hours when I went to bed, and feeling that I could not sleep any more, got up. I had hung my shaving glass by the window, and was just beginning to shave. Suddenly I felt a hand on my shoulder, and heard the Count's voice saying to me, "Good-morning." I started, for it amazed me that I had not seen him, since the reflection of the glass covered the whole room behind me. In starting I had cut myself slightly, but did not notice it at the moment. Having answered the Count's salutation, I turned to the glass again to see how I had been mistaken. This time there could be no error, for the man was close to me, and I could see him over my shoulder. But there was no reflection of him in the mirror! The whole room behind me was displayed; but there was no sign of a man in it, except myself. This was startling, and, coming on the top of so many strange things, was beginning to increase that vague feeling of uneasiness which I always have when the Count is near; but at the instant I saw that the cut had bled a little, and the blood was trickling over my chin. I laid down the razor, turning as I did so half round to look for some sticking plaster. When the Count saw my face, his eyes blazed with a sort of demoniac fury, and he suddenly made a grab at my throat. I drew away, and his hand touched the string of beads which held the crucifix. It made an instant change in him, for the fury passed so quickly that I could hardly believe that it was ever there.

"Take care," he said, "take care how you cut yourself. It is more dangerous than you think in this country." Then seizing the shaving glass, he went on: "And this is the wretched thing that has done the mischief. It is a foul bauble of man's vanity. Away with it!" and opening the heavy window with one wrench of his terrible hand, he flung out the glass, which was shattered into a thousand pieces on the stones of the courtyard far below. Then he withdrew without a word. It is very annoying, for I do not see how I am to shave, unless in my watch-case or the bottom of the shaving-pot, which is fortunately of metal.

When I went into the dining-room, breakfast was prepared; but I could not find the Count anywhere. So I breakfasted alone. It is strange that as yet I have not seen the Count eat or drink. He must be a very peculiar man! After breakfast I did a little exploring in the castle. I went out on the stairs, and found a room looking towards the South. The view was magnificent, and from where I stood there was every opportunity of seeing it. The castle is on the very edge of a terrible precipice. A stone falling from the window would fall a thousand feet without touching anything! As far as the eye can reach is a sea of green tree tops, with occasionally a deep rift where there is a chasm. Here and there are silver threads where the rivers wind in deep gorges through the forests.

But I am not in heart to describe beauty, for when I had seen the view I explored further; doors, doors, doors everywhere, and all locked and bolted. In no place save from the windows in the castle walls is there an available exit.

The castle is a veritable prison, and I am a prisoner!

CHAPTER III

JONATHAN HARKER'S JOURNAL—*continued*

WHEN I found that I was a prisoner a sort of wild feeling came over me. I rushed up and down the stairs, trying every door and peering out of every window I could find; but after a little the conviction of my helplessness overpowered all other feelings. When I look back after a few hours I think I must have been mad for the time, for I behaved much as a rat does in a trap. When, however, the conviction had come to me that I was helpless I sat down quietly—as quietly as I have ever done anything in my life—and began to think over what was best to be done. I am thinking still, and as yet have come to no definite conclusion. Of one thing only am I certain; that it is no use making my ideas known to the Count. He knows well that I am imprisoned; and as he has done it himself, and has doubtless his own motives for it, he would only deceive me if I trusted him fully with the facts. So far as I can see, my only plan will be to keep my knowledge and my fears to myself, and my eyes open. I am, I know, either being deceived, like a baby, by my own fears, or else I am in desperate straits; and if the latter be so, I need, and shall need, all my brains to get through.

I had hardly come to this conclusion when I heard the great door below shut, and knew that the Count had returned. He did not come at once into the library, so I went cautiously to my own room and found him making the bed. This was odd, but only confirmed what I had all along thought—that there were no servants in the house. When later I saw him through the chink of the hinges of the door laying the table in the dining-room, I was assured of it; for if he does himself all these menial offices, surely it is proof that there is no one else to do them. This gave me a fright, for if there is no one else in the castle, it must have been the Count himself who was the driver of the coach that brought me here. This is a terrible thought; for if so, what does it mean that he could control the wolves, as he did, by only holding up his hand in silence. How was it that all the people at Bistritz and on the coach had some terrible fear for me? What meant the giving of the crucifix, of the garlic, of the wild rose, of the mountain ash? Bless that good, good woman who hung the crucifix round my neck! for it is a comfort and a strength to me whenever I touch it. It is odd that a thing which I have been taught to regard with disfavour and as idolatrous should in a time of loneliness and trouble be of help. Is it that there is something in the essence of the thing itself, or that it is a medium, a tangible help, in conveying memories of sympathy and comfort? Some time, if it may be, I must examine this matter and try to make up my mind about it. In the meantime I must find out all I can about Count Dracula, as it may help me to understand. To-night he may talk of himself, if I turn the conversation that way. I must be very careful, however, not to awake his suspicion.

Midnight.—I have had a long talk with the Count. I asked him a few questions on Transylvania history, and he warmed up to the subject wonderfully. In his speaking of things and people, and especially of battles, he spoke as if he had been present at them all. This he afterwards explained by saying that to a *boyar* the pride of his house and name is his own pride, that their glory is his glory, that their fate is his fate. Whenever he spoke of his house he always said "we," and spoke almost in the plural, like a king speaking. I wish I could put down all he said exactly as he said it, for to me it was most fascinating. It seemed to have in it a whole history of the country. He grew excited as he spoke, and walked about the room pulling his great white moustache and grasping anything on which he laid his hands as though he would crush it by main strength. One thing he said which I shall put down as nearly as I can; for it tells in its way the story of his race:—

"We Szekelys have a right to be proud, for in our veins flows the blood of many brave races who fought as the lion fights, for lordship. Here, in the whirlpool of European races, the Ugric tribe bore down from Iceland the fighting spirit which Thor and Wodin gave them, which their Berserkers displayed to such fell intent on the seaboards of Europe, ay, and of Asia and Africa too, till the peoples thought that the were-wolves themselves had come. Here, too, when they came, they found the Huns, whose warlike fury had swept the earth like a living flame, till the dying peoples held that in their veins ran the blood of those old witches, who, expelled from Scythia had mated with the devils in the desert. Fools, fools! What devil or what witch was ever so great as Attila, whose blood is in these veins?" He held up his arms. "Is it a wonder that we were a conquering race; that we were proud; that when the Magyar, the Lombard, the Avar, the Bulgar, or the Turk poured his thousands on our frontiers, we drove them back? Is it strange that when Arpad and his legions swept through the Hungarian fatherland he found us here when he reached the frontier; that the Honfoglalas was completed there? And when the Hungarian flood swept eastward, the Szekelys were claimed as kindred by the victorious Magyars, and to us for centuries was trusted the guarding of the frontier of Turkey-land; ay, and more than that, endless duty of the frontier guard, for, as the Turks say, 'water sleeps, and enemy is sleepless.' Who more gladly than we throughout the Four Nations received the 'bloody sword,' or at its warlike call flocked quicker to the standard of the King? When was redeemed that great shame of my nation, the shame of Cassova, when the flags of the Wallach and the Magyar went down beneath the Crescent? Who was it but one of my own race who as Voivode crossed the Danube and beat the Turk on his own ground? This was a Dracula indeed! Woe was it that his own unworthy brother, when he had fallen, sold his people to the Turk and brought the shame of slavery on them! Was it not this Dracula, indeed, who inspired that other of his race who in a later age again and again brought his forces over the great river into Turkey-land; who, when he was beaten back, came again, and again, and again, though he had to come alone from the bloody field where his troops were being slaughtered, since he knew that he alone could ultimately triumph! They said that he thought only of himself. Bah! what good are peasants without a leader? Where ends the war without a brain and heart to conduct it? Again, when, after the battle of Mohács, we threw off the Hungarian yoke, we of the Dracula blood were amongst their leaders, for our spirit would not brook that we were not free. Ah, young sir, the Szekelys—and the Dracula as their heart's blood, their brains, and their swords—can boast a record that mushroom growths like the Hapsburgs and the Romanoffs can never reach. The warlike days are over. Blood is too precious a thing in these days of dishonourable peace; and the glories of the great races are as a tale that is told."

It was by this time close on morning, and we went to bed. (*Mem.*, this diary seems horribly like the beginning of the "Arabian Nights," for everything has to break off at cockcrow—or like the ghost of Hamlet's father.)

12 May.—Let me begin with facts—bare, meagre facts, verified by books and figures, and of which there can be no doubt. I must not confuse them with experiences which will have to rest on my own observation, or my memory of them. Last evening when the Count came from his room he began by asking me questions on legal matters and on the doing of certain kinds of business. I had spent the day wearily over books, and, simply to keep my mind occupied, went over some of the matters I had been examining at Lincoln's Inn. There was a certain method in the Count's inquiries, so I shall try to put them down in sequence; the knowledge may somehow or some time be useful to me.

First, he asked if a man in England might have two solicitors or more. I told him he might have a dozen if he wished, but that it would not be wise to have more than one solicitor engaged in one transaction, as only one could act at a time, and that to change would be certain to militate against his interest. He seemed thoroughly to understand, and went on to ask if there would be any practical difficulty in having one man to attend, say, to banking, and another to look after shipping, in case local help were needed in a place far from the home of the banking solicitor. I asked him to explain more fully, so that I might not by any chance mislead him, so he said:—

"I shall illustrate. Your friend and mine, Mr. Peter Hawkins, from under the shadow of your beautiful cathedral at Exeter, which is far from London, buys for me through your good self my place at London. Good! Now here let me say frankly, lest you should think it strange that I have sought the services of one so far off from London instead of some one resident there, that my motive was that no local interest might be served save my wish only; and as one of London residence might, perhaps, have some purpose of himself or friend to serve, I went thus afield to seek my agent, whose labours should be only to my interest. Now, suppose I, who have much of affairs, wish to ship goods, say, to Newcastle, or Durham, or Harwich, or Dover, might it not be that it could with more ease be done by consigning to one in these ports?" I answered that certainly it would be most easy, but that we solicitors had a system of agency one for the other, so that local work could be done locally on instruction from any solicitor, so that the client, simply placing himself in the hands of one man, could have his wishes carried out by him without further trouble.

"But," said he, "I could be at liberty to direct myself. Is it not so?"

"Of course," I replied; and "such is often done by men of business, who do not like the whole of their affairs to be known by any one person."

"Good!" he said, and then went on to ask about the means of making consignments and the forms to be gone through, and of all sorts of difficulties which might arise, but by forethought could be guarded against. I explained all these things to him to the best of my ability, and he certainly left me under the impression that he would have made a wonderful solicitor, for there was nothing that he did not think of or foresee. For a man who was never in the country, and who did not evidently do much in the way of business, his knowledge and acumen were wonderful. When he had satisfied himself on these points of which he had spoken, and I had verified all as well as I could by the books available, he suddenly stood up and said:—

"Have you written since your first letter to our friend Mr. Peter Hawkins, or to any other?" It was with some bitterness in my heart that I answered that I had not, that as yet I had not seen any opportunity of sending letters to anybody.

"Then write now, my young friend," he said, laying a heavy hand on my shoulder: "write to our friend and to any other; and say, if it will please you, that you shall stay with me until a month from now."

"Do you wish me to stay so long?" I asked, for my heart grew cold at the thought.

"I desire it much; nay, I will take no refusal. When your master, employer, what you will, engaged that someone should come on his behalf, it was understood that my needs only were to be consulted. I have not stinted. Is it not so?"

What could I do but bow acceptance? It was Mr. Hawkins's interest, not mine, and I had to think of him, not myself; and besides, while Count Dracula was speaking, there was that in his eyes and in his bearing which made me remember that I was a prisoner, and that if I wished it I could have no choice. The Count saw his victory in my bow, and his mastery in the trouble of my face, for he began at once to use them, but in his own smooth, resistless way:—

"I pray you, my good young friend, that you will not discourse of things other than business in your letters. It will doubtless please your friends to know that you are well, and that you look forward to getting home to them. Is it not so?" As he spoke he handed me three sheets of note-paper and three envelopes. They were all of the thinnest foreign post, and looking at them, then at him, and noticing his quiet smile, with the sharp, canine teeth lying over the red underlip, I understood as well as if he had spoken that I should be careful what I wrote, for he would be able to read it. So I determined to write only formal notes now, but to write fully to Mr. Hawkins in secret, and also to Mina, for to her I could write in shorthand, which would puzzle the Count, if he did see it. When I had written my two letters I sat quiet, reading a book whilst the Count wrote several notes, referring as he wrote them to some books on his table. Then he took up my two and placed them with his own, and put by his writing materials, after which, the instant the door had closed behind him, I leaned over and looked at the letters, which were face down on the table. I felt no compunction in doing so, for under the circumstances I felt that I should protect myself in every way I could.

One of the letters was directed to Samuel F. Billington, No. 7, The Crescent, Whitby, another to Herr Leutner, Varna; the third was to Coutts & Co., London, and the fourth to Herren Klopstock & Billreuth, bankers, Buda-Pesth. The second and fourth were unsealed. I was just about to look at them when I saw the door-handle move. I sank back in my seat, having just had time to replace the letters as they had been and to resume my book before the Count, holding still another letter in his hand, entered the room.

He took up the letters on the table and stamped them carefully, and then turning to me, said:—

"I trust you will forgive me, but I have much work to do in private this evening. You will, I hope, find all things as you wish." At the door he turned, and after a moment's pause said:—

"Let me advise you, my dear young friend—nay, let me warn you with all seriousness, that should you leave these rooms you will not by any chance go to sleep in any other part of the castle. It is old, and has many memories, and there are bad dreams for those who sleep unwisely. Be warned! Should sleep now or ever overcome you, or be like to do, then haste to your own chamber or to these rooms, for your rest will then be safe. But if you be not careful in this respect, then"—He finished his speech in a gruesome way, for he motioned with his hands as if he were washing them. I quite understood; my only doubt was as to whether any dream could be more terrible than the unnatural, horrible net of gloom and mystery which seemed closing around me.

Later.—I endorse the last words written, but this time there is no doubt in question. I shall not fear to sleep in any place where he is not. I have placed the crucifix over the head of my bed—I imagine that my rest is thus freer from dreams; and there it shall remain.

When he left me I went to my room. After a little while, not hearing any sound, I came out and went up the stone stair to where I could look out towards the South. There was some sense of freedom in the vast expanse, inaccessible though it was to me, as compared with the narrow darkness of the courtyard. Looking out on this, I felt that I was indeed in prison, and I seemed to want a breath of fresh air, though it were of the night. I am beginning to feel this nocturnal existence tell on me. It is destroying my nerve. I start at my own shadow, and am full of all sorts of horrible imaginings. God knows that there is ground for my terrible fear in this accursed place! I looked out over the beautiful expanse, bathed in soft yellow moonlight till it was almost as light as day. In the soft light the distant hills became melted, and the shadows in the valleys and gorges of velvety blackness. The mere beauty seemed to cheer me; there was peace and comfort in every breath I drew. As I leaned from the window my eye was caught by something moving a storey below me, and somewhat to my left, where I imagined, from the order of the rooms, that the windows of the Count's own room would look out. The window at which I stood was tall and deep, stone-mullioned, and though weatherworn, was still complete; but it was evidently many a day since the case had been there. I drew back behind the stonework, and looked carefully out.

What I saw was the Count's head coming out from the window. I did not see the face, but I knew the man by the neck and the movement of his back and arms. In any case I could not mistake the hands which I had had so many opportunities of studying. I was at first interested and somewhat amused, for it is wonderful how small a matter will interest and amuse a man when he is a prisoner. But my very feelings changed to repulsion and terror when I saw the whole man slowly emerge from the window and begin to crawl down the castle wall over that dreadful abyss, *face down* with his cloak spreading out around him like great wings. At first I could not believe my eyes. I thought it was some trick of the moonlight, some weird effect of shadow; but I kept looking, and it could be no delusion. I saw the fingers and toes grasp the corners of the stones, worn clear of the mortar by the stress of years, and by thus using every projection and inequality move downwards with considerable speed, just as a lizard moves along a wall.

What manner of man is this, or what manner of creature is it in the semblance of man? I feel the dread of this horrible place overpowering me; I am in fear—in awful fear—and there is no escape for me; I am encompassed about with terrors that I dare not think of . . . .

15 May.—Once more have I seen the Count go out in his lizard fashion. He moved downwards in a sidelong way, some hundred feet down, and a good deal to the left. He vanished into some hole or window. When his head had disappeared, I leaned out to try and see more, but without avail—the distance was too great to allow a proper angle of sight. I knew he had left the castle now, and thought to use the opportunity to explore more than I had dared to do as yet. I went back to the room, and taking a lamp, tried all the doors. They were all locked, as I had expected, and the locks were comparatively new; but I went down the stone stairs to the hall where I had entered originally. I found I could pull back the bolts easily enough and unhook the great chains; but the door was locked, and the key was gone! That key must be in the Count's room; I must watch should his door be unlocked, so that I may get it and escape. I went on to make a thorough examination of the various stairs and passages, and to try the doors that opened from them. One or two small rooms near the hall were open, but there was nothing to see in them except old furniture, dusty with age and moth-eaten. At last, however, I found one door at the top of the stairway which, though it seemed to be locked, gave a little under pressure. I tried it harder, and found that it was not really locked, but that the resistance came from the fact that the hinges had fallen somewhat, and the heavy door rested on the floor. Here was an opportunity which I might not have again, so I exerted myself, and with many efforts forced it back so that I could enter. I was now in a wing of the castle further to the right than the rooms I knew and a storey lower down. From the windows I could see that the suite of rooms lay along to the south of the castle, the windows of the end room looking out both west and south. On the latter side, as well as to the former, there was a great precipice. The castle was built on the corner of a great rock, so that on three sides it was quite impregnable, and great windows were placed here where sling, or bow, or culverin could not reach, and consequently light and comfort, impossible to a position which had to be guarded, were secured. To the west was a great valley, and then, rising far away, great jagged mountain fastnesses, rising peak on peak, the sheer rock studded with mountain ash and thorn, whose roots clung in cracks and crevices and crannies of the stone. This was evidently the portion of the castle occupied by the ladies in bygone days, for the furniture had more air of comfort than any I had seen. The windows were curtainless, and the yellow moonlight, flooding in through the diamond panes, enabled one to see even colours, whilst it softened the wealth of dust which lay over all and disguised in some measure the ravages of time and the moth. My lamp seemed to be of little effect in the brilliant moonlight, but I was glad to have it with me, for there was a dread loneliness in the place which chilled my heart and made my nerves tremble. Still, it was better than living alone in the rooms which I had come to hate from the presence of the Count, and after trying a little to school my nerves, I found a soft quietude come over me. Here I am, sitting at a little oak table where in old times possibly some fair lady sat to pen, with much thought and many blushes, her ill-spelt love-letter, and writing in my diary in shorthand all that has happened since I closed it last. It is nineteenth century up-to-date with a vengeance. And yet, unless my senses deceive me, the old centuries had, and have, powers of their own which mere "modernity" cannot kill.

Later: the Morning of 16 May.—God preserve my sanity, for to this I am reduced. Safety and the assurance of safety are things of the past. Whilst I live on here there is but one thing to hope for, that I may not go mad, if, indeed, I be not mad already. If I be sane, then surely it is maddening to think that of all the foul things that lurk in this hateful place the Count is the least dreadful to me; that to him alone I can look for safety, even though this be only whilst I can serve his purpose. Great God! merciful God! Let me be calm, for out of that way lies madness indeed. I begin to get new lights on certain things which have puzzled me. Up to now I never quite knew what Shakespeare meant when he made Hamlet say:—

"My tablets! quick, my tablets!
'Tis meet that I put it down," etc.,

for now, feeling as though my own brain were unhinged or as if the shock
had come which must end in its undoing, I turn to my diary for repose. The
habit of entering accurately must help to soothe me.

The Count's mysterious warning frightened me at the time; it frightens
me more now when I think of it, for in future he has a fearful hold upon me.
I shall fear to doubt what he may say!

When I had written in my diary and had fortunately replaced the book
and pen in my pocket I felt sleepy. The Count's warning came into my mind,
but I took a pleasure in disobeying it. The sense of sleep was upon me, and
with it the obstinacy which sleep brings as outrider. The soft moonlight
soothed, and the wide expanse without gave a sense of freedom which
refreshed me. I determined not to return to-night to the gloom-haunted
rooms, but to sleep here, where, of old, ladies had sat and sung and lived
sweet lives whilst their gentle breasts were sad for their menfolk away in
the midst of remorseless wars. I drew a great couch out of its place near
the corner, so that as I lay, I could look at the lovely view to east and south,
and unthinking of and uncaring for the dust, composed myself for sleep. I
suppose I must have fallen asleep; I hope so, but I fear, for all that followed
was startlingly real—so real that now sitting here in the broad, full sunlight
of the morning, I cannot in the least believe that it was all sleep.

I was not alone. The room was the same, unchanged in any way since I
came into it; I could see along the floor, in the brilliant moonlight, my own
footsteps marked where I had disturbed the long accumulation of dust. In
the moonlight opposite me were three young women, ladies by their dress
and manner. I thought at the time that I must be dreaming when I saw
them, for, though the moonlight was behind them, they threw no shadow
on the floor. They came close to me, and looked at me for some time, and
then whispered together. Two were dark, and had high aquiline noses,
like the Count, and great dark, piercing eyes that seemed to be almost red
when contrasted with the pale yellow moon. The other was fair, as fair as
can be, with great wavy masses of golden hair and eyes like pale sapphires.
I seemed somehow to know her face, and to know it in connection with
some dreamy fear, but I could not recollect at the moment how or where.
All three had brilliant white teeth that shone like pearls against the ruby
of their voluptuous lips. There was something about them that made me
uneasy, some longing and at the same time some deadly fear. I felt in my
heart a wicked, burning desire that they would kiss me with those red lips.

It is not good to note this down, lest some day it should meet Mina's eyes and cause her pain; but it is the truth. They whispered together, and then they all three laughed—such a silvery, musical laugh, but as hard as though the sound never could have come through the softness of human lips. It was like the intolerable, tingling sweetness of water-glasses when played on by a cunning hand. The fair girl shook her head coquettishly, and the other two urged her on. One said:—

"Go on! You are first, and we shall follow; yours is the right to begin." The other added:—

"He is young and strong; there are kisses for us all." I lay quiet, looking out under my eyelashes in an agony of delightful anticipation. The fair girl advanced and bent over me till I could feel the movement of her breath upon me. Sweet it was in one sense, honey-sweet, and sent the same tingling through the nerves as her voice, but with a bitter underlying the sweet, a bitter offensiveness, as one smells in blood.

I was afraid to raise my eyelids, but looked out and saw perfectly under the lashes. The girl went on her knees, and bent over me, simply gloating. There was a deliberate voluptuousness which was both thrilling and repulsive, and as she arched her neck she actually licked her lips like an animal, till I could see in the moonlight the moisture shining on the scarlet lips and on the red tongue as it lapped the white sharp teeth. Lower and lower went her head as the lips went below the range of my mouth and chin and seemed about to fasten on my throat. Then she paused, and I could hear the churning sound of her tongue as it licked her teeth and lips, and could feel the hot breath on my neck. Then the skin of my throat began to tingle as one's flesh does when the hand that is to tickle it approaches nearer—nearer. I could feel the soft, shivering touch of the lips on the super-sensitive skin of my throat, and the hard dents of two sharp teeth, just touching and pausing there. I closed my eyes in a languorous ecstasy and waited—waited with beating heart.

But at that instant, another sensation swept through me as quick as lightning. I was conscious of the presence of the Count, and of his being as if lapped in a storm of fury. As my eyes opened involuntarily I saw his strong hand grasp the slender neck of the fair woman and with giant's power draw it back, the blue eyes transformed with fury, the white teeth champing with rage, and the fair cheeks blazing red with passion. But the Count! Never did I imagine such wrath and fury, even to the demons of the pit. His eyes were positively blazing. The red light in them was lurid, as if the flames of hell-fire blazed behind them. His face was deathly pale, and the lines of it were hard like drawn wires; the thick eyebrows that met over the nose now seemed like a heaving bar of white-hot metal. With a fierce sweep of his arm, he hurled the woman from him, and then motioned to the others, as though he were beating them back; it was the same imperious gesture that I had seen used to the wolves. In a voice which, though low and almost in a whisper seemed to cut through the air and then ring round the room he said:—

"How dare you touch him, any of you? How dare you cast eyes on him when I had forbidden it? Back, I tell you all! This man belongs to me! Beware how you meddle with him, or you'll have to deal with me." The fair girl, with a laugh of ribald coquetry, turned to answer him:—

"You yourself never loved; you never love!" On this the other women joined, and such a mirthless, hard, soulless laughter rang through the room that it almost made me faint to hear; it seemed like the pleasure of fiends. Then the Count turned, after looking at my face attentively, and said in a soft whisper:—

"Yes, I too can love; you yourselves can tell it from the past. Is it not so? Well, now I promise you that when I am done with him you shall kiss him at your will. Now go! go! I must awaken him, for there is work to be done."

"Are we to have nothing to-night?" said one of them, with a low laugh, as she pointed to the bag which he had thrown upon the floor, and which moved as though there were some living thing within it. For answer he nodded his head. One of the women jumped forward and opened it. If my ears did not deceive me there was a gasp and a low wail, as of a half-smothered child. The women closed round, whilst I was aghast with horror; but as I looked they disappeared, and with them the dreadful bag. There was no door near them, and they could not have passed me without my noticing. They simply seemed to fade into the rays of the moonlight and pass out through the window, for I could see outside the dim, shadowy forms for a moment before they entirely faded away.

Then the horror overcame me, and I sank down unconscious.

CHAPTER IV

JONATHAN HARKER'S JOURNAL—*continued*

I AWOKE in my own bed. If it be that I had not dreamt, the Count must have carried me here. I tried to satisfy myself on the subject, but could not arrive at any unquestionable result. To be sure, there were certain small evidences, such as that my clothes were folded and laid by in a manner which was not my habit. My watch was still unwound, and I am rigorously accustomed to wind it the last thing before going to bed, and many such details. But these things are no proof, for they may have been evidences that my mind was not as usual, and, from some cause or another, I had certainly been much upset. I must watch for proof. Of one thing I am glad: if it was that the Count carried me here and undressed me, he must have been hurried in his task, for my pockets are intact. I am sure this diary would have been a mystery to him which he would not have brooked. He would have taken or destroyed it. As I look round this room, although it has been to me so full of fear, it is now a sort of sanctuary, for nothing can be more dreadful than those awful women, who were—who *are*—waiting to suck my blood.

18 May.—I have been down to look at that room again in daylight, for I *must* know the truth. When I got to the doorway at the top of the stairs I found it closed. It had been so forcibly driven against the jamb that part of the woodwork was splintered. I could see that the bolt of the lock had not been shot, but the door is fastened from the inside. I fear it was no dream, and must act on this surmise.

19 May.—I am surely in the toils. Last night the Count asked me in the suavest tones to write three letters, one saying that my work here was nearly done, and that I should start for home within a few days, another that I was starting on the next morning from the time of the letter, and the third that I had left the castle and arrived at Bistritz. I would fain have rebelled, but felt that in the present state of things it would be madness to quarrel openly with the Count whilst I am so absolutely in his power; and to refuse would be to excite his suspicion and to arouse his anger. He knows that I know too much, and that I must not live, lest I be dangerous to him; my only chance is to prolong my opportunities. Something may occur which will give me a chance to escape. I saw in his eyes something of that gathering wrath which was manifest when he hurled that fair woman from him. He explained to me that posts were few and uncertain, and that my writing now would ensure ease of mind to my friends; and he assured me with so much impressiveness that he would countermand the later letters, which would be held over at Bistritz until due time in case chance would admit of my prolonging my stay, that to oppose him would have been to create new suspicion. I therefore pretended to fall in with his views, and asked him what dates I should put on the letters. He calculated a minute, and then said:—

"The first should be June 12, the second June 19, and the third June 29."

I know now the span of my life. God help me!

28 May.—There is a chance of escape, or at any rate of being able to send word home. A band of Szgany have come to the castle, and are encamped in the courtyard. These Szgany are gipsies; I have notes of them in my book. They are peculiar to this part of the world, though allied to the ordinary gipsies all the world over. There are thousands of them in Hungary and Transylvania, who are almost outside all law. They attach themselves as a rule to some great noble or *boyar*, and call themselves by his name. They are fearless and without religion, save superstition, and they talk only their own varieties of the Romany tongue.

I shall write some letters home, and shall try to get them to have them posted. I have already spoken them through my window to begin acquaintanceship. They took their hats off and made obeisance and many signs, which, however, I could not understand any more than I could their spoken language . . . .

I have written the letters. Mina's is in shorthand, and I simply ask Mr. Hawkins to communicate with her. To her I have explained my situation, but without the horrors which I may only surmise. It would shock and frighten her to death were I to expose my heart to her. Should the letters not carry, then the Count shall not yet know my secret or the extent of my knowledge . . . .

I have given the letters; I threw them through the bars of my window with a gold piece, and made what signs I could to have them posted. The man who took them pressed them to his heart and bowed, and then put them in his cap. I could do no more. I stole back to the study, and began to read. As the Count did not come in, I have written here . . . .

The Count has come. He sat down beside me, and said in his smoothest voice as he opened two letters:—

"The Szgany has given me these, of which, though I know not whence they come, I shall, of course, take care. See!"—he must have looked at it—"one is from you, and to my friend Peter Hawkins; the other"—here he caught sight of the strange symbols as he opened the envelope, and the dark look came into his face, and his eyes blazed wickedly—"the other is a vile thing, an outrage upon friendship and hospitality! It is not signed. Well! so it cannot matter to us." And he calmly held letter and envelope in the flame of the lamp till they were consumed. Then he went on:—

"The letter to Hawkins—that I shall, of course, send on, since it is yours. Your letters are sacred to me. Your pardon, my friend, that unknowingly I did break the seal. Will you not cover it again?" He held out the letter to me, and with a courteous bow handed me a clean envelope. I could only redirect it and hand it to him in silence. When he went out of the room I could hear the key turn softly. A minute later I went over and tried it, and the door was locked.

When, an hour or two after, the Count came quietly into the room, his coming awakened me, for I had gone to sleep on the sofa. He was very courteous and very cheery in his manner, and seeing that I had been sleeping, he said:—

"So, my friend, you are tired? Get to bed. There is the surest rest. I may not have the pleasure to talk to-night, since there are many labours to me; but you will sleep, I pray." I passed to my room and went to bed, and, strange to say, slept without dreaming. Despair has its own calms.

31 May.—This morning when I woke I thought I would provide myself with some paper and envelopes from my bag and keep them in my pocket, so that I might write in case I should get an opportunity, but again a surprise, again a shock!

Every scrap of paper was gone, and with it all my notes, my memoranda, relating to railways and travel, my letter of credit, in fact all that might be useful to me were I once outside the castle. I sat and pondered awhile, and then some thought occurred to me, and I made search of my portmanteau and in the wardrobe where I had placed my clothes.

The suit in which I had travelled was gone, and also my overcoat and rug; I could find no trace of them anywhere. This looked like some new scheme of villainy . . . .

17 June.—This morning, as I was sitting on the edge of my bed cudgelling my brains, I heard without a cracking of whips and pounding and scraping of horses' feet up the rocky path beyond the courtyard. With joy I hurried to the window, and saw drive into the yard two great leiter-wagons, each drawn by eight sturdy horses, and at the head of each pair a Slovak, with his wide hat, great nail-studded belt, dirty sheepskin, and high boots. They had also their long staves in hand. I ran to the door, intending to descend and try and join them through the main hall, as I thought that way might be opened for them. Again a shock: my door was fastened on the outside.

Then I ran to the window and cried to them. They looked up at me stupidly and pointed, but just then the "hetman" of the Szgany came out, and seeing them pointing to my window, said something, at which they laughed. Henceforth no effort of mine, no piteous cry or agonised entreaty, would make them even look at me. They resolutely turned away. The leiter-wagons contained great, square boxes, with handles of thick rope; these were evidently empty by the ease with which the Slovaks handled them, and by their resonance as they were roughly moved. When they were all unloaded and packed in a great heap in one corner of the yard, the Slovaks were given some money by the Szgany, and spitting on it for luck, lazily went each to his horse's head. Shortly afterwards, I heard the cracking of their whips die away in the distance.

24 June, before morning.—Last night the Count left me early, and locked himself into his own room. As soon as I dared I ran up the winding stair, and looked out of the window, which opened south. I thought I would watch for the Count, for there is something going on. The Szgany are quartered somewhere in the castle and are doing work of some kind. I know it, for now and then I hear a far-away muffled sound as of mattock and spade, and, whatever it is, it must be the end of some ruthless villainy.

I had been at the window somewhat less than half an hour, when I saw something coming out of the Count's window. I drew back and watched carefully, and saw the whole man emerge. It was a new shock to me to find that he had on the suit of clothes which I had worn whilst travelling here, and slung over his shoulder the terrible bag which I had seen the women take away. There could be no doubt as to his quest, and in my garb, too! This, then, is his new scheme of evil: that he will allow others to see me, as they think, so that he may both leave evidence that I have been seen in the towns or villages posting my own letters, and that any wickedness which he may do shall by the local people be attributed to me.

It makes me rage to think that this can go on, and whilst I am shut up here, a veritable prisoner, but without that protection of the law which is even a criminal's right and consolation.

I thought I would watch for the Count's return, and for a long time sat doggedly at the window. Then I began to notice that there were some quaint little specks floating in the rays of the moonlight. They were like the tiniest grains of dust, and they whirled round and gathered in clusters in a nebulous sort of way. I watched them with a sense of soothing, and a sort of calm stole over me. I leaned back in the embrasure in a more comfortable position, so that I could enjoy more fully the aërial gambolling.

Something made me start up, a low, piteous howling of dogs somewhere far below in the valley, which was hidden from my sight. Louder it seemed to ring in my ears, and the floating motes of dust to take new shapes to the sound as they danced in the moonlight. I felt myself struggling to awake to some call of my instincts; nay, my very soul was struggling, and my half-remembered sensibilities were striving to answer the call. I was becoming hypnotised! Quicker and quicker danced the dust; the moonbeams seemed to quiver as they went by me into the mass of gloom beyond. More and more they gathered till they seemed to take dim phantom shapes. And then I started, broad awake and in full possession of my senses, and ran screaming from the place. The phantom shapes, which were becoming gradually materialised from the moonbeams, were those of the three ghostly women to whom I was doomed. I fled, and felt somewhat safer in my own room, where there was no moonlight and where the lamp was burning brightly.

When a couple of hours had passed I heard something stirring in the Count's room, something like a sharp wail quickly suppressed; and then there was silence, deep, awful silence, which chilled me. With a beating heart, I tried the door; but I was locked in my prison, and could do nothing. I sat down and simply cried.

As I sat I heard a sound in the courtyard without—the agonised cry of a woman. I rushed to the window, and throwing it up, peered out between the bars. There, indeed, was a woman with dishevelled hair, holding her hands over her heart as one distressed with running. She was leaning against a corner of the gateway. When she saw my face at the window she threw herself forward, and shouted in a voice laden with menace:—

"Monster, give me my child!"

She threw herself on her knees, and raising up her hands, cried the same words in tones which wrung my heart. Then she tore her hair and beat her breast, and abandoned herself to all the violences of extravagant emotion. Finally, she threw herself forward, and, though I could not see her, I could hear the beating of her naked hands against the door.

Somewhere high overhead, probably on the tower, I heard the voice of the Count calling in his harsh, metallic whisper. His call seemed to be answered from far and wide by the howling of wolves. Before many minutes had passed a pack of them poured, like a pent-up dam when liberated, through the wide entrance into the courtyard.

There was no cry from the woman, and the howling of the wolves was but short. Before long they streamed away singly, licking their lips.

I could not pity her, for I knew now what had become of her child, and she was better dead.

What shall I do? what can I do? How can I escape from this dreadful thing of night and gloom and fear?

25 June, morning.—No man knows till he has suffered from the night how sweet and how dear to his heart and eye the morning can be. When the sun grew so high this morning that it struck the top of the great gateway opposite my window, the high spot which it touched seemed to me as if the dove from the ark had lighted there. My fear fell from me as if it had been a vaporous garment which dissolved in the warmth. I must take action of some sort whilst the courage of the day is upon me. Last night one of my post-dated letters went to post, the first of that fatal series which is to blot out the very traces of my existence from the earth.

Let me not think of it. Action!

It has always been at night-time that I have been molested or threatened, or in some way in danger or in fear. I have not yet seen the Count in the daylight. Can it be that he sleeps when others wake, that he may be awake whilst they sleep? If I could only get into his room! But there is no possible way. The door is always locked, no way for me.

Yes, there is a way, if one dares to take it. Where his body has gone why may not another body go? I have seen him myself crawl from his window. Why should not I imitate him, and go in by his window? The chances are desperate, but my need is more desperate still. I shall risk it. At the worst it can only be death; and a man's death is not a calf's, and the dreaded Hereafter may still be open to me. God help me in my task! Good-bye, Mina, if I fail; good-bye, my faithful friend and second father; good-bye, all, and last of all Mina!

Same day, later.—I have made the effort, and God, helping me, have come safely back to this room. I must put down every detail in order. I went whilst my courage was fresh straight to the window on the south side, and at once got outside on the narrow ledge of stone which runs around the building on this side. The stones are big and roughly cut, and the mortar has by process of time been washed away between them. I took off my boots, and ventured out on the desperate way. I looked down once, so as to make sure that a sudden glimpse of the awful depth would not overcome me, but after that kept my eyes away from it. I knew pretty well the direction and distance of the Count's window, and made for it as well as I could, having regard to the opportunities available. I did not feel dizzy—I suppose I was too excited— and the time seemed ridiculously short till I found myself standing on the window-sill and trying to raise up the sash. I was filled with agitation, however, when I bent down and slid feet foremost in through the window. Then I looked around for the Count, but, with surprise and gladness, made a discovery. The room was empty! It was barely furnished with odd things, which seemed to have never been used; the furniture was something the same style as that in the south rooms, and was covered with dust. I looked for the key, but it was not in the lock, and I could not find it anywhere. The only thing I found was a great heap of gold in one corner—gold of all kinds, Roman, and British, and Austrian, and Hungarian, and Greek and Turkish money, covered with a film of dust, as though it had lain long in the ground. None of it that I noticed was less than three hundred years old. There were also chains and ornaments, some jewelled, but all of them old and stained.

At one corner of the room was a heavy door. I tried it, for, since I could not find the key of the room or the key of the outer door, which was the main object of my search, I must make further examination, or all my efforts would be in vain. It was open, and led through a stone passage to a circular stairway, which went steeply down. I descended, minding carefully where I went, for the stairs were dark, being only lit by loopholes in the heavy masonry. At the bottom there was a dark, tunnel-like passage, through which came a deathly, sickly odour, the odour of old earth newly turned. As I went through the passage the smell grew closer and heavier. At last I pulled open a heavy door which stood ajar, and found myself in an old, ruined chapel, which had evidently been used as a graveyard. The roof was broken, and in two places were steps leading to vaults, but the ground had recently been dug over, and the earth placed in great wooden boxes, manifestly those which had been brought by the Slovaks. There was nobody about, and I made search for any further outlet, but there was none. Then I went over every inch of the ground, so as not to lose a chance. I went down even into the vaults, where the dim light struggled, although to do so was a dread to my very soul. Into two of these I went, but saw nothing except fragments of old coffins and piles of dust; in the third, however, I made a discovery.

There, in one of the great boxes, of which there were fifty in all, on a pile of newly dug earth, lay the Count! He was either dead or asleep, I could not say which—for the eyes were open and stony, but without the glassiness of death—and the cheeks had the warmth of life through all their pallor; the lips were as red as ever. But there was no sign of movement, no pulse, no breath, no beating of the heart. I bent over him, and tried to find any sign of life, but in vain. He could not have lain there long, for the earthy smell would have passed away in a few hours. By the side of the box was its cover, pierced with holes here and there. I thought he might have the keys on him, but when I went to search I saw the dead eyes, and in them, dead though they were, such a look of hate, though unconscious of me or my presence, that I fled from the place, and leaving the Count's room by the window, crawled again up the castle wall. Regaining my room, I threw myself panting upon the bed and tried to think . . . .

29 June.—To-day is the date of my last letter, and the Count has taken steps to prove that it was genuine, for again I saw him leave the castle by the same window, and in my clothes. As he went down the wall, lizard fashion, I wished I had a gun or some lethal weapon, that I might destroy him; but I fear that no weapon wrought alone by man's hand would have any effect on him. I dared not wait to see him return, for I feared to see those weird sisters. I came back to the library, and read there till I fell asleep.

I was awakened by the Count, who looked at me as grimly as a man can look as he said:—

"To-morrow, my friend, we must part. You return to your beautiful England, I to some work which may have such an end that we may never meet. Your letter home has been despatched; to-morrow I shall not be here, but all shall be ready for your journey. In the morning come the Szgany, who have some labours of their own here, and also come some Slovaks. When they have gone, my carriage shall come for you, and shall bear you to the Borgo Pass to meet the diligence from Bukovina to Bistritz. But I am in hopes that I shall see more of you at Castle Dracula." I suspected him, and determined to test his sincerity. Sincerity! It seems like a profanation of the word to write it in connection with such a monster, so asked him point-blank:—

"Why may I not go to-night?"

"Because, dear sir, my coachman and horses are away on a mission."

"But I would walk with pleasure. I want to get away at once." He smiled, such a soft, smooth, diabolical smile that I knew there was some trick behind his smoothness. He said:—

"And your baggage?"

"I do not care about it. I can send for it some other time."

The Count stood up, and said, with a sweet courtesy which made me rub my eyes, it seemed so real:—

"You English have a saying which is close to my heart, for its spirit is that which rules our *boyars*: 'Welcome the coming; speed the parting guest.' Come with me, my dear young friend. Not an hour shall you wait in my house against your will, though sad am I at your going, and that you so suddenly desire it. Come!" With a stately gravity, he, with the lamp, preceded me down the stairs and along the hall. Suddenly he stopped.

"Hark!"

Close at hand came the howling of many wolves. It was almost as if the sound sprang up at the rising of his hand, just as the music of a great orchestra seems to leap under the bâton of the conductor. After a pause of a moment, he proceeded, in his stately way, to the door, drew back the ponderous bolts, unhooked the heavy chains, and began to draw it open.

To my intense astonishment I saw that it was unlocked. Suspiciously, I looked all round, but could see no key of any kind.

As the door began to open, the howling of the wolves without grew louder and angrier; their red jaws, with champing teeth, and their blunt-clawed feet as they leaped, came in through the opening door. I knew then that to struggle at the moment against the Count was useless. With such allies as these at his command, I could do nothing. But still the door continued slowly to open, and only the Count's body stood in the gap. Suddenly it struck me that this might be the moment and means of my doom; I was to be given to the wolves, and at my own instigation. There was a diabolical wickedness in the idea great enough for the Count, and as a last chance I cried out:—

"Shut the door; I shall wait till morning!" and covered my face with my hands to hide my tears of bitter disappointment. With one sweep of his powerful arm, the Count threw the door shut, and the great bolts clanged and echoed through the hall as they shot back into their places.

In silence we returned to the library, and after a minute or two I went to my own room. The last I saw of Count Dracula was his kissing his hand to me; with a red light of triumph in his eyes, and with a smile that Judas in hell might be proud of.

When I was in my room and about to lie down, I thought I heard a whispering at my door. I went to it softly and listened. Unless my ears deceived me, I heard the voice of the Count:—

"Back, back, to your own place! Your time is not yet come. Wait! Have patience! To-night is mine. To-morrow night is yours!" There was a low, sweet ripple of laughter, and in a rage I threw open the door, and saw without the three terrible women licking their lips. As I appeared they all joined in a horrible laugh, and ran away.

I came back to my room and threw myself on my knees. It is then so near the end? To-morrow! to-morrow! Lord, help me, and those to whom I am dear!

30 June, morning.—These may be the last words I ever write in this diary. I slept till just before the dawn, and when I woke threw myself on my knees, for I determined that if Death came he should find me ready.

At last I felt that subtle change in the air, and knew that the morning had come. Then came the welcome cock-crow, and I felt that I was safe. With a glad heart, I opened my door and ran down to the hall. I had seen that the door was unlocked, and now escape was before me. With hands that trembled with eagerness, I unhooked the chains and drew back the massive bolts.

But the door would not move. Despair seized me. I pulled, and pulled, at the door, and shook it till, massive as it was, it rattled in its casement. I could see the bolt shot. It had been locked after I left the Count.

Then a wild desire took me to obtain that key at any risk, and I determined then and there to scale the wall again and gain the Count's room. He might kill me, but death now seemed the happier choice of evils. Without a pause I rushed up to the east window, and scrambled down the wall, as before, into the Count's room. It was empty, but that was as I expected. I could not see a key anywhere, but the heap of gold remained. I went through the door in the corner and down the winding stair and along the dark passage to the old chapel. I knew now well enough where to find the monster I sought.

The great box was in the same place, close against the wall, but the lid was laid on it, not fastened down, but with the nails ready in their places to be hammered home. I knew I must reach the body for the key, so I raised the lid, and laid it back against the wall; and then I saw something which filled my very soul with horror. There lay the Count, but looking as if his youth had been half renewed, for the white hair and moustache were changed to dark iron-grey; the cheeks were fuller, and the white skin seemed ruby-red underneath; the mouth was redder than ever, for on the lips were gouts of fresh blood, which trickled from the corners of the mouth and ran over the chin and neck. Even the deep, burning eyes seemed set amongst swollen flesh, for the lids and pouches underneath were bloated. It seemed as if the whole awful creature were simply gorged with blood. He lay like a filthy leech, exhausted with his repletion. I shuddered as I bent over to touch him, and every sense in me revolted at the contact; but I had to search, or I was lost. The coming night might see my own body a banquet in a similar way to those horrid three. I felt all over the body, but no sign could I find of the key. Then I stopped and looked at the Count. There was a mocking smile on the bloated face which seemed to drive me mad. This was the being I was helping to transfer to London, where, perhaps, for centuries to come he might, amongst its teeming millions, satiate his lust for blood, and create a new and ever-widening circle of semi-demons to batten on the helpless. The very thought drove me mad. A terrible desire came upon me to rid the world of such a monster. There was no lethal weapon at hand, but I seized a shovel which the workmen had been using to fill the cases, and lifting it high, struck, with the edge downward, at the hateful face. But as I did so the head turned, and the eyes fell full upon me, with all their blaze of basilisk horror. The sight seemed to paralyse me, and the shovel turned in my hand and glanced from the face, merely making a deep gash above the forehead. The shovel fell from my hand across the box, and as I pulled it away the flange of the blade caught the edge of the lid which fell over again, and hid the horrid thing from my sight. The last glimpse I had was of the bloated face, blood-stained and fixed with a grin of malice which would have held its own in the nethermost hell.

I thought and thought what should be my next move, but my brain seemed on fire, and I waited with a despairing feeling growing over me. As I waited I heard in the distance a gipsy song sung by merry voices coming closer, and through their song the rolling of heavy wheels and the cracking of whips; the Szgany and the Slovaks of whom the Count had spoken were coming. With a last look around and at the box which contained the vile body, I ran from the place and gained the Count's room, determined to rush out at the moment the door should be opened. With strained ears, I listened, and heard downstairs the grinding of the key in the great lock and the falling back of the heavy door. There must have been some other means of entry, or some one had a key for one of the locked doors. Then there came the sound of many feet tramping and dying away in some passage which sent up a clanging echo. I turned to run down again towards the vault, where I might find the new entrance; but at the moment there seemed to come a violent puff of wind, and the door to the winding stair blew to with a shock that set the dust from the lintels flying. When I ran to push it open, I found that it was hopelessly fast. I was again a prisoner, and the net of doom was closing round me more closely.

As I write there is in the passage below a sound of many tramping feet and the crash of weights being set down heavily, doubtless the boxes, with their freight of earth. There is a sound of hammering; it is the box being nailed down. Now I can hear the heavy feet tramping again along the hall, with many other idle feet coming behind them.

The door is shut, and the chains rattle; there is a grinding of the key in the lock; I can hear the key withdraw: then another door opens and shuts; I hear the creaking of lock and bolt.

Hark! in the courtyard and down the rocky way the roll of heavy wheels, the crack of whips, and the chorus of the Szgany as they pass into the distance.

I am alone in the castle with those awful women. Faugh! Mina is a woman, and there is nought in common. They are devils of the Pit!

I shall not remain alone with them; I shall try to scale the castle wall farther than I have yet attempted. I shall take some of the gold with me, lest I want it later. I may find a way from this dreadful place.

And then away for home! away to the quickest and nearest train! away from this cursed spot, from this cursed land, where the devil and his children still walk with earthly feet!

At least God's mercy is better than that of these monsters, and the precipice is steep and high. At its foot a man may sleep—as a man. Goodbye, all! Mina!

CHAPTER V

LETTER FROM MISS MINA MURRAY TO MISS LUCY WESTENRA.

"9 May.

"My dearest Lucy,—

"Forgive my long delay in writing, but I have been simply overwhelmed with work. The life of an assistant schoolmistress is sometimes trying. I am longing to be with you, and by the sea, where we can talk together freely and build our castles in the air. I have been working very hard lately, because I want to keep up with Jonathan's studies, and I have been practising shorthand very assiduously. When we are married I shall be able to be useful to Jonathan, and if I can stenograph well enough I can take down what he wants to say in this way and write it out for him on the typewriter, at which also I am practising very hard. He and I sometimes write letters in shorthand, and he is keeping a stenographic journal of his travels abroad. When I am with you I shall keep a diary in the same way. I don't mean one of those two-pages-to-the-week-with-Sunday-squeezed-in-a-corner diaries, but a sort of journal which I can write in whenever I feel inclined. I do not suppose there will be much of interest to other people; but it is not intended for them. I may show it to Jonathan some day if there is in it anything worth sharing, but it is really an exercise book. I shall try to do what I see lady journalists do: interviewing and writing descriptions and trying to remember conversations. I am told that, with a little practice, one can remember all that goes on or that one hears said during a day.

However, we shall see. I will tell you of my little plans when we meet. I have just had a few hurried lines from Jonathan from Transylvania.

He is well, and will be returning in about a week. I am longing to hear all his news. It must be so nice to see strange countries. I wonder if we—I mean Jonathan and I—shall ever see them together. There is the ten o'clock bell ringing. Good-bye.

"Your loving
"MINA.

"Tell me all the news when you write. You have not told me anything for a long time. I hear rumours, and especially of a tall, handsome, curly-haired man???"

LETTER,
LUCY WESTENRA TO MINA MURRAY.

"17, Chatham Street,
"Wednesday.

"MY DEAREST MINA,—

"I must say you tax me *very* unfairly with being a bad correspondent. I wrote to you *twice* since we parted, and your last letter was only your *second*. Besides, I have nothing to tell you. There is really nothing to interest you. Town is very pleasant just now, and we go a good deal to picture-galleries and for walks and rides in the park. As to the tall, curly-haired man, I suppose it was the one who was with me at the last Pop. Some one has evidently been telling tales. That was Mr. Holmwood. He often comes to see us, and he and mamma get on very well together; they have so many things to talk about in common. We met some time ago a man that would just *do for you*, if you were not already engaged to Jonathan. He is an excellent *parti*, being handsome, well off, and of good birth. He is a doctor and really clever. Just fancy! He is only nine-and-twenty, and he has an immense lunatic asylum all under his own care. Mr. Holmwood introduced him to me, and he called here to see us, and often comes now. I think he is one of the most resolute men I ever saw, and yet the most calm. He seems absolutely imperturbable. I can fancy what a wonderful power he must have over his patients. He has a curious habit of looking one straight in the face, as if trying to read one's thoughts. He tries this on very much with me, but I flatter myself he has got a tough nut to crack. I know that from my glass. Do you ever try to read your own face? *I do*, and I can tell you it is not a bad study, and gives you more trouble than you can well fancy if you have never tried it. He says that I afford him a curious psychological study, and I humbly think I do. I do not, as you know, take sufficient interest in dress to be able to describe the new fashions. Dress is a bore. That is slang again, but never mind; Arthur says that every day. There, it is all out. Mina, we have told all our secrets to each other since we were *children*; we have slept together and eaten together, and laughed and cried together; and now, though I have spoken, I would like to speak more. Oh, Mina, couldn't you guess? I love him. I am blushing as I write, for although I *think* he loves me, he has not told me so in words. But oh, Mina, I love him; I love him; I love him! There, that does me good. I wish I were with you, dear, sitting by the fire undressing, as we used to sit; and I would try to tell you what I feel. I do not know how I am writing this even to you. I am afraid to stop, or I should tear up the letter, and I don't want to stop, for I *do* so want to tell you all. Let me hear from you *at once*, and tell me all that you think about it. Mina, I must stop. Good-night. Bless me in your prayers; and, Mina, pray for my happiness.

"Lucy.

"P.S.—I need not tell you this is a secret. Good-night again.
"L."

LETTER,
LUCY WESTENRA TO MINA MURRAY.

"*24 May.*

"My dearest Mina,—

"Thanks, and thanks, and thanks again for your sweet letter. It was so nice to be able to tell you and to have your sympathy.

"My dear, it never rains but it pours. How true the old proverbs are. Here am I, who shall be twenty in September, and yet I never had a proposal till to-day, not a real proposal, and to-day I have had three. Just fancy! THREE proposals in one day! Isn't it awful! I feel sorry, really and truly sorry, for two of the poor fellows. Oh, Mina, I am so happy that I don't know what to do with myself. And three proposals! But, for goodness' sake, don't tell any of the girls, or they would be getting all sorts of extravagant ideas and imagining themselves injured and slighted if in their very first day at home they did not get six at least. Some girls are so vain! You and I, Mina dear, who are engaged and are going to settle down soon soberly into old married women, can despise vanity. Well, I must tell you about the three, but you must keep it a secret, dear, from *every one*, except, of course, Jonathan. You will tell him, because I would, if I were in your place, certainly tell Arthur. A woman ought to tell her husband everything—don't you think so, dear?—and I must be fair. Men like women, certainly their wives, to be quite as fair as they are; and women, I am afraid, are not always quite as fair as they should be. Well, my dear, number One came just before lunch. I told you of him, Dr. John Seward, the lunatic-asylum man, with the strong jaw and the good forehead. He was very cool outwardly, but was nervous all the same. He had evidently been schooling himself as to all sorts of little things, and remembered them; but he almost managed to sit down on his silk hat, which men don't generally do when they are cool, and then when he wanted to appear at ease he kept playing with a lancet in a way that made me nearly scream. He spoke to me, Mina, very straightforwardly. He told me how dear I was to him, though he had known me so little, and what his life would be with me to help and cheer him. He was going to tell me how unhappy he would be if I did not care for him, but when he saw me cry he said that he was a brute and would not add to my present trouble. Then he broke off and asked if I could love him in time; and when I shook my head his hands trembled, and then with some hesitation he asked me if I cared already for any one else. He put it very nicely, saying that he did not want to wring my confidence from me, but only to know, because if a woman's heart was free a man might have hope. And then, Mina, I felt a sort of duty to tell him that there was some one. I only told him that much, and then he stood up, and he looked very strong and very grave as he took both my hands in his and said he hoped I would be happy, and that if I ever wanted a friend I must count him one of my best. Oh, Mina dear, I can't help crying: and you must excuse this letter being all blotted. Being proposed to is all very nice and all that sort of thing, but it isn't at all a happy thing when you have to see a poor fellow, whom you know loves you honestly, going away and looking all broken-hearted, and to know that, no matter what he may say at the moment, you are passing quite out of his life. My dear, I must stop here at present, I feel so miserable, though I am so happy.

"*Evening.*

"Arthur has just gone, and I feel in better spirits than when I left off, so I can go on telling you about the day. Well, my dear, number Two came after lunch. He is such a nice fellow, an American from Texas, and he looks so young and so fresh that it seems almost impossible that he has been to so many places and has had such adventures. I sympathise with poor

Desdemona when she had such a dangerous stream poured in her ear, even by a black man. I suppose that we women are such cowards that we think a man will save us from fears, and we marry him. I know now what I would do if I were a man and wanted to make a girl love me. No, I don't, for there was Mr. Morris telling us his stories, and Arthur never told any, and yet—— My dear, I am somewhat previous. Mr. Quincey P. Morris found me alone. It seems that a man always does find a girl alone. No, he doesn't, for Arthur tried twice to *make* a chance, and I helping him all I could; I am not ashamed to say it now. I must tell you beforehand that Mr. Morris doesn't always speak slang—that is to say, he never does so to strangers or before them, for he is really well educated and has exquisite manners—but he found out that it amused me to hear him talk American slang, and whenever I was present, and there was no one to be shocked, he said such funny things. I am afraid, my dear, he has to invent it all, for it fits exactly into whatever else he has to say. But this is a way slang has. I do not know myself if I shall ever speak slang; I do not know if Arthur likes it, as I have never heard him use any as yet. Well, Mr. Morris sat down beside me and looked as happy and jolly as he could, but I could see all the same that he was very nervous. He took my hand in his, and said ever so sweetly:—

" 'Miss Lucy, I know I ain't good enough to regulate the fixin's of your little shoes, but I guess if you wait till you find a man that is you will go join them seven young women with the lamps when you quit. Won't you just hitch up alongside of me and let us go down the long road together, driving in double harness?'

"Well, he did look so good-humoured and so jolly that it didn't seem half so hard to refuse him as it did poor Dr. Seward; so I said, as lightly as I could, that I did not know anything of hitching, and that I wasn't broken to harness at all yet. Then he said that he had spoken in a light manner, and he hoped that if he had made a mistake in doing so on so grave, so momentous, an occasion for him, I would forgive him. He really did look serious when he was saying it, and I couldn't help feeling a bit serious too—I know, Mina, you will think me a horrid flirt—though I couldn't help feeling a sort of exultation that he was number two in one day. And then, my dear, before I could say a word he began pouring out a perfect torrent of love-making, laying his very heart and soul at my feet. He looked so earnest over it that I shall never again think that a man must be playful always, and never earnest, because he is merry at times. I suppose he saw something in my face which checked him, for he suddenly stopped, and said with a sort of manly fervour that I could have loved him for if I had been free:—

" 'Lucy, you are an honest-hearted girl, I know. I should not be here speaking to you as I am now if I did not believe you clean grit, right through to the very depths of your soul. Tell me, like one good fellow to another, is there any one else that you care for? And if there is I'll never trouble you a hair's breadth again, but will be, if you will let me, a very faithful friend.'

"My dear Mina, why are men so noble when we women are so little worthy of them? Here was I almost making fun of this great-hearted, true gentleman. I burst into tears—I am afraid, my dear, you will think this a very sloppy letter in more ways than one—and I really felt very badly. Why can't they let a girl marry three men, or as many as want her, and save all this trouble? But this is heresy, and I must not say it. I am glad to say that, though I was crying, I was able to look into Mr. Morris's brave eyes, and I told him out straight:—

" 'Yes, there is some one I love, though he has not told me yet that he even loves me.' I was right to speak to him so frankly, for quite a light came into his face, and he put out both his hands and took mine—I think I put them into his—and said in a hearty way:—

" 'That's my brave girl. It's better worth being late for a chance of winning you than being in time for any other girl in the world. Don't cry, my dear. If it's for me, I'm a hard nut to crack; and I take it standing up. If that other fellow doesn't know his happiness, well, he'd better look for it soon, or he'll have to deal with me. Little girl, your honesty and pluck have made me a friend, and that's rarer than a lover; it's more unselfish anyhow. My dear, I'm going to have a pretty lonely walk between this and Kingdom Come. Won't you give me one kiss? It'll be something to keep off the darkness now and then. You can, you know, if you like, for that other good fellow—he must be a good fellow, my dear, and a fine fellow, or you could not love him—hasn't spoken yet.' That quite won me, Mina, for it *was* brave and sweet of him, and noble, too, to a rival—wasn't it?—and he so sad; so I leant over and kissed him. He stood up with my two hands in his, and as he looked down into my face—I am afraid I was blushing very much—he said:—

" 'Little girl, I hold your hand, and you've kissed me, and if these things don't make us friends nothing ever will. Thank you for your sweet honesty to me, and good-bye.' He wrung my hand, and taking up his hat, went straight out of the room without looking back, without a tear or a quiver or a pause; and I am crying like a baby. Oh, why must a man like that be made unhappy when there are lots of girls about who would worship the very ground he trod on? I know I would if I were free—only I don't want to be free. My dear, this quite upset me, and I feel I cannot write of happiness just at once, after telling you of it; and I don't wish to tell of the number three until it can be all happy.

"Ever your loving
"Lucy.

"P.S.—Oh, about number Three—I needn't tell you of number
Three, need I? Besides, it was all so confused; it seemed only a
moment from his coming into the room till both his arms were
round me, and he was kissing me. I am very, very happy, and
I don't know what I have done to deserve it. I must only try in
the future to show that I am not ungrateful to God for all His
goodness to me in sending to me such a lover, such a husband,
and such a friend.

"Good-bye."

DR. SEWARD'S DIARY.

(*Kept in phonograph*)

25 May.—Ebb tide in appetite to-day. Cannot eat, cannot rest, so diary
instead. Since my rebuff of yesterday I have a sort of empty feeling; nothing
in the world seems of sufficient importance to be worth the doing . . . . As I
knew that the only cure for this sort of thing was work, I went down amongst
the patients. I picked out one who has afforded me a study of much interest.
He is so quaint that I am determined to understand him as well as I can.
To-day I seemed to get nearer than ever before to the heart of his mystery.

I questioned him more fully than I had ever done, with a view to making
myself master of the facts of his hallucination. In my manner of doing it
there was, I now see, something of cruelty. I seemed to wish to keep him to
the point of his madness—a thing which I avoid with the patients as I would
the mouth of hell.

(*Mem.*, under what circumstances would I *not* avoid the pit of hell?)
Omnia Romæ venalia sunt. Hell has its price! *verb. sap.* If there be anything
behind this instinct it will be valuable to trace it afterwards *accurately*, so I
had better commence to do so, therefore—

R. M. Renfield, ætat 59.—Sanguine temperament; great physical strength;
morbidly excitable; periods of gloom, ending in some fixed idea which I
cannot make out. I presume that the sanguine temperament itself and the

disturbing influence end in a mentally-accomplished finish; a possibly dangerous man, probably dangerous if unselfish. In selfish men caution is as secure an armour for their foes as for themselves. What I think of on this point is, when self is the fixed point the centripetal force is balanced with the centrifugal; when duty, a cause, etc., is the fixed point, the latter force is paramount, and only accident or a series of accidents can balance it.

LETTER,
QUINCEY P. MORRIS TO
HON. ARTHUR HOLMWOOD.

"25 May.

"My dear Art,—

"We've told yarns by the camp-fire in the prairies; and dressed one another's wounds after trying a landing at the Marquesas; and drunk healths on the shore of Titicaca. There are more yarns to be told, and other wounds to be healed, and another health to be drunk. Won't you let this be at my camp-fire to-morrow night? I have no hesitation in asking you, as I know a certain lady is engaged to a certain dinner-party, and that you are free. There will only be one other, our old pal at the Korea, Jack Seward. He's coming, too, and we both want to mingle our weeps over the wine-cup, and to drink a health with all our hearts to the happiest man in all the wide world, who has won the noblest heart that God has made and the best worth winning. We promise you a hearty welcome, and a loving greeting, and a health as true as your own right hand. We shall both swear to leave you at home if you drink too deep to a certain pair of eyes. Come!

"Yours, as ever and always,
"Quincey P. Morris."

TELEGRAM FROM
ARTHUR HOLMWOOD
TO QUINCEY P. MORRIS.

"26 May.

"Count me in every time. I bear messages which will make both your ears tingle.

"ART."

CHAPTER VI

MINA MURRAY'S JOURNAL

24 July. Whitby.—Lucy met me at the station, looking sweeter and lovelier than ever, and we drove up to the house at the Crescent in which they have rooms. This is a lovely place. The little river, the Esk, runs through a deep valley, which broadens out as it comes near the harbour. A great viaduct runs across, with high piers, through which the view seems somehow further away than it really is. The valley is beautifully green, and it is so steep that when you are on the high land on either side you look right across it, unless you are near enough to see down. The houses of the old town—the side away from us—are all red-roofed, and seem piled up one over the other anyhow, like the pictures we see of Nuremberg. Right over the town is the ruin of Whitby Abbey, which was sacked by the Danes, and which is the scene of part of "Marmion," where the girl was built up in the wall. It is a most noble ruin, of immense size, and full of beautiful and romantic bits; there is a legend that a white lady is seen in one of the windows. Between it and the town there is another church, the parish one, round which is a big graveyard, all full of tombstones. This is to my mind the nicest spot in Whitby, for it lies right over the town, and has a full view of the harbour and all up the bay to where the headland called Kettleness stretches out into the sea. It descends so steeply over the harbour that part of the bank has fallen away, and some of the graves have been destroyed. In one place part of the stonework of the graves stretches out over the sandy pathway far below. There are walks, with seats beside them, through the churchyard; and people go and sit there all day long looking at the beautiful view and enjoying the breeze. I shall come and sit here very often myself and work. Indeed, I am writing now, with my book on my knee, and listening to the talk of three old men who are sitting beside me. They seem to do nothing all day but sit up here and talk.

The harbour lies below me, with, on the far side, one long granite wall stretching out into the sea, with a curve outwards at the end of it, in the middle of which is a lighthouse. A heavy sea-wall runs along outside of it. On the near side, the sea-wall makes an elbow crooked inversely, and its end too has a lighthouse. Between the two piers there is a narrow opening into the harbour, which then suddenly widens.

It is nice at high water; but when the tide is out it shoals away to nothing, and there is merely the stream of the Esk, running between banks of sand, with rocks here and there. Outside the harbour on this side there rises for about half a mile a great reef, the sharp edge of which runs straight out from behind the south lighthouse. At the end of it is a buoy with a bell, which swings in bad weather, and sends in a mournful sound on the wind. They have a legend here that when a ship is lost bells are heard out at sea. I must ask the old man about this; he is coming this way . . . .

He is a funny old man. He must be awfully old, for his face is all gnarled and twisted like the bark of a tree. He tells me that he is nearly a hundred, and that he was a sailor in the Greenland fishing fleet when Waterloo was fought. He is, I am afraid, a very sceptical person, for when I asked him about the bells at sea and the White Lady at the abbey he said very brusquely:—

"I wouldn't fash masel' about them, miss. Them things be all wore out. Mind, I don't say that they never was, but I do say that they wasn't in my time. They be all very well for comers and trippers, an' the like, but not for a nice young lady like you. Them feet-folks from York and Leeds that be always eatin' cured herrin's an' drinkin' tea an' lookin' out to buy cheap jet would creed aught. I wonder masel' who'd be bothered tellin' lies to them— even the newspapers, which is full of fool-talk." I thought he would be a good person to learn interesting things from, so I asked him if he would mind telling me something about the whale-fishing in the old days. He was just settling himself to begin when the clock struck six, whereupon he laboured to get up, and said:—

"I must gang ageeanwards home now, miss. My grand-daughter doesn't like to be kept waitin' when the tea is ready, for it takes me time to crammle aboon the grees, for there be a many of 'em; an', miss, I lack belly-timber sairly by the clock."

He hobbled away, and I could see him hurrying, as well as he could, down the steps. The steps are a great feature on the place. They lead from the town up to the church, there are hundreds of them—I do not know how many— and they wind up in a delicate curve; the slope is so gentle that a horse could easily walk up and down them. I think they must originally have had something to do with the abbey. I shall go home too. Lucy went out visiting with her mother, and as they were only duty calls, I did not go. They will be home by this.

1 August.—I came up here an hour ago with Lucy, and we had a most interesting talk with my old friend and the two others who always come and join him. He is evidently the Sir Oracle of them, and I should think must have been in his time a most dictatorial person. He will not admit anything, and downfaces everybody. If he can't out-argue them he bullies them, and then takes their silence for agreement with his views. Lucy was looking sweetly pretty in her white lawn frock; she has got a beautiful colour since she has been here. I noticed that the old men did not lose any time in coming up and sitting near her when we sat down. She is so sweet with old people; I think they all fell in love with her on the spot. Even my old man succumbed and did not contradict her, but gave me double share instead. I got him on the subject of the legends, and he went off at once into a sort of sermon. I must try to remember it and put it down:—

"It be all fool-talk, lock, stock, and barrel; that's what it be, an' nowt else. These bans an' wafts an' boh-ghosts an' barguests an' bogles an' all anent them is only fit to set bairns an' dizzy women a-belderin'. They be nowt but air-blebs. They, an' all grims an' signs an' warnin's, be all invented by parsons an' illsome beuk-bodies an' railway touters to skeer an' scunner hafflin's, an' to get folks to do somethin' that they don't other incline to. It makes me ireful to think o' them. Why, it's them that, not content with printin' lies on paper an' preachin' them out of pulpits, does want to be cuttin' them on the tombstones. Look here all around you in what airt ye will; all them steans, holdin' up their heads as well as they can out of their pride, is acant—simply tumblin' down with the weight o' the lies wrote on them, 'Here lies the body' or 'Sacred to the memory' wrote on all of them, an' yet in nigh half of them there bean't no bodies at all; an' the memories of them bean't cared a pinch of snuff about, much less sacred. Lies all of them, nothin' but lies of one kind or another! My gog, but it'll be a quare scowderment at the Day of Judgment when they come tumblin' up in their death-sarks, all jouped together an' tryin' to drag their tombsteans with them to prove how good they was; some of them trimmlin' and ditherin', with their hands that dozzened an' slippy from lyin' in the sea that they can't even keep their grup o' them."

I could see from the old fellow's self-satisfied air and the way in which he looked round for the approval of his cronies that he was "showing off," so I put in a word to keep him going:—

"Oh, Mr. Swales, you can't be serious. Surely these tombstones are not all wrong?"

"Yabblins! There may be a poorish few not wrong, savin' where they make out the people too good; for there be folk that do think a balm-bowl be like the sea, if only it be their own. The whole thing be only lies. Now look you here; you come here a stranger, an' you see this kirk-garth." I nodded, for I thought it better to assent, though I did not quite understand his dialect. I knew it had something to do with the church. He went on: "And you consate that all these steans be aboon folk that be happed here, snod an' snog?" I assented again. "Then that be just where the lie comes in. Why, there be scores of these lay-beds that be toom as old Dun's 'bacca-box on Friday night." He nudged one of his companions, and they all laughed. "And my gog! how could they be otherwise? Look at that one, the aftest abaft the bier-bank: read it!" I went over and read:—

"Edward Spencelagh, master mariner, murdered by pirates off the coast of Andres, April, 1854, æt. 30." When I came back Mr. Swales went on:—

"Who brought him home, I wonder, to hap him here? Murdered off the coast of Andres! an' you consated his body lay under! Why, I could name ye a dozen whose bones lie in the Greenland seas above"—he pointed northwards—"or where the currents may have drifted them. There be the steans around ye. Ye can, with your young eyes, read the small-print of the lies from here. This Braithwaite Lowrey—I knew his father, lost in the *Lively* off Greenland in '20; or Andrew Woodhouse, drowned in the same seas in 1777; or John Paxton, drowned off Cape Farewell a year later; or old John Rawlings, whose grandfather sailed with me, drowned in the Gulf of Finland in '50. Do ye think that all these men will have to make a rush to Whitby when the trumpet sounds? I have me antherums aboot it! I tell ye that when they got here they'd be jommlin' an' jostlin' one another that way that it 'ud be like a fight up on the ice in the old days, when we'd be at one another from daylight to dark, an' tryin' to tie up our cuts by the light of the aurora borealis." This was evidently local pleasantry, for the old man cackled over it, and his cronies joined in with gusto.

"But," I said, "surely you are not quite correct, for you start on the assumption that all the poor people, or their spirits, will have to take their tombstones with them on the Day of Judgment. Do you think that will be really necessary?"

"Well, what else be they tombstones for? Answer me that, miss!"

"To please their relatives, I suppose."

"To please their relatives, you suppose!" This he said with intense scorn. "How will it pleasure their relatives to know that lies is wrote over them, and that everybody in the place knows that they be lies?" He pointed to a stone at our feet which had been laid down as a slab, on which the seat was rested, close to the edge of the cliff. "Read the lies on that thruff-stean," he said. The letters were upside down to me from where I sat, but Lucy was more opposite to them, so she leant over and read:—

"Sacred to the memory of George Canon, who died, in the hope of a glorious resurrection, on July, 29, 1873, falling from the rocks at Kettleness.

This tomb was erected by his sorrowing mother to her dearly beloved son. 'He was the only son of his mother, and she was a widow.' Really, Mr. Swales, I don't see anything very funny in that!" She spoke her comment very gravely and somewhat severely.

"Ye don't see aught funny! Ha! ha! But that's because ye don't gawm the sorrowin' mother was a hell-cat that hated him because he was acrewk'd—a regular lamiter he was—an' he hated her so that he committed suicide in order that she mightn't get an insurance she put on his life. He blew nigh the top of his head off with an old musket that they had for scarin' the crows with. 'Twarn't for crows then, for it brought the clegs and the dowps to him. That's the way he fell off the rocks. And, as to hopes of a glorious resurrection, I've often heard him say masel' that he hoped he'd go to hell, for his mother was so pious that she'd be sure to go to heaven, an' he didn't want to addle where she was. Now isn't that stean at any rate"—he hammered it with his stick as he spoke—"a pack of lies? and won't it make Gabriel keckle when Geordie comes pantin' up the grees with the tombstean balanced on his hump, and asks it to be took as evidence!"

I did not know what to say, but Lucy turned the conversation as she said, rising up:—

"Oh, why did you tell us of this? It is my favourite seat, and I cannot leave it; and now I find I must go on sitting over the grave of a suicide."

"That won't harm ye, my pretty; an' it may make poor Geordie gladsome to have so trim a lass sittin' on his lap. That won't hurt ye. Why, I've sat here off an' on for nigh twenty years past, an' it hasn't done me no harm. Don't ye fash about them as lies under ye, or that doesn' lie there either! It'll be time for ye to be getting scart when ye see the tombsteans all run away with, and the place as bare as a stubble-field. There's the clock, an' I must gang. My service to ye, ladies!" And off he hobbled.

Lucy and I sat awhile, and it was all so beautiful before us that we took hands as we sat; and she told me all over again about Arthur and their coming marriage. That made me just a little heart-sick, for I haven't heard from Jonathan for a whole month.

The same day. I came up here alone, for I am very sad. There was no letter for me. I hope there cannot be anything the matter with Jonathan. The clock has just struck nine. I see the lights scattered all over the town, sometimes in rows where the streets are, and sometimes singly; they run right up the Esk and die away in the curve of the valley. To my left the view is cut off by a black line of roof of the old house next the abbey. The sheep and lambs are bleating in the fields away behind me, and there is a clatter of a donkey's hoofs up the paved road below. The band on the pier is playing a harsh waltz in good time, and further along the quay there is a Salvation Army meeting in a back street. Neither of the bands hears the other, but up here I hear and see them both. I wonder where Jonathan is and if he is thinking of me! I wish he were here.

DR. SEWARD'S DIARY.

5 June.—The case of Renfield grows more interesting the more I get to understand the man. He has certain qualities very largely developed; selfishness, secrecy, and purpose. I wish I could get at what is the object of the latter. He seems to have some settled scheme of his own, but what it is I do not yet know. His redeeming quality is a love of animals, though, indeed, he has such curious turns in it that I sometimes imagine he is only abnormally cruel. His pets are of odd sorts. Just now his hobby is catching flies. He has at present such a quantity that I have had myself to expostulate. To my astonishment, he did not break out into a fury, as I expected, but took the matter in simple seriousness. He thought for a moment, and then said: "May I have three days? I shall clear them away." Of course, I said that would do. I must watch him.

18 June.—He has turned his mind now to spiders, and has got several very big fellows in a box. He keeps feeding them with his flies, and the number of the latter is becoming sensibly diminished, although he has used half his food in attracting more flies from outside to his room.

1 July.—His spiders are now becoming as great a nuisance as his flies, and to-day I told him that he must get rid of them. He looked very sad at this, so I said that he must clear out some of them, at all events. He cheerfully acquiesced in this, and I gave him the same time as before for reduction. He disgusted me much while with him, for when a horrid blow-fly, bloated with some carrion food, buzzed into the room, he caught it, held it exultantly for a few moments between his finger and thumb, and, before I knew what he was going to do, put it in his mouth and ate it. I scolded him for it, but he argued quietly that it was very good and very wholesome; that it was life, strong life, and gave life to him. This gave me an idea, or the rudiment of one. I must watch how he gets rid of his spiders. He has evidently some deep problem in his mind, for he keeps a little note-book in which he is always jotting down something. Whole pages of it are filled with masses of figures, generally single numbers added up in batches, and then the totals added in batches again, as though he were "focussing" some account, as the auditors put it.

8 July.—There is a method in his madness, and the rudimentary idea in my mind is growing. It will be a whole idea soon, and then, oh, unconscious cerebration! you will have to give the wall to your conscious brother. I kept away from my friend for a few days, so that I might notice if there were any change. Things remain as they were except that he has parted with some of his pets and got a new one. He has managed to get a sparrow, and has already partially tamed it. His means of taming is simple, for already the spiders have diminished. Those that do remain, however, are well fed, for he still brings in the flies by tempting them with his food.

19 July.—We are progressing. My friend has now a whole colony of sparrows, and his flies and spiders are almost obliterated. When I came in he ran to me and said he wanted to ask me a great favour—a very, very great favour; and as he spoke he fawned on me like a dog. I asked him what it was, and he said, with a sort of rapture in his voice and bearing:—

"A kitten, a nice little, sleek playful kitten, that I can play with, and teach, and feed—and feed—and feed!" I was not unprepared for this request, for I had noticed how his pets went on increasing in size and vivacity, but I did not care that his pretty family of tame sparrows should be wiped out in the same manner as the flies and the spiders; so I said I would see about it, and asked him if he would not rather have a cat than a kitten. His eagerness betrayed him as he answered:—

"Oh, yes, I would like a cat! I only asked for a kitten lest you should refuse me a cat. No one would refuse me a kitten, would they?" I shook my head, and said that at present I feared it would not be possible, but that I would see about it. His face fell, and I could see a warning of danger in it, for there was a sudden fierce, sidelong look which meant killing. The man is an undeveloped homicidal maniac. I shall test him with his present craving and see how it will work out; then I shall know more.

10 p. m.—I have visited him again and found him sitting in a corner brooding. When I came in he threw himself on his knees before me and implored me to let him have a cat; that his salvation depended upon it. I was firm, however, and told him that he could not have it, whereupon he went without a word, and sat down, gnawing his fingers, in the corner where I had found him. I shall see him in the morning early.

20 July.—Visited Renfield very early, before the attendant went his rounds. Found him up and humming a tune. He was spreading out his sugar, which he had saved, in the window, and was manifestly beginning his fly-catching again; and beginning it cheerfully and with a good grace. I looked around for his birds, and not seeing them, asked him where they were. He replied, without turning round, that they had all flown away. There were a few feathers about the room and on his pillow a drop of blood. I said nothing, but went and told the keeper to report to me if there were anything odd about him during the day.

11 a. m.—The attendant has just been to me to say that Renfield has been very sick and has disgorged a whole lot of feathers. "My belief is, doctor," he said, "that he has eaten his birds, and that he just took and ate them raw!"

11 p. m.—I gave Renfield a strong opiate to-night, enough to make even him sleep, and took away his pocket-book to look at it. The thought that has been buzzing about my brain lately is complete, and the theory proved. My homicidal maniac is of a peculiar kind. I shall have to invent a new classification for him, and call him a zoöphagous (life-eating) maniac; what he desires is to absorb as many lives as he can, and he has laid himself out to achieve it in a cumulative way. He gave many flies to one spider and many spiders to one bird, and then wanted a cat to eat the many birds. What would have been his later steps? It would almost be worth while to complete the experiment. It might be done if there were only a sufficient cause. Men sneered at vivisection, and yet look at its results to-day! Why not advance science in its most difficult and vital aspect—the knowledge of the brain? Had I even the secret of one such mind—did I hold the key to the fancy of even one lunatic—I might advance my own branch of science to a pitch compared with which Burdon-Sanderson's physiology or Ferrier's brain-knowledge would be as nothing. If only there were a sufficient cause! I must not think too much of this, or I may be tempted; a good cause might turn the scale with me, for may not I too be of an exceptional brain, congenitally?

How well the man reasoned; lunatics always do within their own scope. I wonder at how many lives he values a man, or if at only one. He has closed the account most accurately, and to-day begun a new record. How many of us begin a new record with each day of our lives?

To me it seems only yesterday that my whole life ended with my new hope, and that truly I began a new record. So it will be until the Great Recorder sums me up and closes my ledger account with a balance to profit or loss. Oh, Lucy, Lucy, I cannot be angry with you, nor can I be angry with my friend whose happiness is yours; but I must only wait on hopeless and work. Work! work!

If I only could have as strong a cause as my poor mad friend there—a good, unselfish cause to make me work—that would be indeed happiness.

MINA MURRAY'S JOURNAL.

26 July.—I am anxious, and it soothes me to express myself here; it is like whispering to one's self and listening at the same time. And there is also something about the shorthand symbols that makes it different from writing. I am unhappy about Lucy and about Jonathan. I had not heard from Jonathan for some time, and was very concerned; but yesterday dear Mr. Hawkins, who is always so kind, sent me a letter from him. I had written asking him if he had heard, and he said the enclosed had just been received. It is only a line dated from Castle Dracula, and says that he is just starting for home. That is not like Jonathan; I do not understand it, and it makes me uneasy. Then, too, Lucy, although she is so well, has lately taken to her old habit of walking in her sleep. Her mother has spoken to me about it, and we have decided that I am to lock the door of our room every night. Mrs. Westenra has got an idea that sleep-walkers always go out on roofs of houses and along the edges of cliffs and then get suddenly wakened and fall over with a despairing cry that echoes all over the place. Poor dear, she is naturally anxious about Lucy, and she tells me that her husband, Lucy's father, had the same habit; that he would get up in the night and dress himself and go out, if he were not stopped. Lucy is to be married in the autumn, and she is already planning out her dresses and how her house is to be arranged. I sympathise with her, for I do the same, only Jonathan and I will start in life in a very simple way, and shall have to try to make both ends meet. Mr. Holmwood— he is the Hon. Arthur Holmwood, only son of Lord Godalming—is coming up here very shortly—as soon as he can leave town, for his father is not very well, and I think dear Lucy is counting the moments till he comes. She wants to take him up to the seat on the churchyard cliff and show him the beauty of Whitby. I daresay it is the waiting which disturbs her; she will be all right when he arrives.

27 July.—No news from Jonathan. I am getting quite uneasy about him, though why I should I do not know; but I do wish that he would write, if it were only a single line. Lucy walks more than ever, and each night I am awakened by her moving about the room. Fortunately, the weather is so hot that she cannot get cold; but still the anxiety and the perpetually being wakened is beginning to tell on me, and I am getting nervous and wakeful myself. Thank God, Lucy's health keeps up. Mr. Holmwood has been suddenly called to Ring to see his father, who has been taken seriously ill. Lucy frets at the postponement of seeing him, but it does not touch her looks; she is a trifle stouter, and her cheeks are a lovely rose-pink. She has lost that anæmic look which she had. I pray it will all last.

3 August.—Another week gone, and no news from Jonathan, not even to Mr. Hawkins, from whom I have heard. Oh, I do hope he is not ill. He surely would have written. I look at that last letter of his, but somehow it does not satisfy me. It does not read like him, and yet it is his writing. There is no mistake of that. Lucy has not walked much in her sleep the last week, but there is an odd concentration about her which I do not understand; even in her sleep she seems to be watching me. She tries the door, and finding it locked, goes about the room searching for the key.

6 August.—Another three days, and no news. This suspense is getting dreadful. If I only knew where to write to or where to go to, I should feel easier; but no one has heard a word of Jonathan since that last letter. I must only pray to God for patience. Lucy is more excitable than ever, but is otherwise well. Last night was very threatening, and the fishermen say that we are in for a storm. I must try to watch it and learn the weather signs. To-day is a grey day, and the sun as I write is hidden in thick clouds, high over Kettleness. Everything is grey—except the green grass, which seems like emerald amongst it; grey earthy rock; grey clouds, tinged with the sunburst at the far edge, hang over the grey sea, into which the sand-points stretch like grey fingers. The sea is tumbling in over the shallows and the sandy flats with a roar, muffled in the sea-mists drifting inland. The horizon is lost in a grey mist. All is vastness; the clouds are piled up like giant rocks, and there is a "brool" over the sea that sounds like some presage of doom. Dark figures are on the beach here and there, sometimes half shrouded in the mist, and seem "men like trees walking." The fishing-boats are racing for home, and rise and dip in the ground swell as they sweep into the harbour, bending to the scuppers. Here comes old Mr. Swales. He is making straight for me, and I can see, by the way he lifts his hat, that he wants to talk . . . .

I have been quite touched by the change in the poor old man. When he sat down beside me, he said in a very gentle way:—

"I want to say something to you, miss." I could see he was not at ease, so I took his poor old wrinkled hand in mine and asked him to speak fully; so he said, leaving his hand in mine:—

"I'm afraid, my deary, that I must have shocked you by all the wicked things I've been sayin' about the dead, and such like, for weeks past; but I didn't mean them, and I want ye to remember that when I'm gone. We aud folks that be daffled, and with one foot abaft the krok-hooal, don't altogether like to think of it, and we don't want to feel scart of it; an' that's why I've took to makin' light of it, so that I'd cheer up my own heart a bit. But, Lord love ye, miss, I ain't afraid of dyin', not a bit; only I don't want to die if I can help it. My time must be nigh at hand now, for I be aud, and a hundred years is too much for any man to expect; and I'm so nigh it that the Aud Man is already whettin' his scythe. Ye see, I can't get out o' the habit of caffin' about it all at once; the chafts will wag as they be used to. Some day soon the Angel of Death will sound his trumpet for me. But don't ye dooal an' greet, my deary!"—for he saw that I was crying—"if he should come this very night I'd not refuse to answer his call. For life be, after all, only a waitin' for somethin' else than what we're doin'; and death be all that we can rightly depend on. But I'm content, for it's comin' to me, my deary, and comin' quick. It may be comin' while we be lookin' and wonderin'. Maybe it's in that wind out over the sea that's bringin' with it loss and wreck, and sore distress, and sad hearts. Look! look!" he cried suddenly. "There's something in that wind and in the hoast beyont that sounds, and looks, and tastes, and smells like death. It's in the air; I feel it comin'. Lord, make me answer cheerful when my call comes!" He held up his arms devoutly, and raised his hat. His mouth moved as though he were praying. After a few minutes' silence, he got up, shook hands with me, and blessed me, and said good-bye, and hobbled off. It all touched me, and upset me very much.

I was glad when the coastguard came along, with his spy-glass under his arm. He stopped to talk with me, as he always does, but all the time kept looking at a strange ship.

"I can't make her out," he said; "she's a Russian, by the look of her; but she's knocking about in the queerest way. She doesn't know her mind a bit; she seems to see the storm coming, but can't decide whether to run up north in the open, or to put in here. Look there again! She is steered mighty strangely, for she doesn't mind the hand on the wheel; changes about with every puff of wind. We'll hear more of her before this time to-morrow."

CHAPTER VII

CUTTING FROM "THE DAILYGRAPH," 8 AUGUST

(Pasted in Mina Murray's Journal.)

From a Correspondent.

Whitby.

ONE greatest and suddenest storms on record has just been experienced here, with results both strange and unique. The weather had been somewhat sultry, but not to any degree uncommon in the month of August. Saturday evening was as fine as was ever known, and the great body of holiday-makers laid out yesterday for visits to Mulgrave Woods, Robin Hood's Bay, Rig Mill, Runswick, Staithes, and the various trips in the neighbourhood of Whitby. The steamers *Emma* and *Scarborough* made trips up and down the coast, and there was an unusual amount of "tripping" both to and from Whitby. The day was unusually fine till the afternoon, when some of the gossips who frequent the East Cliff churchyard, and from that commanding eminence watch the wide sweep of sea visible to the north and east, called attention to a sudden show of "mares'-tails" high in the sky to the north-west. The wind was then blowing from the south-west in the mild degree which in barometrical language is ranked "No. 2: light breeze." The coastguard on duty at once made report, and one old fisherman, who for more than half a century has kept watch on weather signs from the East Cliff, foretold in an emphatic manner the coming of a sudden storm. The approach of sunset was so very beautiful, so grand in its masses of splendidly-coloured clouds, that there was quite an assemblage on the walk along the cliff in the old churchyard to enjoy the beauty. Before the sun dipped below the black mass of Kettleness, standing boldly athwart the western sky, its downward way was marked by myriad clouds of every sunset-colour—flame, purple, pink, green, violet, and all the tints of gold; with here and there masses not large, but of seemingly absolute blackness, in all sorts of shapes, as well outlined as colossal silhouettes. The experience was not lost on the painters, and doubtless some of the sketches of the "Prelude to the Great Storm" will grace the R. A. and R. I. walls in May next. More than one captain made up his mind then and there that his "cobble" or his "mule," as they term the different classes of boats, would remain in the harbour till the storm had passed. The wind fell away entirely during the evening, and at midnight there was a dead calm, a sultry heat, and that prevailing intensity which, on the approach of thunder, affects persons of a sensitive nature. There were but few lights in sight at sea, for even the coasting steamers, which usually "hug" the shore so closely, kept well to seaward, and but few fishing-boats were in sight. The only sail noticeable was a foreign schooner with all sails set, which was seemingly going westwards. The foolhardiness or ignorance of her officers was a prolific theme for comment whilst she remained in sight, and efforts were made to signal her to reduce sail in face of her danger. Before the night shut down she was seen with sails idly flapping as she gently rolled on the undulating swell of the sea,

"As idle as a painted ship upon a painted ocean."

Shortly before ten o'clock the stillness of the air grew quite oppressive, and the silence was so marked that the bleating of a sheep inland or the barking of a dog in the town was distinctly heard, and the band on the pier, with its lively French air, was like a discord in the great harmony of nature's silence. A little after midnight came a strange sound from over the sea, and high overhead the air began to carry a strange, faint, hollow booming.

Then without warning the tempest broke. With a rapidity which, at the time, seemed incredible, and even afterwards is impossible to realize, the whole aspect of nature at once became convulsed. The waves rose in growing fury, each overtopping its fellow, till in a very few minutes the lately glassy sea was like a roaring and devouring monster. White-crested waves beat madly on the level sands and rushed up the shelving cliffs; others broke over the piers, and with their spume swept the lanthorns of the lighthouses which rise from the end of either pier of Whitby Harbour. The wind roared like thunder, and blew with such force that it was with difficulty that even strong men kept their feet, or clung with grim clasp to the iron stanchions. It was found necessary to clear the entire piers from the mass of onlookers, or else the fatalities of the night would have been increased manifold. To add to the difficulties and dangers of the time, masses of sea-fog came drifting inland—white, wet clouds, which swept by in ghostly fashion, so dank and damp and cold that it needed but little effort of imagination to think that the spirits of those lost at sea were touching their living brethren with the clammy hands of death, and many a one shuddered as the wreaths of sea-mist swept by. At times the mist cleared, and the sea for some distance could be seen in the glare of the lightning, which now came thick and fast, followed by such sudden peals of thunder that the whole sky overhead seemed trembling under the shock of the footsteps of the storm.

Some of the scenes thus revealed were of immeasurable grandeur and of absorbing interest—the sea, running mountains high, threw skywards with each wave mighty masses of white foam, which the tempest seemed to snatch at and whirl away into space; here and there a fishing-boat, with a rag of sail, running madly for shelter before the blast; now and again the white wings of a storm-tossed sea-bird. On the summit of the East Cliff the new searchlight was ready for experiment, but had not yet been tried. The officers in charge of it got it into working order, and in the pauses of the inrushing mist swept with it the surface of the sea. Once or twice its service was most effective, as when a fishing-boat, with gunwale under water, rushed into the harbour, able, by the guidance of the sheltering light, to avoid the danger of dashing against the piers. As each boat achieved the safety of the port there was a shout of joy from the mass of people on shore, a shout which for a moment seemed to cleave the gale and was then swept away in its rush.

Before long the searchlight discovered some distance away a schooner with all sails set, apparently the same vessel which had been noticed earlier in the evening. The wind had by this time backed to the east, and there was a shudder amongst the watchers on the cliff as they realized the terrible danger in which she now was. Between her and the port lay the great flat reef on which so many good ships have from time to time suffered, and, with the wind blowing from its present quarter, it would be quite impossible that she should fetch the entrance of the harbour. It was now nearly the hour of high tide, but the waves were so great that in their troughs the shallows of the shore were almost visible, and the schooner, with all sails set, was rushing with such speed that, in the words of one old salt, "she must fetch up somewhere, if it was only in hell." Then came another rush of sea-fog, greater than any hitherto—a mass of dank mist, which seemed to close on all things like a grey pall, and left available to men only the organ of hearing, for the roar of the tempest, and the crash of the thunder, and the booming of the mighty billows came through the damp oblivion even louder than before. The rays of the searchlight were kept fixed on the harbour mouth across the East Pier, where the shock was expected, and men waited breathless. The wind suddenly shifted to the north-east, and the remnant of the sea-fog melted in the blast; and then, *mirabile dictu*, between the piers, leaping from wave to wave as it rushed at headlong speed, swept the strange schooner before the blast, with all sail set, and gained the safety of the harbour. The searchlight followed her, and a shudder ran through all who saw her, for lashed to the helm was a corpse, with drooping head, which swung horribly to and fro at each motion of the ship. No other form could be seen on deck at all. A great awe came on all as they realised that the ship, as if by a miracle, had found the harbour, unsteered save by the hand of a dead man! However, all took place more quickly than it takes to write these words. The schooner paused not, but rushing across the harbour, pitched herself on that accumulation of sand and gravel washed by many tides and many storms into the south-east corner of the pier jutting under the East Cliff, known locally as Tate Hill Pier.

There was of course a considerable concussion as the vessel drove up on the sand heap. Every spar, rope, and stay was strained, and some of the "top-hammer" came crashing down. But, strangest of all, the very instant the shore was touched, an immense dog sprang up on deck from below, as if shot up by the concussion, and running forward, jumped from the bow on the sand. Making straight for the steep cliff, where the churchyard hangs over the laneway to the East Pier so steeply that some of the flat tombstones—"thruff-steans" or "through-stones," as they call them in the Whitby vernacular—actually project over where the sustaining cliff has fallen away, it disappeared in the darkness, which seemed intensified just beyond the focus of the searchlight.

It so happened that there was no one at the moment on Tate Hill Pier, as all those whose houses are in close proximity were either in bed or were out on the heights above. Thus the coastguard on duty on the eastern side of the harbour, who at once ran down to the little pier, was the first to climb on board. The men working the searchlight, after scouring the entrance of the harbour without seeing anything, then turned the light on the derelict and kept it there. The coastguard ran aft, and when he came beside the wheel, bent over to examine it, and recoiled at once as though under some sudden emotion. This seemed to pique general curiosity, and quite a number of people began to run. It is a good way round from the West Cliff by the Drawbridge to Tate Hill Pier, but your correspondent is a fairly good runner, and came well ahead of the crowd. When I arrived, however, I found already assembled on the pier a crowd, whom the coastguard and police refused to allow to come on board. By the courtesy of the chief boatman, I was, as your correspondent, permitted to climb on deck, and was one of a small group who saw the dead seaman whilst actually lashed to the wheel.

It was no wonder that the coastguard was surprised, or even awed, for not often can such a sight have been seen. The man was simply fastened by his hands, tied one over the other, to a spoke of the wheel. Between the inner hand and the wood was a crucifix, the set of beads on which it was fastened being around both wrists and wheel, and all kept fast by the binding cords. The poor fellow may have been seated at one time, but the flapping and buffeting of the sails had worked through the rudder of the wheel and dragged him to and fro, so that the cords with which he was tied had cut the flesh to the bone. Accurate note was made of the state of things, and a doctor—Surgeon J. M. Caffyn, of 33, East Elliot Place—who came immediately after me, declared, after making examination, that the man must have been dead for quite two days. In his pocket was a bottle, carefully corked, empty save for a little roll of paper, which proved to be the addendum to the log. The coastguard said the man must have tied up his own hands, fastening the knots with his teeth. The fact that a coastguard was the first on board may save some complications, later on, in the Admiralty Court; for coastguards cannot claim the salvage which is the right of the first civilian entering on a derelict. Already, however, the legal tongues are wagging, and one young law student is loudly asserting that the rights of the owner are already completely sacrificed, his property being held in contravention of the statutes of mortmain, since the tiller, as emblemship, if not proof, of delegated possession, is held in a *dead hand*. It is needless to say that the dead steersman has been reverently removed from the place where he held his honourable watch and ward till death—a steadfastness as noble as that of the young Casabianca—and placed in the mortuary to await inquest.

Already the sudden storm is passing, and its fierceness is abating; crowds are scattering homeward, and the sky is beginning to redden over the Yorkshire wolds. I shall send, in time for your next issue, further details of the derelict ship which found her way so miraculously into harbour in the storm.

Whitby

9 August.—The sequel to the strange arrival of the derelict in the storm last night is almost more startling than the thing itself. It turns out that the schooner is a Russian from Varna, and is called the *Demeter*. She is almost entirely in ballast of silver sand, with only a small amount of cargo—a number of great wooden boxes filled with mould. This cargo was consigned to a Whitby solicitor, Mr. S. F. Billington, of 7, The Crescent, who this morning went aboard and formally took possession of the goods consigned to him. The Russian consul, too, acting for the charter-party, took formal possession of the ship, and paid all harbour dues, etc. Nothing is talked about here to-day except the strange coincidence; the officials of the Board of Trade have been most exacting in seeing that every compliance has been made with existing regulations. As the matter is to be a "nine days' wonder," they are evidently determined that there shall be no cause of after complaint. A good deal of interest was abroad concerning the dog which landed when the ship struck, and more than a few of the members of the S. P. C. A., which is very strong in Whitby, have tried to befriend the animal. To the general disappointment, however, it was not to be found; it seems to have disappeared entirely from the town. It may be that it was frightened and made its way on to the moors, where it is still hiding in terror. There are some who look with dread on such a possibility, lest later on it should in itself become a danger, for it is evidently a fierce brute. Early this morning a large dog, a half-bred mastiff belonging to a coal merchant close to Tate Hill Pier, was found dead in the roadway opposite to its master's yard. It had been fighting, and manifestly had had a savage opponent, for its throat was torn away, and its belly was slit open as if with a savage claw.

Later.—By the kindness of the Board of Trade inspector, I have been permitted to look over the log-book of the *Demeter*, which was in order up to within three days, but contained nothing of special interest except as to facts of missing men. The greatest interest, however, is with regard to the paper found in the bottle, which was to-day produced at the inquest; and a more strange narrative than the two between them unfold it has not been my lot to come across. As there is no motive for concealment, I am permitted to use them, and accordingly send you a rescript, simply omitting technical details of seamanship and supercargo. It almost seems as though the captain had been seized with some kind of mania before he had got well into blue water, and that this had developed persistently throughout the voyage. Of course my statement must be taken *cum grano*, since I am writing from the dictation of a clerk of the Russian consul, who kindly translated for me, time being short.

LOG OF THE "DEMETER."

Varna to Whitby.

Written 18 July, things so strange happening, that I shall keep accurate note henceforth till we land.

On 6 July we finished taking in cargo, silver sand and boxes of earth. At noon set sail. East wind, fresh. Crew, five hands . . . two mates, cook, and myself (captain).

On 11 July at dawn entered Bosphorus. Boarded by Turkish Customs officers. Backsheesh. All correct. Under way at 4 p. m.

On 12 July through Dardanelles. More Customs officers and flagboat of guarding squadron. Backsheesh again. Work of officers thorough, but quick. Want us off soon. At dark passed into Archipelago.

On 13 July passed Cape Matapan. Crew dissatisfied about something. Seemed scared, but would not speak out.

On 14 July was somewhat anxious about crew. Men all steady fellows, who sailed with me before. Mate could not make out what was wrong; they only told him there was *something*, and crossed themselves. Mate lost temper with one of them that day and struck him. Expected fierce quarrel, but all was quiet.

On 16 July mate reported in the morning that one of crew, Petrofsky, was missing. Could not account for it. Took larboard watch eight bells last night; was relieved by Abramoff, but did not go to bunk. Men more downcast than ever. All said they expected something of the kind, but would not say more than there was *something* aboard. Mate getting very impatient with them; feared some trouble ahead.

On 17 July, yesterday, one of the men, Olgaren, came to my cabin, and in an awestruck way confided to me that he thought there was a strange man aboard the ship. He said that in his watch he had been sheltering behind the deck-house, as there was a rain-storm, when he saw a tall, thin man, who was not like any of the crew, come up the companion-way, and go along the deck forward, and disappear. He followed cautiously, but when he got to bows found no one, and the hatchways were all closed. He was in a panic of superstitious fear, and I am afraid the panic may spread. To allay it, I shall to-day search entire ship carefully from stem to stern.

Later in the day I got together the whole crew, and told them, as they evidently thought there was some one in the ship, we would search from stem to stern. First mate angry; said it was folly, and to yield to such foolish ideas would demoralise the men; said he would engage to keep them out of trouble with a handspike. I let him take the helm, while the rest began thorough search, all keeping abreast, with lanterns: we left no corner unsearched. As there were only the big wooden boxes, there were no odd corners where a man could hide. Men much relieved when search over, and went back to work cheerfully. First mate scowled, but said nothing.

22 July.—Rough weather last three days, and all hands busy with sails— no time to be frightened. Men seem to have forgotten their dread. Mate cheerful again, and all on good terms. Praised men for work in bad weather.

Passed Gibralter and out through Straits. All well.

24 July.—There seems some doom over this ship. Already a hand short, and entering on the Bay of Biscay with wild weather ahead, and yet last night another man lost—disappeared. Like the first, he came off his watch and was not seen again. Men all in a panic of fear; sent a round robin, asking to have double watch, as they fear to be alone. Mate angry. Fear there will be some trouble, as either he or the men will do some violence.

28 July.—Four days in hell, knocking about in a sort of maelstrom, and the wind a tempest. No sleep for any one. Men all worn out. Hardly know how to set a watch, since no one fit to go on. Second mate volunteered to steer and watch, and let men snatch a few hours' sleep. Wind abating; seas still terrific, but feel them less, as ship is steadier.

29 July.—Another tragedy. Had single watch to-night, as crew too tired to double. When morning watch came on deck could find no one except steersman. Raised outcry, and all came on deck. Thorough search, but no one found. Are now without second mate, and crew in a panic. Mate and I agreed to go armed henceforth and wait for any sign of cause.

30 July.—Last night. Rejoiced we are nearing England. Weather fine, all sails set. Retired worn out; slept soundly; awaked by mate telling me that both man of watch and steersman missing. Only self and mate and two hands left to work ship.

1 August.—Two days of fog, and not a sail sighted. Had hoped when in the English Channel to be able to signal for help or get in somewhere. Not having power to work sails, have to run before wind. Dare not lower, as could not raise them again. We seem to be drifting to some terrible doom. Mate now more demoralised than either of men. His stronger nature seems to have worked inwardly against himself. Men are beyond fear, working stolidly and patiently, with minds made up to worst. They are Russian, he Roumanian.

2 August, midnight.—Woke up from few minutes' sleep by hearing a cry, seemingly outside my port. Could see nothing in fog. Rushed on deck, and ran against mate. Tells me heard cry and ran, but no sign of man on watch. One more gone. Lord, help us! Mate says we must be past Straits of Dover, as in a moment of fog lifting he saw North Foreland, just as he heard the man cry out. If so we are now off in the North Sea, and only God can guide us in the fog, which seems to move with us; and God seems to have deserted us.

3 August.—At midnight I went to relieve the man at the wheel, and when I got to it found no one there. The wind was steady, and as we ran before it there was no yawing. I dared not leave it, so shouted for the mate. After a few seconds he rushed up on deck in his flannels. He looked wild-eyed and haggard, and I greatly fear his reason has given way. He came close to me and whispered hoarsely, with his mouth to my ear, as though fearing the very air might hear: "*It* is here; I know it, now. On the watch last night I saw It, like a man, tall and thin, and ghastly pale. It was in the bows, and looking out. I crept behind It, and gave It my knife; but the knife went through It, empty as the air." And as he spoke he took his knife and drove it savagely into space. Then he went on: "But It is here, and I'll find It. It is in the hold, perhaps in one of those boxes. I'll unscrew them one by one and see. You work the helm." And, with a warning look and his finger on his lip, he went below. There was springing up a choppy wind, and I could not leave the helm. I saw him come out on deck again with a tool-chest and a lantern, and go down the forward hatchway. He is mad, stark, raving mad, and it's no use my trying to stop him. He can't hurt those big boxes: they are invoiced as "clay," and to pull them about is as harmless a thing as he can do. So here I stay, and mind the helm, and write these notes. I can only trust in God and wait till the fog clears. Then, if I can't steer to any harbour with the wind that is, I shall cut down sails and lie by, and signal for help . . . .

It is nearly all over now. Just as I was beginning to hope that the mate would come out calmer—for I heard him knocking away at something in the hold, and work is good for him—there came up the hatchway a sudden, startled scream, which made my blood run cold, and up on the deck he came as if shot from a gun—a raging madman, with his eyes rolling and his face convulsed with fear. "Save me! save me!" he cried, and then looked round on the blanket of fog. His horror turned to despair, and in a steady voice he said: "You had better come too, captain, before it is too late. *He* is there. I know the secret now. The sea will save me from Him, and it is all that is left!" Before I could say a word, or move forward to seize him, he sprang on the bulwark and deliberately threw himself into the sea. I suppose I know the secret too, now. It was this madman who had got rid of the men one by one, and now he has followed them himself. God help me! How am I to account for all these horrors when I get to port? *When* I get to port! Will that ever be?

4 August.—Still fog, which the sunrise cannot pierce. I know there is sunrise because I am a sailor, why else I know not. I dared not go below, I dared not leave the helm; so here all night I stayed, and in the dimness of the night I saw It—Him! God forgive me, but the mate was right to jump overboard. It was better to die like a man; to die like a sailor in blue water no man can object. But I am captain, and I must not leave my ship. But I shall baffle this fiend or monster, for I shall tie my hands to the wheel when my strength begins to fail, and along with them I shall tie that which He—

It!—dare not touch; and then, come good wind or foul, I shall save my soul, and my honour as a captain. I am growing weaker, and the night is coming on. If He can look me in the face again, I may not have time to act . . . . If we are wrecked, mayhap this bottle may be found, and those who find it may understand; if not, . . . well, then all men shall know that I have been true to my trust. God and the Blessed Virgin and the saints help a poor ignorant soul trying to do his duty . . . .

Of course the verdict was an open one. There is no evidence to adduce; and whether or not the man himself committed the murders there is now none to say. The folk here hold almost universally that the captain is simply a hero, and he is to be given a public funeral. Already it is arranged that his body is to be taken with a train of boats up the Esk for a piece and then brought back to Tate Hill Pier and up the abbey steps; for he is to be buried in the churchyard on the cliff. The owners of more than a hundred boats have already given in their names as wishing to follow him to the grave.

No trace has ever been found of the great dog; at which there is much mourning, for, with public opinion in its present state, he would, I believe, be adopted by the town. To-morrow will see the funeral; and so will end this one more "mystery of the sea."

MINA MURRAY'S JOURNAL.

8 August.—Lucy was very restless all night, and I, too, could not sleep. The storm was fearful, and as it boomed loudly among the chimney-pots, it made me shudder. When a sharp puff came it seemed to be like a distant gun. Strangely enough, Lucy did not wake; but she got up twice and dressed herself. Fortunately, each time I awoke in time and managed to undress her without waking her, and got her back to bed. It is a very strange thing, this sleep-walking, for as soon as her will is thwarted in any physical way, her intention, if there be any, disappears, and she yields herself almost exactly to the routine of her life.

Early in the morning we both got up and went down to the harbour to see if anything had happened in the night. There were very few people about, and though the sun was bright, and the air clear and fresh, the big, grim-looking waves, that seemed dark themselves because the foam that topped them was like snow, forced themselves in through the narrow mouth of the harbour—like a bullying man going through a crowd. Somehow I felt glad that Jonathan was not on the sea last night, but on land. But, oh, is he on land or sea? Where is he, and how? I am getting fearfully anxious about him. If I only knew what to do, and could do anything!

10 August.—The funeral of the poor sea-captain to-day was most touching. Every boat in the harbour seemed to be there, and the coffin was carried by captains all the way from Tate Hill Pier up to the churchyard. Lucy came with me, and we went early to our old seat, whilst the cortège of boats went up the river to the Viaduct and came down again. We had a lovely view, and saw the procession nearly all the way. The poor fellow was laid to rest quite near our seat so that we stood on it when the time came and saw everything. Poor Lucy seemed much upset. She was restless and uneasy all the time, and I cannot but think that her dreaming at night is telling on her. She is quite odd in one thing: she will not admit to me that there is any cause for restlessness; or if there be, she does not understand it herself. There is an additional cause in that poor old Mr. Swales was found dead this morning on our seat, his neck being broken. He had evidently, as the doctor said, fallen back in the seat in some sort of fright, for there was a look of fear and horror on his face that the men said made them shudder. Poor dear old man! Perhaps he had seen Death with his dying eyes! Lucy is so sweet and sensitive that she feels influences more acutely than other people do. Just now she was quite upset by a little thing which I did not much heed, though I am myself very fond of animals. One of the men who came up here often to look for the boats was followed by his dog. The dog is always with him. They are both quiet persons, and I never saw the man angry, nor heard the dog bark. During the service the dog would not come to its master, who was on the seat with us, but kept a few yards off, barking and howling. Its master spoke to it gently, and then harshly, and then angrily; but it would neither come nor cease to make a noise. It was in a sort of fury, with its eyes savage, and all its hairs bristling out like a cat's tail when puss is on the war-path. Finally the man, too, got angry, and jumped down and kicked the dog, and then took it by the scruff of the neck and half dragged and half threw it on the tombstone on which the seat is fixed. The moment it touched the stone the poor thing became quiet and fell all into a tremble. It did not try to get away, but crouched down, quivering and cowering, and was in such a pitiable state of terror that I tried, though without effect, to comfort it. Lucy was full of pity, too, but she did not attempt to touch the dog, but looked at it in an agonised sort of way. I greatly fear that she is of too super-sensitive a nature to go through the world without trouble. She will be dreaming of this to-night, I am sure. The whole agglomeration of things—the ship steered into port by a dead man; his attitude, tied to the wheel with a crucifix and beads; the touching funeral; the dog, now furious and now in terror—will all afford material for her dreams.

I think it will be best for her to go to bed tired out physically, so I shall take her for a long walk by the cliffs to Robin Hood's Bay and back. She ought not to have much inclination for sleep-walking then.

CHAPTER VIII

MINA MURRAY'S JOURNAL

Same day, 11 o'clock p. m.—Oh, but I am tired! If it were not that I had made my diary a duty I should not open it to-night. We had a lovely walk. Lucy, after a while, was in gay spirits, owing, I think, to some dear cows who came nosing towards us in a field close to the lighthouse, and frightened the wits out of us. I believe we forgot everything except, of course, personal fear, and it seemed to wipe the slate clean and give us a fresh start. We had a capital "severe tea" at Robin Hood's Bay in a sweet little old-fashioned inn, with a bow-window right over the seaweed-covered rocks of the strand. I believe we should have shocked the "New Woman" with our appetites. Men are more tolerant, bless them! Then we walked home with some, or rather many, stoppages to rest, and with our hearts full of a constant dread of wild bulls. Lucy was really tired, and we intended to creep off to bed as soon as we could. The young curate came in, however, and Mrs. Westenra asked him to stay for supper. Lucy and I had both a fight for it with the dusty miller; I know it was a hard fight on my part, and I am quite heroic. I think that some day the bishops must get together and see about breeding up a new class of curates, who don't take supper, no matter how they may be pressed to, and who will know when girls are tired. Lucy is asleep and breathing softly. She has more colour in her cheeks than usual, and looks, oh, so sweet. If Mr. Holmwood fell in love with her seeing her only in the drawing-room, I wonder what he would say if he saw her now. Some of the "New Women" writers will some day start an idea that men and women should be allowed to see each other asleep before proposing or accepting. But I suppose the New Woman won't condescend in future to accept; she will do the proposing herself. And a nice job she will make of it, too! There's some consolation in that. I am so happy to-night, because dear Lucy seems better. I really believe she has turned the corner, and that we are over her troubles with dreaming. I should be quite happy if I only knew if Jonathan . . . . God bless and keep him.

11 August, 3 a. m.—Diary again. No sleep now, so I may as well write. I am too agitated to sleep. We have had such an adventure, such an agonising experience. I fell asleep as soon as I had closed my diary . . . . Suddenly I became broad awake, and sat up, with a horrible sense of fear upon me, and of some feeling of emptiness around me. The room was dark, so I could not see Lucy's bed; I stole across and felt for her. The bed was empty. I lit a match and found that she was not in the room. The door was shut, but not locked, as I had left it. I feared to wake her mother, who has been more than usually ill lately, so threw on some clothes and got ready to look for her. As I was leaving the room it struck me that the clothes she wore might give me some clue to her dreaming intention. Dressing-gown would mean house; dress, outside. Dressing-gown and dress were both in their places. "Thank God," I said to myself, "she cannot be far, as she is only in her nightdress." I ran downstairs and looked in the sitting-room. Not there! Then I looked in all the other open rooms of the house, with an ever-growing fear chilling my heart. Finally I came to the hall door and found it open. It was not wide open, but the catch of the lock had not caught. The people of the house are careful to lock the door every night, so I feared that Lucy must have gone out as she was. There was no time to think of what might happen; a vague, overmastering fear obscured all details. I took a big, heavy shawl and ran out. The clock was striking one as I was in the Crescent, and there was not a soul in sight. I ran along the North Terrace, but could see no sign of the white figure which I expected. At the edge of the West Cliff above the pier I looked across the harbour to the East Cliff, in the hope or fear—I don't know which—of seeing Lucy in our favourite seat. There was a bright full moon, with heavy black, driving clouds, which threw the whole scene into a fleeting diorama of light and shade as they sailed across. For a moment or two I could see nothing, as the shadow of a cloud obscured St. Mary's Church and all around it. Then as the cloud passed I could see the ruins of the abbey coming into view; and as the edge of a narrow band of light as sharp as a sword-cut moved along, the church and the churchyard became gradually visible. Whatever my expectation was, it was not disappointed, for there, on our favourite seat, the silver light of the moon struck a half-reclining figure, snowy white. The coming of the cloud was too quick for me to see much, for shadow shut down on light almost immediately; but it seemed to me as though something dark stood behind the seat where the white figure shone, and bent over it. What it was, whether man or beast, I could not tell; I did not wait to catch another glance, but flew down the steep steps to the pier and along by the fish-market to the bridge, which was the only way to reach the East Cliff. The town seemed as dead, for not a soul did I see; I rejoiced that it was so, for I wanted no witness of poor Lucy's condition. The time and distance seemed endless, and my knees trembled and my breath came laboured as I toiled up the endless steps to the abbey. I must have gone fast, and yet it seemed to me as if my feet were weighted with lead, and as though every joint in my body were rusty. When I got almost to the top I could see the seat and the white figure, for I was now close enough to distinguish it even through the spells of shadow. There was undoubtedly something, long and black, bending over the half-reclining white figure. I called in fright, "Lucy! Lucy!" and something raised a head, and from where I was I could see a white face and red, gleaming eyes. Lucy did not answer, and I ran on to the entrance of the churchyard. As I entered, the church was between me and the seat, and for a minute or so I lost sight of her. When I came in view again the cloud had passed, and the moonlight struck so brilliantly that I could see Lucy half reclining with her head lying over the back of the seat. She was quite alone, and there was not a sign of any living thing about.

When I bent over her I could see that she was still asleep. Her lips were parted, and she was breathing—not softly as usual with her, but in long, heavy gasps, as though striving to get her lungs full at every breath. As I came close, she put up her hand in her sleep and pulled the collar of her nightdress close around her throat. Whilst she did so there came a little shudder through her, as though she felt the cold. I flung the warm shawl over her, and drew the edges tight round her neck, for I dreaded lest she should get some deadly chill from the night air, unclad as she was. I feared to wake her all at once, so, in order to have my hands free that I might help her, I fastened the shawl at her throat with a big safety-pin; but I must have been clumsy in my anxiety and pinched or pricked her with it, for by-and-by, when her breathing became quieter, she put her hand to her throat again and moaned. When I had her carefully wrapped up I put my shoes on her feet and then began very gently to wake her. At first she did not respond; but gradually she became more and more uneasy in her sleep, moaning and sighing occasionally. At last, as time was passing fast, and, for many other reasons, I wished to get her home at once, I shook her more forcibly, till finally she opened her eyes and awoke. She did not seem surprised to see me, as, of course, she did not realise all at once where she was. Lucy always wakes prettily, and even at such a time, when her body must have been chilled with cold, and her mind somewhat appalled at waking unclad in a churchyard at night, she did not lose her grace. She trembled a little, and clung to me; when I told her to come at once with me home she rose without a word, with the obedience of a child. As we passed along, the gravel hurt my feet, and Lucy noticed me wince. She stopped and wanted to insist upon my taking my shoes; but I would not. However, when we got to the pathway outside the churchyard, where there was a puddle of water, remaining from the storm, I daubed my feet with mud, using each foot in turn on the other, so that as we went home, no one, in case we should meet any one, should notice my bare feet.

Fortune favoured us, and we got home without meeting a soul. Once we saw a man, who seemed not quite sober, passing along a street in front of us; but we hid in a door till he had disappeared up an opening such as there are here, steep little closes, or "wynds," as they call them in Scotland. My heart beat so loud all the time that sometimes I thought I should faint. I was filled with anxiety about Lucy, not only for her health, lest she should suffer from the exposure, but for her reputation in case the story should get wind. When we got in, and had washed our feet, and had said a prayer of thankfulness together, I tucked her into bed. Before falling asleep she asked—even implored—me not to say a word to any one, even her mother, about her sleep-walking adventure. I hesitated at first to promise; but on thinking of the state of her mother's health, and how the knowledge of such a thing would fret her, and thinking, too, of how such a story might become distorted—nay, infallibly would—in case it should leak out, I thought it wiser to do so. I hope I did right. I have locked the door, and the key is tied to my wrist, so perhaps I shall not be again disturbed. Lucy is sleeping soundly; the reflex of the dawn is high and far over the sea . . . .

Same day, noon.—All goes well. Lucy slept till I woke her and seemed not to have even changed her side. The adventure of the night does not seem to have harmed her; on the contrary, it has benefited her, for she looks better this morning than she has done for weeks. I was sorry to notice that my clumsiness with the safety-pin hurt her. Indeed, it might have been serious, for the skin of her throat was pierced. I must have pinched up a piece of loose skin and have transfixed it, for there are two little red points like pin-pricks, and on the band of her nightdress was a drop of blood. When I apologised and was concerned about it, she laughed and petted me, and said she did not even feel it. Fortunately it cannot leave a scar, as it is so tiny.

Same day, night.—We passed a happy day. The air was clear, and the sun bright, and there was a cool breeze. We took our lunch to Mulgrave Woods, Mrs. Westenra driving by the road and Lucy and I walking by the cliff-path and joining her at the gate. I felt a little sad myself, for I could not but feel how *absolutely* happy it would have been had Jonathan been with me. But there! I must only be patient. In the evening we strolled in the Casino Terrace, and heard some good music by Spohr and Mackenzie, and went to bed early. Lucy seems more restful than she has been for some time, and fell asleep at once. I shall lock the door and secure the key the same as before, though I do not expect any trouble to-night.

12 August.—My expectations were wrong, for twice during the night I was wakened by Lucy trying to get out. She seemed, even in her sleep, to be a little impatient at finding the door shut, and went back to bed under a sort of protest. I woke with the dawn, and heard the birds chirping outside of the window. Lucy woke, too, and, I was glad to see, was even better than on the previous morning. All her old gaiety of manner seemed to have come back, and she came and snuggled in beside me and told me all about Arthur. I told her how anxious I was about Jonathan, and then she tried to comfort me. Well, she succeeded somewhat, for, though sympathy can't alter facts, it can help to make them more bearable.

13 August.—Another quiet day, and to bed with the key on my wrist as before. Again I awoke in the night, and found Lucy sitting up in bed, still asleep, pointing to the window. I got up quietly, and pulling aside the blind, looked out. It was brilliant moonlight, and the soft effect of the light over the sea and sky—merged together in one great, silent mystery—was beautiful beyond words. Between me and the moonlight flitted a great bat, coming and going in great whirling circles. Once or twice it came quite close, but was, I suppose, frightened at seeing me, and flitted away across the harbour towards the abbey. When I came back from the window Lucy had lain down again, and was sleeping peacefully. She did not stir again all night.

14 August.—On the East Cliff, reading and writing all day. Lucy seems to have become as much in love with the spot as I am, and it is hard to get her away from it when it is time to come home for lunch or tea or dinner. This afternoon she made a funny remark. We were coming home for dinner, and had come to the top of the steps up from the West Pier and stopped to look at the view, as we generally do. The setting sun, low down in the sky, was just dropping behind Kettleness; the red light was thrown over on the East Cliff and the old abbey, and seemed to bathe everything in a beautiful rosy glow. We were silent for a while, and suddenly Lucy murmured as if to herself:—

"His red eyes again! They are just the same." It was such an odd expression, coming *apropos* of nothing, that it quite startled me. I slewed round a little, so as to see Lucy well without seeming to stare at her, and saw that she was in a half-dreamy state, with an odd look on her face that I could not quite make out; so I said nothing, but followed her eyes. She appeared to be looking over at our own seat, whereon was a dark figure seated alone. I was a little startled myself, for it seemed for an instant as if the stranger had great eyes like burning flames; but a second look dispelled the illusion. The red sunlight was shining on the windows of St. Mary's Church behind our seat, and as the sun dipped there was just sufficient change in the refraction and reflection to make it appear as if the light moved. I called Lucy's attention to the peculiar effect, and she became herself with a start, but she looked sad all the same; it may have been that she was thinking of that terrible night up there. We never refer to it; so I said nothing, and we went home to dinner. Lucy had a headache and went early to bed. I saw her asleep, and went out for a little stroll myself; I walked along the cliffs to the westward, and was full of sweet sadness, for I was thinking of Jonathan. When coming home— it was then bright moonlight, so bright that, though the front of our part of the Crescent was in shadow, everything could be well seen—I threw a glance up at our window, and saw Lucy's head leaning out. I thought that perhaps she was looking out for me, so I opened my handkerchief and waved it. She did not notice or make any movement whatever. Just then, the moonlight crept round an angle of the building, and the light fell on the window. There distinctly was Lucy with her head lying up against the side of the window-sill and her eyes shut. She was fast asleep, and by her, seated on the window-sill, was something that looked like a good-sized bird. I was afraid she might get a chill, so I ran upstairs, but as I came into the room she was moving back to her bed, fast asleep, and breathing heavily; she was holding her hand to her throat, as though to protect it from cold.

I did not wake her, but tucked her up warmly; I have taken care that the door is locked and the window securely fastened.

She looks so sweet as she sleeps; but she is paler than is her wont, and there is a drawn, haggard look under her eyes which I do not like. I fear she is fretting about something. I wish I could find out what it is.

15 August.—Rose later than usual. Lucy was languid and tired, and slept on after we had been called. We had a happy surprise at breakfast. Arthur's father is better, and wants the marriage to come off soon. Lucy is full of quiet joy, and her mother is glad and sorry at once. Later on in the day she told me the cause. She is grieved to lose Lucy as her very own, but she is rejoiced that she is soon to have some one to protect her. Poor dear, sweet lady! She confided to me that she has got her death-warrant. She has not told Lucy, and made me promise secrecy; her doctor told her that within a few months, at most, she must die, for her heart is weakening. At any time, even now, a sudden shock would be almost sure to kill her. Ah, we were wise to keep from her the affair of the dreadful night of Lucy's sleep-walking.

17 August.—No diary for two whole days. I have not had the heart to write. Some sort of shadowy pall seems to be coming over our happiness. No news from Jonathan, and Lucy seems to be growing weaker, whilst her mother's hours are numbering to a close. I do not understand Lucy's fading away as she is doing. She eats well and sleeps well, and enjoys the fresh air;

but all the time the roses in her cheeks are fading, and she gets weaker and more languid day by day; at night I hear her gasping as if for air. I keep the key of our door always fastened to my wrist at night, but she gets up and walks about the room, and sits at the open window. Last night I found her leaning out when I woke up, and when I tried to wake her I could not; she was in a faint. When I managed to restore her she was as weak as water, and cried silently between long, painful struggles for breath. When I asked her how she came to be at the window she shook her head and turned away. I trust her feeling ill may not be from that unlucky prick of the safety-pin. I looked at her throat just now as she lay asleep, and the tiny wounds seem not to have healed. They are still open, and, if anything, larger than before, and the edges of them are faintly white. They are like little white dots with red centres. Unless they heal within a day or two, I shall insist on the doctor seeing about them.

**LETTER,
SAMUEL F. BILLINGTON & SON,
SOLICITORS, WHITBY, TO MESSRS. CARTER,
PATERSON & CO., LONDON.**

"*17 August.*

"Dear Sirs,—

"Herewith please receive invoice of goods sent by Great Northern Railway. Same are to be delivered at Carfax, near Purfleet, immediately on receipt at goods station King's Cross. The house is at present empty, but enclosed please find keys, all of which are labelled.

"You will please deposit the boxes, fifty in number, which form the consignment, in the partially ruined building forming part of the house and marked 'A' on rough diagram enclosed. Your agent will easily recognise the locality, as it is the ancient chapel of the mansion. The goods leave by the train at 9:30 to-night, and will be due at King's Cross at 4:30 to-morrow afternoon. As our client wishes the delivery made as soon as possible, we shall be obliged by your having teams ready at King's Cross at the time named and forthwith conveying the goods to destination. In order to obviate any delays possible through any routine requirements as to payment in your departments, we enclose cheque herewith for ten pounds (£10), receipt of which please acknowledge. Should the charge be less than this amount, you can return balance; if greater, we shall at once send cheque for difference on hearing from you. You are to leave the keys on coming away in the main hall of the house, where the proprietor may get them on his entering the house by means of his duplicate key.

"Pray do not take us as exceeding the bounds of business courtesy in pressing you in all ways to use the utmost expedition.

"We are, dear Sirs,
"Faithfully yours,
"SAMUEL F. BILLINGTON & SON."

LETTER,
MESSRS. CARTER, PATERSON & CO.,
LONDON, TO MESSRS. BILLINGTON & SON, WHITBY.

"21 August.

"DEAR SIRS,—

"We beg to acknowledge £10 received and to return cheque £1 17s. 9d, amount of overplus, as shown in receipted account herewith. Goods are delivered in exact accordance with instructions, and keys left in parcel in main hall, as directed.

"We are, dear Sirs,
"Yours respectfully.
"PRO CARTER, PATERSON & CO."

MINA MURRAY'S JOURNAL.

18 August.—I am happy to-day, and write sitting on the seat in the churchyard. Lucy is ever so much better. Last night she slept well all night, and did not disturb me once. The roses seem coming back already to her cheeks, though she is still sadly pale and wan-looking. If she were in any way anæmic I could understand it, but she is not. She is in gay spirits and full of life and cheerfulness. All the morbid reticence seems to have passed from her, and she has just reminded me, as if I needed any reminding, of *that* night, and that it was here, on this very seat, I found her asleep. As she told me she tapped playfully with the heel of her boot on the stone slab and said:—

"My poor little feet didn't make much noise then! I daresay poor old Mr. Swales would have told me that it was because I didn't want to wake up Geordie." As she was in such a communicative humour, I asked her if she had dreamed at all that night. Before she answered, that sweet, puckered look came into her forehead, which Arthur—I call him Arthur from her habit—says he loves; and, indeed, I don't wonder that he does. Then she went on in a half-dreaming kind of way, as if trying to recall it to herself:—

"I didn't quite dream; but it all seemed to be real. I only wanted to be here in this spot—I don't know why, for I was afraid of something—I don't know what. I remember, though I suppose I was asleep, passing through the streets and over the bridge. A fish leaped as I went by, and I leaned over to look at it, and I heard a lot of dogs howling—the whole town seemed as if it must be full of dogs all howling at once—as I went up the steps. Then I had a vague memory of something long and dark with red eyes, just as we saw in the sunset, and something very sweet and very bitter all around me at once; and then I seemed sinking into deep green water, and there was a singing in my ears, as I have heard there is to drowning men; and then everything seemed passing away from me; my soul seemed to go out from my body and float about the air. I seem to remember that once the West Lighthouse was right under me, and then there was a sort of agonising feeling, as if I were in an earthquake, and I came back and found you shaking my body. I saw you do it before I felt you."

Then she began to laugh. It seemed a little uncanny to me, and I listened to her breathlessly. I did not quite like it, and thought it better not to keep her mind on the subject, so we drifted on to other subjects, and Lucy was like her old self again. When we got home the fresh breeze had braced her up, and her pale cheeks were really more rosy. Her mother rejoiced when she saw her, and we all spent a very happy evening together.

19 August.—Joy, joy, joy! although not all joy. At last, news of Jonathan. The dear fellow has been ill; that is why he did not write. I am not afraid to think it or say it, now that I know. Mr. Hawkins sent me on the letter, and wrote himself, oh, so kindly. I am to leave in the morning and go over to Jonathan, and to help to nurse him if necessary, and to bring him home. Mr. Hawkins says it would not be a bad thing if we were to be married out there. I have cried over the good Sister's letter till I can feel it wet against my bosom, where it lies. It is of Jonathan, and must be next my heart, for he is *in* my heart. My journey is all mapped out, and my luggage ready. I am only taking one change of dress; Lucy will bring my trunk to London and keep it till I send for it, for it may be that . . . I must write no more; I must keep it to say to Jonathan, my husband. The letter that he has seen and touched must comfort me till we meet.

**LETTER,
SISTER AGATHA, HOSPITAL OF
ST. JOSEPH AND STE. MARY, BUDA-PESTH,
TO MISS WILHELMINA MURRAY.**

"12 August.

    "Dear Madam,—

    "I write by desire of Mr. Jonathan Harker, who is himself not strong enough to write, though progressing well, thanks to God and St. Joseph and Ste. Mary. He has been under our care for nearly six weeks, suffering from a violent brain fever. He wishes me to convey his love, and to say that by this post I write for him to Mr. Peter Hawkins, Exeter, to say, with his dutiful respects, that he is sorry for his delay, and that all of his work is completed. He will require some few weeks' rest in our sanatorium in the hills, but will then return. He wishes me to say that he has not sufficient money with him, and that he would like to pay for his staying here, so that others who need shall not be wanting for help.

    "Believe me,
    "Yours, with sympathy and all blessings,
    "Sister Agatha.

    "P. S.—My patient being asleep, I open this to let you know something more. He has told me all about you, and that you are shortly to be his wife. All blessings to you both! He has had some fearful shock—so says our doctor—and in his delirium his ravings have been dreadful; of wolves and poison and blood; of ghosts and demons; and I fear to say of what. Be careful with him always that there may be nothing to excite him of this kind for a long time to come; the traces of such an illness as his do not lightly die away. We should have written long ago, but we knew nothing of his friends, and there was on him nothing that any one could understand. He came in the train from Klausenburg, and the guard was told by the station-master there that he rushed into the station shouting for a ticket for home. Seeing from his violent demeanour that he was English, they gave him a ticket for the furthest station on the way thither that the train reached.

"Be assured that he is well cared for. He has won all hearts by his sweetness and gentleness. He is truly getting on well, and I have no doubt will in a few weeks be all himself. But be careful of him for safety's sake. There are, I pray God and St. Joseph and Ste. Mary, many, many, happy years for you both."

DR. SEWARD'S DIARY.

19 August.—Strange and sudden change in Renfield last night. About eight o'clock he began to get excited and sniff about as a dog does when setting. The attendant was struck by his manner, and knowing my interest in him, encouraged him to talk. He is usually respectful to the attendant and at times servile; but to-night, the man tells me, he was quite haughty. Would not condescend to talk with him at all. All he would say was:—

"I don't want to talk to you: you don't count now; the Master is at hand."

The attendant thinks it is some sudden form of religious mania which has seized him. If so, we must look out for squalls, for a strong man with homicidal and religious mania at once might be dangerous. The combination is a dreadful one. At nine o'clock I visited him myself. His attitude to me was the same as that to the attendant; in his sublime self-feeling the difference between myself and attendant seemed to him as nothing. It looks like religious mania, and he will soon think that he himself is God. These infinitesimal distinctions between man and man are too paltry for an Omnipotent Being. How these madmen give themselves away! The real God taketh heed lest a sparrow fall; but the God created from human vanity sees no difference between an eagle and a sparrow. Oh, if men only knew!

For half an hour or more Renfield kept getting excited in greater and greater degree. I did not pretend to be watching him, but I kept strict observation all the same. All at once that shifty look came into his eyes which we always see when a madman has seized an idea, and with it the shifty movement of the head and back which asylum attendants come to know so well. He became quite quiet, and went and sat on the edge of his bed resignedly, and looked into space with lack-lustre eyes. I thought I would find out if his apathy were real or only assumed, and tried to lead him to talk of his pets, a theme which had never failed to excite his attention. At first he made no reply, but at length said testily:—

"Bother them all! I don't care a pin about them."

"What?" I said. "You don't mean to tell me you don't care about spiders?" (Spiders at present are his hobby and the note-book is filling up with columns of small figures.) To this he answered enigmatically:—

"The bride-maidens rejoice the eyes that wait the coming of the bride; but when the bride draweth nigh, then the maidens shine not to the eyes that are filled."

He would not explain himself, but remained obstinately seated on his bed all the time I remained with him.

I am weary to-night and low in spirits. I cannot but think of Lucy, and how different things might have been. If I don't sleep at once, chloral, the modern Morpheus—$C_2HCl_3O. H_2O$! I must be careful not to let it grow into a habit. No, I shall take none to-night! I have thought of Lucy, and I shall not dishonour her by mixing the two. If need be, to-night shall be sleepless . . . .

Later.—Glad I made the resolution; gladder that I kept to it. I had lain tossing about, and had heard the clock strike only twice, when the night-watchman came to me, sent up from the ward, to say that Renfield had escaped. I threw on my clothes and ran down at once; my patient is too dangerous a person to be roaming about. Those ideas of his might work out dangerously with strangers. The attendant was waiting for me. He said he had seen him not ten minutes before, seemingly asleep in his bed, when he had looked through the observation-trap in the door. His attention was called by the sound of the window being wrenched out. He ran back and saw his feet disappear through the window, and had at once sent up for me. He was only in his night-gear, and cannot be far off. The attendant thought it would be more useful to watch where he should go than to follow him, as he might lose sight of him whilst getting out of the building by the door. He is a bulky man, and couldn't get through the window. I am thin, so, with his aid, I got out, but feet foremost, and, as we were only a few feet above ground, landed unhurt. The attendant told me the patient had gone to the left, and had taken a straight line, so I ran as quickly as I could. As I got through the belt of trees I saw a white figure scale the high wall which separates our grounds from those of the deserted house.

I ran back at once, told the watchman to get three or four men immediately and follow me into the grounds of Carfax, in case our friend might be dangerous. I got a ladder myself, and crossing the wall, dropped down on the other side. I could see Renfield's figure just disappearing behind the angle of the house, so I ran after him. On the far side of the house I found him pressed close against the old ironbound oak door of the chapel. He was talking, apparently to some one, but I was afraid to go near enough to hear what he was saying, lest I might frighten him, and he should run off. Chasing an errant swarm of bees is nothing to following a naked lunatic, when the fit of escaping is upon him! After a few minutes, however, I could see that he did not take note of anything around him, and so ventured to draw nearer to him—the more so as my men had now crossed the wall and were closing him in. I heard him say:—

"I am here to do Your bidding, Master. I am Your slave, and You will reward me, for I shall be faithful. I have worshipped You long and afar off. Now that You are near, I await Your commands, and You will not pass me by, will You, dear Master, in Your distribution of good things?"

He *is* a selfish old beggar anyhow. He thinks of the loaves and fishes even when he believes he is in a Real Presence. His manias make a startling combination. When we closed in on him he fought like a tiger. He is immensely strong, for he was more like a wild beast than a man. I never saw a lunatic in such a paroxysm of rage before; and I hope I shall not again. It is a mercy that we have found out his strength and his danger in good time. With strength and determination like his, he might have done wild work before he was caged. He is safe now at any rate. Jack Sheppard himself couldn't get free from the strait-waistcoat that keeps him restrained, and he's chained to the wall in the padded room. His cries are at times awful, but the silences that follow are more deadly still, for he means murder in every turn and movement.

Just now he spoke coherent words for the first time:—

"I shall be patient, Master. It is coming—coming—coming!"

So I took the hint, and came too. I was too excited to sleep, but this diary has quieted me, and I feel I shall get some sleep to-night.

CHAPTER IX

LETTER,
MINA HARKER TO LUCY WESTENRA.

"Buda-Pesth, 24 August.

"MY DEAREST LUCY,—

"I know you will be anxious to hear all that has happened since we parted at the railway station at Whitby. Well, my dear, I got to Hull all right, and caught the boat to Hamburg, and then the train on here. I feel that I can hardly recall anything of the journey, except that I knew I was coming to Jonathan, and, that as I should have to do some nursing, I had better get all the sleep I could . . . . I found my dear one, oh, so thin and pale and weak-looking. All the resolution has gone out of his dear eyes, and that quiet dignity which I told you was in his face has vanished. He is only a wreck of himself, and he does not remember anything that has happened to him for a long time past. At least, he wants me to believe so, and I shall never ask. He has had some terrible shock, and I fear it might tax his poor brain if he were to try to recall it. Sister Agatha, who is a good creature and a born nurse, tells me that he raved of dreadful things whilst he was off his head. I wanted her to tell me what they were; but she would only cross herself, and say she would never tell; that the ravings of the sick were the secrets of God, and that if a nurse through her vocation should hear them, she should respect her trust. She is a sweet, good soul, and the next day, when she saw I was troubled, she opened up the subject again, and after saying that she could never mention what my poor dear raved about, added: 'I can tell you this much, my dear: that it was not about anything which he has done wrong himself; and you, as his wife to be, have no cause to be concerned. He has not forgotten you or what he owes to you. His fear was of great and terrible things, which no mortal can treat of.' I do believe the dear soul thought I might be jealous lest my poor dear should have fallen in love with any other girl. The idea of *my* being jealous about Jonathan! And yet, my dear, let me whisper, I felt a thrill of joy through me when I *knew* that no other woman was a cause of trouble. I am now sitting by his bedside, where I can see his face while he sleeps. He is waking! . . .

"When he woke he asked me for his coat, as he wanted to get something from the pocket; I asked Sister Agatha, and she brought all his things. I saw that amongst them was his note-book, and was going to ask him to let me look at it—for I knew then that I might find some clue to his trouble—but I suppose he must have seen my wish in my eyes, for he sent me over to the window, saying he wanted to be quite alone for a moment. Then he called me back, and when I came he had his hand over the note-book, and he said to me very solemnly:—

" 'Wilhelmina'—I knew then that he was in deadly earnest, for he has never called me by that name since he asked me to marry him—'you know, dear, my ideas of the trust between husband and wife: there should be no secret, no concealment. I have had a great shock, and when I try to think of what it is I feel my head spin round, and I do not know if it was all real or the dreaming of a madman. You know I have had brain fever, and that is to be mad. The secret is here, and I do not want to know it. I want to take up my life here, with our marriage.' For, my dear, we had decided to be married as soon as the formalities are complete. 'Are you willing, Wilhelmina, to share my ignorance? Here is the book. Take it and keep it, read it if you will, but never let me know; unless, indeed, some solemn duty should come upon me to go back to the bitter hours, asleep or awake, sane or mad, recorded here.' He fell back exhausted, and I put the book under his pillow, and kissed him. I have asked Sister Agatha to beg the Superior to let our wedding be this afternoon, and am waiting her reply . . . .

"She has come and told me that the chaplain of the English mission church has been sent for. We are to be married in an hour, or as soon after as Jonathan awakes . . . .

"Lucy, the time has come and gone. I feel very solemn, but very, very happy. Jonathan woke a little after the hour, and all was ready, and he sat up in bed, propped up with pillows. He answered his 'I will' firmly and strongly. I could hardly speak; my heart was so full that even those words seemed to choke me. The dear sisters were so kind. Please God, I shall never, never forget them, nor the grave and sweet responsibilities I have taken upon me. I must tell you of my wedding present. When the chaplain and the sisters had left me alone with my husband—oh, Lucy, it is the first time I have written the words 'my husband'—left me alone with my husband, I took the book from under his pillow, and wrapped it up in white paper, and tied it with a little bit of pale blue ribbon which was round my neck, and sealed it over the knot with sealing-wax, and for my seal I used my wedding ring. Then

I kissed it and showed it to my husband, and told him that I would keep it so, and then it would be an outward and visible sign for us all our lives that we trusted each other; that I would never open it unless it were for his own dear sake or for the sake of some stern duty. Then he took my hand in his, and oh, Lucy, it was the first time he took *his wife's* hand, and said that it was the dearest thing in all the wide world, and that he would go through all the past again to win it, if need be. The poor dear meant to have said a part of the past, but he cannot think of time yet, and I shall not wonder if at first he mixes up not only the month, but the year.

"Well, my dear, what could I say? I could only tell him that I was the happiest woman in all the wide world, and that I had nothing to give him except myself, my life, and my trust, and that with these went my love and duty for all the days of my life. And, my dear, when he kissed me, and drew me to him with his poor weak hands, it was like a very solemn pledge between us . . . .

"Lucy dear, do you know why I tell you all this? It is not only because it is all sweet to me, but because you have been, and are, very dear to me. It was my privilege to be your friend and guide when you came from the schoolroom to prepare for the world of life. I want you to see now, and with the eyes of a very happy wife, whither duty has led me; so that in your own married life you too may be all happy as I am. My dear, please Almighty God, your life may be all it promises: a long day of sunshine, with no harsh wind, no forgetting duty, no distrust. I must not wish you no pain, for that can never be; but I do hope you will be *always* as happy as I am *now*. Good-bye, my dear. I shall post this at once, and, perhaps, write you very soon again. I must stop, for Jonathan is waking—I must attend to my husband!

"Your ever-loving
"MINA HARKER."

LETTER,
LUCY WESTENRA TO MINA HARKER.

"Whitby, 30 August.

"MY DEAREST MINA,—

"Oceans of love and millions of kisses, and may you soon be in your own home with your husband. I wish you could be coming home soon enough to stay with us here. The strong air would soon restore Jonathan; it has quite restored me. I have an appetite like a cormorant, am full of life, and sleep well. You will be glad to know that I have quite given up walking in my sleep. I think I have not stirred out of my bed for a week, that is when I once got into it at night. Arthur says I am getting fat. By the way, I forgot to tell you that Arthur is here. We have such walks and drives, and rides, and rowing, and tennis, and fishing together; and I love him more than ever. He *tells* me that he loves me more, but I doubt that, for at first he told me that he couldn't love me more than he did then. But this is nonsense. There he is, calling to me. So no more just at present from your loving

"LUCY.

"P. S.—Mother sends her love. She seems better, poor dear.
"P. P. S.—We are to be married on 28 September."

DR. SEWARD'S DIARY.

20 August.—The case of Renfield grows even more interesting. He has now so far quieted that there are spells of cessation from his passion. For the first week after his attack he was perpetually violent. Then one night, just as the moon rose, he grew quiet, and kept murmuring to himself: "Now I can wait; now I can wait." The attendant came to tell me, so I ran down at once to have a look at him. He was still in the strait-waistcoat and in the padded room, but the suffused look had gone from his face, and his eyes had something of their old pleading—I might almost say, "cringing"—softness. I was satisfied with his present condition, and directed him to be relieved. The attendants hesitated, but finally carried out my wishes without protest. It was a strange thing that the patient had humour enough to see their distrust, for, coming close to me, he said in a whisper, all the while looking furtively at them:—

"They think I could hurt you! Fancy *me* hurting *you*! The fools!"

It was soothing, somehow, to the feelings to find myself dissociated even in the mind of this poor madman from the others; but all the same I do not follow his thought. Am I to take it that I have anything in common with him, so that we are, as it were, to stand together; or has he to gain from me some good so stupendous that my well-being is needful to him? I must find out later on. To-night he will not speak. Even the offer of a kitten or even a full-grown cat will not tempt him. He will only say: "I don't take any stock in cats. I have more to think of now, and I can wait; I can wait."

After a while I left him. The attendant tells me that he was quiet until just before dawn, and that then he began to get uneasy, and at length violent, until at last he fell into a paroxysm which exhausted him so that he swooned into a sort of coma.

. . . Three nights has the same thing happened—violent all day then quiet from moonrise to sunrise. I wish I could get some clue to the cause. It would almost seem as if there was some influence which came and went. Happy thought! We shall to-night play sane wits against mad ones. He escaped before without our help; to-night he shall escape with it. We shall give him a chance, and have the men ready to follow in case they are required . . . .

23 August.—"The unexpected always happens." How well Disraeli knew life. Our bird when he found the cage open would not fly, so all our subtle arrangements were for nought. At any rate, we have proved one thing; that the spells of quietness last a reasonable time. We shall in future be able to ease his bonds for a few hours each day. I have given orders to the night attendant merely to shut him in the padded room, when once he is quiet, until an hour before sunrise. The poor soul's body will enjoy the relief even if his mind cannot appreciate it. Hark! The unexpected again! I am called; the patient has once more escaped.

Later.—Another night adventure. Renfield artfully waited until the attendant was entering the room to inspect. Then he dashed out past him and flew down the passage. I sent word for the attendants to follow. Again he went into the grounds of the deserted house, and we found him in the same place, pressed against the old chapel door. When he saw me he became furious, and had not the attendants seized him in time, he would have tried to kill me. As we were holding him a strange thing happened. He suddenly redoubled his efforts, and then as suddenly grew calm. I looked round instinctively, but could see nothing. Then I caught the patient's eye and followed it, but could trace nothing as it looked into the moonlit sky except a big bat, which was flapping its silent and ghostly way to the west. Bats usually wheel and flit about, but this one seemed to go straight on, as if it knew where it was bound for or had some intention of its own. The patient grew calmer every instant, and presently said:—

"You needn't tie me; I shall go quietly!" Without trouble we came back to the house. I feel there is something ominous in his calm, and shall not forget this night . . . .

LUCY WESTENRA'S DIARY

Hillingham, 24 August.—I must imitate Mina, and keep writing things down. Then we can have long talks when we do meet. I wonder when it will be. I wish she were with me again, for I feel so unhappy. Last night I seemed to be dreaming again just as I was at Whitby. Perhaps it is the change of air, or getting home again. It is all dark and horrid to me, for I can remember nothing; but I am full of vague fear, and I feel so weak and worn out. When Arthur came to lunch he looked quite grieved when he saw me, and I hadn't the spirit to try to be cheerful. I wonder if I could sleep in mother's room to-night. I shall make an excuse and try.

25 August.—Another bad night. Mother did not seem to take to my proposal. She seems not too well herself, and doubtless she fears to worry me. I tried to keep awake, and succeeded for a while; but when the clock struck twelve it waked me from a doze, so I must have been falling asleep. There was a sort of scratching or flapping at the window, but I did not mind it, and as I remember no more, I suppose I must then have fallen asleep. More bad dreams. I wish I could remember them. This morning I am horribly weak. My face is ghastly pale, and my throat pains me. It must be something wrong with my lungs, for I don't seem ever to get air enough. I shall try to cheer up when Arthur comes, or else I know he will be miserable to see me so.

LETTER,
ARTHUR HOLMWOOD TO DR. SEWARD.

"Albemarle Hotel, 31 August.

"MY DEAR JACK,—

"I want you to do me a favour. Lucy is ill; that is, she has no special disease, but she looks awful, and is getting worse every day. I have asked her if there is any cause; I do not dare to ask her mother, for to disturb the poor lady's mind about her daughter in her present state of health would be fatal. Mrs. Westenra has confided to me that her doom is spoken—disease of the heart—though poor Lucy does not know it yet. I am sure that there is something preying on my dear girl's mind. I am almost distracted when I think of her; to look at her gives me a pang. I told her I should ask you to see her, and though she demurred at first—I know why, old fellow—she finally consented. It will be a painful task for you, I know, old friend, but it is for *her* sake, and I must not hesitate to ask, or you to act. You are to come to lunch at Hillingham to-morrow, two o'clock, so as not to arouse any suspicion in Mrs. Westenra, and after lunch Lucy will take an opportunity of being alone with you. I shall come in for tea, and we can go away together; I am filled with anxiety, and want to consult with you alone as soon as I can after you have seen her. Do not fail!

"ARTHUR."

TELEGRAM,
ARTHUR HOLMWOOD TO SEWARD.

"1 September.

"Am summoned to see my father, who is worse. Am writing. Write me fully by to-night's post to Ring. Wire me if necessary."

LETTER FROM
DR. SEWARD TO ARTHUR HOLMWOOD.

"2 September.

"MY DEAR OLD FELLOW,—

"With regard to Miss Westenra's health I hasten to let you know at once that in my opinion there is not any functional disturbance or any malady that I know of. At the same time, I am not by any means satisfied with her appearance; she is woefully different from what she was when I saw her last. Of course you must bear in mind that I did not have full opportunity of examination such as I should wish; our very friendship makes a little difficulty which not even medical science or custom can bridge over. I had better tell you exactly what happened, leaving you to draw, in a measure, your own conclusions. I shall then say what I have done and propose doing.

"I found Miss Westenra in seemingly gay spirits. Her mother was present, and in a few seconds I made up my mind that she was trying all she knew to mislead her mother and prevent her from being anxious. I have no doubt she guesses, if she does not know, what need of caution there is. We lunched alone, and as we all exerted ourselves to be cheerful, we got, as some kind of reward for our labours, some real cheerfulness amongst us. Then Mrs. Westenra went to lie down, and Lucy was left with me. We went into her boudoir, and till we got there her gaiety remained, for the servants were coming and going. As soon as the door was closed, however, the mask fell from her face, and she sank down into a chair with a great sigh, and hid her eyes with her hand. When I saw that her high spirits had failed, I at once took advantage of her reaction to make a diagnosis. She said to me very sweetly:—

" 'I cannot tell you how I loathe talking about myself.' I reminded her that a doctor's confidence was sacred, but that you were grievously anxious about her. She caught on to my meaning at once, and settled that matter in a word. 'Tell Arthur everything you choose. I do not care for myself, but all for him!' So I am quite free.

"I could easily see that she is somewhat bloodless, but I could not see the usual anæmic signs, and by a chance I was actually able to test the quality of her blood, for in opening a window which was stiff a cord gave way, and she cut her hand slightly with broken glass. It was a slight matter in itself, but it gave me an evident chance, and I secured a few drops of the blood and have analysed them. The qualitative analysis gives a quite normal condition, and shows, I should infer, in itself a vigorous state of health. In other physical matters I was quite satisfied that there is no need for anxiety; but as there must be a cause somewhere, I have come to the conclusion that it must be something mental. She complains of difficulty in breathing satisfactorily at times, and of heavy, lethargic sleep, with dreams that frighten her, but regarding which she can remember nothing. She says that as a child she used to walk in her sleep, and that when in Whitby the habit came back, and that once she walked out in the night and went to East Cliff, where Miss Murray found her; but she assures me that of late the habit has not returned. I am in doubt, and so have done the best thing I know of; I have written to my old friend and master, Professor Van Helsing, of Amsterdam, who knows as much about obscure diseases as any one in the world. I have asked him to come over, and as you told me that all things were to be at your charge, I have mentioned to him who you are and your relations to Miss Westenra. This, my dear fellow, is in obedience to your wishes, for I am only too proud and happy to do anything I can for her. Van Helsing would, I know, do anything for me for a personal reason, so, no matter on what ground he comes, we must accept his wishes. He is a seemingly arbitrary man, but this is because he knows what he is talking about better than any one else. He is a philosopher and a metaphysician, and one of the most advanced scientists of his day; and he has, I believe, an absolutely open mind. This, with an iron nerve, a temper of the ice-brook, an indomitable resolution, self-command, and toleration exalted from virtues to blessings, and the kindliest and truest heart that beats—these form his equipment for the noble work that he is doing for mankind—work both in theory and practice, for his views are as wide as his all-embracing sympathy. I tell you these facts that you may know why I have such confidence in him. I have asked him to come at once. I shall see Miss Westenra to-morrow again. She is to meet me at the Stores, so that I may not alarm her mother by too early a repetition of my call.

"Yours always,
"JOHN SEWARD."

LETTER,
ABRAHAM VAN HELSING, M. D., D. PH., D. LIT., ETC., ETC., TO DR. SEWARD.

"2 September.

"MY GOOD FRIEND,—

"When I have received your letter I am already coming to you. By good fortune I can leave just at once, without wrong to any of those who have trusted me. Were fortune other, then it were bad for those who have trusted, for I come to my friend when he call me to aid those he holds dear. Tell your friend that when that time you suck from my wound so swiftly the poison of the gangrene from that knife that our other friend, too nervous, let slip, you did more for him when he wants my aids and you call for them than all his great fortune could do. But it is pleasure added to do for him, your friend; it is to you that I come. Have then rooms for me at the Great Eastern Hotel, so that I may be near to hand, and please it so arrange that we may see the young lady not too late on to-morrow, for it is likely that I may have to return here that night. But if need be I shall come again in three days, and stay longer if it must. Till then good-bye, my friend John.

"VAN HELSING."

LETTER,
DR. SEWARD TO HON. ARTHUR HOLMWOOD.

"3 September.

"MY DEAR ART,—

"Van Helsing has come and gone. He came on with me to Hillingham, and found that, by Lucy's discretion, her mother was lunching out, so that we were alone with her. Van Helsing made a very careful examination of the patient. He is to report to me, and I shall advise you, for of course I was not present all the time. He is, I fear, much concerned, but says he must think. When I told him of our friendship and how you trust to me in the matter, he said: 'You must tell him all you think. Tell him what I think, if you can guess it, if you will. Nay, I am not jesting. This is no jest, but life and death, perhaps more.' I asked what he meant by that, for he was very serious. This was when we had come back to town, and he was having a cup of tea before starting on his return to Amsterdam. He would not give me any further clue. You must not be angry with me, Art, because his very reticence means that all his brains are working for her good. He will speak plainly enough when the time comes, be sure. So I told him I would simply write an account of our visit, just as if I were doing a descriptive special article for *The Daily Telegraph*. He seemed not to notice, but remarked that the smuts in London were not quite so bad as they used to be when he was a student here. I am to get his report to-morrow if he can possibly make it. In any case I am to have a letter.

"Well, as to the visit. Lucy was more cheerful than on the day I first saw her, and certainly looked better. She had lost something of the ghastly look that so upset you, and her breathing was normal. She was very sweet to the professor (as she always is), and tried to make him feel at ease; though I could see that the poor girl was making a hard struggle for it. I believe Van Helsing saw it, too, for I saw the quick look under his bushy brows that I knew of old. Then he began to chat of all things except ourselves and diseases and with such an infinite geniality that I could see poor Lucy's pretense of animation merge into reality. Then, without any seeming change, he brought the conversation gently round to his visit, and suavely said:—

" 'My dear young miss, I have the so great pleasure because you are so much beloved. That is much, my dear, ever were there that which I do not see. They told me you were down in the spirit, and that you were of a ghastly pale. To them I say: "Pouf!" ' And he snapped his fingers at me and went on: 'But you and I shall show them how wrong they are. How can he'— and he pointed at me with the same look and gesture as that with which once he pointed me out to his class, on, or rather after, a particular occasion which he never fails to remind me of—'know anything of a young ladies? He has his madams to play with, and to bring them back to happiness, and to those that love them. It is much to do, and, oh, but there are rewards, in that we can bestow such happiness. But the young ladies! He has no wife nor daughter, and the young do not tell themselves to the young, but to the old, like me, who have known so many sorrows and the causes of them. So, my dear, we will send him away to smoke the cigarette in the garden, whiles you and I have little talk all to ourselves.' I took the hint, and strolled about, and presently the professor came to the window and called me in. He looked grave, but said: 'I have made careful examination, but there is no functional cause. With you I agree that there has been much blood lost; it has been, but is not. But the conditions of her are in no way anæmic. I have asked her to send me her maid, that I may ask just one or two question, that so I may not chance to miss nothing. I know well what she will say. And yet there is cause; there is always cause for everything. I must go back home and think. You must send to me the telegram every day; and if there be cause I shall come again. The disease—for not to be all well is a disease—interest me, and the sweet young dear, she interest me too. She charm me, and for her, if not for you or disease, I come.'

"As I tell you, he would not say a word more, even when we were alone. And so now, Art, you know all I know. I shall keep stern watch. I trust your poor father is rallying. It must be a terrible thing to you, my dear old fellow, to be placed in such a position between two people who are both so dear to you. I know your idea of duty to your father, and you are right to stick to it; but, if need be, I shall send you word to come at once to Lucy; so do not be over-anxious unless you hear from me."

DR. SEWARD'S DIARY.

4 September.—Zoöphagous patient still keeps up our interest in him. He had only one outburst and that was yesterday at an unusual time. Just before the stroke of noon he began to grow restless. The attendant knew the symptoms, and at once summoned aid. Fortunately the men came at a run, and were just in time, for at the stroke of noon he became so violent that it took all their strength to hold him. In about five minutes, however, he began to get more and more quiet, and finally sank into a sort of melancholy, in which state he has remained up to now. The attendant tells me that his screams whilst in the paroxysm were really appalling; I found my hands full when I got in, attending to some of the other patients who were frightened by him. Indeed, I can quite understand the effect, for the sounds disturbed even me, though I was some distance away. It is now after the dinner-hour of the asylum, and as yet my patient sits in a corner brooding, with a dull, sullen, woe-begone look in his face, which seems rather to indicate than to show something directly. I cannot quite understand it.

Later.—Another change in my patient. At five o'clock I looked in on him, and found him seemingly as happy and contented as he used to be. He was catching flies and eating them, and was keeping note of his capture by making nail-marks on the edge of the door between the ridges of padding. When he saw me, he came over and apologised for his bad conduct, and asked me in a very humble, cringing way to be led back to his own room and to have his note-book again. I thought it well to humour him: so he is back in his room with the window open. He has the sugar of his tea spread out on the window-sill, and is reaping quite a harvest of flies. He is not now eating them, but putting them into a box, as of old, and is already examining the corners of his room to find a spider. I tried to get him to talk about the past few days, for any clue to his thoughts would be of immense help to me; but he would not rise. For a moment or two he looked very sad, and said in a sort of far-away voice, as though saying it rather to himself than to me:—

"All over! all over! He has deserted me. No hope for me now unless I do it for myself!" Then suddenly turning to me in a resolute way, he said: "Doctor, won't you be very good to me and let me have a little more sugar? I think it would be good for me."

"And the flies?" I said.

"Yes! The flies like it, too, and I like the flies; therefore I like it." And there are people who know so little as to think that madmen do not argue. I procured him a double supply, and left him as happy a man as, I suppose, any in the world. I wish I could fathom his mind.

Midnight.—Another change in him. I had been to see Miss Westenra, whom I found much better, and had just returned, and was standing at our own gate looking at the sunset, when once more I heard him yelling. As his room is on this side of the house, I could hear it better than in the morning. It was a shock to me to turn from the wonderful smoky beauty of a sunset over London, with its lurid lights and inky shadows and all the marvellous tints that come on foul clouds even as on foul water, and to realise all the grim sternness of my own cold stone building, with its wealth of breathing misery, and my own desolate heart to endure it all. I reached him just as the sun was going down, and from his window saw the red disc sink. As it sank he became less and less frenzied; and just as it dipped he slid from the hands that held him, an inert mass, on the floor. It is wonderful, however, what intellectual recuperative power lunatics have, for within a few minutes he stood up quite calmly and looked around him. I signalled to the attendants not to hold him, for I was anxious to see what he would do. He went straight over to the window and brushed out the crumbs of sugar; then he took his fly-box, and emptied it outside, and threw away the box; then he shut the window, and crossing over, sat down on his bed. All this surprised me, so I asked him: "Are you not going to keep flies any more?"

"No," said he; "I am sick of all that rubbish!" He certainly is a wonderfully interesting study. I wish I could get some glimpse of his mind or of the cause of his sudden passion. Stop; there may be a clue after all, if we can find why to-day his paroxysms came on at high noon and at sunset. Can it be that there is a malign influence of the sun at periods which affects certain natures—as at times the moon does others? We shall see.

**TELEGRAM,
SEWARD, LONDON,
TO VAN HELSING, AMSTERDAM.**

"*4 September.*—Patient still better to-day."

**TELEGRAM,
SEWARD, LONDON,
TO VAN HELSING, AMSTERDAM.**

"*5 September.*—Patient greatly improved. Good appetite; sleeps naturally; good spirits; colour coming back."

**TELEGRAM,
SEWARD, LONDON,
TO VAN HELSING, AMSTERDAM.**

"*6 September.*—Terrible change for the worse. Come at once; do not lose an hour. I hold over telegram to Holmwood till have seen you."

CHAPTER X

LETTER,
DR. SEWARD TO HON. ARTHUR HOLMWOOD.

"6 September.

"MY DEAR ART,—

"My news to-day is not so good. Lucy this morning had gone back a bit. There is, however, one good thing which has arisen from it; Mrs. Westenra was naturally anxious concerning Lucy, and has consulted me professionally about her. I took advantage of the opportunity, and told her that my old master, Van Helsing, the great specialist, was coming to stay with me, and that I would put her in his charge conjointly with myself; so now we can come and go without alarming her unduly, for a shock to her would mean sudden death, and this, in Lucy's weak condition, might be disastrous to her. We are hedged in with difficulties, all of us, my poor old fellow; but, please God, we shall come through them all right. If any need I shall write, so that, if you do not hear from me, take it for granted that I am simply waiting for news. In haste

Yours ever,
"JOHN SEWARD."

DR. SEWARD'S DIARY.

7 September.—The first thing Van Helsing said to me when we met at Liverpool Street was:—

"Have you said anything to our young friend the lover of her?"

"No," I said. "I waited till I had seen you, as I said in my telegram. I wrote him a letter simply telling him that you were coming, as Miss Westenra was not so well, and that I should let him know if need be."

"Right, my friend," he said, "quite right! Better he not know as yet;

perhaps he shall never know. I pray so; but if it be needed, then he shall know all. And, my good friend John, let me caution you. You deal with the madmen. All men are mad in some way or the other; and inasmuch as you deal discreetly with your madmen, so deal with God's madmen, too—the rest of the world. You tell not your madmen what you do nor why you do it; you tell them not what you think. So you shall keep knowledge in its place, where it may rest—where it may gather its kind around it and breed. You and I shall keep as yet what we know here, and here." He touched me on the heart and on the forehead, and then touched himself the same way. "I have for myself thoughts at the present. Later I shall unfold to you."

"Why not now?" I asked. "It may do some good; we may arrive at some decision." He stopped and looked at me, and said:—

"My friend John, when the corn is grown, even before it has ripened—while the milk of its mother-earth is in him, and the sunshine has not yet begun to paint him with his gold, the husbandman he pull the ear and rub him between his rough hands, and blow away the green chaff, and say to you: 'Look! he's good corn; he will make good crop when the time comes.' " I did not see the application, and told him so. For reply he reached over and took my ear in his hand and pulled it playfully, as he used long ago to do at lectures, and said: "The good husbandman tell you so then because he knows, but not till then. But you do not find the good husbandman dig up his planted corn to see if he grow; that is for the children who play at husbandry, and not for those who take it as of the work of their life. See you now, friend John? I have sown my corn, and Nature has her work to do in making it sprout; if he sprout at all, there's some promise; and I wait till the ear begins to swell." He broke off, for he evidently saw that I understood. Then he went on, and very gravely:—

"You were always a careful student, and your case-book was ever more full than the rest. You were only student then; now you are master, and I trust that good habit have not fail. Remember, my friend, that knowledge is stronger than memory, and we should not trust the weaker. Even if you have not kept the good practise, let me tell you that this case of our dear miss is one that may be—mind, I say *may be*—of such interest to us and others that all the rest may not make him kick the beam, as your peoples say. Take then good note of it. Nothing is too small. I counsel you, put down in record even your doubts and surmises. Hereafter it may be of interest to you to see how true you guess. We learn from failure, not from success!"

When I described Lucy's symptoms—the same as before, but infinitely more marked—he looked very grave, but said nothing. He took with him a bag in which were many instruments and drugs, "the ghastly paraphernalia of our beneficial trade," as he once called, in one of his lectures, the equipment of a professor of the healing craft. When we were shown in, Mrs. Westenra met us. She was alarmed, but not nearly so much as I expected to find her. Nature in one of her beneficent moods has ordained that even death has some antidote to its own terrors. Here, in a case where any shock may prove fatal, matters are so ordered that, from some cause or other, the things not personal—even the terrible change in her daughter to whom she is so attached—do not seem to reach her. It is something like the way Dame Nature gathers round a foreign body an envelope of some insensitive tissue which can protect from evil that which it would otherwise harm by contact. If this be an ordered selfishness, then we should pause before we condemn any one for the vice of egoism, for there may be deeper root for its causes than we have knowledge of.

I used my knowledge of this phase of spiritual pathology, and laid down a rule that she should not be present with Lucy or think of her illness more than was absolutely required. She assented readily, so readily that I saw again the hand of Nature fighting for life. Van Helsing and I were shown up to Lucy's room. If I was shocked when I saw her yesterday, I was horrified when I saw her to-day. She was ghastly, chalkily pale; the red seemed to have gone even from her lips and gums, and the bones of her face stood out prominently; her breathing was painful to see or hear. Van Helsing's face grew set as marble, and his eyebrows converged till they almost touched over his nose. Lucy lay motionless, and did not seem to have strength to speak, so for a while we were all silent. Then Van Helsing beckoned to me, and we went gently out of the room. The instant we had closed the door he stepped quickly along the passage to the next door, which was open. Then he pulled me quickly in with him and closed the door. "My God!" he said; "this is dreadful. There is no time to be lost. She will die for sheer want of blood to keep the heart's action as it should be. There must be transfusion of blood at once. Is it you or me?"

"I am younger and stronger, Professor. It must be me."

"Then get ready at once. I will bring up my bag. I am prepared."

I went downstairs with him, and as we were going there was a knock at the hall-door. When we reached the hall the maid had just opened the door, and Arthur was stepping quickly in. He rushed up to me, saying in an eager whisper:—

"Jack, I was so anxious. I read between the lines of your letter, and have been in an agony. The dad was better, so I ran down here to see for myself. Is not that gentleman Dr. Van Helsing? I am so thankful to you, sir, for coming." When first the Professor's eye had lit upon him he had been angry at his interruption at such a time; but now, as he took in his stalwart proportions and recognised the strong young manhood which seemed to emanate from him, his eyes gleamed. Without a pause he said to him gravely as he held out his hand:—

"Sir, you have come in time. You are the lover of our dear miss. She is bad, very, very bad. Nay, my child, do not go like that." For he suddenly grew pale and sat down in a chair almost fainting. "You are to help her. You can do more than any that live, and your courage is your best help."

"What can I do?" asked Arthur hoarsely. "Tell me, and I shall do it. My life is hers, and I would give the last drop of blood in my body for her." The Professor has a strongly humorous side, and I could from old knowledge detect a trace of its origin in his answer:—

"My young sir, I do not ask so much as that—not the last!"

"What shall I do?" There was fire in his eyes, and his open nostril quivered with intent. Van Helsing slapped him on the shoulder. "Come!" he said. "You are a man, and it is a man we want. You are better than me, better than my friend John." Arthur looked bewildered, and the Professor went on by explaining in a kindly way:—

"Young miss is bad, very bad. She wants blood, and blood she must have or die. My friend John and I have consulted; and we are about to perform what we call transfusion of blood—to transfer from full veins of one to the empty veins which pine for him. John was to give his blood, as he is the more young and strong than me"—here Arthur took my hand and wrung it hard in silence—"but, now you are here, you are more good than us, old or young, who toil much in the world of thought. Our nerves are not so calm and our blood not so bright than yours!" Arthur turned to him and said:—

"If you only knew how gladly I would die for her you would understand——"

He stopped, with a sort of choke in his voice.

"Good boy!" said Van Helsing. "In the not-so-far-off you will be happy that you have done all for her you love. Come now and be silent. You shall kiss her once before it is done, but then you must go; and you must leave at my sign. Say no word to Madame; you know how it is with her! There must be no shock; any knowledge of this would be one. Come!"

We all went up to Lucy's room. Arthur by direction remained outside. Lucy turned her head and looked at us, but said nothing. She was not asleep, but she was simply too weak to make the effort. Her eyes spoke to us; that was all. Van Helsing took some things from his bag and laid them on a little table out of sight. Then he mixed a narcotic, and coming over to the bed, said cheerily:—

"Now, little miss, here is your medicine. Drink it off, like a good child. See, I lift you so that to swallow is easy. Yes." She had made the effort with success.

It astonished me how long the drug took to act. This, in fact, marked the extent of her weakness. The time seemed endless until sleep began to flicker in her eyelids. At last, however, the narcotic began to manifest its potency; and she fell into a deep sleep. When the Professor was satisfied he called Arthur into the room, and bade him strip off his coat. Then he added: "You may take that one little kiss whiles I bring over the table. Friend John, help to me!" So neither of us looked whilst he bent over her.

Van Helsing turning to me, said:

"He is so young and strong and of blood so pure that we need not defibrinate it."

Then with swiftness, but with absolute method, Van Helsing performed the operation. As the transfusion went on something like life seemed to come back to poor Lucy's cheeks, and through Arthur's growing pallor the joy of his face seemed absolutely to shine. After a bit I began to grow anxious, for the loss of blood was telling on Arthur, strong man as he was. It gave me an idea of what a terrible strain Lucy's system must have undergone that what weakened Arthur only partially restored her. But the Professor's face was set, and he stood watch in hand and with his eyes fixed now on the patient and now on Arthur. I could hear my own heart beat. Presently he said in a soft voice: "Do not stir an instant. It is enough. You attend him; I will look to her." When all was over I could see how much Arthur was weakened. I dressed the wound and took his arm to bring him away, when Van Helsing spoke without turning round—the man seems to have eyes in the back of his head:—

"The brave lover, I think, deserve another kiss, which he shall have presently." And as he had now finished his operation, he adjusted the pillow to the patient's head. As he did so the narrow black velvet band which she seems always to wear round her throat, buckled with an old diamond buckle which her lover had given her, was dragged a little up, and showed a red mark on her throat. Arthur did not notice it, but I could hear the deep hiss of indrawn breath which is one of Van Helsing's ways of betraying emotion. He said nothing at the moment, but turned to me, saying: "Now take down our brave young lover, give him of the port wine, and let him lie down a while. He must then go home and rest, sleep much and eat much, that he may be recruited of what he has so given to his love. He must not stay here. Hold! a moment. I may take it, sir, that you are anxious of result. Then bring it with you that in all ways the operation is successful. You have saved her life this time, and you can go home and rest easy in mind that all that can be is. I shall tell her all when she is well; she shall love you none the less for what you have done. Good-bye."

When Arthur had gone I went back to the room. Lucy was sleeping gently, but her breathing was stronger; I could see the counterpane move as her breast heaved. By the bedside sat Van Helsing, looking at her intently. The velvet band again covered the red mark. I asked the Professor in a whisper:—

"What do you make of that mark on her throat?"

"What do you make of it?"

"I have not examined it yet," I answered, and then and there proceeded to loose the band. Just over the external jugular vein there were two punctures, not large, but not wholesome-looking. There was no sign of disease, but the edges were white and worn-looking, as if by some trituration. It at once occurred to me that this wound, or whatever it was, might be the means of that manifest loss of blood; but I abandoned the idea as soon as formed, for such a thing could not be. The whole bed would have been drenched to a scarlet with the blood which the girl must have lost to leave such a pallor as she had before the transfusion.

"Well?" said Van Helsing.

"Well," said I, "I can make nothing of it." The Professor stood up. "I must go back to Amsterdam to-night," he said. "There are books and things there which I want. You must remain here all the night, and you must not let your sight pass from her."

"Shall I have a nurse?" I asked.

"We are the best nurses, you and I. You keep watch all night; see that she is well fed, and that nothing disturbs her. You must not sleep all the night. Later on we can sleep, you and I. I shall be back as soon as possible. And then we may begin."

"May begin?" I said. "What on earth do you mean?"

"We shall see!" he answered, as he hurried out. He came back a moment later and put his head inside the door and said with warning finger held up:—

"Remember, she is your charge. If you leave her, and harm befall, you shall not sleep easy hereafter!"

DR. SEWARD'S DIARY—*continued.*

8 September.—I sat up all night with Lucy. The opiate worked itself off towards dusk, and she waked naturally; she looked a different being from what she had been before the operation. Her spirits even were good, and she was full of a happy vivacity, but I could see evidences of the absolute prostration which she had undergone. When I told Mrs. Westenra that Dr. Van Helsing had directed that I should sit up with her she almost pooh-poohed the idea, pointing out her daughter's renewed strength and excellent spirits. I was firm, however, and made preparations for my long vigil. When her maid had prepared her for the night I came in, having in the meantime had supper, and took a seat by the bedside. She did not in any way make objection, but looked at me gratefully whenever I caught her eye. After a long spell she seemed sinking off to sleep, but with an effort seemed to pull herself together and shook it off. This was repeated several times, with greater effort and with shorter pauses as the time moved on. It was apparent that she did not want to sleep, so I tackled the subject at once:—

"You do not want to go to sleep?"

"No; I am afraid."

"Afraid to go to sleep! Why so? It is the boon we all crave for."

"Ah, not if you were like me—if sleep was to you a presage of horror!"

"A presage of horror! What on earth do you mean?"

"I don't know; oh, I don't know. And that is what is so terrible. All this weakness comes to me in sleep; until I dread the very thought."

"But, my dear girl, you may sleep to-night. I am here watching you, and I can promise that nothing will happen."

"Ah, I can trust you!" I seized the opportunity, and said: "I promise you that if I see any evidence of bad dreams I will wake you at once."

"You will? Oh, will you really? How good you are to me. Then I will sleep!" And almost at the word she gave a deep sigh of relief, and sank back, asleep.

All night long I watched by her. She never stirred, but slept on and on in a deep, tranquil, life-giving, health-giving sleep. Her lips were slightly parted, and her breast rose and fell with the regularity of a pendulum. There was a smile on her face, and it was evident that no bad dreams had come to disturb her peace of mind.

In the early morning her maid came, and I left her in her care and took myself back home, for I was anxious about many things. I sent a short wire to Van Helsing and to Arthur, telling them of the excellent result of the operation. My own work, with its manifold arrears, took me all day to clear off; it was dark when I was able to inquire about my zoöphagous patient. The report was good; he had been quite quiet for the past day and night. A telegram came from Van Helsing at Amsterdam whilst I was at dinner, suggesting that I should be at Hillingham to-night, as it might be well to be at hand, and stating that he was leaving by the night mail and would join me early in the morning.

9 September.—I was pretty tired and worn out when I got to Hillingham. For two nights I had hardly had a wink of sleep, and my brain was beginning to feel that numbness which marks cerebral exhaustion. Lucy was up and in cheerful spirits. When she shook hands with me she looked sharply in my face and said:—

"No sitting up to-night for you. You are worn out. I am quite well again; indeed, I am; and if there is to be any sitting up, it is I who will sit up with you." I would not argue the point, but went and had my supper. Lucy came with me, and, enlivened by her charming presence, I made an excellent meal, and had a couple of glasses of the more than excellent port. Then Lucy took me upstairs, and showed me a room next her own, where a cozy fire was burning. "Now," she said, "you must stay here. I shall leave this door open and my door too. You can lie on the sofa for I know that nothing would induce any of you doctors to go to bed whilst there is a patient above the horizon. If I want anything I shall call out, and you can come to me at once." I could not but acquiesce, for I was "dog-tired," and could not have sat up had I tried. So, on her renewing her promise to call me if she should want anything, I lay on the sofa, and forgot all about everything.

LUCY WESTENRA'S DIARY.

9 September.—I feel so happy to-night. I have been so miserably weak, that to be able to think and move about is like feeling sunshine after a long spell of east wind out of a steel sky. Somehow Arthur feels very, very close to me. I seem to feel his presence warm about me. I suppose it is that sickness and weakness are selfish things and turn our inner eyes and sympathy on ourselves, whilst health and strength give Love rein, and in thought and feeling he can wander where he wills. I know where my thoughts are. If Arthur only knew! My dear, my dear, your ears must tingle as you sleep, as mine do waking. Oh, the blissful rest of last night! How I slept, with that dear, good Dr. Seward watching me. And to-night I shall not fear to sleep, since he is close at hand and within call. Thank everybody for being so good to me! Thank God! Good-night, Arthur.

DR. SEWARD'S DIARY.

10 September.—I was conscious of the Professor's hand on my head, and started awake all in a second. That is one of the things that we learn in an asylum, at any rate.

"And how is our patient?"

"Well, when I left her, or rather when she left me," I answered.

"Come, let us see," he said. And together we went into the room. The blind was down, and I went over to raise it gently, whilst Van Helsing stepped, with his soft, cat-like tread, over to the bed.

As I raised the blind, and the morning sunlight flooded the room, I heard the Professor's low hiss of inspiration, and knowing its rarity, a deadly fear shot through my heart. As I passed over he moved back, and his exclamation of horror, "Gott in Himmel!" needed no enforcement from his agonised face. He raised his hand and pointed to the bed, and his iron face was drawn and ashen white. I felt my knees begin to tremble.

There on the bed, seemingly in a swoon, lay poor Lucy, more horribly white and wan-looking than ever. Even the lips were white, and the gums seemed to have shrunken back from the teeth, as we sometimes see in a corpse after a prolonged illness. Van Helsing raised his foot to stamp in anger, but the instinct of his life and all the long years of habit stood to him, and he put it down again softly. "Quick!" he said. "Bring the brandy." I flew to the dining-room, and returned with the decanter. He wetted the poor white lips with it, and together we rubbed palm and wrist and heart. He felt her heart, and after a few moments of agonising suspense said:—

"It is not too late. It beats, though but feebly. All our work is undone; we must begin again. There is no young Arthur here now; I have to call on you yourself this time, friend John." As he spoke, he was dipping into his bag and producing the instruments for transfusion; I had taken off my coat and rolled up my shirt-sleeve. There was no possibility of an opiate just at present, and no need of one; and so, without a moment's delay, we began the operation. After a time—it did not seem a short time either, for the draining away of one's blood, no matter how willingly it be given, is a terrible feeling—Van Helsing held up a warning finger. "Do not stir," he said, "but I fear that with growing strength she may wake; and that would make danger, oh, so much danger. But I shall precaution take. I shall give hypodermic injection of morphia." He proceeded then, swiftly and deftly, to carry out his intent. The effect on Lucy was not bad, for the faint seemed to merge subtly into the narcotic sleep. It was with a feeling of personal pride that I could see a faint tinge of colour steal back into the pallid cheeks and lips. No man knows, till he experiences it, what it is to feel his own life-blood drawn away into the veins of the woman he loves.

The Professor watched me critically. "That will do," he said. "Already?" I remonstrated. "You took a great deal more from Art." To which he smiled a sad sort of smile as he replied:—

"He is her lover, her *fiancé*. You have work, much work, to do for her and for others; and the present will suffice."

When we stopped the operation, he attended to Lucy, whilst I applied digital pressure to my own incision. I laid down, whilst I waited his leisure to attend to me, for I felt faint and a little sick. By-and-by he bound up my wound, and sent me downstairs to get a glass of wine for myself. As I was leaving the room, he came after me, and half whispered:—

"Mind, nothing must be said of this. If our young lover should turn up unexpected, as before, no word to him. It would at once frighten him and enjealous him, too. There must be none. So!"

When I came back he looked at me carefully, and then said:—

"You are not much the worse. Go into the room, and lie on your sofa, and rest awhile; then have much breakfast, and come here to me."

I followed out his orders, for I knew how right and wise they were. I had done my part, and now my next duty was to keep up my strength. I felt very weak, and in the weakness lost something of the amazement at what had occurred. I fell asleep on the sofa, however, wondering over and over again how Lucy had made such a retrograde movement, and how she could have been drained of so much blood with no sign anywhere to show for it. I think I must have continued my wonder in my dreams, for, sleeping and waking, my thoughts always came back to the little punctures in her throat and the ragged, exhausted appearance of their edges—tiny though they were.

Lucy slept well into the day, and when she woke she was fairly well and strong, though not nearly so much so as the day before. When Van Helsing had seen her, he went out for a walk, leaving me in charge, with strict injunctions that I was not to leave her for a moment. I could hear his voice in the hall, asking the way to the nearest telegraph office.

Lucy chatted with me freely, and seemed quite unconscious that anything had happened. I tried to keep her amused and interested. When her mother came up to see her, she did not seem to notice any change whatever, but said to me gratefully:—

"We owe you so much, Dr. Seward, for all you have done, but you really must now take care not to overwork yourself. You are looking pale yourself. You want a wife to nurse and look after you a bit; that you do!" As she spoke, Lucy turned crimson, though it was only momentarily, for her poor wasted veins could not stand for long such an unwonted drain to the head. The reaction came in excessive pallor as she turned imploring eyes on me. I smiled and nodded, and laid my finger on my lips; with a sigh, she sank back amid her pillows.

Van Helsing returned in a couple of hours, and presently said to me: "Now you go home, and eat much and drink enough. Make yourself strong. I stay here to-night, and I shall sit up with little miss myself. You and I must watch the case, and we must have none other to know. I have grave reasons. No, do not ask them; think what you will. Do not fear to think even the most not-probable. Good-night."

In the hall two of the maids came to me, and asked if they or either of them might not sit up with Miss Lucy. They implored me to let them; and when I said it was Dr. Van Helsing's wish that either he or I should sit up, they asked me quite piteously to intercede with the "foreign gentleman." I was much touched by their kindness. Perhaps it is because I am weak at present, and perhaps because it was on Lucy's account, that their devotion was manifested; for over and over again have I seen similar instances of woman's kindness. I got back here in time for a late dinner; went my rounds—all well; and set this down whilst waiting for sleep. It is coming.

11 September.—This afternoon I went over to Hillingham. Found Van Helsing in excellent spirits, and Lucy much better. Shortly after I had arrived, a big parcel from abroad came for the Professor. He opened it with much impressment—assumed, of course—and showed a great bundle of white flowers.

"These are for you, Miss Lucy," he said.

"For me? Oh, Dr. Van Helsing!"

"Yes, my dear, but not for you to play with. These are medicines." Here Lucy made a wry face. "Nay, but they are not to take in a decoction or in nauseous form, so you need not snub that so charming nose, or I shall point out to my friend Arthur what woes he may have to endure in seeing so much beauty that he so loves so much distort. Aha, my pretty miss, that bring the so nice nose all straight again. This is medicinal, but you do not know how. I put him in your window, I make pretty wreath, and hang him round your neck, so that you sleep well. Oh yes! they, like the lotus flower, make your trouble forgotten. It smell so like the waters of Lethe, and of that fountain of youth that the Conquistadores sought for in the Floridas, and find him all too late."

Whilst he was speaking, Lucy had been examining the flowers and smelling them. Now she threw them down, saying, with half-laughter, and half-disgust:—

"Oh, Professor, I believe you are only putting up a joke on me. Why, these flowers are only common garlic."

To my surprise, Van Helsing rose up and said with all his sternness, his iron jaw set and his bushy eyebrows meeting:—

"No trifling with me! I never jest! There is grim purpose in all I do; and I warn you that you do not thwart me. Take care, for the sake of others if not for your own." Then seeing poor Lucy scared, as she might well be, he went on more gently: "Oh, little miss, my dear, do not fear me. I only do for your good; but there is much virtue to you in those so common flowers. See, I place them myself in your room. I make myself the wreath that you are to wear. But hush! no telling to others that make so inquisitive questions. We must obey, and silence is a part of obedience; and obedience is to bring you strong and well into loving arms that wait for you. Now sit still awhile. Come with me, friend John, and you shall help me deck the room with my garlic, which is all the way from Haarlem, where my friend Vanderpool raise herb in his glass-houses all the year. I had to telegraph yesterday, or they would not have been here."

We went into the room, taking the flowers with us. The Professor's actions were certainly odd and not to be found in any pharmacopœia that I ever heard of. First he fastened up the windows and latched them securely; next, taking a handful of the flowers, he rubbed them all over the sashes, as though to ensure that every whiff of air that might get in would be laden with the garlic smell. Then with the wisp he rubbed all over the jamb of the door, above, below, and at each side, and round the fireplace in the same way. It all seemed grotesque to me, and presently I said:—

"Well, Professor, I know you always have a reason for what you do, but this certainly puzzles me. It is well we have no sceptic here, or he would say that you were working some spell to keep out an evil spirit."

"Perhaps I am!" he answered quietly as he began to make the wreath which Lucy was to wear round her neck.

We then waited whilst Lucy made her toilet for the night, and when she was in bed he came and himself fixed the wreath of garlic round her neck. The last words he said to her were:—

"Take care you do not disturb it; and even if the room feel close, do not to-night open the window or the door."

"I promise," said Lucy, "and thank you both a thousand times for all your kindness to me! Oh, what have I done to be blessed with such friends?"

As we left the house in my fly, which was waiting, Van Helsing said:—

"To-night I can sleep in peace, and sleep I want—two nights of travel, much reading in the day between, and much anxiety on the day to follow, and a night to sit up, without to wink. To-morrow in the morning early you call for me, and we come together to see our pretty miss, so much more strong for my 'spell' which I have work. Ho! ho!"

He seemed so confident that I, remembering my own confidence two nights before and with the baneful result, felt awe and vague terror. It must have been my weakness that made me hesitate to tell it to my friend, but I felt it all the more, like unshed tears.

CHAPTER XI

LUCY WESTENRA'S DIARY.

12 September.—How good they all are to me. I quite love that dear Dr. Van Helsing. I wonder why he was so anxious about these flowers. He positively frightened me, he was so fierce. And yet he must have been right, for I feel comfort from them already. Somehow, I do not dread being alone to-night, and I can go to sleep without fear. I shall not mind any flapping outside the window. Oh, the terrible struggle that I have had against sleep so often of late; the pain of the sleeplessness, or the pain of the fear of sleep, with such unknown horrors as it has for me! How blessed are some people, whose lives have no fears, no dreads; to whom sleep is a blessing that comes nightly, and brings nothing but sweet dreams. Well, here I am to-night, hoping for sleep, and lying like Ophelia in the play, with "virgin crants and maiden strewments." I never liked garlic before, but to-night it is delightful! There is peace in its smell; I feel sleep coming already. Good-night, everybody.

DR. SEWARD'S DIARY.

13 September.—Called at the Berkeley and found Van Helsing, as usual, up to time. The carriage ordered from the hotel was waiting. The Professor took his bag, which he always brings with him now.

Let all be put down exactly. Van Helsing and I arrived at Hillingham at eight o'clock. It was a lovely morning; the bright sunshine and all the fresh feeling of early autumn seemed like the completion of nature's annual work. The leaves were turning to all kinds of beautiful colours, but had not yet begun to drop from the trees. When we entered we met Mrs. Westenra coming out of the morning room. She is always an early riser. She greeted us warmly and said:—

"You will be glad to know that Lucy is better. The dear child is still asleep. I looked into her room and saw her, but did not go in, lest I should disturb her." The Professor smiled, and looked quite jubilant. He rubbed his hands together, and said:—

"Aha! I thought I had diagnosed the case. My treatment is working," to which she answered:—

"You must not take all the credit to yourself, doctor. Lucy's state this morning is due in part to me."

"How you do mean, ma'am?" asked the Professor.

"Well, I was anxious about the dear child in the night, and went into her room. She was sleeping soundly—so soundly that even my coming did not wake her. But the room was awfully stuffy. There were a lot of those horrible, strong-smelling flowers about everywhere, and she had actually a bunch of them round her neck. I feared that the heavy odour would be too much for the dear child in her weak state, so I took them all away and opened a bit of the window to let in a little fresh air. You will be pleased with her, I am sure."

She moved off into her boudoir, where she usually breakfasted early. As she had spoken, I watched the Professor's face, and saw it turn ashen grey. He had been able to retain his self-command whilst the poor lady was present, for he knew her state and how mischievous a shock would be; he actually smiled on her as he held open the door for her to pass into her room. But the instant she had disappeared he pulled me, suddenly and forcibly, into the dining-room and closed the door.

Then, for the first time in my life, I saw Van Helsing break down. He raised his hands over his head in a sort of mute despair, and then beat his palms together in a helpless way; finally he sat down on a chair, and putting his hands before his face, began to sob, with loud, dry sobs that seemed to come from the very racking of his heart. Then he raised his arms again, as though appealing to the whole universe. "God! God! God!" he said. "What have we done, what has this poor thing done, that we are so sore beset? Is there fate amongst us still, sent down from the pagan world of old, that such things must be, and in such way? This poor mother, all unknowing, and all for the best as she think, does such thing as lose her daughter body and soul; and we must not tell her, we must not even warn her, or she die, and then both die. Oh, how we are beset! How are all the powers of the devils against us!" Suddenly he jumped to his feet. "Come," he said, "come, we must see and act. Devils or no devils, or all the devils at once, it matters not; we fight him all the same." He went to the hall-door for his bag; and together we went up to Lucy's room.

Once again I drew up the blind, whilst Van Helsing went towards the bed. This time he did not start as he looked on the poor face with the same awful, waxen pallor as before. He wore a look of stern sadness and infinite pity.

"As I expected," he murmured, with that hissing inspiration of his which meant so much. Without a word he went and locked the door, and then began to set out on the little table the instruments for yet another operation of transfusion of blood. I had long ago recognised the necessity, and begun to take off my coat, but he stopped me with a warning hand. "No!" he said. "To-day you must operate. I shall provide. You are weakened already." As he spoke he took off his coat and rolled up his shirt-sleeve.

Again the operation; again the narcotic; again some return of colour to the ashy cheeks, and the regular breathing of healthy sleep. This time I watched whilst Van Helsing recruited himself and rested.

Presently he took an opportunity of telling Mrs. Westenra that she must not remove anything from Lucy's room without consulting him; that the flowers were of medicinal value, and that the breathing of their odour was a part of the system of cure. Then he took over the care of the case himself, saying that he would watch this night and the next and would send me word when to come.

After another hour Lucy waked from her sleep, fresh and bright and seemingly not much the worse for her terrible ordeal.

What does it all mean? I am beginning to wonder if my long habit of life amongst the insane is beginning to tell upon my own brain.

LUCY WESTENRA'S DIARY.

17 September.—Four days and nights of peace. I am getting so strong again that I hardly know myself. It is as if I had passed through some long nightmare, and had just awakened to see the beautiful sunshine and feel the fresh air of the morning around me. I have a dim half-remembrance of long, anxious times of waiting and fearing; darkness in which there was not even the pain of hope to make present distress more poignant: and then long spells of oblivion, and the rising back to life as a diver coming up through a great press of water. Since, however, Dr. Van Helsing has been with me, all this bad dreaming seems to have passed away; the noises that used to frighten me out of my wits—the flapping against the windows, the distant voices which seemed so close to me, the harsh sounds that came from I know not where and commanded me to do I know not what—have all ceased. I go to bed now without any fear of sleep. I do not even try to keep awake. I have grown quite fond of the garlic, and a boxful arrives for me every day from Haarlem. To-night Dr. Van Helsing is going away, as he has to be for a day in Amsterdam. But I need not be watched; I am well enough to be left alone. Thank God for mother's sake, and dear Arthur's, and for all our friends who have been so kind! I shall not even feel the change, for last night Dr. Van

Helsing slept in his chair a lot of the time. I found him asleep twice when I awoke; but I did not fear to go to sleep again, although the boughs or bats or something napped almost angrily against the window-panes.

"The Pall Mall Gazette," 18 September.

THE ESCAPED WOLF.
PERILOUS ADVENTURE OF OUR INTERVIEWER.

INTERVIEW WITH THE
KEEPER IN THE ZOÖLOGICAL GARDENS.

After many inquiries and almost as many refusals, and perpetually using the words "Pall Mall Gazette" as a sort of talisman, I managed to find the keeper of the section of the Zoölogical Gardens in which the wolf department is included. Thomas Bilder lives in one of the cottages in the enclosure behind the elephant-house, and was just sitting down to his tea when I found him. Thomas and his wife are hospitable folk, elderly, and without children, and if the specimen I enjoyed of their hospitality be of the average kind, their lives must be pretty comfortable. The keeper would not enter on what he called "business" until the supper was over, and we were all satisfied. Then when the table was cleared, and he had lit his pipe, he said:—

"Now, sir, you can go on and arsk me what you want. You'll excoose me refoosin' to talk of perfeshunal subjects afore meals. I gives the wolves and the jackals and the hyenas in all our section their tea afore I begins to arsk them questions."

"How do you mean, ask them questions?" I queried, wishful to get him into a talkative humour.

" 'Ittin' of them over the 'ead with a pole is one way; scratchin' of their hears is another, when gents as is flush wants a bit of a show-orf to their gals. I don't so much mind the fust—the 'ittin' with a pole afore I chucks in their dinner; but I waits till they've 'ad their sherry and kawffee, so to speak, afore I tries on with the ear-scratchin'. Mind you," he added philosophically, "there's a deal of the same nature in us as in them theer animiles. Here's you a-comin' and arskin' of me questions about my business, and I that grumpy-like that only for your bloomin' 'arf-quid I'd 'a' seen you blowed fust 'fore I'd answer. Not even when you arsked me sarcastic-like if I'd like you to arsk the Superintendent if you might arsk me questions. Without offence did I tell yer to go to 'ell?"

"You did."

"An' when you said you'd report me for usin' of obscene language that was 'ittin' me over the 'ead; but the 'arf-quid made that all right. I weren't a-goin' to fight, so I waited for the food, and did with my 'owl as the wolves, and lions, and tigers does. But, Lor' love yer 'art, now that the old 'ooman has stuck a chunk of her tea-cake in me, an' rinsed me out with her bloomin' old teapot, and I've lit hup, you may scratch my ears for all you're worth, and won't git even a growl out of me. Drive along with your questions. I know what yer a-comin' at, that 'ere escaped wolf."

"Exactly. I want you to give me your view of it. Just tell me how it happened; and when I know the facts I'll get you to say what you consider was the cause of it, and how you think the whole affair will end."

"All right, guv'nor. This 'ere is about the 'ole story. That 'ere wolf what we called Bersicker was one of three grey ones that came from Norway to Jamrach's, which we bought off him four years ago. He was a nice well-behaved wolf, that never gave no trouble to talk of. I'm more surprised at 'im for wantin' to get out nor any other animile in the place. But, there, you can't trust wolves no more nor women."

"Don't you mind him, sir!" broke in Mrs. Tom, with a cheery laugh. " 'E's got mindin' the animiles so long that blest if he ain't like a old wolf 'isself! But there ain't no 'arm in 'im."

"Well, sir, it was about two hours after feedin' yesterday when I first hear my disturbance. I was makin' up a litter in the monkey-house for a young puma which is ill; but when I heard the yelpin' and 'owlin' I kem away straight. There was Bersicker a-tearin' like a mad thing at the bars as if he wanted to get out. There wasn't much people about that day, and close at hand was only one man, a tall, thin chap, with a 'ook nose and a pointed beard, with a few white hairs runnin' through it. He had a 'ard, cold look and red eyes, and I took a sort of mislike to him, for it seemed as if it was 'im as they was hirritated at. He 'ad white kid gloves on 'is 'ands, and he pointed out the animiles to me and says: 'Keeper, these wolves seem upset at something.'

" 'Maybe it's you,' says I, for I did not like the airs as he give 'isself. He didn't git angry, as I 'oped he would, but he smiled a kind of insolent smile, with a mouth full of white, sharp teeth. 'Oh no, they wouldn't like me,' 'e says.

" 'Ow yes, they would,' says I, a-imitatin' of him. 'They always likes a bone or two to clean their teeth on about tea-time, which you 'as a bagful.'

"Well, it was a odd thing, but when the animiles see us a-talkin' they lay down, and when I went over to Bersicker he let me stroke his ears same as ever. That there man kem over, and blessed but if he didn't put in his hand and stroke the old wolf's ears too!

" 'Tyke care,' says I. 'Bersicker is quick.'

" 'Never mind,' he says. 'I'm used to 'em!'

" 'Are you in the business yourself?' I says, tyking off my 'at, for a man what trades in wolves, anceterer, is a good friend to keepers.

" 'No' says he, 'not exactly in the business, but I 'ave made pets of several.' And with that he lifts his 'at as perlite as a lord, and walks away. Old Bersicker kep' a-lookin' arter 'im till 'e was out of sight, and then went and lay down in a corner and wouldn't come hout the 'ole hevening. Well, larst night, so soon as the moon was hup, the wolves here all began a-'owling. There warn't nothing for them to 'owl at. There warn't no one near, except some one that was evidently a-callin' a dog somewheres out back of the gardings in the Park road. Once or twice I went out to see that all was right, and it was, and then the 'owling stopped. Just before twelve o'clock I just took a look round afore turnin' in, an', bust me, but when I kem opposite to old Bersicker's cage I see the rails broken and twisted about and the cage empty. And that's all I know for certing."

"Did any one else see anything?"

"One of our gard'ners was a-comin' 'ome about that time from a 'armony, when he sees a big grey dog comin' out through the garding 'edges. At least, so he says, but I don't give much for it myself, for if he did 'e never said a word about it to his missis when 'e got 'ome, and it was only after the escape of the wolf was made known, and we had been up all night-a-huntin' of the Park for Bersicker, that he remembered seein' anything. My own belief was that the 'armony 'ad got into his 'ead."

"Now, Mr. Bilder, can you account in any way for the escape of the wolf?"

"Well, sir," he said, with a suspicious sort of modesty, "I think I can; but I don't know as 'ow you'd be satisfied with the theory."

"Certainly I shall. If a man like you, who knows the animals from experience, can't hazard a good guess at any rate, who is even to try?"

"Well then, sir, I accounts for it this way; it seems to me that 'ere wolf escaped—simply because he wanted to get out."

From the hearty way that both Thomas and his wife laughed at the joke I could see that it had done service before, and that the whole explanation was simply an elaborate sell. I couldn't cope in badinage with the worthy Thomas, but I thought I knew a surer way to his heart, so I said:—

"Now, Mr. Bilder, we'll consider that first half-sovereign worked off, and this brother of his is waiting to be claimed when you've told me what you think will happen."

"Right y'are, sir," he said briskly. "Ye'll excoose me, I know, for a-chaffin' of ye, but the old woman here winked at me, which was as much as telling me to go on."

"Well, I never!" said the old lady.

"My opinion is this: that 'ere wolf is a-'idin' of, somewheres. The gard'ner wot didn't remember said he was a-gallopin' northward faster than a horse could go; but I don't believe him, for, yer see, sir, wolves don't gallop no more nor dogs does, they not bein' built that way. Wolves is fine things in a storybook, and I dessay when they gets in packs and does be chivyin' somethin' that's more afeared than they is they can make a devil of a noise and chop it up, whatever it is. But, Lor' bless you, in real life a wolf is only a low creature, not half so clever or bold as a good dog; and not half a quarter so much fight in 'im. This one ain't been used to fightin' or even to providin' for hisself, and more like he's somewhere round the Park a-'idin' an' a-shiverin' of, and, if he thinks at all, wonderin' where he is to get his breakfast from; or maybe he's got down some area and is in a coal-cellar. My eye, won't some cook get a rum start when she sees his green eyes a-shining at her out of the dark! If he can't get food he's bound to look for it, and mayhap he may chance to light on a butcher's shop in time. If he doesn't, and some nursemaid goes a-walkin' orf with a soldier, leavin' of the hinfant in the perambulator—well, then I shouldn't be surprised if the census is one babby the less. That's all."

I was handing him the half-sovereign, when something came bobbing up against the window, and Mr. Bilder's face doubled its natural length with surprise.

"God bless me!" he said. "If there ain't old Bersicker come back by 'isself!"

He went to the door and opened it; a most unnecessary proceeding it seemed to me. I have always thought that a wild animal never looks so well as when some obstacle of pronounced durability is between us; a personal experience has intensified rather than diminished that idea.

After all, however, there is nothing like custom, for neither Bilder nor his wife thought any more of the wolf than I should of a dog. The animal itself was as peaceful and well-behaved as that father of all picture-wolves— Red Riding Hood's quondam friend, whilst moving her confidence in masquerade.

The whole scene was an unutterable mixture of comedy and pathos. The wicked wolf that for half a day had paralysed London and set all the children in the town shivering in their shoes, was there in a sort of penitent mood, and was received and petted like a sort of vulpine prodigal son. Old Bilder examined him all over with most tender solicitude, and when he had finished with his penitent said:—

"There, I knew the poor old chap would get into some kind of trouble; didn't I say it all along? Here's his head all cut and full of broken glass. 'E's been a-gettin' over some bloomin' wall or other. It's a shyme that people are allowed to top their walls with broken bottles. This 'ere's what comes of it. Come along, Bersicker."

He took the wolf and locked him up in a cage, with a piece of meat that satisfied, in quantity at any rate, the elementary conditions of the fatted calf, and went off to report.

I came off, too, to report the only exclusive information that is given to-day regarding the strange escapade at the Zoo.

DR. SEWARD'S DIARY.

17 September.—I was engaged after dinner in my study posting up my books, which, through press of other work and the many visits to Lucy, had fallen sadly into arrear. Suddenly the door was burst open, and in rushed my patient, with his face distorted with passion. I was thunderstruck, for such a thing as a patient getting of his own accord into the Superintendent's study is almost unknown. Without an instant's pause he made straight at me. He had a dinner-knife in his hand, and, as I saw he was dangerous, I tried to keep the table between us. He was too quick and too strong for me, however; for before I could get my balance he had struck at me and cut my left wrist rather severely. Before he could strike again, however, I got in my right and he was sprawling on his back on the floor. My wrist bled freely, and quite a little pool trickled on to the carpet. I saw that my friend was not intent on further effort, and occupied myself binding up my wrist, keeping a wary eye on the prostrate figure all the time. When the attendants rushed in, and we turned our attention to him, his employment positively sickened me. He was lying on his belly on the floor licking up, like a dog, the blood which had fallen from my wounded wrist. He was easily secured, and, to my surprise, went with the attendants quite placidly, simply repeating over and over again: "The blood is the life! The blood is the life!"

I cannot afford to lose blood just at present; I have lost too much of late for my physical good, and then the prolonged strain of Lucy's illness and its horrible phases is telling on me. I am over-excited and weary, and I need rest, rest, rest. Happily Van Helsing has not summoned me, so I need not forego my sleep; to-night I could not well do without it.

TELEGRAM, VAN HELSING,
ANTWERP, TO SEWARD, CARFAX.

*(Sent to Carfax, Sussex, as no county
given; delivered late by twenty-two hours.)*

"*17 September.*—Do not fail to be at Hillingham to-night. If not watching all the time frequently, visit and see that flowers are as placed; very important; do not fail. Shall be with you as soon as possible after arrival."

DR. SEWARD'S DIARY.

18 September.—Just off for train to London. The arrival of Van Helsing's telegram filled me with dismay. A whole night lost, and I know by bitter experience what may happen in a night. Of course it is possible that all may be well, but what *may* have happened? Surely there is some horrible doom hanging over us that every possible accident should thwart us in all we try to do. I shall take this cylinder with me, and then I can complete my entry on Lucy's phonograph.

MEMORANDUM LEFT BY LUCY WESTENRA.

17 September. Night.—I write this and leave it to be seen, so that no one may by any chance get into trouble through me. This is an exact record of what took place to-night. I feel I am dying of weakness, and have barely strength to write, but it must be done if I die in the doing.

I went to bed as usual, taking care that the flowers were placed as Dr. Van Helsing directed, and soon fell asleep.

I was waked by the flapping at the window, which had begun after that sleep-walking on the cliff at Whitby when Mina saved me, and which now I know so well. I was not afraid, but I did wish that Dr. Seward was in the next room—as Dr. Van Helsing said he would be—so that I might have called him. I tried to go to sleep, but could not. Then there came to me the old fear of sleep, and I determined to keep awake. Perversely sleep would try to come then when I did not want it; so, as I feared to be alone, I opened my door and called out: "Is there anybody there?" There was no answer. I was afraid to wake mother, and so closed my door again. Then outside in the shrubbery I heard a sort of howl like a dog's, but more fierce and deeper. I went to the window and looked out, but could see nothing, except a big bat, which had evidently been buffeting its wings against the window. So I went back to bed again, but determined not to go to sleep. Presently the door opened, and mother looked in; seeing by my moving that I was not asleep, came in, and sat by me. She said to me even more sweetly and softly than her wont:—

"I was uneasy about you, darling, and came in to see that you were all right."

I feared she might catch cold sitting there, and asked her to come in and sleep with me, so she came into bed, and lay down beside me; she did not take off her dressing gown, for she said she would only stay a while and then go back to her own bed. As she lay there in my arms, and I in hers, the flapping and buffeting came to the window again. She was startled and a little frightened, and cried out: "What is that?" I tried to pacify her, and at last succeeded, and she lay quiet; but I could hear her poor dear heart still beating terribly. After a while there was the low howl again out in the shrubbery, and shortly after there was a crash at the window, and a lot of broken glass was hurled on the floor. The window blind blew back with the wind that rushed in, and in the aperture of the broken panes there was the head of a great, gaunt grey wolf. Mother cried out in a fright, and struggled up into a sitting posture, and clutched wildly at anything that would help her. Amongst other things, she clutched the wreath of flowers that Dr. Van Helsing insisted on my wearing round my neck, and tore it away from me. For a second or two she sat up, pointing at the wolf, and there was a strange and horrible gurgling in her throat; then she fell over—as if struck with lightning, and her head hit my forehead and made me dizzy for a moment or two. The room and all round seemed to spin round. I kept my eyes fixed on the window, but the wolf drew his head back, and a whole myriad of little specks seemed to come blowing in through the broken window, and wheeling and circling round like the pillar of dust that travellers describe when there is a simoon in the desert. I tried to stir, but there was some spell upon me, and dear mother's poor body, which seemed to grow cold already—for her dear heart had ceased to beat—weighed me down; and I remembered no more for a while.

The time did not seem long, but very, very awful, till I recovered consciousness again. Somewhere near, a passing bell was tolling; the dogs all round the neighbourhood were howling; and in our shrubbery, seemingly just outside, a nightingale was singing. I was dazed and stupid with pain and terror and weakness, but the sound of the nightingale seemed like the voice of my dead mother come back to comfort me. The sounds seemed to have awakened the maids, too, for I could hear their bare feet pattering outside my door. I called to them, and they came in, and when they saw what had happened, and what it was that lay over me on the bed, they screamed out. The wind rushed in through the broken window, and the door slammed to. They lifted off the body of my dear mother, and laid her, covered up with a sheet, on the bed after I had got up. They were all so frightened and nervous that I directed them to go to the dining-room and have each a glass of wine. The door flew open for an instant and closed again. The maids shrieked, and then went in a body to the dining-room; and I laid what flowers I had on my dear mother's breast. When they were there I remembered what Dr. Van Helsing had told me, but I didn't like to remove them, and, besides, I would have some of the servants to sit up with me now. I was surprised that the maids did not come back. I called them, but got no answer, so I went to the dining-room to look for them.

My heart sank when I saw what had happened. They all four lay helpless on the floor, breathing heavily. The decanter of sherry was on the table half full, but there was a queer, acrid smell about. I was suspicious, and examined the decanter. It smelt of laudanum, and looking on the sideboard, I found that the bottle which mother's doctor uses for her—oh! did use—was empty. What am I to do? what am I to do? I am back in the room with mother. I cannot leave her, and I am alone, save for the sleeping servants, whom some one has drugged. Alone with the dead! I dare not go out, for I can hear the low howl of the wolf through the broken window.

The air seems full of specks, floating and circling in the draught from the window, and the lights burn blue and dim. What am I to do? God shield me from harm this night! I shall hide this paper in my breast, where they shall find it when they come to lay me out. My dear mother gone! It is time that I go too. Good-bye, dear Arthur, if I should not survive this night. God keep you, dear, and God help me!

CHAPTER XII

DR. SEWARD'S DIARY

18 September.—I drove at once to Hillingham and arrived early. Keeping my cab at the gate, I went up the avenue alone. I knocked gently and rang as quietly as possible, for I feared to disturb Lucy or her mother, and hoped to only bring a servant to the door. After a while, finding no response, I knocked and rang again; still no answer. I cursed the laziness of the servants that they should lie abed at such an hour—for it was now ten o'clock—and so rang and knocked again, but more impatiently, but still without response. Hitherto I had blamed only the servants, but now a terrible fear began to assail me. Was this desolation but another link in the chain of doom which seemed drawing tight around us? Was it indeed a house of death to which I had come, too late? I knew that minutes, even seconds of delay, might mean hours of danger to Lucy, if she had had again one of those frightful relapses; and I went round the house to try if I could find by chance an entry anywhere.

I could find no means of ingress. Every window and door was fastened and locked, and I returned baffled to the porch. As I did so, I heard the rapid pit-pat of a swiftly driven horse's feet. They stopped at the gate, and a few seconds later I met Van Helsing running up the avenue. When he saw me, he gasped out:—

"Then it was you, and just arrived. How is she? Are we too late? Did you not get my telegram?"

I answered as quickly and coherently as I could that I had only got his telegram early in the morning, and had not lost a minute in coming here, and that I could not make any one in the house hear me. He paused and raised his hat as he said solemnly:—

"Then I fear we are too late. God's will be done!" With his usual recuperative energy, he went on: "Come. If there be no way open to get in, we must make one. Time is all in all to us now."

We went round to the back of the house, where there was a kitchen window. The Professor took a small surgical saw from his case, and handing it to me, pointed to the iron bars which guarded the window. I attacked them at once and had very soon cut through three of them. Then with a long, thin knife we pushed back the fastening of the sashes and opened the window. I helped the Professor in, and followed him. There was no one in the kitchen or in the servants' rooms, which were close at hand. We tried all the rooms as we went along, and in the dining-room, dimly lit by rays of light through the shutters, found four servant-women lying on the floor. There was no need to think them dead, for their stertorous breathing and the acrid smell of laudanum in the room left no doubt as to their condition. Van Helsing and I looked at each other, and as we moved away he said: "We can attend to them later." Then we ascended to Lucy's room. For an instant or two we paused at the door to listen, but there was no sound that we could hear. With white faces and trembling hands, we opened the door gently, and entered the room.

How shall I describe what we saw? On the bed lay two women, Lucy and her mother. The latter lay farthest in, and she was covered with a white sheet, the edge of which had been blown back by the draught through the broken window, showing the drawn, white face, with a look of terror fixed upon it. By her side lay Lucy, with face white and still more drawn. The flowers which had been round her neck we found upon her mother's bosom, and her throat was bare, showing the two little wounds which we had noticed before, but looking horribly white and mangled. Without a word the Professor bent over the bed, his head almost touching poor Lucy's breast; then he gave a quick turn of his head, as of one who listens, and leaping to his feet, he cried out to me:—

"It is not yet too late! Quick! quick! Bring the brandy!"

I flew downstairs and returned with it, taking care to smell and taste it, lest it, too, were drugged like the decanter of sherry which I found on the table. The maids were still breathing, but more restlessly, and I fancied that the narcotic was wearing off. I did not stay to make sure, but returned to Van Helsing. He rubbed the brandy, as on another occasion, on her lips and gums and on her wrists and the palms of her hands. He said to me:—

"I can do this, all that can be at the present. You go wake those maids. Flick them in the face with a wet towel, and flick them hard. Make them get heat and fire and a warm bath. This poor soul is nearly as cold as that beside her. She will need be heated before we can do anything more."

I went at once, and found little difficulty in waking three of the women. The fourth was only a young girl, and the drug had evidently affected her more strongly, so I lifted her on the sofa and let her sleep. The others were dazed at first, but as remembrance came back to them they cried and sobbed in a hysterical manner. I was stern with them, however, and would not let them talk. I told them that one life was bad enough to lose, and that if they delayed they would sacrifice Miss Lucy. So, sobbing and crying, they went about their way, half clad as they were, and prepared fire and water. Fortunately, the kitchen and boiler fires were still alive, and there was no lack of hot water. We got a bath and carried Lucy out as she was and placed her in it. Whilst we were busy chafing her limbs there was a knock at the hall door. One of the maids ran off, hurried on some more clothes, and opened it. Then she returned and whispered to us that there was a gentleman who had come with a message from Mr. Holmwood. I bade her simply tell him that he must wait, for we could see no one now. She went away with the message, and, engrossed with our work, I clean forgot all about him.

I never saw in all my experience the Professor work in such deadly earnest. I knew—as he knew—that it was a stand-up fight with death, and in a pause told him so. He answered me in a way that I did not understand, but with the sternest look that his face could wear:—

"If that were all, I would stop here where we are now, and let her fade away into peace, for I see no light in life over her horizon." He went on with his work with, if possible, renewed and more frenzied vigour.

Presently we both began to be conscious that the heat was beginning to be of some effect. Lucy's heart beat a trifle more audibly to the stethoscope, and her lungs had a perceptible movement. Van Helsing's face almost beamed, and as we lifted her from the bath and rolled her in a hot sheet to dry her he said to me:—

"The first gain is ours! Check to the King!"

We took Lucy into another room, which had by now been prepared, and laid her in bed and forced a few drops of brandy down her throat. I noticed that Van Helsing tied a soft silk handkerchief round her throat. She was still unconscious, and was quite as bad as, if not worse than, we had ever seen her.

Van Helsing called in one of the women, and told her to stay with her and not to take her eyes off her till we returned, and then beckoned me out of the room.

"We must consult as to what is to be done," he said as we descended the stairs. In the hall he opened the dining-room door, and we passed in, he closing the door carefully behind him. The shutters had been opened, but the blinds were already down, with that obedience to the etiquette of death which the British woman of the lower classes always rigidly observes. The room was, therefore, dimly dark. It was, however, light enough for our purposes. Van Helsing's sternness was somewhat relieved by a look of perplexity. He was evidently torturing his mind about something, so I waited for an instant, and he spoke:—

"What are we to do now? Where are we to turn for help? We must have another transfusion of blood, and that soon, or that poor girl's life won't be worth an hour's purchase. You are exhausted already; I am exhausted too. I fear to trust those women, even if they would have courage to submit. What are we to do for some one who will open his veins for her?"

"What's the matter with me, anyhow?"

The voice came from the sofa across the room, and its tones brought relief and joy to my heart, for they were those of Quincey Morris. Van Helsing started angrily at the first sound, but his face softened and a glad look came into his eyes as I cried out: "Quincey Morris!" and rushed towards him with outstretched hands.

"What brought you here?" I cried as our hands met.

"I guess Art is the cause."

He handed me a telegram:—

"Have not heard from Seward for three days, and am terribly anxious. Cannot leave. Father still in same condition. Send me word how Lucy is. Do not delay.—HOLMWOOD."

"I think I came just in the nick of time. You know you have only to tell me what to do."

Van Helsing strode forward, and took his hand, looking him straight in the eyes as he said:—

"A brave man's blood is the best thing on this earth when a woman is in trouble. You're a man and no mistake. Well, the devil may work against us for all he's worth, but God sends us men when we want them."

Once again we went through that ghastly operation. I have not the heart to go through with the details. Lucy had got a terrible shock and it told on her more than before, for though plenty of blood went into her veins, her body did not respond to the treatment as well as on the other occasions. Her struggle back into life was something frightful to see and hear. However, the action of both heart and lungs improved, and Van Helsing made a subcutaneous injection of morphia, as before, and with good effect. Her faint became a profound slumber. The Professor watched whilst I went downstairs with Quincey Morris, and sent one of the maids to pay off one of the cabmen who were waiting. I left Quincey lying down after having a glass of wine, and told the cook to get ready a good breakfast. Then a thought struck me, and I went back to the room where Lucy now was. When I came softly in, I found Van Helsing with a sheet or two of note-paper in his hand.

He had evidently read it, and was thinking it over as he sat with his hand to his brow. There was a look of grim satisfaction in his face, as of one who has had a doubt solved. He handed me the paper saying only: "It dropped from Lucy's breast when we carried her to the bath."

When I had read it, I stood looking at the Professor, and after a pause asked him: "In God's name, what does it all mean? Was she, or is she, mad; or what sort of horrible danger is it?" I was so bewildered that I did not know what to say more. Van Helsing put out his hand and took the paper, saying:—

"Do not trouble about it now. Forget it for the present. You shall know and understand it all in good time; but it will be later. And now what is it that you came to me to say?" This brought me back to fact, and I was all myself again.

"I came to speak about the certificate of death. If we do not act properly and wisely, there may be an inquest, and that paper would have to be produced. I am in hopes that we need have no inquest, for if we had it would surely kill poor Lucy, if nothing else did. I know, and you know, and the other doctor who attended her knows, that Mrs. Westenra had disease of the heart, and we can certify that she died of it. Let us fill up the certificate at once, and I shall take it myself to the registrar and go on to the undertaker."

"Good, oh my friend John! Well thought of! Truly Miss Lucy, if she be sad in the foes that beset her, is at least happy in the friends that love her. One, two, three, all open their veins for her, besides one old man. Ah yes, I know, friend John; I am not blind! I love you all the more for it! Now go."

In the hall I met Quincey Morris, with a telegram for Arthur telling him that Mrs. Westenra was dead; that Lucy also had been ill, but was now going on better; and that Van Helsing and I were with her. I told him where I was going, and he hurried me out, but as I was going said:—

"When you come back, Jack, may I have two words with you all to ourselves?" I nodded in reply and went out. I found no difficulty about the registration, and arranged with the local undertaker to come up in the evening to measure for the coffin and to make arrangements.

When I got back Quincey was waiting for me. I told him I would see him as soon as I knew about Lucy, and went up to her room. She was still sleeping, and the Professor seemingly had not moved from his seat at her side. From his putting his finger to his lips, I gathered that he expected her to wake before long and was afraid of forestalling nature. So I went down to Quincey and took him into the breakfast-room, where the blinds were not drawn down, and which was a little more cheerful, or rather less cheerless, than the other rooms. When we were alone, he said to me:—

"Jack Seward, I don't want to shove myself in anywhere where I've no right to be; but this is no ordinary case. You know I loved that girl and wanted to marry her; but, although that's all past and gone, I can't help feeling anxious about her all the same. What is it that's wrong with her? The Dutchman—and a fine old fellow he is; I can see that—said, that time you two came into the room, that you must have *another* transfusion of blood, and that both you and he were exhausted. Now I know well that you medical men speak *in camera*, and that a man must not expect to know what they consult about in private. But this is no common matter, and, whatever it is, I have done my part. Is not that so?"

"That's so," I said, and he went on:—

"I take it that both you and Van Helsing had done already what I did to-day. Is not that so?"

"That's so."

"And I guess Art was in it too. When I saw him four days ago down at his own place he looked queer. I have not seen anything pulled down so quick since I was on the Pampas and had a mare that I was fond of go to grass all in a night. One of those big bats that they call vampires had got at her in the night, and what with his gorge and the vein left open, there wasn't enough blood in her to let her stand up, and I had to put a bullet through her as she lay. Jack, if you may tell me without betraying confidence, Arthur was the first, is not that so?" As he spoke the poor fellow looked terribly anxious. He was in a torture of suspense regarding the woman he loved, and his utter ignorance of the terrible mystery which seemed to surround her intensified his pain. His very heart was bleeding, and it took all the manhood of him— and there was a royal lot of it, too—to keep him from breaking down. I paused before answering, for I felt that I must not betray anything which the Professor wished kept secret; but already he knew so much, and guessed so much, that there could be no reason for not answering, so I answered in the same phrase: "That's so."

"And how long has this been going on?"

"About ten days."

"Ten days! Then I guess, Jack Seward, that that poor pretty creature that we all love has had put into her veins within that time the blood of four strong men. Man alive, her whole body wouldn't hold it." Then, coming close to me, he spoke in a fierce half-whisper: "What took it out?"

I shook my head. "That," I said, "is the crux. Van Helsing is simply frantic about it, and I am at my wits' end. I can't even hazard a guess. There has been a series of little circumstances which have thrown out all our calculations as to Lucy being properly watched. But these shall not occur again. Here we stay until all be well—or ill." Quincey held out his hand. "Count me in," he said. "You and the Dutchman will tell me what to do, and I'll do it."

When she woke late in the afternoon, Lucy's first movement was to feel in her breast, and, to my surprise, produced the paper which Van Helsing had given me to read. The careful Professor had replaced it where it had come from, lest on waking she should be alarmed. Her eye then lit on Van Helsing and on me too, and gladdened. Then she looked around the room, and seeing where she was, shuddered; she gave a loud cry, and put her poor thin hands before her pale face. We both understood what that meant—that she had realised to the full her mother's death; so we tried what we could to comfort her. Doubtless sympathy eased her somewhat, but she was very low in thought and spirit, and wept silently and weakly for a long time. We told her that either or both of us would now remain with her all the time, and that seemed to comfort her. Towards dusk she fell into a doze. Here a very odd thing occurred. Whilst still asleep she took the paper from her breast and tore it in two. Van Helsing stepped over and took the pieces from her. All the same, however, she went on with the action of tearing, as though the material were still in her hands; finally she lifted her hands and opened them as though scattering the fragments. Van Helsing seemed surprised, and his brows gathered as if in thought, but he said nothing.

19 September.—All last night she slept fitfully, being always afraid to sleep, and something weaker when she woke from it. The Professor and I took it in turns to watch, and we never left her for a moment unattended. Quincey Morris said nothing about his intention, but I knew that all night long he patrolled round and round the house.

When the day came, its searching light showed the ravages in poor Lucy's strength. She was hardly able to turn her head, and the little nourishment which she could take seemed to do her no good. At times she slept, and both Van Helsing and I noticed the difference in her, between sleeping and waking. Whilst asleep she looked stronger, although more haggard, and her breathing was softer; her open mouth showed the pale gums drawn back from the teeth, which thus looked positively longer and sharper than usual; when she woke the softness of her eyes evidently changed the expression, for she looked her own self, although a dying one. In the afternoon she asked for Arthur, and we telegraphed for him. Quincey went off to meet him at the station.

When he arrived it was nearly six o'clock, and the sun was setting full and warm, and the red light streamed in through the window and gave more colour to the pale cheeks. When he saw her, Arthur was simply choking with emotion, and none of us could speak. In the hours that had passed, the fits of sleep, or the comatose condition that passed for it, had grown more frequent, so that the pauses when conversation was possible were shortened. Arthur's presence, however, seemed to act as a stimulant; she rallied a little, and spoke to him more brightly than she had done since we arrived. He too pulled himself together, and spoke as cheerily as he could, so that the best was made of everything.

It was now nearly one o'clock, and he and Van Helsing are sitting with her. I am to relieve them in a quarter of an hour, and I am entering this on Lucy's phonograph. Until six o'clock they are to try to rest. I fear that to-morrow will end our watching, for the shock has been too great; the poor child cannot rally. God help us all.

LETTER,
MINA HARKER TO LUCY WESTENRA.

(Unopened by her.)

                                                                    "17 September.

"My dearest Lucy,—

"It seems *an age* since I heard from you, or indeed since I wrote. You will pardon me, I know, for all my faults when you have read all my budget of news. Well, I got my husband back all right; when we arrived at Exeter there was a carriage waiting for us, and in it, though he had an attack of gout, Mr. Hawkins. He took us to his house, where there were rooms for us all nice and comfortable, and we dined together. After dinner Mr. Hawkins said:—

" 'My dears, I want to drink your health and prosperity; and may every blessing attend you both. I know you both from children, and have, with love and pride, seen you grow up. Now I want you to make your home here with me. I have left to me neither chick nor child; all are gone, and in my will I have left you everything.' I cried, Lucy dear, as Jonathan and the old man clasped hands. Our evening was a very, very happy one.

"So here we are, installed in this beautiful old house, and from both my bedroom and the drawing-room I can see the great elms of the cathedral close, with their great black stems standing out against the old yellow stone of the cathedral and I can hear the rooks overhead cawing and cawing and chattering and gossiping all day, after the manner of rooks—and humans. I am busy, I need not tell you, arranging things and housekeeping. Jonathan and Mr. Hawkins are busy all day; for, now that Jonathan is a partner, Mr.

Hawkins wants to tell him all about the clients.

"How is your dear mother getting on? I wish I could run up to town for a day or two to see you, dear, but I dare not go yet, with so much on my shoulders; and Jonathan wants looking after still. He is beginning to put some flesh on his bones again, but he was terribly weakened by the long illness; even now he sometimes starts out of his sleep in a sudden way and awakes all trembling until I can coax him back to his usual placidity. However, thank God, these occasions grow less frequent as the days go on, and they will in time pass away altogether, I trust. And now I have told you my news, let me ask yours. When are you to be married, and where, and who is to perform the ceremony, and what are you to wear, and is it to be a public or a private wedding? Tell me all about it, dear; tell me all about everything, for there is nothing which interests you which will not be dear to me. Jonathan asks me to send his 'respectful duty,' but I do not think that is good enough from the junior partner of the important firm Hawkins & Harker; and so, as you love me, and he loves me, and I love you with all the moods and tenses of the verb, I send you simply his 'love' instead. Good-bye, my dearest Lucy, and all blessings on you.

"Yours,
"Mina Harker."

**REPORT FROM
PATRICK HENNESSEY,
M. D., M. R. C. S. L. K. Q. C. P. I., ETC., ETC.,
TO JOHN SEWARD, M. D.**

"20 September.

"My dear Sir,—

"In accordance with your wishes, I enclose report of the conditions of everything left in my charge . . . . With regard to patient, Renfield, there is more to say. He has had another outbreak, which might have had a dreadful ending, but which, as it fortunately happened, was unattended with any unhappy results. This afternoon a carrier's cart with two men made a call at the empty house whose grounds abut on ours—the house to which, you will remember, the patient twice ran away. The men stopped at our gate to ask the porter their way, as they were strangers. I was myself looking out of the

study window, having a smoke after dinner, and saw one of them come up
to the house. As he passed the window of Renfield's room, the patient began
to rate him from within, and called him all the foul names he could lay his
tongue to. The man, who seemed a decent fellow enough, contented himself
by telling him to "shut up for a foul-mouthed beggar," whereon our man
accused him of robbing him and wanting to murder him and said that he
would hinder him if he were to swing for it. I opened the window and signed
to the man not to notice, so he contented himself after looking the place
over and making up his mind as to what kind of a place he had got to by
saying: 'Lor' bless yer, sir, I wouldn't mind what was said to me in a bloomin'
madhouse. I pity ye and the guv'nor for havin' to live in the house with a
wild beast like that.' Then he asked his way civilly enough, and I told him
where the gate of the empty house was; he went away, followed by threats
and curses and revilings from our man. I went down to see if I could make
out any cause for his anger, since he is usually such a well-behaved man,
and except his violent fits nothing of the kind had ever occurred. I found
him, to my astonishment, quite composed and most genial in his manner.
I tried to get him to talk of the incident, but he blandly asked me questions
as to what I meant, and led me to believe that he was completely oblivious
of the affair. It was, I am sorry to say, however, only another instance of
his cunning, for within half an hour I heard of him again. This time he
had broken out through the window of his room, and was running down
the avenue. I called to the attendants to follow me, and ran after him, for
I feared he was intent on some mischief. My fear was justified when I saw
the same cart which had passed before coming down the road, having on
it some great wooden boxes. The men were wiping their foreheads, and
were flushed in the face, as if with violent exercise. Before I could get up to
him the patient rushed at them, and pulling one of them off the cart, began
to knock his head against the ground. If I had not seized him just at the
moment I believe he would have killed the man there and then. The other
fellow jumped down and struck him over the head with the butt-end of his
heavy whip. It was a terrible blow; but he did not seem to mind it, but seized
him also, and struggled with the three of us, pulling us to and fro as if we
were kittens. You know I am no light weight, and the others were both burly
men. At first he was silent in his fighting; but as we began to master him, and
the attendants were putting a strait-waistcoat on him, he began to shout: 'I'll
frustrate them! They shan't rob me! they shan't murder me by inches! I'll
fight for my Lord and Master!' and all sorts of similar incoherent ravings.
It was with very considerable difficulty that they got him back to the house
and put him in the padded room. One of the attendants, Hardy, had a finger

broken. However, I set it all right; and he is going on well.

"The two carriers were at first loud in their threats of actions for damages, and promised to rain all the penalties of the law on us. Their threats were, however, mingled with some sort of indirect apology for the defeat of the two of them by a feeble madman. They said that if it had not been for the way their strength had been spent in carrying and raising the heavy boxes to the cart they would have made short work of him. They gave as another reason for their defeat the extraordinary state of drouth to which they had been reduced by the dusty nature of their occupation and the reprehensible distance from the scene of their labours of any place of public entertainment. I quite understood their drift, and after a stiff glass of grog, or rather more of the same, and with each a sovereign in hand, they made light of the attack, and swore that they would encounter a worse madman any day for the pleasure of meeting so 'bloomin' good a bloke' as your correspondent. I took their names and addresses, in case they might be needed. They are as follows:—Jack Smollet, of Dudding's Rents, King George's Road, Great Walworth, and Thomas Snelling, Peter Farley's Row, Guide Court, Bethnal Green. They are both in the employment of Harris & Sons, Moving and Shipment Company, Orange Master's Yard, Soho.

"I shall report to you any matter of interest occurring here, and shall wire you at once if there is anything of importance.

> "Believe me, dear Sir,
> "Yours faithfully,
> "Patrick Hennessey."

LETTER,
MINA HARKER TO LUCY WESTENRA.

(Unopened by her.)

"18 September.

"My dearest Lucy,—

"Such a sad blow has befallen us. Mr. Hawkins has died very suddenly. Some may not think it so sad for us, but we had both come to so love him that it really seems as though we had lost a father. I never knew either father or mother, so that the dear old man's death is a real blow to me. Jonathan is greatly distressed. It is not only that he feels sorrow, deep sorrow, for the dear, good man who has befriended him all his life, and now at the end has treated him like his own son and left him a fortune which to people of our modest bringing up is wealth beyond the dream of avarice, but Jonathan feels it on another account. He says the amount of responsibility which it puts upon him makes him nervous. He begins to doubt himself. I try to cheer him up, and *my* belief in *him* helps him to have a belief in himself. But it is here that the grave shock that he experienced tells upon him the most. Oh, it is too hard that a sweet, simple, noble, strong nature such as his—a nature which enabled him by our dear, good friend's aid to rise from clerk to master in a few years—should be so injured that the very essence of its strength is gone. Forgive me, dear, if I worry you with my troubles in the midst of your own happiness; but, Lucy dear, I must tell some one, for the strain of keeping up a brave and cheerful appearance to Jonathan tries me, and I have no one here that I can confide in. I dread coming up to London, as we must do the day after to-morrow; for poor Mr. Hawkins left in his will that he was to be buried in the grave with his father. As there are no relations at all, Jonathan will have to be chief mourner. I shall try to run over to see you, dearest, if only for a few minutes. Forgive me for troubling you. With all blessings,

"Your loving
"Mina Harker."

DR. SEWARD'S DIARY.

20 September.—Only resolution and habit can let me make an entry to-night. I am too miserable, too low-spirited, too sick of the world and all in it, including life itself, that I would not care if I heard this moment the flapping of the wings of the angel of death. And he has been flapping those grim wings to some purpose of late—Lucy's mother and Arthur's father, and now . . . . Let me get on with my work.

I duly relieved Van Helsing in his watch over Lucy. We wanted Arthur to go to rest also, but he refused at first. It was only when I told him that we should want him to help us during the day, and that we must not all break down for want of rest, lest Lucy should suffer, that he agreed to go. Van Helsing was very kind to him. "Come, my child," he said; "come with me. You are sick and weak, and have had much sorrow and much mental pain, as well as that tax on your strength that we know of. You must not be alone;

for to be alone is to be full of fears and alarms. Come to the drawing-room, where there is a big fire, and there are two sofas. You shall lie on one, and I on the other, and our sympathy will be comfort to each other, even though we do not speak, and even if we sleep." Arthur went off with him, casting back a longing look on Lucy's face, which lay in her pillow, almost whiter than the lawn. She lay quite still, and I looked round the room to see that all was as it should be. I could see that the Professor had carried out in this room, as in the other, his purpose of using the garlic; the whole of the window-sashes reeked with it, and round Lucy's neck, over the silk handkerchief which Van Helsing made her keep on, was a rough chaplet of the same odorous flowers. Lucy was breathing somewhat stertorously, and her face was at its worst, for the open mouth showed the pale gums. Her teeth, in the dim, uncertain light, seemed longer and sharper than they had been in the morning. In particular, by some trick of the light, the canine teeth looked longer and sharper than the rest. I sat down by her, and presently she moved uneasily. At the same moment there came a sort of dull flapping or buffeting at the window. I went over to it softly, and peeped out by the corner of the blind. There was a full moonlight, and I could see that the noise was made by a great bat, which wheeled round—doubtless attracted by the light, although so dim—and every now and again struck the window with its wings. When I came back to my seat, I found that Lucy had moved slightly, and had torn away the garlic flowers from her throat. I replaced them as well as I could, and sat watching her.

Presently she woke, and I gave her food, as Van Helsing had prescribed. She took but a little, and that languidly. There did not seem to be with her now the unconscious struggle for life and strength that had hitherto so marked her illness. It struck me as curious that the moment she became conscious she pressed the garlic flowers close to her. It was certainly odd that whenever she got into that lethargic state, with the stertorous breathing, she put the flowers from her; but that when she waked she clutched them close. There was no possibility of making any mistake about this, for in the long hours that followed, she had many spells of sleeping and waking and repeated both actions many times.

At six o'clock Van Helsing came to relieve me. Arthur had then fallen into a doze, and he mercifully let him sleep on. When he saw Lucy's face I could hear the sissing indraw of his breath, and he said to me in a sharp whisper: "Draw up the blind; I want light!" Then he bent down, and, with his face almost touching Lucy's, examined her carefully. He removed the flowers and lifted the silk handkerchief from her throat. As he did so he started back, and I could hear his ejaculation, "Mein Gott!" as it was smothered in his throat. I bent over and looked, too, and as I noticed some queer chill came over me.

The wounds on the throat had absolutely disappeared.

For fully five minutes Van Helsing stood looking at her, with his face at its sternest. Then he turned to me and said calmly:—

"She is dying. It will not be long now. It will be much difference, mark me, whether she dies conscious or in her sleep. Wake that poor boy, and let him come and see the last; he trusts us, and we have promised him."

I went to the dining-room and waked him. He was dazed for a moment, but when he saw the sunlight streaming in through the edges of the shutters he thought he was late, and expressed his fear. I assured him that Lucy was still asleep, but told him as gently as I could that both Van Helsing and I feared that the end was near. He covered his face with his hands, and slid down on his knees by the sofa, where he remained, perhaps a minute, with his head buried, praying, whilst his shoulders shook with grief. I took him by the hand and raised him up. "Come," I said, "my dear old fellow, summon all your fortitude: it will be best and easiest for her."

When we came into Lucy's room I could see that Van Helsing had, with his usual forethought, been putting matters straight and making everything look as pleasing as possible. He had even brushed Lucy's hair, so that it lay on the pillow in its usual sunny ripples. When we came into the room she opened her eyes, and seeing him, whispered softly:—

"Arthur! Oh, my love, I am so glad you have come!" He was stooping to kiss her, when Van Helsing motioned him back. "No," he whispered, "not yet! Hold her hand; it will comfort her more."

So Arthur took her hand and knelt beside her, and she looked her best, with all the soft lines matching the angelic beauty of her eyes. Then gradually her eyes closed, and she sank to sleep. For a little bit her breast heaved softly, and her breath came and went like a tired child's.

And then insensibly there came the strange change which I had noticed in the night. Her breathing grew stertorous, the mouth opened, and the pale gums, drawn back, made the teeth look longer and sharper than ever. In a sort of sleep-waking, vague, unconscious way she opened her eyes, which were now dull and hard at once, and said in a soft, voluptuous voice, such as I had never heard from her lips:—

"Arthur! Oh, my love, I am so glad you have come! Kiss me!" Arthur bent eagerly over to kiss her; but at that instant Van Helsing, who, like me, had been startled by her voice, swooped upon him, and catching him by the neck with both hands, dragged him back with a fury of strength which I never thought he could have possessed, and actually hurled him almost across the room.

"Not for your life!" he said; "not for your living soul and hers!" And he stood between them like a lion at bay.

Arthur was so taken aback that he did not for a moment know what to do or say; and before any impulse of violence could seize him he realised the place and the occasion, and stood silent, waiting.

I kept my eyes fixed on Lucy, as did Van Helsing, and we saw a spasm as of rage flit like a shadow over her face; the sharp teeth champed together. Then her eyes closed, and she breathed heavily.

Very shortly after she opened her eyes in all their softness, and putting out her poor, pale, thin hand, took Van Helsing's great brown one; drawing it to her, she kissed it. "My true friend," she said, in a faint voice, but with untellable pathos, "My true friend, and his! Oh, guard him, and give me peace!"

"I swear it!" he said solemnly, kneeling beside her and holding up his hand, as one who registers an oath. Then he turned to Arthur, and said to him: "Come, my child, take her hand in yours, and kiss her on the forehead, and only once."

Their eyes met instead of their lips; and so they parted.

Lucy's eyes closed; and Van Helsing, who had been watching closely, took Arthur's arm, and drew him away.

And then Lucy's breathing became stertorous again, and all at once it ceased.

"It is all over," said Van Helsing. "She is dead!"

I took Arthur by the arm, and led him away to the drawing-room, where he sat down, and covered his face with his hands, sobbing in a way that nearly broke me down to see.

I went back to the room, and found Van Helsing looking at poor Lucy, and his face was sterner than ever. Some change had come over her body. Death had given back part of her beauty, for her brow and cheeks had recovered some of their flowing lines; even the lips had lost their deadly pallor. It was as if the blood, no longer needed for the working of the heart, had gone to make the harshness of death as little rude as might be.

> "We thought her dying whilst she slept,
> And sleeping when she died."

I stood beside Van Helsing, and said:—
"Ah, well, poor girl, there is peace for her at last. It is the end!"
He turned to me, and said with grave solemnity:—

"Not so; alas! not so. It is only the beginning!"
When I asked him what he meant, he only shook his head and answered:—
"We can do nothing as yet. Wait and see."

CHAPTER XIII

DR. SEWARD'S DIARY—*continued.*

THE funeral was arranged for the next succeeding day, so that Lucy and her mother might be buried together. I attended to all the ghastly formalities, and the urbane undertaker proved that his staff were afflicted—or blessed—with something of his own obsequious suavity. Even the woman who performed the last offices for the dead remarked to me, in a confidential, brother-professional way, when she had come out from the death-chamber:—

"She makes a very beautiful corpse, sir. It's quite a privilege to attend on her. It's not too much to say that she will do credit to our establishment!"

I noticed that Van Helsing never kept far away. This was possible from the disordered state of things in the household. There were no relatives at hand; and as Arthur had to be back the next day to attend at his father's funeral, we were unable to notify any one who should have been bidden. Under the circumstances, Van Helsing and I took it upon ourselves to examine papers, etc. He insisted upon looking over Lucy's papers himself. I asked him why, for I feared that he, being a foreigner, might not be quite aware of English legal requirements, and so might in ignorance make some unnecessary trouble. He answered me:—

"I know; I know. You forget that I am a lawyer as well as a doctor. But this is not altogether for the law. You knew that, when you avoided the coroner. I have more than him to avoid. There may be papers more—such as this."

As he spoke he took from his pocket-book the memorandum which had been in Lucy's breast, and which she had torn in her sleep.

"When you find anything of the solicitor who is for the late Mrs. Westenra, seal all her papers, and write him to-night. For me, I watch here in the room and in Miss Lucy's old room all night, and I myself search for what may be. It is not well that her very thoughts go into the hands of strangers."

I went on with my part of the work, and in another half hour had found the name and address of Mrs. Westenra's solicitor and had written to him. All the poor lady's papers were in order; explicit directions regarding the place of burial were given. I had hardly sealed the letter, when, to my surprise, Van Helsing walked into the room, saying:—

"Can I help you, friend John? I am free, and if I may, my service is to you."

"Have you got what you looked for?" I asked, to which he replied:—

"I did not look for any specific thing. I only hoped to find, and find I have, all that there was—only some letters and a few memoranda, and a diary new begun. But I have them here, and we shall for the present say nothing of them. I shall see that poor lad to-morrow evening, and, with his sanction, I shall use some."

When we had finished the work in hand, he said to me:—

"And now, friend John, I think we may to bed. We want sleep, both you and I, and rest to recuperate. To-morrow we shall have much to do, but for the to-night there is no need of us. Alas!"

Before turning in we went to look at poor Lucy. The undertaker had certainly done his work well, for the room was turned into a small *chapelle ardente*. There was a wilderness of beautiful white flowers, and death was made as little repulsive as might be. The end of the winding-sheet was laid over the face; when the Professor bent over and turned it gently back, we both started at the beauty before us, the tall wax candles showing a sufficient light to note it well. All Lucy's loveliness had come back to her in death, and the hours that had passed, instead of leaving traces of "decay's effacing fingers," had but restored the beauty of life, till positively I could not believe my eyes that I was looking at a corpse.

The Professor looked sternly grave. He had not loved her as I had, and there was no need for tears in his eyes. He said to me: "Remain till I return," and left the room. He came back with a handful of wild garlic from the box waiting in the hall, but which had not been opened, and placed the flowers amongst the others on and around the bed. Then he took from his neck, inside his collar, a little gold crucifix, and placed it over the mouth. He restored the sheet to its place, and we came away.

I was undressing in my own room, when, with a premonitory tap at the door, he entered, and at once began to speak:—

"To-morrow I want you to bring me, before night, a set of post-mortem knives."

"Must we make an autopsy?" I asked.

"Yes and no. I want to operate, but not as you think. Let me tell you now, but not a word to another. I want to cut off her head and take out her heart. Ah! you a surgeon, and so shocked! You, whom I have seen with no tremble of hand or heart, do operations of life and death that make the rest shudder. Oh, but I must not forget, my dear friend John, that you loved her; and I have not forgotten it, for it is I that shall operate, and you must only help. I would like to do it to-night, but for Arthur I must not; he will be free after his father's funeral to-morrow, and he will want to see her—to see *it*. Then, when she is coffined ready for the next day, you and I shall come when all sleep. We shall unscrew the coffin-lid, and shall do our operation: and then replace all, so that none know, save we alone."

"But why do it at all? The girl is dead. Why mutilate her poor body without need? And if there is no necessity for a post-mortem and nothing to gain by it—no good to her, to us, to science, to human knowledge—why do it? Without such it is monstrous."

For answer he put his hand on my shoulder, and said, with infinite tenderness:—

"Friend John, I pity your poor bleeding heart; and I love you the more because it does so bleed. If I could, I would take on myself the burden that you do bear. But there are things that you know not, but that you shall know, and bless me for knowing, though they are not pleasant things. John, my child, you have been my friend now many years, and yet did you ever know me to do any without good cause? I may err—I am but man; but I believe in all I do. Was it not for these causes that you send for me when the great trouble came? Yes! Were you not amazed, nay horrified, when I would not let Arthur kiss his love—though she was dying—and snatched him away by all my strength? Yes! And yet you saw how she thanked me, with her so beautiful dying eyes, her voice, too, so weak, and she kiss my rough old hand and bless me? Yes! And did you not hear me swear promise to her, that so she closed her eyes grateful? Yes!

"Well, I have good reason now for all I want to do. You have for many years trust me; you have believe me weeks past, when there be things so strange that you might have well doubt. Believe me yet a little, friend John. If you trust me not, then I must tell what I think; and that is not perhaps well. And if I work—as work I shall, no matter trust or no trust—without my friend trust in me, I work with heavy heart and feel, oh! so lonely when I want all help and courage that may be!" He paused a moment and went on solemnly: "Friend John, there are strange and terrible days before us. Let us not be two, but one, that so we work to a good end. Will you not have faith in me?"

I took his hand, and promised him. I held my door open as he went away, and watched him go into his room and close the door. As I stood without moving, I saw one of the maids pass silently along the passage—she had her back towards me, so did not see me—and go into the room where Lucy lay. The sight touched me. Devotion is so rare, and we are so grateful to those who show it unasked to those we love. Here was a poor girl putting aside the terrors which she naturally had of death to go watch alone by the bier of the mistress whom she loved, so that the poor clay might not be lonely till laid to eternal rest . . . .

* * * * *

I must have slept long and soundly, for it was broad daylight when Van Helsing waked me by coming into my room. He came over to my bedside and said:—

"You need not trouble about the knives; we shall not do it."

"Why not?" I asked. For his solemnity of the night before had greatly impressed me.

"Because," he said sternly, "it is too late—or too early. See!" Here he held up the little golden crucifix. "This was stolen in the night."

"How, stolen," I asked in wonder, "since you have it now?"

"Because I get it back from the worthless wretch who stole it, from the woman who robbed the dead and the living. Her punishment will surely come, but not through me; she knew not altogether what she did and thus unknowing, she only stole. Now we must wait."

He went away on the word, leaving me with a new mystery to think of, a new puzzle to grapple with.

The forenoon was a dreary time, but at noon the solicitor came: Mr. Marquand, of Wholeman, Sons, Marquand & Lidderdale. He was very genial and very appreciative of what we had done, and took off our hands all cares as to details. During lunch he told us that Mrs. Westenra had for some time expected sudden death from her heart, and had put her affairs in absolute order; he informed us that, with the exception of a certain entailed property of Lucy's father's which now, in default of direct issue, went back to a distant branch of the family, the whole estate, real and personal, was left absolutely to Arthur Holmwood. When he had told us so much he went on:—

"Frankly we did our best to prevent such a testamentary disposition, and pointed out certain contingencies that might leave her daughter either penniless or not so free as she should be to act regarding a matrimonial alliance. Indeed, we pressed the matter so far that we almost came into collision, for she asked us if we were or were not prepared to carry out her wishes. Of course, we had then no alternative but to accept. We were right in principle, and ninety-nine times out of a hundred we should have proved, by the logic of events, the accuracy of our judgment. Frankly, however, I must admit that in this case any other form of disposition would have rendered impossible the carrying out of her wishes. For by her predeceasing her daughter the latter would have come into possession of the property, and, even had she only survived her mother by five minutes, her property would, in case there were no will—and a will was a practical impossibility in such a case—have been treated at her decease as under intestacy. In which case Lord Godalming, though so dear a friend, would have had no claim in the world; and the inheritors, being remote, would not be likely to abandon their just rights, for sentimental reasons regarding an entire stranger. I assure you, my dear sirs, I am rejoiced at the result, perfectly rejoiced."

He was a good fellow, but his rejoicing at the one little part—in which he was officially interested—of so great a tragedy, was an object-lesson in the limitations of sympathetic understanding.

He did not remain long, but said he would look in later in the day and see Lord Godalming. His coming, however, had been a certain comfort to us, since it assured us that we should not have to dread hostile criticism as to any of our acts. Arthur was expected at five o'clock, so a little before that time we visited the death-chamber. It was so in very truth, for now both mother and daughter lay in it. The undertaker, true to his craft, had made the best display he could of his goods, and there was a mortuary air about the place that lowered our spirits at once. Van Helsing ordered the former arrangement to be adhered to, explaining that, as Lord Godalming was coming very soon, it would be less harrowing to his feelings to see all that was left of his *fiancée* quite alone. The undertaker seemed shocked at his own stupidity and exerted himself to restore things to the condition in which we left them the night before, so that when Arthur came such shocks to his feelings as we could avoid were saved.

Poor fellow! He looked desperately sad and broken; even his stalwart manhood seemed to have shrunk somewhat under the strain of his much-tried emotions. He had, I knew, been very genuinely and devotedly attached to his father; and to lose him, and at such a time, was a bitter blow to him. With me he was warm as ever, and to Van Helsing he was sweetly courteous; but I could not help seeing that there was some constraint with him. The Professor noticed it, too, and motioned me to bring him upstairs. I did so, and left him at the door of the room, as I felt he would like to be quite alone with her, but he took my arm and led me in, saying huskily:—

"You loved her too, old fellow; she told me all about it, and there was no friend had a closer place in her heart than you. I don't know how to thank you for all you have done for her. I can't think yet . . . ."

Here he suddenly broke down, and threw his arms round my shoulders and laid his head on my breast, crying:—

"Oh, Jack! Jack! What shall I do! The whole of life seems gone from me all at once, and there is nothing in the wide world for me to live for."

I comforted him as well as I could. In such cases men do not need much expression. A grip of the hand, the tightening of an arm over the shoulder, a sob in unison, are expressions of sympathy dear to a man's heart. I stood still and silent till his sobs died away, and then I said softly to him:—

"Come and look at her."

Together we moved over to the bed, and I lifted the lawn from her face. God! how beautiful she was. Every hour seemed to be enhancing her loveliness. It frightened and amazed me somewhat; and as for Arthur, he fell a-trembling, and finally was shaken with doubt as with an ague. At last, after a long pause, he said to me in a faint whisper:—

"Jack, is she really dead?"

I assured him sadly that it was so, and went on to suggest—for I felt that such a horrible doubt should not have life for a moment longer than I could help—that it often happened that after death faces became softened and even resolved into their youthful beauty; that this was especially so when death had been preceded by any acute or prolonged suffering. It seemed to quite do away with any doubt, and, after kneeling beside the couch for a while and looking at her lovingly and long, he turned aside. I told him that that must be good-bye, as the coffin had to be prepared; so he went back and took her dead hand in his and kissed it, and bent over and kissed her forehead. He came away, fondly looking back over his shoulder at her as he came.

I left him in the drawing-room, and told Van Helsing that he had said good-bye; so the latter went to the kitchen to tell the undertaker's men to proceed with the preparations and to screw up the coffin. When he came out of the room again I told him of Arthur's question, and he replied:—

"I am not surprised. Just now I doubted for a moment myself!"

We all dined together, and I could see that poor Art was trying to make the best of things. Van Helsing had been silent all dinner-time; but when we had lit our cigars he said—

"Lord——"; but Arthur interrupted him:—

"No, no, not that, for God's sake! not yet at any rate. Forgive me, sir: I did not mean to speak offensively; it is only because my loss is so recent."

The Professor answered very sweetly:—

"I only used that name because I was in doubt. I must not call you 'Mr.,' and I have grown to love you—yes, my dear boy, to love you—as Arthur."

Arthur held out his hand, and took the old man's warmly.

"Call me what you will," he said. "I hope I may always have the title of a friend. And let me say that I am at a loss for words to thank you for your goodness to my poor dear." He paused a moment, and went on: "I know that she understood your goodness even better than I do; and if I was rude or in any way wanting at that time you acted so—you remember"—the Professor nodded—"you must forgive me."

He answered with a grave kindness:—

"I know it was hard for you to quite trust me then, for to trust such violence needs to understand; and I take it that you do not—that you cannot—trust me now, for you do not yet understand. And there may be more times when I shall want you to trust when you cannot—and may not—and must not yet understand. But the time will come when your trust shall be whole and complete in me, and when you shall understand as though the sunlight himself shone through. Then you shall bless me from first to last for your own sake, and for the sake of others and for her dear sake to whom I swore to protect."

"And, indeed, indeed, sir," said Arthur warmly, "I shall in all ways trust you. I know and believe you have a very noble heart, and you are Jack's friend, and you were hers. You shall do what you like."

The Professor cleared his throat a couple of times, as though about to speak, and finally said:—

"May I ask you something now?"

"Certainly."

"You know that Mrs. Westenra left you all her property?"

"No, poor dear; I never thought of it."

"And as it is all yours, you have a right to deal with it as you will. I want you to give me permission to read all Miss Lucy's papers and letters. Believe me, it is no idle curiosity. I have a motive of which, be sure, she would have approved. I have them all here. I took them before we knew that all was yours, so that no strange hand might touch them—no strange eye look through words into her soul. I shall keep them, if I may; even you may not see them yet, but I shall keep them safe. No word shall be lost; and in the good time I shall give them back to you. It's a hard thing I ask, but you will do it, will you not, for Lucy's sake?"

Arthur spoke out heartily, like his old self:—

"Dr. Van Helsing, you may do what you will. I feel that in saying this I am doing what my dear one would have approved. I shall not trouble you with questions till the time comes."

The old Professor stood up as he said solemnly:—

"And you are right. There will be pain for us all; but it will not be all pain, nor will this pain be the last. We and you too—you most of all, my dear boy—will have to pass through the bitter water before we reach the sweet. But we must be brave of heart and unselfish, and do our duty, and all will be well!"

I slept on a sofa in Arthur's room that night. Van Helsing did not go to bed at all. He went to and fro, as if patrolling the house, and was never out of sight of the room where Lucy lay in her coffin, strewn with the wild garlic flowers, which sent, through the odour of lily and rose, a heavy, overpowering smell into the night.

MINA HARKER'S JOURNAL.

22 September.—In the train to Exeter. Jonathan sleeping.

It seems only yesterday that the last entry was made, and yet how much between then, in Whitby and all the world before me, Jonathan away and no news of him; and now, married to Jonathan, Jonathan a solicitor, a partner, rich, master of his business, Mr. Hawkins dead and buried, and Jonathan with another attack that may harm him. Some day he may ask me about it. Down it all goes. I am rusty in my shorthand—see what unexpected prosperity does for us—so it may be as well to freshen it up again with an exercise anyhow . . . .

The service was very simple and very solemn. There were only ourselves and the servants there, one or two old friends of his from Exeter, his London agent, and a gentleman representing Sir John Paxton, the President of the Incorporated Law Society. Jonathan and I stood hand in hand, and we felt that our best and dearest friend was gone from us . . . .

We came back to town quietly, taking a 'bus to Hyde Park Corner. Jonathan thought it would interest me to go into the Row for a while, so we sat down; but there were very few people there, and it was sad-looking and desolate to see so many empty chairs. It made us think of the empty chair at home; so we got up and walked down Piccadilly. Jonathan was holding me by the arm, the way he used to in old days before I went to school. I felt it very improper, for you can't go on for some years teaching etiquette and decorum to other girls without the pedantry of it biting into yourself a bit; but it was Jonathan, and he was my husband, and we didn't know anybody who saw us—and we didn't care if they did—so on we walked. I was looking at a very beautiful girl, in a big cart-wheel hat, sitting in a victoria outside Guiliano's, when I felt Jonathan clutch my arm so tight that he hurt me, and he said under his breath: "My God!" I am always anxious about Jonathan, for I fear that some nervous fit may upset him again; so I turned to him quickly, and asked him what it was that disturbed him.

He was very pale, and his eyes seemed bulging out as, half in terror and half in amazement, he gazed at a tall, thin man, with a beaky nose and black moustache and pointed beard, who was also observing the pretty girl. He was looking at her so hard that he did not see either of us, and so I had a good view of him. His face was not a good face; it was hard, and cruel, and sensual, and his big white teeth, that looked all the whiter because his lips were so red, were pointed like an animal's. Jonathan kept staring at him, till I was afraid he would notice. I feared he might take it ill, he looked so fierce and nasty. I asked Jonathan why he was disturbed, and he answered, evidently thinking that I knew as much about it as he did: "Do you see who it is?"

"No, dear," I said; "I don't know him; who is it?" His answer seemed to shock and thrill me, for it was said as if he did not know that it was to me, Mina, to whom he was speaking:—

"It is the man himself!"

The poor dear was evidently terrified at something—very greatly terrified; I do believe that if he had not had me to lean on and to support him he would have sunk down. He kept staring; a man came out of the shop with a small parcel, and gave it to the lady, who then drove off. The dark man kept his eyes fixed on her, and when the carriage moved up Piccadilly he followed in the same direction, and hailed a hansom. Jonathan kept looking after him, and said, as if to himself:—

"I believe it is the Count, but he has grown young. My God, if this be so! Oh, my God! my God! If I only knew! if I only knew!" He was distressing himself so much that I feared to keep his mind on the subject by asking him any questions, so I remained silent. I drew him away quietly, and he, holding my arm, came easily. We walked a little further, and then went in and sat for a while in the Green Park. It was a hot day for autumn, and there was a comfortable seat in a shady place. After a few minutes' staring at nothing, Jonathan's eyes closed, and he went quietly into a sleep, with his head on my shoulder. I thought it was the best thing for him, so did not disturb him. In about twenty minutes he woke up, and said to me quite cheerfully:—

"Why, Mina, have I been asleep! Oh, do forgive me for being so rude. Come, and we'll have a cup of tea somewhere." He had evidently forgotten all about the dark stranger, as in his illness he had forgotten all that this episode had reminded him of. I don't like this lapsing into forgetfulness; it may make or continue some injury to the brain. I must not ask him, for fear I shall do more harm than good; but I must somehow learn the facts of his journey abroad. The time is come, I fear, when I must open that parcel, and know what is written. Oh, Jonathan, you will, I know, forgive me if I do wrong, but it is for your own dear sake.

Later.—A sad home-coming in every way—the house empty of the dear soul who was so good to us; Jonathan still pale and dizzy under a slight relapse of his malady; and now a telegram from Van Helsing, whoever he may be:—

"You will be grieved to hear that Mrs. Westenra died five days ago, and that Lucy died the day before yesterday. They were both buried to-day."

Oh, what a wealth of sorrow in a few words! Poor Mrs. Westenra! poor Lucy! Gone, gone, never to return to us! And poor, poor Arthur, to have lost such sweetness out of his life! God help us all to bear our troubles.

DR. SEWARD'S DIARY.

22 September.—It is all over. Arthur has gone back to Ring, and has taken Quincey Morris with him. What a fine fellow is Quincey! I believe in my heart of hearts that he suffered as much about Lucy's death as any of us; but he bore himself through it like a moral Viking. If America can go on breeding men like that, she will be a power in the world indeed. Van Helsing is lying down, having a rest preparatory to his journey. He goes over to Amsterdam to-night, but says he returns to-morrow night; that he only wants to make some arrangements which can only be made personally. He is to stop with me then, if he can; he says he has work to do in London which may take him some time. Poor old fellow! I fear that the strain of the past week has broken down even his iron strength. All the time of the burial he was, I could see, putting some terrible restraint on himself. When it was all over, we were standing beside Arthur, who, poor fellow, was speaking of his part in the operation where his blood had been transfused to his Lucy's veins; I could see Van Helsing's face grow white and purple by turns. Arthur was saying that he felt since then as if they two had been really married and that she was his wife in the sight of God. None of us said a word of the other operations, and none of us ever shall. Arthur and Quincey went away together to the station, and Van Helsing and I came on here. The moment we were alone in the carriage he gave way to a regular fit of hysterics. He has denied to me since that it was hysterics, and insisted that it was only his sense of humour asserting itself under very terrible conditions. He laughed till he cried, and I had to draw down the blinds lest any one should see us and misjudge; and then he cried, till he laughed again; and laughed and cried together, just as a woman does. I tried to be stern with him, as one is to a woman under the circumstances; but it had no effect. Men and women are so different in manifestations of nervous strength or weakness! Then when his face grew grave and stern again I asked him why his mirth, and why at such a time. His reply was in a way characteristic of him, for it was logical and forceful and mysterious. He said:—

"Ah, you don't comprehend, friend John. Do not think that I am not sad, though I laugh. See, I have cried even when the laugh did choke me. But no more think that I am all sorry when I cry, for the laugh he come just the same. Keep it always with you that laughter who knock at your door and say, 'May I come in?' is not the true laughter. No! he is a king, and he come when and how he like. He ask no person; he choose no time of suitability. He say, 'I am here.' Behold, in example I grieve my heart out for that so sweet young girl; I give my blood for her, though I am old and worn; I give my time, my skill, my sleep; I let my other sufferers want that so she may have all. And yet I can laugh at her very grave—laugh when the clay from the spade of the sexton drop upon her coffin and say 'Thud! thud!' to my heart, till it send back the blood from my cheek. My heart bleed for that poor boy—that dear boy, so of the age of mine own boy had I been so blessed that he live, and with his hair and eyes the same. There, you know now why I love him so. And yet when he say things that touch my husband-heart to the quick, and make my father-heart yearn to him as to no other man—not even to you, friend John, for we are more level in experiences than father and son—yet even at such moment King Laugh he come to me and shout and bellow in my ear, 'Here I am! here I am!' till the blood come dance back and bring some of the sunshine that he carry with him to my cheek. Oh, friend John, it is a strange world, a sad world, a world full of miseries, and woes, and troubles; and yet when King Laugh come he make them all dance to the tune he play. Bleeding hearts, and dry bones of the churchyard, and tears that burn as they fall—all dance together to the music that he make with that smileless mouth of him. And believe me, friend John, that he is good to come, and kind. Ah, we men and women are like ropes drawn tight with strain that pull us different ways. Then tears come; and, like the rain on the ropes, they brace us up, until perhaps the strain become too great, and we break. But King Laugh he come like the sunshine, and he ease off the strain again; and we bear to go on with our labour, what it may be."

I did not like to wound him by pretending not to see his idea; but, as I did not yet understand the cause of his laughter, I asked him. As he answered me his face grew stern, and he said in quite a different tone:—

"Oh, it was the grim irony of it all—this so lovely lady garlanded with flowers, that looked so fair as life, till one by one we wondered if she were truly dead; she laid in that so fine marble house in that lonely churchyard, where rest so many of her kin, laid there with the mother who loved her, and whom she loved; and that sacred bell going 'Toll! toll! toll!' so sad and slow; and those holy men, with the white garments of the angel, pretending to read books, and yet all the time their eyes never on the page; and all of us with the bowed head. And all for what? She is dead; so! Is it not?"

"Well, for the life of me, Professor," I said, "I can't see anything to laugh at in all that. Why, your explanation makes it a harder puzzle than before. But even if the burial service was comic, what about poor Art and his trouble? Why, his heart was simply breaking."

"Just so. Said he not that the transfusion of his blood to her veins had made her truly his bride?"

"Yes, and it was a sweet and comforting idea for him."

"Quite so. But there was a difficulty, friend John. If so that, then what about the others? Ho, ho! Then this so sweet maid is a polyandrist, and me, with my poor wife dead to me, but alive by Church's law, though no wits, all gone—even I, who am faithful husband to this now-no-wife, am bigamist."

"I don't see where the joke comes in there either!" I said; and I did not feel particularly pleased with him for saying such things. He laid his hand on my arm, and said:—

"Friend John, forgive me if I pain. I showed not my feeling to others when it would wound, but only to you, my old friend, whom I can trust. If you could have looked into my very heart then when I want to laugh; if you could have done so when the laugh arrived; if you could do so now, when King Laugh have pack up his crown, and all that is to him—for he go far, far away from me, and for a long, long time—maybe you would perhaps pity me the most of all."

I was touched by the tenderness of his tone, and asked why.

"Because I know!"

And now we are all scattered; and for many a long day loneliness will sit over our roofs with brooding wings. Lucy lies in the tomb of her kin, a lordly death-house in a lonely churchyard, away from teeming London; where the air is fresh, and the sun rises over Hampstead Hill, and where wild flowers grow of their own accord.

So I can finish this diary; and God only knows if I shall ever begin another. If I do, or if I even open this again, it will be to deal with different people and different themes; for here at the end, where the romance of my life is told, ere I go back to take up the thread of my life-work, I say sadly and without hope,

"FINIS."

"The Westminster Gazette," 25 September.

A HAMPSTEAD MYSTERY.

The neighbourhood of Hampstead is just at present exercised with a series of events which seem to run on lines parallel to those of what was known to the writers of headlines as "The Kensington Horror," or "The Stabbing Woman," or "The Woman in Black." During the past two or three days several cases have occurred of young children straying from home or neglecting to return from their playing on the Heath. In all these cases the children were too young to give any properly intelligible account of themselves, but the consensus of their excuses is that they had been with a "bloofer lady." It has always been late in the evening when they have been missed, and on two occasions the children have not been found until early in the following morning. It is generally supposed in the neighbourhood that, as the first child missed gave as his reason for being away that a "bloofer lady" had asked him to come for a walk, the others had picked up the phrase and used it as occasion served. This is the more natural as the favourite game of the little ones at present is luring each other away by wiles. A correspondent writes us that to see some of the tiny tots pretending to be the "bloofer lady" is supremely funny. Some of our caricaturists might, he says, take a lesson in the irony of grotesque by comparing the reality and the picture. It is only in accordance with general principles of human nature that the "bloofer lady" should be the popular rôle at these *al fresco* performances. Our correspondent naïvely says that even Ellen Terry could not be so winningly attractive as some of these grubby-faced little children pretend—and even imagine themselves—to be.

There is, however, possibly a serious side to the question, for some of the children, indeed all who have been missed at night, have been slightly torn or wounded in the throat. The wounds seem such as might be made by a rat or a small dog, and although of not much importance individually, would tend to show that whatever animal inflicts them has a system or method of its own. The police of the division have been instructed to keep a sharp look-out for straying children, especially when very young, in and around Hampstead Heath, and for any stray dog which may be about.

"The Westminster Gazette," 25 September.
Extra Special.

THE HAMPSTEAD HORROR.
ANOTHER CHILD INJURED.
The "Bloofer Lady."

We have just received intelligence that another child, missed last night, was only discovered late in the morning under a furze bush at the Shooter's Hill side of Hampstead Heath, which is, perhaps, less frequented than the other parts. It has the same tiny wound in the throat as has been noticed in other cases. It was terribly weak, and looked quite emaciated. It too, when partially restored, had the common story to tell of being lured away by the "bloofer lady."

CHAPTER XIV

MINA HARKER'S JOURNAL

23 September.—Jonathan is better after a bad night. I am so glad that he has plenty of work to do, for that keeps his mind off the terrible things; and oh, I am rejoiced that he is not now weighed down with the responsibility of his new position. I knew he would be true to himself, and now how proud I am to see my Jonathan rising to the height of his advancement and keeping pace in all ways with the duties that come upon him. He will be away all day till late, for he said he could not lunch at home. My household work is done, so I shall take his foreign journal, and lock myself up in my room and read it . . . .

24 September.—I hadn't the heart to write last night; that terrible record of Jonathan's upset me so. Poor dear! How he must have suffered, whether it be true or only imagination. I wonder if there is any truth in it at all. Did he get his brain fever, and then write all those terrible things, or had he some cause for it all? I suppose I shall never know, for I dare not open the subject to him . . . . And yet that man we saw yesterday! He seemed quite certain of him . . . . Poor fellow! I suppose it was the funeral upset him and sent his mind back on some train of thought . . . . He believes it all himself. I remember how on our wedding-day he said: "Unless some solemn duty come upon me to go back to the bitter hours, asleep or awake, mad or sane." There seems to be through it all some thread of continuity . . . . That fearful Count was coming to London . . . . If it should be, and he came to London, with his teeming millions . . . . There may be a solemn duty; and if it come we must not shrink from it . . . . I shall be prepared. I shall get my typewriter this very hour and begin transcribing. Then we shall be ready for other eyes if required. And if it be wanted; then, perhaps, if I am ready, poor Jonathan may not be upset, for I can speak for him and never let him be troubled or worried with it at all. If ever Jonathan quite gets over the nervousness he may want to tell me of it all, and I can ask him questions and find out things, and see how I may comfort him.

LETTER,
VAN HELSING TO MRS. HARKER.

"24 September.
(Confidence)

"DEAR MADAM,—

"I pray you to pardon my writing, in that I am so far friend as that I sent to you sad news of Miss Lucy Westenra's death. By the kindness of Lord Godalming, I am empowered to read her letters and papers, for I am deeply concerned about certain matters vitally important. In them I find some letters from you, which show how great friends you were and how you love her. Oh, Madam Mina, by that love, I implore you, help me. It is for others' good that I ask—to redress great wrong, and to lift much and terrible troubles—that may be more great than you can know. May it be that I see you? You can trust me. I am friend of Dr. John Seward and of Lord Godalming (that was Arthur of Miss Lucy). I must keep it private for the present from all. I should come to Exeter to see you at once if you tell me I am privilege to come, and where and when. I implore your pardon, madam. I have read your letters to poor Lucy, and know how good you are and how your husband suffer; so I pray you, if it may be, enlighten him not, lest it may harm. Again your pardon, and forgive me.

"VAN HELSING."

TELEGRAM,
MRS. HARKER TO VAN HELSING.

"25 September.—Come to-day by quarter-past ten train if you can catch it. Can see you any time you call.

"WILHELMINA HARKER."

MINA HARKER'S JOURNAL.

25 September.—I cannot help feeling terribly excited as the time draws near for the visit of Dr. Van Helsing, for somehow I expect that it will throw some light upon Jonathan's sad experience; and as he attended poor dear Lucy in her last illness, he can tell me all about her. That is the reason of his coming; it is concerning Lucy and her sleep-walking, and not about Jonathan. Then I shall never know the real truth now! How silly I am. That awful journal gets hold of my imagination and tinges everything with something of its own colour. Of course it is about Lucy. That habit came back to the poor dear, and that awful night on the cliff must have made her ill. I had almost forgotten in my own affairs how ill she was afterwards. She must have told him of her sleep-walking adventure on the cliff, and that I knew all about it; and now he wants me to tell him what she knows, so that he may understand. I hope I did right in not saying anything of it to Mrs. Westenra; I should never forgive myself if any act of mine, were it even a negative one, brought harm on poor dear Lucy. I hope, too, Dr. Van Helsing will not blame me; I have had so much trouble and anxiety of late that I feel I cannot bear more just at present.

I suppose a cry does us all good at times—clears the air as other rain does. Perhaps it was reading the journal yesterday that upset me, and then Jonathan went away this morning to stay away from me a whole day and night, the first time we have been parted since our marriage. I do hope the dear fellow will take care of himself, and that nothing will occur to upset him. It is two o'clock, and the doctor will be here soon now. I shall say nothing of Jonathan's journal unless he asks me. I am so glad I have type-written out my own journal, so that, in case he asks about Lucy, I can hand it to him; it will save much questioning.

Later.—He has come and gone. Oh, what a strange meeting, and how it all makes my head whirl round! I feel like one in a dream. Can it be all possible, or even a part of it? If I had not read Jonathan's journal first, I should never have accepted even a possibility. Poor, poor, dear Jonathan! How he must have suffered. Please the good God, all this may not upset him again. I shall try to save him from it; but it may be even a consolation and a help to him—terrible though it be and awful in its consequences—to know for certain that his eyes and ears and brain did not deceive him, and that it is all true. It may be that it is the doubt which haunts him; that when the doubt is removed, no matter which—waking or dreaming—may prove the truth, he will be more satisfied and better able to bear the shock. Dr. Van Helsing must be a good man as well as a clever one if he is Arthur's friend and Dr. Seward's, and if they brought him all the way from Holland to look after Lucy. I feel from having seen him that he *is* good and kind and of a noble nature. When he comes to-morrow I shall ask him about Jonathan; and then, please God, all this sorrow and anxiety may lead to a good end. I used to think I would like to practise interviewing; Jonathan's friend on "The Exeter News" told him that memory was everything in such work—that you must be able to put down exactly almost every word spoken, even if you had to refine some of it afterwards. Here was a rare interview; I shall try to record it *verbatim*.

It was half-past two o'clock when the knock came. I took my courage *à deux mains* and waited. In a few minutes Mary opened the door, and announced "Dr. Van Helsing."

I rose and bowed, and he came towards me; a man of medium weight, strongly built, with his shoulders set back over a broad, deep chest and a neck well balanced on the trunk as the head is on the neck. The poise of the head strikes one at once as indicative of thought and power; the head is noble, well-sized, broad, and large behind the ears. The face, clean-shaven, shows a hard, square chin, a large, resolute, mobile mouth, a good-sized nose, rather straight, but with quick, sensitive nostrils, that seem to broaden as the big, bushy brows come down and the mouth tightens. The forehead is broad and fine, rising at first almost straight and then sloping back above two bumps or ridges wide apart; such a forehead that the reddish hair cannot possibly tumble over it, but falls naturally back and to the sides. Big, dark blue eyes are set widely apart, and are quick and tender or stern with the man's moods. He said to me:—

"Mrs. Harker, is it not?" I bowed assent.

"That was Miss Mina Murray?" Again I assented.

"It is Mina Murray that I came to see that was friend of that poor dear child Lucy Westenra. Madam Mina, it is on account of the dead I come."

"Sir," I said, "you could have no better claim on me than that you were a friend and helper of Lucy Westenra." And I held out my hand. He took it and said tenderly:—

"Oh, Madam Mina, I knew that the friend of that poor lily girl must be good, but I had yet to learn——" He finished his speech with a courtly bow. I asked him what it was that he wanted to see me about, so he at once began:—

"I have read your letters to Miss Lucy. Forgive me, but I had to begin to inquire somewhere, and there was none to ask. I know that you were with her at Whitby. She sometimes kept a diary—you need not look surprised, Madam Mina; it was begun after you had left, and was in imitation of you—and in that diary she traces by inference certain things to a sleep-walking in which she puts down that you saved her. In great perplexity then I come to you, and ask you out of your so much kindness to tell me all of it that you can remember."

"I can tell you, I think, Dr. Van Helsing, all about it."

"Ah, then you have good memory for facts, for details? It is not always so with young ladies."

"No, doctor, but I wrote it all down at the time. I can show it to you if you like."

"Oh, Madam Mina, I will be grateful; you will do me much favour." I could not resist the temptation of mystifying him a bit—I suppose it is some of the taste of the original apple that remains still in our mouths—so I handed him the shorthand diary. He took it with a grateful bow, and said:—

"May I read it?"

"If you wish," I answered as demurely as I could. He opened it, and for an instant his face fell. Then he stood up and bowed.

"Oh, you so clever woman!" he said. "I knew long that Mr. Jonathan was a man of much thankfulness; but see, his wife have all the good things. And will you not so much honour me and so help me as to read it for me? Alas! I know not the shorthand." By this time my little joke was over, and I was almost ashamed; so I took the typewritten copy from my workbasket and handed it to him.

"Forgive me," I said: "I could not help it; but I had been thinking that it was of dear Lucy that you wished to ask, and so that you might not have time to wait—not on my account, but because I know your time must be precious—I have written it out on the typewriter for you."

He took it and his eyes glistened. "You are so good," he said. "And may I read it now? I may want to ask you some things when I have read."

"By all means," I said, "read it over whilst I order lunch; and then you can ask me questions whilst we eat." He bowed and settled himself in a chair with his back to the light, and became absorbed in the papers, whilst I went to see after lunch chiefly in order that he might not be disturbed. When I came back, I found him walking hurriedly up and down the room, his face all ablaze with excitement. He rushed up to me and took me by both hands.

"Oh, Madam Mina," he said, "how can I say what I owe to you? This paper is as sunshine. It opens the gate to me. I am daze, I am dazzle, with so much light, and yet clouds roll in behind the light every time. But that you do not, cannot, comprehend. Oh, but I am grateful to you, you so clever woman. Madam"—he said this very solemnly—"if ever Abraham Van Helsing can do anything for you or yours, I trust you will let me know. It will be pleasure and delight if I may serve you as a friend; as a friend, but all I have ever learned, all I can ever do, shall be for you and those you love. There are darknesses in life, and there are lights; you are one of the lights. You will have happy life and good life, and your husband will be blessed in you."

"But, doctor, you praise me too much, and—and you do not know me."

"Not know you—I, who am old, and who have studied all my life men and women; I, who have made my specialty the brain and all that belongs to him and all that follow from him! And I have read your diary that you have so goodly written for me, and which breathes out truth in every line. I, who have read your so sweet letter to poor Lucy of your marriage and your trust, not know you! Oh, Madam Mina, good women tell all their lives, and by day and by hour and by minute, such things that angels can read; and we men who wish to know have in us something of angels' eyes. Your husband is noble nature, and you are noble too, for you trust, and trust cannot be where there is mean nature. And your husband—tell me of him. Is he quite well? Is all that fever gone, and is he strong and hearty?" I saw here an opening to ask him about Jonathan, so I said:—

"He was almost recovered, but he has been greatly upset by Mr. Hawkins's death." He interrupted:—

"Oh, yes, I know, I know. I have read your last two letters." I went on:—

"I suppose this upset him, for when we were in town on Thursday last he had a sort of shock."

"A shock, and after brain fever so soon! That was not good. What kind of a shock was it?"

"He thought he saw some one who recalled something terrible, something which led to his brain fever." And here the whole thing seemed to overwhelm me in a rush. The pity for Jonathan, the horror which he experienced, the whole fearful mystery of his diary, and the fear that has been brooding over me ever since, all came in a tumult. I suppose I was hysterical, for I threw myself on my knees and held up my hands to him, and implored him to make my husband well again. He took my hands and raised me up, and made me sit on the sofa, and sat by me; he held my hand in his, and said to me with, oh, such infinite sweetness:—

"My life is a barren and lonely one, and so full of work that I have not had much time for friendships; but since I have been summoned to here by my friend John Seward I have known so many good people and seen such nobility that I feel more than ever—and it has grown with my advancing years—the loneliness of my life. Believe, me, then, that I come here full of respect for you, and you have given me hope—hope, not in what I am seeking of, but that there are good women still left to make life happy— good women, whose lives and whose truths may make good lesson for the children that are to be. I am glad, glad, that I may here be of some use to you; for if your husband suffer, he suffer within the range of my study and experience. I promise you that I will gladly do *all* for him that I can—all to make his life strong and manly, and your life a happy one. Now you must eat. You are overwrought and perhaps over-anxious. Husband Jonathan would not like to see you so pale; and what he like not where he love, is not to his good. Therefore for his sake you must eat and smile. You have told me all about Lucy, and so now we shall not speak of it, lest it distress. I shall stay in Exeter to-night, for I want to think much over what you have told me, and when I have thought I will ask you questions, if I may. And then, too, you will tell me of husband Jonathan's trouble so far as you can, but not yet. You must eat now; afterwards you shall tell me all."

After lunch, when we went back to the drawing-room, he said to me:—

"And now tell me all about him." When it came to speaking to this great learned man, I began to fear that he would think me a weak fool, and Jonathan a madman—that journal is all so strange—and I hesitated to go on. But he was so sweet and kind, and he had promised to help, and I trusted him, so I said:—

"Dr. Van Helsing, what I have to tell you is so queer that you must not laugh at me or at my husband. I have been since yesterday in a sort of fever of doubt; you must be kind to me, and not think me foolish that I have even half believed some very strange things." He reassured me by his manner as well as his words when he said:—

"Oh, my dear, if you only know how strange is the matter regarding which I am here, it is you who would laugh. I have learned not to think little of any one's belief, no matter how strange it be. I have tried to keep an open mind; and it is not the ordinary things of life that could close it, but the strange things, the extraordinary things, the things that make one doubt if they be mad or sane."

"Thank you, thank you, a thousand times! You have taken a weight off my mind. If you will let me, I shall give you a paper to read. It is long, but I have typewritten it out. It will tell you my trouble and Jonathan's. It is the copy of his journal when abroad, and all that happened. I dare not say anything of it; you will read for yourself and judge. And then when I see you, perhaps, you will be very kind and tell me what you think."

"I promise," he said as I gave him the papers; "I shall in the morning, so soon as I can, come to see you and your husband, if I may."

"Jonathan will be here at half-past eleven, and you must come to lunch with us and see him then; you could catch the quick 3:34 train, which will leave you at Paddington before eight." He was surprised at my knowledge of the trains off-hand, but he does not know that I have made up all the trains to and from Exeter, so that I may help Jonathan in case he is in a hurry.

So he took the papers with him and went away, and I sit here thinking—thinking I don't know what.

LETTER (*by hand*),
VAN HELSING TO MRS. HARKER.

"25 September, 6 o'clock.

"Dear Madam Mina,—

"I have read your husband's so wonderful diary. You may sleep without doubt. Strange and terrible as it is, it is *true*! I will pledge my life on it. It may be worse for others; but for him and you there is no dread. He is a noble fellow; and let me tell you from experience of men, that one who would do as he did in going down that wall and to that room—ay, and going a second time—is not one to be injured in permanence by a shock. His brain and his heart are all right; this I swear, before I have even seen him; so be at rest. I shall have much to ask him of other things. I am blessed that to-day I come to see you, for I have learn all at once so much that again I am dazzle—dazzle more than ever, and I must think.

"Yours the most faithful,
"Abraham Van Helsing."

LETTER,
MRS. HARKER TO VAN HELSING.

"25 September, 6:30 p. m.

"My dear Dr. Van Helsing,—

"A thousand thanks for your kind letter, which has taken a great weight off my mind. And yet, if it be true, what terrible things there are in the world, and what an awful thing if that man, that monster, be really in London! I fear to think. I have this moment, whilst writing, had a wire from Jonathan, saying that he leaves by the 6:25 to-night from Launceston and will be here at 10:18, so that I shall have no fear to-night. Will you, therefore, instead of lunching with us, please come to breakfast at eight o'clock, if this be not too early for you? You can get away, if you are in a hurry, by the 10:30 train, which will bring you to Paddington by 2:35. Do not answer this, as I shall take it that, if I do not hear, you will come to breakfast.

> "Believe me,
> "Your faithful and grateful friend,
> "MINA HARKER."

JONATHAN HARKER'S JOURNAL.

26 September.—I thought never to write in this diary again, but the time has come. When I got home last night Mina had supper ready, and when we had supped she told me of Van Helsing's visit, and of her having given him the two diaries copied out, and of how anxious she has been about me. She showed me in the doctor's letter that all I wrote down was true. It seems to have made a new man of me. It was the doubt as to the reality of the whole thing that knocked me over. I felt impotent, and in the dark, and distrustful. But, now that I *know*, I am not afraid, even of the Count. He has succeeded after all, then, in his design in getting to London, and it was he I saw. He has got younger, and how? Van Helsing is the man to unmask him and hunt him out, if he is anything like what Mina says. We sat late, and talked it all over. Mina is dressing, and I shall call at the hotel in a few minutes and bring him over . . . .

He was, I think, surprised to see me. When I came into the room where he was, and introduced myself, he took me by the shoulder, and turned my face round to the light, and said, after a sharp scrutiny:—

"But Madam Mina told me you were ill, that you had had a shock." It was so funny to hear my wife called "Madam Mina" by this kindly, strong-faced old man. I smiled, and said:—

"I *was* ill, I *have* had a shock; but you have cured me already."

"And how?"

"By your letter to Mina last night. I was in doubt, and then everything took a hue of unreality, and I did not know what to trust, even the evidence of my own senses. Not knowing what to trust, I did not know what to do; and so had only to keep on working in what had hitherto been the groove of my life. The groove ceased to avail me, and I mistrusted myself. Doctor, you don't know what it is to doubt everything, even yourself. No, you don't;

you couldn't with eyebrows like yours." He seemed pleased, and laughed as he said:—

"So! You are physiognomist. I learn more here with each hour. I am with so much pleasure coming to you to breakfast; and, oh, sir, you will pardon praise from an old man, but you are blessed in your wife." I would listen to him go on praising Mina for a day, so I simply nodded and stood silent.

"She is one of God's women, fashioned by His own hand to show us men and other women that there is a heaven where we can enter, and that its light can be here on earth. So true, so sweet, so noble, so little an egoist—and that, let me tell you, is much in this age, so sceptical and selfish. And you, sir—I have read all the letters to poor Miss Lucy, and some of them speak of you, so I know you since some days from the knowing of others; but I have seen your true self since last night. You will give me your hand, will you not? And let us be friends for all our lives."

We shook hands, and he was so earnest and so kind that it made me quite choky.

"And now," he said, "may I ask you for some more help? I have a great task to do, and at the beginning it is to know. You can help me here. Can you tell me what went before your going to Transylvania? Later on I may ask more help, and of a different kind; but at first this will do."

"Look here, sir," I said, "does what you have to do concern the Count?"

"It does," he said solemnly.

"Then I am with you heart and soul. As you go by the 10:30 train, you will not have time to read them; but I shall get the bundle of papers. You can take them with you and read them in the train."

After breakfast I saw him to the station. When we were parting he said:—

"Perhaps you will come to town if I send to you, and take Madam Mina too."

"We shall both come when you will," I said.

I had got him the morning papers and the London papers of the previous night, and while we were talking at the carriage window, waiting for the train to start, he was turning them over. His eyes suddenly seemed to catch something in one of them, "The Westminster Gazette"—I knew it by the colour—and he grew quite white. He read something intently, groaning to himself: "Mein Gott! Mein Gott! So soon! so soon!" I do not think he remembered me at the moment. Just then the whistle blew, and the train moved off. This recalled him to himself, and he leaned out of the window and waved his hand, calling out: "Love to Madam Mina; I shall write so soon as ever I can."

DR. SEWARD'S DIARY.

26 September.—Truly there is no such thing as finality. Not a week since I said "Finis," and yet here I am starting fresh again, or rather going on with the same record. Until this afternoon I had no cause to think of what is done. Renfield had become, to all intents, as sane as he ever was. He was already well ahead with his fly business; and he had just started in the spider line also; so he had not been of any trouble to me. I had a letter from Arthur, written on Sunday, and from it I gather that he is bearing up wonderfully well. Quincey Morris is with him, and that is much of a help, for he himself is a bubbling well of good spirits. Quincey wrote me a line too, and from him I hear that Arthur is beginning to recover something of his old buoyancy; so as to them all my mind is at rest. As for myself, I was settling down to my work with the enthusiasm which I used to have for it, so that I might fairly have said that the wound which poor Lucy left on me was becoming cicatrised. Everything is, however, now reopened; and what is to be the end God only knows. I have an idea that Van Helsing thinks he knows, too, but he will only let out enough at a time to whet curiosity. He went to Exeter yesterday, and stayed there all night. To-day he came back, and almost bounded into the room at about half-past five o'clock, and thrust last night's "Westminster Gazette" into my hand.

"What do you think of that?" he asked as he stood back and folded his arms.

I looked over the paper, for I really did not know what he meant; but he took it from me and pointed out a paragraph about children being decoyed away at Hampstead. It did not convey much to me, until I reached a passage where it described small punctured wounds on their throats. An idea struck me, and I looked up. "Well?" he said.

"It is like poor Lucy's."

"And what do you make of it?"

"Simply that there is some cause in common. Whatever it was that injured her has injured them." I did not quite understand his answer:—

"That is true indirectly, but not directly."

"How do you mean, Professor?" I asked. I was a little inclined to take his seriousness lightly—for, after all, four days of rest and freedom from burning, harrowing anxiety does help to restore one's spirits—but when I saw his face, it sobered me. Never, even in the midst of our despair about poor Lucy, had he looked more stern.

"Tell me!" I said. "I can hazard no opinion. I do not know what to think, and I have no data on which to found a conjecture."

"Do you mean to tell me, friend John, that you have no suspicion as to what poor Lucy died of; not after all the hints given, not only by events, but by me?"

"Of nervous prostration following on great loss or waste of blood."

"And how the blood lost or waste?" I shook my head. He stepped over and sat down beside me, and went on:—

"You are clever man, friend John; you reason well, and your wit is bold; but you are too prejudiced. You do not let your eyes see nor your ears hear, and that which is outside your daily life is not of account to you. Do you not think that there are things which you cannot understand, and yet which are; that some people see things that others cannot? But there are things old and new which must not be contemplate by men's eyes, because they know—or think they know—some things which other men have told them. Ah, it is the fault of our science that it wants to explain all; and if it explain not, then it says there is nothing to explain. But yet we see around us every day the growth of new beliefs, which think themselves new; and which are yet but the old, which pretend to be young—like the fine ladies at the opera. I suppose now you do not believe in corporeal transference. No? Nor in materialisation. No? Nor in astral bodies. No? Nor in the reading of thought. No? Nor in hypnotism——"

"Yes," I said. "Charcot has proved that pretty well." He smiled as he went on: "Then you are satisfied as to it. Yes? And of course then you understand how it act, and can follow the mind of the great Charcot—alas that he is no more!—into the very soul of the patient that he influence. No? Then, friend John, am I to take it that you simply accept fact, and are satisfied to let from premise to conclusion be a blank? No? Then tell me—for I am student of the brain—how you accept the hypnotism and reject the thought reading. Let me tell you, my friend, that there are things done to-day in electrical science which would have been deemed unholy by the very men who discovered electricity—who would themselves not so long before have been burned as wizards. There are always mysteries in life. Why was it that Methuselah lived nine hundred years, and 'Old Parr' one hundred and sixty-nine, and yet that poor Lucy, with four men's blood in her poor veins, could not live even one day? For, had she live one more day, we could have save her. Do you know all the mystery of life and death? Do you know the altogether of comparative anatomy and can say wherefore the qualities of brutes are in some men, and not in others? Can you tell me why, when other spiders die small and soon, that one great spider lived for centuries in the tower of the old Spanish church and grew and grew, till, on descending, he could drink the oil of all the church lamps? Can you tell me why in the Pampas, ay and elsewhere, there are bats that come at night and open the veins of cattle and horses and suck dry their veins; how in some islands of the Western seas there are bats which hang on the trees all day, and those who have seen describe as like giant nuts or pods, and that when the sailors sleep on the deck, because that it is hot, flit down on them, and then—and then in the morning are found dead men, white as even Miss Lucy was?"

"Good God, Professor!" I said, starting up. "Do you mean to tell me that Lucy was bitten by such a bat; and that such a thing is here in London in the nineteenth century?" He waved his hand for silence, and went on:—

"Can you tell me why the tortoise lives more long than generations of men; why the elephant goes on and on till he have seen dynasties; and why the parrot never die only of bite of cat or dog or other complaint? Can you tell me why men believe in all ages and places that there are some few who live on always if they be permit; that there are men and women who cannot die? We all know—because science has vouched for the fact—that there have been toads shut up in rocks for thousands of years, shut in one so small hole that only hold him since the youth of the world. Can you tell me how the Indian fakir can make himself to die and have been buried, and his grave sealed and corn sowed on it, and the corn reaped and be cut and sown and reaped and cut again, and then men come and take away the unbroken seal and that there lie the Indian fakir, not dead, but that rise up and walk amongst them as before?" Here I interrupted him. I was getting bewildered; he so crowded on my mind his list of nature's eccentricities and possible impossibilities that my imagination was getting fired. I had a dim idea that he was teaching me some lesson, as long ago he used to do in his study at Amsterdam; but he used then to tell me the thing, so that I could have the object of thought in mind all the time. But now I was without this help, yet I wanted to follow him, so I said:—

"Professor, let me be your pet student again. Tell me the thesis, so that I may apply your knowledge as you go on. At present I am going in my mind from point to point as a mad man, and not a sane one, follows an idea. I feel like a novice lumbering through a bog in a mist, jumping from one tussock to another in the mere blind effort to move on without knowing where I am going."

"That is good image," he said. "Well, I shall tell you. My thesis is this: I want you to believe."

"To believe what?"

"To believe in things that you cannot. Let me illustrate. I heard once of an American who so defined faith: 'that faculty which enables us to believe things which we know to be untrue.' For one, I follow that man. He meant that we shall have an open mind, and not let a little bit of truth check the rush of a big truth, like a small rock does a railway truck. We get the small truth first. Good! We keep him, and we value him; but all the same we must not let him think himself all the truth in the universe."

"Then you want me not to let some previous conviction injure the receptivity of my mind with regard to some strange matter. Do I read your lesson aright?"

"Ah, you are my favourite pupil still. It is worth to teach you. Now that you are willing to understand, you have taken the first step to understand. You think then that those so small holes in the children's throats were made by the same that made the hole in Miss Lucy?"

"I suppose so." He stood up and said solemnly:—

"Then you are wrong. Oh, would it were so! but alas! no. It is worse, far, far worse."

"In God's name, Professor Van Helsing, what do you mean?" I cried.

He threw himself with a despairing gesture into a chair, and placed his elbows on the table, covering his face with his hands as he spoke:—

"They were made by Miss Lucy!"

CHAPTER XV

DR. SEWARD'S DIARY—*continued*.

FOR a while sheer anger mastered me; it was as if he had during her life struck Lucy on the face. I smote the table hard and rose up as I said to him:—

"Dr. Van Helsing, are you mad?" He raised his head and looked at me, and somehow the tenderness of his face calmed me at once. "Would I were!" he said. "Madness were easy to bear compared with truth like this. Oh, my friend, why, think you, did I go so far round, why take so long to tell you so simple a thing? Was it because I hate you and have hated you all my life? Was it because I wished to give you pain? Was it that I wanted, now so late, revenge for that time when you saved my life, and from a fearful death? Ah no!"

"Forgive me," said I. He went on:—

"My friend, it was because I wished to be gentle in the breaking to you, for I know you have loved that so sweet lady. But even yet I do not expect you to believe. It is so hard to accept at once any abstract truth, that we may doubt such to be possible when we have always believed the 'no' of it; it is more hard still to accept so sad a concrete truth, and of such a one as Miss Lucy. To-night I go to prove it. Dare you come with me?"

This staggered me. A man does not like to prove such a truth; Byron excepted from the category, jealousy.

"And prove the very truth he most abhorred."

He saw my hesitation, and spoke:—

"The logic is simple, no madman's logic this time, jumping from tussock to tussock in a misty bog. If it be not true, then proof will be relief; at worst it will not harm. If it be true! Ah, there is the dread; yet very dread should help my cause, for in it is some need of belief. Come, I tell you what I propose: first, that we go off now and see that child in the hospital. Dr. Vincent, of the North Hospital, where the papers say the child is, is friend of mine, and I think of yours since you were in class at Amsterdam. He will let two scientists see his case, if he will not let two friends. We shall tell him nothing, but only that we wish to learn. And then——"

"And then?" He took a key from his pocket and held it up. "And then we spend the night, you and I, in the churchyard where Lucy lies. This is the key that lock the tomb. I had it from the coffin-man to give to Arthur." My heart sank within me, for I felt that there was some fearful ordeal before us. I could do nothing, however, so I plucked up what heart I could and said that we had better hasten, as the afternoon was passing . . . .

We found the child awake. It had had a sleep and taken some food, and altogether was going on well. Dr. Vincent took the bandage from its throat, and showed us the punctures. There was no mistaking the similarity to those which had been on Lucy's throat. They were smaller, and the edges looked fresher; that was all. We asked Vincent to what he attributed them, and he replied that it must have been a bite of some animal, perhaps a rat; but, for his own part, he was inclined to think that it was one of the bats which are so numerous on the northern heights of London. "Out of so many harmless ones," he said, "there may be some wild specimen from the South of a more malignant species. Some sailor may have brought one home, and it managed to escape; or even from the Zoölogical Gardens a young one may have got loose, or one be bred there from a vampire. These things do occur, you know. Only ten days ago a wolf got out, and was, I believe, traced up in this direction. For a week after, the children were playing nothing but Red Riding Hood on the Heath and in every alley in the place until this 'bloofer lady' scare came along, since when it has been quite a gala-time with them. Even this poor little mite, when he woke up to-day, asked the nurse if he might go away. When she asked him why he wanted to go, he said he wanted to play with the 'bloofer lady.' "

"I hope," said Van Helsing, "that when you are sending the child home you will caution its parents to keep strict watch over it. These fancies to stray are most dangerous; and if the child were to remain out another night, it would probably be fatal. But in any case I suppose you will not let it away for some days?"

"Certainly not, not for a week at least; longer if the wound is not healed."

Our visit to the hospital took more time than we had reckoned on, and the sun had dipped before we came out. When Van Helsing saw how dark it was, he said:—

"There is no hurry. It is more late than I thought. Come, let us seek somewhere that we may eat, and then we shall go on our way."

We dined at "Jack Straw's Castle" along with a little crowd of bicyclists and others who were genially noisy. About ten o'clock we started from the inn. It was then very dark, and the scattered lamps made the darkness greater when we were once outside their individual radius. The Professor had evidently noted the road we were to go, for he went on unhesitatingly; but, as for me, I was in quite a mixup as to locality. As we went further, we met fewer and fewer people, till at last we were somewhat surprised when we met even the patrol of horse police going their usual suburban round. At last we reached the wall of the churchyard, which we climbed over. With some little difficulty—for it was very dark, and the whole place seemed so strange to us—we found the Westenra tomb. The Professor took the key, opened the creaky door, and standing back, politely, but quite unconsciously, motioned me to precede him. There was a delicious irony in the offer, in the courtliness of giving preference on such a ghastly occasion. My companion followed me quickly, and cautiously drew the door to, after carefully ascertaining that the lock was a falling, and not a spring, one. In the latter case we should have been in a bad plight. Then he fumbled in his bag, and taking out a matchbox and a piece of candle, proceeded to make a light. The tomb in the day-time, and when wreathed with fresh flowers, had looked grim and gruesome enough; but now, some days afterwards, when the flowers hung lank and dead, their whites turning to rust and their greens to browns; when the spider and the beetle had resumed their accustomed dominance; when time-discoloured stone, and dust-encrusted mortar, and rusty, dank iron, and tarnished brass, and clouded silver-plating gave back the feeble glimmer of a candle, the effect was more miserable and sordid than could have been imagined. It conveyed irresistibly the idea that life—animal life— was not the only thing which could pass away.

Van Helsing went about his work systematically. Holding his candle so that he could read the coffin plates, and so holding it that the sperm dropped in white patches which congealed as they touched the metal, he made assurance of Lucy's coffin. Another search in his bag, and he took out a turnscrew.

"What are you going to do?" I asked.

"To open the coffin. You shall yet be convinced." Straightway he began taking out the screws, and finally lifted off the lid, showing the casing of lead beneath. The sight was almost too much for me. It seemed to be as much an affront to the dead as it would have been to have stripped off her clothing in her sleep whilst living; I actually took hold of his hand to stop him. He only said: "You shall see," and again fumbling in his bag, took out a tiny fret-saw. Striking the turnscrew through the lead with a swift downward stab, which made me wince, he made a small hole, which was, however, big enough to admit the point of the saw. I had expected a rush of gas from the week-old corpse. We doctors, who have had to study our dangers, have to become accustomed to such things, and I drew back towards the door. But the Professor never stopped for a moment; he sawed down a couple of feet along one side of the lead coffin, and then across, and down the other side. Taking the edge of the loose flange, he bent it back towards the foot of the coffin, and holding up the candle into the aperture, motioned to me to look.

I drew near and looked. The coffin was empty.

It was certainly a surprise to me, and gave me a considerable shock, but Van Helsing was unmoved. He was now more sure than ever of his ground, and so emboldened to proceed in his task. "Are you satisfied now, friend John?" he asked.

I felt all the dogged argumentativeness of my nature awake within me as I answered him:—

"I am satisfied that Lucy's body is not in that coffin; but that only proves one thing."

"And what is that, friend John?"

"That it is not there."

"That is good logic," he said, "so far as it goes. But how do you—how can you—account for it not being there?"

"Perhaps a body-snatcher," I suggested. "Some of the undertaker's people may have stolen it." I felt that I was speaking folly, and yet it was the only real cause which I could suggest. The Professor sighed. "Ah well!" he said, "we must have more proof. Come with me."

He put on the coffin-lid again, gathered up all his things and placed them in the bag, blew out the light, and placed the candle also in the bag. We opened the door, and went out. Behind us he closed the door and locked it. He handed me the key, saying: "Will you keep it? You had better be assured." I laughed—it was not a very cheerful laugh, I am bound to say—as I motioned him to keep it. "A key is nothing," I said; "there may be duplicates; and anyhow it is not difficult to pick a lock of that kind." He said nothing, but put the key in his pocket. Then he told me to watch at one side of the churchyard whilst he would watch at the other. I took up my place behind a yew-tree, and I saw his dark figure move until the intervening headstones and trees hid it from my sight.

It was a lonely vigil. Just after I had taken my place I heard a distant clock strike twelve, and in time came one and two. I was chilled and unnerved, and angry with the Professor for taking me on such an errand and with myself for coming. I was too cold and too sleepy to be keenly observant, and not sleepy enough to betray my trust so altogether I had a dreary, miserable time.

Suddenly, as I turned round, I thought I saw something like a white streak, moving between two dark yew-trees at the side of the churchyard farthest from the tomb; at the same time a dark mass moved from the Professor's side of the ground, and hurriedly went towards it. Then I too moved; but I had to go round headstones and railed-off tombs, and I stumbled over graves. The sky was overcast, and somewhere far off an early cock crew. A little way off, beyond a line of scattered juniper-trees, which marked the pathway to the church, a white, dim figure flitted in the direction of the tomb. The tomb itself was hidden by trees, and I could not see where the figure disappeared. I heard the rustle of actual movement where I had first seen the white figure, and coming over, found the Professor holding in his arms a tiny child. When he saw me he held it out to me, and said:—

"Are you satisfied now?"

"No," I said, in a way that I felt was aggressive.

"Do you not see the child?"

"Yes, it is a child, but who brought it here? And is it wounded?" I asked.

"We shall see," said the Professor, and with one impulse we took our way out of the churchyard, he carrying the sleeping child.

When we had got some little distance away, we went into a clump of trees, and struck a match, and looked at the child's throat. It was without a scratch or scar of any kind.

"Was I right?" I asked triumphantly.

"We were just in time," said the Professor thankfully.

We had now to decide what we were to do with the child, and so consulted about it. If we were to take it to a police-station we should have to give some account of our movements during the night; at least, we should have had to make some statement as to how we had come to find the child. So finally we decided that we would take it to the Heath, and when we heard a policeman coming, would leave it where he could not fail to find it; we would then seek our way home as quickly as we could. All fell out well. At the edge of Hampstead Heath we heard a policeman's heavy tramp, and laying the child on the pathway, we waited and watched until he saw it as he flashed his lantern to and fro. We heard his exclamation of astonishment, and then we went away silently. By good chance we got a cab near the "Spaniards," and drove to town.

I cannot sleep, so I make this entry. But I must try to get a few hours' sleep, as Van Helsing is to call for me at noon. He insists that I shall go with him on another expedition.

27 September.—It was two o'clock before we found a suitable opportunity for our attempt. The funeral held at noon was all completed, and the last stragglers of the mourners had taken themselves lazily away, when, looking carefully from behind a clump of alder-trees, we saw the sexton lock the gate after him. We knew then that we were safe till morning did we desire it; but the Professor told me that we should not want more than an hour at most. Again I felt that horrid sense of the reality of things, in which any effort of imagination seemed out of place; and I realised distinctly the perils of the law which we were incurring in our unhallowed work. Besides, I felt it was all so useless. Outrageous as it was to open a leaden coffin, to see if a woman dead nearly a week were really dead, it now seemed the height of folly to open the tomb again, when we knew, from the evidence of our own eyesight, that the coffin was empty. I shrugged my shoulders, however, and rested silent, for Van Helsing had a way of going on his own road, no matter who remonstrated. He took the key, opened the vault, and again courteously motioned me to precede. The place was not so gruesome as last night, but oh, how unutterably mean-looking when the sunshine streamed in. Van Helsing walked over to Lucy's coffin, and I followed. He bent over and again forced back the leaden flange; and then a shock of surprise and dismay shot through me.

There lay Lucy, seemingly just as we had seen her the night before her funeral. She was, if possible, more radiantly beautiful than ever; and I could not believe that she was dead. The lips were red, nay redder than before; and on the cheeks was a delicate bloom.

"Is this a juggle?" I said to him.

"Are you convinced now?" said the Professor in response, and as he spoke he put over his hand, and in a way that made me shudder, pulled back the dead lips and showed the white teeth.

"See," he went on, "see, they are even sharper than before. With this and this"—and he touched one of the canine teeth and that below it—"the little children can be bitten. Are you of belief now, friend John?" Once more, argumentative hostility woke within me. I *could* not accept such an overwhelming idea as he suggested; so, with an attempt to argue of which I was even at the moment ashamed, I said:—

"She may have been placed here since last night."

"Indeed? That is so, and by whom?"

"I do not know. Some one has done it."

"And yet she has been dead one week. Most peoples in that time would not look so." I had no answer for this, so was silent. Van Helsing did not seem to notice my silence; at any rate, he showed neither chagrin nor triumph. He was looking intently at the face of the dead woman, raising the eyelids and looking at the eyes, and once more opening the lips and examining the teeth. Then he turned to me and said:—

"Here, there is one thing which is different from all recorded; here is some dual life that is not as the common. She was bitten by the vampire when she was in a trance, sleep-walking—oh, you start; you do not know that, friend John, but you shall know it all later—and in trance could he best come to take more blood. In trance she died, and in trance she is Un-Dead, too. So it is that she differ from all other. Usually when the Un-Dead sleep at home"—as he spoke he made a comprehensive sweep of his arm to designate what to a vampire was "home"—"their face show what they are, but this so sweet that was when she not Un-Dead she go back to the nothings of the common dead. There is no malign there, see, and so it make hard that I must kill her in her sleep." This turned my blood cold, and it began to dawn upon me that I was accepting Van Helsing's theories; but if she were really dead, what was there of terror in the idea of killing her? He looked up at me, and evidently saw the change in my face, for he said almost joyously:—

"Ah, you believe now?"

I answered: "Do not press me too hard all at once. I am willing to accept. How will you do this bloody work?"

"I shall cut off her head and fill her mouth with garlic, and I shall drive a stake through her body." It made me shudder to think of so mutilating the body of the woman whom I had loved. And yet the feeling was not so strong as I had expected. I was, in fact, beginning to shudder at the presence of this being, this Un-Dead, as Van Helsing called it, and to loathe it. Is it possible that love is all subjective, or all objective?

I waited a considerable time for Van Helsing to begin, but he stood as if wrapped in thought. Presently he closed the catch of his bag with a snap, and said:—

"I have been thinking, and have made up my mind as to what is best. If I did simply follow my inclining I would do now, at this moment, what is to be done; but there are other things to follow, and things that are thousand times more difficult in that them we do not know. This is simple. She have yet no life taken, though that is of time; and to act now would be to take danger from her for ever. But then we may have to want Arthur, and how shall we tell him of this? If you, who saw the wounds on Lucy's throat, and saw the wounds so similar on the child's at the hospital; if you, who saw the coffin empty last night and full to-day with a woman who have not change only to be more rose and more beautiful in a whole week, after she die—if you know of this and know of the white figure last night that brought the child to the churchyard, and yet of your own senses you did not believe, how, then, can I expect Arthur, who know none of those things, to believe? He doubted me when I took him from her kiss when she was dying. I know he has forgiven me because in some mistaken idea I have done things that prevent him say good-bye as he ought; and he may think that in some more mistaken idea this woman was buried alive; and that in most mistake of all we have killed her. He will then argue back that it is we, mistaken ones, that have killed her by our ideas; and so he will be much unhappy always. Yet he never can be sure; and that is the worst of all. And he will sometimes think that she he loved was buried alive, and that will paint his dreams with horrors of what she must have suffered; and again, he will think that we may be right, and that his so beloved was, after all, an Un-Dead. No! I told him once, and since then I learn much. Now, since I know it is all true, a hundred thousand times more do I know that he must pass through the bitter waters to reach the sweet. He, poor fellow, must have one hour that will make the very face of heaven grow black to him; then we can act for good all round and send him peace. My mind is made up. Let us go. You return home for to-night to your asylum, and see that all be well. As for me, I shall spend the night here in this churchyard in my own way. To-morrow night you will come to me to the Berkeley Hotel at ten of the clock. I shall send for Arthur to come too, and also that so fine young man of America that gave his blood. Later we shall all have work to do. I come with you so far as Piccadilly and there dine, for I must be back here before the sun set."

So we locked the tomb and came away, and got over the wall of the churchyard, which was not much of a task, and drove back to Piccadilly.

NOTE LEFT BY
VAN HELSING IN HIS PORTMANTEAU,
BERKELEY HOTEL DIRECTED TO JOHN SEWARD, M. D.

(Not delivered.)

"*27 September.*

"Friend John,—

"I write this in case anything should happen. I go alone to watch in that churchyard. It pleases me that the Un-Dead, Miss Lucy, shall not leave to-night, that so on the morrow night she may be more eager. Therefore I shall fix some things she like not—garlic and a crucifix—and so seal up the door of the tomb. She is young as Un-Dead, and will heed. Moreover, these are only to prevent her coming out; they may not prevail on her wanting to get in; for then the Un-Dead is desperate, and must find the line of least resistance, whatsoever it may be. I shall be at hand all the night from sunset till after the sunrise, and if there be aught that may be learned I shall learn it. For Miss Lucy or from her, I have no fear; but that other to whom is there that she is Un-Dead, he have now the power to seek her tomb and find shelter. He is cunning, as I know from Mr. Jonathan and from the way that all along he have fooled us when he played with us for Miss Lucy's life, and we lost; and in many ways the Un-Dead are strong. He have always the strength in his hand of twenty men; even we four who gave our strength to Miss Lucy it also is all to him. Besides, he can summon his wolf and I know not what. So if it be that he come thither on this night he shall find me; but none other shall—until it be too late. But it may be that he will not attempt the place. There is no reason why he should; his hunting ground is more full of game than the churchyard where the Un-Dead woman sleep, and the one old man watch.

"Therefore I write this in case . . . . Take the papers that are with this, the diaries of Harker and the rest, and read them, and then find this great Un-Dead, and cut off his head and burn his heart or drive a stake through it, so that the world may rest from him.

"If it be so, farewell.

"VAN HELSING."

DR. SEWARD'S DIARY.

28 September.—It is wonderful what a good night's sleep will do for one. Yesterday I was almost willing to accept Van Helsing's monstrous ideas; but now they seem to start out lurid before me as outrages on common sense. I have no doubt that he believes it all. I wonder if his mind can have become in any way unhinged. Surely there must be *some* rational explanation of all these mysterious things. Is it possible that the Professor can have done it himself? He is so abnormally clever that if he went off his head he would carry out his intent with regard to some fixed idea in a wonderful way. I am loath to think it, and indeed it would be almost as great a marvel as the other to find that Van Helsing was mad; but anyhow I shall watch him carefully. I may get some light on the mystery.

29 September, morning . . . . . . Last night, at a little before ten o'clock, Arthur and Quincey came into Van Helsing's room; he told us all that he wanted us to do, but especially addressing himself to Arthur, as if all our wills were centred in his. He began by saying that he hoped we would all come with him too, "for," he said, "there is a grave duty to be done there. You were doubtless surprised at my letter?" This query was directly addressed to Lord Godalming.

"I was. It rather upset me for a bit. There has been so much trouble around my house of late that I could do without any more. I have been curious, too, as to what you mean. Quincey and I talked it over; but the more we talked, the more puzzled we got, till now I can say for myself that I'm about up a tree as to any meaning about anything."

"Me too," said Quincey Morris laconically.

"Oh," said the Professor, "then you are nearer the beginning, both of you, than friend John here, who has to go a long way back before he can even get so far as to begin."

It was evident that he recognised my return to my old doubting frame of mind without my saying a word. Then, turning to the other two, he said with intense gravity:—

"I want your permission to do what I think good this night. It is, I know, much to ask; and when you know what it is I propose to do you will know, and only then, how much. Therefore may I ask that you promise me in the dark, so that afterwards, though you may be angry with me for a time—I must not disguise from myself the possibility that such may be—you shall not blame yourselves for anything."

"That's frank anyhow," broke in Quincey. "I'll answer for the Professor. I don't quite see his drift, but I swear he's honest; and that's good enough for me."

"I thank you, sir," said Van Helsing proudly. "I have done myself the honour of counting you one trusting friend, and such endorsement is dear to me." He held out a hand, which Quincey took.

Then Arthur spoke out:—

"Dr. Van Helsing, I don't quite like to 'buy a pig in a poke,' as they say in Scotland, and if it be anything in which my honour as a gentleman or my faith as a Christian is concerned, I cannot make such a promise. If you can assure me that what you intend does not violate either of these two, then I give my consent at once; though for the life of me, I cannot understand what you are driving at."

"I accept your limitation," said Van Helsing, "and all I ask of you is that if you feel it necessary to condemn any act of mine, you will first consider it well and be satisfied that it does not violate your reservations."

"Agreed!" said Arthur; "that is only fair. And now that the *pourparlers* are over, may I ask what it is we are to do?"

"I want you to come with me, and to come in secret, to the churchyard at Kingstead."

Arthur's face fell as he said in an amazed sort of way:—

"Where poor Lucy is buried?" The Professor bowed. Arthur went on: "And when there?"

"To enter the tomb!" Arthur stood up.

"Professor, are you in earnest; or it is some monstrous joke? Pardon me, I see that you are in earnest." He sat down again, but I could see that he sat firmly and proudly, as one who is on his dignity. There was silence until he asked again:—

"And when in the tomb?"

"To open the coffin."

"This is too much!" he said, angrily rising again. "I am willing to be patient in all things that are reasonable; but in this—this desecration of the grave—of one who——" He fairly choked with indignation. The Professor looked pityingly at him.

"If I could spare you one pang, my poor friend," he said, "God knows I would. But this night our feet must tread in thorny paths; or later, and for ever, the feet you love must walk in paths of flame!"

Arthur looked up with set white face and said:—

"Take care, sir, take care!"

"Would it not be well to hear what I have to say?" said Van Helsing. "And then you will at least know the limit of my purpose. Shall I go on?"

"That's fair enough," broke in Morris.

After a pause Van Helsing went on, evidently with an effort:—

"Miss Lucy is dead; is it not so? Yes! Then there can be no wrong to her. But if she be not dead——"

Arthur jumped to his feet.

"Good God!" he cried. "What do you mean? Has there been any mistake; has she been buried alive?" He groaned in anguish that not even hope could soften.

"I did not say she was alive, my child; I did not think it. I go no further than to say that she might be Un-Dead."

"Un-Dead! Not alive! What do you mean? Is this all a nightmare, or what is it?"

"There are mysteries which men can only guess at, which age by age they may solve only in part. Believe me, we are now on the verge of one. But I have not done. May I cut off the head of dead Miss Lucy?"

"Heavens and earth, no!" cried Arthur in a storm of passion. "Not for the wide world will I consent to any mutilation of her dead body. Dr. Van

Helsing, you try me too far. What have I done to you that you should torture me so? What did that poor, sweet girl do that you should want to cast such dishonour on her grave? Are you mad to speak such things, or am I mad to listen to them? Don't dare to think more of such a desecration; I shall not give my consent to anything you do. I have a duty to do in protecting her grave from outrage; and, by God, I shall do it!"

Van Helsing rose up from where he had all the time been seated, and said, gravely and sternly:—

"My Lord Godalming, I, too, have a duty to do, a duty to others, a duty to you, a duty to the dead; and, by God, I shall do it! All I ask you now is that you come with me, that you look and listen; and if when later I make the same request you do not be more eager for its fulfilment even than I am, then—then I shall do my duty, whatever it may seem to me. And then, to follow of your Lordship's wishes I shall hold myself at your disposal to render an account to you, when and where you will." His voice broke a little, and he went on with a voice full of pity:—

"But, I beseech you, do not go forth in anger with me. In a long life of acts which were often not pleasant to do, and which sometimes did wring my heart, I have never had so heavy a task as now. Believe me that if the time comes for you to change your mind towards me, one look from you will wipe away all this so sad hour, for I would do what a man can to save you from sorrow. Just think. For why should I give myself so much of labour and so much of sorrow? I have come here from my own land to do what I can of good; at the first to please my friend John, and then to help a sweet young lady, whom, too, I came to love. For her—I am ashamed to say so much, but I say it in kindness—I gave what you gave; the blood of my veins; I gave it, I, who was not, like you, her lover, but only her physician and her friend. I gave to her my nights and days—before death, after death; and if my death can do her good even now, when she is the dead Un-Dead, she shall have it freely." He said this with a very grave, sweet pride, and Arthur was much affected by it. He took the old man's hand and said in a broken voice:—

"Oh, it is hard to think of it, and I cannot understand; but at least I shall go with you and wait."

CHAPTER XVI

DR. SEWARD'S DIARY—*continued*

IT was just a quarter before twelve o'clock when we got into the churchyard over the low wall. The night was dark with occasional gleams of moonlight between the rents of the heavy clouds that scudded across the sky. We all kept somehow close together, with Van Helsing slightly in front as he led the way. When we had come close to the tomb I looked well at Arthur, for I feared that the proximity to a place laden with so sorrowful a memory would upset him; but he bore himself well. I took it that the very mystery of the proceeding was in some way a counteractant to his grief. The Professor unlocked the door, and seeing a natural hesitation amongst us for various reasons, solved the difficulty by entering first himself. The rest of us followed, and he closed the door. He then lit a dark lantern and pointed to the coffin. Arthur stepped forward hesitatingly; Van Helsing said to me:—

"You were with me here yesterday. Was the body of Miss Lucy in that coffin?"

"It was." The Professor turned to the rest saying:—

"You hear; and yet there is no one who does not believe with me." He took his screwdriver and again took off the lid of the coffin. Arthur looked on, very pale but silent; when the lid was removed he stepped forward. He evidently did not know that there was a leaden coffin, or, at any rate, had not thought of it. When he saw the rent in the lead, the blood rushed to his face for an instant, but as quickly fell away again, so that he remained of a ghastly whiteness; he was still silent. Van Helsing forced back the leaden flange, and we all looked in and recoiled.

The coffin was empty!

For several minutes no one spoke a word. The silence was broken by Quincey Morris:—

"Professor, I answered for you. Your word is all I want. I wouldn't ask such a thing ordinarily—I wouldn't so dishonour you as to imply a doubt; but this is a mystery that goes beyond any honour or dishonour. Is this your doing?"

"I swear to you by all that I hold sacred that I have not removed nor touched her. What happened was this: Two nights ago my friend Seward and I came here—with good purpose, believe me. I opened that coffin, which was then sealed up, and we found it, as now, empty. We then waited, and saw something white come through the trees. The next day we came here in day-time, and she lay there. Did she not, friend John?"

"Yes."

"That night we were just in time. One more so small child was missing, and we find it, thank God, unharmed amongst the graves. Yesterday I came here before sundown, for at sundown the Un-Dead can move. I waited here all the night till the sun rose, but I saw nothing. It was most probable that it was because I had laid over the clamps of those doors garlic, which the Un-Dead cannot bear, and other things which they shun. Last night there was no exodus, so to-night before the sundown I took away my garlic and other things. And so it is we find this coffin empty. But bear with me. So far there is much that is strange. Wait you with me outside, unseen and unheard, and things much stranger are yet to be. So"—here he shut the dark slide of his lantern—"now to the outside." He opened the door, and we filed out, he coming last and locking the door behind him.

Oh! but it seemed fresh and pure in the night air after the terror of that vault. How sweet it was to see the clouds race by, and the passing gleams of the moonlight between the scudding clouds crossing and passing—like the gladness and sorrow of a man's life; how sweet it was to breathe the fresh air, that had no taint of death and decay; how humanising to see the red lighting of the sky beyond the hill, and to hear far away the muffled roar that marks the life of a great city. Each in his own way was solemn and overcome. Arthur was silent, and was, I could see, striving to grasp the purpose and the inner meaning of the mystery. I was myself tolerably patient, and half inclined again to throw aside doubt and to accept Van Helsing's conclusions. Quincey Morris was phlegmatic in the way of a man who accepts all things, and accepts them in the spirit of cool bravery, with hazard of all he has to stake. Not being able to smoke, he cut himself a good-sized plug of tobacco and began to chew. As to Van Helsing, he was employed in a definite way. First he took from his bag a mass of what looked like thin, wafer-like biscuit, which was carefully rolled up in a white napkin; next he took out a double-handful of some whitish stuff, like dough or putty. He crumbled the wafer up fine and worked it into the mass between his hands. This he then took, and rolling it into thin strips, began to lay them into the crevices between the door and its setting in the tomb. I was somewhat puzzled at this, and being close, asked him what it was that he was doing. Arthur and Quincey drew near also, as they too were curious. He answered:—

"I am closing the tomb, so that the Un-Dead may not enter."

"And is that stuff you have put there going to do it?" asked Quincey. "Great Scott! Is this a game?"

"It is."

"What is that which you are using?" This time the question was by Arthur. Van Helsing reverently lifted his hat as he answered:—

"The Host. I brought it from Amsterdam. I have an Indulgence." It was an answer that appalled the most sceptical of us, and we felt individually that in the presence of such earnest purpose as the Professor's, a purpose which could thus use the to him most sacred of things, it was impossible to distrust. In respectful silence we took the places assigned to us close round the tomb, but hidden from the sight of any one approaching. I pitied the others, especially Arthur. I had myself been apprenticed by my former visits to this watching horror; and yet I, who had up to an hour ago repudiated the proofs, felt my heart sink within me. Never did tombs look so ghastly white; never did cypress, or yew, or juniper so seem the embodiment of funereal gloom; never did tree or grass wave or rustle so ominously; never did bough creak so mysteriously; and never did the far-away howling of dogs send such a woeful presage through the night.

There was a long spell of silence, a big, aching void, and then from the Professor a keen "S-s-s-s!" He pointed; and far down the avenue of yews we saw a white figure advance—a dim white figure, which held something dark at its breast. The figure stopped, and at the moment a ray of moonlight fell upon the masses of driving clouds and showed in startling prominence a dark-haired woman, dressed in the cerements of the grave. We could not see the face, for it was bent down over what we saw to be a fair-haired child. There was a pause and a sharp little cry, such as a child gives in sleep, or a dog as it lies before the fire and dreams. We were starting forward, but the Professor's warning hand, seen by us as he stood behind a yew-tree, kept us back; and then as we looked the white figure moved forwards again. It was now near enough for us to see clearly, and the moonlight still held. My own heart grew cold as ice, and I could hear the gasp of Arthur, as we recognised the features of Lucy Westenra. Lucy Westenra, but yet how changed. The sweetness was turned to adamantine, heartless cruelty, and the purity to voluptuous wantonness. Van Helsing stepped out, and, obedient to his gesture, we all advanced too; the four of us ranged in a line before the door of the tomb. Van Helsing raised his lantern and drew the slide; by the concentrated light that fell on Lucy's face we could see that the lips were crimson with fresh blood, and that the stream had trickled over her chin and stained the purity of her lawn death-robe.

We shuddered with horror. I could see by the tremulous light that even Van Helsing's iron nerve had failed. Arthur was next to me, and if I had not seized his arm and held him up, he would have fallen.

When Lucy—I call the thing that was before us Lucy because it bore her shape—saw us she drew back with an angry snarl, such as a cat gives when taken unawares; then her eyes ranged over us. Lucy's eyes in form and colour; but Lucy's eyes unclean and full of hell-fire, instead of the pure, gentle orbs we knew. At that moment the remnant of my love passed into hate and loathing; had she then to be killed, I could have done it with savage delight. As she looked, her eyes blazed with unholy light, and the face became wreathed with a voluptuous smile. Oh, God, how it made me shudder to see it! With a careless motion, she flung to the ground, callous as a devil, the child that up to now she had clutched strenuously to her breast, growling over it as a dog growls over a bone. The child gave a sharp cry, and lay there moaning. There was a cold-bloodedness in the act which wrung a groan from Arthur; when she advanced to him with outstretched arms and a wanton smile he fell back and hid his face in his hands.

She still advanced, however, and with a languorous, voluptuous grace, said:—

"Come to me, Arthur. Leave these others and come to me. My arms are hungry for you. Come, and we can rest together. Come, my husband, come!"

There was something diabolically sweet in her tones—something of the tingling of glass when struck—which rang through the brains even of us who heard the words addressed to another. As for Arthur, he seemed under a spell; moving his hands from his face, he opened wide his arms. She was leaping for them, when Van Helsing sprang forward and held between them his little golden crucifix. She recoiled from it, and, with a suddenly distorted face, full of rage, dashed past him as if to enter the tomb.

When within a foot or two of the door, however, she stopped, as if arrested by some irresistible force. Then she turned, and her face was shown in the clear burst of moonlight and by the lamp, which had now no quiver from Van Helsing's iron nerves. Never did I see such baffled malice on a face; and never, I trust, shall such ever be seen again by mortal eyes. The beautiful colour became livid, the eyes seemed to throw out sparks of hell-fire, the brows were wrinkled as though the folds of the flesh were the coils of Medusa's snakes, and the lovely, blood-stained mouth grew to an open square, as in the passion masks of the Greeks and Japanese. If ever a face meant death—if looks could kill—we saw it at that moment.

And so for full half a minute, which seemed an eternity, she remained between the lifted crucifix and the sacred closing of her means of entry. Van

Helsing broke the silence by asking Arthur:—

"Answer me, oh my friend! Am I to proceed in my work?"

Arthur threw himself on his knees, and hid his face in his hands, as he answered:—

"Do as you will, friend; do as you will. There can be no horror like this ever any more;" and he groaned in spirit. Quincey and I simultaneously moved towards him, and took his arms. We could hear the click of the closing lantern as Van Helsing held it down; coming close to the tomb, he began to remove from the chinks some of the sacred emblem which he had placed there. We all looked on in horrified amazement as we saw, when he stood back, the woman, with a corporeal body as real at that moment as our own, pass in through the interstice where scarce a knife-blade could have gone. We all felt a glad sense of relief when we saw the Professor calmly restoring the strings of putty to the edges of the door.

When this was done, he lifted the child and said:

"Come now, my friends; we can do no more till to-morrow. There is a funeral at noon, so here we shall all come before long after that. The friends of the dead will all be gone by two, and when the sexton lock the gate we shall remain. Then there is more to do; but not like this of to-night. As for this little one, he is not much harm, and by to-morrow night he shall be well. We shall leave him where the police will find him, as on the other night; and then to home." Coming close to Arthur, he said:—

"My friend Arthur, you have had a sore trial; but after, when you look back, you will see how it was necessary. You are now in the bitter waters, my child. By this time to-morrow you will, please God, have passed them, and have drunk of the sweet waters; so do not mourn overmuch. Till then I shall not ask you to forgive me."

Arthur and Quincey came home with me, and we tried to cheer each other on the way. We had left the child in safety, and were tired; so we all slept with more or less reality of sleep.

29 September, night.—A little before twelve o'clock we three—Arthur, Quincey Morris, and myself—called for the Professor. It was odd to notice that by common consent we had all put on black clothes. Of course, Arthur wore black, for he was in deep mourning, but the rest of us wore it by instinct. We got to the churchyard by half-past one, and strolled about, keeping out of official observation, so that when the gravediggers had completed their task and the sexton under the belief that every one had gone, had locked the gate, we had the place all to ourselves. Van Helsing, instead of his little black bag, had with him a long leather one, something like a cricketing bag; it was manifestly of fair weight.

When we were alone and had heard the last of the footsteps die out up the road, we silently, and as if by ordered intention, followed the Professor to the tomb. He unlocked the door, and we entered, closing it behind us. Then he took from his bag the lantern, which he lit, and also two wax candles, which, when lighted, he stuck, by melting their own ends, on other coffins, so that they might give light sufficient to work by. When he again lifted the lid off Lucy's coffin we all looked—Arthur trembling like an aspen—and saw that the body lay there in all its death-beauty. But there was no love in my own heart, nothing but loathing for the foul Thing which had taken Lucy's shape without her soul. I could see even Arthur's face grow hard as he looked. Presently he said to Van Helsing:—

"Is this really Lucy's body, or only a demon in her shape?"

"It is her body, and yet not it. But wait a while, and you all see her as she was, and is."

She seemed like a nightmare of Lucy as she lay there; the pointed teeth, the bloodstained, voluptuous mouth—which it made one shudder to see—the whole carnal and unspiritual appearance, seeming like a devilish mockery of Lucy's sweet purity. Van Helsing, with his usual methodicalness, began taking the various contents from his bag and placing them ready for use. First he took out a soldering iron and some plumbing solder, and then a small oil-lamp, which gave out, when lit in a corner of the tomb, gas which burned at fierce heat with a blue flame; then his operating knives, which he placed to hand; and last a round wooden stake, some two and a half or three inches thick and about three feet long. One end of it was hardened by charring in the fire, and was sharpened to a fine point. With this stake came a heavy hammer, such as in households is used in the coal-cellar for breaking the lumps. To me, a doctor's preparations for work of any kind are stimulating and bracing, but the effect of these things on both Arthur and Quincey was to cause them a sort of consternation. They both, however, kept their courage, and remained silent and quiet.

When all was ready, Van Helsing said:—

"Before we do anything, let me tell you this; it is out of the lore and experience of the ancients and of all those who have studied the powers of the Un-Dead. When they become such, there comes with the change the curse of immortality; they cannot die, but must go on age after age adding new victims and multiplying the evils of the world; for all that die from the preying of the Un-Dead becomes themselves Un-Dead, and prey on their kind. And so the circle goes on ever widening, like as the ripples from a stone thrown in the water. Friend Arthur, if you had met that kiss which you know of before poor Lucy die; or again, last night when you open your arms to her, you would in time, when you had died, have become *nosferatu*, as they call it in Eastern Europe, and would all time make more of those Un-Deads that so have fill us with horror. The career of this so unhappy dear lady is but just begun. Those children whose blood she suck are not as yet so much the worse; but if she live on, Un-Dead, more and more they lose their blood and by her power over them they come to her; and so she draw their blood with that so wicked mouth. But if she die in truth, then all cease; the tiny wounds of the throats disappear, and they go back to their plays unknowing ever of what has been. But of the most blessed of all, when this now Un-Dead be made to rest as true dead, then the soul of the poor lady whom we love shall again be free. Instead of working wickedness by night and growing more debased in the assimilating of it by day, she shall take her place with the other Angels. So that, my friend, it will be a blessed hand for her that shall strike the blow that sets her free. To this I am willing; but is there none amongst us who has a better right? Will it be no joy to think of hereafter in the silence of the night when sleep is not: 'It was my hand that sent her to the stars; it was the hand of him that loved her best; the hand that of all she would herself have chosen, had it been to her to choose?' Tell me if there be such a one amongst us?"

We all looked at Arthur. He saw, too, what we all did, the infinite kindness which suggested that his should be the hand which would restore Lucy to us as a holy, and not an unholy, memory; he stepped forward and said bravely, though his hand trembled, and his face was as pale as snow:—

"My true friend, from the bottom of my broken heart I thank you. Tell me what I am to do, and I shall not falter!" Van Helsing laid a hand on his shoulder, and said:—

"Brave lad! A moment's courage, and it is done. This stake must be driven through her. It will be a fearful ordeal—be not deceived in that—but it will be only a short time, and you will then rejoice more than your pain was great; from this grim tomb you will emerge as though you tread on air. But you must not falter when once you have begun. Only think that we, your true friends, are round you, and that we pray for you all the time."

"Go on," said Arthur hoarsely. "Tell me what I am to do."

"Take this stake in your left hand, ready to place the point over the heart, and the hammer in your right. Then when we begin our prayer for the dead—I shall read him, I have here the book, and the others shall follow— strike in God's name, that so all may be well with the dead that we love and that the Un-Dead pass away."

Arthur took the stake and the hammer, and when once his mind was set on action his hands never trembled nor even quivered. Van Helsing opened his missal and began to read, and Quincey and I followed as well as we could. Arthur placed the point over the heart, and as I looked I could see its dint in the white flesh. Then he struck with all his might.

The Thing in the coffin writhed; and a hideous, blood-curdling screech came from the opened red lips. The body shook and quivered and twisted in wild contortions; the sharp white teeth champed together till the lips were cut, and the mouth was smeared with a crimson foam. But Arthur never faltered. He looked like a figure of Thor as his untrembling arm rose and fell, driving deeper and deeper the mercy-bearing stake, whilst the blood from the pierced heart welled and spurted up around it. His face was set, and high duty seemed to shine through it; the sight of it gave us courage so that our voices seemed to ring through the little vault.

And then the writhing and quivering of the body became less, and the teeth seemed to champ, and the face to quiver. Finally it lay still. The terrible task was over.

The hammer fell from Arthur's hand. He reeled and would have fallen had we not caught him. The great drops of sweat sprang from his forehead, and his breath came in broken gasps. It had indeed been an awful strain on him; and had he not been forced to his task by more than human considerations he could never have gone through with it. For a few minutes we were so taken up with him that we did not look towards the coffin. When we did, however, a murmur of startled surprise ran from one to the other of us. We gazed so eagerly that Arthur rose, for he had been seated on the ground, and came and looked too; and then a glad, strange light broke over his face and dispelled altogether the gloom of horror that lay upon it.

There, in the coffin lay no longer the foul Thing that we had so dreaded and grown to hate that the work of her destruction was yielded as a privilege to the one best entitled to it, but Lucy as we had seen her in her life, with her face of unequalled sweetness and purity. True that there were there, as we had seen them in life, the traces of care and pain and waste; but these were all dear to us, for they marked her truth to what we knew. One and all we felt that the holy calm that lay like sunshine over the wasted face and form was only an earthly token and symbol of the calm that was to reign for ever.

Van Helsing came and laid his hand on Arthur's shoulder, and said to him:—

"And now, Arthur my friend, dear lad, am I not forgiven?"

The reaction of the terrible strain came as he took the old man's hand in his, and raising it to his lips, pressed it, and said:—

"Forgiven! God bless you that you have given my dear one her soul again, and me peace." He put his hands on the Professor's shoulder, and laying his head on his breast, cried for a while silently, whilst we stood unmoving. When he raised his head Van Helsing said to him:—

"And now, my child, you may kiss her. Kiss her dead lips if you will, as she would have you to, if for her to choose. For she is not a grinning devil now—not any more a foul Thing for all eternity. No longer she is the devil's Un-Dead. She is God's true dead, whose soul is with Him!"

Arthur bent and kissed her, and then we sent him and Quincey out of the tomb; the Professor and I sawed the top off the stake, leaving the point of it in the body. Then we cut off the head and filled the mouth with garlic. We soldered up the leaden coffin, screwed on the coffin-lid, and gathering up our belongings, came away. When the Professor locked the door he gave the key to Arthur.

Outside the air was sweet, the sun shone, and the birds sang, and it seemed as if all nature were tuned to a different pitch. There was gladness and mirth and peace everywhere, for we were at rest ourselves on one account, and we were glad, though it was with a tempered joy.

Before we moved away Van Helsing said:—

"Now, my friends, one step of our work is done, one the most harrowing to ourselves. But there remains a greater task: to find out the author of all this our sorrow and to stamp him out. I have clues which we can follow; but it is a long task, and a difficult, and there is danger in it, and pain. Shall you not all help me? We have learned to believe, all of us—is it not so? And since so, do we not see our duty? Yes! And do we not promise to go on to the bitter end?"

Each in turn, we took his hand, and the promise was made. Then said the Professor as we moved off:—

"Two nights hence you shall meet with me and dine together at seven of the clock with friend John. I shall entreat two others, two that you know not as yet; and I shall be ready to all our work show and our plans unfold. Friend John, you come with me home, for I have much to consult about, and you can help me. To-night I leave for Amsterdam, but shall return to-morrow night. And then begins our great quest. But first I shall have much to say, so that you may know what is to do and to dread. Then our promise shall be made to each other anew; for there is a terrible task before us, and once our feet are on the ploughshare we must not draw back."

CHAPTER XVII

DR. SEWARD'S DIARY—*continued*

WHEN we arrived at the Berkeley Hotel, Van Helsing found a telegram waiting for him:—

"Am coming up by train. Jonathan at Whitby. Important news.—MINA HARKER."

The Professor was delighted. "Ah, that wonderful Madam Mina," he said, "pearl among women! She arrive, but I cannot stay. She must go to your house, friend John. You must meet her at the station. Telegraph her *en route*, so that she may be prepared."

When the wire was despatched he had a cup of tea; over it he told me of a diary kept by Jonathan Harker when abroad, and gave me a typewritten copy of it, as also of Mrs. Harker's diary at Whitby. "Take these," he said, "and study them well. When I have returned you will be master of all the facts, and we can then better enter on our inquisition. Keep them safe, for there is in them much of treasure. You will need all your faith, even you who have had such an experience as that of to-day. What is here told," he laid his hand heavily and gravely on the packet of papers as he spoke, "may be the beginning of the end to you and me and many another; or it may sound the knell of the Un-Dead who walk the earth. Read all, I pray you, with the open mind; and if you can add in any way to the story here told do so, for it is all-important. You have kept diary of all these so strange things; is it not so? Yes! Then we shall go through all these together when we meet." He then made ready for his departure, and shortly after drove off to Liverpool Street. I took my way to Paddington, where I arrived about fifteen minutes before the train came in.

The crowd melted away, after the bustling fashion common to arrival platforms; and I was beginning to feel uneasy, lest I might miss my guest, when a sweet-faced, dainty-looking girl stepped up to me, and, after a quick glance, said: "Dr. Seward, is it not?"

"And you are Mrs. Harker!" I answered at once; whereupon she held out her hand.

"I knew you from the description of poor dear Lucy; but——" She stopped suddenly, and a quick blush overspread her face.

The blush that rose to my own cheeks somehow set us both at ease, for it was a tacit answer to her own. I got her luggage, which included a typewriter, and we took the Underground to Fenchurch Street, after I had sent a wire to my housekeeper to have a sitting-room and bedroom prepared at once for Mrs. Harker.

In due time we arrived. She knew, of course, that the place was a lunatic asylum, but I could see that she was unable to repress a shudder when we entered.

She told me that, if she might, she would come presently to my study, as she had much to say. So here I am finishing my entry in my phonograph diary whilst I await her. As yet I have not had the chance of looking at the papers which Van Helsing left with me, though they lie open before me. I must get her interested in something, so that I may have an opportunity of reading them. She does not know how precious time is, or what a task we have in hand. I must be careful not to frighten her. Here she is!

MINA HARKER'S JOURNAL.

29 September.—After I had tidied myself, I went down to Dr. Seward's study. At the door I paused a moment, for I thought I heard him talking with some one. As, however, he had pressed me to be quick, I knocked at the door, and on his calling out, "Come in," I entered.

To my intense surprise, there was no one with him. He was quite alone, and on the table opposite him was what I knew at once from the description to be a phonograph. I had never seen one, and was much interested.

"I hope I did not keep you waiting," I said; "but I stayed at the door as I heard you talking, and thought there was some one with you."

"Oh," he replied with a smile, "I was only entering my diary."

"Your diary?" I asked him in surprise.

"Yes," he answered. "I keep it in this." As he spoke he laid his hand on the phonograph. I felt quite excited over it, and blurted out:—

"Why, this beats even shorthand! May I hear it say something?"

"Certainly," he replied with alacrity, and stood up to put it in train for speaking. Then he paused, and a troubled look overspread his face.

"The fact is," he began awkwardly, "I only keep my diary in it; and as it is entirely—almost entirely—about my cases, it may be awkward—that is, I mean——" He stopped, and I tried to help him out of his embarrassment:—

"You helped to attend dear Lucy at the end. Let me hear how she died; for all that I know of her, I shall be very grateful. She was very, very dear to me."

To my surprise, he answered, with a horrorstruck look in his face:—

"Tell you of her death? Not for the wide world!"

"Why not?" I asked, for some grave, terrible feeling was coming over me. Again he paused, and I could see that he was trying to invent an excuse. At length he stammered out:—

"You see, I do not know how to pick out any particular part of the diary." Even while he was speaking an idea dawned upon him, and he said with unconscious simplicity, in a different voice, and with the naïveté of a child: "That's quite true, upon my honour. Honest Indian!" I could not but smile, at which he grimaced. "I gave myself away that time!" he said. "But do you know that, although I have kept the diary for months past, it never once struck me how I was going to find any particular part of it in case I wanted to look it up?" By this time my mind was made up that the diary of a doctor who attended Lucy might have something to add to the sum of our knowledge of that terrible Being, and I said boldly:—

"Then, Dr. Seward, you had better let me copy it out for you on my typewriter." He grew to a positively deathly pallor as he said:—

"No! no! no! For all the world, I wouldn't let you know that terrible story!"

Then it was terrible; my intuition was right! For a moment I thought, and as my eyes ranged the room, unconsciously looking for something or some opportunity to aid me, they lit on a great batch of typewriting on the table. His eyes caught the look in mine, and, without his thinking, followed their direction. As they saw the parcel he realised my meaning.

"You do not know me," I said. "When you have read those papers—my own diary and my husband's also, which I have typed—you will know me better. I have not faltered in giving every thought of my own heart in this cause; but, of course, you do not know me—yet; and I must not expect you to trust me so far."

He is certainly a man of noble nature; poor dear Lucy was right about him. He stood up and opened a large drawer, in which were arranged in order a number of hollow cylinders of metal covered with dark wax, and said:—

"You are quite right. I did not trust you because I did not know you. But I know you now; and let me say that I should have known you long ago. I know that Lucy told you of me; she told me of you too. May I make the only atonement in my power? Take the cylinders and hear them—the first half-dozen of them are personal to me, and they will not horrify you; then you will know me better. Dinner will by then be ready. In the meantime I shall read over some of these documents, and shall be better able to understand certain things." He carried the phonograph himself up to my sitting-room and adjusted it for me. Now I shall learn something pleasant, I am sure; for it will tell me the other side of a true love episode of which I know one side already . . . .

DR. SEWARD'S DIARY.

29 September.—I was so absorbed in that wonderful diary of Jonathan Harker and that other of his wife that I let the time run on without thinking. Mrs. Harker was not down when the maid came to announce dinner, so I said: "She is possibly tired; let dinner wait an hour," and I went on with my work. I had just finished Mrs. Harker's diary, when she came in. She looked sweetly pretty, but very sad, and her eyes were flushed with crying. This somehow moved me much. Of late I have had cause for tears, God knows! but the relief of them was denied me; and now the sight of those sweet eyes, brightened with recent tears, went straight to my heart. So I said as gently as I could:—

"I greatly fear I have distressed you."

"Oh, no, not distressed me," she replied, "but I have been more touched than I can say by your grief. That is a wonderful machine, but it is cruelly true. It told me, in its very tones, the anguish of your heart. It was like a soul crying out to Almighty God. No one must hear them spoken ever again! See, I have tried to be useful. I have copied out the words on my typewriter, and none other need now hear your heart beat, as I did."

"No one need ever know, shall ever know," I said in a low voice. She laid her hand on mine and said very gravely:—

"Ah, but they must!"

"Must! But why?" I asked.

"Because it is a part of the terrible story, a part of poor dear Lucy's death and all that led to it; because in the struggle which we have before us to rid the earth of this terrible monster we must have all the knowledge and all the help which we can get. I think that the cylinders which you gave me contained more than you intended me to know; but I can see that there are in your record many lights to this dark mystery. You will let me help, will you not? I know all up to a certain point; and I see already, though your diary only took me to 7 September, how poor Lucy was beset, and how her terrible doom was being wrought out. Jonathan and I have been working day and night since Professor Van Helsing saw us. He is gone to Whitby to get more information, and he will be here to-morrow to help us. We need have no secrets amongst us; working together and with absolute trust, we can surely be stronger than if some of us were in the dark." She looked at me so appealingly, and at the same time manifested such courage and resolution in her bearing, that I gave in at once to her wishes. "You shall," I said, "do as you like in the matter. God forgive me if I do wrong! There are terrible things yet to learn of; but if you have so far travelled on the road to poor Lucy's death, you will not be content, I know, to remain in the dark. Nay, the end—the very end—may give you a gleam of peace. Come, there is dinner. We must keep one another strong for what is before us; we have a cruel and dreadful task. When you have eaten you shall learn the rest, and I shall answer any questions you ask—if there be anything which you do not understand, though it was apparent to us who were present."

MINA HARKER'S JOURNAL.

29 September.—After dinner I came with Dr. Seward to his study. He brought back the phonograph from my room, and I took my typewriter. He placed me in a comfortable chair, and arranged the phonograph so that I could touch it without getting up, and showed me how to stop it in case I should want to pause. Then he very thoughtfully took a chair, with his back to me, so that I might be as free as possible, and began to read. I put the forked metal to my ears and listened.

When the terrible story of Lucy's death, and—and all that followed, was done, I lay back in my chair powerless. Fortunately I am not of a fainting disposition. When Dr. Seward saw me he jumped up with a horrified exclamation, and hurriedly taking a case-bottle from a cupboard, gave me some brandy, which in a few minutes somewhat restored me. My brain was all in a whirl, and only that there came through all the multitude of horrors, the holy ray of light that my dear, dear Lucy was at last at peace, I do not think I could have borne it without making a scene. It is all so wild, and mysterious, and strange that if I had not known Jonathan's experience in Transylvania I could not have believed. As it was, I didn't know what to believe, and so got out of my difficulty by attending to something else. I took the cover off my typewriter, and said to Dr. Seward:—

"Let me write this all out now. We must be ready for Dr. Van Helsing when he comes. I have sent a telegram to Jonathan to come on here when he arrives in London from Whitby. In this matter dates are everything, and I think that if we get all our material ready, and have every item put in chronological order, we shall have done much. You tell me that Lord Godalming and Mr. Morris are coming too. Let us be able to tell him when they come." He accordingly set the phonograph at a slow pace, and I began to typewrite from the beginning of the seventh cylinder. I used manifold, and so took three copies of the diary, just as I had done with all the rest. It was late when I got through, but Dr. Seward went about his work of going his round of the patients; when he had finished he came back and sat near me, reading, so that I did not feel too lonely whilst I worked. How good and thoughtful he is; the world seems full of good men—even if there *are* monsters in it. Before I left him I remembered what Jonathan put in his diary of the Professor's perturbation at reading something in an evening paper at the station at Exeter; so, seeing that Dr. Seward keeps his newspapers, I borrowed the files of "The Westminster Gazette" and "The Pall Mall Gazette," and took them to my room. I remember how much "The Dailygraph" and "The Whitby Gazette," of which I had made cuttings, helped us to understand the terrible events at Whitby when Count Dracula landed, so I shall look through the evening papers since then, and perhaps I shall get some new light. I am not sleepy, and the work will help to keep me quiet.

DR. SEWARD'S DIARY.

30 September.—Mr. Harker arrived at nine o'clock. He had got his wife's wire just before starting. He is uncommonly clever, if one can judge from his face, and full of energy. If this journal be true—and judging by one's own wonderful experiences, it must be—he is also a man of great nerve. That going down to the vault a second time was a remarkable piece of daring. After reading his account of it I was prepared to meet a good specimen of manhood, but hardly the quiet, business-like gentleman who came here to-day.

Later.—After lunch Harker and his wife went back to their own room, and as I passed a while ago I heard the click of the typewriter. They are hard at it. Mrs. Harker says that they are knitting together in chronological order every scrap of evidence they have. Harker has got the letters between the consignee of the boxes at Whitby and the carriers in London who took charge of them. He is now reading his wife's typescript of my diary. I wonder what they make out of it. Here it is . . . .

Strange that it never struck me that the very next house might be the Count's hiding-place! Goodness knows that we had enough clues from the conduct of the patient Renfield! The bundle of letters relating to the purchase of the house were with the typescript. Oh, if we had only had them earlier we might have saved poor Lucy! Stop; that way madness lies! Harker has gone back, and is again collating his material. He says that by dinner-time they will be able to show a whole connected narrative. He thinks that in the meantime I should see Renfield, as hitherto he has been a sort of index to the coming and going of the Count. I hardly see this yet, but when I get at the dates I suppose I shall. What a good thing that Mrs. Harker put my cylinders into type! We never could have found the dates otherwise . . . .

I found Renfield sitting placidly in his room with his hands folded, smiling benignly. At the moment he seemed as sane as any one I ever saw. I sat down and talked with him on a lot of subjects, all of which he treated naturally. He then, of his own accord, spoke of going home, a subject he has never mentioned to my knowledge during his sojourn here. In fact, he spoke quite confidently of getting his discharge at once. I believe that, had I not had the chat with Harker and read the letters and the dates of his outbursts, I should have been prepared to sign for him after a brief time of observation. As it is, I am darkly suspicious. All those outbreaks were in some way linked with the proximity of the Count. What then does this absolute content mean? Can it be that his instinct is satisfied as to the vampire's ultimate triumph? Stay; he is himself zoöphagous, and in his wild ravings outside the chapel door of the deserted house he always spoke of "master." This all seems confirmation of our idea. However, after a while I came away; my friend is just a little too sane at present to make it safe to probe him too deep with questions. He might begin to think, and then—! So I came away. I mistrust these quiet moods of his; so I have given the attendant a hint to look closely after him, and to have a strait-waistcoat ready in case of need.

JONATHAN HARKER'S JOURNAL.

29 September, in train to London.—When I received Mr. Billington's courteous message that he would give me any information in his power I thought it best to go down to Whitby and make, on the spot, such inquiries as I wanted. It was now my object to trace that horrid cargo of the Count's to its place in London. Later, we may be able to deal with it. Billington junior, a nice lad, met me at the station, and brought me to his father's house, where they had decided that I must stay the night. They are hospitable, with true Yorkshire hospitality: give a guest everything, and leave him free to do as he likes. They all knew that I was busy, and that my stay was short, and Mr.

Billington had ready in his office all the papers concerning the consignment of boxes. It gave me almost a turn to see again one of the letters which I had seen on the Count's table before I knew of his diabolical plans. Everything had been carefully thought out, and done systematically and with precision. He seemed to have been prepared for every obstacle which might be placed by accident in the way of his intentions being carried out. To use an Americanism, he had "taken no chances," and the absolute accuracy with which his instructions were fulfilled, was simply the logical result of his care. I saw the invoice, and took note of it: "Fifty cases of common earth, to be used for experimental purposes." Also the copy of letter to Carter Paterson, and their reply; of both of these I got copies. This was all the information Mr. Billington could give me, so I went down to the port and saw the coastguards, the Customs officers and the harbour-master. They had all something to say of the strange entry of the ship, which is already taking its place in local tradition; but no one could add to the simple description "Fifty cases of common earth." I then saw the station-master, who kindly put me in communication with the men who had actually received the boxes. Their tally was exact with the list, and they had nothing to add except that the boxes were "main and mortal heavy," and that shifting them was dry work. One of them added that it was hard lines that there wasn't any gentleman "such-like as yourself, squire," to show some sort of appreciation of their efforts in a liquid form; another put in a rider that the thirst then generated was such that even the time which had elapsed had not completely allayed it. Needless to add, I took care before leaving to lift, for ever and adequately, this source of reproach.

30 September.—The station-master was good enough to give me a line to his old companion the station-master at King's Cross, so that when I arrived there in the morning I was able to ask him about the arrival of the boxes. He, too, put me at once in communication with the proper officials, and I saw that their tally was correct with the original invoice. The opportunities of acquiring an abnormal thirst had been here limited; a noble use of them had, however, been made, and again I was compelled to deal with the result in an *ex post facto* manner.

From thence I went on to Carter Paterson's central office, where I met with the utmost courtesy. They looked up the transaction in their day-book and letter-book, and at once telephoned to their King's Cross office for more details. By good fortune, the men who did the teaming were waiting for work, and the official at once sent them over, sending also by one of them the way-bill and all the papers connected with the delivery of the boxes at Carfax. Here again I found the tally agreeing exactly; the carriers' men were able to supplement the paucity of the written words with a few details. These were, I shortly found, connected almost solely with the dusty nature of the job, and of the consequent thirst engendered in the operators. On my affording an opportunity, through the medium of the currency of the realm, of the allaying, at a later period, this beneficial evil, one of the men remarked:—

"That 'ere 'ouse, guv'nor, is the rummiest I ever was in. Blyme! but it ain't been touched sence a hundred years. There was dust that thick in the place that you might have slep' on it without 'urtin' of yer bones; an' the place was that neglected that yer might 'ave smelled ole Jerusalem in it. But the ole chapel—that took the cike, that did! Me and my mate, we thort we wouldn't never git out quick enough. Lor', I wouldn't take less nor a quid a moment to stay there arter dark."

Having been in the house, I could well believe him; but if he knew what I know, he would, I think, have raised his terms.

Of one thing I am now satisfied: that *all* the boxes which arrived at Whitby from Varna in the *Demeter* were safely deposited in the old chapel at Carfax. There should be fifty of them there, unless any have since been removed—as from Dr. Seward's diary I fear.

I shall try to see the carter who took away the boxes from Carfax when Renfield attacked them. By following up this clue we may learn a good deal.

Later.—Mina and I have worked all day, and we have put all the papers into order.

MINA HARKER'S JOURNAL

30 September.—I am so glad that I hardly know how to contain myself. It is, I suppose, the reaction from the haunting fear which I have had: that this terrible affair and the reopening of his old wound might act detrimentally on Jonathan. I saw him leave for Whitby with as brave a face as I could, but I was sick with apprehension. The effort has, however, done him good. He was never so resolute, never so strong, never so full of volcanic energy, as at present. It is just as that dear, good Professor Van Helsing said: he is true grit, and he improves under strain that would kill a weaker nature. He came back full of life and hope and determination; we have got everything in order for to-night. I feel myself quite wild with excitement. I suppose one ought to pity any thing so hunted as is the Count.

That is just it: this Thing is not human—not even beast. To read Dr. Seward's account of poor Lucy's death, and what followed, is enough to dry up the springs of pity in one's heart.

Later.—Lord Godalming and Mr. Morris arrived earlier than we expected. Dr. Seward was out on business, and had taken Jonathan with him, so I had to see them. It was to me a painful meeting, for it brought back all poor dear Lucy's hopes of only a few months ago. Of course they had heard Lucy speak of me, and it seemed that Dr. Van Helsing, too, has been quite "blowing my trumpet," as Mr. Morris expressed it. Poor fellows, neither of them is aware that I know all about the proposals they made to Lucy. They did not quite know what to say or do, as they were ignorant of the amount of my knowledge; so they had to keep on neutral subjects. However, I thought the matter over, and came to the conclusion that the best thing I could do would be to post them in affairs right up to date. I knew from Dr. Seward's diary that they had been at Lucy's death—her real death—and that I need not fear to betray any secret before the time. So I told them, as well as I could, that I had read all the papers and diaries, and that my husband and I, having typewritten them, had just finished putting them in order. I gave them each a copy to read in the library. When Lord Godalming got his and turned it over—it does make a pretty good pile—he said:—

"Did you write all this, Mrs. Harker?"

I nodded, and he went on:—

"I don't quite see the drift of it; but you people are all so good and kind, and have been working so earnestly and so energetically, that all I can do is to accept your ideas blindfold and try to help you. I have had one lesson already in accepting facts that should make a man humble to the last hour of his life. Besides, I know you loved my poor Lucy—" Here he turned away and covered his face with his hands. I could hear the tears in his voice. Mr. Morris, with instinctive delicacy, just laid a hand for a moment on his shoulder, and then walked quietly out of the room. I suppose there is something in woman's nature that makes a man free to break down before her and express his feelings on the tender or emotional side without feeling it derogatory to his manhood; for when Lord Godalming found himself alone with me he sat down on the sofa and gave way utterly and openly. I sat down beside him and took his hand. I hope he didn't think it forward of me, and that if he ever thinks of it afterwards he never will have such a thought. There I wrong him; I *know* he never will—he is too true a gentleman. I said to him, for I could see that his heart was breaking:—

"I loved dear Lucy, and I know what she was to you, and what you were to her. She and I were like sisters; and now she is gone, will you not let me be like a sister to you in your trouble? I know what sorrows you have had, though I cannot measure the depth of them. If sympathy and pity can help in your affliction, won't you let me be of some little service—for Lucy's sake?"

In an instant the poor dear fellow was overwhelmed with grief. It seemed to me that all that he had of late been suffering in silence found a vent at once. He grew quite hysterical, and raising his open hands, beat his palms together in a perfect agony of grief. He stood up and then sat down again, and the tears rained down his cheeks. I felt an infinite pity for him, and opened my arms unthinkingly. With a sob he laid his head on my shoulder and cried like a wearied child, whilst he shook with emotion.

We women have something of the mother in us that makes us rise above smaller matters when the mother-spirit is invoked; I felt this big sorrowing man's head resting on me, as though it were that of the baby that some day may lie on my bosom, and I stroked his hair as though he were my own child. I never thought at the time how strange it all was.

After a little bit his sobs ceased, and he raised himself with an apology, though he made no disguise of his emotion. He told me that for days and nights past—weary days and sleepless nights—he had been unable to speak with any one, as a man must speak in his time of sorrow. There was no woman whose sympathy could be given to him, or with whom, owing to the terrible circumstance with which his sorrow was surrounded, he could speak freely. "I know now how I suffered," he said, as he dried his eyes, "but I do not know even yet—and none other can ever know—how much your sweet sympathy has been to me to-day. I shall know better in time; and believe me that, though I am not ungrateful now, my gratitude will grow with my understanding. You will let me be like a brother, will you not, for all our lives—for dear Lucy's sake?"

"For dear Lucy's sake," I said as we clasped hands. "Ay, and for your own sake," he added, "for if a man's esteem and gratitude are ever worth the winning, you have won mine to-day. If ever the future should bring to you a time when you need a man's help, believe me, you will not call in vain. God grant that no such time may ever come to you to break the sunshine of your life; but if it should ever come, promise me that you will let me know." He was so earnest, and his sorrow was so fresh, that I felt it would comfort him, so I said:—

"I promise."

As I came along the corridor I saw Mr. Morris looking out of a window. He turned as he heard my footsteps. "How is Art?" he said. Then noticing my red eyes, he went on: "Ah, I see you have been comforting him. Poor old fellow! he needs it. No one but a woman can help a man when he is in trouble of the heart; and he had no one to comfort him."

He bore his own trouble so bravely that my heart bled for him. I saw the manuscript in his hand, and I knew that when he read it he would realise how much I knew; so I said to him:—

"I wish I could comfort all who suffer from the heart. Will you let me be your friend, and will you come to me for comfort if you need it? You will know, later on, why I speak." He saw that I was in earnest, and stooping, took my hand, and raising it to his lips, kissed it. It seemed but poor comfort to so brave and unselfish a soul, and impulsively I bent over and kissed him. The tears rose in his eyes, and there was a momentary choking in his throat; he said quite calmly:—

"Little girl, you will never regret that true-hearted kindness, so long as ever you live!" Then he went into the study to his friend.

"Little girl!"—the very words he had used to Lucy, and oh, but he proved himself a friend!

CHAPTER XVIII

DR. SEWARD'S DIARY

30 September.—I got home at five o'clock, and found that Godalming and Morris had not only arrived, but had already studied the transcript of the various diaries and letters which Harker and his wonderful wife had made and arranged. Harker had not yet returned from his visit to the carriers' men, of whom Dr. Hennessey had written to me. Mrs. Harker gave us a cup of tea, and I can honestly say that, for the first time since I have lived in it, this old house seemed like *home.* When we had finished, Mrs. Harker said:—

"Dr. Seward, may I ask a favour? I want to see your patient, Mr. Renfield. Do let me see him. What you have said of him in your diary interests me so much!" She looked so appealing and so pretty that I could not refuse her, and there was no possible reason why I should; so I took her with me. When I went into the room, I told the man that a lady would like to see him; to which he simply answered: "Why?"

"She is going through the house, and wants to see every one in it," I answered. "Oh, very well," he said; "let her come in, by all means; but just wait a minute till I tidy up the place." His method of tidying was peculiar: he simply swallowed all the flies and spiders in the boxes before I could stop him. It was quite evident that he feared, or was jealous of, some interference. When he had got through his disgusting task, he said cheerfully: "Let the lady come in," and sat down on the edge of his bed with his head down, but with his eyelids raised so that he could see her as she entered. For a moment I thought that he might have some homicidal intent; I remembered how quiet he had been just before he attacked me in my own study, and I took care to stand where I could seize him at once if he attempted to make a spring at her. She came into the room with an easy gracefulness which would at once command the respect of any lunatic—for easiness is one of the qualities mad people most respect. She walked over to him, smiling pleasantly, and held out her hand.

"Good-evening, Mr. Renfield," said she. "You see, I know you, for Dr. Seward has told me of you." He made no immediate reply, but eyed her all over intently with a set frown on his face. This look gave way to one of wonder, which merged in doubt; then, to my intense astonishment, he said:—

"You're not the girl the doctor wanted to marry, are you? You can't be, you know, for she's dead." Mrs. Harker smiled sweetly as she replied:—

"Oh no! I have a husband of my own, to whom I was married before I ever saw Dr. Seward, or he me. I am Mrs. Harker."

"Then what are you doing here?"

"My husband and I are staying on a visit with Dr. Seward."

"Then don't stay."

"But why not?" I thought that this style of conversation might not be pleasant to Mrs. Harker, any more than it was to me, so I joined in:—

"How did you know I wanted to marry any one?" His reply was simply contemptuous, given in a pause in which he turned his eyes from Mrs. Harker to me, instantly turning them back again:—

"What an asinine question!"

"I don't see that at all, Mr. Renfield," said Mrs. Harker, at once championing me. He replied to her with as much courtesy and respect as he had shown contempt to me:—

"You will, of course, understand, Mrs. Harker, that when a man is so loved and honoured as our host is, everything regarding him is of interest in our little community. Dr. Seward is loved not only by his household and his friends, but even by his patients, who, being some of them hardly in mental equilibrium, are apt to distort causes and effects. Since I myself have been an inmate of a lunatic asylum, I cannot but notice that the sophistic tendencies of some of its inmates lean towards the errors of *non causa* and *ignoratio elenchi*." I positively opened my eyes at this new development. Here was my own pet lunatic—the most pronounced of his type that I had ever met with—talking elemental philosophy, and with the manner of a polished gentleman. I wonder if it was Mrs. Harker's presence which had touched some chord in his memory. If this new phase was spontaneous, or in any way due to her unconscious influence, she must have some rare gift or power.

We continued to talk for some time; and, seeing that he was seemingly quite reasonable, she ventured, looking at me questioningly as she began, to lead him to his favourite topic. I was again astonished, for he addressed himself to the question with the impartiality of the completest sanity; he even took himself as an example when he mentioned certain things.

"Why, I myself am an instance of a man who had a strange belief. Indeed, it was no wonder that my friends were alarmed, and insisted on my being put under control. I used to fancy that life was a positive and perpetual entity, and that by consuming a multitude of live things, no matter how low in the scale of creation, one might indefinitely prolong life. At times I held the belief so strongly that I actually tried to take human life. The doctor here will bear me out that on one occasion I tried to kill him for the purpose of strengthening my vital powers by the assimilation with my own body of his life through the medium of his blood—relying, of course, upon the Scriptural phrase, 'For the blood is the life.' Though, indeed, the vendor of a certain nostrum has vulgarised the truism to the very point of contempt. Isn't that true, doctor?" I nodded assent, for I was so amazed that I hardly knew what to either think or say; it was hard to imagine that I had seen him eat up his spiders and flies not five minutes before. Looking at my watch, I saw that I should go to the station to meet Van Helsing, so I told Mrs. Harker that it was time to leave. She came at once, after saying pleasantly to Mr. Renfield: "Good-bye, and I hope I may see you often, under auspices pleasanter to yourself," to which, to my astonishment, he replied:—

"Good-bye, my dear. I pray God I may never see your sweet face again. May He bless and keep you!"

When I went to the station to meet Van Helsing I left the boys behind me. Poor Art seemed more cheerful than he has been since Lucy first took ill, and Quincey is more like his own bright self than he has been for many a long day.

Van Helsing stepped from the carriage with the eager nimbleness of a boy. He saw me at once, and rushed up to me, saying:—

"Ah, friend John, how goes all? Well? So! I have been busy, for I come here to stay if need be. All affairs are settled with me, and I have much to tell. Madam Mina is with you? Yes. And her so fine husband? And Arthur and my friend Quincey, they are with you, too? Good!"

As I drove to the house I told him of what had passed, and of how my own diary had come to be of some use through Mrs. Harker's suggestion; at which the Professor interrupted me:—

"Ah, that wonderful Madam Mina! She has man's brain—a brain that a man should have were he much gifted—and a woman's heart. The good God fashioned her for a purpose, believe me, when He made that so good combination. Friend John, up to now fortune has made that woman of help to us; after to-night she must not have to do with this so terrible affair. It is not good that she run a risk so great. We men are determined—nay, are we not pledged?—to destroy this monster; but it is no part for a woman. Even if she be not harmed, her heart may fail her in so much and so many horrors; and hereafter she may suffer—both in waking, from her nerves, and in sleep, from her dreams. And, besides, she is young woman and not so long married; there may be other things to think of some time, if not now.

You tell me she has wrote all, then she must consult with us; but to-morrow she say good-bye to this work, and we go alone." I agreed heartily with him, and then I told him what we had found in his absence: that the house which Dracula had bought was the very next one to my own. He was amazed, and a great concern seemed to come on him. "Oh that we had known it before!" he said, "for then we might have reached him in time to save poor Lucy. However, 'the milk that is spilt cries not out afterwards,' as you say. We shall not think of that, but go on our way to the end." Then he fell into a silence that lasted till we entered my own gateway. Before we went to prepare for dinner he said to Mrs. Harker:—

"I am told, Madam Mina, by my friend John that you and your husband have put up in exact order all things that have been, up to this moment."

"Not up to this moment, Professor," she said impulsively, "but up to this morning."

"But why not up to now? We have seen hitherto how good light all the little things have made. We have told our secrets, and yet no one who has told is the worse for it."

Mrs. Harker began to blush, and taking a paper from her pockets, she said:—

"Dr. Van Helsing, will you read this, and tell me if it must go in. It is my record of to-day. I too have seen the need of putting down at present everything, however trivial; but there is little in this except what is personal. Must it go in?" The Professor read it over gravely, and handed it back, saying:—

"It need not go in if you do not wish it; but I pray that it may. It can but make your husband love you the more, and all us, your friends, more honour you—as well as more esteem and love." She took it back with another blush and a bright smile.

And so now, up to this very hour, all the records we have are complete and in order. The Professor took away one copy to study after dinner, and before our meeting, which is fixed for nine o'clock. The rest of us have already read everything; so when we meet in the study we shall all be informed as to facts, and can arrange our plan of battle with this terrible and mysterious enemy.

MINA HARKER'S JOURNAL.

30 September.—When we met in Dr. Seward's study two hours after dinner, which had been at six o'clock, we unconsciously formed a sort of board or committee. Professor Van Helsing took the head of the table, to which Dr. Seward motioned him as he came into the room. He made me sit next to him on his right, and asked me to act as secretary; Jonathan sat next to me. Opposite us were Lord Godalming, Dr. Seward, and Mr. Morris—Lord Godalming being next the Professor, and Dr. Seward in the centre. The Professor said:—

"I may, I suppose, take it that we are all acquainted with the facts that are in these papers." We all expressed assent, and he went on:—

"Then it were, I think good that I tell you something of the kind of enemy with which we have to deal. I shall then make known to you something of the history of this man, which has been ascertained for me. So we then can discuss how we shall act, and can take our measure according.

"There are such beings as vampires; some of us have evidence that they exist. Even had we not the proof of our own unhappy experience, the teachings and the records of the past give proof enough for sane peoples. I admit that at the first I was sceptic. Were it not that through long years I have train myself to keep an open mind, I could not have believe until such time as that fact thunder on my ear. 'See! see! I prove; I prove.' Alas! Had I known at the first what now I know—nay, had I even guess at him—one so precious life had been spared to many of us who did love her. But that is gone; and we must so work, that other poor souls perish not, whilst we can save. The *nosferatu* do not die like the bee when he sting once. He is only stronger; and being stronger, have yet more power to work evil. This vampire which is amongst us is of himself so strong in person as twenty men; he is of cunning more than mortal, for his cunning be the growth of ages; he have still the aids of necromancy, which is, as his etymology imply, the divination by the dead, and all the dead that he can come nigh to are for him at command; he is brute, and more than brute; he is devil in callous, and the heart of him is not; he can, within limitations, appear at will when, and where, and in any of the forms that are to him; he can, within his range, direct the elements; the storm, the fog, the thunder; he can command all the meaner things: the rat, and the owl, and the bat—the moth, and the fox, and the wolf; he can grow and become small; and he can at times vanish and come unknown. How then are we to begin our strike to destroy him? How shall we find his where; and having found it, how can we destroy? My friends, this is much; it is a terrible task that we undertake, and there may be consequence to make the brave shudder. For if we fail in this our fight he must surely win; and then where end we? Life is nothings; I heed him not. But to fail here, is not mere life or death. It is that we become as him; that we henceforward become foul things of the night like him—without heart or conscience, preying on the bodies and the souls of those we love best. To us for ever are the gates of heaven shut; for who shall open them to us again? We go on for all time abhorred by all; a blot on the face of God's sunshine; an arrow in the side of Him who died for man. But we are face to face with duty; and in such case must we shrink? For me, I say, no; but then I am old, and life, with his sunshine, his fair places, his song of birds, his music and his love, lie far behind. You others are young. Some have seen sorrow; but there are fair days yet in store. What say you?"

Whilst he was speaking, Jonathan had taken my hand. I feared, oh so much, that the appalling nature of our danger was overcoming him when I saw his hand stretch out; but it was life to me to feel its touch—so strong, so self-reliant, so resolute. A brave man's hand can speak for itself; it does not even need a woman's love to hear its music.

When the Professor had done speaking my husband looked in my eyes, and I in his; there was no need for speaking between us.

"I answer for Mina and myself," he said.

"Count me in, Professor," said Mr. Quincey Morris, laconically as usual.

"I am with you," said Lord Godalming, "for Lucy's sake, if for no other reason."

Dr. Seward simply nodded. The Professor stood up and, after laying his golden crucifix on the table, held out his hand on either side. I took his right hand, and Lord Godalming his left; Jonathan held my right with his left and stretched across to Mr. Morris. So as we all took hands our solemn compact was made. I felt my heart icy cold, but it did not even occur to me to draw back. We resumed our places, and Dr. Van Helsing went on with a sort of cheerfulness which showed that the serious work had begun. It was to be taken as gravely, and in as businesslike a way, as any other transaction of life:—

"Well, you know what we have to contend against; but we, too, are not without strength. We have on our side power of combination—a power denied to the vampire kind; we have sources of science; we are free to act and think; and the hours of the day and the night are ours equally. In fact, so far as our powers extend, they are unfettered, and we are free to use them. We have self-devotion in a cause, and an end to achieve which is not a selfish one. These things are much.

"Now let us see how far the general powers arrayed against us are restrict, and how the individual cannot. In fine, let us consider the limitations of the vampire in general, and of this one in particular.

"All we have to go upon are traditions and superstitions. These do not at the first appear much, when the matter is one of life and death—nay of more than either life or death. Yet must we be satisfied; in the first place because we have to be—no other means is at our control—and secondly, because, after all, these things—tradition and superstition—are everything. Does not the belief in vampires rest for others—though not, alas! for us—on them? A year ago which of us would have received such a possibility, in the midst of our scientific, sceptical, matter-of-fact nineteenth century? We even scouted a belief that we saw justified under our very eyes. Take it, then, that the vampire, and the belief in his limitations and his cure, rest for the moment on the same base. For, let me tell you, he is known everywhere that men have been. In old Greece, in old Rome; he flourish in Germany all over, in France, in India, even in the Chernosese; and in China, so far from us in all ways, there even is he, and the peoples fear him at this day. He have follow the wake of the berserker Icelander, the devil-begotten Hun, the Slav, the Saxon, the Magyar. So far, then, we have all we may act upon; and let me tell you that very much of the beliefs are justified by what we have seen in our own so unhappy experience. The vampire live on, and cannot die by mere passing of the time; he can flourish when that he can fatten on the blood of the living. Even more, we have seen amongst us that he can even grow younger; that his vital faculties grow strenuous, and seem as though they refresh themselves when his special pabulum is plenty. But he cannot flourish without this diet; he eat not as others. Even friend Jonathan, who lived with him for weeks, did never see him to eat, never! He throws no shadow; he make in the mirror no reflect, as again Jonathan observe. He has the strength of many of his hand—witness again Jonathan when he shut the door against the wolfs, and when he help him from the diligence too. He can transform himself to wolf, as we gather from the ship arrival in Whitby, when he tear open the dog; he can be as bat, as Madam Mina saw him on the window at Whitby, and as friend John saw him fly from this so near house, and as my friend Quincey saw him at the window of Miss Lucy. He can come in mist which he create—that noble ship's captain proved him of this; but, from what we know, the distance he can make this mist is limited, and it can only be round himself. He come on moonlight rays as elemental dust—as again Jonathan saw those sisters in the castle of Dracula. He become so small—we ourselves saw Miss Lucy, ere she was at peace, slip through a hairbreadth space at the tomb door. He can, when once he find his way, come out from anything or into anything, no matter how close it be bound or even fused up with fire—solder you call it. He can see in the dark—no small power this, in a world which is one half shut from the light. Ah, but hear me through. He can do all these things, yet he is not free. Nay; he is even more prisoner than the slave of the galley, than the madman in his cell. He cannot go where he lists; he who is not of nature has yet to obey some of nature's laws—why we know not. He may not enter anywhere at the first, unless there be some one of the household who bid him to come; though afterwards he can come as he please. His power ceases, as does that of all evil things, at the coming of the day. Only at certain times can he have limited freedom. If he be not at the place whither he is bound, he can only change himself at noon or at exact sunrise or sunset. These things are we told, and in this record of ours we have proof by inference. Thus, whereas he can do as he will within his limit, when he have his earth-home, his coffin-home, his hell-home, the place unhallowed, as we saw when he went to the grave of the suicide at Whitby; still at other time he can only change when the time come. It is said, too, that he can only pass running water at the slack or the flood of the tide. Then there are things which so afflict him that he has no power, as the garlic that we know of; and as for things sacred, as this symbol, my crucifix, that was amongst us even now when we resolve, to them he is nothing, but in their presence he take his place far off and silent with respect. There are others, too, which I shall tell you of, lest in our seeking we may need them. The branch of wild rose on his coffin keep him that he move not from it; a sacred bullet fired into the coffin kill him so that he be true dead; and as for the stake through him, we know already of its peace; or the cut-off head that giveth rest. We have seen it with our eyes.

"Thus when we find the habitation of this man-that-was, we can confine him to his coffin and destroy him, if we obey what we know. But he is clever. I have asked my friend Arminius, of Buda-Pesth University, to make his record; and, from all the means that are, he tell me of what he has been. He must, indeed, have been that Voivode Dracula who won his name against the Turk, over the great river on the very frontier of Turkey-land. If it be so, then was he no common man; for in that time, and for centuries after, he was spoken of as the cleverest and the most cunning, as well as the bravest of the sons of the 'land beyond the forest.' That mighty brain and that iron resolution went with him to his grave, and are even now arrayed against us. The Draculas were, says Arminius, a great and noble race, though now and again were scions who were held by their coevals to have had dealings with the Evil One. They learned his secrets in the Scholomance, amongst the mountains over Lake Hermanstadt, where the devil claims the tenth scholar as his due. In the records are such words as 'stregoica'—witch, 'ordog,' and 'pokol'—Satan and hell; and in one manuscript this very Dracula is spoken of as 'wampyr,' which we all understand too well. There have been from the loins of this very one great men and good women, and their graves make sacred the earth where alone this foulness can dwell. For it is not the least of its terrors that this evil thing is rooted deep in all good; in soil barren of holy memories it cannot rest."

Whilst they were talking Mr. Morris was looking steadily at the window, and he now got up quietly, and went out of the room. There was a little pause, and then the Professor went on:—

"And now we must settle what we do. We have here much data, and we must proceed to lay out our campaign. We know from the inquiry of Jonathan that from the castle to Whitby came fifty boxes of earth, all of which were delivered at Carfax; we also know that at least some of these boxes have been removed. It seems to me, that our first step should be to ascertain whether all the rest remain in the house beyond that wall where we look to-day; or whether any more have been removed. If the latter, we must trace——"

Here we were interrupted in a very startling way. Outside the house came the sound of a pistol-shot; the glass of the window was shattered with a bullet, which, ricochetting from the top of the embrasure, struck the far wall of the room. I am afraid I am at heart a coward, for I shrieked out. The men all jumped to their feet; Lord Godalming flew over to the window and threw up the sash. As he did so we heard Mr. Morris's voice without:—

"Sorry! I fear I have alarmed you. I shall come in and tell you about it." A minute later he came in and said:—

"It was an idiotic thing of me to do, and I ask your pardon, Mrs. Harker, most sincerely; I fear I must have frightened you terribly. But the fact is that whilst the Professor was talking there came a big bat and sat on the window-sill. I have got such a horror of the damned brutes from recent events that I cannot stand them, and I went out to have a shot, as I have been doing of late of evenings, whenever I have seen one. You used to laugh at me for it then, Art."

"Did you hit it?" asked Dr. Van Helsing.

"I don't know; I fancy not, for it flew away into the wood." Without saying any more he took his seat, and the Professor began to resume his statement:—

"We must trace each of these boxes; and when we are ready, we must either capture or kill this monster in his lair; or we must, so to speak, sterilise the earth, so that no more he can seek safety in it. Thus in the end we may find him in his form of man between the hours of noon and sunset, and so engage with him when he is at his most weak.

"And now for you, Madam Mina, this night is the end until all be well. You are too precious to us to have such risk. When we part to-night, you no more must question. We shall tell you all in good time. We are men and are able to bear; but you must be our star and our hope, and we shall act all the more free that you are not in the danger, such as we are."

All the men, even Jonathan, seemed relieved; but it did not seem to me good that they should brave danger and, perhaps, lessen their safety—strength being the best safety—through care of me; but their minds were made up, and, though it was a bitter pill for me to swallow, I could say nothing, save to accept their chivalrous care of me.

Mr. Morris resumed the discussion:—

"As there is no time to lose, I vote we have a look at his house right now. Time is everything with him; and swift action on our part may save another victim."

I own that my heart began to fail me when the time for action came so close, but I did not say anything, for I had a greater fear that if I appeared as a drag or a hindrance to their work, they might even leave me out of their counsels altogether. They have now gone off to Carfax, with means to get into the house.

Manlike, they had told me to go to bed and sleep; as if a woman can sleep when those she loves are in danger! I shall lie down and pretend to sleep, lest Jonathan have added anxiety about me when he returns.

DR. SEWARD'S DIARY.

1 October, 4 a. m.—Just as we were about to leave the house, an urgent message was brought to me from Renfield to know if I would see him at once, as he had something of the utmost importance to say to me. I told the messenger to say that I would attend to his wishes in the morning; I was busy just at the moment. The attendant added:—

"He seems very importunate, sir. I have never seen him so eager. I don't know but what, if you don't see him soon, he will have one of his violent fits." I knew the man would not have said this without some cause, so I said: "All right; I'll go now"; and I asked the others to wait a few minutes for me, as I had to go and see my "patient."

"Take me with you, friend John," said the Professor. "His case in your diary interest me much, and it had bearing, too, now and again on *our* case. I should much like to see him, and especial when his mind is disturbed."

"May I come also?" asked Lord Godalming.

"Me too?" said Quincey Morris. "May I come?" said Harker. I nodded, and we all went down the passage together.

We found him in a state of considerable excitement, but far more rational in his speech and manner than I had ever seen him. There was an unusual understanding of himself, which was unlike anything I had ever met with in a lunatic; and he took it for granted that his reasons would prevail with others entirely sane. We all four went into the room, but none of the others at first said anything. His request was that I would at once release him from the asylum and send him home. This he backed up with arguments regarding his complete recovery, and adduced his own existing sanity. "I appeal to your friends," he said, "they will, perhaps, not mind sitting in judgment on my case. By the way, you have not introduced me." I was so much astonished, that the oddness of introducing a madman in an asylum did not strike me at the moment; and, besides, there was a certain dignity in the man's manner, so much of the habit of equality, that I at once made the introduction: "Lord Godalming; Professor Van Helsing; Mr. Quincey Morris, of Texas; Mr. Renfield." He shook hands with each of them, saying in turn:—

"Lord Godalming, I had the honour of seconding your father at the Windham; I grieve to know, by your holding the title, that he is no more. He was a man loved and honoured by all who knew him; and in his youth was, I have heard, the inventor of a burnt rum punch, much patronised on Derby night. Mr. Morris, you should be proud of your great state. Its reception into the Union was a precedent which may have far-reaching effects hereafter, when the Pole and the Tropics may hold alliance to the Stars and Stripes. The power of Treaty may yet prove a vast engine of enlargement, when the Monroe doctrine takes its true place as a political fable. What shall any man say of his pleasure at meeting Van Helsing? Sir, I make no apology for dropping all forms of conventional prefix. When an individual has revolutionised therapeutics by his discovery of the continuous evolution of brain-matter, conventional forms are unfitting, since they would seem to limit him to one of a class. You, gentlemen, who by nationality, by heredity, or by the possession of natural gifts, are fitted to hold your respective places in the moving world, I take to witness that I am as sane as at least the majority of men who are in full possession of their liberties. And I am sure that you, Dr. Seward, humanitarian and medico-jurist as well as scientist, will deem it a moral duty to deal with me as one to be considered as under exceptional circumstances." He made this last appeal with a courtly air of conviction which was not without its own charm.

I think we were all staggered. For my own part, I was under the conviction, despite my knowledge of the man's character and history, that his reason had been restored; and I felt under a strong impulse to tell him that I was satisfied as to his sanity, and would see about the necessary formalities for his release in the morning. I thought it better to wait, however, before making so grave a statement, for of old I knew the sudden changes to which this particular patient was liable. So I contented myself with making a general statement that he appeared to be improving very rapidly; that I would have a longer chat with him in the morning, and would then see what I could do in the direction of meeting his wishes. This did not at all satisfy him, for he said quickly:—

"But I fear, Dr. Seward, that you hardly apprehend my wish. I desire to go at once—here—now—this very hour—this very moment, if I may. Time presses, and in our implied agreement with the old scytheman it is of the essence of the contract. I am sure it is only necessary to put before so admirable a practitioner as Dr. Seward so simple, yet so momentous a wish, to ensure its fulfilment." He looked at me keenly, and seeing the negative in my face, turned to the others, and scrutinised them closely. Not meeting any sufficient response, he went on:—

"Is it possible that I have erred in my supposition?"

"You have," I said frankly, but at the same time, as I felt, brutally. There was a considerable pause, and then he said slowly:—

"Then I suppose I must only shift my ground of request. Let me ask for this concession—boon, privilege, what you will. I am content to implore in such a case, not on personal grounds, but for the sake of others. I am not at liberty to give you the whole of my reasons; but you may, I assure you, take it from me that they are good ones, sound and unselfish, and spring from the highest sense of duty. Could you look, sir, into my heart, you would approve to the full the sentiments which animate me. Nay, more, you would count me amongst the best and truest of your friends." Again he looked at us all keenly. I had a growing conviction that this sudden change of his entire intellectual method was but yet another form or phase of his madness, and so determined to let him go on a little longer, knowing from experience that he would, like all lunatics, give himself away in the end. Van Helsing was gazing at him with a look of utmost intensity, his bushy eyebrows almost meeting with the fixed concentration of his look. He said to Renfield in a tone which did not surprise me at the time, but only when I thought of it afterwards—for it was as of one addressing an equal:—

"Can you not tell frankly your real reason for wishing to be free to-night? I will undertake that if you will satisfy even me—a stranger, without prejudice, and with the habit of keeping an open mind—Dr. Seward will give you, at his own risk and on his own responsibility, the privilege you seek." He shook his head sadly, and with a look of poignant regret on his face. The Professor went on:—

"Come, sir, bethink yourself. You claim the privilege of reason in the highest degree, since you seek to impress us with your complete reasonableness. You do this, whose sanity we have reason to doubt, since you are not yet released from medical treatment for this very defect. If you will not help us in our effort to choose the wisest course, how can we perform the duty which you yourself put upon us? Be wise, and help us; and if we can we shall aid you to achieve your wish." He still shook his head as he said:—

"Dr. Van Helsing, I have nothing to say. Your argument is complete, and if I were free to speak I should not hesitate a moment; but I am not my own master in the matter. I can only ask you to trust me. If I am refused, the responsibility does not rest with me." I thought it was now time to end the scene, which was becoming too comically grave, so I went towards the door, simply saying:—

"Come, my friends, we have work to do. Good-night."

As, however, I got near the door, a new change came over the patient. He moved towards me so quickly that for the moment I feared that he was about to make another homicidal attack. My fears, however, were groundless, for he held up his two hands imploringly, and made his petition in a moving manner. As he saw that the very excess of his emotion was militating against him, by restoring us more to our old relations, he became still more demonstrative. I glanced at Van Helsing, and saw my conviction reflected in his eyes; so I became a little more fixed in my manner, if not more stern, and motioned to him that his efforts were unavailing. I had previously seen something of the same constantly growing excitement in him when he had to make some request of which at the time he had thought much, such, for instance, as when he wanted a cat; and I was prepared to see the collapse into the same sullen acquiescence on this occasion. My expectation was not realised, for, when he found that his appeal would not be successful, he got into quite a frantic condition. He threw himself on his knees, and held up his hands, wringing them in plaintive supplication, and poured forth a torrent of entreaty, with the tears rolling down his cheeks, and his whole face and form expressive of the deepest emotion:—

"Let me entreat you, Dr. Seward, oh, let me implore you, to let me out of this house at once. Send me away how you will and where you will; send keepers with me with whips and chains; let them take me in a strait-waistcoat, manacled and leg-ironed, even to a gaol; but let me go out of this. You don't know what you do by keeping me here. I am speaking from the depths of my heart—of my very soul. You don't know whom you wrong, or how; and I may not tell. Woe is me! I may not tell. By all you hold sacred—by all you hold dear—by your love that is lost—by your hope that lives—for the sake of the Almighty, take me out of this and save my soul from guilt! Can't you hear me, man? Can't you understand? Will you never learn? Don't you know that I am sane and earnest now; that I am no lunatic in a mad fit, but a sane man fighting for his soul? Oh, hear me! hear me! Let me go! let me go! let me go!"

I thought that the longer this went on the wilder he would get, and so would bring on a fit; so I took him by the hand and raised him up.

"Come," I said sternly, "no more of this; we have had quite enough already. Get to your bed and try to behave more discreetly."

He suddenly stopped and looked at me intently for several moments. Then, without a word, he rose and moving over, sat down on the side of the bed. The collapse had come, as on former occasion, just as I had expected.

When I was leaving the room, last of our party, he said to me in a quiet, well-bred voice:—

"You will, I trust, Dr. Seward, do me the justice to bear in mind, later on, that I did what I could to convince you to-night."

CHAPTER XIX

JONATHAN HARKER'S JOURNAL

1 October, 5 a. m.—I went with the party to the search with an easy mind, for I think I never saw Mina so absolutely strong and well. I am so glad that she consented to hold back and let us men do the work. Somehow, it was a dread to me that she was in this fearful business at all; but now that her work is done, and that it is due to her energy and brains and foresight that the whole story is put together in such a way that every point tells, she may well feel that her part is finished, and that she can henceforth leave the rest to us. We were, I think, all a little upset by the scene with Mr. Renfield. When we came away from his room we were silent till we got back to the study. Then Mr. Morris said to Dr. Seward:—

"Say, Jack, if that man wasn't attempting a bluff, he is about the sanest lunatic I ever saw. I'm not sure, but I believe that he had some serious purpose, and if he had, it was pretty rough on him not to get a chance." Lord Godalming and I were silent, but Dr. Van Helsing added:—

"Friend John, you know more of lunatics than I do, and I'm glad of it, for I fear that if it had been to me to decide I would before that last hysterical outburst have given him free. But we live and learn, and in our present task we must take no chance, as my friend Quincey would say. All is best as they are." Dr. Seward seemed to answer them both in a dreamy kind of way:—

"I don't know but that I agree with you. If that man had been an ordinary lunatic I would have taken my chance of trusting him; but he seems so mixed up with the Count in an indexy kind of way that I am afraid of doing anything wrong by helping his fads. I can't forget how he prayed with almost equal fervour for a cat, and then tried to tear my throat out with his teeth. Besides, he called the Count 'lord and master,' and he may want to get out to help him in some diabolical way. That horrid thing has the wolves and the rats and his own kind to help him, so I suppose he isn't above trying to use a respectable lunatic. He certainly did seem earnest, though. I only hope we have done what is best. These things, in conjunction with the wild work we have in hand, help to unnerve a man." The Professor stepped over, and laying his hand on his shoulder, said in his grave, kindly way:—

"Friend John, have no fear. We are trying to do our duty in a very sad and terrible case; we can only do as we deem best. What else have we to hope for, except the pity of the good God?" Lord Godalming had slipped away for a few minutes, but now he returned. He held up a little silver whistle, as he remarked:—

"That old place may be full of rats, and if so, I've got an antidote on call." Having passed the wall, we took our way to the house, taking care to keep in the shadows of the trees on the lawn when the moonlight shone out. When we got to the porch the Professor opened his bag and took out a lot of things, which he laid on the step, sorting them into four little groups, evidently one for each. Then he spoke:—

"My friends, we are going into a terrible danger, and we need arms of many kinds. Our enemy is not merely spiritual. Remember that he has the strength of twenty men, and that, though our necks or our windpipes are of the common kind—and therefore breakable or crushable—his are not amenable to mere strength. A stronger man, or a body of men more strong in all than him, can at certain times hold him; but they cannot hurt him as we can be hurt by him. We must, therefore, guard ourselves from his touch. Keep this near your heart"—as he spoke he lifted a little silver crucifix and held it out to me, I being nearest to him—"put these flowers round your neck"—here he handed to me a wreath of withered garlic blossoms—"for other enemies more mundane, this revolver and this knife; and for aid in all, these so small electric lamps, which you can fasten to your breast; and for all, and above all at the last, this, which we must not desecrate needless." This was a portion of Sacred Wafer, which he put in an envelope and handed to me. Each of the others was similarly equipped. "Now," he said, "friend John, where are the skeleton keys? If so that we can open the door, we need not break house by the window, as before at Miss Lucy's."

Dr. Seward tried one or two skeleton keys, his mechanical dexterity as a surgeon standing him in good stead. Presently he got one to suit; after a little play back and forward the bolt yielded, and, with a rusty clang, shot back. We pressed on the door, the rusty hinges creaked, and it slowly opened. It was startlingly like the image conveyed to me in Dr. Seward's diary of the opening of Miss Westenra's tomb; I fancy that the same idea seemed to strike the others, for with one accord they shrank back. The Professor was the first to move forward, and stepped into the open door.

"*In manus tuas, Domine!*" he said, crossing himself as he passed over the threshold. We closed the door behind us, lest when we should have lit our lamps we should possibly attract attention from the road. The Professor carefully tried the lock, lest we might not be able to open it from within should we be in a hurry making our exit. Then we all lit our lamps and proceeded on our search.

The light from the tiny lamps fell in all sorts of odd forms, as the rays crossed each other, or the opacity of our bodies threw great shadows. I could not for my life get away from the feeling that there was some one else amongst us. I suppose it was the recollection, so powerfully brought home to me by the grim surroundings, of that terrible experience in Transylvania. I think the feeling was common to us all, for I noticed that the others kept looking over their shoulders at every sound and every new shadow, just as I felt myself doing.

The whole place was thick with dust. The floor was seemingly inches deep, except where there were recent footsteps, in which on holding down my lamp I could see marks of hobnails where the dust was cracked. The walls were fluffy and heavy with dust, and in the corners were masses of spider's webs, whereon the dust had gathered till they looked like old tattered rags as the weight had torn them partly down. On a table in the hall was a great bunch of keys, with a time-yellowed label on each. They had been used several times, for on the table were several similar rents in the blanket of dust, similar to that exposed when the Professor lifted them. He turned to me and said:—

"You know this place, Jonathan. You have copied maps of it, and you know it at least more than we do. Which is the way to the chapel?" I had an idea of its direction, though on my former visit I had not been able to get admission to it; so I led the way, and after a few wrong turnings found myself opposite a low, arched oaken door, ribbed with iron bands. "This is the spot," said the Professor as he turned his lamp on a small map of the house, copied from the file of my original correspondence regarding the purchase. With a little trouble we found the key on the bunch and opened the door. We were prepared for some unpleasantness, for as we were opening the door a faint, malodorous air seemed to exhale through the gaps, but none of us ever expected such an odour as we encountered. None of the others had met the Count at all at close quarters, and when I had seen him he was either in the fasting stage of his existence in his rooms or, when he was gloated with fresh blood, in a ruined building open to the air; but here the place was small and close, and the long disuse had made the air stagnant and foul. There was an earthy smell, as of some dry miasma, which came through the fouler air. But as to the odour itself, how shall I describe it? It was not alone that it was composed of all the ills of mortality and with the pungent, acrid smell of blood, but it seemed as though corruption had become itself corrupt. Faugh! it sickens me to think of it. Every breath exhaled by that monster seemed to have clung to the place and intensified its loathsomeness.

Under ordinary circumstances such a stench would have brought our enterprise to an end; but this was no ordinary case, and the high and terrible purpose in which we were involved gave us a strength which rose above merely physical considerations. After the involuntary shrinking consequent on the first nauseous whiff, we one and all set about our work as though that loathsome place were a garden of roses.

We made an accurate examination of the place, the Professor saying as we began:—

"The first thing is to see how many of the boxes are left; we must then examine every hole and corner and cranny and see if we cannot get some clue as to what has become of the rest." A glance was sufficient to show how many remained, for the great earth chests were bulky, and there was no mistaking them.

There were only twenty-nine left out of the fifty! Once I got a fright, for, seeing Lord Godalming suddenly turn and look out of the vaulted door into the dark passage beyond, I looked too, and for an instant my heart stood still. Somewhere, looking out from the shadow, I seemed to see the high lights of the Count's evil face, the ridge of the nose, the red eyes, the red lips, the awful pallor. It was only for a moment, for, as Lord Godalming said, "I thought I saw a face, but it was only the shadows," and resumed his inquiry, I turned my lamp in the direction, and stepped into the passage. There was no sign of any one; and as there were no corners, no doors, no aperture of any kind, but only the solid walls of the passage, there could be no hiding-place even for *him*. I took it that fear had helped imagination, and said nothing.

A few minutes later I saw Morris step suddenly back from a corner, which he was examining. We all followed his movements with our eyes, for undoubtedly some nervousness was growing on us, and we saw a whole mass of phosphorescence, which twinkled like stars. We all instinctively drew back. The whole place was becoming alive with rats.

For a moment or two we stood appalled, all save Lord Godalming, who was seemingly prepared for such an emergency. Rushing over to the great iron-bound oaken door, which Dr. Seward had described from the outside, and which I had seen myself, he turned the key in the lock, drew the huge bolts, and swung the door open. Then, taking his little silver whistle from his pocket, he blew a low, shrill call. It was answered from behind Dr. Seward's house by the yelping of dogs, and after about a minute three terriers came dashing round the corner of the house. Unconsciously we had all moved towards the door, and as we moved I noticed that the dust had been much disturbed: the boxes which had been taken out had been brought this way.

But even in the minute that had elapsed the number of the rats had vastly increased. They seemed to swarm over the place all at once, till the lamplight, shining on their moving dark bodies and glittering, baleful eyes, made the place look like a bank of earth set with fireflies. The dogs dashed on, but at the threshold suddenly stopped and snarled, and then, simultaneously lifting their noses, began to howl in most lugubrious fashion. The rats were multiplying in thousands, and we moved out.

Lord Godalming lifted one of the dogs, and carrying him in, placed him on the floor. The instant his feet touched the ground he seemed to recover his courage, and rushed at his natural enemies. They fled before him so fast that before he had shaken the life out of a score, the other dogs, who had by now been lifted in the same manner, had but small prey ere the whole mass had vanished.

With their going it seemed as if some evil presence had departed, for the dogs frisked about and barked merrily as they made sudden darts at their prostrate foes, and turned them over and over and tossed them in the air with vicious shakes. We all seemed to find our spirits rise. Whether it was the purifying of the deadly atmosphere by the opening of the chapel door, or the relief which we experienced by finding ourselves in the open I know not; but most certainly the shadow of dread seemed to slip from us like a robe, and the occasion of our coming lost something of its grim significance, though we did not slacken a whit in our resolution. We closed the outer door and barred and locked it, and bringing the dogs with us, began our search of the house. We found nothing throughout except dust in extraordinary proportions, and all untouched save for my own footsteps when I had made my first visit. Never once did the dogs exhibit any symptom of uneasiness, and even when we returned to the chapel they frisked about as though they had been rabbit-hunting in a summer wood.

The morning was quickening in the east when we emerged from the front. Dr. Van Helsing had taken the key of the hall-door from the bunch, and locked the door in orthodox fashion, putting the key into his pocket when he had done.

"So far," he said, "our night has been eminently successful. No harm has come to us such as I feared might be and yet we have ascertained how many boxes are missing. More than all do I rejoice that this, our first—and perhaps our most difficult and dangerous—step has been accomplished without the bringing thereinto our most sweet Madam Mina or troubling her waking or sleeping thoughts with sights and sounds and smells of horror which she might never forget. One lesson, too, we have learned, if it be allowable to argue *a particulari*: that the brute beasts which are to the Count's command are yet themselves not amenable to his spiritual power; for look, these rats that would come to his call, just as from his castle top he summon the wolves to your going and to that poor mother's cry, though they come to him, they run pell-mell from the so little dogs of my friend Arthur. We have other matters before us, other dangers, other fears; and that monster—he has not used his power over the brute world for the only or the last time to-night. So be it that he has gone elsewhere. Good! It has given us opportunity to cry 'check' in some ways in this chess game, which we play for the stake of human souls. And now let us go home. The dawn is close at hand, and we have reason to be content with our first night's work. It may be ordained that we have many nights and days to follow, if full of peril; but we must go on, and from no danger shall we shrink."

The house was silent when we got back, save for some poor creature who was screaming away in one of the distant wards, and a low, moaning sound from Renfield's room. The poor wretch was doubtless torturing himself, after the manner of the insane, with needless thoughts of pain.

I came tiptoe into our own room, and found Mina asleep, breathing so softly that I had to put my ear down to hear it. She looks paler than usual. I hope the meeting to-night has not upset her. I am truly thankful that she is to be left out of our future work, and even of our deliberations. It is too great a strain for a woman to bear. I did not think so at first, but I know better now. Therefore I am glad that it is settled. There may be things which would frighten her to hear; and yet to conceal them from her might be worse than to tell her if once she suspected that there was any concealment. Henceforth our work is to be a sealed book to her, till at least such time as we can tell her that all is finished, and the earth free from a monster of the nether world. I daresay it will be difficult to begin to keep silence after such confidence as ours; but I must be resolute, and to-morrow I shall keep dark over to-night's doings, and shall refuse to speak of anything that has happened. I rest on the sofa, so as not to disturb her.

1 October, later.—I suppose it was natural that we should have all overslept ourselves, for the day was a busy one, and the night had no rest at all. Even Mina must have felt its exhaustion, for though I slept till the sun was high, I was awake before her, and had to call two or three times before she awoke. Indeed, she was so sound asleep that for a few seconds she did not recognize me, but looked at me with a sort of blank terror, as one looks who has been waked out of a bad dream. She complained a little of being tired, and I let her rest till later in the day. We now know of twenty-one boxes having been removed, and if it be that several were taken in any of these removals we may be able to trace them all. Such will, of course, immensely simplify our labour, and the sooner the matter is attended to the better. I shall look up Thomas Snelling to-day.

DR. SEWARD'S DIARY.

1 October.—It was towards noon when I was awakened by the Professor walking into my room. He was more jolly and cheerful than usual, and it is quite evident that last night's work has helped to take some of the brooding weight off his mind. After going over the adventure of the night he suddenly said:—

"Your patient interests me much. May it be that with you I visit him this morning? Or if that you are too occupy, I can go alone if it may be. It is a new experience to me to find a lunatic who talk philosophy, and reason so sound." I had some work to do which pressed, so I told him that if he would go alone I would be glad, as then I should not have to keep him waiting; so I called an attendant and gave him the necessary instructions. Before the Professor left the room I cautioned him against getting any false impression from my patient. "But," he answered, "I want him to talk of himself and of his delusion as to consuming live things. He said to Madam Mina, as I see in your diary of yesterday, that he had once had such a belief. Why do you smile, friend John?"

"Excuse me," I said, "but the answer is here." I laid my hand on the type-written matter. "When our sane and learned lunatic made that very statement of how he *used* to consume life, his mouth was actually nauseous with the flies and spiders which he had eaten just before Mrs. Harker entered the room." Van Helsing smiled in turn. "Good!" he said. "Your memory is true, friend John. I should have remembered. And yet it is this very obliquity of thought and memory which makes mental disease such a fascinating study. Perhaps I may gain more knowledge out of the folly of this madman than I shall from the teaching of the most wise. Who knows?" I went on with my work, and before long was through that in hand. It seemed that the time had been very short indeed, but there was Van Helsing back in the study. "Do I interrupt?" he asked politely as he stood at the door.

"Not at all," I answered. "Come in. My work is finished, and I am free. I can go with you now, if you like.

"It is needless; I have seen him!"

"Well?"

"I fear that he does not appraise me at much. Our interview was short. When I entered his room he was sitting on a stool in the centre, with his elbows on his knees, and his face was the picture of sullen discontent. I spoke to him as cheerfully as I could, and with such a measure of respect as I could assume. He made no reply whatever. "Don't you know me?" I asked. His answer was not reassuring: "I know you well enough; you are the old fool Van Helsing. I wish you would take yourself and your idiotic brain theories somewhere else. Damn all thick-headed Dutchmen!" Not a word more would he say, but sat in his implacable sullenness as indifferent to me as though I had not been in the room at all. Thus departed for this time my chance of much learning from this so clever lunatic; so I shall go, if I may, and cheer myself with a few happy words with that sweet soul Madam Mina. Friend John, it does rejoice me unspeakable that she is no more to be pained, no more to be worried with our terrible things. Though we shall much miss her help, it is better so."

"I agree with you with all my heart," I answered earnestly, for I did not want him to weaken in this matter. "Mrs. Harker is better out of it. Things are quite bad enough for us, all men of the world, and who have been in many tight places in our time; but it is no place for a woman, and if she had remained in touch with the affair, it would in time infallibly have wrecked her."

So Van Helsing has gone to confer with Mrs. Harker and Harker; Quincey and Art are all out following up the clues as to the earth-boxes. I shall finish my round of work and we shall meet to-night.

MINA HARKER'S JOURNAL.

1 October.—It is strange to me to be kept in the dark as I am to-day; after Jonathan's full confidence for so many years, to see him manifestly avoid certain matters, and those the most vital of all. This morning I slept late after the fatigues of yesterday, and though Jonathan was late too, he was the earlier. He spoke to me before he went out, never more sweetly or tenderly, but he never mentioned a word of what had happened in the visit to the Count's house. And yet he must have known how terribly anxious I was. Poor dear fellow! I suppose it must have distressed him even more than it did me. They all agreed that it was best that I should not be drawn further into this awful work, and I acquiesced. But to think that he keeps anything from me! And now I am crying like a silly fool, when I *know* it comes from my husband's great love and from the good, good wishes of those other strong men.

That has done me good. Well, some day Jonathan will tell me all; and lest it should ever be that he should think for a moment that I kept anything from him, I still keep my journal as usual. Then if he has feared of my trust I shall show it to him, with every thought of my heart put down for his dear eyes to read. I feel strangely sad and low-spirited to-day. I suppose it is the reaction from the terrible excitement.

Last night I went to bed when the men had gone, simply because they told me to. I didn't feel sleepy, and I did feel full of devouring anxiety. I kept thinking over everything that has been ever since Jonathan came to see me in London, and it all seems like a horrible tragedy, with fate pressing on relentlessly to some destined end. Everything that one does seems, no matter how right it may be, to bring on the very thing which is most to be deplored. If I hadn't gone to Whitby, perhaps poor dear Lucy would be with us now. She hadn't taken to visiting the churchyard till I came, and if she hadn't come there in the day-time with me she wouldn't have walked there in her sleep; and if she hadn't gone there at night and asleep, that monster couldn't have destroyed her as he did. Oh, why did I ever go to Whitby? There now, crying again! I wonder what has come over me to-day. I must hide it from Jonathan, for if he knew that I had been crying twice in one morning—I, who never cried on my own account, and whom he has never caused to shed a tear—the dear fellow would fret his heart out. I shall put a bold face on, and if I do feel weepy, he shall never see it. I suppose it is one of the lessons that we poor women have to learn . . . .

I can't quite remember how I fell asleep last night. I remember hearing the sudden barking of the dogs and a lot of queer sounds, like praying on a very tumultuous scale, from Mr. Renfield's room, which is somewhere under this. And then there was silence over everything, silence so profound that it startled me, and I got up and looked out of the window. All was dark and silent, the black shadows thrown by the moonlight seeming full of a silent mystery of their own. Not a thing seemed to be stirring, but all to be grim and fixed as death or fate; so that a thin streak of white mist, that crept with almost imperceptible slowness across the grass towards the house, seemed to have a sentience and a vitality of its own. I think that the digression of my thoughts must have done me good, for when I got back to bed I found a lethargy creeping over me. I lay a while, but could not quite sleep, so I got out and looked out of the window again. The mist was spreading, and was now close up to the house, so that I could see it lying thick against the wall, as though it were stealing up to the windows. The poor man was more loud than ever, and though I could not distinguish a word he said, I could in some way recognise in his tones some passionate entreaty on his part. Then there was the sound of a struggle, and I knew that the attendants were dealing with him. I was so frightened that I crept into bed, and pulled the clothes over my head, putting my fingers in my ears. I was not then a bit sleepy, at least so I thought; but I must have fallen asleep, for, except dreams, I do not remember anything until the morning, when Jonathan woke me. I think that it took me an effort and a little time to realise where I was, and that it was Jonathan who was bending over me. My dream was very peculiar, and was almost typical of the way that waking thoughts become merged in, or continued in, dreams.

I thought that I was asleep, and waiting for Jonathan to come back. I was very anxious about him, and I was powerless to act; my feet, and my hands, and my brain were weighted, so that nothing could proceed at the usual pace. And so I slept uneasily and thought. Then it began to dawn upon me that the air was heavy, and dank, and cold. I put back the clothes from my face, and found, to my surprise, that all was dim around. The gaslight which I had left lit for Jonathan, but turned down, came only like a tiny red spark through the fog, which had evidently grown thicker and poured into the room. Then it occurred to me that I had shut the window before I had come to bed. I would have got out to make certain on the point, but some leaden lethargy seemed to chain my limbs and even my will. I lay still and endured; that was all. I closed my eyes, but could still see through my eyelids. (It is wonderful what tricks our dreams play us, and how conveniently we can imagine.) The mist grew thicker and thicker and I could see now how it came in, for I could see it like smoke—or with the white energy of boiling water—pouring in, not through the window, but through the joinings of the door. It got thicker and thicker, till it seemed as if it became concentrated into a sort of pillar of cloud in the room, through the top of which I could see the light of the gas shining like a red eye. Things began to whirl through my brain just as the cloudy column was now whirling in the room, and through it all came the scriptural words "a pillar of cloud by day and of fire by night." Was it indeed some such spiritual guidance that was coming to me in my sleep? But the pillar was composed of both the day and the night-guiding, for the fire was in the red eye, which at the thought got a new fascination for me; till, as I looked, the fire divided, and seemed to shine on me through the fog like two red eyes, such as Lucy told me of in her momentary mental wandering when, on the cliff, the dying sunlight struck the windows of St. Mary's Church. Suddenly the horror burst upon me that it was thus that Jonathan had seen those awful women growing into reality through the whirling mist in the moonlight, and in my dream I must have fainted, for all became black darkness. The last conscious effort which imagination made was to show me a livid white face bending over me out of the mist. I must be careful of such dreams, for they would unseat one's reason if there were too much of them. I would get Dr. Van Helsing or Dr. Seward to prescribe something for me which would make me sleep, only that I fear to alarm them. Such a dream at the present time would become woven into their fears for me. To-night I shall strive hard to sleep naturally. If I do not, I shall to-morrow night get them to give me a dose of chloral; that cannot hurt me for once, and it will give me a good night's sleep. Last night tired me more than if I had not slept at all.

2 October 10 p. m.—Last night I slept, but did not dream. I must have slept soundly, for I was not waked by Jonathan coming to bed; but the sleep has not refreshed me, for to-day I feel terribly weak and spiritless. I spent all yesterday trying to read, or lying down dozing. In the afternoon Mr. Renfield asked if he might see me. Poor man, he was very gentle, and when I came away he kissed my hand and bade God bless me. Some way it affected me much; I am crying when I think of him. This is a new weakness, of which I must be careful. Jonathan would be miserable if he knew I had been crying. He and the others were out till dinner-time, and they all came in tired. I did what I could to brighten them up, and I suppose that the effort did me good, for I forgot how tired I was. After dinner they sent me to bed, and all went off to smoke together, as they said, but I knew that they wanted to tell each other of what had occurred to each during the day; I could see from Jonathan's manner that he had something important to communicate. I was not so sleepy as I should have been; so before they went I asked Dr. Seward to give me a little opiate of some kind, as I had not slept well the night before. He very kindly made me up a sleeping draught, which he gave to me, telling me that it would do me no harm, as it was very mild . . . . I have taken it, and am waiting for sleep, which still keeps aloof. I hope I have not done wrong, for as sleep begins to flirt with me, a new fear comes: that I may have been foolish in thus depriving myself of the power of waking. I might want it. Here comes sleep. Good-night.

CHAPTER XX

JONATHAN HARKER'S JOURNAL

1 October, evening.—I found Thomas Snelling in his house at Bethnal Green, but unhappily he was not in a condition to remember anything. The very prospect of beer which my expected coming had opened to him had proved too much, and he had begun too early on his expected debauch. I learned, however, from his wife, who seemed a decent, poor soul, that he was only the assistant to Smollet, who of the two mates was the responsible person. So off I drove to Walworth, and found Mr. Joseph Smollet at home and in his shirtsleeves, taking a late tea out of a saucer. He is a decent, intelligent fellow, distinctly a good, reliable type of workman, and with a headpiece of his own. He remembered all about the incident of the boxes, and from a wonderful dog's-eared notebook, which he produced from some mysterious receptacle about the seat of his trousers, and which had hieroglyphical entries in thick, half-obliterated pencil, he gave me the destinations of the boxes. There were, he said, six in the cartload which he took from Carfax and left at 197, Chicksand Street, Mile End New Town, and another six which he deposited at Jamaica Lane, Bermondsey. If then the Count meant to scatter these ghastly refuges of his over London, these places were chosen as the first of delivery, so that later he might distribute more fully. The systematic manner in which this was done made me think that he could not mean to confine himself to two sides of London. He was now fixed on the far east of the northern shore, on the east of the southern shore, and on the south. The north and west were surely never meant to be left out of his diabolical scheme—let alone the City itself and the very heart of fashionable London in the south-west and west. I went back to Smollet, and asked him if he could tell us if any other boxes had been taken from Carfax.

He replied:—

"Well, guv'nor, you've treated me wery 'an'some"—I had given him half a sovereign—"an' I'll tell yer all I know. I heard a man by the name of Bloxam say four nights ago in the 'Are an' 'Ounds, in Pincher's Alley, as 'ow he an' his mate 'ad 'ad a rare dusty job in a old 'ouse at Purfect. There ain't a-many such jobs as this 'ere, an' I'm thinkin' that maybe Sam Bloxam could tell ye summut." I asked if he could tell me where to find him. I told him that if he could get me the address it would be worth another half-sovereign to him. So he gulped down the rest of his tea and stood up, saying that he was going to begin the search then and there. At the door he stopped, and said:—

"Look 'ere, guv'nor, there ain't no sense in me a-keepin' you 'ere. I may find Sam soon, or I mayn't; but anyhow he ain't like to be in a way to tell ye much to-night. Sam is a rare one when he starts on the booze. If you can give me a envelope with a stamp on it, and put yer address on it, I'll find out where Sam is to be found and post it ye to-night. But ye'd better be up arter 'im soon in the mornin', or maybe ye won't ketch 'im; for Sam gets off main early, never mind the booze the night afore."

This was all practical, so one of the children went off with a penny to buy an envelope and a sheet of paper, and to keep the change. When she came back, I addressed the envelope and stamped it, and when Smollet had again faithfully promised to post the address when found, I took my way to home. We're on the track anyhow. I am tired to-night, and want sleep. Mina is fast asleep, and looks a little too pale; her eyes look as though she had been crying. Poor dear, I've no doubt it frets her to be kept in the dark, and it may make her doubly anxious about me and the others. But it is best as it is. It is better to be disappointed and worried in such a way now than to have her nerve broken. The doctors were quite right to insist on her being kept out of this dreadful business. I must be firm, for on me this particular burden of silence must rest. I shall not ever enter on the subject with her under any circumstances. Indeed, it may not be a hard task, after all, for she herself has become reticent on the subject, and has not spoken of the Count or his doings ever since we told her of our decision.

2 October, evening.—A long and trying and exciting day. By the first post I got my directed envelope with a dirty scrap of paper enclosed, on which was written with a carpenter's pencil in a sprawling hand:—

"Sam Bloxam, Korkrans, 4, Poters Cort, Bartel Street, Walworth. Arsk for the depite."

I got the letter in bed, and rose without waking Mina. She looked heavy and sleepy and pale, and far from well. I determined not to wake her, but that, when I should return from this new search, I would arrange for her going back to Exeter. I think she would be happier in our own home, with her daily tasks to interest her, than in being here amongst us and in ignorance. I only saw Dr. Seward for a moment, and told him where I was off to, promising to come back and tell the rest so soon as I should have found out anything. I drove to Walworth and found, with some difficulty, Potter's

Court. Mr. Smollet's spelling misled me, as I asked for Poter's Court instead of Potter's Court. However, when I had found the court, I had no difficulty in discovering Corcoran's lodging-house. When I asked the man who came to the door for the "depite," he shook his head, and said: "I dunno 'im. There ain't no such a person 'ere; I never 'eard of 'im in all my bloomin' days. Don't believe there ain't nobody of that kind livin' ere or anywheres." I took out Smollet's letter, and as I read it it seemed to me that the lesson of the spelling of the name of the court might guide me. "What are you?" I asked.

"I'm the depity," he answered. I saw at once that I was on the right track; phonetic spelling had again misled me. A half-crown tip put the deputy's knowledge at my disposal, and I learned that Mr. Bloxam, who had slept off the remains of his beer on the previous night at Corcoran's, had left for his work at Poplar at five o'clock that morning. He could not tell me where the place of work was situated, but he had a vague idea that it was some kind of a "new-fangled ware'us"; and with this slender clue I had to start for Poplar. It was twelve o'clock before I got any satisfactory hint of such a building, and this I got at a coffee-shop, where some workmen were having their dinner. One of these suggested that there was being erected at Cross Angel Street a new "cold storage" building; and as this suited the condition of a "new-fangled ware'us," I at once drove to it. An interview with a surly gatekeeper and a surlier foreman, both of whom were appeased with the coin of the realm, put me on the track of Bloxam; he was sent for on my suggesting that I was willing to pay his day's wages to his foreman for the privilege of asking him a few questions on a private matter. He was a smart enough fellow, though rough of speech and bearing. When I had promised to pay for his information and given him an earnest, he told me that he had made two journeys between Carfax and a house in Piccadilly, and had taken from this house to the latter nine great boxes—"main heavy ones"—with a horse and cart hired by him for this purpose. I asked him if he could tell me the number of the house in Piccadilly, to which he replied:—

"Well, guv'nor, I forgits the number, but it was only a few doors from a big white church or somethink of the kind, not long built. It was a dusty old 'ouse, too, though nothin' to the dustiness of the 'ouse we tooked the bloomin' boxes from."

"How did you get into the houses if they were both empty?"

"There was the old party what engaged me a-waitin' in the 'ouse at Purfleet. He 'elped me to lift the boxes and put them in the dray. Curse me, but he was the strongest chap I ever struck, an' him a old feller, with a white moustache, one that thin you would think he couldn't throw a shadder."

How this phrase thrilled through me!

"Why, 'e took up 'is end o' the boxes like they was pounds of tea, and me a-puffin' an' a-blowin' afore I could up-end mine anyhow—an' I'm no chicken, neither."

"How did you get into the house in Piccadilly?" I asked.

"He was there too. He must 'a' started off and got there afore me, for when I rung of the bell he kem an' opened the door 'isself an' 'elped me to carry the boxes into the 'all."

"The whole nine?" I asked.

"Yus; there was five in the first load an' four in the second. It was main dry work, an' I don't so well remember 'ow I got 'ome." I interrupted him:—

"Were the boxes left in the hall?"

"Yus; it was a big 'all, an' there was nothin' else in it." I made one more attempt to further matters:—

"You didn't have any key?"

"Never used no key nor nothink. The old gent, he opened the door 'isself an' shut it again when I druv off. I don't remember the last time—but that was the beer."

"And you can't remember the number of the house?"

"No, sir. But ye needn't have no difficulty about that. It's a 'igh 'un with a stone front with a bow on it, an' 'igh steps up to the door. I know them steps, 'avin' 'ad to carry the boxes up with three loafers what come round to earn a copper. The old gent give them shillin's, an' they seein' they got so much, they wanted more; but 'e took one of them by the shoulder and was like to throw 'im down the steps, till the lot of them went away cussin'." I thought that with this description I could find the house, so, having paid my friend for his information, I started off for Piccadilly. I had gained a new painful experience; the Count could, it was evident, handle the earth-boxes himself. If so, time was precious; for, now that he had achieved a certain amount of distribution, he could, by choosing his own time, complete the task unobserved. At Piccadilly Circus I discharged my cab, and walked westward; beyond the Junior Constitutional I came across the house described, and was satisfied that this was the next of the lairs arranged by Dracula. The house looked as though it had been long untenanted. The windows were encrusted with dust, and the shutters were up. All the framework was black with time, and from the iron the paint had mostly scaled away. It was evident that up to lately there had been a large notice-board in front of the balcony; it had, however, been roughly torn away, the uprights which had supported it still remaining. Behind the rails of the balcony I saw there were some loose boards, whose raw edges looked white. I would have given a good deal to have been able to see the notice-board intact, as it would, perhaps, have given some clue to the ownership of the house. I remembered my experience of the investigation and purchase of Carfax, and I could not but feel that if I could find the former owner there might be some means discovered of gaining access to the house.

There was at present nothing to be learned from the Piccadilly side, and nothing could be done; so I went round to the back to see if anything could be gathered from this quarter. The mews were active, the Piccadilly houses being mostly in occupation. I asked one or two of the grooms and helpers whom I saw around if they could tell me anything about the empty house. One of them said that he heard it had lately been taken, but he couldn't say from whom. He told me, however, that up to very lately there had been a notice-board of "For Sale" up, and that perhaps Mitchell, Sons, & Candy, the house agents, could tell me something, as he thought he remembered seeing the name of that firm on the board. I did not wish to seem too eager, or to let my informant know or guess too much, so, thanking him in the usual manner, I strolled away. It was now growing dusk, and the autumn night was closing in, so I did not lose any time. Having learned the address of Mitchell, Sons, & Candy from a directory at the Berkeley, I was soon at their office in Sackville Street.

The gentleman who saw me was particularly suave in manner, but uncommunicative in equal proportion. Having once told me that the Piccadilly house—which throughout our interview he called a "mansion"—was sold, he considered my business as concluded. When I asked who had purchased it, he opened his eyes a thought wider, and paused a few seconds before replying:—

"It is sold, sir."

"Pardon me," I said, with equal politeness, "but I have a special reason for wishing to know who purchased it."

Again he paused longer, and raised his eyebrows still more. "It is sold, sir," was again his laconic reply.

"Surely," I said, "you do not mind letting me know so much."

"But I do mind," he answered. "The affairs of their clients are absolutely safe in the hands of Mitchell, Sons, & Candy." This was manifestly a prig of the first water, and there was no use arguing with him. I thought I had best meet him on his own ground, so I said:—

"Your clients, sir, are happy in having so resolute a guardian of their confidence. I am myself a professional man." Here I handed him my card. "In this instance I am not prompted by curiosity; I act on the part of Lord Godalming, who wishes to know something of the property which was, he understood, lately for sale." These words put a different complexion on affairs. He said:—

"I would like to oblige you if I could, Mr. Harker, and especially would I like to oblige his lordship. We once carried out a small matter of renting some chambers for him when he was the Honourable Arthur Holmwood. If you will let me have his lordship's address I will consult the House on the subject, and will, in any case, communicate with his lordship by to-night's post. It will be a pleasure if we can so far deviate from our rules as to give the required information to his lordship."

I wanted to secure a friend, and not to make an enemy, so I thanked him, gave the address at Dr. Seward's and came away. It was now dark, and I was tired and hungry. I got a cup of tea at the Aërated Bread Company and came down to Purfleet by the next train.

I found all the others at home. Mina was looking tired and pale, but she made a gallant effort to be bright and cheerful, it wrung my heart to think that I had had to keep anything from her and so caused her inquietude. Thank God, this will be the last night of her looking on at our conferences, and feeling the sting of our not showing our confidence. It took all my courage to hold to the wise resolution of keeping her out of our grim task. She seems somehow more reconciled; or else the very subject seems to have become repugnant to her, for when any accidental allusion is made she actually shudders. I am glad we made our resolution in time, as with such a feeling as this, our growing knowledge would be torture to her.

I could not tell the others of the day's discovery till we were alone; so after dinner—followed by a little music to save appearances even amongst ourselves—I took Mina to her room and left her to go to bed. The dear girl was more affectionate with me than ever, and clung to me as though she would detain me; but there was much to be talked of and I came away. Thank God, the ceasing of telling things has made no difference between us.

When I came down again I found the others all gathered round the fire in the study. In the train I had written my diary so far, and simply read it off to them as the best means of letting them get abreast of my own information; when I had finished Van Helsing said:—

"This has been a great day's work, friend Jonathan. Doubtless we are on the track of the missing boxes. If we find them all in that house, then our work is near the end. But if there be some missing, we must search until we find them. Then shall we make our final *coup*, and hunt the wretch to his real death." We all sat silent awhile and all at once Mr. Morris spoke:—

"Say! how are we going to get into that house?"

"We got into the other," answered Lord Godalming quickly.

"But, Art, this is different. We broke house at Carfax, but we had night and a walled park to protect us. It will be a mighty different thing to commit burglary in Piccadilly, either by day or night. I confess I don't see how we are going to get in unless that agency duck can find us a key of some sort; perhaps we shall know when you get his letter in the morning." Lord Godalming's brows contracted, and he stood up and walked about the room. By-and-by he stopped and said, turning from one to another of us:—

"Quincey's head is level. This burglary business is getting serious; we got off once all right; but we have now a rare job on hand—unless we can find the Count's key basket."

As nothing could well be done before morning, and as it would be at least advisable to wait till Lord Godalming should hear from Mitchell's, we decided not to take any active step before breakfast time. For a good while we sat and smoked, discussing the matter in its various lights and bearings; I took the opportunity of bringing this diary right up to the moment. I am very sleepy and shall go to bed . . . .

Just a line. Mina sleeps soundly and her breathing is regular. Her forehead is puckered up into little wrinkles, as though she thinks even in her sleep. She is still too pale, but does not look so haggard as she did this morning. To-morrow will, I hope, mend all this; she will be herself at home in Exeter. Oh, but I am sleepy!

DR. SEWARD'S DIARY.

1 October.—I am puzzled afresh about Renfield. His moods change so rapidly that I find it difficult to keep touch of them, and as they always mean something more than his own well-being, they form a more than interesting study. This morning, when I went to see him after his repulse of Van Helsing, his manner was that of a man commanding destiny. He was, in fact, commanding destiny—subjectively. He did not really care for any of the things of mere earth; he was in the clouds and looked down on all the weaknesses and wants of us poor mortals. I thought I would improve the occasion and learn something, so I asked him:—

"What about the flies these times?" He smiled on me in quite a superior sort of way—such a smile as would have become the face of Malvolio—as he answered me:—

"The fly, my dear sir, has one striking feature; its wings are typical of the aërial powers of the psychic faculties. The ancients did well when they typified the soul as a butterfly!"

I thought I would push his analogy to its utmost logically, so I said quickly:—

"Oh, it is a soul you are after now, is it?" His madness foiled his reason, and a puzzled look spread over his face as, shaking his head with a decision which I had but seldom seen in him, he said:—

"Oh, no, oh no! I want no souls. Life is all I want." Here he brightened up; "I am pretty indifferent about it at present. Life is all right; I have all I want. You must get a new patient, doctor, if you wish to study zoöphagy!"

This puzzled me a little, so I drew him on:—

"Then you command life; you are a god, I suppose?" He smiled with an ineffably benign superiority.

"Oh no! Far be it from me to arrogate to myself the attributes of the Deity. I am not even concerned in His especially spiritual doings. If I may state my intellectual position I am, so far as concerns things purely terrestrial, somewhat in the position which Enoch occupied spiritually!" This was a poser to me. I could not at the moment recall Enoch's appositeness; so I had to ask a simple question, though I felt that by so doing I was lowering myself in the eyes of the lunatic:—

"And why with Enoch?"

"Because he walked with God." I could not see the analogy, but did not like to admit it; so I harked back to what he had denied:—

"So you don't care about life and you don't want souls. Why not?" I put my question quickly and somewhat sternly, on purpose to disconcert him. The effort succeeded; for an instant he unconsciously relapsed into his old servile manner, bent low before me, and actually fawned upon me as he replied:—

"I don't want any souls, indeed, indeed! I don't. I couldn't use them if I had them; they would be no manner of use to me. I couldn't eat them or——" He suddenly stopped and the old cunning look spread over his face, like a wind-sweep on the surface of the water. "And doctor, as to life, what is it after all? When you've got all you require, and you know that you will never want, that is all. I have friends—good friends—like you, Dr. Seward"; this was said with a leer of inexpressible cunning. "I know that I shall never lack the means of life!"

I think that through the cloudiness of his insanity he saw some antagonism in me, for he at once fell back on the last refuge of such as he—a dogged silence. After a short time I saw that for the present it was useless to speak to him. He was sulky, and so I came away.

Later in the day he sent for me. Ordinarily I would not have come without special reason, but just at present I am so interested in him that I would gladly make an effort. Besides, I am glad to have anything to help to pass the time. Harker is out, following up clues; and so are Lord Godalming and Quincey. Van Helsing sits in my study poring over the record prepared by the Harkers; he seems to think that by accurate knowledge of all details he will light upon some clue. He does not wish to be disturbed in the work, without cause. I would have taken him with me to see the patient, only I thought that after his last repulse he might not care to go again. There was also another reason: Renfield might not speak so freely before a third person as when he and I were alone.

I found him sitting out in the middle of the floor on his stool, a pose which is generally indicative of some mental energy on his part. When I came in, he said at once, as though the question had been waiting on his lips:—

"What about souls?" It was evident then that my surmise had been correct. Unconscious cerebration was doing its work, even with the lunatic. I determined to have the matter out. "What about them yourself?" I asked. He did not reply for a moment but looked all round him, and up and down, as though he expected to find some inspiration for an answer.

"I don't want any souls!" he said in a feeble, apologetic way. The matter seemed preying on his mind, and so I determined to use it—to "be cruel only to be kind." So I said:—

"You like life, and you want life?"

"Oh yes! but that is all right; you needn't worry about that!"

"But," I asked, "how are we to get the life without getting the soul also?" This seemed to puzzle him, so I followed it up:—

"A nice time you'll have some time when you're flying out there, with the souls of thousands of flies and spiders and birds and cats buzzing and twittering and miauing all round you. You've got their lives, you know, and you must put up with their souls!" Something seemed to affect his imagination, for he put his fingers to his ears and shut his eyes, screwing them up tightly just as a small boy does when his face is being soaped. There was something pathetic in it that touched me; it also gave me a lesson, for it seemed that before me was a child—only a child, though the features were worn, and the stubble on the jaws was white. It was evident that he was undergoing some process of mental disturbance, and, knowing how his past moods had interpreted things seemingly foreign to himself, I thought I would enter into his mind as well as I could and go with him. The first step was to restore confidence, so I asked him, speaking pretty loud so that he would hear me through his closed ears:—

"Would you like some sugar to get your flies round again?" He seemed to wake up all at once, and shook his head. With a laugh he replied:—

"Not much! flies are poor things, after all!" After a pause he added, "But

I don't want their souls buzzing round me, all the same."

"Or spiders?" I went on.

"Blow spiders! What's the use of spiders? There isn't anything in them to eat or"—he stopped suddenly, as though reminded of a forbidden topic.

"So, so!" I thought to myself, "this is the second time he has suddenly stopped at the word 'drink'; what does it mean?" Renfield seemed himself aware of having made a lapse, for he hurried on, as though to distract my attention from it:—

"I don't take any stock at all in such matters. 'Rats and mice and such small deer,' as Shakespeare has it, 'chicken-feed of the larder' they might be called. I'm past all that sort of nonsense. You might as well ask a man to eat molecules with a pair of chop-sticks, as to try to interest me about the lesser carnivora, when I know of what is before me."

"I see," I said. "You want big things that you can make your teeth meet in? How would you like to breakfast on elephant?"

"What ridiculous nonsense you are talking!" He was getting too wide awake, so I thought I would press him hard. "I wonder," I said reflectively, "what an elephant's soul is like!"

The effect I desired was obtained, for he at once fell from his high-horse and became a child again.

"I don't want an elephant's soul, or any soul at all!" he said. For a few moments he sat despondently. Suddenly he jumped to his feet, with his eyes blazing and all the signs of intense cerebral excitement. "To hell with you and your souls!" he shouted. "Why do you plague me about souls? Haven't I got enough to worry, and pain, and distract me already, without thinking of souls!" He looked so hostile that I thought he was in for another homicidal fit, so I blew my whistle. The instant, however, that I did so he became calm, and said apologetically:—

"Forgive me, Doctor; I forgot myself. You do not need any help. I am so worried in my mind that I am apt to be irritable. If you only knew the problem I have to face, and that I am working out, you would pity, and tolerate, and pardon me. Pray do not put me in a strait-waistcoat. I want to think and I cannot think freely when my body is confined. I am sure you will understand!" He had evidently self-control; so when the attendants came I told them not to mind, and they withdrew. Renfield watched them go; when the door was closed he said, with considerable dignity and sweetness:—

"Dr. Seward, you have been very considerate towards me. Believe me that I am very, very grateful to you!" I thought it well to leave him in this mood, and so I came away. There is certainly something to ponder over in this man's state. Several points seem to make what the American interviewer calls "a story," if one could only get them in proper order. Here they are:—

Will not mention "drinking."

Fears the thought of being burdened with the "soul" of anything.

Has no dread of wanting "life" in the future.

Despises the meaner forms of life altogether, though he dreads being haunted by their souls.

Logically all these things point one way! he has assurance of some kind that he will acquire some higher life. He dreads the consequence—the burden of a soul. Then it is a human life he looks to!

And the assurance—?

Merciful God! the Count has been to him, and there is some new scheme of terror afoot!

Later.—I went after my round to Van Helsing and told him my suspicion. He grew very grave; and, after thinking the matter over for a while asked me to take him to Renfield. I did so. As we came to the door we heard the lunatic within singing gaily, as he used to do in the time which now seems so long ago. When we entered we saw with amazement that he had spread out his sugar as of old; the flies, lethargic with the autumn, were beginning to buzz into the room. We tried to make him talk of the subject of our previous conversation, but he would not attend. He went on with his singing, just as though we had not been present. He had got a scrap of paper and was folding it into a note-book. We had to come away as ignorant as we went in.

His is a curious case indeed; we must watch him to-night.

LETTER,
MITCHELL, SONS AND CANDY
TO LORD GODALMING.

"1 October.

"My Lord,

"We are at all times only too happy to meet your wishes. We beg, with regard to the desire of your Lordship, expressed by Mr. Harker on your behalf, to supply the following information concerning the sale and purchase of No. 347, Piccadilly. The original vendors are the executors of the late Mr. Archibald Winter-Suffield. The purchaser is a foreign nobleman, Count de Ville, who effected the purchase himself paying the purchase money in notes 'over the counter,' if your Lordship will pardon us using so vulgar an expression. Beyond this we know nothing whatever of him.

"We are, my Lord,
"Your Lordship's humble servants,
"MITCHELL, SONS & CANDY."

DR. SEWARD'S DIARY.

2 October.—I placed a man in the corridor last night, and told him to make an accurate note of any sound he might hear from Renfield's room, and gave him instructions that if there should be anything strange he was to call me. After dinner, when we had all gathered round the fire in the study—Mrs. Harker having gone to bed—we discussed the attempts and discoveries of the day. Harker was the only one who had any result, and we are in great hopes that his clue may be an important one.

Before going to bed I went round to the patient's room and looked in through the observation trap. He was sleeping soundly, and his heart rose and fell with regular respiration.

This morning the man on duty reported to me that a little after midnight he was restless and kept saying his prayers somewhat loudly. I asked him if that was all; he replied that it was all he heard. There was something about his manner so suspicious that I asked him point blank if he had been asleep. He denied sleep, but admitted to having "dozed" for a while. It is too bad that men cannot be trusted unless they are watched.

To-day Harker is out following up his clue, and Art and Quincey are looking after horses. Godalming thinks that it will be well to have horses always in readiness, for when we get the information which we seek there will be no time to lose. We must sterilise all the imported earth between sunrise and sunset; we shall thus catch the Count at his weakest, and without a refuge to fly to. Van Helsing is off to the British Museum looking up some authorities on ancient medicine. The old physicians took account of things which their followers do not accept, and the Professor is searching for witch and demon cures which may be useful to us later.

I sometimes think we must be all mad and that we shall wake to sanity in strait-waistcoats.

Later.—We have met again. We seem at last to be on the track, and our work of to-morrow may be the beginning of the end. I wonder if Renfield's quiet has anything to do with this. His moods have so followed the doings of the Count, that the coming destruction of the monster may be carried to him in some subtle way. If we could only get some hint as to what passed in his mind, between the time of my argument with him to-day and his resumption of fly-catching, it might afford us a valuable clue. He is now seemingly quiet for a spell . . . . Is he?—— That wild yell seemed to come from his room . . . .

The attendant came bursting into my room and told me that Renfield had somehow met with some accident. He had heard him yell; and when he went to him found him lying on his face on the floor, all covered with blood. I must go at once . . . .

CHAPTER XXI

DR. SEWARD'S DIARY

3 October.—Let me put down with exactness all that happened, as well as I can remember it, since last I made an entry. Not a detail that I can recall must be forgotten; in all calmness I must proceed.

When I came to Renfield's room I found him lying on the floor on his left side in a glittering pool of blood. When I went to move him, it became at once apparent that he had received some terrible injuries; there seemed none of that unity of purpose between the parts of the body which marks even lethargic sanity. As the face was exposed I could see that it was horribly bruised, as though it had been beaten against the floor—indeed it was from the face wounds that the pool of blood originated. The attendant who was kneeling beside the body said to me as we turned him over:—

"I think, sir, his back is broken. See, both his right arm and leg and the whole side of his face are paralysed." How such a thing could have happened puzzled the attendant beyond measure. He seemed quite bewildered, and his brows were gathered in as he said:—

"I can't understand the two things. He could mark his face like that by beating his own head on the floor. I saw a young woman do it once at the Eversfield Asylum before anyone could lay hands on her. And I suppose he might have broke his neck by falling out of bed, if he got in an awkward kink. But for the life of me I can't imagine how the two things occurred. If his back was broke, he couldn't beat his head; and if his face was like that before the fall out of bed, there would be marks of it." I said to him:—

"Go to Dr. Van Helsing, and ask him to kindly come here at once. I want him without an instant's delay." The man ran off, and within a few minutes the Professor, in his dressing gown and slippers, appeared. When he saw Renfield on the ground, he looked keenly at him a moment, and then turned to me. I think he recognised my thought in my eyes, for he said very quietly, manifestly for the ears of the attendant:—

"Ah, a sad accident! He will need very careful watching, and much attention. I shall stay with you myself; but I shall first dress myself. If you will remain I shall in a few minutes join you."

The patient was now breathing stertorously and it was easy to see that he had suffered some terrible injury. Van Helsing returned with extraordinary celerity, bearing with him a surgical case. He had evidently been thinking and had his mind made up; for, almost before he looked at the patient, he whispered to me:—

"Send the attendant away. We must be alone with him when he becomes conscious, after the operation." So I said:—

"I think that will do now, Simmons. We have done all that we can at present. You had better go your round, and Dr. Van Helsing will operate. Let me know instantly if there be anything unusual anywhere."

The man withdrew, and we went into a strict examination of the patient. The wounds of the face was superficial; the real injury was a depressed fracture of the skull, extending right up through the motor area. The Professor thought a moment and said:—

"We must reduce the pressure and get back to normal conditions, as far as can be; the rapidity of the suffusion shows the terrible nature of his injury. The whole motor area seems affected. The suffusion of the brain will increase quickly, so we must trephine at once or it may be too late." As he was speaking there was a soft tapping at the door. I went over and opened it and found in the corridor without, Arthur and Quincey in pajamas and slippers: the former spoke:—

"I heard your man call up Dr. Van Helsing and tell him of an accident. So I woke Quincey or rather called for him as he was not asleep. Things are moving too quickly and too strangely for sound sleep for any of us these times. I've been thinking that to-morrow night will not see things as they have been. We'll have to look back—and forward a little more than we have done. May we come in?" I nodded, and held the door open till they had entered; then I closed it again. When Quincey saw the attitude and state of the patient, and noted the horrible pool on the floor, he said softly:—

"My God! what has happened to him? Poor, poor devil!" I told him briefly, and added that we expected he would recover consciousness after the operation—for a short time, at all events. He went at once and sat down on the edge of the bed, with Godalming beside him; we all watched in patience.

"We shall wait," said Van Helsing, "just long enough to fix the best spot for trephining, so that we may most quickly and perfectly remove the blood clot; for it is evident that the hæmorrhage is increasing."

The minutes during which we waited passed with fearful slowness. I had a horrible sinking in my heart, and from Van Helsing's face I gathered that he felt some fear or apprehension as to what was to come. I dreaded the words that Renfield might speak. I was positively afraid to think; but the conviction of what was coming was on me, as I have read of men who have heard the death-watch. The poor man's breathing came in uncertain gasps. Each instant he seemed as though he would open his eyes and speak; but then would follow a prolonged stertorous breath, and he would relapse into a more fixed insensibility. Inured as I was to sick beds and death, this suspense grew, and grew upon me. I could almost hear the beating of my own heart; and the blood surging through my temples sounded like blows from a hammer. The silence finally became agonising. I looked at my companions, one after another, and saw from their flushed faces and damp brows that they were enduring equal torture. There was a nervous suspense over us all, as though overhead some dread bell would peal out powerfully when we should least expect it.

At last there came a time when it was evident that the patient was sinking fast; he might die at any moment. I looked up at the Professor and caught his eyes fixed on mine. His face was sternly set as he spoke:—

"There is no time to lose. His words may be worth many lives; I have been thinking so, as I stood here. It may be there is a soul at stake! We shall operate just above the ear."

Without another word he made the operation. For a few moments the breathing continued to be stertorous. Then there came a breath so prolonged that it seemed as though it would tear open his chest. Suddenly his eyes opened, and became fixed in a wild, helpless stare. This was continued for a few moments; then it softened into a glad surprise, and from the lips came a sigh of relief. He moved convulsively, and as he did so, said:—

"I'll be quiet, Doctor. Tell them to take off the strait-waistcoat. I have had a terrible dream, and it has left me so weak that I cannot move. What's wrong with my face? it feels all swollen, and it smarts dreadfully." He tried to turn his head; but even with the effort his eyes seemed to grow glassy again so I gently put it back. Then Van Helsing said in a quiet grave tone:—

"Tell us your dream, Mr. Renfield." As he heard the voice his face brightened, through its mutilation, and he said:—

"That is Dr. Van Helsing. How good it is of you to be here. Give me some water, my lips are dry; and I shall try to tell you. I dreamed"—he stopped and seemed fainting, I called quietly to Quincey—"The brandy—it is in my study—quick!" He flew and returned with a glass, the decanter of brandy and a carafe of water. We moistened the parched lips, and the patient quickly revived. It seemed, however, that his poor injured brain had been working in the interval, for, when he was quite conscious, he looked at me piercingly with an agonised confusion which I shall never forget, and said:—

"I must not deceive myself; it was no dream, but all a grim reality." Then his eyes roved round the room; as they caught sight of the two figures sitting patiently on the edge of the bed he went on:—

"If I were not sure already, I would know from them." For an instant his eyes closed—not with pain or sleep but voluntarily, as though he were bringing all his faculties to bear; when he opened them he said, hurriedly, and with more energy than he had yet displayed:—

"Quick, Doctor, quick. I am dying! I feel that I have but a few minutes; and then I must go back to death—or worse! Wet my lips with brandy again. I have something that I must say before I die; or before my poor crushed brain dies anyhow. Thank you! It was that night after you left me, when I implored you to let me go away. I couldn't speak then, for I felt my tongue was tied; but I was as sane then, except in that way, as I am now. I was in an agony of despair for a long time after you left me; it seemed hours. Then there came a sudden peace to me. My brain seemed to become cool again, and I realised where I was. I heard the dogs bark behind our house, but not where He was!" As he spoke, Van Helsing's eyes never blinked, but his hand came out and met mine and gripped it hard. He did not, however, betray himself; he nodded slightly and said: "Go on," in a low voice. Renfield proceeded:—

"He came up to the window in the mist, as I had seen him often before; but he was solid then—not a ghost, and his eyes were fierce like a man's when angry. He was laughing with his red mouth; the sharp white teeth glinted in the moonlight when he turned to look back over the belt of trees, to where the dogs were barking. I wouldn't ask him to come in at first, though I knew he wanted to—just as he had wanted all along. Then he began promising me things—not in words but by doing them." He was interrupted by a word from the Professor:—

"How?"

"By making them happen; just as he used to send in the flies when the sun was shining. Great big fat ones with steel and sapphire on their wings; and big moths, in the night, with skull and cross-bones on their backs." Van Helsing nodded to him as he whispered to me unconsciously:—

"The *Acherontia Aitetropos of the Sphinges*—what you call the 'Death's-head Moth'?" The patient went on without stopping.

"Then he began to whisper: 'Rats, rats, rats! Hundreds, thousands, millions of them, and every one a life; and dogs to eat them, and cats too. All lives! all red blood, with years of life in it; and not merely buzzing flies!' I laughed at him, for I wanted to see what he could do. Then the dogs howled, away beyond the dark trees in His house. He beckoned me to the window. I got up and looked out, and He raised his hands, and seemed to call out without using any words. A dark mass spread over the grass, coming on like the shape of a flame of fire; and then He moved the mist to the right and left, and I could see that there were thousands of rats with their eyes blazing red—like His, only smaller. He held up his hand, and they all stopped; and I thought he seemed to be saying: 'All these lives will I give you, ay, and many more and greater, through countless ages, if you will fall down and worship me!' And then a red cloud, like the colour of blood, seemed to close over my eyes; and before I knew what I was doing, I found myself opening the sash and saying to Him: 'Come in, Lord and Master!' The rats were all gone, but He slid into the room through the sash, though it was only open an inch wide—just as the Moon herself has often come in through the tiniest crack and has stood before me in all her size and splendour."

His voice was weaker, so I moistened his lips with the brandy again, and he continued; but it seemed as though his memory had gone on working in the interval for his story was further advanced. I was about to call him back to the point, but Van Helsing whispered to me: "Let him go on. Do not interrupt him; he cannot go back, and maybe could not proceed at all if once he lost the thread of his thought." He proceeded:—

"All day I waited to hear from him, but he did not send me anything, not even a blow-fly, and when the moon got up I was pretty angry with him. When he slid in through the window, though it was shut, and did not even knock, I got mad with him. He sneered at me, and his white face looked out of the mist with his red eyes gleaming, and he went on as though he owned the whole place, and I was no one. He didn't even smell the same as he went by me. I couldn't hold him. I thought that, somehow, Mrs. Harker had come into the room."

The two men sitting on the bed stood up and came over, standing behind him so that he could not see them, but where they could hear better. They were both silent, but the Professor started and quivered; his face, however, grew grimmer and sterner still. Renfield went on without noticing:—

"When Mrs. Harker came in to see me this afternoon she wasn't the same; it was like tea after the teapot had been watered." Here we all moved, but no one said a word; he went on:—

"I didn't know that she was here till she spoke; and she didn't look the same. I don't care for the pale people; I like them with lots of blood in them, and hers had all seemed to have run out. I didn't think of it at the time; but when she went away I began to think, and it made me mad to know that He had been taking the life out of her." I could feel that the rest quivered, as I did, but we remained otherwise still. "So when He came to-night I was ready for Him. I saw the mist stealing in, and I grabbed it tight. I had heard that madmen have unnatural strength; and as I knew I was a madman—at times anyhow—I resolved to use my power. Ay, and He felt it too, for He had to come out of the mist to struggle with me. I held tight; and I thought I was going to win, for I didn't mean Him to take any more of her life, till I saw His eyes. They burned into me, and my strength became like water. He slipped through it, and when I tried to cling to Him, He raised me up and flung me down. There was a red cloud before me, and a noise like thunder, and the mist seemed to steal away under the door." His voice was becoming fainter and his breath more stertorous. Van Helsing stood up instinctively.

"We know the worst now," he said. "He is here, and we know his purpose. It may not be too late. Let us be armed—the same as we were the other night, but lose no time; there is not an instant to spare." There was no need to put our fear, nay our conviction, into words—we shared them in common. We all hurried and took from our rooms the same things that we had when we entered the Count's house. The Professor had his ready, and as we met in the corridor he pointed to them significantly as he said:—

"They never leave me; and they shall not till this unhappy business is over. Be wise also, my friends. It is no common enemy that we deal with. Alas! alas! that that dear Madam Mina should suffer!" He stopped; his voice was breaking, and I do not know if rage or terror predominated in my own heart.

Outside the Harkers' door we paused. Art and Quincey held back, and the latter said:—

"Should we disturb her?"

"We must," said Van Helsing grimly. "If the door be locked, I shall break it in."

"May it not frighten her terribly? It is unusual to break into a lady's room!"

Van Helsing said solemnly, "You are always right; but this is life and death. All chambers are alike to the doctor; and even were they not they are all as one to me to-night. Friend John, when I turn the handle, if the door does not open, do you put your shoulder down and shove; and you too, my friends. Now!"

He turned the handle as he spoke, but the door did not yield. We threw ourselves against it; with a crash it burst open, and we almost fell headlong into the room. The Professor did actually fall, and I saw across him as he gathered himself up from hands and knees. What I saw appalled me. I felt my hair rise like bristles on the back of my neck, and my heart seemed to stand still.

The moonlight was so bright that through the thick yellow blind the room was light enough to see. On the bed beside the window lay Jonathan Harker, his face flushed and breathing heavily as though in a stupor. Kneeling on the near edge of the bed facing outwards was the white-clad figure of his wife. By her side stood a tall, thin man, clad in black. His face was turned from us, but the instant we saw we all recognised the Count—in every way, even to the scar on his forehead. With his left hand he held both Mrs. Harker's hands, keeping them away with her arms at full tension; his right hand gripped her by the back of the neck, forcing her face down on his bosom. Her white nightdress was smeared with blood, and a thin stream trickled down the man's bare breast which was shown by his torn-open dress. The attitude of the two had a terrible resemblance to a child forcing a kitten's nose into a saucer of milk to compel it to drink. As we burst into the room, the Count turned his face, and the hellish look that I had heard described seemed to leap into it. His eyes flamed red with devilish passion; the great nostrils of the white aquiline nose opened wide and quivered at the edge; and the white sharp teeth, behind the full lips of the blood-dripping mouth, champed together like those of a wild beast. With a wrench, which threw his victim back upon the bed as though hurled from a height, he turned and sprang at us. But by this time the Professor had gained his feet, and was holding towards him the envelope which contained the Sacred Wafer. The Count suddenly stopped, just as poor Lucy had done outside the tomb, and cowered back. Further and further back he cowered, as we, lifting our crucifixes, advanced. The moonlight suddenly failed, as a great black cloud sailed across the sky; and when the gaslight sprang up under Quincey's match, we saw nothing but a faint vapour. This, as we looked, trailed under the door, which with the recoil from its bursting open, had swung back to its old position. Van Helsing, Art, and I moved forward to Mrs. Harker, who by this time had drawn her breath and with it had given a scream so wild, so ear-piercing, so despairing that it seems to me now that it will ring in my ears till my dying day. For a few seconds she lay in her helpless attitude and disarray. Her face was ghastly, with a pallor which was accentuated by the blood which smeared her lips and cheeks and chin; from her throat trickled a thin stream of blood; her eyes were mad with terror. Then she put before her face her poor crushed hands, which bore on their whiteness the red mark of the Count's terrible grip, and from behind them came a low desolate wail which made the terrible scream seem only the quick expression of an endless grief. Van Helsing stepped forward and drew the coverlet gently over her body, whilst Art, after looking at her face for an instant despairingly, ran out of the room. Van Helsing whispered to me:—

"Jonathan is in a stupor such as we know the Vampire can produce. We can do nothing with poor Madam Mina for a few moments till she recovers herself; I must wake him!" He dipped the end of a towel in cold water and with it began to flick him on the face, his wife all the while holding her face between her hands and sobbing in a way that was heart-breaking to hear. I raised the blind, and looked out of the window. There was much moonshine; and as I looked I could see Quincey Morris run across the lawn and hide himself in the shadow of a great yew-tree. It puzzled me to think why he was doing this; but at the instant I heard Harker's quick exclamation as he woke to partial consciousness, and turned to the bed. On his face, as there might well be, was a look of wild amazement. He seemed dazed for a few seconds, and then full consciousness seemed to burst upon him all at once, and he started up. His wife was aroused by the quick movement, and turned to him with her arms stretched out, as though to embrace him; instantly, however, she drew them in again, and putting her elbows together, held her hands before her face, and shuddered till the bed beneath her shook.

"In God's name what does this mean?" Harker cried out. "Dr. Seward, Dr. Van Helsing, what is it? What has happened? What is wrong? Mina, dear, what is it? What does that blood mean? My God, my God! has it come to this!" and, raising himself to his knees, he beat his hands wildly together. "Good God help us! help her! oh, help her!" With a quick movement he jumped from bed, and began to pull on his clothes,—all the man in him awake at the need for instant exertion. "What has happened? Tell me all about it!" he cried without pausing. "Dr. Van Helsing, you love Mina, I know. Oh, do something to save her. It cannot have gone too far yet. Guard her while I look for *him*!" His wife, through her terror and horror and distress, saw some sure danger to him: instantly forgetting her own grief, she seized hold of him and cried out:—

"No! no! Jonathan, you must not leave me. I have suffered enough to-night, God knows, without the dread of his harming you. You must stay with me. Stay with these friends who will watch over you!" Her expression became frantic as she spoke; and, he yielding to her, she pulled him down sitting on the bed side, and clung to him fiercely.

Van Helsing and I tried to calm them both. The Professor held up his little golden crucifix, and said with wonderful calmness:—

"Do not fear, my dear. We are here; and whilst this is close to you no foul thing can approach. You are safe for to-night; and we must be calm and take counsel together." She shuddered and was silent, holding down her head on her husband's breast. When she raised it, his white night-robe was stained with blood where her lips had touched, and where the thin open wound in her neck had sent forth drops. The instant she saw it she drew back, with a low wail, and whispered, amidst choking sobs:—

"Unclean, unclean! I must touch him or kiss him no more. Oh, that it should be that it is I who am now his worst enemy, and whom he may have most cause to fear." To this he spoke out resolutely:—

"Nonsense, Mina. It is a shame to me to hear such a word. I would not hear it of you; and I shall not hear it from you. May God judge me by my deserts, and punish me with more bitter suffering than even this hour, if by any act or will of mine anything ever come between us!" He put out his arms and folded her to his breast; and for a while she lay there sobbing. He looked at us over her bowed head, with eyes that blinked damply above his quivering nostrils; his mouth was set as steel. After a while her sobs became less frequent and more faint, and then he said to me, speaking with a studied calmness which I felt tried his nervous power to the utmost:—

"And now, Dr. Seward, tell me all about it. Too well I know the broad fact; tell me all that has been." I told him exactly what had happened, and he listened with seeming impassiveness; but his nostrils twitched and his eyes blazed as I told how the ruthless hands of the Count had held his wife in that terrible and horrid position, with her mouth to the open wound in his breast. It interested me, even at that moment, to see, that, whilst the face of white set passion worked convulsively over the bowed head, the hands tenderly and lovingly stroked the ruffled hair. Just as I had finished, Quincey and Godalming knocked at the door. They entered in obedience to our summons. Van Helsing looked at me questioningly. I understood him to mean if we were to take advantage of their coming to divert if possible the thoughts of the unhappy husband and wife from each other and from themselves; so on nodding acquiescence to him he asked them what they had seen or done. To which Lord Godalming answered:—

"I could not see him anywhere in the passage, or in any of our rooms. I looked in the study but, though he had been there, he had gone. He had, however——" He stopped suddenly, looking at the poor drooping figure on the bed. Van Helsing said gravely:—

"Go on, friend Arthur. We want here no more concealments. Our hope now is in knowing all. Tell freely!" So Art went on:—

"He had been there, and though it could only have been for a few seconds, he made rare hay of the place. All the manuscript had been burned, and the blue flames were flickering amongst the white ashes; the cylinders of your phonograph too were thrown on the fire, and the wax had helped the flames." Here I interrupted. "Thank God there is the other copy in the safe!" His face lit for a moment, but fell again as he went on: "I ran downstairs then, but could see no sign of him. I looked into Renfield's room; but there was no trace there except——!" Again he paused. "Go on," said Harker hoarsely; so he bowed his head and moistening his lips with his tongue, added: "except that the poor fellow is dead." Mrs. Harker raised her head, looking from one to the other of us she said solemnly:—

"God's will be done!" I could not but feel that Art was keeping back something; but, as I took it that it was with a purpose, I said nothing. Van Helsing turned to Morris and asked:—

"And you, friend Quincey, have you any to tell?"

"A little," he answered. "It may be much eventually, but at present I can't say. I thought it well to know if possible where the Count would go when he left the house. I did not see him; but I saw a bat rise from Renfield's window, and flap westward. I expected to see him in some shape go back to Carfax; but he evidently sought some other lair. He will not be back to-night; for the sky is reddening in the east, and the dawn is close. We must work to-morrow!"

He said the latter words through his shut teeth. For a space of perhaps a couple of minutes there was silence, and I could fancy that I could hear the sound of our hearts beating; then Van Helsing said, placing his hand very tenderly on Mrs. Harker's head:—

"And now, Madam Mina—poor, dear, dear Madam Mina—tell us exactly what happened. God knows that I do not want that you be pained; but it is need that we know all. For now more than ever has all work to be done quick and sharp, and in deadly earnest. The day is close to us that must end all, if it may be so; and now is the chance that we may live and learn."

The poor, dear lady shivered, and I could see the tension of her nerves as she clasped her husband closer to her and bent her head lower and lower still on his breast. Then she raised her head proudly, and held out one hand to Van Helsing who took it in his, and, after stooping and kissing it reverently, held it fast. The other hand was locked in that of her husband, who held his other arm thrown round her protectingly. After a pause in which she was evidently ordering her thoughts, she began:—

"I took the sleeping draught which you had so kindly given me, but for a long time it did not act. I seemed to become more wakeful, and myriads of horrible fancies began to crowd in upon my mind—all of them connected with death, and vampires; with blood, and pain, and trouble." Her husband involuntarily groaned as she turned to him and said lovingly: "Do not fret, dear. You must be brave and strong, and help me through the horrible task. If you only knew what an effort it is to me to tell of this fearful thing at all, you would understand how much I need your help. Well, I saw I must try to help the medicine to its work with my will, if it was to do me any good, so I resolutely set myself to sleep. Sure enough sleep must soon have come to me, for I remember no more. Jonathan coming in had not waked me, for he lay by my side when next I remember. There was in the room the same thin white mist that I had before noticed. But I forget now if you know of this; you will find it in my diary which I shall show you later. I felt the same vague terror which had come to me before and the same sense of some presence. I turned to wake Jonathan, but found that he slept so soundly that it seemed as if it was he who had taken the sleeping draught, and not I. I tried, but I could not wake him. This caused me a great fear, and I looked around terrified. Then indeed, my heart sank within me: beside the bed, as if he had stepped out of the mist—or rather as if the mist had turned into his figure, for it had entirely disappeared—stood a tall, thin man, all in black. I knew him at once from the description of the others. The waxen face; the high aquiline nose, on which the light fell in a thin white line; the parted red lips, with the sharp white teeth showing between; and the red eyes that I had seemed to see in the sunset on the windows of St. Mary's Church at Whitby. I knew, too, the red scar on his forehead where Jonathan had struck him. For an instant my heart stood still, and I would have screamed out, only that I was paralysed. In the pause he spoke in a sort of keen, cutting whisper, pointing as he spoke to Jonathan:—

" 'Silence! If you make a sound I shall take him and dash his brains out before your very eyes.' I was appalled and was too bewildered to do or say anything. With a mocking smile, he placed one hand upon my shoulder and, holding me tight, bared my throat with the other, saying as he did so, 'First, a little refreshment to reward my exertions. You may as well be quiet; it is not the first time, or the second, that your veins have appeased my thirst!' I was bewildered, and, strangely enough, I did not want to hinder him. I suppose it is a part of the horrible curse that such is, when his touch is on his victim. And oh, my God, my God, pity me! He placed his reeking lips upon my throat!" Her husband groaned again. She clasped his hand harder, and looked at him pityingly, as if he were the injured one, and went on:—

"I felt my strength fading away, and I was in a half swoon. How long this horrible thing lasted I know not; but it seemed that a long time must have passed before he took his foul, awful, sneering mouth away. I saw it drip with the fresh blood!" The remembrance seemed for a while to overpower her, and she drooped and would have sunk down but for her husband's sustaining arm. With a great effort she recovered herself and went on:—

"Then he spoke to me mockingly, 'And so you, like the others, would play your brains against mine. You would help these men to hunt me and frustrate me in my designs! You know now, and they know in part already, and will know in full before long, what it is to cross my path. They should have kept their energies for use closer to home. Whilst they played wits against me—against me who commanded nations, and intrigued for them, and fought for them, hundreds of years before they were born—I was countermining them. And you, their best beloved one, are now to me, flesh of my flesh; blood of my blood; kin of my kin; my bountiful wine-press for a while; and shall be later on my companion and my helper. You shall be avenged in turn; for not one of them but shall minister to your needs. But as yet you are to be punished for what you have done. You have aided in thwarting me; now you shall come to my call. When my brain says "Come!" to you, you shall cross land or sea to do my bidding; and to that end this!' With that he pulled open his shirt, and with his long sharp nails opened a vein in his breast. When the blood began to spurt out, he took my hands in one of his, holding them tight, and with the other seized my neck and pressed my mouth to the wound, so that I must either suffocate or swallow some of the—— Oh my God! my God! what have I done? What have I done to deserve such a fate, I who have tried to walk in meekness and righteousness all my days. God pity me! Look down on a poor soul in worse than mortal peril; and in mercy pity those to whom she is dear!" Then she began to rub her lips as though to cleanse them from pollution.

As she was telling her terrible story, the eastern sky began to quicken, and everything became more and more clear. Harker was still and quiet; but over his face, as the awful narrative went on, came a grey look which deepened and deepened in the morning light, till when the first red streak of the coming dawn shot up, the flesh stood darkly out against the whitening hair.

We have arranged that one of us is to stay within call of the unhappy pair till we can meet together and arrange about taking action.

Of this I am sure: the sun rises to-day on no more miserable house in all the great round of its daily course.

CHAPTER XXII

JONATHAN HARKER'S JOURNAL

3 October.—As I must do something or go mad, I write this diary. It is now six o'clock, and we are to meet in the study in half an hour and take something to eat; for Dr. Van Helsing and Dr. Seward are agreed that if we do not eat we cannot work our best. Our best will be, God knows, required to-day. I must keep writing at every chance, for I dare not stop to think. All, big and little, must go down; perhaps at the end the little things may teach us most. The teaching, big or little, could not have landed Mina or me anywhere worse than we are to-day. However, we must trust and hope. Poor Mina told me just now, with the tears running down her dear cheeks, that it is in trouble and trial that our faith is tested—that we must keep on trusting; and that God will aid us up to the end. The end! oh my God! what end? . . . To work! To work!

When Dr. Van Helsing and Dr. Seward had come back from seeing poor Renfield, we went gravely into what was to be done. First, Dr. Seward told us that when he and Dr. Van Helsing had gone down to the room below they had found Renfield lying on the floor, all in a heap. His face was all bruised and crushed in, and the bones of the neck were broken.

Dr. Seward asked the attendant who was on duty in the passage if he had heard anything. He said that he had been sitting down—he confessed to half dozing—when he heard loud voices in the room, and then Renfield had called out loudly several times, "God! God! God!" after that there was a sound of falling, and when he entered the room he found him lying on the floor, face down, just as the doctors had seen him. Van Helsing asked if he had heard "voices" or "a voice," and he said he could not say; that at first it had seemed to him as if there were two, but as there was no one in the room it could have been only one. He could swear to it, if required, that the word "God" was spoken by the patient. Dr. Seward said to us, when we were alone, that he did not wish to go into the matter; the question of an inquest had to be considered, and it would never do to put forward the truth, as no one would believe it. As it was, he thought that on the attendant's evidence he could give a certificate of death by misadventure in falling from bed. In case the coroner should demand it, there would be a formal inquest, necessarily to the same result.

When the question began to be discussed as to what should be our next step, the very first thing we decided was that Mina should be in full confidence; that nothing of any sort—no matter how painful—should be kept from her. She herself agreed as to its wisdom, and it was pitiful to see her so brave and yet so sorrowful, and in such a depth of despair. "There must be no concealment," she said, "Alas! we have had too much already. And besides there is nothing in all the world that can give me more pain than I have already endured—than I suffer now! Whatever may happen, it must be of new hope or of new courage to me!" Van Helsing was looking at her fixedly as she spoke, and said, suddenly but quietly:—

"But dear Madam Mina, are you not afraid; not for yourself, but for others from yourself, after what has happened?" Her face grew set in its lines, but her eyes shone with the devotion of a martyr as she answered:—

"Ah no! for my mind is made up!"

"To what?" he asked gently, whilst we were all very still; for each in our own way we had a sort of vague idea of what she meant. Her answer came with direct simplicity, as though she were simply stating a fact:—

"Because if I find in myself—and I shall watch keenly for it—a sign of harm to any that I love, I shall die!"

"You would not kill yourself?" he asked, hoarsely.

"I would; if there were no friend who loved me, who would save me such a pain, and so desperate an effort!" She looked at him meaningly as she spoke. He was sitting down; but now he rose and came close to her and put his hand on her head as he said solemnly:

"My child, there is such an one if it were for your good. For myself I could hold it in my account with God to find such an euthanasia for you, even at this moment if it were best. Nay, were it safe! But my child——" For a moment he seemed choked, and a great sob rose in his throat; he gulped it down and went on:—

"There are here some who would stand between you and death. You must not die. You must not die by any hand; but least of all by your own. Until the other, who has fouled your sweet life, is true dead you must not die; for if he is still with the quick Un-Dead, your death would make you even as he is. No, you must live! You must struggle and strive to live, though death would seem a boon unspeakable. You must fight Death himself, though he come to you in pain or in joy; by the day, or the night; in safety or in peril! On your living soul I charge you that you do not die—nay, nor think of death—till this great evil be past." The poor dear grew white as death, and shock and shivered, as I have seen a quicksand shake and shiver at the incoming of the tide. We were all silent; we could do nothing. At length she grew more calm and turning to him said, sweetly, but oh! so sorrowfully, as she held out her hand:—

"I promise you, my dear friend, that if God will let me live, I shall strive to do so; till, if it may be in His good time, this horror may have passed away from me." She was so good and brave that we all felt that our hearts were strengthened to work and endure for her, and we began to discuss what we were to do. I told her that she was to have all the papers in the safe, and all the papers or diaries and phonographs we might hereafter use; and was to keep the record as she had done before. She was pleased with the prospect of anything to do—if "pleased" could be used in connection with so grim an interest.

As usual Van Helsing had thought ahead of everyone else, and was prepared with an exact ordering of our work.

"It is perhaps well," he said, "that at our meeting after our visit to Carfax we decided not to do anything with the earth-boxes that lay there. Had we done so, the Count must have guessed our purpose, and would doubtless have taken measures in advance to frustrate such an effort with regard to the others; but now he does not know our intentions. Nay, more, in all probability, he does not know that such a power exists to us as can sterilise his lairs, so that he cannot use them as of old. We are now so much further advanced in our knowledge as to their disposition that, when we have examined the house in Piccadilly, we may track the very last of them. To-day, then, is ours; and in it rests our hope. The sun that rose on our sorrow this morning guards us in its course. Until it sets to-night, that monster must retain whatever form he now has. He is confined within the limitations of his earthly envelope. He cannot melt into thin air nor disappear through cracks or chinks or crannies. If he go through a doorway, he must open the door like a mortal. And so we have this day to hunt out all his lairs and sterilise them. So we shall, if we have not yet catch him and destroy him, drive him to bay in some place where the catching and the destroying shall be, in time, sure." Here I started up for I could not contain myself at the thought that the minutes and seconds so preciously laden with Mina's life and happiness were flying from us, since whilst we talked action was impossible. But Van Helsing held up his hand warningly. "Nay, friend Jonathan," he said, "in this, the quickest way home is the longest way, so your proverb say. We shall all act and act with desperate quick, when the time has come. But think, in all probable the key of the situation is in that house in Piccadilly. The Count may have many houses which he has bought. Of them he will have deeds of purchase, keys and other things. He will have paper that he write on; he will have his book of cheques. There are many belongings that he must have somewhere; why not in this place so central, so quiet, where he come and go by the front or the back at all hour, when in the very vast of the traffic there is none to notice. We shall go there and search that house; and when we learn what it holds, then we do what our friend Arthur call, in his phrases of hunt 'stop the earths' and so we run down our old fox—so? is it not?"

"Then let us come at once," I cried, "we are wasting the precious, precious time!" The Professor did not move, but simply said:—

"And how are we to get into that house in Piccadilly?"

"Any way!" I cried. "We shall break in if need be."

"And your police; where will they be, and what will they say?"

I was staggered; but I knew that if he wished to delay he had a good reason for it. So I said, as quietly as I could:—

"Don't wait more than need be; you know, I am sure, what torture I am in."

"Ah, my child, that I do; and indeed there is no wish of me to add to your anguish. But just think, what can we do, until all the world be at movement. Then will come our time. I have thought and thought, and it seems to me that the simplest way is the best of all. Now we wish to get into the house, but we have no key; is it not so?" I nodded.

"Now suppose that you were, in truth, the owner of that house, and could not still get in; and think there was to you no conscience of the housebreaker, what would you do?"

"I should get a respectable locksmith, and set him to work to pick the lock for me."

"And your police, they would interfere, would they not?"

"Oh, no! not if they knew the man was properly employed."

"Then," he looked at me as keenly as he spoke, "all that is in doubt is the conscience of the employer, and the belief of your policemen as to whether or no that employer has a good conscience or a bad one. Your police must indeed be zealous men and clever—oh, so clever!—in reading the heart, that they trouble themselves in such matter. No, no, my friend Jonathan, you go take the lock off a hundred empty house in this your London, or of any city in the world; and if you do it as such things are rightly done, and at the time such things are rightly done, no one will interfere. I have read of a gentleman who owned a so fine house in London, and when he went for months of summer to Switzerland and lock up his house, some burglar came and broke window at back and got in. Then he went and made open the shutters in front and walk out and in through the door, before the very eyes of the police. Then he have an auction in that house, and advertise it, and put up big notice; and when the day come he sell off by a great auctioneer all the goods of that other man who own them. Then he go to a builder, and he sell him that house, making an agreement that he pull it down and take all away within a certain time. And your police and other authority help him all they can. And when that owner come back from his holiday in Switzerland he find only an empty hole where his house had been. This was all done *en règle*; and in our work we shall be *en règle* too. We shall not go so early that the policemen who have then little to think of, shall deem it strange; but we shall go after ten o'clock, when there are many about, and such things would be done were we indeed owners of the house."

I could not but see how right he was and the terrible despair of Mina's face became relaxed a thought; there was hope in such good counsel. Van Helsing went on:—

"When once within that house we may find more clues; at any rate some of us can remain there whilst the rest find the other places where there be more earth-boxes—at Bermondsey and Mile End."

Lord Godalming stood up. "I can be of some use here," he said. "I shall wire to my people to have horses and carriages where they will be most convenient."

"Look here, old fellow," said Morris, "it is a capital idea to have all ready in case we want to go horsebacking; but don't you think that one of your snappy carriages with its heraldic adornments in a byway of Walworth or Mile End would attract too much attention for our purposes? It seems to me that we ought to take cabs when we go south or east; and even leave them somewhere near the neighbourhood we are going to."

"Friend Quincey is right!" said the Professor. "His head is what you call in plane with the horizon. It is a difficult thing that we go to do, and we do not want no peoples to watch us if so it may."

Mina took a growing interest in everything and I was rejoiced to see that the exigency of affairs was helping her to forget for a time the terrible experience of the night. She was very, very pale—almost ghastly, and so thin that her lips were drawn away, showing her teeth in somewhat of prominence. I did not mention this last, lest it should give her needless pain; but it made my blood run cold in my veins to think of what had occurred with poor Lucy when the Count had sucked her blood. As yet there was no sign of the teeth growing sharper; but the time as yet was short, and there was time for fear.

When we came to the discussion of the sequence of our efforts and of the disposition of our forces, there were new sources of doubt. It was finally agreed that before starting for Piccadilly we should destroy the Count's lair close at hand. In case he should find it out too soon, we should thus be still ahead of him in our work of destruction; and his presence in his purely material shape, and at his weakest, might give us some new clue.

As to the disposal of forces, it was suggested by the Professor that, after our visit to Carfax, we should all enter the house in Piccadilly; that the two doctors and I should remain there, whilst Lord Godalming and Quincey found the lairs at Walworth and Mile End and destroyed them. It was possible, if not likely, the Professor urged, that the Count might appear in Piccadilly during the day, and that if so we might be able to cope with him then and there. At any rate, we might be able to follow him in force. To this plan I strenuously objected, and so far as my going was concerned, for I said that I intended to stay and protect Mina, I thought that my mind was made up on the subject; but Mina would not listen to my objection. She said that there might be some law matter in which I could be useful; that amongst the Count's papers might be some clue which I could understand out of my experience in Transylvania; and that, as it was, all the strength we could muster was required to cope with the Count's extraordinary power. I had to give in, for Mina's resolution was fixed; she said that it was the last hope for *her* that we should all work together. "As for me," she said, "I have no fear. Things have been as bad as they can be; and whatever may happen must have in it some element of hope or comfort. Go, my husband! God can, if He wishes it, guard me as well alone as with any one present." So I started up crying out: "Then in God's name let us come at once, for we are losing time. The Count may come to Piccadilly earlier than we think."

"Not so!" said Van Helsing, holding up his hand.

"But why?" I asked.

"Do you forget," he said, with actually a smile, "that last night he banqueted heavily, and will sleep late?"

Did I forget! shall I ever—can I ever! Can any of us ever forget that terrible scene! Mina struggled hard to keep her brave countenance; but the pain overmastered her and she put her hands before her face, and shuddered whilst she moaned. Van Helsing had not intended to recall her frightful experience. He had simply lost sight of her and her part in the affair in his intellectual effort. When it struck him what he said, he was horrified at his thoughtlessness and tried to comfort her. "Oh, Madam Mina," he said, "dear, dear Madam Mina, alas! that I of all who so reverence you should have said anything so forgetful. These stupid old lips of mine and this stupid old head do not deserve so; but you will forget it, will you not?" He bent low beside her as he spoke; she took his hand, and looking at him through her tears, said hoarsely:—

"No, I shall not forget, for it is well that I remember; and with it I have so much in memory of you that is sweet, that I take it all together. Now, you must all be going soon. Breakfast is ready, and we must all eat that we may be strong."

Breakfast was a strange meal to us all. We tried to be cheerful and encourage each other, and Mina was the brightest and most cheerful of us. When it was over, Van Helsing stood up and said:—

"Now, my dear friends, we go forth to our terrible enterprise. Are we all armed, as we were on that night when first we visited our enemy's lair; armed against ghostly as well as carnal attack?" We all assured him. "Then it is well. Now, Madam Mina, you are in any case *quite* safe here until the sunset; and before then we shall return—if—— We shall return! But before we go let me see you armed against personal attack. I have myself, since you came down, prepared your chamber by the placing of things of which we know, so that He may not enter. Now let me guard yourself. On your forehead I touch this piece of Sacred Wafer in the name of the Father, the Son, and——"

There was a fearful scream which almost froze our hearts to hear. As he had placed the Wafer on Mina's forehead, it had seared it—had burned into the flesh as though it had been a piece of white-hot metal. My poor darling's brain had told her the significance of the fact as quickly as her nerves received the pain of it; and the two so overwhelmed her that her overwrought nature had its voice in that dreadful scream. But the words to her thought came quickly; the echo of the scream had not ceased to ring on the air when there came the reaction, and she sank on her knees on the floor in an agony of abasement. Pulling her beautiful hair over her face, as the leper of old his mantle, she wailed out:—

"Unclean! Unclean! Even the Almighty shuns my polluted flesh! I must bear this mark of shame upon my forehead until the Judgment Day." They all paused. I had thrown myself beside her in an agony of helpless grief, and putting my arms around held her tight. For a few minutes our sorrowful hearts beat together, whilst the friends around us turned away their eyes that ran tears silently. Then Van Helsing turned and said gravely; so gravely that I could not help feeling that he was in some way inspired, and was stating things outside himself:—

"It may be that you may have to bear that mark till God himself see fit, as He most surely shall, on the Judgment Day, to redress all wrongs of the earth and of His children that He has placed thereon. And oh, Madam Mina, my dear, my dear, may we who love you be there to see, when that red scar, the sign of God's knowledge of what has been, shall pass away, and leave your forehead as pure as the heart we know. For so surely as we live, that scar shall pass away when God sees right to lift the burden that is hard upon us. Till then we bear our Cross, as His Son did in obedience to His Will. It may be that we are chosen instruments of His good pleasure, and that we ascend to His bidding as that other through stripes and shame; through tears and blood; through doubts and fears, and all that makes the difference between God and man."

There was hope in his words, and comfort; and they made for resignation. Mina and I both felt so, and simultaneously we each took one of the old man's hands and bent over and kissed it. Then without a word we all knelt down together, and, all holding hands, swore to be true to each other. We men pledged ourselves to raise the veil of sorrow from the head of her whom, each in his own way, we loved; and we prayed for help and guidance in the terrible task which lay before us.

It was then time to start. So I said farewell to Mina, a parting which neither of us shall forget to our dying day; and we set out.

To one thing I have made up my mind: if we find out that Mina must be a vampire in the end, then she shall not go into that unknown and terrible land alone. I suppose it is thus that in old times one vampire meant many; just as their hideous bodies could only rest in sacred earth, so the holiest love was the recruiting sergeant for their ghastly ranks.

We entered Carfax without trouble and found all things the same as on the first occasion. It was hard to believe that amongst so prosaic surroundings of neglect and dust and decay there was any ground for such fear as already we knew. Had not our minds been made up, and had there not been terrible memories to spur us on, we could hardly have proceeded with our task. We found no papers, or any sign of use in the house; and in the old chapel the great boxes looked just as we had seen them last. Dr. Van Helsing said to us solemnly as we stood before them:—

"And now, my friends, we have a duty here to do. We must sterilise this earth, so sacred of holy memories, that he has brought from a far distant land for such fell use. He has chosen this earth because it has been holy. Thus we defeat him with his own weapon, for we make it more holy still. It was sanctified to such use of man, now we sanctify it to God." As he spoke he took from his bag a screwdriver and a wrench, and very soon the top of one of the cases was thrown open. The earth smelled musty and close; but we did not somehow seem to mind, for our attention was concentrated on the Professor. Taking from his box a piece of the Sacred Wafer he laid it reverently on the earth, and then shutting down the lid began to screw it home, we aiding him as he worked.

One by one we treated in the same way each of the great boxes, and left them as we had found them to all appearance; but in each was a portion of the Host.

When we closed the door behind us, the Professor said solemnly:—

"So much is already done. If it may be that with all the others we can be so successful, then the sunset of this evening may shine on Madam Mina's forehead all white as ivory and with no stain!"

As we passed across the lawn on our way to the station to catch our train we could see the front of the asylum. I looked eagerly, and in the window of my own room saw Mina. I waved my hand to her, and nodded to tell that our work there was successfully accomplished. She nodded in reply to show that she understood. The last I saw, she was waving her hand in farewell. It was with a heavy heart that we sought the station and just caught the train, which was steaming in as we reached the platform.

I have written this in the train.

Piccadilly, 12:30 o'clock.—Just before we reached Fenchurch Street Lord Godalming said to me:—

"Quincey and I will find a locksmith. You had better not come with us in case there should be any difficulty; for under the circumstances it wouldn't seem so bad for us to break into an empty house. But you are a solicitor and the Incorporated Law Society might tell you that you should have known better." I demurred as to my not sharing any danger even of odium, but he went on: "Besides, it will attract less attention if there are not too many of us. My title will make it all right with the locksmith, and with any policeman that may come along. You had better go with Jack and the Professor and stay in the Green Park, somewhere in sight of the house; and when you see the door opened and the smith has gone away, do you all come across. We shall be on the lookout for you, and shall let you in."

"The advice is good!" said Van Helsing, so we said no more. Godalming and Morris hurried off in a cab, we following in another. At the corner of Arlington Street our contingent got out and strolled into the Green Park. My heart beat as I saw the house on which so much of our hope was centred, looming up grim and silent in its deserted condition amongst its more lively and spruce-looking neighbours. We sat down on a bench within good view, and began to smoke cigars so as to attract as little attention as possible. The minutes seemed to pass with leaden feet as we waited for the coming of the others.

At length we saw a four-wheeler drive up. Out of it, in leisurely fashion, got Lord Godalming and Morris; and down from the box descended a thick-set working man with his rush-woven basket of tools. Morris paid the cabman, who touched his hat and drove away. Together the two ascended the steps, and Lord Godalming pointed out what he wanted done. The workman took off his coat leisurely and hung it on one of the spikes of the rail, saying something to a policeman who just then sauntered along. The policeman nodded acquiescence, and the man kneeling down placed his bag beside him. After searching through it, he took out a selection of tools which he produced to lay beside him in orderly fashion. Then he stood up, looked into the keyhole, blew into it, and turning to his employers, made some remark. Lord Godalming smiled, and the man lifted a good-sized bunch of keys; selecting one of them, he began to probe the lock, as if feeling his way with it. After fumbling about for a bit he tried a second, and then a third. All at once the door opened under a slight push from him, and he and the two others entered the hall. We sat still; my own cigar burnt furiously, but Van Helsing's went cold altogether. We waited patiently as we saw the workman come out and bring in his bag. Then he held the door partly open, steadying it with his knees, whilst he fitted a key to the lock. This he finally handed to Lord Godalming, who took out his purse and gave him something. The man touched his hat, took his bag, put on his coat and departed; not a soul took the slightest notice of the whole transaction.

When the man had fairly gone, we three crossed the street and knocked at the door. It was immediately opened by Quincey Morris, beside whom stood Lord Godalming lighting a cigar.

"The place smells so vilely," said the latter as we came in. It did indeed smell vilely—like the old chapel at Carfax—and with our previous experience it was plain to us that the Count had been using the place pretty freely. We moved to explore the house, all keeping together in case of attack; for we knew we had a strong and wily enemy to deal with, and as yet we did not know whether the Count might not be in the house. In the dining-room, which lay at the back of the hall, we found eight boxes of earth. Eight boxes only out of the nine, which we sought! Our work was not over, and would never be until we should have found the missing box. First we opened the shutters of the window which looked out across a narrow stone-flagged yard at the blank face of a stable, pointed to look like the front of a miniature house. There were no windows in it, so we were not afraid of being over-looked. We did not lose any time in examining the chests. With the tools which we had brought with us we opened them, one by one, and treated them as we had treated those others in the old chapel. It was evident to us that the Count was not at present in the house, and we proceeded to search for any of his effects.

After a cursory glance at the rest of the rooms, from basement to attic, we came to the conclusion that the dining-room contained any effects which might belong to the Count; and so we proceeded to minutely examine them. They lay in a sort of orderly disorder on the great dining-room table. There were title deeds of the Piccadilly house in a great bundle; deeds of the purchase of the houses at Mile End and Bermondsey; note-paper, envelopes, and pens and ink. All were covered up in thin wrapping paper to keep them from the dust. There were also a clothes brush, a brush and comb, and a jug and basin—the latter containing dirty water which was reddened as if with blood. Last of all was a little heap of keys of all sorts and sizes, probably those belonging to the other houses. When we had examined this last find, Lord Godalming and Quincey Morris taking accurate notes of the various addresses of the houses in the East and the South, took with them the keys in a great bunch, and set out to destroy the boxes in these places. The rest of us are, with what patience we can, waiting their return—or the coming of the Count.

CHAPTER XXIII

DR. SEWARD'S DIARY

3 October.—The time seemed terrible long whilst we were waiting for the coming of Godalming and Quincey Morris. The Professor tried to keep our minds active by using them all the time. I could see his beneficent purpose, by the side glances which he threw from time to time at Harker. The poor fellow is overwhelmed in a misery that is appalling to see. Last night he was a frank, happy-looking man, with strong, youthful face, full of energy, and with dark brown hair. To-day he is a drawn, haggard old man, whose white hair matches well with the hollow burning eyes and grief-written lines of his face. His energy is still intact; in fact, he is like a living flame. This may yet be his salvation, for, if all go well, it will tide him over the despairing period; he will then, in a kind of way, wake again to the realities of life. Poor fellow, I thought my own trouble was bad enough, but his——! The Professor knows this well enough, and is doing his best to keep his mind active. What he has been saying was, under the circumstances, of absorbing interest. So well as I can remember, here it is:—

"I have studied, over and over again since they came into my hands, all the papers relating to this monster; and the more I have studied, the greater seems the necessity to utterly stamp him out. All through there are signs of his advance; not only of his power, but of his knowledge of it. As I learned from the researches of my friend Arminus of Buda-Pesth, he was in life a most wonderful man. Soldier, statesman, and alchemist—which latter was the highest development of the science-knowledge of his time. He had a mighty brain, a learning beyond compare, and a heart that knew no fear and no remorse. He dared even to attend the Scholomance, and there was no branch of knowledge of his time that he did not essay. Well, in him the brain powers survived the physical death; though it would seem that memory was not all complete. In some faculties of mind he has been, and is, only a child; but he is growing, and some things that were childish at the first are now of man's stature. He is experimenting, and doing it well; and if it had not been that we have crossed his path he would be yet—he may be yet if we fail—the father or furtherer of a new order of beings, whose road must lead through

Death, not Life."

Harker groaned and said, "And this is all arrayed against my darling! But how is he experimenting? The knowledge may help us to defeat him!"

"He has all along, since his coming, been trying his power, slowly but surely; that big child-brain of his is working. Well for us, it is, as yet, a child-brain; for had he dared, at the first, to attempt certain things he would long ago have been beyond our power. However, he means to succeed, and a man who has centuries before him can afford to wait and to go slow. *Festina lente* may well be his motto."

"I fail to understand," said Harker wearily. "Oh, do be more plain to me! Perhaps grief and trouble are dulling my brain."

The Professor laid his hand tenderly on his shoulder as he spoke:—

"Ah, my child, I will be plain. Do you not see how, of late, this monster has been creeping into knowledge experimentally. How he has been making use of the zoöphagous patient to effect his entry into friend John's home; for your Vampire, though in all afterwards he can come when and how he will, must at the first make entry only when asked thereto by an inmate. But these are not his most important experiments. Do we not see how at the first all these so great boxes were moved by others. He knew not then but that must be so. But all the time that so great child-brain of his was growing, and he began to consider whether he might not himself move the box. So he began to help; and then, when he found that this be all-right, he try to move them all alone. And so he progress, and he scatter these graves of him; and none but he know where they are hidden. He may have intend to bury them deep in the ground. So that he only use them in the night, or at such time as he can change his form, they do him equal well; and none may know these are his hiding-place! But, my child, do not despair; this knowledge come to him just too late! Already all of his lairs but one be sterilise as for him; and before the sunset this shall be so. Then he have no place where he can move and hide. I delayed this morning that so we might be sure. Is there not more at stake for us than for him? Then why we not be even more careful than him? By my clock it is one hour and already, if all be well, friend Arthur and Quincey are on their way to us. To-day is our day, and we must go sure, if slow, and lose no chance. See! there are five of us when those absent ones return."

Whilst he was speaking we were startled by a knock at the hall door, the double postman's knock of the telegraph boy. We all moved out to the hall with one impulse, and Van Helsing, holding up his hand to us to keep silence, stepped to the door and opened it.

The boy handed in a despatch. The Professor closed the door again, and, after looking at the direction, opened it and read aloud.

> "Look out for D. He has just now, 12:45, come from Carfax hurriedly and hastened towards the South. He seems to be going the round and may want to see you: MINA."

There was a pause, broken by Jonathan Harker's voice:—

"Now, God be thanked, we shall soon meet!" Van Helsing turned to him quickly and said:—

"God will act in His own way and time. Do not fear, and do not rejoice as yet; for what we wish for at the moment may be our undoings."

"I care for nothing now," he answered hotly, "except to wipe out this brute from the face of creation. I would sell my soul to do it!"

"Oh, hush, hush, my child!" said Van Helsing. "God does not purchase souls in this wise; and the Devil, though he may purchase, does not keep faith. But God is merciful and just, and knows your pain and your devotion to that dear Madam Mina. Think you, how her pain would be doubled, did she but hear your wild words. Do not fear any of us, we are all devoted to this cause, and to-day shall see the end. The time is coming for action; to-day this Vampire is limit to the powers of man, and till sunset he may not change. It will take him time to arrive here—see, it is twenty minutes past one—and there are yet some times before he can hither come, be he never so quick. What we must hope for is that my Lord Arthur and Quincey arrive first."

About half an hour after we had received Mrs. Harker's telegram, there came a quiet, resolute knock at the hall door. It was just an ordinary knock, such as is given hourly by thousands of gentlemen, but it made the Professor's heart and mine beat loudly. We looked at each other, and together moved out into the hall; we each held ready to use our various armaments—the spiritual in the left hand, the mortal in the right. Van Helsing pulled back the latch, and, holding the door half open, stood back, having both hands ready for action. The gladness of our hearts must have shown upon our faces when on the step, close to the door, we saw Lord Godalming and Quincey Morris. They came quickly in and closed the door behind them, the former saying, as they moved along the hall:—

"It is all right. We found both places; six boxes in each and we destroyed them all!"

"Destroyed?" asked the Professor.

"For him!" We were silent for a minute, and then Quincey said:—

"There's nothing to do but to wait here. If, however, he doesn't turn up by five o'clock, we must start off; for it won't do to leave Mrs. Harker alone after sunset."

"He will be here before long now," said Van Helsing, who had been consulting his pocket-book. "*Nota bene*, in Madam's telegram he went south from Carfax, that means he went to cross the river, and he could only do so at slack of tide, which should be something before one o'clock. That he went south has a meaning for us. He is as yet only suspicious; and he went from Carfax first to the place where he would suspect interference least. You must have been at Bermondsey only a short time before him. That he is not here already shows that he went to Mile End next. This took him some time; for he would then have to be carried over the river in some way. Believe me, my friends, we shall not have long to wait now. We should have ready some plan of attack, so that we may throw away no chance. Hush, there is no time now. Have all your arms! Be ready!" He held up a warning hand as he spoke, for we all could hear a key softly inserted in the lock of the hall door.

I could not but admire, even at such a moment, the way in which a dominant spirit asserted itself. In all our hunting parties and adventures in different parts of the world, Quincey Morris had always been the one to arrange the plan of action, and Arthur and I had been accustomed to obey him implicitly. Now, the old habit seemed to be renewed instinctively. With a swift glance around the room, he at once laid out our plan of attack, and, without speaking a word, with a gesture, placed us each in position. Van Helsing, Harker, and I were just behind the door, so that when it was opened the Professor could guard it whilst we two stepped between the incomer and the door. Godalming behind and Quincey in front stood just out of sight ready to move in front of the window. We waited in a suspense that made the seconds pass with nightmare slowness. The slow, careful steps came along the hall; the Count was evidently prepared for some surprise—at least he feared it.

Suddenly with a single bound he leaped into the room, winning a way past us before any of us could raise a hand to stay him. There was something so panther-like in the movement—something so unhuman, that it seemed to sober us all from the shock of his coming. The first to act was Harker, who, with a quick movement, threw himself before the door leading into the room in the front of the house. As the Count saw us, a horrible sort of snarl passed over his face, showing the eye-teeth long and pointed; but the evil smile as quickly passed into a cold stare of lion-like disdain. His expression again changed as, with a single impulse, we all advanced upon him. It was a pity that we had not some better organised plan of attack, for even at the moment I wondered what we were to do. I did not myself know whether our lethal weapons would avail us anything. Harker evidently meant to try the matter, for he had ready his great Kukri knife and made a fierce and sudden cut at him. The blow was a powerful one; only the diabolical quickness of the Count's leap back saved him. A second less and the trenchant blade had shorne through his heart. As it was, the point just cut the cloth of his coat, making a wide gap whence a bundle of bank-notes and a stream of gold fell out. The expression of the Count's face was so hellish, that for a moment I feared for Harker, though I saw him throw the terrible knife aloft again for another stroke. Instinctively I moved forward with a protective impulse, holding the Crucifix and Wafer in my left hand. I felt a mighty power fly along my arm; and it was without surprise that I saw the monster cower back before a similar movement made spontaneously by each one of us. It would be impossible to describe the expression of hate and baffled malignity—of anger and hellish rage—which came over the Count's face. His waxen hue became greenish-yellow by the contrast of his burning eyes, and the red scar on the forehead showed on the pallid skin like a palpitating wound. The next instant, with a sinuous dive he swept under Harker's arm, ere his blow could fall, and, grasping a handful of the money from the floor, dashed across the room, threw himself at the window. Amid the crash and glitter of the falling glass, he tumbled into the flagged area below. Through the sound of the shivering glass I could hear the "ting" of the gold, as some of the sovereigns fell on the flagging.

We ran over and saw him spring unhurt from the ground. He, rushing up the steps, crossed the flagged yard, and pushed open the stable door. There he turned and spoke to us:—

"You think to baffle me, you—with your pale faces all in a row, like sheep in a butcher's. You shall be sorry yet, each one of you! You think you have left me without a place to rest; but I have more. My revenge is just begun! I spread it over centuries, and time is on my side. Your girls that you all love are mine already; and through them you and others shall yet be mine— my creatures, to do my bidding and to be my jackals when I want to feed. Bah!" With a contemptuous sneer, he passed quickly through the door, and we heard the rusty bolt creak as he fastened it behind him. A door beyond opened and shut. The first of us to speak was the Professor, as, realising the difficulty of following him through the stable, we moved toward the hall.

"We have learnt something—much! Notwithstanding his brave words, he fears us; he fear time, he fear want! For if not, why he hurry so? His very tone betray him, or my ears deceive. Why take that money? You follow quick. You are hunters of wild beast, and understand it so. For me, I make sure that nothing here may be of use to him, if so that he return." As he spoke he put the money remaining into his pocket; took the title-deeds in the bundle as Harker had left them, and swept the remaining things into the open fireplace, where he set fire to them with a match.

Godalming and Morris had rushed out into the yard, and Harker had lowered himself from the window to follow the Count. He had, however, bolted the stable door; and by the time they had forced it open there was no sign of him. Van Helsing and I tried to make inquiry at the back of the house; but the mews was deserted and no one had seen him depart.

It was now late in the afternoon, and sunset was not far off. We had to recognise that our game was up; with heavy hearts we agreed with the Professor when he said:—

"Let us go back to Madam Mina—poor, poor dear Madam Mina. All we can do just now is done; and we can there, at least, protect her. But we need not despair. There is but one more earth-box, and we must try to find it; when that is done all may yet be well." I could see that he spoke as bravely as he could to comfort Harker. The poor fellow was quite broken down; now and again he gave a low groan which he could not suppress—he was thinking of his wife.

With sad hearts we came back to my house, where we found Mrs. Harker waiting us, with an appearance of cheerfulness which did honour to her bravery and unselfishness. When she saw our faces, her own became as pale as death: for a second or two her eyes were closed as if she were in secret prayer; and then she said cheerfully:—

"I can never thank you all enough. Oh, my poor darling!" As she spoke, she took her husband's grey head in her hands and kissed it—"Lay your poor head here and rest it. All will yet be well, dear! God will protect us if He so will it in His good intent." The poor fellow groaned. There was no place for words in his sublime misery.

We had a sort of perfunctory supper together, and I think it cheered us all up somewhat. It was, perhaps, the mere animal heat of food to hungry people—for none of us had eaten anything since breakfast—or the sense of companionship may have helped us; but anyhow we were all less miserable, and saw the morrow as not altogether without hope. True to our promise, we told Mrs. Harker everything which had passed; and although she grew snowy white at times when danger had seemed to threaten her husband, and red at others when his devotion to her was manifested, she listened bravely and with calmness. When we came to the part where Harker had rushed at the Count so recklessly, she clung to her husband's arm, and held it tight as though her clinging could protect him from any harm that might come.

She said nothing, however, till the narration was all done, and matters had been brought right up to the present time. Then without letting go her husband's hand she stood up amongst us and spoke. Oh, that I could give any idea of the scene; of that sweet, sweet, good, good woman in all the radiant beauty of her youth and animation, with the red scar on her forehead, of which she was conscious, and which we saw with grinding of our teeth—remembering whence and how it came; her loving kindness against our grim hate; her tender faith against all our fears and doubting; and we, knowing that so far as symbols went, she with all her goodness and purity and faith, was outcast from God.

"Jonathan," she said, and the word sounded like music on her lips it was so full of love and tenderness, "Jonathan dear, and you all my true, true friends, I want you to bear something in mind through all this dreadful time. I know that you must fight—that you must destroy even as you destroyed the false Lucy so that the true Lucy might live hereafter; but it is not a work of hate. That poor soul who has wrought all this misery is the saddest case of all. Just think what will be his joy when he, too, is destroyed in his worser part that his better part may have spiritual immortality. You must be pitiful to him, too, though it may not hold your hands from his destruction."

As she spoke I could see her husband's face darken and draw together, as though the passion in him were shrivelling his being to its core. Instinctively the clasp on his wife's hand grew closer, till his knuckles looked white. She did not flinch from the pain which I knew she must have suffered, but looked at him with eyes that were more appealing than ever. As she stopped speaking he leaped to his feet, almost tearing his hand from hers as he spoke:—

"May God give him into my hand just for long enough to destroy that earthly life of him which we are aiming at. If beyond it I could send his soul for ever and ever to burning hell I would do it!"

"Oh, hush! oh, hush! in the name of the good God. Don't say such things, Jonathan, my husband; or you will crush me with fear and horror. Just think, my dear—I have been thinking all this long, long day of it—that . . . perhaps . . . some day . . . I, too, may need such pity; and that some other like you—and with equal cause for anger—may deny it to me! Oh, my husband! my husband, indeed I would have spared you such a thought had there been another way; but I pray that God may not have treasured your wild words, except as the heart-broken wail of a very loving and sorely stricken man. Oh, God, let these poor white hairs go in evidence of what he has suffered, who all his life has done no wrong, and on whom so many sorrows have come."

We men were all in tears now. There was no resisting them, and we wept openly. She wept, too, to see that her sweeter counsels had prevailed. Her husband flung himself on his knees beside her, and putting his arms round her, hid his face in the folds of her dress. Van Helsing beckoned to us and we stole out of the room, leaving the two loving hearts alone with their God.

Before they retired the Professor fixed up the room against any coming of the Vampire, and assured Mrs. Harker that she might rest in peace. She tried to school herself to the belief, and, manifestly for her husband's sake, tried to seem content. It was a brave struggle; and was, I think and believe, not without its reward. Van Helsing had placed at hand a bell which either of them was to sound in case of any emergency. When they had retired, Quincey, Godalming, and I arranged that we should sit up, dividing the night between us, and watch over the safety of the poor stricken lady. The first watch falls to Quincey, so the rest of us shall be off to bed as soon as we can. Godalming has already turned in, for his is the second watch. Now that my work is done I, too, shall go to bed.

JONATHAN HARKER'S JOURNAL.

3-4 October, close to midnight.—I thought yesterday would never end. There was over me a yearning for sleep, in some sort of blind belief that to wake would be to find things changed, and that any change must now be for the better. Before we parted, we discussed what our next step was to be, but we could arrive at no result. All we knew was that one earth-box remained, and that the Count alone knew where it was. If he chooses to lie hidden, he may baffle us for years; and in the meantime!—the thought is too horrible, I dare not think of it even now. This I know: that if ever there was a woman who was all perfection, that one is my poor wronged darling. I love her a thousand times more for her sweet pity of last night, a pity that made my own hate of the monster seem despicable. Surely God will not permit the world to be the poorer by the loss of such a creature. This is hope to me. We are all drifting reefwards now, and faith is our only anchor. Thank God! Mina is sleeping, and sleeping without dreams. I fear what her dreams might be like, with such terrible memories to ground them in. She has not been so calm, within my seeing, since the sunset. Then, for a while, there came over her face a repose which was like spring after the blasts of March. I thought at the time that it was the softness of the red sunset on her face, but somehow now I think it has a deeper meaning. I am not sleepy myself, though I am weary—weary to death. However, I must try to sleep; for there is to-morrow to think of, and there is no rest for me until . . . .

Later.—I must have fallen asleep, for I was awaked by Mina, who was sitting up in bed, with a startled look on her face. I could see easily, for we did not leave the room in darkness; she had placed a warning hand over my mouth, and now she whispered in my ear:—

"Hush! there is someone in the corridor!" I got up softly, and crossing the room, gently opened the door.

Just outside, stretched on a mattress, lay Mr. Morris, wide awake. He raised a warning hand for silence as he whispered to me:—

"Hush! go back to bed; it is all right. One of us will be here all night. We don't mean to take any chances!"

His look and gesture forbade discussion, so I came back and told Mina. She sighed and positively a shadow of a smile stole over her poor, pale face as she put her arms round me and said softly:—

"Oh, thank God for good brave men!" With a sigh she sank back again to sleep. I write this now as I am not sleepy, though I must try again.

4 October, morning.—Once again during the night I was wakened by Mina. This time we had all had a good sleep, for the grey of the coming dawn was making the windows into sharp oblongs, and the gas flame was like a speck rather than a disc of light. She said to me hurriedly:—

"Go, call the Professor. I want to see him at once."

"Why?" I asked.

"I have an idea. I suppose it must have come in the night, and matured without my knowing it. He must hypnotise me before the dawn, and then I shall be able to speak. Go quick, dearest; the time is getting close." I went to the door. Dr. Seward was resting on the mattress, and, seeing me, he sprang to his feet.

"Is anything wrong?" he asked, in alarm.

"No," I replied; "but Mina wants to see Dr. Van Helsing at once."

"I will go," he said, and hurried into the Professor's room.

In two or three minutes later Van Helsing was in the room in his dressing-gown, and Mr. Morris and Lord Godalming were with Dr. Seward at the door asking questions. When the Professor saw Mina smile—a positive smile ousted the anxiety of his face; he rubbed his hands as he said:—

"Oh, my dear Madam Mina, this is indeed a change. See! friend Jonathan, we have got our dear Madam Mina, as of old, back to us to-day!" Then turning to her, he said, cheerfully: "And what am I do for you? For at this hour you do not want me for nothings."

"I want you to hypnotise me!" she said. "Do it before the dawn, for I feel that then I can speak, and speak freely. Be quick, for the time is short!" Without a word he motioned her to sit up in bed.

Looking fixedly at her, he commenced to make passes in front of her, from over the top of her head downward, with each hand in turn. Mina gazed at him fixedly for a few minutes, during which my own heart beat like a trip hammer, for I felt that some crisis was at hand. Gradually her eyes closed, and she sat, stock still; only by the gentle heaving of her bosom could one know that she was alive. The Professor made a few more passes and then stopped, and I could see that his forehead was covered with great beads of perspiration. Mina opened her eyes; but she did not seem the same woman. There was a far-away look in her eyes, and her voice had a sad dreaminess which was new to me. Raising his hand to impose silence, the Professor motioned to me to bring the others in. They came on tip-toe, closing the door behind them, and stood at the foot of the bed, looking on. Mina appeared not to see them. The stillness was broken by Van Helsing's voice speaking in a low level tone which would not break the current of her thoughts:—

"Where are you?" The answer came in a neutral way:—

"I do not know. Sleep has no place it can call its own." For several minutes there was silence. Mina sat rigid, and the Professor stood staring at her fixedly; the rest of us hardly dared to breathe. The room was growing lighter; without taking his eyes from Mina's face, Dr. Van Helsing motioned me to pull up the blind. I did so, and the day seemed just upon us. A red streak shot up, and a rosy light seemed to diffuse itself through the room. On the instant the Professor spoke again:—

"Where are you now?" The answer came dreamily, but with intention; it were as though she were interpreting something. I have heard her use the same tone when reading her shorthand notes.

"I do not know. It is all strange to me!"

"What do you see?"

"I can see nothing; it is all dark."

"What do you hear?" I could detect the strain in the Professor's patient voice.

"The lapping of water. It is gurgling by, and little waves leap. I can hear them on the outside."

"Then you are on a ship?" We all looked at each other, trying to glean something each from the other. We were afraid to think. The answer came quick:—

"Oh, yes!"

"What else do you hear?"

"The sound of men stamping overhead as they run about. There is the creaking of a chain, and the loud tinkle as the check of the capstan falls into the rachet."

"What are you doing?"

"I am still—oh, so still. It is like death!" The voice faded away into a deep breath as of one sleeping, and the open eyes closed again.

By this time the sun had risen, and we were all in the full light of day. Dr. Van Helsing placed his hands on Mina's shoulders, and laid her head down softly on her pillow. She lay like a sleeping child for a few moments, and then, with a long sigh, awoke and stared in wonder to see us all around her. "Have I been talking in my sleep?" was all she said. She seemed, however, to know the situation without telling, though she was eager to know what she had told. The Professor repeated the conversation, and she said:—

"Then there is not a moment to lose: it may not be yet too late!" Mr. Morris and Lord Godalming started for the door but the Professor's calm voice called them back:—

"Stay, my friends. That ship, wherever it was, was weighing anchor whilst she spoke. There are many ships weighing anchor at the moment in your so great Port of London. Which of them is it that you seek? God be thanked that we have once again a clue, though whither it may lead us we know not. We have been blind somewhat; blind after the manner of men, since when we can look back we see what we might have seen looking forward if we had been able to see what we might have seen! Alas, but that sentence is a puddle; is it not? We can know now what was in the Count's mind, when he seize that money, though Jonathan's so fierce knife put him in the danger that even he dread. He meant escape. Hear me, ESCAPE! He saw that with but one earth-box left, and a pack of men following like dogs after a fox, this London was no place for him. He have take his last earth-box on board a ship, and he leave the land. He think to escape, but no! we follow him. Tally Ho! as friend Arthur would say when he put on his red frock! Our old fox is wily; oh! so wily, and we must follow with wile. I, too, am wily and I think his mind in a little while. In meantime we may rest and in peace, for there are waters between us which he do not want to pass, and which he could not if he would—unless the ship were to touch the land, and then only at full or slack tide. See, and the sun is just rose, and all day to sunset is to us. Let us take bath, and dress, and have breakfast which we all need, and which we can eat comfortably since he be not in the same land with us." Mina looked at him appealingly as she asked:—

"But why need we seek him further, when he is gone away from us?" He took her hand and patted it as he replied:—

"Ask me nothings as yet. When we have breakfast, then I answer all questions." He would say no more, and we separated to dress.

After breakfast Mina repeated her question. He looked at her gravely for a minute and then said sorrowfully:—

"Because my dear, dear Madam Mina, now more than ever must we find him even if we have to follow him to the jaws of Hell!" She grew paler as she asked faintly:—

"Why?"

"Because," he answered solemnly, "he can live for centuries, and you are but mortal woman. Time is now to be dreaded—since once he put that mark upon your throat."

I was just in time to catch her as she fell forward in a faint.

CHAPTER XXIV

DR. SEWARD'S
PHONOGRAPH DIARY,
SPOKEN BY VAN HELSING

THIS to Jonathan Harker.

You are to stay with your dear Madam Mina. We shall go to make our search—if I can call it so, for it is not search but knowing, and we seek confirmation only. But do you stay and take care of her to-day. This is your best and most holiest office. This day nothing can find him here. Let me tell you that so you will know what we four know already, for I have tell them. He, our enemy, have gone away; he have gone back to his Castle in Transylvania. I know it so well, as if a great hand of fire wrote it on the wall. He have prepare for this in some way, and that last earth-box was ready to ship somewheres. For this he took the money; for this he hurry at the last, lest we catch him before the sun go down. It was his last hope, save that he might hide in the tomb that he think poor Miss Lucy, being as he thought like him, keep open to him. But there was not of time. When that fail he make straight for his last resource—his last earth-work I might say did I wish *double entente*. He is clever, oh, so clever! he know that his game here was finish; and so he decide he go back home. He find ship going by the route he came, and he go in it. We go off now to find what ship, and whither bound; when we have discover that, we come back and tell you all. Then we will comfort you and poor dear Madam Mina with new hope. For it will be hope when you think it over: that all is not lost. This very creature that we pursue, he take hundreds of years to get so far as London; and yet in one day, when we know of the disposal of him we drive him out. He is finite, though he is powerful to do much harm and suffers not as we do. But we are strong, each in our purpose; and we are all more strong together. Take heart afresh, dear husband of Madam Mina. This battle is but begun, and in the end we shall win—so sure as that God sits on high to watch over His children. Therefore be of much comfort till we return.

VAN HELSING.

JONATHAN HARKER'S JOURNAL.

4 October.—When I read to Mina, Van Helsing's message in the phonograph, the poor girl brightened up considerably. Already the certainty that the Count is out of the country has given her comfort; and comfort is strength to her. For my own part, now that his horrible danger is not face to face with us, it seems almost impossible to believe in it. Even my own terrible experiences in Castle Dracula seem like a long-forgotten dream. Here in the crisp autumn air in the bright sunlight——

Alas! how can I disbelieve! In the midst of my thought my eye fell on the red scar on my poor darling's white forehead. Whilst that lasts, there can be no disbelief. And afterwards the very memory of it will keep faith crystal clear. Mina and I fear to be idle, so we have been over all the diaries again and again. Somehow, although the reality seems greater each time, the pain and the fear seem less. There is something of a guiding purpose manifest throughout, which is comforting. Mina says that perhaps we are the instruments of ultimate good. It may be! I shall try to think as she does. We have never spoken to each other yet of the future. It is better to wait till we see the Professor and the others after their investigations.

The day is running by more quickly than I ever thought a day could run for me again. It is now three o'clock.

MINA HARKER'S JOURNAL.

5 October, 5 p. m.—Our meeting for report. Present: Professor Van Helsing, Lord Godalming, Dr. Seward, Mr. Quincey Morris, Jonathan Harker, Mina Harker.

Dr. Van Helsing described what steps were taken during the day to discover on what boat and whither bound Count Dracula made his escape:—

"As I knew that he wanted to get back to Transylvania, I felt sure that he must go by the Danube mouth; or by somewhere in the Black Sea, since by that way he come. It was a dreary blank that was before us. *Omne ignotum pro magnifico*; and so with heavy hearts we start to find what ships leave for the Black Sea last night. He was in sailing ship, since Madam Mina tell of sails being set. These not so important as to go in your list of the shipping in the *Times*, and so we go, by suggestion of Lord Godalming, to your Lloyd's, where are note of all ships that sail, however so small. There we find that only one Black-Sea-bound ship go out with the tide. She is the *Czarina Catherine*, and she sail from Doolittle's Wharf for Varna, and thence on to other parts and up the Danube. 'Soh!' said I, 'this is the ship whereon is the Count.' So off we go to Doolittle's Wharf, and there we find a man in an office of wood so small that the man look bigger than the office. From him we inquire of the goings of the *Czarina Catherine*. He swear much, and he red face and loud of voice, but he good fellow all the same; and when Quincey give him something from his pocket which crackle as he roll it up, and put it in a so small bag which he have hid deep in his clothing, he still better fellow and humble servant to us. He come with us, and ask many men who are rough and hot; these be better fellows too when they have been no more thirsty. They say much of blood and bloom, and of others which I comprehend not, though I guess what they mean; but nevertheless they tell us all things which we want to know.

"They make known to us among them, how last afternoon at about five o'clock comes a man so hurry. A tall man, thin and pale, with high nose and teeth so white, and eyes that seem to be burning. That he be all in black, except that he have a hat of straw which suit not him or the time. That he scatter his money in making quick inquiry as to what ship sails for the Black Sea and for where. Some took him to the office and then to the ship, where he will not go aboard but halt at shore end of gang-plank, and ask that the captain come to him. The captain come, when told that he will be pay well; and though he swear much at the first he agree to term. Then the thin man go and some one tell him where horse and cart can be hired. He go there and soon he come again, himself driving cart on which a great box; this he himself lift down, though it take several to put it on truck for the ship. He give much talk to captain as to how and where his box is to be place; but the captain like it not and swear at him in many tongues, and tell him that if he like he can come and see where it shall be. But he say 'no'; that he come not yet, for that he have much to do. Whereupon the captain tell him that he had better be quick—with blood—for that his ship will leave the place—of blood—before the turn of the tide—with blood. Then the thin man smile and say that of course he must go when he think fit; but he will be surprise if he go quite so soon. The captain swear again, polyglot, and the thin man make him bow, and thank him, and say that he will so far intrude on his kindness as to come aboard before the sailing. Final the captain, more red than ever, and in more tongues tell him that he doesn't want no Frenchmen—with bloom upon them and also with blood—in his ship—with blood on her also. And so, after asking where there might be close at hand a ship where he might purchase ship forms, he departed.

"No one knew where he went 'or bloomin' well cared,' as they said, for they had something else to think of—well with blood again; for it soon became apparent to all that the *Czarina Catherine* would not sail as was expected. A thin mist began to creep up from the river, and it grew, and grew; till soon a dense fog enveloped the ship and all around her. The captain swore polyglot—very polyglot—polyglot with bloom and blood; but he could do nothing. The water rose and rose; and he began to fear that he would lose the tide altogether. He was in no friendly mood, when just at full tide, the thin man came up the gang-plank again and asked to see where his box had been stowed. Then the captain replied that he wished that he and his box—old and with much bloom and blood—were in hell. But the thin man did not be offend, and went down with the mate and saw where it was place, and came up and stood awhile on deck in fog. He must have come off by himself, for none notice him. Indeed they thought not of him; for soon the fog begin to melt away, and all was clear again. My friends of the thirst and the language that was of bloom and blood laughed, as they told how the captain's swears exceeded even his usual polyglot, and was more than ever full of picturesque, when on questioning other mariners who were on movement up and down on the river that hour, he found that few of them had seen any of fog at all, except where it lay round the wharf. However, the ship went out on the ebb tide; and was doubtless by morning far down the river mouth. She was by then, when they told us, well out to sea.

"And so, my dear Madam Mina, it is that we have to rest for a time, for our enemy is on the sea, with the fog at his command, on his way to the Danube mouth. To sail a ship takes time, go she never so quick; and when we start we go on land more quick, and we meet him there. Our best hope is to come on him when in the box between sunrise and sunset; for then he can make no struggle, and we may deal with him as we should. There are days for us, in which we can make ready our plan. We know all about where he go; for we have seen the owner of the ship, who have shown us invoices and all papers that can be. The box we seek is to be landed in Varna, and to be given to an agent, one Ristics who will there present his credentials; and so our merchant friend will have done his part. When he ask if there be any wrong, for that so, he can telegraph and have inquiry made at Varna, we say 'no'; for what is to be done is not for police or of the customs. It must be done by us alone and in our own way."

When Dr. Van Helsing had done speaking, I asked him if he were certain that the Count had remained on board the ship. He replied: "We have the best proof of that: your own evidence, when in the hypnotic trance this morning." I asked him again if it were really necessary that they should pursue the Count, for oh! I dread Jonathan leaving me, and I know that he would surely go if the others went. He answered in growing passion, at first quietly. As he went on, however, he grew more angry and more forceful, till in the end we could not but see wherein was at least some of that personal dominance which made him so long a master amongst men:—

"Yes, it is necessary—necessary—necessary! For your sake in the first, and then for the sake of humanity. This monster has done much harm already, in the narrow scope where he find himself, and in the short time when as yet he was only as a body groping his so small measure in darkness and not knowing. All this have I told these others; you, my dear Madam Mina, will learn it in the phonograph of my friend John, or in that of your husband. I have told them how the measure of leaving his own barren land—barren of peoples—and coming to a new land where life of man teems till they are like the multitude of standing corn, was the work of centuries. Were another of the Un-Dead, like him, to try to do what he has done, perhaps not all the centuries of the world that have been, or that will be, could aid him. With this one, all the forces of nature that are occult and deep and strong must have worked together in some wondrous way. The very place, where he have been alive, Un-Dead for all these centuries, is full of strangeness of the geologic and chemical world. There are deep caverns and fissures that reach none know whither. There have been volcanoes, some of whose openings still send out waters of strange properties, and gases that kill or make to vivify. Doubtless, there is something magnetic or electric in some of these combinations of occult forces which work for physical life in strange way; and in himself were from the first some great qualities. In a hard and warlike time he was celebrate that he have more iron nerve, more subtle brain, more braver heart, than any man. In him some vital principle have in strange way found their utmost; and as his body keep strong and grow and thrive, so his brain grow too. All this without that diabolic aid which is surely to him; for it have to yield to the powers that come from, and are, symbolic of good. And now this is what he is to us. He have infect you—oh, forgive me, my dear, that I must say such; but it is for good of you that I speak. He infect you in such wise, that even if he do no more, you have only to live—to live in your own old, sweet way; and so in time, death, which is of man's common lot and with God's sanction, shall make you like to him. This must not be! We have sworn together that it must not. Thus are we ministers of God's own wish: that the world, and men for whom His Son die, will not be given over to monsters, whose very existence would defame Him. He have allowed us to redeem one soul already, and we go out as the old knights of the Cross to redeem more. Like them we shall travel towards the sunrise; and like them, if we fall, we fall in good cause." He paused and I said:—

"But will not the Count take his rebuff wisely? Since he has been driven from England, will he not avoid it, as a tiger does the village from which he has been hunted?"

"Aha!" he said, "your simile of the tiger good, for me, and I shall adopt him. Your man-eater, as they of India call the tiger who has once tasted blood of the human, care no more for the other prey, but prowl unceasing till he get him. This that we hunt from our village is a tiger, too, a man-eater, and he never cease to prowl. Nay, in himself he is not one to retire and stay afar. In his life, his living life, he go over the Turkey frontier and attack his enemy on his own ground; he be beaten back, but did he stay? No! He come again, and again, and again. Look at his persistence and endurance. With the child-brain that was to him he have long since conceive the idea of coming to a great city. What does he do? He find out the place of all the world most of promise for him. Then he deliberately set himself down to prepare for the task. He find in patience just how is his strength, and what are his powers. He study new tongues. He learn new social life; new environment of old ways, the politic, the law, the finance, the science, the habit of a new land and a new people who have come to be since he was. His glimpse that he have had, whet his appetite only and enkeen his desire. Nay, it help him to grow as to his brain; for it all prove to him how right he was at the first in his surmises. He have done this alone; all alone! from a ruin tomb in a forgotten land. What more may he not do when the greater world of thought is open to him. He that can smile at death, as we know him; who can flourish in the midst of diseases that kill off whole peoples. Oh, if such an one was to come from God, and not the Devil, what a force for good might he not be in this old world of ours. But we are pledged to set the world free. Our toil must be in silence, and our efforts all in secret; for in this enlightened age, when men believe not even what they see, the doubting of wise men would be his greatest strength. It would be at once his sheath and his armour, and his weapons to destroy us, his enemies, who are willing to peril even our own souls for the safety of one we love—for the good of mankind, and for the honour and glory of God."

After a general discussion it was determined that for to-night nothing be definitely settled; that we should all sleep on the facts, and try to think out the proper conclusions. To-morrow, at breakfast, we are to meet again, and, after making our conclusions known to one another, we shall decide on some definite cause of action.

* * * * *

I feel a wonderful peace and rest to-night. It is as if some haunting presence were removed from me. Perhaps . . .

My surmise was not finished, could not be; for I caught sight in the mirror of the red mark upon my forehead; and I knew that I was still unclean.

DR. SEWARD'S DIARY.

5 October.—We all rose early, and I think that sleep did much for each and all of us. When we met at early breakfast there was more general cheerfulness than any of us had ever expected to experience again.

It is really wonderful how much resilience there is in human nature. Let any obstructing cause, no matter what, be removed in any way—even by death—and we fly back to first principles of hope and enjoyment. More than once as we sat around the table, my eyes opened in wonder whether the whole of the past days had not been a dream. It was only when I caught sight of the red blotch on Mrs. Harker's forehead that I was brought back to reality. Even now, when I am gravely revolving the matter, it is almost impossible to realise that the cause of all our trouble is still existent. Even Mrs. Harker seems to lose sight of her trouble for whole spells; it is only now and again, when something recalls it to her mind, that she thinks of her terrible scar. We are to meet here in my study in half an hour and decide on our course of action. I see only one immediate difficulty, I know it by instinct rather than reason: we shall all have to speak frankly; and yet I fear that in some mysterious way poor Mrs. Harker's tongue is tied. I *know* that she forms conclusions of her own, and from all that has been I can guess how brilliant and how true they must be; but she will not, or cannot, give them utterance. I have mentioned this to Van Helsing, and he and I are to talk it over when we are alone. I suppose it is some of that horrid poison which has got into her veins beginning to work. The Count had his own purposes when he gave her what Van Helsing called "the Vampire's baptism of blood." Well, there may be a poison that distils itself out of good things; in an age when the existence of ptomaines is a mystery we should not wonder at anything! One thing I know: that if my instinct be true regarding poor Mrs. Harker's silences, then there is a terrible difficulty—an unknown danger—in the work before us. The same power that compels her silence may compel her speech. I dare not think further; for so I should in my thoughts dishonour a noble woman!

Van Helsing is coming to my study a little before the others. I shall try to open the subject with him.

Later.—When the Professor came in, we talked over the state of things. I could see that he had something on his mind which he wanted to say, but felt some hesitancy about broaching the subject. After beating about the bush a little, he said suddenly:—

"Friend John, there is something that you and I must talk of alone, just at the first at any rate. Later, we may have to take the others into our confidence"; then he stopped, so I waited; he went on:—

"Madam Mina, our poor, dear Madam Mina is changing." A cold shiver ran through me to find my worst fears thus endorsed. Van Helsing continued:—

"With the sad experience of Miss Lucy, we must this time be warned before things go too far. Our task is now in reality more difficult than ever, and this new trouble makes every hour of the direst importance. I can see the characteristics of the vampire coming in her face. It is now but very, very slight; but it is to be seen if we have eyes to notice without to prejudge. Her teeth are some sharper, and at times her eyes are more hard. But these are not all, there is to her the silence now often; as so it was with Miss Lucy. She did not speak, even when she wrote that which she wished to be known later. Now my fear is this. If it be that she can, by our hypnotic trance, tell what the Count see and hear, is it not more true that he who have hypnotise her first, and who have drink of her very blood and make her drink of his, should, if he will, compel her mind to disclose to him that which she know?" I nodded acquiescence; he went on:—

"Then, what we must do is to prevent this; we must keep her ignorant of our intent, and so she cannot tell what she know not. This is a painful task! Oh, so painful that it heart-break me to think of; but it must be. When to-day we meet, I must tell her that for reason which we will not to speak she must not more be of our council, but be simply guarded by us." He wiped his forehead, which had broken out in profuse perspiration at the thought of the pain which he might have to inflict upon the poor soul already so tortured. I knew that it would be some sort of comfort to him if I told him that I also had come to the same conclusion; for at any rate it would take away the pain of doubt. I told him, and the effect was as I expected.

It is now close to the time of our general gathering. Van Helsing has gone away to prepare for the meeting, and his painful part of it. I really believe his purpose is to be able to pray alone.

Later.—At the very outset of our meeting a great personal relief was experienced by both Van Helsing and myself. Mrs. Harker had sent a message by her husband to say that she would not join us at present, as she thought it better that we should be free to discuss our movements without her presence to embarrass us. The Professor and I looked at each other for an instant, and somehow we both seemed relieved. For my own part, I thought that if Mrs. Harker realised the danger herself, it was much pain as well as much danger averted. Under the circumstances we agreed, by a questioning look and answer, with finger on lip, to preserve silence in our suspicions, until we should have been able to confer alone again. We went at once into our Plan of Campaign. Van Helsing roughly put the facts before us first:—

"The *Czarina Catherine* left the Thames yesterday morning. It will take her at the quickest speed she has ever made at least three weeks to reach Varna; but we can travel overland to the same place in three days. Now, if we allow for two days less for the ship's voyage, owing to such weather influences as we know that the Count can bring to bear; and if we allow a whole day and night for any delays which may occur to us, then we have a margin of nearly two weeks. Thus, in order to be quite safe, we must leave here on 17th at latest. Then we shall at any rate be in Varna a day before the ship arrives, and able to make such preparations as may be necessary. Of course we shall all go armed—armed against evil things, spiritual as well as physical." Here Quincey Morris added:—

"I understand that the Count comes from a wolf country, and it may be that he shall get there before us. I propose that we add Winchesters to our armament. I have a kind of belief in a Winchester when there is any trouble of that sort around. Do you remember, Art, when we had the pack after us at Tobolsk? What wouldn't we have given then for a repeater apiece!"

"Good!" said Van Helsing, "Winchesters it shall be. Quincey's head is level at all times, but most so when there is to hunt, metaphor be more dishonour to science than wolves be of danger to man. In the meantime we can do nothing here; and as I think that Varna is not familiar to any of us, why not go there more soon? It is as long to wait here as there. To-night and to-morrow we can get ready, and then, if all be well, we four can set out on our journey."

"We four?" said Harker interrogatively, looking from one to another of us.

"Of course!" answered the Professor quickly, "you must remain to take care of your so sweet wife!" Harker was silent for awhile and then said in a hollow voice:—

"Let us talk of that part of it in the morning. I want to consult with Mina." I thought that now was the time for Van Helsing to warn him not to disclose our plans to her; but he took no notice. I looked at him significantly and coughed. For answer he put his finger on his lips and turned away.

JONATHAN HARKER'S JOURNAL.

5 October, afternoon.—For some time after our meeting this morning I could not think. The new phases of things leave my mind in a state of wonder which allows no room for active thought. Mina's determination not to take any part in the discussion set me thinking; and as I could not argue the matter with her, I could only guess. I am as far as ever from a solution now. The way the others received it, too, puzzled me; the last time we talked of the subject we agreed that there was to be no more concealment of anything amongst us. Mina is sleeping now, calmly and sweetly like a little child. Her lips are curved and her face beams with happiness. Thank God, there are such moments still for her.

Later.—How strange it all is. I sat watching Mina's happy sleep, and came as near to being happy myself as I suppose I shall ever be. As the evening drew on, and the earth took its shadows from the sun sinking lower, the silence of the room grew more and more solemn to me. All at once Mina opened her eyes, and looking at me tenderly, said:—

"Jonathan, I want you to promise me something on your word of honour. A promise made to me, but made holily in God's hearing, and not to be broken though I should go down on my knees and implore you with bitter tears. Quick, you must make it to me at once."

"Mina," I said, "a promise like that, I cannot make at once. I may have no right to make it."

"But, dear one," she said, with such spiritual intensity that her eyes were like pole stars, "it is I who wish it; and it is not for myself. You can ask Dr. Van Helsing if I am not right; if he disagrees you may do as you will. Nay, more, if you all agree, later, you are absolved from the promise."

"I promise!" I said, and for a moment she looked supremely happy; though to me all happiness for her was denied by the red scar on her forehead. She said:—

"Promise me that you will not tell me anything of the plans formed for the campaign against the Count. Not by word, or inference, or implication; not at any time whilst this remains to me!" and she solemnly pointed to the scar. I saw that she was in earnest, and said solemnly:—

"I promise!" and as I said it I felt that from that instant a door had been shut between us.

Later, midnight.—Mina has been bright and cheerful all the evening. So much so that all the rest seemed to take courage, as if infected somewhat with her gaiety; as a result even I myself felt as if the pall of gloom which weighs us down were somewhat lifted. We all retired early. Mina is now sleeping like a little child; it is a wonderful thing that her faculty of sleep remains to her in the midst of her terrible trouble. Thank God for it, for then at least she can forget her care. Perhaps her example may affect me as her gaiety did to-night. I shall try it. Oh! for a dreamless sleep.

6 October, morning.—Another surprise. Mina woke me early, about the same time as yesterday, and asked me to bring Dr. Van Helsing. I thought that it was another occasion for hypnotism, and without question went for the Professor. He had evidently expected some such call, for I found him dressed in his room. His door was ajar, so that he could hear the opening of the door of our room. He came at once; as he passed into the room, he asked Mina if the others might come, too.

"No," she said quite simply, "it will not be necessary. You can tell them just as well. I must go with you on your journey."

Dr. Van Helsing was as startled as I was. After a moment's pause he asked:—

"But why?"

"You must take me with you. I am safer with you, and you shall be safer, too."

"But why, dear Madam Mina? You know that your safety is our solemnest duty. We go into danger, to which you are, or may be, more liable than any of us from—from circumstances—things that have been." He paused, embarrassed.

As she replied, she raised her finger and pointed to her forehead:—

"I know. That is why I must go. I can tell you now, whilst the sun is coming up; I may not be able again. I know that when the Count wills me I must go. I know that if he tells me to come in secret, I must come by wile; by any device to hoodwink—even Jonathan." God saw the look that she turned on me as she spoke, and if there be indeed a Recording Angel that look is noted to her everlasting honour. I could only clasp her hand. I could not speak; my emotion was too great for even the relief of tears. She went on:—

"You men are brave and strong. You are strong in your numbers, for you can defy that which would break down the human endurance of one who had to guard alone. Besides, I may be of service, since you can hypnotise me and so learn that which even I myself do not know." Dr. Van Helsing said very gravely:—

"Madam Mina, you are, as always, most wise. You shall with us come; and together we shall do that which we go forth to achieve." When he had spoken, Mina's long spell of silence made me look at her. She had fallen back on her pillow asleep; she did not even wake when I had pulled up the blind and let in the sunlight which flooded the room. Van Helsing motioned to me to come with him quietly. We went to his room, and within a minute Lord Godalming, Dr. Seward, and Mr. Morris were with us also. He told them what Mina had said, and went on:—

"In the morning we shall leave for Varna. We have now to deal with a new factor: Madam Mina. Oh, but her soul is true. It is to her an agony to tell us so much as she has done; but it is most right, and we are warned in time. There must be no chance lost, and in Varna we must be ready to act the instant when that ship arrives."

"What shall we do exactly?" asked Mr. Morris laconically. The Professor paused before replying:—

"We shall at the first board that ship; then, when we have identified the box, we shall place a branch of the wild rose on it. This we shall fasten, for when it is there none can emerge; so at least says the superstition. And to superstition must we trust at the first; it was man's faith in the early, and it have its root in faith still. Then, when we get the opportunity that we seek, when none are near to see, we shall open the box, and—and all will be well."

"I shall not wait for any opportunity," said Morris. "When I see the box I shall open it and destroy the monster, though there were a thousand men looking on, and if I am to be wiped out for it the next moment!" I grasped his hand instinctively and found it as firm as a piece of steel. I think he understood my look; I hope he did.

"Good boy," said Dr. Van Helsing. "Brave boy. Quincey is all man. God bless him for it. My child, believe me none of us shall lag behind or pause from any fear. I do but say what we may do—what we must do. But, indeed, indeed we cannot say what we shall do. There are so many things which may happen, and their ways and their ends are so various that until the moment we may not say. We shall all be armed, in all ways; and when the time for the end has come, our effort shall not be lack. Now let us to-day put all our affairs in order. Let all things which touch on others dear to us, and who on us depend, be complete; for none of us can tell what, or when, or how, the end may be. As for me, my own affairs are regulate; and as I have nothing else to do, I shall go make arrangements for the travel. I shall have all tickets and so forth for our journey."

There was nothing further to be said, and we parted. I shall now settle up all my affairs of earth, and be ready for whatever may come . . . .

Later.—It is all done; my will is made, and all complete. Mina if she survive is my sole heir. If it should not be so, then the others who have been so good to us shall have remainder.

It is now drawing towards the sunset; Mina's uneasiness calls my attention to it. I am sure that there is something on her mind which the time of exact sunset will reveal. These occasions are becoming harrowing times for us all, for each sunrise and sunset opens up some new danger—some new pain, which, however, may in God's will be means to a good end. I write all these things in the diary since my darling must not hear them now; but if it may be that she can see them again, they shall be ready.

She is calling to me.

CHAPTER XXV

DR. SEWARD'S DIARY

11 October, Evening.—Jonathan Harker has asked me to note this, as he says he is hardly equal to the task, and he wants an exact record kept.

I think that none of us were surprised when we were asked to see Mrs. Harker a little before the time of sunset. We have of late come to understand that sunrise and sunset are to her times of peculiar freedom; when her old self can be manifest without any controlling force subduing or restraining her, or inciting her to action. This mood or condition begins some half hour or more before actual sunrise or sunset, and lasts till either the sun is high, or whilst the clouds are still aglow with the rays streaming above the horizon. At first there is a sort of negative condition, as if some tie were loosened, and then the absolute freedom quickly follows; when, however, the freedom ceases the change-back or relapse comes quickly, preceded only by a spell of warning silence.

To-night, when we met, she was somewhat constrained, and bore all the signs of an internal struggle. I put it down myself to her making a violent effort at the earliest instant she could do so. A very few minutes, however, gave her complete control of herself; then, motioning her husband to sit beside her on the sofa where she was half reclining, she made the rest of us bring chairs up close. Taking her husband's hand in hers began:—

"We are all here together in freedom, for perhaps the last time! I know, dear; I know that you will always be with me to the end." This was to her husband whose hand had, as we could see, tightened upon hers. "In the morning we go out upon our task, and God alone knows what may be in store for any of us. You are going to be so good to me as to take me with you. I know that all that brave earnest men can do for a poor weak woman, whose soul perhaps is lost—no, no, not yet, but is at any rate at stake—you will do. But you must remember that I am not as you are. There is a poison in my blood, in my soul, which may destroy me; which must destroy me, unless some relief comes to us. Oh, my friends, you know as well as I do, that my soul is at stake; and though I know there is one way out for me, you must not and I must not take it!" She looked appealingly to us all in turn, beginning and ending with her husband.

"What is that way?" asked Van Helsing in a hoarse voice. "What is that way, which we must not—may not—take?"

"That I may die now, either by my own hand or that of another, before the greater evil is entirely wrought. I know, and you know, that were I once dead you could and would set free my immortal spirit, even as you did my poor Lucy's. Were death, or the fear of death, the only thing that stood in the way I would not shrink to die here, now, amidst the friends who love me. But death is not all. I cannot believe that to die in such a case, when there is hope before us and a bitter task to be done, is God's will. Therefore, I, on my part, give up here the certainty of eternal rest, and go out into the dark where may be the blackest things that the world or the nether world holds!" We were all silent, for we knew instinctively that this was only a prelude. The faces of the others were set and Harker's grew ashen grey; perhaps he guessed better than any of us what was coming. She continued:—

"This is what I can give into the hotch-pot." I could not but note the quaint legal phrase which she used in such a place, and with all seriousness. "What will each of you give? Your lives I know," she went on quickly, "that is easy for brave men. Your lives are God's, and you can give them back to Him; but what will you give to me?" She looked again questioningly, but this time avoided her husband's face. Quincey seemed to understand; he nodded, and her face lit up. "Then I shall tell you plainly what I want, for there must be no doubtful matter in this connection between us now. You must promise me, one and all—even you, my beloved husband—that, should the time come, you will kill me."

"What is that time?" The voice was Quincey's, but it was low and strained.

"When you shall be convinced that I am so changed that it is better that I die than I may live. When I am thus dead in the flesh, then you will, without a moment's delay, drive a stake through me and cut off my head; or do whatever else may be wanting to give me rest!"

Quincey was the first to rise after the pause. He knelt down before her and taking her hand in his said solemnly:—

"I'm only a rough fellow, who hasn't, perhaps, lived as a man should to win such a distinction, but I swear to you by all that I hold sacred and dear that, should the time ever come, I shall not flinch from the duty that you have set us. And I promise you, too, that I shall make all certain, for if I am only doubtful I shall take it that the time has come!"

"My true friend!" was all she could say amid her fast-falling tears, as, bending over, she kissed his hand.

"I swear the same, my dear Madam Mina!" said Van Helsing.

"And I!" said Lord Godalming, each of them in turn kneeling to her to take the oath. I followed, myself. Then her husband turned to her wan-eyed and with a greenish pallor which subdued the snowy whiteness of his hair, and asked:—

"And must I, too, make such a promise, oh, my wife?"

"You too, my dearest," she said, with infinite yearning of pity in her voice and eyes. "You must not shrink. You are nearest and dearest and all the world to me; our souls are knit into one, for all life and all time. Think, dear, that there have been times when brave men have killed their wives and their womenkind, to keep them from falling into the hands of the enemy. Their hands did not falter any the more because those that they loved implored them to slay them. It is men's duty towards those whom they love, in such times of sore trial! And oh, my dear, if it is to be that I must meet death at any hand, let it be at the hand of him that loves me best. Dr. Van Helsing, I have not forgotten your mercy in poor Lucy's case to him who loved"—she stopped with a flying blush, and changed her phrase—"to him who had best right to give her peace. If that time shall come again, I look to you to make it a happy memory of my husband's life that it was his loving hand which set me free from the awful thrall upon me."

"Again I swear!" came the Professor's resonant voice. Mrs. Harker smiled, positively smiled, as with a sigh of relief she leaned back and said:—

"And now one word of warning, a warning which you must never forget: this time, if it ever come, may come quickly and unexpectedly, and in such case you must lose no time in using your opportunity. At such a time I myself might be—nay! if the time ever comes, *shall be*—leagued with your enemy against you."

"One more request;" she became very solemn as she said this, "it is not vital and necessary like the other, but I want you to do one thing for me, if you will." We all acquiesced, but no one spoke; there was no need to speak:—

"I want you to read the Burial Service." She was interrupted by a deep groan from her husband; taking his hand in hers, she held it over her heart, and continued: "You must read it over me some day. Whatever may be the issue of all this fearful state of things, it will be a sweet thought to all or some of us. You, my dearest, will I hope read it, for then it will be in your voice in my memory for ever—come what may!"

"But oh, my dear one," he pleaded, "death is afar off from you."

"Nay," she said, holding up a warning hand. "I am deeper in death at this moment than if the weight of an earthly grave lay heavy upon me!"

"Oh, my wife, must I read it?" he said, before he began.

"It would comfort me, my husband!" was all she said; and he began to read when she had got the book ready.

"How can I—how could any one—tell of that strange scene, its solemnity, its gloom, its sadness, its horror; and, withal, its sweetness. Even a sceptic, who can see nothing but a travesty of bitter truth in anything holy or emotional, would have been melted to the heart had he seen that little group of loving and devoted friends kneeling round that stricken and sorrowing lady; or heard the tender passion of her husband's voice, as in tones so broken with emotion that often he had to pause, he read the simple and beautiful service from the Burial of the Dead. I—I cannot go on—words—and—v-voice—f-fail m-me!"

She was right in her instinct. Strange as it all was, bizarre as it may hereafter seem even to us who felt its potent influence at the time, it comforted us much; and the silence, which showed Mrs. Harker's coming relapse from her freedom of soul, did not seem so full of despair to any of us as we had dreaded.

JONATHAN HARKER'S JOURNAL.

15 October, Varna.—We left Charing Cross on the morning of the 12th, got to Paris the same night, and took the places secured for us in the Orient Express. We travelled night and day, arriving here at about five o'clock. Lord Godalming went to the Consulate to see if any telegram had arrived for him, whilst the rest of us came on to this hotel—"the Odessus." The journey may have had incidents; I was, however, too eager to get on, to care for them. Until the *Czarina Catherine* comes into port there will be no interest for me in anything in the wide world. Thank God! Mina is well, and looks to be getting stronger; her colour is coming back. She sleeps a great deal; throughout the journey she slept nearly all the time. Before sunrise and sunset, however, she is very wakeful and alert; and it has become a habit for Van Helsing to hypnotise her at such times. At first, some effort was needed, and he had to make many passes; but now, she seems to yield at once, as if by habit, and scarcely any action is needed. He seems to have power at these particular moments to simply will, and her thoughts obey him. He always asks her what she can see and hear. She answers to the first:—

"Nothing; all is dark." And to the second:—

"I can hear the waves lapping against the ship, and the water rushing by. Canvas and cordage strain and masts and yards creak. The wind is high—I can hear it in the shrouds, and the bow throws back the foam." It is evident that the *Czarina Catherine* is still at sea, hastening on her way to Varna.

Lord Godalming has just returned. He had four telegrams, one each day since we started, and all to the same effect: that the *Czarina Catherine* had not been reported to Lloyd's from anywhere. He had arranged before leaving London that his agent should send him every day a telegram saying if the ship had been reported. He was to have a message even if she were not reported, so that he might be sure that there was a watch being kept at the other end of the wire.

We had dinner and went to bed early. To-morrow we are to see the Vice-Consul, and to arrange, if we can, about getting on board the ship as soon as she arrives. Van Helsing says that our chance will be to get on the boat between sunrise and sunset. The Count, even if he takes the form of a bat, cannot cross the running water of his own volition, and so cannot leave the ship. As he dare not change to man's form without suspicion—which he evidently wishes to avoid—he must remain in the box. If, then, we can come on board after sunrise, he is at our mercy; for we can open the box and make sure of him, as we did of poor Lucy, before he wakes. What mercy he shall get from us will not count for much. We think that we shall not have much trouble with officials or the seamen. Thank God! this is the country where bribery can do anything, and we are well supplied with money. We have only to make sure that the ship cannot come into port between sunset and sunrise without our being warned, and we shall be safe. Judge Moneybag will settle this case, I think!

16 October.—Mina's report still the same: lapping waves and rushing water, darkness and favouring winds. We are evidently in good time, and when we hear of the *Czarina Catherine* we shall be ready. As she must pass the Dardanelles we are sure to have some report.

* * * * *

17 October.—Everything is pretty well fixed now, I think, to welcome the Count on his return from his tour. Godalming told the shippers that he fancied that the box sent aboard might contain something stolen from a friend of his, and got a half consent that he might open it at his own risk. The owner gave him a paper telling the Captain to give him every facility in doing whatever he chose on board the ship, and also a similar authorisation to his agent at Varna. We have seen the agent, who was much impressed with Godalming's kindly manner to him, and we are all satisfied that whatever he can do to aid our wishes will be done. We have already arranged what to do in case we get the box open. If the Count is there, Van Helsing and Seward will cut off his head at once and drive a stake through his heart. Morris and Godalming and I shall prevent interference, even if we have to use the arms which we shall have ready. The Professor says that if we can so treat the Count's body, it will soon after fall into dust. In such case there would be no evidence against us, in case any suspicion of murder were aroused. But even if it were not, we should stand or fall by our act, and perhaps some day this very script may be evidence to come between some of us and a rope. For myself, I should take the chance only too thankfully if it were to come. We mean to leave no stone unturned to carry out our intent. We have arranged with certain officials that the instant the *Czarina Catherine* is seen, we are to be informed by a special messenger.

24 October.—A whole week of waiting. Daily telegrams to Godalming, but only the same story: "Not yet reported." Mina's morning and evening hypnotic answer is unvaried: lapping waves, rushing water, and creaking masts.

RUFUS SMITH, LLOYD'S, LONDON, TO LORD GODALMING, CARE OF H. B. M. VICE-CONSUL, VARNA.

Telegram, October 24th.

"*Czarina Catherine* reported this morning from Dardanelles."

DR. SEWARD'S DIARY.

25 October.—How I miss my phonograph! To write diary with a pen is irksome to me; but Van Helsing says I must. We were all wild with excitement yesterday when Godalming got his telegram from Lloyd's. I know now what men feel in battle when the call to action is heard. Mrs. Harker, alone of our party, did not show any signs of emotion. After all, it is not strange that she did not; for we took special care not to let her know anything about it, and we all tried not to show any excitement when we were in her presence. In old days she would, I am sure, have noticed, no matter how we might have tried to conceal it; but in this way she is greatly changed during the past three weeks. The lethargy grows upon her, and though she seems strong and well, and is getting back some of her colour, Van Helsing and I are not satisfied. We talk of her often; we have not, however, said a word to the others. It would break poor Harker's heart—certainly his nerve—if he knew that we had even a suspicion on the subject. Van Helsing examines, he tells me, her teeth very carefully, whilst she is in the hypnotic condition, for he says that so long as they do not begin to sharpen there is no active danger of a change in her. If this change should come, it would be necessary to take steps! . . . We both know what those steps would have to be, though we do not mention our thoughts to each other. We should neither of us shrink from the task—awful though it be to contemplate. "Euthanasia" is an excellent and a comforting word! I am grateful to whoever invented it.

It is only about 24 hours' sail from the Dardanelles to here, at the rate the *Czarina Catherine* has come from London. She should therefore arrive some time in the morning; but as she cannot possibly get in before then, we are all about to retire early. We shall get up at one o'clock, so as to be ready.

25 October, Noon.—No news yet of the ship's arrival. Mrs. Harker's hypnotic report this morning was the same as usual, so it is possible that we may get news at any moment. We men are all in a fever of excitement, except Harker, who is calm; his hands are cold as ice, and an hour ago I found him whetting the edge of the great Ghoorka knife which he now always carries with him. It will be a bad lookout for the Count if the edge of that "Kukri" ever touches his throat, driven by that stern, ice-cold hand!

Van Helsing and I were a little alarmed about Mrs. Harker to-day. About noon she got into a sort of lethargy which we did not like; although we kept silence to the others, we were neither of us happy about it. She had been restless all the morning, so that we were at first glad to know that she was sleeping. When, however, her husband mentioned casually that she was sleeping so soundly that he could not wake her, we went to her room to see for ourselves. She was breathing naturally and looked so well and peaceful that we agreed that the sleep was better for her than anything else. Poor girl, she has so much to forget that it is no wonder that sleep, if it brings oblivion to her, does her good.

Later.—Our opinion was justified, for when after a refreshing sleep of some hours she woke up, she seemed brighter and better than she had been for days. At sunset she made the usual hypnotic report. Wherever he may be in the Black Sea, the Count is hurrying to his destination. To his doom, I trust!

26 October.—Another day and no tidings of the *Czarina Catherine.* She ought to be here by now. That she is still journeying *somewhere* is apparent, for Mrs. Harker's hypnotic report at sunrise was still the same. It is possible that the vessel may be lying by, at times, for fog; some of the steamers which came in last evening reported patches of fog both to north and south of the port. We must continue our watching, as the ship may now be signalled any moment.

27 October, Noon.—Most strange; no news yet of the ship we wait for. Mrs. Harker reported last night and this morning as usual: "lapping waves and rushing water," though she added that "the waves were very faint." The telegrams from London have been the same: "no further report." Van Helsing is terribly anxious, and told me just now that he fears the Count is escaping us. He added significantly:—

"I did not like that lethargy of Madam Mina's. Souls and memories can do strange things during trance." I was about to ask him more, but Harker just then came in, and he held up a warning hand. We must try to-night at sunset to make her speak more fully when in her hypnotic state.

TELEGRAM.
RUFUS SMITH, LONDON, TO LORD GODALMING, CARE H. B. M. VICE CONSUL, VARNA

28 October.

"*Czarina Catherine* reported entering Galatz at one o'clock to-day."

DR. SEWARD'S DIARY.

28 October.—When the telegram came announcing the arrival in Galatz I do not think it was such a shock to any of us as might have been expected. True, we did not know whence, or how, or when, the bolt would come; but I think we all expected that something strange would happen. The delay of arrival at Varna made us individually satisfied that things would not be just as we had expected; we only waited to learn where the change would occur. None the less, however, was it a surprise. I suppose that nature works on such a hopeful basis that we believe against ourselves that things will be as they ought to be, not as we should know that they will be. Transcendentalism is a beacon to the angels, even if it be a will-o'-the-wisp to man. It was an odd experience and we all took it differently. Van Helsing raised his hand over his head for a moment, as though in remonstrance with the Almighty; but he said not a word, and in a few seconds stood up with his face sternly set. Lord Godalming grew very pale, and sat breathing heavily. I was myself half stunned and looked in wonder at one after another. Quincey Morris tightened his belt with that quick movement which I knew so well; in our old wandering days it meant "action." Mrs. Harker grew ghastly white, so that the scar on her forehead seemed to burn, but she folded her hands meekly and looked up in prayer. Harker smiled—actually smiled—the dark, bitter smile of one who is without hope; but at the same time his action belied his words, for his hands instinctively sought the hilt of the great Kukri knife and rested there. "When does the next train start for Galatz?" said Van Helsing to us generally.

"At 6:30 to-morrow morning!" We all started, for the answer came from Mrs. Harker.

"How on earth do you know?" said Art.

"You forget—or perhaps you do not know, though Jonathan does and so does Dr. Van Helsing—that I am the train fiend. At home in Exeter I always used to make up the time-tables, so as to be helpful to my husband. I found it so useful sometimes, that I always make a study of the time-tables now. I knew that if anything were to take us to Castle Dracula we should go by Galatz, or at any rate through Bucharest, so I learned the times very carefully. Unhappily there are not many to learn, as the only train to-morrow leaves as I say."

"Wonderful woman!" murmured the Professor.

"Can't we get a special?" asked Lord Godalming. Van Helsing shook his head: "I fear not. This land is very different from yours or mine; even if we did have a special, it would probably not arrive as soon as our regular train. Moreover, we have something to prepare. We must think. Now let us organize. You, friend Arthur, go to the train and get the tickets and arrange that all be ready for us to go in the morning. Do you, friend Jonathan, go to the agent of the ship and get from him letters to the agent in Galatz, with authority to make search the ship just as it was here. Morris Quincey, you see the Vice-Consul, and get his aid with his fellow in Galatz and all he can do to make our way smooth, so that no times be lost when over the Danube. John will stay with Madam Mina and me, and we shall consult. For so if time be long you may be delayed; and it will not matter when the sun set, since I am here with Madam to make report."

"And I," said Mrs. Harker brightly, and more like her old self than she had been for many a long day, "shall try to be of use in all ways, and shall think and write for you as I used to do. Something is shifting from me in some strange way, and I feel freer than I have been of late!" The three younger men looked happier at the moment as they seemed to realise the significance of her words; but Van Helsing and I, turning to each other, met each a grave and troubled glance. We said nothing at the time, however.

When the three men had gone out to their tasks Van Helsing asked Mrs. Harker to look up the copy of the diaries and find him the part of Harker's journal at the Castle. She went away to get it; when the door was shut upon her he said to me:—

"We mean the same! speak out!"

"There is some change. It is a hope that makes me sick, for it may deceive us."

"Quite so. Do you know why I asked her to get the manuscript?"

"No!" said I, "unless it was to get an opportunity of seeing me alone."

"You are in part right, friend John, but only in part. I want to tell you something. And oh, my friend, I am taking a great—a terrible—risk; but I believe it is right. In the moment when Madam Mina said those words that arrest both our understanding, an inspiration came to me. In the trance of three days ago the Count sent her his spirit to read her mind; or more like he took her to see him in his earth-box in the ship with water rushing, just as it go free at rise and set of sun. He learn then that we are here; for she have more to tell in her open life with eyes to see and ears to hear than he, shut, as he is, in his coffin-box. Now he make his most effort to escape us. At present he want her not.

"He is sure with his so great knowledge that she will come at his call; but he cut her off—take her, as he can do, out of his own power, that so she come not to him. Ah! there I have hope that our man-brains that have been of man so long and that have not lost the grace of God, will come higher than his child-brain that lie in his tomb for centuries, that grow not yet to our stature, and that do only work selfish and therefore small. Here comes Madam Mina; not a word to her of her trance! She know it not; and it would overwhelm her and make despair just when we want all her hope, all her courage; when most we want all her great brain which is trained like man's brain, but is of sweet woman and have a special power which the Count give her, and which he may not take away altogether—though he think not so. Hush! let me speak, and you shall learn. Oh, John, my friend, we are in awful straits. I fear, as I never feared before. We can only trust the good God. Silence! here she comes!"

I thought that the Professor was going to break down and have hysterics, just as he had when Lucy died, but with a great effort he controlled himself and was at perfect nervous poise when Mrs. Harker tripped into the room, bright and happy-looking and, in the doing of work, seemingly forgetful of her misery. As she came in, she handed a number of sheets of typewriting to Van Helsing. He looked over them gravely, his face brightening up as he read. Then holding the pages between his finger and thumb he said:—

"Friend John, to you with so much of experience already—and you, too, dear Madam Mina, that are young—here is a lesson: do not fear ever to think. A half-thought has been buzzing often in my brain, but I fear to let him loose his wings. Here now, with more knowledge, I go back to where that half-thought come from and I find that he be no half-thought at all; that be a whole thought, though so young that he is not yet strong to use his little wings. Nay, like the "Ugly Duck" of my friend Hans Andersen, he be no duck-thought at all, but a big swan-thought that sail nobly on big wings, when the time come for him to try them. See I read here what Jonathan have written:—

"That other of his race who, in a later age, again and again, brought his forces over The Great River into Turkey Land; who, when he was beaten back, came again, and again, and again, though he had to come alone from the bloody field where his troops were being slaughtered, since he knew that he alone could ultimately triumph."

"What does this tell us? Not much? no! The Count's child-thought see nothing; therefore he speak so free. Your man-thought see nothing; my man-thought see nothing, till just now. No! But there comes another word from some one who speak without thought because she, too, know not what it mean—what it *might* mean. Just as there are elements which rest, yet when in nature's course they move on their way and they touch—then pouf! and there comes a flash of light, heaven wide, that blind and kill and destroy some; but that show up all earth below for leagues and leagues. Is it not so? Well, I shall explain. To begin, have you ever study the philosophy of crime? 'Yes' and 'No.' You, John, yes; for it is a study of insanity. You, no, Madam Mina; for crime touch you not—not but once. Still, your mind works true, and argues not *a particulari ad universale.* There is this peculiarity in criminals. It is so constant, in all countries and at all times, that even police, who know not much from philosophy, come to know it empirically, that *it is.* That is to be empiric. The criminal always work at one crime—that is the true criminal who seems predestinate to crime, and who will of none other. This criminal has not full man-brain. He is clever and cunning and resourceful; but he be not of man-stature as to brain. He be of child-brain in much. Now this criminal of ours is predestinate to crime also; he, too, have child-brain, and it is of the child to do what he have done. The little bird, the little fish, the little animal learn not by principle, but empirically; and when he learn to do, then there is to him the ground to start from to do more. 'Dos pou sto,' said Archimedes. 'Give me a fulcrum, and I shall move the world!' To do once, is the fulcrum whereby child-brain become man-brain; and until he have the purpose to do more, he continue to do the same again every time, just as he have done before! Oh, my dear, I see that your eyes are opened, and that to you the lightning flash show all the leagues," for Mrs.

Harker began to clap her hands and her eyes sparkled. He went on:—

"Now you shall speak. Tell us two dry men of science what you see with those so bright eyes." He took her hand and held it whilst she spoke. His finger and thumb closed on her pulse, as I thought instinctively and unconsciously, as she spoke:—

"The Count is a criminal and of criminal type. Nordau and Lombroso would so classify him, and *quâ* criminal he is of imperfectly formed mind. Thus, in a difficulty he has to seek resource in habit. His past is a clue, and the one page of it that we know—and that from his own lips—tells that once before, when in what Mr. Morris would call a 'tight place,' he went back to his own country from the land he had tried to invade, and thence, without losing purpose, prepared himself for a new effort. He came again better equipped for his work; and won. So he came to London to invade a new land. He was beaten, and when all hope of success was lost, and his existence in danger, he fled back over the sea to his home; just as formerly he had fled back over the Danube from Turkey Land."

"Good, good! oh, you so clever lady!" said Van Helsing, enthusiastically, as he stooped and kissed her hand. A moment later he said to me, as calmly as though we had been having a sick-room consultation:—

"Seventy-two only; and in all this excitement. I have hope." Turning to her again, he said with keen expectation:—

"But go on. Go on! there is more to tell if you will. Be not afraid; John and I know. I do in any case, and shall tell you if you are right. Speak, without fear!"

"I will try to; but you will forgive me if I seem egotistical."

"Nay! fear not, you must be egotist, for it is of you that we think."

"Then, as he is criminal he is selfish; and as his intellect is small and his action is based on selfishness, he confines himself to one purpose. That purpose is remorseless. As he fled back over the Danube, leaving his forces to be cut to pieces, so now he is intent on being safe, careless of all. So his own selfishness frees my soul somewhat from the terrible power which he acquired over me on that dreadful night. I felt it! Oh, I felt it! Thank God, for His great mercy! My soul is freer than it has been since that awful hour; and all that haunts me is a fear lest in some trance or dream he may have used my knowledge for his ends." The Professor stood up:—

"He has so used your mind; and by it he has left us here in Varna, whilst the ship that carried him rushed through enveloping fog up to Galatz, where, doubtless, he had made preparation for escaping from us. But his child-mind only saw so far; and it may be that, as ever is in God's Providence, the very thing that the evil-doer most reckoned on for his selfish good, turns out to be his chiefest harm. The hunter is taken in his own snare, as the great Psalmist says. For now that he think he is free from every trace of us all, and that he has escaped us with so many hours to him, then his selfish child-brain will whisper him to sleep. He think, too, that as he cut himself off from knowing your mind, there can be no knowledge of him to you; there is where he fail! That terrible baptism of blood which he give you makes you free to go to him in spirit, as you have as yet done in your times of freedom, when the sun rise and set. At such times you go by my volition and not by his; and this power to good of you and others, as you have won from your suffering at his hands. This is now all the more precious that he know it not, and to guard himself have even cut himself off from his knowledge of our where. We, however, are not selfish, and we believe that God is with us through all this blackness, and these many dark hours. We shall follow him; and we shall not flinch; even if we peril ourselves that we become like him. Friend John, this has been a great hour; and it have done much to advance us on our way. You must be scribe and write him all down, so that when the others return from their work you can give it to them; then they shall know as we do."

And so I have written it whilst we wait their return, and Mrs. Harker has written with her typewriter all since she brought the MS. to us.

CHAPTER XXVI

DR. SEWARD'S DIARY

29 October.—This is written in the train from Varna to Galatz. Last night we all assembled a little before the time of sunset. Each of us had done his work as well as he could; so far as thought, and endeavour, and opportunity go, we are prepared for the whole of our journey, and for our work when we get to Galatz. When the usual time came round Mrs. Harker prepared herself for her hypnotic effort; and after a longer and more serious effort on the part of Van Helsing than has been usually necessary, she sank into the trance. Usually she speaks on a hint; but this time the Professor had to ask her questions, and to ask them pretty resolutely, before we could learn anything; at last her answer came:—

"I can see nothing; we are still; there are no waves lapping, but only a steady swirl of water softly running against the hawser. I can hear men's voices calling, near and far, and the roll and creak of oars in the rowlocks. A gun is fired somewhere; the echo of it seems far away. There is tramping of feet overhead, and ropes and chains are dragged along. What is this? There is a gleam of light; I can feel the air blowing upon me."

Here she stopped. She had risen, as if impulsively, from where she lay on the sofa, and raised both her hands, palms upwards, as if lifting a weight. Van Helsing and I looked at each other with understanding. Quincey raised his eyebrows slightly and looked at her intently, whilst Harker's hand instinctively closed round the hilt of his Kukri. There was a long pause. We all knew that the time when she could speak was passing; but we felt that it was useless to say anything. Suddenly she sat up, and, as she opened her eyes, said sweetly:—

"Would none of you like a cup of tea? You must all be so tired!" We could only make her happy, and so acquiesced. She bustled off to get tea; when she had gone Van Helsing said:—

"You see, my friends. *He* is close to land: he has left his earth-chest. But he has yet to get on shore. In the night he may lie hidden somewhere; but if he be not carried on shore, or if the ship do not touch it, he cannot achieve the land. In such case he can, if it be in the night, change his form and can jump or fly on shore, as he did at Whitby. But if the day come before he get on shore, then, unless he be carried he cannot escape. And if he be carried, then the customs men may discover what the box contain. Thus, in fine, if he escape not on shore to-night, or before dawn, there will be the whole day lost to him. We may then arrive in time; for if he escape not at night we shall come on him in daytime, boxed up and at our mercy; for he dare not be his true self, awake and visible, lest he be discovered."

There was no more to be said, so we waited in patience until the dawn; at which time we might learn more from Mrs. Harker.

Early this morning we listened, with breathless anxiety, for her response in her trance. The hypnotic stage was even longer in coming than before; and when it came the time remaining until full sunrise was so short that we began to despair. Van Helsing seemed to throw his whole soul into the effort; at last, in obedience to his will she made reply:—

"All is dark. I hear lapping water, level with me, and some creaking as of wood on wood." She paused, and the red sun shot up. We must wait till to-night.

And so it is that we are travelling towards Galatz in an agony of expectation. We are due to arrive between two and three in the morning; but already, at Bucharest, we are three hours late, so we cannot possibly get in till well after sun-up. Thus we shall have two more hypnotic messages from Mrs. Harker; either or both may possibly throw more light on what is happening.

Later.—Sunset has come and gone. Fortunately it came at a time when there was no distraction; for had it occurred whilst we were at a station, we might not have secured the necessary calm and isolation. Mrs. Harker yielded to the hypnotic influence even less readily than this morning. I am in fear that her power of reading the Count's sensations may die away, just when we want it most. It seems to me that her imagination is beginning to work. Whilst she has been in the trance hitherto she has confined herself to the simplest of facts. If this goes on it may ultimately mislead us. If I thought that the Count's power over her would die away equally with her power of knowledge it would be a happy thought; but I am afraid that it may not be so. When she did speak, her words were enigmatical:—

"Something is going out; I can feel it pass me like a cold wind. I can hear, far off, confused sounds—as of men talking in strange tongues, fierce-falling water, and the howling of wolves." She stopped and a shudder ran through her, increasing in intensity for a few seconds, till, at the end, she shook as though in a palsy. She said no more, even in answer to the Professor's imperative questioning. When she woke from the trance, she was cold, and exhausted, and languid; but her mind was all alert. She could not remember anything, but asked what she had said; when she was told, she pondered over it deeply for a long time and in silence.

30 October, 7 a. m.—We are near Galatz now, and I may not have time to write later. Sunrise this morning was anxiously looked for by us all. Knowing of the increasing difficulty of procuring the hypnotic trance, Van Helsing began his passes earlier than usual. They produced no effect, however, until the regular time, when she yielded with a still greater difficulty, only a minute before the sun rose. The Professor lost no time in his questioning; her answer came with equal quickness:—

"All is dark. I hear water swirling by, level with my ears, and the creaking of wood on wood. Cattle low far off. There is another sound, a queer one like——" She stopped and grew white, and whiter still.

"Go on; go on! Speak, I command you!" said Van Helsing in an agonised voice. At the same time there was despair in his eyes, for the risen sun was reddening even Mrs. Harker's pale face. She opened her eyes, and we all started as she said, sweetly and seemingly with the utmost unconcern:—

"Oh, Professor, why ask me to do what you know I can't? I don't remember anything." Then, seeing the look of amazement on our faces, she said, turning from one to the other with a troubled look:—

"What have I said? What have I done? I know nothing, only that I was lying here, half asleep, and heard you say go on! speak, I command you!' It seemed so funny to hear you order me about, as if I were a bad child!"

"Oh, Madam Mina," he said, sadly, "it is proof, if proof be needed, of how I love and honour you, when a word for your good, spoken more earnest than ever, can seem so strange because it is to order her whom I am proud to obey!"

The whistles are sounding; we are nearing Galatz. We are on fire with anxiety and eagerness.

MINA HARKER'S JOURNAL.

30 October.—Mr. Morris took me to the hotel where our rooms had been ordered by telegraph, he being the one who could best be spared, since he does not speak any foreign language. The forces were distributed much as they had been at Varna, except that Lord Godalming went to the Vice-Consul, as his rank might serve as an immediate guarantee of some sort to the official, we being in extreme hurry.

Jonathan and the two doctors went to the shipping agent to learn particulars of the arrival of the *Czarina Catherine.*

Later.—Lord Godalming has returned. The Consul is away, and the Vice-Consul sick; so the routine work has been attended to by a clerk. He was very obliging, and offered to do anything in his power.

JONATHAN HARKER'S JOURNAL.

30 October.—At nine o'clock Dr. Van Helsing, Dr. Seward, and I called on Messrs. Mackenzie & Steinkoff, the agents of the London firm of Hapgood. They had received a wire from London, in answer to Lord Godalming's telegraphed request, asking us to show them any civility in their power. They were more than kind and courteous, and took us at once on board the *Czarina Catherine*, which lay at anchor out in the river harbour. There we saw the Captain, Donelson by name, who told us of his voyage. He said that in all his life he had never had so favourable a run.

"Man!" he said, "but it made us afeard, for we expeckit that we should have to pay for it wi' some rare piece o' ill luck, so as to keep up the average. It's no canny to run frae London to the Black Sea wi' a wind ahint ye, as though the Deil himself were blawin' on yer sail for his ain purpose. An' a' the time we could no speer a thing. Gin we were nigh a ship, or a port, or a headland, a fog fell on us and travelled wi' us, till when after it had lifted and we looked out, the deil a thing could we see. We ran by Gibraltar wi'oot bein' able to signal; an' till we came to the Dardanelles and had to wait to get our permit to pass, we never were within hail o' aught. At first I inclined to slack off sail and beat about till the fog was lifted; but whiles, I thocht that if the Deil was minded to get us into the Black Sea quick, he was like to do it whether we would or no. If we had a quick voyage it would be no to our miscredit wi' the owners, or no hurt to our traffic; an' the Old Mon who had served his ain purpose wad be decently grateful to us for no hinderin' him." This mixture of simplicity and cunning, of superstition and commercial reasoning, aroused Van Helsing, who said:—

"Mine friend, that Devil is more clever than he is thought by some; and he know when he meet his match!" The skipper was not displeased with the compliment, and went on:—

"When we got past the Bosphorus the men began to grumble; some o' them, the Roumanians, came and asked me to heave overboard a big box which had been put on board by a queer lookin' old man just before we had started frae London. I had seen them speer at the fellow, and put out their twa fingers when they saw him, to guard against the evil eye. Man! but the supersteetion of foreigners is pairfectly rideeculous! I sent them aboot their business pretty quick; but as just after a fog closed in on us I felt a wee bit as they did anent something, though I wouldn't say it was agin the big box. Well, on we went, and as the fog didn't let up for five days I joost let the wind carry us; for if the Deil wanted to get somewheres—well, he would fetch it up a'reet. An' if he didn't, well, we'd keep a sharp lookout anyhow. Sure eneuch, we had a fair way and deep water all the time; and two days ago, when the mornin' sun came through the fog, we found ourselves just in the river opposite Galatz. The Roumanians were wild, and wanted me right or wrong to take out the box and fling it in the river. I had to argy wi' them aboot it wi' a handspike; an' when the last o' them rose off the deck wi' his head in his hand, I had convinced them that, evil eye or no evil eye, the property and the trust of my owners were better in my hands than in the river Danube. They had, mind ye, taken the box on the deck ready to fling in, and as it was marked Galatz *via* Varna, I thocht I'd let it lie till we discharged in the port an' get rid o't althegither. We didn't do much clearin' that day, an' had to remain the nicht at anchor; but in the mornin', braw an' airly, an hour before sun-up, a man came aboard wi' an order, written to him from England, to receive a box marked for one Count Dracula. Sure eneuch the matter was one ready to his hand. He had his papers a' reet, an' glad I was to be rid o' the dam' thing, for I was beginnin' masel' to feel uneasy at it. If the Deil did have any luggage aboord the ship, I'm thinkin' it was nane ither than that same!"

"What was the name of the man who took it?" asked Dr. Van Helsing with restrained eagerness.

"I'll be tellin' ye quick!" he answered, and, stepping down to his cabin, produced a receipt signed "Immanuel Hildesheim." Burgen-strasse 16 was the address. We found out that this was all the Captain knew; so with thanks we came away.

We found Hildesheim in his office, a Hebrew of rather the Adelphi Theatre type, with a nose like a sheep, and a fez. His arguments were pointed with specie—we doing the punctuation—and with a little bargaining he told us what he knew. This turned out to be simple but important. He had received a letter from Mr. de Ville of London, telling him to receive, if possible before sunrise so as to avoid customs, a box which would arrive at Galatz in the *Czarina Catherine*. This he was to give in charge to a certain Petrof Skinsky, who dealt with the Slovaks who traded down the river to the port. He had been paid for his work by an English bank note, which had been duly cashed for gold at the Danube International Bank. When Skinsky had come to him, he had taken him to the ship and handed over the box, so as to save porterage. That was all he knew.

We then sought for Skinsky, but were unable to find him. One of his neighbours, who did not seem to bear him any affection, said that he had gone away two days before, no one knew whither. This was corroborated by his landlord, who had received by messenger the key of the house together with the rent due, in English money. This had been between ten and eleven o'clock last night. We were at a standstill again.

Whilst we were talking one came running and breathlessly gasped out that the body of Skinsky had been found inside the wall of the churchyard of St. Peter, and that the throat had been torn open as if by some wild animal. Those we had been speaking with ran off to see the horror, the women crying out "This is the work of a Slovak!" We hurried away lest we should have been in some way drawn into the affair, and so detained.

As we came home we could arrive at no definite conclusion. We were all convinced that the box was on its way, by water, to somewhere; but where that might be we would have to discover. With heavy hearts we came home to the hotel to Mina.

When we met together, the first thing was to consult as to taking Mina again into our confidence. Things are getting desperate, and it is at least a chance, though a hazardous one. As a preliminary step, I was released from my promise to her.

MINA HARKER'S JOURNAL.

30 October, evening.—They were so tired and worn out and dispirited that there was nothing to be done till they had some rest; so I asked them all to lie down for half an hour whilst I should enter everything up to the moment. I feel so grateful to the man who invented the "Traveller's" typewriter, and to Mr. Morris for getting this one for me. I should have felt quite astray doing the work if I had to write with a pen . . . .

It is all done; poor dear, dear Jonathan, what he must have suffered, what must he be suffering now. He lies on the sofa hardly seeming to breathe, and his whole body appears in collapse. His brows are knit; his face is drawn with pain. Poor fellow, maybe he is thinking, and I can see his face all wrinkled up with the concentration of his thoughts. Oh! if I could only help at all . . . . I shall do what I can.

I have asked Dr. Van Helsing, and he has got me all the papers that I have not yet seen . . . . Whilst they are resting, I shall go over all carefully, and perhaps I may arrive at some conclusion. I shall try to follow the Professor's example, and think without prejudice on the facts before me . . . .

I do believe that under God's providence I have made a discovery. I shall get the maps and look over them . . . .

I am more than ever sure that I am right. My new conclusion is ready, so I shall get our party together and read it. They can judge it; it is well to be accurate, and every minute is precious.

MINA HARKER'S MEMORANDUM.

(Entered in her Journal.)

Ground of inquiry.—Count Dracula's problem is to get back to his own place.

(*a*) He must be *brought back* by some one. This is evident; for had he power to move himself as he wished he could go either as man, or wolf, or bat, or in some other way. He evidently fears discovery or interference, in the state of helplessness in which he must be—confined as he is between dawn and sunset in his wooden box.

(*b*) *How is he to be taken?*—Here a process of exclusions may help us. By road, by rail, by water?

1. *By Road.*—There are endless difficulties, especially in leaving the city.

(*x*) There are people; and people are curious, and investigate. A hint, a surmise, a doubt as to what might be in the box, would destroy him.

(*y*) There are, or there may be, customs and octroi officers to pass.

(*z*) His pursuers might follow. This is his highest fear; and in order to prevent his being betrayed he has repelled, so far as he can, even his victim—me!

2. *By Rail.*—There is no one in charge of the box. It would have to take its chance of being delayed; and delay would be fatal, with enemies on the track. True, he might escape at night; but what would he be, if left in a strange place with no refuge that he could fly to? This is not what he intends; and he does not mean to risk it.

3. *By Water.*—Here is the safest way, in one respect, but with most danger in another. On the water he is powerless except at night; even then he can only summon fog and storm and snow and his wolves. But were he wrecked, the living water would engulf him, helpless; and he would indeed be lost. He could have the vessel drive to land; but if it were unfriendly land, wherein he was not free to move, his position would still be desperate.

We know from the record that he was on the water; so what we have to do is to ascertain *what* water.

The first thing is to realise exactly what he has done as yet; we may, then, get a light on what his later task is to be.

Firstly.—We must differentiate between what he did in London as part of his general plan of action, when he was pressed for moments and had to arrange as best he could.

Secondly we must see, as well as we can surmise it from the facts we know of, what he has done here.

As to the first, he evidently intended to arrive at Galatz, and sent invoice to Varna to deceive us lest we should ascertain his means of exit from England; his immediate and sole purpose then was to escape. The proof of this, is the letter of instructions sent to Immanuel Hildesheim to clear and take away the box *before sunrise.* There is also the instruction to Petrof Skinsky. These we must only guess at; but there must have been some letter or message, since Skinsky came to Hildesheim.

That, so far, his plans were successful we know. The *Czarina Catherine* made a phenomenally quick journey—so much so that Captain Donelson's suspicions were aroused; but his superstition united with his canniness played the Count's game for him, and he ran with his favouring wind through fogs and all till he brought up blindfold at Galatz. That the Count's arrangements were well made, has been proved. Hildesheim cleared the box, took it off, and gave it to Skinsky. Skinsky took it—and here we lose the trail. We only know that the box is somewhere on the water, moving along. The customs and the octroi, if there be any, have been avoided.

Now we come to what the Count must have done after his arrival—*on land*, at Galatz.

The box was given to Skinsky before sunrise. At sunrise the Count could appear in his own form. Here, we ask why Skinsky was chosen at all to aid in the work? In my husband's diary, Skinsky is mentioned as dealing with the Slovaks who trade down the river to the port; and the man's remark, that the murder was the work of a Slovak, showed the general feeling against his class. The Count wanted isolation.

My surmise is, this: that in London the Count decided to get back to his castle by water, as the most safe and secret way. He was brought from the castle by Szgany, and probably they delivered their cargo to Slovaks who took the boxes to Varna, for there they were shipped for London. Thus the Count had knowledge of the persons who could arrange this service. When the box was on land, before sunrise or after sunset, he came out from his box, met Skinsky and instructed him what to do as to arranging the carriage of the box up some river. When this was done, and he knew that all was in train, he blotted out his traces, as he thought, by murdering his agent.

I have examined the map and find that the river most suitable for the Slovaks to have ascended is either the Pruth or the Sereth. I read in the typescript that in my trance I heard cows low and water swirling level with my ears and the creaking of wood. The Count in his box, then, was on a river in an open boat—propelled probably either by oars or poles, for the banks are near and it is working against stream. There would be no such sound if floating down stream.

Of course it may not be either the Sereth or the Pruth, but we may possibly investigate further. Now of these two, the Pruth is the more easily navigated, but the Sereth is, at Fundu, joined by the Bistritza which runs up round the Borgo Pass. The loop it makes is manifestly as close to Dracula's castle as can be got by water.

MINA HARKER'S JOURNAL—*continued.*

When I had done reading, Jonathan took me in his arms and kissed me. The others kept shaking me by both hands, and Dr. Van Helsing said:—

"Our dear Madam Mina is once more our teacher. Her eyes have been where we were blinded. Now we are on the track once again, and this time we may succeed. Our enemy is at his most helpless; and if we can come on him by day, on the water, our task will be over. He has a start, but he is powerless to hasten, as he may not leave his box lest those who carry him may suspect; for them to suspect would be to prompt them to throw him in the stream where he perish. This he knows, and will not. Now men, to our Council of War; for, here and now, we must plan what each and all shall do."

"I shall get a steam launch and follow him," said Lord Godalming.

"And I, horses to follow on the bank lest by chance he land," said Mr. Morris.

"Good!" said the Professor, "both good. But neither must go alone. There must be force to overcome force if need be; the Slovak is strong and rough, and he carries rude arms." All the men smiled, for amongst them they carried a small arsenal. Said Mr. Morris:—

"I have brought some Winchesters; they are pretty handy in a crowd, and there may be wolves. The Count, if you remember, took some other precautions; he made some requisitions on others that Mrs. Harker could not quite hear or understand. We must be ready at all points." Dr. Seward said:—

"I think I had better go with Quincey. We have been accustomed to hunt together, and we two, well armed, will be a match for whatever may come along. You must not be alone, Art. It may be necessary to fight the Slovaks, and a chance thrust—for I don't suppose these fellows carry guns—would undo all our plans. There must be no chances, this time; we shall not rest until the Count's head and body have been separated, and we are sure that he cannot re-incarnate." He looked at Jonathan as he spoke, and Jonathan looked at me. I could see that the poor dear was torn about in his mind. Of course he wanted to be with me; but then the boat service would, most likely, be the one which would destroy the . . . the . . . the . . . Vampire. (Why did I hesitate to write the word?) He was silent awhile, and during his silence Dr. Van Helsing spoke:—

"Friend Jonathan, this is to you for twice reasons. First, because you are young and brave and can fight, and all energies may be needed at the last; and again that it is your right to destroy him—that—which has wrought such woe to you and yours. Be not afraid for Madam Mina; she will be my care, if I may. I am old. My legs are not so quick to run as once; and I am not used to ride so long or to pursue as need be, or to fight with lethal weapons. But I can be of other service; I can fight in other way. And I can die, if need be, as well as younger men. Now let me say that what I would is this: while you, my Lord Godalming and friend Jonathan go in your so swift little steamboat up the river, and whilst John and Quincey guard the bank where perchance he might be landed, I will take Madam Mina right into the heart of the enemy's country. Whilst the old fox is tied in his box, floating on the running stream whence he cannot escape to land—where he dares not raise the lid of his coffin-box lest his Slovak carriers should in fear leave him to perish—we shall go in the track where Jonathan went,—from Bistritz over the Borgo, and find our way to the Castle of Dracula. Here, Madam Mina's hypnotic power will surely help, and we shall find our way—all dark and unknown otherwise—after the first sunrise when we are near that fateful place. There is much to be done, and other places to be made sanctify, so that that nest of vipers be obliterated." Here Jonathan interrupted him hotly:—

"Do you mean to say, Professor Van Helsing, that you would bring Mina, in her sad case and tainted as she is with that devil's illness, right into the jaws of his death-trap? Not for the world! Not for Heaven or Hell!" He became almost speechless for a minute, and then went on:—

"Do you know what the place is? Have you seen that awful den of hellish infamy—with the very moonlight alive with grisly shapes, and every speck of dust that whirls in the wind a devouring monster in embryo? Have you felt the Vampire's lips upon your throat?" Here he turned to me, and as his eyes lit on my forehead he threw up his arms with a cry: "Oh, my God, what have we done to have this terror upon us!" and he sank down on the sofa in a collapse of misery. The Professor's voice, as he spoke in clear, sweet tones, which seemed to vibrate in the air, calmed us all:—

"Oh, my friend, it is because I would save Madam Mina from that awful place that I would go. God forbid that I should take her into that place. There is work—wild work—to be done there, that her eyes may not see. We men here, all save Jonathan, have seen with their own eyes what is to be done before that place can be purify. Remember that we are in terrible straits. If the Count escape us this time—and he is strong and subtle and cunning—he may choose to sleep him for a century, and then in time our dear one"—he took my hand—"would come to him to keep him company, and would be as those others that you, Jonathan, saw. You have told us of their gloating lips; you heard their ribald laugh as they clutched the moving bag that the Count threw to them. You shudder; and well may it be. Forgive me that I make you so much pain, but it is necessary. My friend, is it not a dire need for the which I am giving, possibly my life? If it were that any one went into that place to stay, it is I who would have to go to keep them company."

"Do as you will," said Jonathan, with a sob that shook him all over, "we are in the hands of God!"

Later.—Oh, it did me good to see the way that these brave men worked. How can women help loving men when they are so earnest, and so true, and so brave! And, too, it made me think of the wonderful power of money! What can it not do when it is properly applied; and what might it do when basely used. I felt so thankful that Lord Godalming is rich, and that both he and Mr. Morris, who also has plenty of money, are willing to spend it so freely. For if they did not, our little expedition could not start, either so promptly or so well equipped, as it will within another hour. It is not three hours since it was arranged what part each of us was to do; and now Lord Godalming and Jonathan have a lovely steam launch, with steam up ready to start at a moment's notice. Dr. Seward and Mr. Morris have half a dozen good horses, well appointed. We have all the maps and appliances of various kinds that can be had. Professor Van Helsing and I are to leave by the 11:40 train to-night for Veresti, where we are to get a carriage to drive to the Borgo Pass. We are bringing a good deal of ready money, as we are to buy a carriage and horses. We shall drive ourselves, for we have no one whom we can trust in the matter. The Professor knows something of a great many languages, so we shall get on all right. We have all got arms, even for me a large-bore revolver; Jonathan would not be happy unless I was armed like the rest. Alas! I cannot carry one arm that the rest do; the scar on my forehead forbids that. Dear Dr. Van Helsing comforts me by telling me that

I am fully armed as there may be wolves; the weather is getting colder every hour, and there are snow-flurries which come and go as warnings.

Later.—It took all my courage to say good-bye to my darling. We may never meet again. Courage, Mina! the Professor is looking at you keenly; his look is a warning. There must be no tears now—unless it may be that God will let them fall in gladness.

JONATHAN HARKER'S JOURNAL.

October 30. Night.—I am writing this in the light from the furnace door of the steam launch: Lord Godalming is firing up. He is an experienced hand at the work, as he has had for years a launch of his own on the Thames, and another on the Norfolk Broads. Regarding our plans, we finally decided that Mina's guess was correct, and that if any waterway was chosen for the Count's escape back to his Castle, the Sereth and then the Bistritza at its junction, would be the one. We took it, that somewhere about the 47th degree, north latitude, would be the place chosen for the crossing the country between the river and the Carpathians. We have no fear in running at good speed up the river at night; there is plenty of water, and the banks are wide enough apart to make steaming, even in the dark, easy enough. Lord Godalming tells me to sleep for a while, as it is enough for the present for one to be on watch. But I cannot sleep—how can I with the terrible danger hanging over my darling, and her going out into that awful place . . . . My only comfort is that we are in the hands of God. Only for that faith it would be easier to die than to live, and so be quit of all the trouble. Mr. Morris and Dr. Seward were off on their long ride before we started; they are to keep up the right bank, far enough off to get on higher lands where they can see a good stretch of river and avoid the following of its curves. They have, for the first stages, two men to ride and lead their spare horses—four in all, so as not to excite curiosity. When they dismiss the men, which shall be shortly, they shall themselves look after the horses. It may be necessary for us to join forces; if so they can mount our whole party. One of the saddles has a movable horn, and can be easily adapted for Mina, if required.

It is a wild adventure we are on. Here, as we are rushing along through the darkness, with the cold from the river seeming to rise up and strike us; with all the mysterious voices of the night around us, it all comes home. We seem to be drifting into unknown places and unknown ways; into a whole world of dark and dreadful things. Godalming is shutting the furnace door . . . .

31 October.—Still hurrying along. The day has come, and Godalming is sleeping. I am on watch. The morning is bitterly cold; the furnace heat is grateful, though we have heavy fur coats. As yet we have passed only a few open boats, but none of them had on board any box or package of anything like the size of the one we seek. The men were scared every time we turned our electric lamp on them, and fell on their knees and prayed.

1 November, evening.—No news all day; we have found nothing of the kind we seek. We have now passed into the Bistritza; and if we are wrong in our surmise our chance is gone. We have over-hauled every boat, big and little. Early this morning, one crew took us for a Government boat, and treated us accordingly. We saw in this a way of smoothing matters, so at Fundu, where the Bistritza runs into the Sereth, we got a Roumanian flag which we now fly conspicuously. With every boat which we have over-hauled since then this trick has succeeded; we have had every deference shown to us, and not once any objection to whatever we chose to ask or do. Some of the Slovaks tell us that a big boat passed them, going at more than usual speed as she had a double crew on board. This was before they came to Fundu, so they could not tell us whether the boat turned into the Bistritza or continued on up the Sereth. At Fundu we could not hear of any such boat, so she must have passed there in the night. I am feeling very sleepy; the cold is perhaps beginning to tell upon me, and nature must have rest some time. Godalming insists that he shall keep the first watch. God bless him for all his goodness to poor dear Mina and me.

2 November, morning.—It is broad daylight. That good fellow would not wake me. He says it would have been a sin to, for I slept peacefully and was forgetting my trouble. It seems brutally selfish to me to have slept so long, and let him watch all night; but he was quite right. I am a new man this morning; and, as I sit here and watch him sleeping, I can do all that is necessary both as to minding the engine, steering, and keeping watch. I can feel that my strength and energy are coming back to me. I wonder where Mina is now, and Van Helsing. They should have got to Veresti about noon on Wednesday. It would take them some time to get the carriage and horses; so if they had started and travelled hard, they would be about now at the Borgo Pass. God guide and help them! I am afraid to think what may happen. If we could only go faster! but we cannot; the engines are throbbing and doing their utmost. I wonder how Dr. Seward and Mr. Morris are getting on. There seem to be endless streams running down the mountains into this river, but as none of them are very large—at present, at all events, though they are terrible doubtless in winter and when the snow melts—the horsemen may not have met much obstruction. I hope that before we get to Strasba we may see them; for if by that time we have not overtaken the Count, it may be necessary to take counsel together what to do next.

DR. SEWARD'S DIARY.

2 November.—Three days on the road. No news, and no time to write it if there had been, for every moment is precious. We have had only the rest needful for the horses; but we are both bearing it wonderfully. Those adventurous days of ours are turning up useful. We must push on; we shall never feel happy till we get the launch in sight again.

3 November.—We heard at Fundu that the launch had gone up the Bistritza. I wish it wasn't so cold. There are signs of snow coming; and if it falls heavy it will stop us. In such case we must get a sledge and go on, Russian fashion.

4 November.—To-day we heard of the launch having been detained by an accident when trying to force a way up the rapids. The Slovak boats get up all right, by aid of a rope and steering with knowledge. Some went up only a few hours before. Godalming is an amateur fitter himself, and evidently it was he who put the launch in trim again. Finally, they got up the rapids all right, with local help, and are off on the chase afresh. I fear that the boat is not any better for the accident; the peasantry tell us that after she got upon smooth water again, she kept stopping every now and again so long as she was in sight. We must push on harder than ever; our help may be wanted soon.

MINA HARKER'S JOURNAL.

31 October.—Arrived at Veresti at noon. The Professor tells me that this morning at dawn he could hardly hypnotise me at all, and that all I could say was: "dark and quiet." He is off now buying a carriage and horses. He says that he will later on try to buy additional horses, so that we may be able to change them on the way. We have something more than 70 miles before us. The country is lovely, and most interesting; if only we were under different conditions, how delightful it would be to see it all. If Jonathan and I were driving through it alone what a pleasure it would be. To stop and see people, and learn something of their life, and to fill our minds and memories with all the colour and picturesqueness of the whole wild, beautiful country and the quaint people! But, alas!—

Later.—Dr. Van Helsing has returned. He has got the carriage and horses;

we are to have some dinner, and to start in an hour. The landlady is putting us up a huge basket of provisions; it seems enough for a company of soldiers. The Professor encourages her, and whispers to me that it may be a week before we can get any good food again. He has been shopping too, and has sent home such a wonderful lot of fur coats and wraps, and all sorts of warm things. There will not be any chance of our being cold.

* * * * *

We shall soon be off. I am afraid to think what may happen to us. We are truly in the hands of God. He alone knows what may be, and I pray Him, with all the strength of my sad and humble soul, that He will watch over my beloved husband; that whatever may happen, Jonathan may know that I loved him and honoured him more than I can say, and that my latest and truest thought will be always for him.

CHAPTER XXVII

MINA HARKER'S JOURNAL

1 November.—All day long we have travelled, and at a good speed. The horses seem to know that they are being kindly treated, for they go willingly their full stage at best speed. We have now had so many changes and find the same thing so constantly that we are encouraged to think that the journey will be an easy one. Dr. Van Helsing is laconic; he tells the farmers that he is hurrying to Bistritz, and pays them well to make the exchange of horses. We get hot soup, or coffee, or tea; and off we go. It is a lovely country; full of beauties of all imaginable kinds, and the people are brave, and strong, and simple, and seem full of nice qualities. They are *very, very* superstitious. In the first house where we stopped, when the woman who served us saw the scar on my forehead, she crossed herself and put out two fingers towards me, to keep off the evil eye. I believe they went to the trouble of putting an extra amount of garlic into our food; and I can't abide garlic. Ever since then I have taken care not to take off my hat or veil, and so have escaped their suspicions. We are travelling fast, and as we have no driver with us to carry tales, we go ahead of scandal; but I daresay that fear of the evil eye will follow hard behind us all the way. The Professor seems tireless; all day he would not take any rest, though he made me sleep for a long spell. At sunset time he hypnotised me, and he says that I answered as usual "darkness, lapping water and creaking wood"; so our enemy is still on the river. I am afraid to think of Jonathan, but somehow I have now no fear for him, or for myself. I write this whilst we wait in a farmhouse for the horses to be got ready. Dr. Van Helsing is sleeping, Poor dear, he looks very tired and old and grey, but his mouth is set as firmly as a conqueror's; even in his sleep he is instinct with resolution. When we have well started I must make him rest whilst I drive. I shall tell him that we have days before us, and we must not break down when most of all his strength will be needed . . . . All is ready; we are off shortly.

2 November, morning.—I was successful, and we took turns driving all night; now the day is on us, bright though cold. There is a strange heaviness in the air—I say heaviness for want of a better word; I mean that it oppresses us both. It is very cold, and only our warm furs keep us comfortable. At dawn Van Helsing hypnotised me; he says I answered "darkness, creaking wood and roaring water," so the river is changing as they ascend. I do hope that my darling will not run any chance of danger—more than need be; but we are in God's hands.

2 November, night.—All day long driving. The country gets wilder as we go, and the great spurs of the Carpathians, which at Veresti seemed so far from us and so low on the horizon, now seem to gather round us and tower in front. We both seem in good spirits; I think we make an effort each to cheer the other; in the doing so we cheer ourselves. Dr. Van Helsing says that by morning we shall reach the Borgo Pass. The houses are very few here now, and the Professor says that the last horse we got will have to go on with us, as we may not be able to change. He got two in addition to the two we changed, so that now we have a rude four-in-hand. The dear horses are patient and good, and they give us no trouble. We are not worried with other travellers, and so even I can drive. We shall get to the Pass in daylight; we do not want to arrive before. So we take it easy, and have each a long rest in turn. Oh, what will to-morrow bring to us? We go to seek the place where my poor darling suffered so much. God grant that we may be guided aright, and that He will deign to watch over my husband and those dear to us both, and who are in such deadly peril. As for me, I am not worthy in His sight. Alas! I am unclean to His eyes, and shall be until He may deign to let me stand forth in His sight as one of those who have not incurred His wrath.

MEMORANDUM BY ABRAHAM VAN HELSING.

4 November.—This to my old and true friend John Seward, M.D., of Purfleet, London, in case I may not see him. It may explain. It is morning, and I write by a fire which all the night I have kept alive—Madam Mina aiding me. It is cold, cold; so cold that the grey heavy sky is full of snow, which when it falls will settle for all winter as the ground is hardening to receive it. It seems to have affected Madam Mina; she has been so heavy of head all day that she was not like herself. She sleeps, and sleeps, and sleeps! She who is usual so alert, have done literally nothing all the day; she even have lost her appetite. She make no entry into her little diary, she who write so faithful at every pause. Something whisper to me that all is not well. However, to-night she is more *vif.* Her long sleep all day have refresh and restore her, for now she is all sweet and bright as ever. At sunset I try to hypnotise her, but alas! with no effect; the power has grown less and less with each day, and to-night it fail me altogether. Well, God's will be done—whatever it may be, and whithersoever it may lead!

Now to the historical, for as Madam Mina write not in her stenography, I must, in my cumbrous old fashion, that so each day of us may not go unrecorded.

We got to the Borgo Pass just after sunrise yesterday morning. When I saw the signs of the dawn I got ready for the hypnotism. We stopped our carriage, and got down so that there might be no disturbance. I made a couch with furs, and Madam Mina, lying down, yield herself as usual, but more slow and more short time than ever, to the hypnotic sleep. As before, came the answer: "darkness and the swirling of water." Then she woke, bright and radiant and we go on our way and soon reach the Pass. At this time and place, she become all on fire with zeal; some new guiding power be in her manifested, for she point to a road and say:—

"This is the way."

"How know you it?" I ask.

"Of course I know it," she answer, and with a pause, add: "Have not my Jonathan travelled it and wrote of his travel?"

At first I think somewhat strange, but soon I see that there be only one such by-road. It is used but little, and very different from the coach road from the Bukovina to Bistritz, which is more wide and hard, and more of use.

So we came down this road; when we meet other ways—not always were we sure that they were roads at all, for they be neglect and light snow have fallen—the horses know and they only. I give rein to them, and they go on so patient. By-and-by we find all the things which Jonathan have note in that wonderful diary of him. Then we go on for long, long hours and hours. At the first, I tell Madam Mina to sleep; she try, and she succeed. She sleep all the time; till at the last, I feel myself to suspicious grow, and attempt to wake her. But she sleep on, and I may not wake her though I try. I do not wish to try too hard lest I harm her; for I know that she have suffer much, and sleep at times be all-in-all to her. I think I drowse myself, for all of sudden I feel guilt, as though I have done something; I find myself bolt up, with the reins in my hand, and the good horses go along jog, jog, just as ever. I look down and find Madam Mina still sleep. It is now not far off sunset time, and over the snow the light of the sun flow in big yellow flood, so that we throw great long shadow on where the mountain rise so steep. For we are going up, and up; and all is oh! so wild and rocky, as though it were the end of the world.

Then I arouse Madam Mina. This time she wake with not much trouble, and then I try to put her to hypnotic sleep. But she sleep not, being as though I were not. Still I try and try, till all at once I find her and myself in dark; so

I look round, and find that the sun have gone down. Madam Mina laugh, and I turn and look at her. She is now quite awake, and look so well as I never saw her since that night at Carfax when we first enter the Count's house. I am amaze, and not at ease then; but she is so bright and tender and thoughtful for me that I forget all fear. I light a fire, for we have brought supply of wood with us, and she prepare food while I undo the horses and set them, tethered in shelter, to feed. Then when I return to the fire she have my supper ready. I go to help her; but she smile, and tell me that she have eat already—that she was so hungry that she would not wait. I like it not, and I have grave doubts; but I fear to affright her, and so I am silent of it. She help me and I eat alone; and then we wrap in fur and lie beside the fire, and I tell her to sleep while I watch. But presently I forget all of watching; and when I sudden remember that I watch, I find her lying quiet, but awake, and looking at me with so bright eyes. Once, twice more the same occur, and I get much sleep till before morning. When I wake I try to hypnotise her; but alas! though she shut her eyes obedient, she may not sleep. The sun rise up, and up, and up; and then sleep come to her too late, but so heavy that she will not wake. I have to lift her up, and place her sleeping in the carriage when I have harnessed the horses and made all ready. Madam still sleep, and she look in her sleep more healthy and more redder than before. And I like it not. And I am afraid, afraid, afraid!—I am afraid of all things—even to think but I must go on my way. The stake we play for is life and death, or more than these, and we must not flinch.

5 November, morning.—Let me be accurate in everything, for though you and I have seen some strange things together, you may at the first think that I, Van Helsing, am mad—that the many horrors and the so long strain on nerves has at the last turn my brain.

All yesterday we travel, ever getting closer to the mountains, and moving into a more and more wild and desert land. There are great, frowning precipices and much falling water, and Nature seem to have held sometime her carnival. Madam Mina still sleep and sleep; and though I did have hunger and appeased it, I could not waken her—even for food. I began to fear that the fatal spell of the place was upon her, tainted as she is with that Vampire baptism. "Well," said I to myself, "if it be that she sleep all the day, it shall also be that I do not sleep at night." As we travel on the rough road, for a road of an ancient and imperfect kind there was, I held down my head and slept. Again I waked with a sense of guilt and of time passed, and found Madam Mina still sleeping, and the sun low down. But all was indeed changed; the frowning mountains seemed further away, and we were near the top of a steep-rising hill, on summit of which was such a castle as

Jonathan tell of in his diary. At once I exulted and feared; for now, for good or ill, the end was near.

I woke Madam Mina, and again tried to hypnotise her; but alas! unavailing till too late. Then, ere the great dark came upon us—for even after down-sun the heavens reflected the gone sun on the snow, and all was for a time in a great twilight—I took out the horses and fed them in what shelter I could. Then I make a fire; and near it I make Madam Mina, now awake and more charming than ever, sit comfortable amid her rugs. I got ready food: but she would not eat, simply saying that she had not hunger. I did not press her, knowing her unavailingness. But I myself eat, for I must needs now be strong for all. Then, with the fear on me of what might be, I drew a ring so big for her comfort, round where Madam Mina sat; and over the ring I passed some of the wafer, and I broke it fine so that all was well guarded. She sat still all the time—so still as one dead; and she grew whiter and ever whiter till the snow was not more pale; and no word she said. But when I drew near, she clung to me, and I could know that the poor soul shook her from head to feet with a tremor that was pain to feel. I said to her presently, when she had grown more quiet:—

"Will you not come over to the fire?" for I wished to make a test of what she could. She rose obedient, but when she have made a step she stopped, and stood as one stricken.

"Why not go on?" I asked. She shook her head, and, coming back, sat down in her place. Then, looking at me with open eyes, as of one waked from sleep, she said simply:—

"I cannot!" and remained silent. I rejoiced, for I knew that what she could not, none of those that we dreaded could. Though there might be danger to her body, yet her soul was safe!

Presently the horses began to scream, and tore at their tethers till I came to them and quieted them. When they did feel my hands on them, they whinnied low as in joy, and licked at my hands and were quiet for a time. Many times through the night did I come to them, till it arrive to the cold hour when all nature is at lowest; and every time my coming was with quiet of them. In the cold hour the fire began to die, and I was about stepping forth to replenish it, for now the snow came in flying sweeps and with it a chill mist. Even in the dark there was a light of some kind, as there ever is over snow; and it seemed as though the snow-flurries and the wreaths of mist took shape as of women with trailing garments. All was in dead, grim silence only that the horses whinnied and cowered, as if in terror of the worst. I began to fear—horrible fears; but then came to me the sense of safety in that ring wherein I stood. I began, too, to think that my imaginings were of the night, and the gloom, and the unrest that I have gone through, and all the terrible anxiety. It was as though my memories of all Jonathan's horrid experience were befooling me; for the snow flakes and the mist began to wheel and circle round, till I could get as though a shadowy glimpse of those women that would have kissed him. And then the horses cowered lower and lower, and moaned in terror as men do in pain. Even the madness of fright was not to them, so that they could break away. I feared for my dear Madam Mina when these weird figures drew near and circled round. I looked at her, but she sat calm, and smiled at me; when I would have stepped to the fire to replenish it, she caught me and held me back, and whispered, like a voice that one hears in a dream, so low it was:—

"No! No! Do not go without. Here you are safe!" I turned to her, and looking in her eyes, said:—

"But you? It is for you that I fear!" whereat she laughed—a laugh, low and unreal, and said:—

"Fear for *me*! Why fear for me? None safer in all the world from them than I am," and as I wondered at the meaning of her words, a puff of wind made the flame leap up, and I see the red scar on her forehead. Then, alas! I knew. Did I not, I would soon have learned, for the wheeling figures of mist and snow came closer, but keeping ever without the Holy circle. Then they began to materialise till—if God have not take away my reason, for I saw it through my eyes—there were before me in actual flesh the same three women that Jonathan saw in the room, when they would have kissed his throat. I knew the swaying round forms, the bright hard eyes, the white teeth, the ruddy colour, the voluptuous lips. They smiled ever at poor dear Madam Mina; and as their laugh came through the silence of the night, they twined their arms and pointed to her, and said in those so sweet tingling tones that Jonathan said were of the intolerable sweetness of the water-glasses:—

"Come, sister. Come to us. Come! Come!" In fear I turned to my poor Madam Mina, and my heart with gladness leapt like flame; for oh! the terror in her sweet eyes, the repulsion, the horror, told a story to my heart that was all of hope. God be thanked she was not, yet, of them. I seized some of the firewood which was by me, and holding out some of the Wafer, advanced on them towards the fire. They drew back before me, and laughed their low horrid laugh. I fed the fire, and feared them not; for I knew that we were safe within our protections. They could not approach, me, whilst so armed, nor Madam Mina whilst she remained within the ring, which she could not leave no more than they could enter. The horses had ceased to moan, and lay still on the ground; the snow fell on them softly, and they grew whiter. I knew that there was for the poor beasts no more of terror.

And so we remained till the red of the dawn to fall through the snow-gloom. I was desolate and afraid, and full of woe and terror; but when that beautiful sun began to climb the horizon life was to me again. At the first coming of the dawn the horrid figures melted in the whirling mist and snow; the wreaths of transparent gloom moved away towards the castle, and were lost. Instinctively, with the dawn coming, I turned to Madam Mina, intending to hypnotise her; but she lay in a deep and sudden sleep, from which I could not wake her. I tried to hypnotise through her sleep, but she made no response, none at all; and the day broke. I fear yet to stir. I have made my fire and have seen the horses, they are all dead. To-day I have much to do here, and I keep waiting till the sun is up high; for there may be places where I must go, where that sunlight, though snow and mist obscure it, will be to me a safety. I will strengthen me with breakfast, and then I will to my terrible work. Madam Mina still sleeps; and, God be thanked! she is calm in her sleep . . . .

JONATHAN HARKER'S JOURNAL.

4 November, evening.—The accident to the launch has been a terrible thing for us. Only for it we should have overtaken the boat long ago; and by now my dear Mina would have been free. I fear to think of her, off on the wolds near that horrid place. We have got horses, and we follow on the track. I note this whilst Godalming is getting ready. We have our arms. The Szgany must look out if they mean fight. Oh, if only Morris and Seward were with us. We must only hope! If I write no more Good-bye, Mina! God bless and keep you.

DR. SEWARD'S DIARY.

5 November.—With the dawn we saw the body of Szgany before us dashing away from the river with their leiter-wagon. They surrounded it in a cluster, and hurried along as though beset. The snow is falling lightly and there is a strange excitement in the air. It may be our own feelings, but the depression is strange. Far off I hear the howling of wolves; the snow brings them down from the mountains, and there are dangers to all of us, and from all sides. The horses are nearly ready, and we are soon off. We ride to death of some one. God alone knows who, or where, or what, or when, or how it may be . . . .

DR. VAN HELSING'S MEMORANDUM.

5 November, afternoon.—I am at least sane. Thank God for that mercy at all events, though the proving it has been dreadful. When I left Madam Mina sleeping within the Holy circle, I took my way to the castle. The blacksmith hammer which I took in the carriage from Veresti was useful; though the doors were all open I broke them off the rusty hinges, lest some ill-intent or ill-chance should close them, so that being entered I might not get out. Jonathan's bitter experience served me here. By memory of his diary I found my way to the old chapel, for I knew that here my work lay. The air was oppressive; it seemed as if there was some sulphurous fume, which at times made me dizzy. Either there was a roaring in my ears or I heard afar off the howl of wolves. Then I bethought me of my dear Madam Mina, and I was in terrible plight. The dilemma had me between his horns.

Her, I had not dare to take into this place, but left safe from the Vampire in that Holy circle; and yet even there would be the wolf! I resolve me that my work lay here, and that as to the wolves we must submit, if it were God's will. At any rate it was only death and freedom beyond. So did I choose for her. Had it but been for myself the choice had been easy, the maw of the wolf were better to rest in than the grave of the Vampire! So I make my choice to go on with my work.

I knew that there were at least three graves to find—graves that are inhabit; so I search, and search, and I find one of them. She lay in her Vampire sleep, so full of life and voluptuous beauty that I shudder as though I have come to do murder. Ah, I doubt not that in old time, when such things were, many a man who set forth to do such a task as mine, found at the last his heart fail him, and then his nerve. So he delay, and delay, and delay, till the mere beauty and the fascination of the wanton Un-Dead have hypnotise him; and he remain on and on, till sunset come, and the Vampire sleep be over. Then the beautiful eyes of the fair woman open and look love, and the voluptuous mouth present to a kiss—and man is weak. And there remain one more victim in the Vampire fold; one more to swell the grim and grisly ranks of the Un-Dead! . . .

There is some fascination, surely, when I am moved by the mere presence of such an one, even lying as she lay in a tomb fretted with age and heavy with the dust of centuries, though there be that horrid odour such as the lairs of the Count have had. Yes, I was moved—I, Van Helsing, with all my purpose and with my motive for hate—I was moved to a yearning for delay which seemed to paralyse my faculties and to clog my very soul. It may have been that the need of natural sleep, and the strange oppression of the air were beginning to overcome me. Certain it was that I was lapsing into sleep, the open-eyed sleep of one who yields to a sweet fascination, when there came through the snow-stilled air a long, low wail, so full of woe and pity that it woke me like the sound of a clarion. For it was the voice of my dear Madam Mina that I heard.

Then I braced myself again to my horrid task, and found by wrenching away tomb-tops one other of the sisters, the other dark one. I dared not pause to look on her as I had on her sister, lest once more I should begin to be enthrall; but I go on searching until, presently, I find in a high great tomb as if made to one much beloved that other fair sister which, like Jonathan I had seen to gather herself out of the atoms of the mist. She was so fair to look on, so radiantly beautiful, so exquisitely voluptuous, that the very instinct of man in me, which calls some of my sex to love and to protect one of hers, made my head whirl with new emotion. But God be thanked, that soul-wail of my dear Madam Mina had not died out of my ears; and, before the spell could be wrought further upon me, I had nerved myself to my wild work. By this time I had searched all the tombs in the chapel, so far as I could tell; and as there had been only three of these Un-Dead phantoms around us in the night, I took it that there were no more of active Un-Dead existent. There was one great tomb more lordly than all the rest; huge it was, and nobly proportioned. On it was but one word

DRACULA.

This then was the Un-Dead home of the King-Vampire, to whom so many more were due. Its emptiness spoke eloquent to make certain what I knew. Before I began to restore these women to their dead selves through my awful work, I laid in Dracula's tomb some of the Wafer, and so banished him from it, Un-Dead, for ever.

Then began my terrible task, and I dreaded it. Had it been but one, it had been easy, comparative. But three! To begin twice more after I had been through a deed of horror; for if it was terrible with the sweet Miss Lucy, what would it not be with these strange ones who had survived through centuries, and who had been strengthened by the passing of the years; who would, if they could, have fought for their foul lives . . . .

Oh, my friend John, but it was butcher work; had I not been nerved by thoughts of other dead, and of the living over whom hung such a pall of fear, I could not have gone on. I tremble and tremble even yet, though till all was over, God be thanked, my nerve did stand. Had I not seen the repose in the first place, and the gladness that stole over it just ere the final dissolution came, as realisation that the soul had been won, I could not have gone further with my butchery. I could not have endured the horrid screeching as the stake drove home; the plunging of writhing form, and lips of bloody foam. I should have fled in terror and left my work undone. But it is over! And the poor souls, I can pity them now and weep, as I think of them placid each in her full sleep of death for a short moment ere fading. For, friend John, hardly had my knife severed the head of each, before the whole body began to melt away and crumble in to its native dust, as though the death that should have come centuries agone had at last assert himself and say at once and loud "I am here!"

Before I left the castle I so fixed its entrances that never more can the Count enter there Un-Dead.

When I stepped into the circle where Madam Mina slept, she woke from her sleep, and, seeing, me, cried out in pain that I had endured too much.

"Come!" she said, "come away from this awful place! Let us go to meet my husband who is, I know, coming towards us." She was looking thin and pale and weak; but her eyes were pure and glowed with fervour. I was glad to see her paleness and her illness, for my mind was full of the fresh horror of that ruddy vampire sleep.

And so with trust and hope, and yet full of fear, we go eastward to meet our friends—and *him*—whom Madam Mina tell me that she *know* are coming to meet us.

MINA HARKER'S JOURNAL.

6 November.—It was late in the afternoon when the Professor and I took our way towards the east whence I knew Jonathan was coming. We did not go fast, though the way was steeply downhill, for we had to take heavy rugs and wraps with us; we dared not face the possibility of being left without warmth in the cold and the snow. We had to take some of our provisions, too, for we were in a perfect desolation, and, so far as we could see through the snowfall, there was not even the sign of habitation. When we had gone about a mile, I was tired with the heavy walking and sat down to rest. Then we looked back and saw where the clear line of Dracula's castle cut the sky; for we were so deep under the hill whereon it was set that the angle of perspective of the Carpathian mountains was far below it. We saw it in all its grandeur, perched a thousand feet on the summit of a sheer precipice, and with seemingly a great gap between it and the steep of the adjacent mountain on any side. There was something wild and uncanny about the place. We could hear the distant howling of wolves. They were far off, but the sound, even though coming muffled through the deadening snowfall, was full of terror. I knew from the way Dr. Van Helsing was searching about that he was trying to seek some strategic point, where we would be less exposed in case of attack. The rough roadway still led downwards; we could trace it through the drifted snow.

In a little while the Professor signalled to me, so I got up and joined him. He had found a wonderful spot, a sort of natural hollow in a rock, with an entrance like a doorway between two boulders. He took me by the hand and drew me in: "See!" he said, "here you will be in shelter; and if the wolves do come I can meet them one by one." He brought in our furs, and made a snug nest for me, and got out some provisions and forced them upon me. But I could not eat; to even try to do so was repulsive to me, and, much as I would have liked to please him, I could not bring myself to the attempt. He looked very sad, but did not reproach me. Taking his field-glasses from the case, he stood on the top of the rock, and began to search the horizon. Suddenly he called out:—

"Look! Madam Mina, look! look!" I sprang up and stood beside him on the rock; he handed me his glasses and pointed. The snow was now falling more heavily, and swirled about fiercely, for a high wind was beginning to blow. However, there were times when there were pauses between the snow flurries and I could see a long way round. From the height where we were it was possible to see a great distance; and far off, beyond the white waste of snow, I could see the river lying like a black ribbon in kinks and curls as it wound its way. Straight in front of us and not far off—in fact, so near that I wondered we had not noticed before—came a group of mounted men hurrying along. In the midst of them was a cart, a long leiter-wagon which swept from side to side, like a dog's tail wagging, with each stern inequality of the road. Outlined against the snow as they were, I could see from the men's clothes that they were peasants or gypsies of some kind.

On the cart was a great square chest. My heart leaped as I saw it, for I felt that the end was coming. The evening was now drawing close, and well I knew that at sunset the Thing, which was till then imprisoned there, would take new freedom and could in any of many forms elude all pursuit. In fear I turned to the Professor; to my consternation, however, he was not there. An instant later, I saw him below me. Round the rock he had drawn a circle, such as we had found shelter in last night. When he had completed it he stood beside me again, saying:—

"At least you shall be safe here from *him*!" He took the glasses from me, and at the next lull of the snow swept the whole space below us. "See," he said, "they come quickly; they are flogging the horses, and galloping as hard as they can." He paused and went on in a hollow voice:—

"They are racing for the sunset. We may be too late. God's will be done!" Down came another blinding rush of driving snow, and the whole landscape was blotted out. It soon passed, however, and once more his glasses were fixed on the plain. Then came a sudden cry:—

"Look! Look! Look! See, two horsemen follow fast, coming up from the south. It must be Quincey and John. Take the glass. Look before the snow blots it all out!" I took it and looked. The two men might be Dr. Seward and Mr. Morris. I knew at all events that neither of them was Jonathan. At the same time I *knew* that Jonathan was not far off; looking around I saw on the north side of the coming party two other men, riding at break-neck speed. One of them I knew was Jonathan, and the other I took, of course, to be Lord Godalming. They, too, were pursuing the party with the cart. When I told the Professor he shouted in glee like a schoolboy, and, after looking intently till a snow fall made sight impossible, he laid his Winchester rifle ready for use against the boulder at the opening of our shelter. "They are all converging," he said. "When the time comes we shall have gypsies on all sides." I got out my revolver ready to hand, for whilst we were speaking the howling of wolves came louder and closer. When the snow storm abated a moment we looked again. It was strange to see the snow falling in such heavy flakes close to us, and beyond, the sun shining more and more brightly as it sank down towards the far mountain tops. Sweeping the glass all around us I could see here and there dots moving singly and in twos and threes and larger numbers—the wolves were gathering for their prey.

Every instant seemed an age whilst we waited. The wind came now in fierce bursts, and the snow was driven with fury as it swept upon us in circling eddies. At times we could not see an arm's length before us; but at others, as the hollow-sounding wind swept by us, it seemed to clear the air-space around us so that we could see afar off. We had of late been so accustomed to watch for sunrise and sunset, that we knew with fair accuracy when it would be; and we knew that before long the sun would set. It was hard to believe that by our watches it was less than an hour that we waited in that rocky shelter before the various bodies began to converge close upon us. The wind came now with fiercer and more bitter sweeps, and more steadily from the north. It seemingly had driven the snow clouds from us, for, with only occasional bursts, the snow fell. We could distinguish clearly the individuals of each party, the pursued and the pursuers. Strangely enough those pursued did not seem to realise, or at least to care, that they were pursued; they seemed, however, to hasten with redoubled speed as the sun dropped lower and lower on the mountain tops.

Closer and closer they drew. The Professor and I crouched down behind our rock, and held our weapons ready; I could see that he was determined that they should not pass. One and all were quite unaware of our presence.

All at once two voices shouted out to: "Halt!" One was my Jonathan's, raised in a high key of passion; the other Mr. Morris' strong resolute tone of quiet command. The gypsies may not have known the language, but there was no mistaking the tone, in whatever tongue the words were spoken. Instinctively they reined in, and at the instant Lord Godalming and Jonathan dashed up at one side and Dr. Seward and Mr. Morris on the other. The leader of the gypsies, a splendid-looking fellow who sat his horse like a centaur, waved them back, and in a fierce voice gave to his companions some word to proceed. They lashed the horses which sprang forward; but the four men raised their Winchester rifles, and in an unmistakable way commanded them to stop. At the same moment Dr. Van Helsing and I rose behind the rock and pointed our weapons at them. Seeing that they were surrounded the men tightened their reins and drew up. The leader turned to them and gave a word at which every man of the gypsy party drew what weapon he carried, knife or pistol, and held himself in readiness to attack. Issue was joined in an instant.

The leader, with a quick movement of his rein, threw his horse out in front, and pointing first to the sun—now close down on the hill tops—and then to the castle, said something which I did not understand. For answer, all four men of our party threw themselves from their horses and dashed towards the cart. I should have felt terrible fear at seeing Jonathan in such danger, but that the ardour of battle must have been upon me as well as the rest of them; I felt no fear, but only a wild, surging desire to do something. Seeing the quick movement of our parties, the leader of the gypsies gave a command; his men instantly formed round the cart in a sort of undisciplined endeavour, each one shouldering and pushing the other in his eagerness to carry out the order.

In the midst of this I could see that Jonathan on one side of the ring of men, and Quincey on the other, were forcing a way to the cart; it was evident that they were bent on finishing their task before the sun should set. Nothing seemed to stop or even to hinder them. Neither the levelled weapons nor the flashing knives of the gypsies in front, nor the howling of the wolves behind, appeared to even attract their attention. Jonathan's impetuosity, and the manifest singleness of his purpose, seemed to overawe those in front of him; instinctively they cowered, aside and let him pass. In an instant he had jumped upon the cart, and, with a strength which seemed incredible, raised the great box, and flung it over the wheel to the ground. In the meantime, Mr. Morris had had to use force to pass through his side of the ring of Szgany. All the time I had been breathlessly watching Jonathan I had, with the tail of my eye, seen him pressing desperately forward, and had seen the knives of the gypsies flash as he won a way through them, and they cut at him. He had parried with his great bowie knife, and at first I thought that he too had come through in safety; but as he sprang beside Jonathan, who had by now jumped from the cart, I could see that with his left hand he was clutching at his side, and that the blood was spurting through his fingers. He did not delay notwithstanding this, for as Jonathan, with desperate energy, attacked one end of the chest, attempting to prize off the lid with his great Kukri knife, he attacked the other frantically with his bowie. Under the efforts of both men the lid began to yield; the nails drew with a quick screeching sound, and the top of the box was thrown back.

By this time the gypsies, seeing themselves covered by the Winchesters, and at the mercy of Lord Godalming and Dr. Seward, had given in and made no resistance. The sun was almost down on the mountain tops, and the shadows of the whole group fell long upon the snow. I saw the Count lying within the box upon the earth, some of which the rude falling from the cart had scattered over him. He was deathly pale, just like a waxen image, and the red eyes glared with the horrible vindictive look which I knew too well.

As I looked, the eyes saw the sinking sun, and the look of hate in them turned to triumph.

But, on the instant, came the sweep and flash of Jonathan's great knife. I shrieked as I saw it shear through the throat; whilst at the same moment Mr. Morris's bowie knife plunged into the heart.

It was like a miracle; but before our very eyes, and almost in the drawing of a breath, the whole body crumble into dust and passed from our sight.

I shall be glad as long as I live that even in that moment of final dissolution, there was in the face a look of peace, such as I never could have imagined might have rested there.

The Castle of Dracula now stood out against the red sky, and every stone of its broken battlements was articulated against the light of the setting sun.

The gypsies, taking us as in some way the cause of the extraordinary disappearance of the dead man, turned, without a word, and rode away as if for their lives. Those who were unmounted jumped upon the leiter-wagon and shouted to the horsemen not to desert them. The wolves, which had withdrawn to a safe distance, followed in their wake, leaving us alone.

Mr. Morris, who had sunk to the ground, leaned on his elbow, holding his hand pressed to his side; the blood still gushed through his fingers. I flew to him, for the Holy circle did not now keep me back; so did the two doctors. Jonathan knelt behind him and the wounded man laid back his head on his shoulder. With a sigh he took, with a feeble effort, my hand in that of his own which was unstained. He must have seen the anguish of my heart in my face, for he smiled at me and said:—

"I am only too happy to have been of any service! Oh, God!" he cried suddenly, struggling up to a sitting posture and pointing to me, "It was worth for this to die! Look! look!"

The sun was now right down upon the mountain top, and the red gleams fell upon my face, so that it was bathed in rosy light. With one impulse the men sank on their knees and a deep and earnest "Amen" broke from all as their eyes followed the pointing of his finger. The dying man spoke:—

"Now God be thanked that all has not been in vain! See! the snow is not more stainless than her forehead! The curse has passed away!"

And, to our bitter grief, with a smile and in silence, he died, a gallant gentleman.

NOTE

Seven years ago we all went through the flames; and the happiness of some of us since then is, we think, well worth the pain we endured. It is an added joy to Mina and to me that our boy's birthday is the same day as that on which Quincey Morris died. His mother holds, I know, the secret belief that some of our brave friend's spirit has passed into him. His bundle of names links all our little band of men together; but we call him Quincey.

In the summer of this year we made a journey to Transylvania, and went over the old ground which was, and is, to us so full of vivid and terrible memories. It was almost impossible to believe that the things which we had seen with our own eyes and heard with our own ears were living truths. Every trace of all that had been was blotted out. The castle stood as before, reared high above a waste of desolation.

When we got home we were talking of the old time—which we could all look back on without despair, for Godalming and Seward are both happily married. I took the papers from the safe where they had been ever since our return so long ago. We were struck with the fact, that in all the mass of material of which the record is composed, there is hardly one authentic document; nothing but a mass of typewriting, except the later note-books of Mina and Seward and myself, and Van Helsing's memorandum. We could hardly ask any one, even did we wish to, to accept these as proofs of so wild a story. Van Helsing summed it all up as he said, with our boy on his knee:—

"We want no proofs; we ask none to believe us! This boy will some day know what a brave and gallant woman his mother is. Already he knows her sweetness and loving care; later on he will understand how some men so loved her, that they did dare much for her sake."

JONATHAN HARKER.

THE PHANTOM OF THE OPERA

By Gaston Leroux

First Published in 1909

Gaston Leroux

Gaston Louis Alfred Leroux was born in Paris, France in 1868. In his youth he enjoyed sailing and fishing, and attended school in Caen, where he began writing poetry and short stories while studying the works of Victor Hugo and Alexandre Dumas. He then travelled to Paris to study law, obtaining his degree in 1889 despite the fact that he had largely lost interest in the profession. When his father died in that same year, Leroux inherited a large amount of money, and lived wildly for a while, developing a taste for expensive wine and high-stakes gambling. In 1890, he started working as a court reporter and theatre critic for *L'Écho de Paris,* and then went on to become international correspondent for the Parisian newspaper *Le Matin.*

As a noted reporter, Leroux attended trials, interviewed prisoners, and observed executions by guillotine. He also travelled widely, finding himself in Russia during the 1905 revolution, and even exploring as far as Asia and Africa, witnessing first-hand some remarkable events of his time. Leroux began to dabble in fiction, producing *Seeking of the Morning's Treasures* in 1903, and four years later he abandoned journalism altogether to focus on his fiction. In 1908, he published *The Mystery of the Yellow Room,* starring the amateur detective Joseph Rouletabille. Rouletabille went on to feature in a number of hugely popular novels, and Leroux's contribution to French detective fiction is now viewed as parallel to Sir Arthur Conan Doyle's in the United Kingdom. Aside from his detective fiction, Leroux is best-remembered in the English-speaking world for his 1910 novel *The Phantom of the Opera,* which has spawned a number of well-known adaptations.

Leroux died in Nice, France in 1927, having published almost fifty novels.

PROLOGUE

IN WHICH THE AUTHOR OF THIS SINGULAR WORK INFORMS THE READER HOW HE ACQUIRED THE CERTAINTY THAT THE OPERA GHOST REALLY EXISTED

The Opera ghost really existed. He was not, as was long believed, a creature of the imagination of the artists, the superstition of the managers, or a product of the absurd and impressionable brains of the young ladies of the ballet, their mothers, the box-keepers, the cloak-room attendants or the concierge. Yes, he existed in flesh and blood, although he assumed the complete appearance of a real phantom; that is to say, of a spectral shade.

When I began to ransack the archives of the National Academy of Music I was at once struck by the surprising coincidences between the phenomena ascribed to the "ghost" and the most extraordinary and fantastic tragedy that ever excited the Paris upper classes; and I soon conceived the idea that this tragedy might reasonably be explained by the phenomena in question. The events do not date more than thirty years back; and it would not be difficult to find at the present day, in the foyer of the ballet, old men of the highest respectability, men upon whose word one could absolutely rely, who would remember as though they happened yesterday the mysterious and dramatic conditions that attended the kidnapping of Christine Daae, the disappearance of the Vicomte de Chagny and the death of his elder brother, Count Philippe, whose body was found on the bank of the lake that exists in the lower cellars of the Opera on the Rue-Scribe side. But none of those witnesses had until that day thought that there was any reason for connecting the more or less legendary figure of the Opera ghost with that terrible story.

The truth was slow to enter my mind, puzzled by an inquiry that at every moment was complicated by events which, at first sight, might be looked upon as superhuman; and more than once I was within an ace of abandoning a task in which I was exhausting myself in the hopeless pursuit of a vain image. At last, I received the proof that my presentiments had not deceived me, and I was rewarded for all my efforts on the day when I acquired the certainty that the Opera ghost was more than a mere shade.

On that day, I had spent long hours over *The Memoirs of a Manager*, the light and frivolous work of the too-skeptical Moncharmin, who, during his term at the Opera, understood nothing of the mysterious behavior of the ghost and who was making all the fun of it that he could at the very moment when he became the first victim of the curious financial operation that went on inside the "magic envelope."

I had just left the library in despair, when I met the delightful acting-manager of our National Academy, who stood chatting on a landing with a lively and well-groomed little old man, to whom he introduced me gaily. The acting-manager knew all about my investigations and how eagerly and unsuccessfully I had been trying to discover the whereabouts of the examining magistrate in the famous Chagny case, M. Faure. Nobody knew what had become of him, alive or dead; and here he was back from Canada, where he had spent fifteen years, and the first thing he had done, on his return to Paris, was to come to the secretarial offices at the Opera and ask for a free seat. The little old man was M. Faure himself.

We spent a good part of the evening together and he told me the whole Chagny case as he had understood it at the time. He was bound to conclude in favor of the madness of the viscount and the accidental death of the elder brother, for lack of evidence to the contrary; but he was nevertheless persuaded that a terrible tragedy had taken place between the two brothers in connection with Christine Daae. He could not tell me what became of Christine or the viscount. When I mentioned the ghost, he only laughed. He, too, had been told of the curious manifestations that seemed to point to the existence of an abnormal being, residing in one of the most mysterious corners of the Opera, and he knew the story of the envelope; but he had never seen anything in it worthy of his attention as magistrate in charge of the Chagny case, and it was as much as he had done to listen to the evidence of a witness who appeared of his own accord and declared that he had often met the ghost. This witness was none other than the man whom all Paris called the "Persian" and who was well-known to every subscriber to the Opera. The magistrate took him for a visionary.

I was immensely interested by this story of the Persian. I wanted, if there were still time, to find this valuable and eccentric witness. My luck began to improve and I discovered him in his little flat in the Rue de Rivoli, where he had lived ever since and where he died five months after my visit. I was at first inclined to be suspicious; but when the Persian had told me, with child-like candor, all that he knew about the ghost and had handed me the proofs of the ghost's existence—including the strange correspondence of Christine Daae—to do as I pleased with, I was no longer able to doubt.

No, the ghost was not a myth!

I have, I know, been told that this correspondence may have been forged from first to last by a man whose imagination had certainly been fed on the most seductive tales; but fortunately I discovered some of Christine's writing outside the famous bundle of letters and, on a comparison between the two, all my doubts were removed. I also went into the past history of the Persian and found that he was an upright man, incapable of inventing a story that might have defeated the ends of justice.

This, moreover, was the opinion of the more serious people who, at one time or other, were mixed up in the Chagny case, who were friends of the Chagny family, to whom I showed all my documents and set forth all my inferences. In this connection, I should like to print a few lines which I received from General D——:

SIR:

I can not urge you too strongly to publish the results of your inquiry. I remember perfectly that, a few weeks before the disappearance of that great singer, Christine Daae, and the tragedy which threw the whole of the Faubourg Saint-Germain into mourning, there was a great deal of talk, in the foyer of the ballet, on the subject of the "ghost;" and I believe that it only ceased to be discussed in consequence of the later affair that excited us all so greatly. But, if it be possible—as, after hearing you, I believe—to explain the tragedy through the ghost, then I beg you sir, to talk to us about the ghost again.

Mysterious though the ghost may at first appear, he will always be more easily explained than the dismal story in which malevolent people have tried to picture two brothers killing each other who had worshiped each other all their lives.

Believe me, etc.

Lastly, with my bundle of papers in hand, I once more went over the ghost's vast domain, the huge building which he had made his kingdom. All that my eyes saw, all that my mind perceived, corroborated the Persian's documents precisely; and a wonderful discovery crowned my labors in a very definite fashion. It will be remembered that, later, when digging in the substructure of the Opera, before burying the phonographic records of the artist's voice, the workmen laid bare a corpse. Well, I was at once able to prove that this corpse was that of the Opera ghost. I made the acting-manager put this proof to the test with his own hand; and it is now a matter of supreme indifference to me if the papers pretend that the body was that of a victim of the Commune.

The wretches who were massacred, under the Commune, in the cellars of the Opera, were not buried on this side; I will tell where their skeletons can be found in a spot not very far from that immense crypt which was stocked during the siege with all sorts of provisions. I came upon this track just when I was looking for the remains of the Opera ghost, which I should never have discovered but for the unheard-of chance described above.

But we will return to the corpse and what ought to be done with it. For the present, I must conclude this very necessary introduction by thanking M. Mifroid (who was the commissary of police called in for the first investigations after the disappearance of Christine Daae), M. Remy, the late secretary, M. Mercier, the late acting-manager, M. Gabriel, the late chorus-master, and more particularly Mme. la Baronne de Castelot-Barbezac, who was once the "little Meg" of the story (and who is not ashamed of it), the most charming star of our admirable corps de ballet, the eldest daughter of the worthy Mme. Giry, now deceased, who had charge of the ghost's private box. All these were of the greatest assistance to me; and, thanks to them, I shall be able to reproduce those hours of sheer love and terror, in their smallest details, before the reader's eyes.

And I should be ungrateful indeed if I omitted, while standing on the threshold of this dreadful and veracious story, to thank the present management the Opera, which has so kindly assisted me in all my inquiries, and M. Messager in particular, together with M. Gabion, the acting-manager, and that most amiable of men, the architect intrusted with the preservation of the building, who did not hesitate to lend me the works of Charles Garnier, although he was almost sure that I would never return them to him. Lastly, I must pay a public tribute to the generosity of my friend and former collaborator, M. J. Le Croze, who allowed me to dip into his splendid theatrical library and to borrow the rarest editions of books by which he set great store.

GASTON LEROUX.

CHAPTER I

IS IT THE GHOST?

It was the evening on which MM. Debienne and Poligny, the managers of the Opera, were giving a last gala performance to mark their retirement. Suddenly the dressing-room of La Sorelli, one of the principal dancers, was invaded by half-a-dozen young ladies of the ballet, who had come up from the stage after "dancing" Polyeucte. They rushed in amid great confusion, some giving vent to forced and unnatural laughter, others to cries of terror. Sorelli, who wished to be alone for a moment to "run through" the speech which she was to make to the resigning managers, looked around angrily at the mad and tumultuous crowd. It was little Jammes—the girl with the tip-tilted nose, the forget-me-not eyes, the rose-red cheeks and the lily-white neck and shoulders—who gave the explanation in a trembling voice:

"It's the ghost!" And she locked the door.

Sorelli's dressing-room was fitted up with official, commonplace elegance. A pier-glass, a sofa, a dressing-table and a cupboard or two provided the necessary furniture. On the walls hung a few engravings, relics of the mother, who had known the glories of the old Opera in the Rue le Peletier; portraits of Vestris, Gardel, Dupont, Bigottini. But the room seemed a palace to the brats of the corps de ballet, who were lodged in common dressing-rooms where they spent their time singing, quarreling, smacking the dressers and hair-dressers and buying one another glasses of cassis, beer, or even rhum, until the call-boy's bell rang.

Sorelli was very superstitious. She shuddered when she heard little Jammes speak of the ghost, called her a "silly little fool" and then, as she was the first to believe in ghosts in general, and the Opera ghost in particular, at once asked for details:

"Have you seen him?"

"As plainly as I see you now!" said little Jammes, whose legs were giving way beneath her, and she dropped with a moan into a chair.

Thereupon little Giry—the girl with eyes black as sloes, hair black as ink, a swarthy complexion and a poor little skin stretched over poor little bones—little Giry added:

"If that's the ghost, he's very ugly!"

"Oh, yes!" cried the chorus of ballet-girls.

And they all began to talk together. The ghost had appeared to them in the shape of a gentleman in dress-clothes, who had suddenly stood before them in the passage, without their knowing where he came from. He seemed to have come straight through the wall.

"Pooh!" said one of them, who had more or less kept her head. "You see the ghost everywhere!"

And it was true. For several months, there had been nothing discussed at the Opera but this ghost in dress-clothes who stalked about the building, from top to bottom, like a shadow, who spoke to nobody, to whom nobody dared speak and who vanished as soon as he was seen, no one knowing how or where. As became a real ghost, he made no noise in walking. People began by laughing and making fun of this specter dressed like a man of fashion or an undertaker; but the ghost legend soon swelled to enormous proportions among the corps de ballet. All the girls pretended to have met this supernatural being more or less often. And those who laughed the loudest were not the most at ease. When he did not show himself, he betrayed his presence or his passing by accident, comic or serious, for which the general superstition held him responsible. Had any one met with a fall, or suffered a practical joke at the hands of one of the other girls, or lost a powderpuff, it was at once the fault of the ghost, of the Opera ghost.

After all, who had seen him? You meet so many men in dress-clothes at the Opera who are not ghosts. But this dress-suit had a peculiarity of its own. It covered a skeleton. At least, so the ballet-girls said. And, of course, it had a death's head.

Was all this serious? The truth is that the idea of the skeleton came from the description of the ghost given by Joseph Buquet, the chief scene-shifter, who had really seen the ghost. He had run up against the ghost on the little staircase, by the footlights, which leads to "the cellars." He had seen him for a second—for the ghost had fled—and to any one who cared to listen to him he said:

"He is extraordinarily thin and his dress-coat hangs on a skeleton frame. His eyes are so deep that you can hardly see the fixed pupils. You just see two big black holes, as in a dead man's skull. His skin, which is stretched across his bones like a drumhead, is not white, but a nasty yellow. His nose is so little worth talking about that you can't see it side-face; and *the absence of that nose is a horrible thing to look at.* All the hair he has is three or four long dark locks on his forehead and behind his ears."

This chief scene-shifter was a serious, sober, steady man, very slow at imagining things. His words were received with interest and amazement;

and soon there were other people to say that they too had met a man in dress-clothes with a death's head on his shoulders. Sensible men who had wind of the story began by saying that Joseph Buquet had been the victim of a joke played by one of his assistants. And then, one after the other, there came a series of incidents so curious and so inexplicable that the very shrewdest people began to feel uneasy.

For instance, a fireman is a brave fellow! He fears nothing, least of all fire! Well, the fireman in question, who had gone to make a round of inspection in the cellars and who, it seems, had ventured a little farther than usual, suddenly reappeared on the stage, pale, scared, trembling, with his eyes starting out of his head, and practically fainted in the arms of the proud mother of little Jammes.[1] And why? Because he had seen coming toward him, *at the level of his head, but without a body attached to it, a head of fire!* And, as I said, a fireman is not afraid of fire.

The fireman's name was Pampin.

The corps de ballet was flung into consternation. At first sight, this fiery head in no way corresponded with Joseph Buquet's description of the ghost. But the young ladies soon persuaded themselves that the ghost had several heads, which he changed about as he pleased. And, of course, they at once imagined that they were in the greatest danger. Once a fireman did not hesitate to faint, leaders and front-row and back-row girls alike had plenty of excuses for the fright that made them quicken their pace when passing some dark corner or ill-lighted corridor. Sorelli herself, on the day after the adventure of the fireman, placed a horseshoe on the table in front of the stage-door-keeper's box, which every one who entered the Opera otherwise than as a spectator must touch before setting foot on the first tread of the staircase. This horse-shoe was not invented by me—any more than any other part of this story, alas!—and may still be seen on the table in the passage outside the stage-door-keeper's box, when you enter the Opera through the court known as the Cour de l'Administration.

To return to the evening in question.

"It's the ghost!" little Jammes had cried.

An agonizing silence now reigned in the dressing-room. Nothing was heard but the hard breathing of the girls. At last, Jammes, flinging herself upon the farthest corner of the wall, with every mark of real terror on her face, whispered:

"Listen!"

---

1   I have the anecdote, which is quite authentic, from M. Pedro Gailhard himself, the late manager of the Opera.

Everybody seemed to hear a rustling outside the door. There was no sound of footsteps. It was like light silk sliding over the panel. Then it stopped.

Sorelli tried to show more pluck than the others. She went up to the door and, in a quavering voice, asked:

"Who's there?"

But nobody answered. Then feeling all eyes upon her, watching her last movement, she made an effort to show courage, and said very loudly:

"Is there any one behind the door?"

"Oh, yes, yes! Of course there is!" cried that little dried plum of a Meg Giry, heroically holding Sorelli back by her gauze skirt. "Whatever you do, don't open the door! Oh, Lord, don't open the door!"

But Sorelli, armed with a dagger that never left her, turned the key and drew back the door, while the ballet-girls retreated to the inner dressing-room and Meg Giry sighed:

"Mother! Mother!"

Sorelli looked into the passage bravely. It was empty; a gas-flame, in its glass prison, cast a red and suspicious light into the surrounding darkness, without succeeding in dispelling it. And the dancer slammed the door again, with a deep sigh.

"No," she said, "there is no one there."

"Still, we saw him!" Jammes declared, returning with timid little steps to her place beside Sorelli. "He must be somewhere prowling about. I shan't go back to dress. We had better all go down to the foyer together, at once, for the 'speech,' and we will come up again together."

And the child reverently touched the little coral finger-ring which she wore as a charm against bad luck, while Sorelli, stealthily, with the tip of her pink right thumb-nail, made a St. Andrew's cross on the wooden ring which adorned the fourth finger of her left hand. She said to the little ballet-girls:

"Come, children, pull yourselves together! I dare say no one has ever seen the ghost."

"Yes, yes, we saw him—we saw him just now!" cried the girls. "He had his death's head and his dress-coat, just as when he appeared to Joseph Buquet!"

"And Gabriel saw him too!" said Jammes. "Only yesterday! Yesterday afternoon—in broad day-light——"

"Gabriel, the chorus-master?"

"Why, yes, didn't you know?"

"And he was wearing his dress-clothes, in broad daylight?"

"Who? Gabriel?"

"Why, no, the ghost!"

"Certainly! Gabriel told me so himself. That's what he knew him by.

Gabriel was in the stage-manager's office. Suddenly the door opened and the Persian entered. You know the Persian has the evil eye——"

"Oh, yes!" answered the little ballet-girls in chorus, warding off ill-luck by pointing their forefinger and little finger at the absent Persian, while their second and third fingers were bent on the palm and held down by the thumb.

"And you know how superstitious Gabriel is," continued Jammes. "However, he is always polite. When he meets the Persian, he just puts his hand in his pocket and touches his keys. Well, the moment the Persian appeared in the doorway, Gabriel gave one jump from his chair to the lock of the cupboard, so as to touch iron! In doing so, he tore a whole skirt of his overcoat on a nail. Hurrying to get out of the room, he banged his forehead against a hat-peg and gave himself a huge bump; then, suddenly stepping back, he skinned his arm on the screen, near the piano; he tried to lean on the piano, but the lid fell on his hands and crushed his fingers; he rushed out of the office like a madman, slipped on the staircase and came down the whole of the first flight on his back. I was just passing with mother. We picked him up. He was covered with bruises and his face was all over blood. We were frightened out of our lives, but, all at once, he began to thank Providence that he had got off so cheaply. Then he told us what had frightened him. He had seen the ghost behind the Persian, *the ghost with the death's head* just like Joseph Buquet's description!"

Jammes had told her story ever so quickly, as though the ghost were at her heels, and was quite out of breath at the finish. A silence followed, while Sorelli polished her nails in great excitement. It was broken by little Giry, who said:

"Joseph Buquet would do better to hold his tongue."

"Why should he hold his tongue?" asked somebody.

"That's mother's opinion," replied Meg, lowering her voice and looking all about her as though fearing lest other ears than those present might overhear.

"And why is it your mother's opinion?"

"Hush! Mother says the ghost doesn't like being talked about."

"And why does your mother say so?"

"Because—because—nothing—"

This reticence exasperated the curiosity of the young ladies, who crowded round little Giry, begging her to explain herself. They were there, side by side, leaning forward simultaneously in one movement of entreaty and fear, communicating their terror to one another, taking a keen pleasure in feeling their blood freeze in their veins.

"I swore not to tell!" gasped Meg.

But they left her no peace and promised to keep the secret, until Meg, burning to say all she knew, began, with her eyes fixed on the door:

"Well, it's because of the private box."

"What private box?"

"The ghost's box!"

"Has the ghost a box? Oh, do tell us, do tell us!"

"Not so loud!" said Meg. "It's Box Five, you know, the box on the grand tier, next to the stage-box, on the left."

"Oh, nonsense!"

"I tell you it is. Mother has charge of it. But you swear you won't say a word?"

"Of course, of course."

"Well, that's the ghost's box. No one has had it for over a month, except the ghost, and orders have been given at the box-office that it must never be sold."

"And does the ghost really come there?"

"Yes."

"Then somebody does come?"

"Why, no! The ghost comes, but there is nobody there."

The little ballet-girls exchanged glances. If the ghost came to the box, he must be seen, because he wore a dress-coat and a death's head. This was what they tried to make Meg understand, but she replied:

"That's just it! The ghost is not seen. And he has no dress-coat and no head! All that talk about his death's head and his head of fire is nonsense! There's nothing in it. You only hear him when he is in the box. Mother has never seen him, but she has heard him. Mother knows, because she gives him his program."

Sorelli interfered.

"Giry, child, you're getting at us!"

Thereupon little Giry began to cry.

"I ought to have held my tongue—if mother ever came to know! But I was quite right, Joseph Buquet had no business to talk of things that don't concern him—it will bring him bad luck—mother was saying so last night——"

There was a sound of hurried and heavy footsteps in the passage and a breathless voice cried:

"Cecile! Cecile! Are you there?"

"It's mother's voice," said Jammes. "What's the matter?"

She opened the door. A respectable lady, built on the lines of a Pomeranian grenadier, burst into the dressing-room and dropped groaning into a vacant arm-chair. Her eyes rolled madly in her brick-dust colored face.

"How awful!" she said. "How awful!"

"What? What?"

"Joseph Buquet!"

"What about him?"

"Joseph Buquet is dead!"

The room became filled with exclamations, with astonished outcries, with scared requests for explanations.

"Yes, he was found hanging in the third-floor cellar!"

"It's the ghost!" little Giry blurted, as though in spite of herself; but she at once corrected herself, with her hands pressed to her mouth: "No, no!—I, didn't say it!—I didn't say it!——"

All around her, her panic-stricken companions repeated under their breaths:

"Yes—it must be the ghost!"

Sorelli was very pale.

"I shall never be able to recite my speech," she said.

Ma Jammes gave her opinion, while she emptied a glass of liqueur that happened to be standing on a table; the ghost must have something to do with it.

The truth is that no one ever knew how Joseph Buquet met his death. The verdict at the inquest was "natural suicide." In his Memoirs of Manager, M. Moncharmin, one of the joint managers who succeeded MM. Debienne and Poligny, describes the incident as follows:

"A grievous accident spoiled the little party which MM. Debienne and Poligny gave to celebrate their retirement. I was in the manager's office, when Mercier, the acting-manager, suddenly came darting in. He seemed half mad and told me that the body of a scene-shifter had been found hanging in the third cellar under the stage, between a farm-house and a scene from the Roi de Lahore. I shouted:

"'Come and cut him down!'

"By the time I had rushed down the staircase and the Jacob's ladder, the man was no longer hanging from his rope!"

So this is an event which M. Moncharmin thinks natural. A man hangs at the end of a rope; they go to cut him down; the rope has disappeared. Oh, M. Moncharmin found a very simple explanation! Listen to him:

"It was just after the ballet; and leaders and dancing-girls lost no time in taking their precautions against the evil eye."

There you are! Picture the corps de ballet scuttling down the Jacob's ladder and dividing the suicide's rope among themselves in less time than it takes to write! When, on the other hand, I think of the exact spot where the body was discovered—the third cellar underneath the stage!—imagine that

SOMEBODY must have been interested in seeing that the rope disappeared after it had effected its purpose; and time will show if I am wrong.

The horrid news soon spread all over the Opera, where Joseph Buquet was very popular. The dressing-rooms emptied and the ballet-girls, crowding around Sorelli like timid sheep around their shepherdess, made for the foyer through the ill-lit passages and staircases, trotting as fast as their little pink legs could carry them.

CHAPTER II

THE NEW MARGARITA

On the first landing, Sorelli ran against the Comte de Chagny, who was coming up-stairs. The count, who was generally so calm, seemed greatly excited.

"I was just going to you," he said, taking off his hat. "Oh, Sorelli, what an evening! And Christine Daae: what a triumph!"

"Impossible!" said Meg Giry. "Six months ago, she used to sing like a CROCK! But do let us get by, my dear count," continues the brat, with a saucy curtsey. "We are going to inquire after a poor man who was found hanging by the neck."

Just then the acting-manager came fussing past and stopped when he heard this remark.

"What!" he exclaimed roughly. "Have you girls heard already? Well, please forget about it for tonight—and above all don't let M. Debienne and M. Poligny hear; it would upset them too much on their last day."

They all went on to the foyer of the ballet, which was already full of people. The Comte de Chagny was right; no gala performance ever equalled this one. All the great composers of the day had conducted their own works in turns. Faure and Krauss had sung; and, on that evening, Christine Daae had revealed her true self, for the first time, to the astonished and enthusiastic audience. Gounod had conducted the Funeral March of a Marionnette; Reyer, his beautiful overture to Siguar; Saint Saens, the Danse Macabre and a Reverie Orientale; Massenet, an unpublished Hungarian march; Guiraud, his Carnaval; Delibes, the Valse Lente from Sylvia and the Pizzicati from Coppelia. Mlle. Krauss had sung the bolero in the Vespri Siciliani; and Mlle. Denise Bloch the drinking song in Lucrezia Borgia.

But the real triumph was reserved for Christine Daae, who had begun by singing a few passages from Romeo and Juliet. It was the first time that the young artist sang in this work of Gounod, which had not been transferred to the Opera and which was revived at the Opera Comique after it had been produced at the old Theatre Lyrique by Mme. Carvalho. Those who heard her say that her voice, in these passages, was seraphic; but this was nothing to the superhuman notes that she gave forth in the prison scene and the final trio in FAUST, which she sang in the place of La Carlotta, who was ill. No one had ever heard or seen anything like it.

Daae revealed a new Margarita that night, a Margarita of a splendor, a radiance hitherto unsuspected. The whole house went mad, rising to its feet, shouting, cheering, clapping, while Christine sobbed and fainted in the arms of her fellow-singers and had to be carried to her dressing-room. A few subscribers, however, protested. Why had so great a treasure been kept from them all that time? Till then, Christine Daae had played a good Siebel to Carlotta's rather too splendidly material Margarita. And it had needed Carlotta's incomprehensible and inexcusable absence from this gala night for the little Daae, at a moment's warning, to show all that she could do in a part of the program reserved for the Spanish diva! Well, what the subscribers wanted to know was, why had Debienne and Poligny applied to Daae, when Carlotta was taken ill? Did they know of her hidden genius? And, if they knew of it, why had they kept it hidden? And why had she kept it hidden? Oddly enough, she was not known to have a professor of singing at that moment. She had often said she meant to practise alone for the future. The whole thing was a mystery.

The Comte de Chagny, standing up in his box, listened to all this frenzy and took part in it by loudly applauding. Philippe Georges Marie Comte de Chagny was just forty-one years of age. He was a great aristocrat and a good-looking man, above middle height and with attractive features, in spite of his hard forehead and his rather cold eyes. He was exquisitely polite to the women and a little haughty to the men, who did not always forgive him for his successes in society. He had an excellent heart and an irreproachable conscience. On the death of old Count Philibert, he became the head of one of the oldest and most distinguished families in France, whose arms dated back to the fourteenth century. The Chagnys owned a great deal of property; and, when the old count, who was a widower, died, it was no easy task for Philippe to accept the management of so large an estate. His two sisters and his brother, Raoul, would not hear of a division and waived their claim to their shares, leaving themselves entirely in Philippe's hands, as though the right of primogeniture had never ceased to exist. When the two sisters married, on the same day, they received their portion from their brother, not as a thing rightfully belonging to them, but as a dowry for which they thanked him.

The Comtesse de Chagny, nee de Moerogis de La Martyniere, had died in giving birth to Raoul, who was born twenty years after his elder brother. At the time of the old count's death, Raoul was twelve years of age. Philippe busied himself actively with the youngster's education. He was admirably assisted in this work first by his sisters and afterward by an old aunt, the widow of a naval officer, who lived at Brest and gave young Raoul a taste for the sea. The lad entered the Borda training-ship, finished his course with honors and quietly made his trip round the world. Thanks to powerful influence, he had just been appointed a member of the official expedition on board the Requin, which was to be sent to the Arctic Circle in search of the survivors of the D'Artoi's expedition, of whom nothing had been heard for three years. Meanwhile, he was enjoying a long furlough which would not be over for six months; and already the dowagers of the Faubourg Saint-Germain were pitying the handsome and apparently delicate stripling for the hard work in store for him.

The shyness of the sailor-lad—I was almost saying his innocence—was remarkable. He seemed to have but just left the women's apron-strings. As a matter of fact, petted as he was by his two sisters and his old aunt, he had retained from this purely feminine education manners that were almost candid and stamped with a charm that nothing had yet been able to sully. He was a little over twenty-one years of age and looked eighteen. He had a small, fair mustache, beautiful blue eyes and a complexion like a girl's.

Philippe spoiled Raoul. To begin with, he was very proud of him and pleased to foresee a glorious career for his junior in the navy in which one of their ancestors, the famous Chagny de La Roche, had held the rank of admiral. He took advantage of the young man's leave of absence to show him Paris, with all its luxurious and artistic delights. The count considered that, at Raoul's age, it is not good to be too good. Philippe himself had a character that was very well-balanced in work and pleasure alike; his demeanor was always faultless; and he was incapable of setting his brother a bad example. He took him with him wherever he went. He even introduced him to the foyer of the ballet. I know that the count was said to be "on terms" with Sorelli. But it could hardly be reckoned as a crime for this nobleman, a bachelor, with plenty of leisure, especially since his sisters were settled, to come and spend an hour or two after dinner in the company of a dancer, who, though not so very, very witty, had the finest eyes that ever were seen! And, besides, there are places where a true Parisian, when he has the rank of the Comte de Chagny, is bound to show himself; and at that time the foyer of the ballet at the Opera was one of those places.

Lastly, Philippe would perhaps not have taken his brother behind the scenes of the Opera if Raoul had not been the first to ask him, repeatedly renewing his request with a gentle obstinacy which the count remembered at a later date.

On that evening, Philippe, after applauding the Daae, turned to Raoul and saw that he was quite pale.

"Don't you see," said Raoul, "that the woman's fainting?"

"You look like fainting yourself," said the count. "What's the matter?"

But Raoul had recovered himself and was standing up.

"Let's go and see," he said, "she never sang like that before."

The count gave his brother a curious smiling glance and seemed quite pleased. They were soon at the door leading from the house to the stage. Numbers of subscribers were slowly making their way through. Raoul tore his gloves without knowing what he was doing and Philippe had much too kind a heart to laugh at him for his impatience. But he now understood why Raoul was absent-minded when spoken to and why he always tried to turn every conversation to the subject of the Opera.

They reached the stage and pushed through the crowd of gentlemen, scene-shifters, supers and chorus-girls, Raoul leading the way, feeling that his heart no longer belonged to him, his face set with passion, while Count Philippe followed him with difficulty and continued to smile. At the back of the stage, Raoul had to stop before the inrush of the little troop of ballet-girls who blocked the passage which he was trying to enter. More than one chaffing phrase darted from little made-up lips, to which he did not reply; and at last he was able to pass, and dived into the semi-darkness of a corridor ringing with the name of "Daae! Daae!" The count was surprised to find that Raoul knew the way. He had never taken him to Christine's himself and came to the conclusion that Raoul must have gone there alone while the count stayed talking in the foyer with Sorelli, who often asked him to wait until it was her time to "go on" and sometimes handed him the little gaiters in which she ran down from her dressing-room to preserve the spotlessness of her satin dancing-shoes and her flesh-colored tights. Sorelli had an excuse; she had lost her mother.

Postponing his usual visit to Sorelli for a few minutes, the count followed his brother down the passage that led to Daae's dressing-room and saw that it had never been so crammed as on that evening, when the whole house seemed excited by her success and also by her fainting fit. For the girl had not yet come to; and the doctor of the theater had just arrived at the moment when Raoul entered at his heels. Christine, therefore, received the first aid of the one, while opening her eyes in the arms of the other. The count and many more remained crowding in the doorway.

"Don't you think, Doctor, that those gentlemen had better clear the room?" asked Raoul coolly. "There's no breathing here."

"You're quite right," said the doctor.

And he sent every one away, except Raoul and the maid, who looked at

Raoul with eyes of the most undisguised astonishment. She had never seen him before and yet dared not question him; and the doctor imagined that the young man was only acting as he did because he had the right to. The viscount, therefore, remained in the room watching Christine as she slowly returned to life, while even the joint managers, Debienne and Poligny, who had come to offer their sympathy and congratulations, found themselves thrust into the passage among the crowd of dandies. The Comte de Chagny, who was one of those standing outside, laughed:

"Oh, the rogue, the rogue!" And he added, under his breath: "Those youngsters with their school-girl airs! So he's a Chagny after all!"

He turned to go to Sorelli's dressing-room, but met her on the way, with her little troop of trembling ballet-girls, as we have seen.

Meanwhile, Christine Daae uttered a deep sigh, which was answered by a groan. She turned her head, saw Raoul and started. She looked at the doctor, on whom she bestowed a smile, then at her maid, then at Raoul again.

"Monsieur," she said, in a voice not much above a whisper, "who are you?"

"Mademoiselle," replied the young man, kneeling on one knee and pressing a fervent kiss on the diva's hand, "I AM THE LITTLE BOY WHO WENT INTO THE SEA TO RESCUE YOUR SCARF."

Christine again looked at the doctor and the maid; and all three began to laugh.

Raoul turned very red and stood up.

"Mademoiselle," he said, "since you are pleased not to recognize me, I should like to say something to you in private, something very important."

"When I am better, do you mind?" And her voice shook. "You have been very good."

"Yes, you must go," said the doctor, with his pleasantest smile. "Leave me to attend to mademoiselle."

"I am not ill now," said Christine suddenly, with strange and unexpected energy.

She rose and passed her hand over her eyelids.

"Thank you, Doctor. I should like to be alone. Please go away, all of you. Leave me. I feel very restless this evening."

The doctor tried to make a short protest, but, perceiving the girl's evident agitation, he thought the best remedy was not to thwart her. And he went away, saying to Raoul, outside:

"She is not herself to-night. She is usually so gentle."

Then he said good night and Raoul was left alone. The whole of this part of the theater was now deserted. The farewell ceremony was no doubt taking place in the foyer of the ballet. Raoul thought that Daae might go to it and he waited in the silent solitude, even hiding in the favoring shadow of a doorway. He felt a terrible pain at his heart and it was of this that he wanted to speak to Daae without delay.

Suddenly the dressing-room door opened and the maid came out by herself, carrying bundles. He stopped her and asked how her mistress was. The woman laughed and said that she was quite well, but that he must not disturb her, for she wished to be left alone. And she passed on. One idea alone filled Raoul's burning brain: of course, Daae wished to be left alone *for him!* Had he not told her that he wanted to speak to her privately?

Hardly breathing, he went up to the dressing-room and, with his ear to the door to catch her reply, prepared to knock. But his hand dropped. He had heard *a man's voice* in the dressing-room, saying, in a curiously masterful tone:

"Christine, you must love me!"

And Christine's voice, infinitely sad and trembling, as though accompanied by tears, replied:

"How can you talk like that? WHEN I SING ONLY FOR YOU!"

Raoul leaned against the panel to ease his pain. His heart, which had seemed gone for ever, returned to his breast and was throbbing loudly. The whole passage echoed with its beating and Raoul's ears were deafened. Surely, if his heart continued to make such a noise, they would hear it inside, they would open the door and the young man would be turned away in disgrace. What a position for a Chagny! To be caught listening behind a door! He took his heart in his two hands to make it stop.

The man's voice spoke again: "Are you very tired?"

"Oh, to-night I gave you my soul and I am dead!" Christine replied.

"Your soul is a beautiful thing, child," replied the grave man's voice, "and I thank you. No emperor ever received so fair a gift. *The angels wept tonight.*"

Raoul heard nothing after that. Nevertheless, he did not go away, but, as though he feared lest he should be caught, he returned to his dark corner, determined to wait for the man to leave the room. At one and the same time, he had learned what love meant, and hatred. He knew that he loved. He wanted to know whom he hated. To his great astonishment, the door opened and Christine Daae appeared, wrapped in furs, with her face hidden in a lace veil, alone. She closed the door behind her, but Raoul observed that she did not lock it. She passed him. He did not even follow her with his eyes, for his eyes were fixed on the door, which did not open again.

When the passage was once more deserted, he crossed it, opened the door of the dressing-room, went in and shut the door. He found himself in absolute darkness. The gas had been turned out.

"There is some one here!" said Raoul, with his back against the closed door, in a quivering voice. "What are you hiding for?"

All was darkness and silence. Raoul heard only the sound of his own breathing. He quite failed to see that the indiscretion of his conduct was exceeding all bounds.

"You shan't leave this until I let you!" he exclaimed. "If you don't answer, you are a coward! But I'll expose you!"

And he struck a match. The blaze lit up the room. There was no one in the room! Raoul, first turning the key in the door, lit the gas-jets. He went into the dressing-closet, opened the cupboards, hunted about, felt the walls with his moist hands. Nothing!

"Look here!" he said, aloud. "Am I going mad?"

He stood for ten minutes listening to the gas flaring in the silence of the empty room; lover though he was, he did not even think of stealing a ribbon that would have given him the perfume of the woman he loved. He went out, not knowing what he was doing nor where he was going. At a given moment in his wayward progress, an icy draft struck him in the face. He found himself at the bottom of a staircase, down which, behind him, a procession of workmen were carrying a sort of stretcher, covered with a white sheet.

"Which is the way out, please?" he asked of one of the men.

"Straight in front of you, the door is open. But let us pass."

Pointing to the stretcher, he asked mechanically: "What's that?"

The workmen answered:

"'That' is Joseph Buquet, who was found in the third cellar, hanging between a farm-house and a scene from the *Roi De Lahore*."

He took off his hat, fell back to make room for the procession and went out.

CHAPTER III

THE MYSTERIOUS REASON

During this time, the farewell ceremony was taking place. I have already said that this magnificent function was being given on the occasion of the retirement of M. Debienne and M. Poligny, who had determined to "die game," as we say nowadays. They had been assisted in the realization of their ideal, though melancholy, program by all that counted in the social and artistic world of Paris. All these people met, after the performance, in the foyer of the ballet, where Sorelli waited for the arrival of the retiring managers with a glass of champagne in her hand and a little prepared speech at the tip of her tongue. Behind her, the members of the Corps de Ballet, young and old, discussed the events of the day in whispers or exchanged discreet signals with their friends, a noisy crowd of whom surrounded the supper-tables arranged along the slanting floor.

A few of the dancers had already changed into ordinary dress; but most of them wore their skirts of gossamer gauze; and all had thought it the right thing to put on a special face for the occasion: all, that is, except little Jammes, whose fifteen summers—happy age!—seemed already to have forgotten the ghost and the death of Joseph Buquet. She never ceased to laugh and chatter, to hop about and play practical jokes, until Mm. Debienne and Poligny appeared on the steps of the foyer, when she was severely called to order by the impatient Sorelli.

Everybody remarked that the retiring managers looked cheerful, as is the Paris way. None will ever be a true Parisian who has not learned to wear a mask of gaiety over his sorrows and one of sadness, boredom or indifference over his inward joy. You know that one of your friends is in trouble; do not try to console him: he will tell you that he is already comforted; but, should he have met with good fortune, be careful how you congratulate him: he thinks it so natural that he is surprised that you should speak of it. In Paris, our lives are one masked ball; and the foyer of the ballet is the last place in which two men so "knowing" as M. Debienne and M. Poligny would have made the mistake of betraying their grief, however genuine it might be. And they were already smiling rather too broadly upon Sorelli, who had begun to recite her speech, when an exclamation from that little madcap of a Jammes broke the smile of the managers so brutally that the expression of distress and dismay that lay beneath it became apparent to all eyes:

"The Opera ghost!"

Jammes yelled these words in a tone of unspeakable terror; and her finger pointed, among the crowd of dandies, to a face so pallid, so lugubrious and so ugly, with two such deep black cavities under the straddling eyebrows, that the death's head in question immediately scored a huge success.

"The Opera ghost! The Opera ghost!" Everybody laughed and pushed his neighbor and wanted to offer the Opera ghost a drink, but he was gone. He had slipped through the crowd; and the others vainly hunted for him, while two old gentlemen tried to calm little Jammes and while little Giry stood screaming like a peacock.

Sorelli was furious; she had not been able to finish her speech; the managers, had kissed her, thanked her and run away as fast as the ghost himself. No one was surprised at this, for it was known that they were to go through the same ceremony on the floor above, in the foyer of the singers, and that finally they were themselves to receive their personal friends, for the last time, in the great lobby outside the managers' office, where a regular supper would be served.

Here they found the new managers, M. Armand Moncharmin and M. Firmin Richard, whom they hardly knew; nevertheless, they were lavish in protestations of friendship and received a thousand flattering compliments in reply, so that those of the guests who had feared that they had a rather tedious evening in store for them at once put on brighter faces. The supper was almost gay and a particularly clever speech of the representative of the government, mingling the glories of the past with the successes of the future, caused the greatest cordiality to prevail.

The retiring managers had already handed over to their successors the two tiny master-keys which opened all the doors—thousands of doors—of the Opera house. And those little keys, the object of general curiosity, were being passed from hand to hand, when the attention of some of the guests was diverted by their discovery, at the end of the table, of that strange, wan and fantastic face, with the hollow eyes, which had already appeared in the foyer of the ballet and been greeted by little Jammes' exclamation:

"The Opera ghost!"

There sat the ghost, as natural as could be, except that he neither ate nor drank. Those who began by looking at him with a smile ended by turning away their heads, for the sight of him at once provoked the most funereal thoughts. No one repeated the joke of the foyer, no one exclaimed:

"There's the Opera ghost!"

He himself did not speak a word and his very neighbors could not have stated at what precise moment he had sat down between them; but every one felt that if the dead did ever come and sit at the table of the living, they could not cut a more ghastly figure. The friends of Firmin Richard and Armand Moncharmin thought that this lean and skinny guest was an acquaintance of Debienne's or Poligny's, while Debienne's and Poligny's friends believed that the cadaverous individual belonged to Firmin Richard and Armand Moncharmin's party.

The result was that no request was made for an explanation; no unpleasant remark; no joke in bad taste, which might have offended this visitor from the tomb. A few of those present who knew the story of the ghost and the description of him given by the chief scene-shifter—they did not know of Joseph Buquet's death—thought, in their own minds, that the man at the end of the table might easily have passed for him; and yet, according to the story, the ghost had no nose and the person in question had. But M. Moncharmin declares, in his Memoirs, that the guest's nose was transparent: "long, thin and transparent" are his exact words. I, for my part, will add that this might very well apply to a false nose. M. Moncharmin may have taken for transparency what was only shininess. Everybody knows that orthopaedic science provides beautiful false noses for those who have lost their noses naturally or as the result of an operation.

Did the ghost really take a seat at the managers' supper-table that night, uninvited? And can we be sure that the figure was that of the Opera ghost himself? Who would venture to assert as much? I mention the incident, not because I wish for a second to make the reader believe—or even to try to make him believe—that the ghost was capable of such a sublime piece of impudence; but because, after all, the thing is impossible.

M. Armand Moncharmin, in chapter eleven of his Memoirs, says:

"When I think of this first evening, I can not separate the secret confided to us by MM. Debienne and Poligny in their office from the presence at our supper of that *ghostly* person whom none of us knew."

What happened was this: Mm. Debienne and Poligny, sitting at the center of the table, had not seen the man with the death's head. Suddenly he began to speak.

"The ballet-girls are right," he said. "The death of that poor Buquet is perhaps not so natural as people think."

Debienne and Poligny gave a start.

"Is Buquet dead?" they cried.

"Yes," replied the man, or the shadow of a man, quietly. "He was found, this evening, hanging in the third cellar, between a farm-house and a scene from the *Roi De Lahore*."

The two managers, or rather ex-managers, at once rose and stared strangely at the speaker. They were more excited than they need have been, that is to say, more excited than any one need be by the announcement of the suicide of a chief scene-shifter. They looked at each other. They, had both turned whiter than the table-cloth. At last, Debienne made a sign to Mm. Richard and Moncharmin; Poligny muttered a few words of excuse to the guests; and all four went into the managers' office. I leave M. Moncharmin to complete the story. In his Memoirs, he says:

"Mm. Debienne and Poligny seemed to grow more and more excited, and they appeared to have something very difficult to tell us. First, they asked us if we knew the man, sitting at the end of the table, who had told them of the death of Joseph Buquet; and, when we answered in the negative, they looked still more concerned. They took the master-keys from our hands, stared at them for a moment and advised us to have new locks made, with the greatest secrecy, for the rooms, closets and presses that we might wish to have hermetically closed. They said this so funnily that we began to laugh and to ask if there were thieves at the Opera. They replied that there was something worse, which was the *ghost*. We began to laugh again, feeling sure that they were indulging in some joke that was intended to crown our little entertainment. Then, at their request, we became 'serious,' resolving to humor them and to enter into the spirit of the game. They told us that they never would have spoken to us of the ghost, if they had not received formal orders from the ghost himself to ask us to be pleasant to him and to grant any request that he might make. However, in their relief at leaving a domain where that tyrannical shade held sway, they had hesitated until the last moment to tell us this curious story, which our skeptical minds were certainly not prepared to entertain. But the announcement of the death of Joseph Buquet had served them as a brutal reminder that, whenever they had disregarded the ghost's wishes, some fantastic or disastrous event had brought them to a sense of their dependence.

"During these unexpected utterances made in a tone of the most secret and important confidence, I looked at Richard. Richard, in his student days, had acquired a great reputation for practical joking, and he seemed to relish the dish which was being served up to him in his turn. He did not miss a morsel of it, though the seasoning was a little gruesome because of the death of Buquet. He nodded his head sadly, while the others spoke, and his features assumed the air of a man who bitterly regretted having taken over the Opera, now that he knew that there was a ghost mixed up in the business. I could think of nothing better than to give him a servile imitation of this attitude of despair. However, in spite of all our efforts, we could not, at the finish, help bursting out laughing in the faces of MM. Debienne and Poligny, who, seeing us pass straight from the gloomiest state of mind to one of the most insolent merriment, acted as though they thought that we had gone mad.

"The joke became a little tedious; and Richard asked half-seriously and half in jest:

"'But, after all, what does this ghost of yours want?'

"M. Poligny went to his desk and returned with a copy of the memorandum-book. The memorandum-book begins with the well-known words saying that 'the management of the Opera shall give to the performance of the National Academy of Music the splendor that becomes the first lyric stage in France' and ends with Clause 98, which says that the privilege can be withdrawn if the manager infringes the conditions stipulated in the memorandum-book. This is followed by the conditions, which are four in number.

"The copy produced by M. Poligny was written in black ink and exactly similar to that in our possession, except that, at the end, it contained a paragraph in red ink and in a queer, labored handwriting, as though it had been produced by dipping the heads of matches into the ink, the writing of a child that has never got beyond the down-strokes and has not learned to join its letters. This paragraph ran, word for word, as follows:

"'5. Or if the manager, in any month, delay for more than a fortnight the payment of the allowance which he shall make to the Opera ghost, an allowance of twenty thousand francs a month, say two hundred and forty thousand francs a year.'

"M. Poligny pointed with a hesitating finger to this last clause, which we certainly did not expect.

"'Is this all? Does he not want anything else?' asked Richard, with the greatest coolness.

"'Yes, he does,' replied Poligny.

"And he turned over the pages of the memorandum-book until he came to the clause specifying the days on which certain private boxes were to be reserved for the free use of the president of the republic, the ministers and so on. At the end of this clause, a line had been added, also in red ink:

"'Box Five on the grand tier shall be placed at the disposal of the Opera ghost for every performance.'

"When we saw this, there was nothing else for us to do but to rise from our chairs, shake our two predecessors warmly by the hand and congratulate them on thinking of this charming little joke, which proved that the old

French sense of humor was never likely to become extinct. Richard added that he now understood why MM. Debienne and Poligny were retiring from the management of the National Academy of Music. Business was impossible with so unreasonable a ghost.

"'Certainly, two hundred and forty thousand francs are not be picked up for the asking,' said M. Poligny, without moving a muscle of his face. 'And have you considered what the loss over Box Five meant to us? We did not sell it once; and not only that, but we had to return the subscription: why, it's awful! We really can't work to keep ghosts! We prefer to go away!'

"'Yes,' echoed M. Debienne, 'we prefer to go away. Let us go.'"

"And he stood up. Richard said: 'But, after all all, it seems to me that you were much too kind to the ghost. If I had such a troublesome ghost as that, I should not hesitate to have him arrested.'

"'But how? Where?' they cried, in chorus. 'We have never seen him!'

"'But when he comes to his box?'

"'*We have never seen him in his box.*'

"'Then sell it.'

"'Sell the Opera ghost's box! Well, gentlemen, try it.'

"Thereupon we all four left the office. Richard and I had 'never laughed so much in our lives.'"

CHAPTER IV

BOX FIVE

Armand Moncharmin wrote such voluminous Memoirs during the fairly long period of his co-management that we may well ask if he ever found time to attend to the affairs of the Opera otherwise than by telling what went on there. M. Moncharmin did not know a note of music, but he called the minister of education and fine arts by his Christian name, had dabbled a little in society journalism and enjoyed a considerable private income. Lastly, he was a charming fellow and showed that he was not lacking in intelligence, for, as soon as he made up his mind to be a sleeping partner in the Opera, he selected the best possible active manager and went straight to Firmin Richard.

Firmin Richard was a very distinguished composer, who had published a number of successful pieces of all kinds and who liked nearly every form of music and every sort of musician. Clearly, therefore, it was the duty of every sort of musician to like M. Firmin Richard. The only things to be said against him were that he was rather masterful in his ways and endowed with a very hasty temper.

The first few days which the partners spent at the Opera were given over to the delight of finding themselves the head of so magnificent an enterprise; and they had forgotten all about that curious, fantastic story of the ghost, when an incident occurred that proved to them that the joke—if joke it were—was not over. M. Firmin Richard reached his office that morning at eleven o'clock. His secretary, M. Remy, showed him half a dozen letters which he had not opened because they were marked "private." One of the letters had at once attracted Richard's attention not only because the envelope was addressed in red ink, but because he seemed to have seen the writing before. He soon remembered that it was the red handwriting in which the memorandum-book had been so curiously completed. He recognized the clumsy childish hand.

He opened the letter and read:

Dear Mr. Manager:

I am sorry to have to trouble you at a time when you must be so very busy, renewing important engagements, signing fresh ones and generally displaying your excellent taste. I know what you have done for Carlotta, Sorelli and little Jammes and for a few others whose admirable qualities of talent or genius you have suspected.

Of course, when I use these words, I do not mean to apply them to La Carlotta, who sings like a squirt and who ought never to have been allowed to leave the Ambassadeurs and the Cafe Jacquin; nor to La Sorelli, who owes her success mainly to the coach-builders; nor to little Jammes, who dances like a calf in a field. And I am not speaking of Christine Daae either, though her genius is certain, whereas your jealousy prevents her from creating any important part. When all is said, you are free to conduct your little business as you think best, are you not?

All the same, I should like to take advantage of the fact that you have not yet turned Christine Daae out of doors by hearing her this evening in the part of Siebel, as that of Margarita has been forbidden her since her triumph of the other evening; and I will ask you not to dispose of my box to-day nor on the *following days*, for I can not end this letter without telling you how disagreeably surprised I have been once or twice, to hear, on arriving at the Opera, that my box had been sold, at the box-office, by your orders.

I did not protest, first, because I dislike scandal, and, second, because I thought that your predecessors, MM. Debienne and Poligny, who were always charming to me, had neglected, before leaving, to mention my little fads to you. I have now received a reply from those gentlemen to my letter asking for an explanation, and this reply proves that you know all about my Memorandum-Book and, consequently, that you are treating me with outrageous contempt. *If you wish to live in peace, you must not begin by taking away my private box.*

Believe me to be, dear Mr. Manager, without prejudice to these little observations,

    Your Most Humble and Obedient Servant,
    Opera Ghost.

The letter was accompanied by a cutting from the agony-column of the Revue Theatrale, which ran:

O. G.—There is no excuse for R. and M. We told them and left your memorandum-book in their hands. Kind regards.

M. Firmin Richard had hardly finished reading this letter when M. Armand Moncharmin entered, carrying one exactly similar. They looked at each other and burst out laughing.

"They are keeping up the joke," said M. Richard, "but I don't call it funny."

"What does it all mean?" asked M. Moncharmin. "Do they imagine that, because they have been managers of the Opera, we are going to let them have a box for an indefinite period?"

"I am not in the mood to let myself be laughed at long," said Firmin Richard.

"It's harmless enough," observed Armand Moncharmin. "What is it they really want? A box for to-night?"

M. Firmin Richard told his secretary to send Box Five on the grand tier to Mm. Debienne and Poligny, if it was not sold. It was not. It was sent off to them. Debienne lived at the corner of the Rue Scribe and the Boulevard des Capucines; Poligny, in the Rue Auber. O. Ghost's two letters had been posted at the Boulevard des Capucines post-office, as Moncharmin remarked after examining the envelopes.

"You see!" said Richard.

They shrugged their shoulders and regretted that two men of that age should amuse themselves with such childish tricks.

"They might have been civil, for all that!" said Moncharmin. "Did you notice how they treat us with regard to Carlotta, Sorelli and Little Jammes?"

"Why, my dear fellow, these two are mad with jealousy! To think that they went to the expense of, an advertisement in the Revue Theatrale! Have they nothing better to do?"

"By the way," said Moncharmin, "they seem to be greatly interested in that little Christine Daae!"

"You know as well as I do that she has the reputation of being quite good," said Richard.

"Reputations are easily obtained," replied Moncharmin. "Haven't I a reputation for knowing all about music? And I don't know one key from another."

"Don't be afraid: you never had that reputation," Richard declared.

Thereupon he ordered the artists to be shown in, who, for the last two hours, had been walking up and down outside the door behind which fame and fortune—or dismissal—awaited them.

The whole day was spent in discussing, negotiating, signing or cancelling contracts; and the two overworked managers went to bed early, without so much as casting a glance at Box Five to see whether M. Debienne and M. Poligny were enjoying the performance.

Next morning, the managers received a card of thanks from the ghost:

Dear, Mr. Manager:

Thanks. Charming evening. Daae exquisite. Choruses want waking up. Carlotta a splendid commonplace instrument. Will write you soon for the 240,000 francs, or 233,424 fr. 70 c., to be correct. Mm. Debienne and Poligny have sent me the 6,575 fr. 30 c. representing the first ten days of my allowance for the current year; their privileges finished on the evening of the tenth inst.

Kind regards. O. G.

On the other hand, there was a letter from Mm. Debienne and Poligny:

Gentlemen:

We are much obliged for your kind thought of us, but you will easily understand that the prospect of again hearing Faust, pleasant though it is to ex-managers of the Opera, can not make us forget that we have no right to occupy Box Five on the grand tier, which is the exclusive property of *him* of whom we spoke to you when we went through the memorandum-book with you for the last time. See Clause 98, final paragraph.

Accept, gentlemen, etc.

"Oh, those fellows are beginning to annoy me!" shouted Firmin Richard, snatching up the letter.

And that evening Box Five was sold.

The next morning, Mm. Richard and Moncharmin, on reaching their office, found an inspector's report relating to an incident that had happened, the night before, in Box Five. I give the essential part of the report:

I was obliged to call in a municipal guard twice, this evening, to clear Box Five on the grand tier, once at the beginning and once in the middle of the second act. The occupants, who arrived as the curtain rose on the second act, created a regular scandal by their laughter and their ridiculous observations. There were cries of "Hush!" all around them and the whole house was beginning to protest, when the box-keeper came to fetch me. I entered the box and said what I thought necessary. The people did not seem to me to be in their right mind; and they made stupid remarks. I said that, if the noise was repeated, I should be compelled to clear the box. The moment I left, I heard the laughing again, with fresh protests from the house. I returned with a municipal guard, who turned them out. They protested, still laughing, saying they would not go unless they had their money back. At last, they became quiet and I allowed them to enter the box again. The laughter at once recommenced; and, this time, I had them turned out definitely.

"Send for the inspector," said Richard to his secretary, who had already read the report and marked it with blue pencil.

M. Remy, the secretary, had foreseen the order and called the inspector at once.

"Tell us what happened," said Richard bluntly.

The inspector began to splutter and referred to the report.

"Well, but what were those people laughing at?" asked Moncharmin.

"They must have been dining, sir, and seemed more inclined to lark about than to listen to good music. The moment they entered the box, they came out again and called the box-keeper, who asked them what they wanted. They said, 'Look in the box: there's no one there, is there?' 'No,' said the woman. 'Well,' said they, 'when we went in, we heard a voice saying THAT THE BOX WAS TAKEN!'"

M. Moncharmin could not help smiling as he looked at M. Richard; but M. Richard did not smile. He himself had done too much in that way in his time not to recognize, in the inspector's story, all the marks of one of those practical jokes which begin by amusing and end by enraging the victims. The inspector, to curry favor with M. Moncharmin, who was smiling, thought it best to give a smile too. A most unfortunate smile! M. Richard glared at his subordinate, who thenceforth made it his business to display a face of utter consternation.

"However, when the people arrived," roared Richard, "there was no one in the box, was there?"

"Not a soul, sir, not a soul! Nor in the box on the right, nor in the box on the left: not a soul, sir, I swear! The box-keeper told it me often enough, which proves that it was all a joke."

"Oh, you agree, do you?" said Richard. "You agree! It's a joke! And you think it funny, no doubt?"

"I think it in very bad taste, sir."

"And what did the box-keeper say?"

"Oh, she just said that it was the Opera ghost. That's all she said!"

And the inspector grinned. But he soon found that he had made a mistake in grinning, for the words had no sooner left his mouth than M. Richard, from gloomy, became furious.

"Send for the box-keeper!" he shouted. "Send for her! This minute! This minute! And bring her in to me here! And turn all those people out!"

The inspector tried to protest, but Richard closed his mouth with an angry order to hold his tongue. Then, when the wretched man's lips seemed shut for ever, the manager commanded him to open them once more.

"Who is this 'Opera ghost?'" he snarled.

But the inspector was by this time incapable of speaking a word. He managed to convey, by a despairing gesture, that he knew nothing about it, or rather that he did not wish to know.

"Have you ever seen him, have you seen the Opera ghost?"

The inspector, by means of a vigorous shake of the head, denied ever having seen the ghost in question.

"Very well!" said M. Richard coldly.

The inspector's eyes started out of his head, as though to ask why the manager had uttered that ominous "Very well!"

"Because I'm going to settle the account of any one who has not seen him!" explained the manager. "As he seems to be everywhere, I can't have people telling me that they see him nowhere. I like people to work for me when I employ them!"

Having said this, M. Richard paid no attention to the inspector and discussed various matters of business with his acting-manager, who had entered the room meanwhile. The inspector thought he could go and was gently—oh, so gently!—sidling toward the door, when M. Richard nailed the man to the floor with a thundering:

"Stay where you are!"

M. Remy had sent for the box-keeper to the Rue de Provence, close to the Opera, where she was engaged as a porteress. She soon made her appearance.

"What's your name?"

"Mme. Giry. You know me well enough, sir; I'm the mother of little Giry, little Meg, what!"

This was said in so rough and solemn a tone that, for a moment, M. Richard was impressed. He looked at Mme. Giry, in her faded shawl, her worn shoes, her old taffeta dress and dingy bonnet. It was quite evident from the manager's attitude, that he either did not know or could not remember having met Mme. Giry, nor even little Giry, nor even "little Meg!" But Mme. Giry's pride was so great that the celebrated box-keeper imagined that everybody knew her.

"Never heard of her!" the manager declared. "But that's no reason, Mme. Giry, why I shouldn't ask you what happened last night to make you and the inspector call in a municipal guard."

"I was just wanting to see you, sir, and talk to you about it, so that you mightn't have the same unpleasantness as M. Debienne and M. Poligny.

They wouldn't listen to me either, at first."

"I'm not asking you about all that. I'm asking what happened last night."

Mme. Giry turned purple with indignation. Never had she been spoken to like that. She rose as though to go, gathering up the folds of her skirt and waving the feathers of her dingy bonnet with dignity, but, changing her mind, she sat down again and said, in a haughty voice:

"I'll tell you what happened. The ghost was annoyed again!"

Thereupon, as M. Richard was on the point of bursting out, M. Moncharmin interfered and conducted the interrogatory, whence it appeared that Mme. Giry thought it quite natural that a voice should be heard to say that a box was taken, when there was nobody in the box. She was unable to explain this phenomenon, which was not new to her, except by the intervention of the ghost. Nobody could see the ghost in his box, but everybody could hear him. She had often heard him; and they could believe her, for she always spoke the truth. They could ask M. Debienne and M. Poligny, and anybody who knew her; and also M. Isidore Saack, who had had a leg broken by the ghost!

"Indeed!" said Moncharmin, interrupting her. "Did the ghost break poor Isidore Saack's leg?"

Mme. Giry opened her eyes with astonishment at such ignorance. However, she consented to enlighten those two poor innocents. The thing had happened in M. Debienne and M. Poligny's time, also in Box Five and also during a performance of *Faust*. Mme. Giry coughed, cleared her throat—it sounded as though she were preparing to sing the whole of Gounod's score—and began:

"It was like this, sir. That night, M. Maniera and his lady, the jewelers in the Rue Mogador, were sitting in the front of the box, with their great friend, M. Isidore Saack, sitting behind Mme. Maniera. Mephistopheles was singing"—Mme. Giry here burst into song herself—"'Catarina, while you play at sleeping,' and then M. Maniera heard a voice in his right ear (his wife was on his left) saying, 'Ha, ha! Julie's not playing at sleeping!' His wife happened to be called Julie. So. M. Maniera turns to the right to see who was talking to him like that. Nobody there! He rubs his ear and asks himself, if he's dreaming. Then Mephistopheles went on with his serenade . . . But, perhaps I'm boring you gentlemen?"

"No, no, go on."

"You are too good, gentlemen," with a smirk. "Well, then, Mephistopheles went on with his serenade"—Mme. Giry, burst into song again—"'Saint, unclose thy portals holy and accord the bliss, to a mortal bending lowly, of a pardon-kiss.' And then M. Maniera again hears the voice in his right ear,

saying, this time, 'Ha, ha! Julie wouldn't mind according a kiss to Isidore!'
Then he turns round again, but, this time, to the left; and what do you think
he sees? Isidore, who had taken his lady's hand and was covering it with
kisses through the little round place in the glove—like this, gentlemen"—
rapturously kissing the bit of palm left bare in the middle of her thread
gloves. "Then they had a lively time between them! Bang! Bang! M. Maniera,
who was big and strong, like you, M. Richard, gave two blows to M. Isidore
Saack, who was small and weak like M. Moncharmin, saving his presence.
There was a great uproar. People in the house shouted, 'That will do! Stop
them! He'll kill him!' Then, at last, M. Isidore Saack managed to run away."

"Then the ghost had not broken his leg?" asked M. Moncharmin, a little
vexed that his figure had made so little impression on Mme. Giry.

"He did break it for him, sir," replied Mme. Giry haughtily. "He broke it
for him on the grand staircase, which he ran down too fast, sir, and it will be
long before the poor gentleman will be able to go up it again!"

"Did the ghost tell you what he said in M. Maniera's right ear?" asked M.
Moncharmin, with a gravity which he thought exceedingly humorous.

"No, sir, it was M. Maniera himself. So——"

"But you have spoken to the ghost, my good lady?"

"As I'm speaking to you now, my good sir!" Mme. Giry replied.

"And, when the ghost speaks to you, what does he say?"

"Well, he tells me to bring him a footstool!"

This time, Richard burst out laughing, as did Moncharmin and Remy,
the secretary. Only the inspector, warned by experience, was careful not to
laugh, while Mme. Giry ventured to adopt an attitude that was positively
threatening.

"Instead of laughing," she cried indignantly, "you'd do better to do as M.
Poligny did, who found out for himself."

"Found out about what?" asked Moncharmin, who had never been so
much amused in his life.

"About the ghost, of course! . . . Look here . . . "

She suddenly calmed herself, feeling that this was a solemn moment
in her life:

"*Look here*," she repeated. "They were playing La Juive. M. Poligny
thought he would watch the performance from the ghost's box . . . Well,
when Leopold cries, 'Let us fly!'—you know—and Eleazer stops them and
says, 'Whither go ye?' . . . well, M. Poligny—I was watching him from the
back of the next box, which was empty—M. Poligny got up and walked out
quite stiffly, like a statue, and before I had time to ask him, 'Whither go ye?'
like Eleazer, he was down the staircase, but without breaking his leg.

"Still, that doesn't let us know how the Opera ghost came to ask you for a footstool," insisted M. Moncharmin.

"Well, from that evening, no one tried to take the ghost's private box from him. The manager gave orders that he was to have it at each performance. And, whenever he came, he asked me for a footstool."

"Tut, tut! A ghost asking for a footstool! Then this ghost of yours is a woman?"

"No, the ghost is a man."

"How do you know?"

"He has a man's voice, oh, such a lovely man's voice! This is what happens: When he comes to the opera, it's usually in the middle of the first act. He gives three little taps on the door of Box Five. The first time I heard those three taps, when I knew there was no one in the box, you can think how puzzled I was! I opened the door, listened, looked; nobody! And then I heard a voice say, 'Mme. Jules' my poor husband's name was Jules—'a footstool, please.' Saving your presence, gentlemen, it made me feel all-overish like. But the voice went on, 'Don't be frightened, Mme. Jules, I'm the Opera ghost!' And the voice was so soft and kind that I hardly felt frightened. *The voice was sitting in the corner chair, on the right, in the front row.*"

"Was there any one in the box on the right of Box Five?" asked Moncharmin.

"No; Box Seven, and Box Three, the one on the left, were both empty. The curtain had only just gone up."

"And what did you do?"

"Well, I brought the footstool. Of course, it wasn't for himself he wanted it, but for his lady! But I never heard her nor saw her."

"Eh? What? So now the ghost is married!" The eyes of the two managers traveled from Mme. Giry to the inspector, who, standing behind the box-keeper, was waving his arms to attract their attention. He tapped his forehead with a distressful forefinger, to convey his opinion that the widow Jules Giry was most certainly mad, a piece of pantomime which confirmed M. Richard in his determination to get rid of an inspector who kept a lunatic in his service. Meanwhile, the worthy lady went on about her ghost, now painting his generosity:

"At the end of the performance, he always gives me two francs, sometimes five, sometimes even ten, when he has been many days without coming. Only, since people have begun to annoy him again, he gives me nothing at all."

"Excuse me, my good woman," said Moncharmin, while Mme. Giry tossed the feathers in her dingy hat at this persistent familiarity, "excuse me, how does the ghost manage to give you your two francs?"

"Why, he leaves them on the little shelf in the box, of course. I find them with the program, which I always give him. Some evenings, I find flowers in the box, a rose that must have dropped from his lady's bodice . . . for he brings a lady with him sometimes; one day, they left a fan behind them."

"Oh, the ghost left a fan, did he? And what did you do with it?"

"Well, I brought it back to the box next night."

Here the inspector's voice was raised.

"You've broken the rules; I shall have to fine you, Mme. Giry."

"Hold your tongue, you fool!" muttered M. Firmin Richard.

"You brought back the fan. And then?"

"Well, then, they took it away with them, sir; it was not there at the end of the performance; and in its place they left me a box of English sweets, which I'm very fond of. That's one of the ghost's pretty thoughts."

"That will do, Mme. Giry. You can go."

When Mme. Giry had bowed herself out, with the dignity that never deserted her, the manager told the inspector that they had decided to dispense with that old madwoman's services; and, when he had gone in his turn, they instructed the acting-manager to make up the inspector's accounts. Left alone, the managers told each other of the idea which they both had in mind, which was that they should look into that little matter of Box Five themselves.

CHAPTER V

THE ENCHANTED VIOLIN

Christine Daae, owing to intrigues to which I will return later, did not immediately continue her triumph at the Opera. After the famous gala night, she sang once at the Duchess de Zurich's; but this was the last occasion on which she was heard in private. She refused, without plausible excuse, to appear at a charity concert to which she had promised her assistance. She acted throughout as though she were no longer the mistress of her own destiny and as though she feared a fresh triumph.

She knew that the Comte de Chagny, to please his brother, had done his best on her behalf with M. Richard; and she wrote to thank him and also to ask him to cease speaking in her favor. Her reason for this curious attitude was never known. Some pretended that it was due to overweening pride; others spoke of her heavenly modesty. But people on the stage are not so modest as all that; and I think that I shall not be far from the truth if I ascribe her action simply to fear. Yes, I believe that Christine Daae was frightened by what had happened to her. I have a letter of Christine's (it forms part of the Persian's collection), relating to this period, which suggests a feeling of absolute dismay:

"I don't know myself when I sing," writes the poor child.

She showed herself nowhere; and the Vicomte de Chagny tried in vain to meet her.

He wrote to her, asking to call upon her, but despaired of receiving a reply when, one morning, she sent him the following note:

Monsieur:

I have not forgotten the little boy who went into the sea to rescue my scarf. I feel that I must write to you to-day, when I am going to Perros, in fulfilment of a sacred duty. To-morrow is the anniversary of the death of my poor father, whom you knew and who was very fond of you. He is buried there, with his violin, in the graveyard of the little church, at the bottom of the slope where we used to play as children, beside the road where, when we were a little bigger, we said good-by for the last time.

The Vicomte de Chagny hurriedly consulted a railway guide, dressed as quickly as he could, wrote a few lines for his valet to take to his brother and jumped into a cab which brought him to the Gare Montparnasse just in time to miss the morning train. He spent a dismal day in town and did not recover his spirits until the evening, when he was seated in his compartment in the Brittany express. He read Christine's note over and over again, smelling its perfume, recalling the sweet pictures of his childhood, and spent the rest of that tedious night journey in feverish dreams that began and ended with Christine Daae. Day was breaking when he alighted at Lannion. He hurried to the diligence for Perros-Guirec. He was the only passenger. He questioned the driver and learned that, on the evening of the previous day, a young lady who looked like a Parisian had gone to Perros and put up at the inn known as the Setting Sun.

The nearer he drew to her, the more fondly he remembered the story of the little Swedish singer. Most of the details are still unknown to the public.

There was once, in a little market-town not far from Upsala, a peasant who lived there with his family, digging the earth during the week and singing in the choir on Sundays. This peasant had a little daughter to whom he taught the musical alphabet before she knew how to read. Daae's father was a great musician, perhaps without knowing it. Not a fiddler throughout the length and breadth of Scandinavia played as he did. His reputation was widespread and he was always invited to set the couples dancing at weddings and other festivals. His wife died when Christine was entering upon her sixth year. Then the father, who cared only for his daughter and his music, sold his patch of ground and went to Upsala in search of fame and fortune. He found nothing but poverty.

He returned to the country, wandering from fair to fair, strumming his Scandinavian melodies, while his child, who never left his side, listened to him in ecstasy or sang to his playing. One day, at Ljimby Fair, Professor Valerius heard them and took them to Gothenburg. He maintained that the father was the first violinist in the world and that the daughter had the making of a great artist. Her education and instruction were provided for. She made rapid progress and charmed everybody with her prettiness, her grace of manner and her genuine eagerness to please.

When Valerius and his wife went to settle in France, they took Daae and Christine with them. "Mamma" Valerius treated Christine as her daughter. As for Daae, he began to pine away with homesickness. He never went out of doors in Paris, but lived in a sort of dream which he kept up with his violin. For hours at a time, he remained locked up in his bedroom with his daughter, fiddling and singing, very, very softly. Sometimes Mamma Valerius would come and listen behind the door, wipe away a tear and go down-stairs again on tiptoe, sighing for her Scandinavian skies.

Daae seemed not to recover his strength until the summer, when the whole family went to stay at Perros-Guirec, in a far-away corner of Brittany, where the sea was of the same color as in his own country. Often he would play his saddest tunes on the beach and pretend that the sea stopped its roaring to listen to them. And then he induced Mamma Valerius to indulge a queer whim of his. At the time of the "pardons," or Breton pilgrimages, the village festival and dances, he went off with his fiddle, as in the old days, and was allowed to take his daughter with him for a week. They gave the smallest hamlets music to last them for a year and slept at night in a barn, refusing a bed at the inn, lying close together on the straw, as when they were so poor in Sweden. At the same time, they were very neatly dressed, made no collection, refused the halfpence offered them; and the people around could not understand the conduct of this rustic fiddler, who tramped the roads with that pretty child who sang like an angel from Heaven. They followed them from village to village.

One day, a little boy, who was out with his governess, made her take a longer walk than he intended, for he could not tear himself from the little girl whose pure, sweet voice seemed to bind him to her. They came to the shore of an inlet which is still called Trestraou, but which now, I believe, harbors a casino or something of the sort. At that time, there was nothing but sky and sea and a stretch of golden beach. Only, there was also a high wind, which blew Christine's scarf out to sea. Christine gave a cry and put out her arms, but the scarf was already far on the waves. Then she heard a voice say:

"It's all right, I'll go and fetch your scarf out of the sea."

And she saw a little boy running fast, in spite of the outcries and the indignant protests of a worthy lady in black. The little boy ran into the sea, dressed as he was, and brought her back her scarf. Boy and scarf were both soaked through. The lady in black made a great fuss, but Christine laughed merrily and kissed the little boy, who was none other than the Vicomte Raoul de Chagny, staying at Lannion with his aunt.

During the season, they saw each other and played together almost every day. At the aunt's request, seconded by Professor Valerius, Daae consented to give the young viscount some violin lessons. In this way, Raoul learned to love the same airs that had charmed Christine's childhood. They also both had the same calm and dreamy little cast of mind. They delighted in stories, in old Breton legends; and their favorite sport was to go and ask for them at the cottage-doors, like beggars:

"Ma'am . . . " or, "Kind gentleman . . . have you a little story to tell us, please?"

And it seldom happened that they did not have one "given" them; for nearly every old Breton grandame has, at least once in her life, seen the "korrigans" dance by moonlight on the heather.

But their great treat was, in the twilight, in the great silence of the evening, after the sun had set in the sea, when Daae came and sat down by them on the roadside and, in a low voice, as though fearing lest he should frighten the ghosts whom he evoked, told them the legends of the land of the North. And, the moment he stopped, the children would ask for more.

There was one story that began:

"A king sat in a little boat on one of those deep, still lakes that open like a bright eye in the midst of the Norwegian mountains . . . "

And another:

"Little Lotte thought of everything and nothing. Her hair was golden as the sun's rays and her soul as clear and blue as her eyes. She wheedled her mother, was kind to her doll, took great care of her frock and her little red shoes and her fiddle, but most of all loved, when she went to sleep, to hear the Angel of Music."

While the old man told this story, Raoul looked at Christine's blue eyes and golden hair; and Christine thought that Lotte was very lucky to hear the Angel of Music when she went to sleep. The Angel of Music played a part in all Daddy Daae's tales; and he maintained that every great musician, every great artist received a visit from the Angel at least once in his life. Sometimes the Angel leans over their cradle, as happened to Lotte, and that is how there are little prodigies who play the fiddle at six better than men at fifty, which, you must admit, is very wonderful. Sometimes, the Angel comes much later, because the children are naughty and won't learn their lessons or practise their scales. And, sometimes, he does not come at all, because the children have a bad heart or a bad conscience.

No one ever sees the Angel; but he is heard by those who are meant to hear him. He often comes when they least expect him, when they are sad and disheartened. Then their ears suddenly perceive celestial harmonies, a divine voice, which they remember all their lives. Persons who are visited by the Angel quiver with a thrill unknown to the rest of mankind. And they can not touch an instrument, or open their mouths to sing, without producing sounds that put all other human sounds to shame. Then people who do not know that the Angel has visited those persons say that they have genius.

Little Christine asked her father if he had heard the Angel of Music. But Daddy Daae shook his head sadly; and then his eyes lit up, as he said:

"You will hear him one day, my child! When I am in Heaven, I will send him to you!"

Daddy was beginning to cough at that time.

Three years later, Raoul and Christine met again at Perros. Professor Valerius was dead, but his widow remained in France with Daddy Daae and his daughter, who continued to play the violin and sing, wrapping in their dream of harmony their kind patroness, who seemed henceforth to live on music alone. The young man, as he now was, had come to Perros on the chance of finding them and went straight to the house in which they used to stay. He first saw the old man; and then Christine entered, carrying the tea-tray. She flushed at the sight of Raoul, who went up to her and kissed her. She asked him a few questions, performed her duties as hostess prettily, took up the tray again and left the room. Then she ran into the garden and took refuge on a bench, a prey to feelings that stirred her young heart for the first time. Raoul followed her and they talked till the evening, very shyly. They were quite changed, cautious as two diplomatists, and told each other things that had nothing to do with their budding sentiments. When they took leave of each other by the roadside, Raoul, pressing a kiss on Christine's trembling hand, said:

"Mademoiselle, I shall never forget you!"

And he went away regretting his words, for he knew that Christine could not be the wife of the Vicomte de Chagny.

As for Christine, she tried not to think of him and devoted herself wholly to her art. She made wonderful progress and those who heard her prophesied that she would be the greatest singer in the world. Meanwhile, the father died; and, suddenly, she seemed to have lost, with him, her voice, her soul and her genius. She retained just, but only just, enough of this to enter the *conservatoire*, where she did not distinguish herself at all, attending the classes without enthusiasm and taking a prize only to please old Mamma Valerius, with whom she continued to live.

The first time that Raoul saw Christine at the Opera, he was charmed by the girl's beauty and by the sweet images of the past which it evoked, but was rather surprised at the negative side of her art. He returned to listen to her. He followed her in the wings. He waited for her behind a Jacob's ladder. He tried to attract her attention. More than once, he walked after her to the door of her box, but she did not see him. She seemed, for that matter, to see nobody. She was all indifference. Raoul suffered, for she was very beautiful and he was shy and dared not confess his love, even to himself. And then came the lightning-flash of the gala performance: the heavens torn asunder and an angel's voice heard upon earth for the delight of mankind and the utter capture of his heart.

And then . . . and then there was that man's voice behind the door—"You must love me!"—and no one in the room . . .

Why did she laugh when he reminded her of the incident of the scarf? Why did she not recognize him? And why had she written to him? . . .

Perros was reached at last. Raoul walked into the smoky sitting-room of the Setting Sun and at once saw Christine standing before him, smiling and showing no astonishment.

"So you have come," she said. "I felt that I should find you here, when I came back from mass. Some one told me so, at the church."

"Who?" asked Raoul, taking her little hand in his.

"Why, my poor father, who is dead."

There was a silence; and then Raoul asked:

"Did your father tell you that I love you, Christine, and that I can not live without you?"

Christine blushed to the eyes and turned away her head. In a trembling voice, she said:

"Me? You are dreaming, my friend!"

And she burst out laughing, to put herself in countenance.

"Don't laugh, Christine; I am quite serious," Raoul answered.

And she replied gravely: "I did not make you come to tell me such things as that."

"You 'made me come,' Christine; you knew that your letter would not leave me indignant and that I should hasten to Perros. How can you have thought that, if you did not think I loved you?"

"I thought you would remember our games here, as children, in which my father so often joined. I really don't know what I thought . . . Perhaps I was wrong to write to you . . . This anniversary and your sudden appearance in my room at the Opera, the other evening, reminded me of the time long past and made me write to you as the little girl that I then was . . ."

There was something in Christine's attitude that seemed to Raoul not natural. He did not feel any hostility in her; far from it: the distressed affection shining in her eyes told him that. But why was this affection distressed? That was what he wished to know and what was irritating him.

"When you saw me in your dressing-room, was that the first time you noticed me, Christine?"

She was incapable of lying.

"No," she said, "I had seen you several times in your brother's box. And also on the stage."

"I thought so!" said Raoul, compressing his lips. "But then why, when you saw me in your room, at your feet, reminding you that I had rescued your scarf from the sea, why did you answer as though you did not know me and also why did you laugh?"

The tone of these questions was so rough that Christine stared at Raoul without replying. The young man himself was aghast at the sudden quarrel which he had dared to raise at the very moment when he had resolved to speak words of gentleness, love and submission to Christine. A husband, a lover with all rights, would talk no differently to a wife, a mistress who had offended him. But he had gone too far and saw no other way out of the ridiculous position than to behave odiously.

"You don't answer!" he said angrily and unhappily. "Well, I will answer for you. It was because there was some one in the room who was in your way, Christine, some one that you did not wish to know that you could be interested in any one else!"

"If any one was in my way, my friend," Christine broke in coldly, "if any one was in my way, that evening, it was yourself, since I told you to leave the room!"

"Yes, so that you might remain with the other!"

"What are you saying, monsieur?" asked the girl excitedly. "And to what other do you refer?"

"To the man to whom you said, 'I sing only for you! . . . to-night I gave you my soul and I am dead!'"

Christine seized Raoul's arm and clutched it with a strength which no one would have suspected in so frail a creature.

"Then you were listening behind the door?"

"Yes, because I love you everything . . . And I heard everything . . . "

"You heard what?"

And the young girl, becoming strangely calm, released Raoul's arm.

"He said to you, 'Christine, you must love me!'"

At these words, a deathly pallor spread over Christine's face, dark rings formed round her eyes, she staggered and seemed on the point of swooning. Raoul darted forward, with arms outstretched, but Christine had overcome her passing faintness and said, in a low voice:

"Go on! Go on! Tell me all you heard!"

At an utter loss to understand, Raoul answered: "I heard him reply, when you said you had given him your soul, 'Your soul is a beautiful thing, child, and I thank you. No emperor ever received so fair a gift. The angels wept tonight.'"

Christine carried her hand to her heart, a prey to indescribable emotion. Her eyes stared before her like a madwoman's. Raoul was terror-stricken. But suddenly Christine's eyes moistened and two great tears trickled, like two pearls, down her ivory cheeks.

"Christine!"

"Raoul!"

The young man tried to take her in his arms, but she escaped and fled in great disorder.

While Christine remained locked in her room, Raoul was at his wit's end what to do. He refused to breakfast. He was terribly concerned and bitterly grieved to see the hours, which he had hoped to find so sweet, slip past without the presence of the young Swedish girl. Why did she not come to roam with him through the country where they had so many memories in common? He heard that she had had a mass said, that morning, for the repose of her father's soul and spent a long time praying in the little church and on the fiddler's tomb. Then, as she seemed to have nothing more to do at Perros and, in fact, was doing nothing there, why did she not go back to Paris at once?

Raoul walked away, dejectedly, to the graveyard in which the church stood and was indeed alone among the tombs, reading the inscriptions; but, when he turned behind the apse, he was suddenly struck by the dazzling note of the flowers that straggled over the white ground. They were marvelous red roses that had blossomed in the morning, in the snow, giving a glimpse of life among the dead, for death was all around him. It also, like the flowers, issued from the ground, which had flung back a number of its corpses. Skeletons and skulls by the hundred were heaped against the wall of the church, held in position by a wire that left the whole gruesome stack visible. Dead men's bones, arranged in rows, like bricks, to form the first course upon which the walls of the sacristy had been built. The door of the sacristy opened in the middle of that bony structure, as is often seen in old Breton churches.

Raoul said a prayer for Daae and then, painfully impressed by all those eternal smiles on the mouths of skulls, he climbed the slope and sat down on the edge of the heath overlooking the sea. The wind fell with the evening. Raoul was surrounded by icy darkness, but he did not feel the cold. It was here, he remembered, that he used to come with little Christine to see the Korrigans dance at the rising of the moon. He had never seen any, though his eyes were good, whereas Christine, who was a little shortsighted, pretended that she had seen many. He smiled at the thought and then suddenly gave a start. A voice behind him said:

"Do you think the Korrigans will come this evening?"

It was Christine. He tried to speak. She put her gloved hand on his mouth.

"Listen, Raoul. I have decided to tell you something serious, very serious . . . Do you remember the legend of the Angel of Music?"

"I do indeed," he said. "I believe it was here that your father first told it to us."

"And it was here that he said, 'When I am in Heaven, my child, I will send him to you.' Well, Raoul, my father is in Heaven, and I have been visited by the Angel of Music."

"I have no doubt of it," replied the young man gravely, for it seemed to him that his friend, in obedience to a pious thought, was connecting the memory of her father with the brilliancy of her last triumph.

Christine appeared astonished at the Vicomte de Chagny's coolness:

"How do you understand it?" she asked, bringing her pale face so close to his that he might have thought that Christine was going to give him a kiss; but she only wanted to read his eyes in spite of the dark.

"I understand," he said, "that no human being can sing as you sang the other evening without the intervention of some miracle. No professor on earth can teach you such accents as those. You have heard the Angel of Music, Christine."

"Yes," she said solemnly, "*In my dressing-room*. That is where he comes to give me my lessons daily."

"In your dressing-room?" he echoed stupidly.

"Yes, that is where I have heard him; and I have not been the only one to hear him."

"Who else heard him, Christine?"

"You, my friend."

"I? I heard the Angel of Music?"

"Yes, the other evening, it was he who was talking when you were listening behind the door. It was he who said, 'You must love me.' But I then thought that I was the only one to hear his voice. Imagine my astonishment when you told me, this morning, that you could hear him too."

Raoul burst out laughing. The first rays of the moon came and shrouded the two young people in their light. Christine turned on Raoul with a hostile air. Her eyes, usually so gentle, flashed fire.

"What are you laughing at? *You* think you heard a man's voice, I suppose?"

"Well! . . . " replied the young man, whose ideas began to grow confused in the face of Christine's determined attitude.

"It's you, Raoul, who say that? You, an old playfellow of my own! A friend of my father's! But you have changed since those days. What are you thinking of? I am an honest girl, M. le Vicomte de Chagny, and I don't lock myself up in my dressing-room with men's voices. If you had opened the door, you would have seen that there was nobody in the room!"

"That's true! I did open the door, when you were gone, and I found no one in the room."

"So you see! . . . Well?"

The viscount summoned up all his courage.

"Well, Christine, I think that somebody is making game of you."

She gave a cry and ran away. He ran after her, but, in a tone of fierce anger, she called out: "Leave me! Leave me!" And she disappeared.

Raoul returned to the inn feeling very weary, very low-spirited and very sad. He was told that Christine had gone to her bedroom saying that she would not be down to dinner. Raoul dined alone, in a very gloomy mood. Then he went to his room and tried to read, went to bed and tried to sleep. There was no sound in the next room.

The hours passed slowly. It was about half-past eleven when he distinctly heard some one moving, with a light, stealthy step, in the room next to his. Then Christine had not gone to bed! Without troubling for a reason, Raoul dressed, taking care not to make a sound, and waited. Waited for what? How could he tell? But his heart thumped in his chest when he heard Christine's door turn slowly on its hinges. Where could she be going, at this hour, when every one was fast asleep at Perros? Softly opening the door, he saw Christine's white form, in the moonlight, slipping along the passage. She went down the stairs and he leaned over the baluster above her. Suddenly he heard two voices in rapid conversation. He caught one sentence: "Don't lose the key."

It was the landlady's voice. The door facing the sea was opened and locked again. Then all was still.

Raoul ran back to his room and threw back the window. Christine's white form stood on the deserted quay.

The first floor of the Setting Sun was at no great height and a tree growing against the wall held out its branches to Raoul's impatient arms and enabled him to climb down unknown to the landlady. Her amazement, therefore, was all the greater when, the next morning, the young man was brought back to her half frozen, more dead than alive, and when she learned that he had been found stretched at full length on the steps of the high altar of the little church. She ran at once to tell Christine, who hurried down and, with the help of the landlady, did her best to revive him. He soon opened his eyes and was not long in recovering when he saw his friend's charming face leaning over him.

A few weeks later, when the tragedy at the Opera compelled the intervention of the public prosecutor, M. Mifroid, the commissary of police, examined the Vicomte de Chagny touching the events of the night at Perros. I quote the questions and answers as given in the official report pp. 150 et seq.:

Q. "Did Mlle. Daae not see you come down from your room by the curious road which you selected?"

R. "No, monsieur, no, although, when walking behind her, I took no pains to deaden the sound of my footsteps. In fact, I was anxious that she should turn round and see me. I realized that I had no excuse for following her and that this way of spying on her was unworthy of me. But she seemed not to hear me and acted exactly as though I were not there. She quietly left the quay and then suddenly walked quickly up the road. The church-clock had struck a quarter to twelve and I thought that this must have made her hurry, for she began almost to run and continued hastening until she came to the church."

Q. "Was the gate open?"

R. "Yes, monsieur, and this surprised me, but did not seem to surprise Mlle. Daae."

Q. "Was there no one in the churchyard?"

R. "I did not see any one; and, if there had been, I must have seen him. The moon was shining on the snow and made the night quite light."

Q. "Was it possible for any one to hide behind the tombstones?"

R. "No, monsieur. They were quite small, poor tombstones, partly hidden under the snow, with their crosses just above the level of the ground. The only shadows were those of the crosses and ourselves. The church stood out quite brightly. I never saw so clear a night. It was very fine and very cold and one could see everything."

Q. "Are you at all superstitious?"

R. "No, monsieur, I am a practising Catholic,"

Q. "In what condition of mind were you?"

R. "Very healthy and peaceful, I assure you. Mlle. Daae's curious action in going out at that hour had worried me at first; but, as soon as I saw her go to the churchyard, I thought that she meant to fulfil some pious duty on her father's grave and I considered this so natural that I recovered all my calmness. I was only surprised that she had not heard me walking behind her, for my footsteps were quite audible on the hard snow. But she must have been taken up with her intentions and I resolved not to disturb her. She knelt down by her father's grave, made the sign of the cross and began to pray. At that moment, it struck midnight. At the last stroke, I saw Mlle. Daae life{sic} her eyes to the sky and stretch out her arms as though in ecstasy. I was wondering what the reason could be, when I myself raised my head and everything within me seemed drawn toward the invisible, **which was playing the most perfect music**! Christine and I knew that music; we had heard it as children. But it had never been executed with such divine art, even by M. Daae. I remembered all that Christine had told me of the Angel of Music. The air was The Resurrection of Lazarus, which old M. Daae used to play to us in his hours of melancholy and of faith. If Christine's Angel had existed, he could not have played better, that night, on the late musician's violin. When the music stopped, I seemed to hear a noise from the skulls in the heap of bones; it was as though they were chuckling and I could not help shuddering."

Q. "Did it not occur to you that the musician might be hiding behind that very heap of bones?"

R. "It was the one thought that did occur to me, monsieur, so much so that I omitted to follow Mlle. Daae, when she stood up and walked slowly to the gate. She was so much absorbed just then that I am not surprised that she did not see me."

Q. "Then what happened that you were found in the morning lying half-dead on the steps of the high altar?"

R. "First a skull rolled to my feet . . . then another . . . then another . . . It was as if I were the mark of that ghastly game of bowls. And I had an idea that false step must have destroyed the balance of the structure behind which our musician was concealed. This surmise seemed to be confirmed when I saw a shadow suddenly glide along the sacristy wall. I ran up. The shadow had already pushed open the door and entered the church. But I was quicker than the shadow and caught hold of a corner of its cloak. At that moment, we were just in front of the high altar; and the moonbeams fell straight upon us through the stained-glass windows of the apse. As I did not let go of the cloak, the shadow turned round; and I saw a terrible death's head, which darted a look at me from a pair of scorching eyes. I felt as if I were face to face with Satan; and, in the presence of this unearthly apparition, my heart gave way, my courage failed me . . . and I remember nothing more until I recovered consciousness at the Setting Sun."

CHAPTER VI

A VISIT TO BOX FIVE

We left M. Firmin Richard and M. Armand Moncharmin at the moment when they were deciding "to look into that little matter of Box Five."

Leaving behind them the broad staircase which leads from the lobby outside the managers' offices to the stage and its dependencies, they crossed the stage, went out by the subscribers' door and entered the house through the first little passage on the left. Then they made their way through the front rows of stalls and looked at Box Five on the grand tier, They could not see it well, because it was half in darkness and because great covers were flung over the red velvet of the ledges of all the boxes.

They were almost alone in the huge, gloomy house; and a great silence surrounded them. It was the time when most of the stage-hands go out for a drink. The staff had left the boards for the moment, leaving a scene half set. A few rays of light, a wan, sinister light, that seemed to have been stolen from an expiring luminary, fell through some opening or other upon an old tower that raised its pasteboard battlements on the stage; everything, in this deceptive light, adopted a fantastic shape. In the orchestra stalls, the drugget covering them looked like an angry sea, whose glaucous waves had been suddenly rendered stationary by a secret order from the storm phantom, who, as everybody knows, is called Adamastor. MM. Moncharmin and Richard were the shipwrecked mariners amid this motionless turmoil of a calico sea. They made for the left boxes, plowing their way like sailors who leave their ship and try to struggle to the shore. The eight great polished columns stood up in the dusk like so many huge piles supporting the threatening, crumbling, big-bellied cliffs whose layers were represented by the circular, parallel, waving lines of the balconies of the grand, first and second tiers of boxes. At the top, right on top of the cliff, lost in M. Lenepveu's copper ceiling, figures grinned and grimaced, laughed and jeered at MM. Richard and Moncharmin's distress. And yet these figures were usually very serious. Their names were Isis, Amphitrite, Hebe, Pandora, Psyche, Thetis, Pomona, Daphne, Clytie, Galatea and Arethusa. Yes, Arethusa herself and Pandora, whom we all know by her box, looked down upon the two new managers of the Opera, who ended by clutching at some piece of wreckage and from there stared silently at Box Five on the grand tier.

I have said that they were distressed. At least, I presume so. M. Moncharmin, in any case, admits that he was impressed. To quote his own words, in his Memoirs:

"This moonshine about the Opera ghost in which, since we first took over the duties of MM. Poligny and Debienne, we had been so nicely steeped"—Moncharmin's style is not always irreproachable—"had no doubt ended by blinding my imaginative and also my visual faculties. It may be that the exceptional surroundings in which we found ourselves, in the midst of an incredible silence, impressed us to an unusual extent. It may be that we were the sport of a kind of hallucination brought about by the semi-darkness of the theater and the partial gloom that filled Box Five. At any rate, I saw and Richard also saw a shape in the box. Richard said nothing, nor I either. But we spontaneously seized each other's hand. We stood like that for some minutes, without moving, with our eyes fixed on the same point; but the figure had disappeared. Then we went out and, in the lobby, communicated our impressions to each other and talked about 'the shape.' The misfortune was that my shape was not in the least like Richard's. I had seen a thing like a death's head resting on the ledge of the box, whereas Richard saw the shape of an old woman who looked like Mme. Giry. We soon discovered that we had really been the victims of an illusion, whereupon, without further delay and laughing like madmen, we ran to Box Five on the grand tier, went inside and found no shape of any kind."

Box Five is just like all the other grand tier boxes. There is nothing to distinguish it from any of the others. M. Moncharmin and M. Richard, ostensibly highly amused and laughing at each other, moved the furniture of the box, lifted the cloths and the chairs and particularly examined the arm-chair in which "the man's voice" used to sit. But they saw that it was a respectable arm-chair, with no magic about it. Altogether, the box was the most ordinary box in the world, with its red hangings, its chairs, its carpet and its ledge covered in red velvet. After, feeling the carpet in the most serious manner possible, and discovering nothing more here or anywhere else, they went down to the corresponding box on the pit tier below. In Box Five on the pit tier, which is just inside the first exit from the stalls on the left, they found nothing worth mentioning either.

"Those people are all making fools of us!" Firmin Richard ended by exclaiming. "It will be *Faust* on Saturday: let us both see the performance from Box Five on the grand tier!"

CHAPTER VII

FAUST AND WHAT FOLLOWED

On the Saturday morning, on reaching their office, the joint managers found a letter from O. G. worded in these terms:

My Dear Managers:

So it is to be war between us?

If you still care for peace, here is my ultimatum. It consists of the four following conditions:

1. You must give me back my private box; and I wish it to be at my free disposal from henceforward.

2. The part of Margarita shall be sung this evening by Christine Daae. Never mind about Carlotta; she will be ill.

3. I absolutely insist upon the good and loyal services of Mme. Giry, my box-keeper, whom you will reinstate in her functions forthwith.

4. Let me know by a letter handed to Mme. Giry, who will see that it reaches me, that you accept, as your predecessors did, the conditions in my memorandum-book relating to my monthly allowance. I will inform you later how you are to pay it to me.

If you refuse, you will give *Faust* to-night in a house with a curse upon it.

Take my advice and be warned in time. O. G.

"Look here, I'm getting sick of him, sick of him!" shouted Richard, bringing his fists down on his office-table.

Just then, Mercier, the acting-manager, entered.

"Lachenel would like to see one of you gentlemen," he said. "He says that his business is urgent and he seems quite upset."

"Who's Lachenel?" asked Richard.

"He's your stud-groom."

"What do you mean? My stud-groom?"

"Yes, sir," explained Mercier, "there are several grooms at the Opera and M. Lachenel is at the head of them."

"And what does this groom do?"

"He has the chief management of the stable."

"What stable?"

"Why, yours, sir, the stable of the Opera."

"Is there a stable at the Opera? Upon my word, I didn't know. Where is it?"

"In the cellars, on the Rotunda side. It's a very important department; we have twelve horses."

"Twelve horses! And what for, in Heaven's name?"

"Why, we want trained horses for the processions in the Juive, The Profeta and so on; horses 'used to the boards.' It is the grooms' business to teach them. M. Lachenel is very clever at it. He used to manage Franconi's stables."

"Very well . . . but what does he want?"

"I don't know; I never saw him in such a state."

"He can come in."

M. Lachenel came in, carrying a riding-whip, with which he struck his right boot in an irritable manner.

"Good morning, M. Lachenel," said Richard, somewhat impressed. "To what do we owe the honor of your visit?"

"Mr. Manager, I have come to ask you to get rid of the whole stable."

"What, you want to get rid of our horses?"

"I'm not talking of the horses, but of the stablemen."

"How many stablemen have you, M. Lachenel?"

"Six stablemen! That's at least two too many."

"These are 'places,'" Mercier interposed, "created and forced upon us by the under-secretary for fine arts. They are filled by protegees of the government and, if I may venture to . . . "

"I don't care a hang for the government!" roared Richard. "We don't need more than four stablemen for twelve horses."

"Eleven," said the head riding-master, correcting him.

"Twelve," repeated Richard.

"Eleven," repeated Lachenel.

"Oh, the acting-manager told me that you had twelve horses!"

"I did have twelve, but I have only eleven since Cesar was stolen."

And M. Lachenel gave himself a great smack on the boot with his whip.

"Has Cesar been stolen?" cried the acting-manager. "Cesar, the white horse in the Profeta?"

"There are not two Cesars," said the stud-groom dryly. "I was ten years at Franconi's and I have seen plenty of horses in my time. Well, there are not two Cesars. And he's been stolen."

"How?"

"I don't know. Nobody knows. That's why I have come to ask you to sack the whole stable."

"What do your stablemen say?"

"All sorts of nonsense. Some of them accuse the supers. Others pretend that it's the acting-manager's doorkeeper . . . "

"My doorkeeper? I'll answer for him as I would for myself!" protested Mercier.

"But, after all, M. Lachenel," cried Richard, "you must have some idea."

"Yes, I have," M. Lachenel declared. "I have an idea and I'll tell you what it is. There's no doubt about it in my mind." He walked up to the two managers and whispered. "It's the ghost who did the trick!"

Richard gave a jump.

"What, you too! You too!"

"How do you mean, I too? Isn't it natural, after what I saw?"

"What did you see?"

"I saw, as clearly as I now see you, a black shadow riding a white horse that was as like Cesar as two peas!"

"And did you run after them?"

"I did and I shouted, but they were too fast for me and disappeared in the darkness of the underground gallery."

M. Richard rose. "That will do, M. Lachenel. You can go . . . We will lodge a complaint against *The Ghost*."

"And sack my stable?"

"Oh, of course! Good morning."

M. Lachenel bowed and withdrew. Richard foamed at the mouth.

"Settle that idiot's account at once, please."

"He is a friend of the government representative's!" Mercier ventured to say.

"And he takes his vermouth at Tortoni's with Lagrene, Scholl and Pertuiset, the lion-hunter," added Moncharmin. "We shall have the whole press against us! He'll tell the story of the ghost; and everybody will be laughing at our expense! We may as well be dead as ridiculous!"

"All right, say no more about it."

At that moment the door opened. It must have been deserted by its usual Cerberus, for Mme. Giry entered without ceremony, holding a letter in her hand, and said hurriedly:

"I beg your pardon, excuse me, gentlemen, but I had a letter this morning from the Opera ghost. He told me to come to you, that you had something to . . . "

She did not complete the sentence. She saw Firmin Richard's face; and it was a terrible sight. He seemed ready to burst. He said nothing, he could not speak. But suddenly he acted. First, his left arm seized upon the quaint person of Mme. Giry and made her describe so unexpected a semicircle that she uttered a despairing cry. Next, his right foot imprinted its sole on the black taffeta of a skirt which certainly had never before undergone a similar outrage in a similar place. The thing happened so quickly that Mme. Giry, when in the passage, was still quite bewildered and seemed not to understand. But, suddenly, she understood; and the Opera rang with her indignant yells, her violent protests and threats.

About the same time, Carlotta, who had a small house of her own in the Rue du Faubourg St. Honore, rang for her maid, who brought her letters to her bed. Among them was an anonymous missive, written in red ink, in a hesitating, clumsy hand, which ran:

If you appear to-night, you must be prepared for a great misfortune at the moment when you open your mouth to sing . . . a misfortune worse than death.

The letter took away Carlotta's appetite for breakfast. She pushed back her chocolate, sat up in bed and thought hard. It was not the first letter of the kind which she had received, but she never had one couched in such threatening terms.

She thought herself, at that time, the victim of a thousand jealous attempts and went about saying that she had a secret enemy who had sworn to ruin her. She pretended that a wicked plot was being hatched against her, a cabal which would come to a head one of those days; but she added that she was not the woman to be intimidated.

The truth is that, if there was a cabal, it was led by Carlotta herself against poor Christine, who had no suspicion of it. Carlotta had never forgiven Christine for the triumph which she had achieved when taking her place at a moment's notice. When Carlotta heard of the astounding reception bestowed upon her understudy, she was at once cured of an incipient attack of bronchitis and a bad fit of sulking against the management and lost the slightest inclination to shirk her duties. From that time, she worked with all her might to "smother" her rival, enlisting the services of influential friends to persuade the managers not to give Christine an opportunity for a fresh triumph. Certain newspapers which had begun to extol the talent of Christine now interested themselves only in the fame of Carlotta. Lastly, in the theater itself, the celebrated, but heartless and soulless diva made the most scandalous remarks about Christine and tried to cause her endless minor unpleasantnesses.

When Carlotta had finished thinking over the threat contained in the strange letter, she got up.

"We shall see," she said, adding a few oaths in her native Spanish with a very determined air.

The first thing she saw, when looking out of her window, was a hearse. She was very superstitious; and the hearse and the letter convinced her that she was running the most serious dangers that evening. She collected all her supporters, told them that she was threatened at that evening's performance with a plot organized by Christine Daae and declared that they must play a trick upon that chit by filling the house with her, Carlotta's, admirers. She had no lack of them, had she? She relied upon them to hold themselves prepared for any eventuality and to silence the adversaries, if, as she feared, they created a disturbance.

M. Richard's private secretary called to ask after the diva's health and returned with the assurance that she was perfectly well and that, "were she dying," she would sing the part of Margarita that evening. The secretary urged her, in his chief's name, to commit no imprudence, to stay at home all day and to be careful of drafts; and Carlotta could not help, after he had gone, comparing this unusual and unexpected advice with the threats contained in the letter.

It was five o'clock when the post brought a second anonymous letter in the same hand as the first. It was short and said simply:

You have a bad cold. If you are wise, you will see that it is madness to try to sing to-night.

Carlotta sneered, shrugged her handsome shoulders and sang two or three notes to reassure herself.

Her friends were faithful to their promise. They were all at the Opera that night, but looked round in vain for the fierce conspirators whom they were instructed to suppress. The only unusual thing was the presence of M. Richard and M. Moncharmin in Box Five. Carlotta's friends thought that, perhaps, the managers had wind, on their side, of the proposed disturbance and that they had determined to be in the house, so as to stop it then and there; but this was unjustifiable supposition, as the reader knows. M. Richard and M. Moncharmin were thinking of nothing but their ghost.

"Vain! In vain do I call, through my vigil weary, On creation and its Lord! Never reply will break the silence dreary! No sign! No single word!"

The famous baritone, Carolus Fonta, had hardly finished Doctor Faust's first appeal to the powers of darkness, when M. Firmin Richard, who was sitting in the ghost's own chair, the front chair on the right, leaned over to his partner and asked him chaffingly:

"Well, has the ghost whispered a word in your ear yet?"

"Wait, don't be in such a hurry," replied M. Armand Moncharmin, in the same gay tone. "The performance has only begun and you know that the ghost does not usually come until the middle of the first act."

The first act passed without incident, which did not surprise Carlotta's friends, because Margarita does not sing in this act. As for the managers, they looked at each other, when the curtain fell.

"That's one!" said Moncharmin.

"Yes, the ghost is late," said Firmin Richard.

"It's not a bad house," said Moncharmin, "for 'a house with a curse on it.'"

M. Richard smiled and pointed to a fat, rather vulgar woman, dressed in black, sitting in a stall in the middle of the auditorium with a man in a broadcloth frock-coat on either side of her.

"Who on earth are 'those?'" asked Moncharmin.

"'Those,' my dear fellow, are my concierge, her husband and her brother."

"Did you give them their tickets?"

"I did . . . My concierge had never been to the Opera—this is, the first time—and, as she is now going to come every night, I wanted her to have a good seat, before spending her time showing other people to theirs."

Moncharmin asked what he meant and Richard answered that he had persuaded his concierge, in whom he had the greatest confidence, to come and take Mme. Giry's place. Yes, he would like to see if, with that woman instead of the old lunatic, Box Five would continue to astonish the natives?

"By the way," said Moncharmin, "you know that Mother Giry is going to lodge a complaint against you."

"With whom? The ghost?"

The ghost! Moncharmin had almost forgotten him. However, that mysterious person did nothing to bring himself to the memory of the managers; and they were just saying so to each other for the second time, when the door of the box suddenly opened to admit the startled stage-manager.

"What's the matter?" they both asked, amazed at seeing him there at such a time.

"It seems there's a plot got up by Christine Daae's friends against Carlotta. Carlotta's furious."

"What on earth . . . ?" said Richard, knitting his brows.

But the curtain rose on the kermess scene and Richard made a sign to the stage-manager to go away. When the two were alone again, Moncharmin leaned over to Richard:

"Then Daae has friends?" he asked.

"Yes, she has."

"Whom?"

Richard glanced across at a box on the grand tier containing no one but two men.

"The Comte de Chagny?"

"Yes, he spoke to me in her favor with such warmth that, if I had not known him to be Sorelli's friend . . . "

"Really? Really?" said Moncharmin. "And who is that pale young man beside him?"

"That's his brother, the viscount."

"He ought to be in his bed. He looks ill."

The stage rang with gay song:

> "Red or white liquor,
> Coarse or fine!
> What can it matter,
> So we have wine?"

Students, citizens, soldiers, girls and matrons whirled light-heartedly before the inn with the figure of Bacchus for a sign. Siebel made her entrance. Christine Daae looked charming in her boy's clothes; and Carlotta's partisans expected to hear her greeted with an ovation which would have enlightened them as to the intentions of her friends. But nothing happened.

On the other hand, when Margarita crossed the stage and sang the only two lines allotted her in this second act:

> "No, my lord, not a lady am I, nor yet a beauty,
> And do not need an arm to help me on my way,"

Carlotta was received with enthusiastic applause. It was so unexpected and so uncalled for that those who knew nothing about the rumors looked at one another and asked what was happening. And this act also was finished without incident.

Then everybody said: "Of course, it will be during the next act."

Some, who seemed to be better informed than the rest, declared that the "row" would begin with the ballad of the *King Of Thule* and rushed to the subscribers' entrance to warn Carlotta. The managers left the box during the entr'acte to find out more about the cabal of which the stage-manager had spoken; but they soon returned to their seats, shrugging their shoulders and treating the whole affair as silly.

The first thing they saw, on entering the box, was a box of English sweets on the little shelf of the ledge. Who had put it there? They asked the box-keepers, but none of them knew. Then they went back to the shelf and, next to the box of sweets, found an opera glass. They looked at each other. They had no inclination to laugh. All that Mme. Giry had told them returned to their memory . . . and then . . . and then . . . they seemed to feel a curious sort of draft around them . . . They sat down in silence.

The scene represented Margarita's garden:

> "Gentle flow'rs in the dew,
> Be message from me . . . "

As she sang these first two lines, with her bunch of roses and lilacs in her hand, Christine, raising her head, saw the Vicomte de Chagny in his box; and, from that moment, her voice seemed less sure, less crystal-clear than usual. Something seemed to deaden and dull her singing . . .

"What a queer girl she is!" said one of Carlotta's friends in the stalls, almost aloud. "The other day she was divine; and to-night she's simply bleating. She has no experience, no training."

> "Gentle flow'rs, lie ye there
> And tell her from me . . . "

The viscount put his head under his hands and wept. The count, behind him, viciously gnawed his mustache, shrugged his shoulders and frowned. For him, usually so cold and correct, to betray his inner feelings like that, by outward signs, the count must be very angry. He was. He had seen his brother return from a rapid and mysterious journey in an alarming state of health. The explanation that followed was unsatisfactory and the count asked Christine Daae for an appointment. She had the audacity to reply that she could not see either him or his brother . . .

> "Would she but deign to hear me
> And with one smile to cheer me . . . "

"The little baggage!" growled the count.

And he wondered what she wanted. What she was hoping for . . . She was a virtuous girl, she was said to have no friend, no protector of any sort . . .

That angel from the North must be very artful!

Raoul, behind the curtain of his hands that veiled his boyish tears, thought only of the letter which he received on his return to Paris, where Christine, fleeing from Perros like a thief in the night, had arrived before him:

My Dear Little Playfellow:

You must have the courage not to see me again, not to speak of me again. If you love me just a little, do this for me, for me who will never forget you, my dear Raoul. My life depends upon it. Your life depends upon it.

Your Little Christine.

Thunders of applause. Carlotta made her entrance.

"I wish I could but know who was he
That addressed me,
If he was noble, or, at least, what his name is . . . "

When Margarita had finished singing the ballad of the KING OF THULE, she was loudly cheered and again when she came to the end of the jewel song:

"Ah, the joy of past compare
These jewels bright to wear! . . . "

Thenceforth, certain of herself, certain of her friends in the house, certain of her voice and her success, fearing nothing, Carlotta flung herself into her part without restraint of modesty . . . She was no longer Margarita, she was Carmen. She was applauded all the more; and her debut with Faust seemed about to bring her a new success, when suddenly . . . a terrible thing happened.

Faust had knelt on one knee:

"Let me gaze on the form below me,
     While from yonder ether blue
Look how the star of eve, bright and tender,
     lingers o'er me,
     To love thy beauty too!"

And Margarita replied:

"Oh, how strange!
    Like a spell does the evening bind me!
And a deep languid charm
I feel without alarm
    With its melody enwind me
And all my heart subdue."

At that moment, at that identical moment, the terrible thing happened .
. Carlotta croaked like a toad:

"Co-ack!"

There was consternation on Carlotta's face and consternation on the faces of all the audience. The two managers in their box could not suppress an exclamation of horror. Every one felt that the thing was not natural, that there was witchcraft behind it. That toad smelt of brimstone. Poor, wretched, despairing, crushed Carlotta!

The uproar in the house was indescribable. If the thing had happened to any one but Carlotta, she would have been hooted. But everybody knew how perfect an instrument her voice was; and there was no display of anger, but only of horror and dismay, the sort of dismay which men would have felt if they had witnessed the catastrophe that broke the arms of the Venus de Milo . . . And even then they would have seen . . . and understood . . .

But here that toad was incomprehensible! So much so that, after some seconds spent in asking herself if she had really heard that note, that sound, that infernal noise issue from her throat, she tried to persuade herself that it was not so, that she was the victim of an illusion, an illusion of the ear, and not of an act of treachery on the part of her voice . . . .

Meanwhile, in Box Five, Moncharmin and Richard had turned very pale. This extraordinary and inexplicable incident filled them with a dread which was the more mysterious inasmuch as for some little while, they had fallen within the direct influence of the ghost. They had felt his breath. Moncharmin's hair stood on end. Richard wiped the perspiration from his forehead. Yes, the ghost was there, around them, behind them, beside them; they felt his presence without seeing him, they heard his breath, close, close, close to them! . . . They were sure that there were three people in the box . . . They trembled . . . They thought of running away . . . They dared not . . . They dared not make a movement or exchange a word that would have told the ghost that they knew that he was there! . . . What was going to happen?

This happened.

"Co-ack!" Their joint exclamation of horror was heard all over the house. *They felt that they were smarting under the ghost's attacks.* Leaning over the ledge of their box, they stared at Carlotta as though they did not recognize her. That infernal girl must have given the signal for some catastrophe. Ah, they were waiting for the catastrophe! The ghost had told them it would come! The house had a curse upon it! The two managers gasped and panted under the weight of the catastrophe. Richard's stifled voice was heard calling to Carlotta:

"Well, go on!"

No, Carlotta did not go on . . . Bravely, heroically, she started afresh on the fatal line at the end of which the toad had appeared.

An awful silence succeeded the uproar. Carlotta's voice alone once more filled the resounding house:

"I feel without alarm . . ."

The audience also felt, but not without alarm. . . .

> "I feel without alarm . . .
> I feel without alarm—co-ack!
> With its melody enwind me—co-ack!
> And all my heart sub—co-ack!"

The toad also had started afresh!

The house broke into a wild tumult.

The two managers collapsed in their chairs and dared not even turn round; they had not the strength; the ghost was chuckling behind their backs! And, at last, they distinctly heard his voice in their right ears, the impossible voice, the mouthless voice, saying:

"SHE IS SINGING TONIGHT TO BRING THE CHANDELIER DOWN!"

With one accord, they raised their eyes to the ceiling and uttered a terrible cry. The chandelier, the immense mass of the chandelier was slipping down, coming toward them, at the call of that fiendish voice. Released from its hook, it plunged from the ceiling and came smashing into the middle of the stalls, amid a thousand shouts of terror. A wild rush for the doors followed.

The papers of the day state that there were numbers wounded and one killed. The chandelier had crashed down upon the head of the wretched woman who had come to the Opera for the first time in her life, the one whom M. Richard had appointed to succeed Mme. Giry, the ghost's box-keeper, in her functions! She died on the spot and, the next morning, a newspaper appeared with this heading:

TWO HUNDRED KILOS ON
THE HEAD OF A CONCIERGE

That was her sole epitaph!

CHAPTER VIII

THE MYSTERIOUS BROUGHAM

That tragic evening was bad for everybody. Carlotta fell ill. As for Christine Daae, she disappeared after the performance. A fortnight elapsed during which she was seen neither at the Opera nor outside.

Raoul, of course, was the first to be astonished at the prima donna's absence. He wrote to her at Mme. Valerius' flat and received no reply. His grief increased and he ended by being seriously alarmed at never seeing her name on the program. *Faust* was played without her.

One afternoon he went to the managers' office to ask the reason of Christine's disappearance. He found them both looking extremely worried. Their own friends did not recognize them: they had lost all their gaiety and spirits. They were seen crossing the stage with hanging heads, care-worn brows, pale cheeks, as though pursued by some abominable thought or a prey to some persistent sport of fate.

The fall of the chandelier had involved them in no little responsibility; but it was difficult to make them speak about it. The inquest had ended in a verdict of accidental death, caused by the wear and tear of the chains by which the chandelier was hung from the ceiling; but it was the duty of both the old and the new managers to have discovered this wear and tear and to have remedied it in time. And I feel bound to say that MM. Richard and Moncharmin at this time appeared so changed, so absent-minded, so mysterious, so incomprehensible that many of the subscribers thought that some event even more horrible than the fall of the chandelier must have affected their state of mind.

In their daily intercourse, they showed themselves very impatient, except with Mme. Giry, who had been reinstated in her functions. And their reception of the Vicomte de Chagny, when he came to ask about Christine, was anything but cordial. They merely told him that she was taking a holiday. He asked how long the holiday was for, and they replied curtly that it was for an unlimited period, as Mlle. Daae had requested leave of absence for reasons of health.

"Then she is ill!" he cried. "What is the matter with her?"

"We don't know."

"Didn't you send the doctor of the Opera to see her?"

"No, she did not ask for him; and, as we trust her, we took her word."

Raoul left the building a prey to the gloomiest thoughts. He resolved, come what might, to go and inquire of Mamma Valerius. He remembered the strong phrases in Christine's letter, forbidding him to make any attempt to see her. But what he had seen at Perros, what he had heard behind the dressing-room door, his conversation with Christine at the edge of the moor made him suspect some machination which, devilish though it might be, was none the less human. The girl's highly strung imagination, her affectionate and credulous mind, the primitive education which had surrounded her childhood with a circle of legends, the constant brooding over her dead father and, above all, the state of sublime ecstasy into which music threw her from the moment that this art was made manifest to her in certain exceptional conditions, as in the churchyard at Perros; all this seemed to him to constitute a moral ground only too favorable for the malevolent designs of some mysterious and unscrupulous person. Of whom was Christine Daae the victim? This was the very reasonable question which Raoul put to himself as he hurried off to Mamma Valerius.

He trembled as he rang at a little flat in the Rue Notre-Dame-des-Victoires. The door was opened by the maid whom he had seen coming out of Christine's dressing-room one evening. He asked if he could speak to Mme. Valerius. He was told that she was ill in bed and was not receiving visitors.

"Take in my card, please," he said.

The maid soon returned and showed him into a small and scantily furnished drawing-room, in which portraits of Professor Valerius and old Daae hung on opposite walls.

"Madame begs Monsieur le Vicomte to excuse her," said the servant. "She can only see him in her bedroom, because she can no longer stand on her poor legs."

Five minutes later, Raoul was ushered into an ill-lit room where he at once recognized the good, kind face of Christine's benefactress in the semi-darkness of an alcove. Mamma Valerius' hair was now quite white, but her eyes had grown no older; never, on the contrary, had their expression been so bright, so pure, so child-like.

"M. de Chagny!" she cried gaily, putting out both her hands to her visitor. "Ah, it's Heaven that sends you here! . . . We can talk of *her.*"

This last sentence sounded very gloomily in the young man's ears. He at once asked:

"Madame . . . where is Christine?"

And the old lady replied calmly:

"She is with her good genius!"

"What good genius?" exclaimed poor Raoul.

"Why, the Angel of Music!"

The viscount dropped into a chair. Really? Christine was with the Angel of Music? And there lay Mamma Valerius in bed, smiling to him and putting her finger to her lips, to warn him to be silent! And she added:

"You must not tell anybody!"

"You can rely on me," said Raoul.

He hardly knew what he was saying, for his ideas about Christine, already greatly confused, were becoming more and more entangled; and it seemed as if everything was beginning to turn around him, around the room, around that extraordinary good lady with the white hair and forget-me-not eyes.

"I know! I know I can!" she said, with a happy laugh. "But why don't you come near me, as you used to do when you were a little boy? Give me your hands, as when you brought me the story of little Lotte, which Daddy Daae had told you. I am very fond of you, M. Raoul, you know. And so is Christine too!"

"She is fond of me!" sighed the young man. He found a difficulty in collecting his thoughts and bringing them to bear on Mamma Valerius' "good genius," on the Angel of Music of whom Christine had spoken to him so strangely, on the death's head which he had seen in a sort of nightmare on the high altar at Perros and also on the Opera ghost, whose fame had come to his ears one evening when he was standing behind the scenes, within hearing of a group of scene-shifters who were repeating the ghastly description which the hanged man, Joseph Buquet, had given of the ghost before his mysterious death.

He asked in a low voice: "What makes you think that Christine is fond of me, madame?"

"She used to speak of you every day."

"Really? . . . And what did she tell you?"

"She told me that you had made her a proposal!"

And the good old lady began laughing wholeheartedly. Raoul sprang from his chair, flushing to the temples, suffering agonies.

"What's this? Where are you going? Sit down again at once, will you? . . . Do you think I will let you go like that? . . . If you're angry with me for laughing, I beg your pardon . . . After all, what has happened isn't your fault . . . Didn't you know? . . . Did you think that Christine was free? . . . "

"Is Christine engaged to be married?" the wretched Raoul asked, in a choking voice.

"Why no! Why no! . . . You know as well as I do that Christine couldn't marry, even if she wanted to!"

"But I don't know anything about it! . . . And why can't Christine marry?"

"Because of the Angel of Music, of course! . . . "

"I don't follow . . . "

"Yes, he forbids her to! . . . "

"He forbids her! . . . The Angel of Music forbids her to marry!"

"Oh, he forbids her . . . without forbidding her. It's like this: he tells her that, if she got married, she would never hear him again. That's all! . . . And that he would go away for ever! . . . So, you understand, she can't let the Angel of Music go. It's quite natural."

"Yes, yes," echoed Raoul submissively, "it's quite natural."

"Besides, I thought Christine had told you all that, when she met you at Perros, where she went with her good genius."

"Oh, she went to Perros with her good genius, did she?"

"That is to say, he arranged to meet her down there, in Perros churchyard, at Daae's grave. He promised to play her The Resurrection of Lazarus on her father's violin!"

Raoul de Chagny rose and, with a very authoritative air, pronounced these peremptory words:

"Madame, you will have the goodness to tell me where that genius lives."

The old lady did not seem surprised at this indiscreet command. She raised her eyes and said:

"In Heaven!"

Such simplicity baffled him. He did not know what to say in the presence of this candid and perfect faith in a genius who came down nightly from Heaven to haunt the dressing-rooms at the Opera.

He now realized the possible state of mind of a girl brought up between a superstitious fiddler and a visionary old lady and he shuddered when he thought of the consequences of it all.

"Is Christine still a good girl?" he asked suddenly, in spite of himself.

"I swear it, as I hope to be saved!" exclaimed the old woman, who, this time, seemed to be incensed. "And, if you doubt it, sir, I don't know what you are here for!"

Raoul tore at his gloves.

"How long has she known this 'genius?'"

"About three months . . . Yes, it's quite three months since he began to give her lessons."

The viscount threw up his arms with a gesture of despair.

"The genius gives her lessons! . . . And where, pray?"

"Now that she has gone away with him, I can't say; but, up to a fortnight ago, it was in Christine's dressing-room. It would be impossible in this little flat. The whole house would hear them. Whereas, at the Opera, at eight o'clock in the morning, there is no one about, do you see!"

"Yes, I see! I see!" cried the viscount.

And he hurriedly took leave of Mme. Valerius, who asked herself if the young nobleman was not a little off his head.

He walked home to his brother's house in a pitiful state. He could have struck himself, banged his head against the walls! To think that he had believed in her innocence, in her purity! The Angel of Music! He knew him now! He saw him! It was beyond a doubt some unspeakable tenor, a good-looking jackanapes, who mouthed and simpered as he sang! He thought himself as absurd and as wretched as could be. Oh, what a miserable, little, insignificant, silly young man was M. le Vicomte de Chagny! thought Raoul, furiously. And she, what a bold and damnable sly creature!

His brother was waiting for him and Raoul fell into his arms, like a child. The count consoled him, without asking for explanations; and Raoul would certainly have long hesitated before telling him the story of the Angel of Music. His brother suggested taking him out to dinner. Overcome as he was with despair, Raoul would probably have refused any invitation that evening, if the count had not, as an inducement, told him that the lady of his thoughts had been seen, the night before, in company of the other sex in the Bois. At first, the viscount refused to believe; but he received such exact details that he ceased protesting. She had been seen, it appeared, driving in a brougham, with the window down. She seemed to be slowly taking in the icy night air. There was a glorious moon shining. She was recognized beyond a doubt. As for her companion, only his shadowy outline was distinguished leaning back in the dark. The carriage was going at a walking pace in a lonely drive behind the grand stand at Longchamp.

Raoul dressed in frantic haste, prepared to forget his distress by flinging himself, as people say, into "the vortex of pleasure." Alas, he was a very sorry guest and, leaving his brother early, found himself, by ten o'clock in the evening, in a cab, behind the Longchamp race-course.

It was bitterly cold. The road seemed deserted and very bright under the moonlight. He told the driver to wait for him patiently at the corner of a near turning and, hiding himself as well as he could, stood stamping his feet to keep warm. He had been indulging in this healthy exercise for half an hour or so, when a carriage turned the corner of the road and came quietly in his direction, at a walking pace.

As it approached, he saw that a woman was leaning her head from the window. And, suddenly, the moon shed a pale gleam over her features.

"Christine!"

The sacred name of his love had sprung from his heart and his lips. He could not keep it back . . . He would have given anything to withdraw it, for that name, proclaimed in the stillness of the night, had acted as though it were the preconcerted signal for a furious rush on the part of the whole turn-out, which dashed past him before he could put into execution his plan of leaping at the horses' heads. The carriage window had been closed and the girl's face had disappeared. And the brougham, behind which he was now running, was no more than a black spot on the white road.

He called out again: "Christine!"

No reply. And he stopped in the midst of the silence.

With a lack-luster eye, he stared down that cold, desolate road and into the pale, dead night. Nothing was colder than his heart, nothing half so dead: he had loved an angel and now he despised a woman!

Raoul, how that little fairy of the North has trifled with you! Was it really, was it really necessary to have so fresh and young a face, a forehead so shy and always ready to cover itself with the pink blush of modesty in order to pass in the lonely night, in a carriage and pair, accompanied by a mysterious lover? Surely there should be some limit to hypocrisy and lying! . . .

She had passed without answering his cry . . . And he was thinking of dying; and he was twenty years old! . . .

His valet found him in the morning sitting on his bed. He had not undressed and the servant feared, at the sight of his face, that some disaster had occurred. Raoul snatched his letters from the man's hands. He had recognized Christine's paper and hand-writing. She said:

DEAR:

Go to the masked ball at the Opera on the night after to-morrow. At twelve o'clock, be in the little room behind the chimney-place of the big crush-room. Stand near the door that leads to the Rotunda. Don't mention this appointment to any one on earth. Wear a white domino and be carefully masked. As you love me, do not let yourself be recognized.

CHRISTINE.

CHAPTER IX

AT THE MASKED BALL

The envelope was covered with mud and unstamped. It bore the words "To be handed to M. le Vicomte Raoul de Chagny," with the address in pencil. It must have been flung out in the hope that a passer-by would pick up the note and deliver it, which was what happened. The note had been picked up on the pavement of the Place de l'Opera.

Raoul read it over again with fevered eyes. No more was needed to revive his hope. The somber picture which he had for a moment imagined of a Christine forgetting her duty to herself made way for his original conception of an unfortunate, innocent child, the victim of imprudence and exaggerated sensibility. To what extent, at this time, was she really a victim? Whose prisoner was she? Into what whirlpool had she been dragged? He asked himself these questions with a cruel anguish; but even this pain seemed endurable beside the frenzy into which he was thrown at the thought of a lying and deceitful Christine. What had happened? What influence had she undergone? What monster had carried her off and by what means? . . .

By what means indeed but that of music? He knew Christine's story. After her father's death, she acquired a distaste of everything in life, including her art. She went through the *conservatoire* like a poor soulless singing-machine. And, suddenly, she awoke as though through the intervention of a god. The Angel of Music appeared upon the scene! She sang Margarita in FAUST and triumphed! . . .

The Angel of Music! . . . For three months the Angel of Music had been giving Christine lessons . . . Ah, he was a punctual singing-master! . . . And now he was taking her for drives in the Bois! . . .

Raoul's fingers clutched at his flesh, above his jealous heart. In his inexperience, he now asked himself with terror what game the girl was playing? Up to what point could an opera-singer make a fool of a good-natured young man, quite new to love? O misery! . . .

Thus did Raoul's thoughts fly from one extreme to the other. He no longer knew whether to pity Christine or to curse her; and he pitied and cursed her turn and turn about. At all events, he bought a white domino.

The hour of the appointment came at last. With his face in a mask trimmed with long, thick lace, looking like a pierrot in his white wrap, the viscount thought himself very ridiculous. Men of the world do not go to the Opera ball in fancy-dress! It was absurd. One thought, however, consoled the viscount: he would certainly never be recognized!

This ball was an exceptional affair, given some time before Shrovetide, in honor of the anniversary of the birth of a famous draftsman; and it was expected to be much gayer, noisier, more Bohemian than the ordinary masked ball. Numbers of artists had arranged to go, accompanied by a whole cohort of models and pupils, who, by midnight, began to create a tremendous din. Raoul climbed the grand staircase at five minutes to twelve, did not linger to look at the motley dresses displayed all the way up the marble steps, one of the richest settings in the world, allowed no facetious mask to draw him into a war of wits, replied to no jests and shook off the bold familiarity of a number of couples who had already become a trifle too gay. Crossing the big crush-room and escaping from a mad whirl of dancers in which he was caught for a moment, he at last entered the room mentioned in Christine's letter. He found it crammed; for this small space was the point where all those who were going to supper in the Rotunda crossed those who were returning from taking a glass of champagne. The fun, here, waxed fast and furious.

Raoul leaned against a door-post and waited. He did not wait long. A black domino passed and gave a quick squeeze to the tips of his fingers. He understood that it was she and followed her:

"Is that you, Christine?" he asked, between his teeth.

The black domino turned round promptly and raised her finger to her lips, no doubt to warn him not to mention her name again. Raoul continued to follow her in silence.

He was afraid of losing her, after meeting her again in such strange circumstances. His grudge against her was gone. He no longer doubted that she had "nothing to reproach herself with," however peculiar and inexplicable her conduct might seem. He was ready to make any display of clemency, forgiveness or cowardice. He was in love. And, no doubt, he would soon receive a very natural explanation of her curious absence.

The black domino turned back from time to time to see if the white domino was still following.

As Raoul once more passed through the great crush-room, this time in the wake of his guide, he could not help noticing a group crowding round a person whose disguise, eccentric air and gruesome appearance were causing a sensation. It was a man dressed all in scarlet, with a huge hat and feathers on the top of a wonderful death's head. From his shoulders hung an immense red-velvet cloak, which trailed along the floor like a king's train; and on this cloak was embroidered, in gold letters, which every one read and repeated aloud, "Don't touch me! I am Red Death stalking abroad!"

Then one, greatly daring, did try to touch him . . . but a skeleton hand shot out of a crimson sleeve and violently seized the rash one's wrist; and he, feeling the clutch of the knucklebones, the furious grasp of Death, uttered a cry of pain and terror. When Red Death released him at last, he ran away like a very madman, pursued by the jeers of the bystanders.

It was at this moment that Raoul passed in front of the funereal masquerader, who had just happened to turn in his direction. And he nearly exclaimed:

"The death's head of Perros-Guirec!"

He had recognized him! . . . He wanted to dart forward, forgetting Christine; but the black domino, who also seemed a prey to some strange excitement, caught him by the arm and dragged him from the crush-room, far from the mad crowd through which Red Death was stalking . . .

The black domino kept on turning back and, apparently, on two occasions saw something that startled her, for she hurried her pace and Raoul's as though they were being pursued.

They went up two floors. Here, the stairs and corridors were almost deserted. The black domino opened the door of a private box and beckoned to the white domino to follow her. Then Christine, whom he recognized by the sound of her voice, closed the door behind them and warned him, in a whisper, to remain at the back of the box and on no account to show himself. Raoul took off his mask. Christine kept hers on. And, when Raoul was about to ask her to remove it, he was surprised to see her put her ear to the partition and listen eagerly for a sound outside. Then she opened the door ajar, looked out into the corridor and, in a low voice, said:

"He must have gone up higher." Suddenly she exclaimed: "He is coming down again!"

She tried to close the door, but Raoul prevented her; for he had seen, on the top step of the staircase that led to the floor above, A *red foot*, followed by another . . . and slowly, majestically, the whole scarlet dress of Red Death met his eyes. And he once more saw the death's head of Perros-Guirec.

"It's he!" he exclaimed. "This time, he shall not escape me! . . . "

But Christian{sic} had slammed the door at the moment when Raoul was on the point of rushing out. He tried to push her aside.

"Whom do you mean by 'he'?" she asked, in a changed voice. "Who shall not escape you?"

Raoul tried to overcome the girl's resistance by force, but she repelled him with a strength which he would not have suspected in her. He understood, or thought he understood, and at once lost his temper.

"Who?" he repeated angrily. "Why, he, the man who hides behind that hideous mask of death! . . . The evil genius of the churchyard at Perros! . . . Red Death! . . . In a word, madam, your friend . . . your Angel of Music! . . . But I shall snatch off his mask, as I shall snatch off my own; and, this time, we shall look each other in the face, he and I, with no veil and no lies between us; and I shall know whom you love and who loves you!"

He burst into a mad laugh, while Christine gave a disconsolate moan behind her velvet mask. With a tragic gesture, she flung out her two arms, which fixed a barrier of white flesh against the door.

"In the name of our love, Raoul, you shall not pass! . . . "

He stopped. What had she said? . . . In the name of their love? . . . Never before had she confessed that she loved him. And yet she had had opportunities enough . . . Pooh, her only object was to gain a few seconds! . . . She wished to give the Red Death time to escape . . . And, in accents of childish hatred, he said:

"You lie, madam, for you do not love me and you have never loved me! What a poor fellow I must be to let you mock and flout me as you have done! Why did you give me every reason for hope, at Perros . . . for honest hope, madam, for I am an honest man and I believed you to be an honest woman, when your only intention was to deceive me! Alas, you have deceived us all! You have taken a shameful advantage of the candid affection of your benefactress herself, who continues to believe in your sincerity while you go about the Opera ball with Red Death! . . . I despise you! . . . "

And he burst into tears. She allowed him to insult her. She thought of but one thing, to keep him from leaving the box.

"You will beg my pardon, one day, for all those ugly words, Raoul, and when you do I shall forgive you!"

He shook his head. "No, no, you have driven me mad! When I think that I had only one object in life: to give my name to an opera wench!"

"Raoul! . . . How can you?"

"I shall die of shame!"

"No, dear, live!" said Christine's grave and changed voice. "And . . . good-by. Good-by, Raoul . . . "

The boy stepped forward, staggering as he went. He risked one more sarcasm:

"Oh, you must let me come and applaud you from time to time!"

"I shall never sing again, Raoul! . . . "

"Really?" he replied, still more satirically. "So he is taking you off the stage: I congratulate you! . . . But we shall meet in the Bois, one of these evenings!"

"Not in the Bois nor anywhere, Raoul: you shall not see me again . . ."

"May one ask at least to what darkness you are returning? . . . For what hell are you leaving, mysterious lady . . . or for what paradise?"

"I came to tell you, dear, but I can't tell you now . . . you would not believe me! You have lost faith in me, Raoul; it is finished!"

She spoke in such a despairing voice that the lad began to feel remorse for his cruelty.

"But look here!" he cried. "Can't you tell me what all this means! . . . You are free, there is no one to interfere with you . . . You go about Paris . . . You put on a domino to come to the ball . . . Why do you not go home? . . . What have you been doing this past fortnight? . . . What is this tale about the Angel of Music, which you have been telling Mamma Valerius? Some one may have taken you in, played upon your innocence. I was a witness of it myself, at Perros . . . but you know what to believe now! You seem to me quite sensible, Christine. You know what you are doing . . . And meanwhile Mamma Valerius lies waiting for you at home and appealing to your 'good genius!' . . . Explain yourself, Christine, I beg of you! Any one might have been deceived as I was. What is this farce?"

Christine simply took off her mask and said: "Dear, it is a tragedy!"

Raoul now saw her face and could not restrain an exclamation of surprise and terror. The fresh complexion of former days was gone. A mortal pallor covered those features, which he had known so charming and so gentle, and sorrow had furrowed them with pitiless lines and traced dark and unspeakably sad shadows under her eyes.

"My dearest! My dearest!" he moaned, holding out his arms. "You promised to forgive me . . ."

"Perhaps! . . . Some day, perhaps!" she said, resuming her mask; and she went away, forbidding him, with a gesture, to follow her.

He tried to disobey her; but she turned round and repeated her gesture of farewell with such authority that he dared not move a step.

He watched her till she was out of sight. Then he also went down among the crowd, hardly knowing what he was doing, with throbbing temples and an aching heart; and, as he crossed the dancing-floor, he asked if anybody had seen Red Death. Yes, every one had seen Red Death; but Raoul could not find him; and, at two o'clock in the morning, he turned down the passage, behind the scenes, that led to Christine Daae's dressing-room.

His footsteps took him to that room where he had first known suffering. He tapped at the door. There was no answer. He entered, as he had entered when he looked everywhere for "the man's voice." The room was empty. A gas-jet was burning, turned down low. He saw some writing-paper on a little desk. He thought of writing to Christine, but he heard steps in the passage. He had only time to hide in the inner room, which was separated from the dressing-room by a curtain.

Christine entered, took off her mask with a weary movement and flung it on the table. She sighed and let her pretty head fall into her two hands. What was she thinking of? Of Raoul? No, for Raoul heard her murmur: "Poor Erik!"

At first, he thought he must be mistaken. To begin with, he was persuaded that, if any one was to be pitied, it was he, Raoul. It would have been quite natural if she had said, "Poor Raoul," after what had happened between them. But, shaking her head, she repeated: "Poor Erik!"

What had this Erik to do with Christine's sighs and why was she pitying Erik when Raoul was so unhappy?

Christine began to write, deliberately, calmly and so placidly that Raoul, who was still trembling from the effects of the tragedy that separated them, was painfully impressed.

"What coolness!" he said to himself.

She wrote on, filling two, three, four sheets. Suddenly, she raised her head and hid the sheets in her bodice . . . She seemed to be listening . . . Raoul also listened . . . Whence came that strange sound, that distant rhythm? . . . A faint singing seemed to issue from the walls . . . yes, it was as though the walls themselves were singing! . . . The song became plainer . . . the words were now distinguishable . . . he heard a voice, a very beautiful, very soft, very captivating voice . . . but, for all its softness, it remained a male voice . . . The voice came nearer and nearer . . . it came through the wall . . . it approached . . . and now the voice was *in the room*, in front of Christine. Christine rose and addressed the voice, as though speaking to some one:

"Here I am, Erik," she said. "I am ready. But you are late."

Raoul, peeping from behind the curtain, could not believe his eyes, which showed him nothing. Christine's face lit up. A smile of happiness appeared upon her bloodless lips, a smile like that of sick people when they receive the first hope of recovery.

The voice without a body went on singing; and certainly Raoul had never in his life heard anything more absolutely and heroically sweet, more gloriously insidious, more delicate, more powerful, in short, more irresistibly triumphant. He listened to it in a fever and he now began to understand how Christine Daae was able to appear one evening, before the stupefied audience, with accents of a beauty hitherto unknown, of a superhuman exaltation, while doubtless still under the influence of the mysterious and invisible master.

The voice was singing the Wedding-night Song from Romeo and Juliet. Raoul saw Christine stretch out her arms to the voice as she had done, in Perros churchyard, to the invisible violin playing The Resurrection of Lazarus. And nothing could describe the passion with which the voice sang:

"Fate links thee to me for ever and a day!"

The strains went through Raoul's heart. Struggling against the charm that seemed to deprive him of all his will and all his energy and of almost all his lucidity at the moment when he needed them most, he succeeded in drawing back the curtain that hid him and he walked to where Christine stood. She herself was moving to the back of the room, the whole wall of which was occupied by a great mirror that reflected her image, but not his, for he was just behind her and entirely covered by her.

"Fate links thee to me for ever and a day!"

Christine walked toward her image in the glass and the image came toward her. The two Christines—the real one and the reflection—ended by touching; and Raoul put out his arms to clasp the two in one embrace. But, by a sort of dazzling miracle that sent him staggering, Raoul was suddenly flung back, while an icy blast swept over his face; he saw, not two, but four, eight, twenty Christines spinning round him, laughing at him and fleeing so swiftly that he could not touch one of them. At last, everything stood still again; and he saw himself in the glass. But Christine had disappeared.

He rushed up to the glass. He struck at the walls. Nobody! And meanwhile the room still echoed with a distant passionate singing:

"Fate links thee to me for ever and a day!"

Which way, which way had Christine gone? . . . Which way would she return? . . .

Would she return? Alas, had she not declared to him that everything was finished? And was the voice not repeating:

"Fate links thee to me for ever and a day!"

To me? To whom?

Then, worn out, beaten, empty-brained, he sat down on the chair which Christine had just left. Like her, he let his head fall into his hands. When he raised it, the tears were streaming down his young cheeks, real, heavy tears like those which jealous children shed, tears that wept for a sorrow which was in no way fanciful, but which is common to all the lovers on earth and which he expressed aloud:

"Who is this Erik?" he said.

CHAPTER X

FORGET THE NAME OF THE MAN'S VOICE

The day after Christine had vanished before his eyes in a sort of dazzlement that still made him doubt the evidence of his senses, M. le Vicomte de Chagny called to inquire at Mamma Valerius'. He came upon a charming picture. Christine herself was seated by the bedside of the old lady, who was sitting up against the pillows, knitting. The pink and white had returned to the young girl's cheeks. The dark rings round her eyes had disappeared. Raoul no longer recognized the tragic face of the day before. If the veil of melancholy over those adorable features had not still appeared to the young man as the last trace of the weird drama in whose toils that mysterious child was struggling, he could have believed that Christine was not its heroine at all.

She rose, without showing any emotion, and offered him her hand. But Raoul's stupefaction was so great that he stood there dumfounded, without a gesture, without a word.

"Well, M. de Chagny," exclaimed Mamma Valerius, "don't you know our Christine? Her good genius has sent her back to us!"

"Mamma!" the girl broke in promptly, while a deep blush mantled to her eyes. "I thought, mamma, that there was to be no more question of that! . . . You know there is no such thing as the Angel of Music!"

"But, child, he gave you lessons for three months!"

"Mamma, I have promised to explain everything to you one of these days; and I hope to do so but you have promised me, until that day, to be silent and to ask me no more questions whatever!"

"Provided that you promised never to leave me again! But have you promised that, Christine?"

"Mamma, all this can not interest M. de Chagny."

"On the contrary, mademoiselle," said the young man, in a voice which he tried to make firm and brave, but which still trembled, "anything that concerns you interests me to an extent which perhaps you will one day understand. I do not deny that my surprise equals my pleasure at finding you with your adopted mother and that, after what happened between us yesterday, after what you said and what I was able to guess, I hardly expected to see you here so soon. I should be the first to delight at your return, if you were not so bent on preserving a secrecy that may be fatal to you . . . and I have been your friend too long not to be alarmed, with Mme. Valerius, at a disastrous adventure which will remain dangerous so long as we have not unraveled its threads and of which you will certainly end by being the victim, Christine."

At these words, Mamma Valerius tossed about in her bed.

"What does this mean?" she cried. "Is Christine in danger?"

"Yes, madame," said Raoul courageously, notwithstanding the signs which Christine made to him.

"My God!" exclaimed the good, simple old woman, gasping for breath. "You must tell me everything, Christine! Why did you try to reassure me? And what danger is it, M. de Chagny?"

"An impostor is abusing her good faith."

"Is the Angel of Music an impostor?"

"She told you herself that there is no Angel of Music."

"But then what is it, in Heaven's name? You will be the death of me!"

"There is a terrible mystery around us, madame, around you, around Christine, a mystery much more to be feared than any number of ghosts or genii!"

Mamma Valerius turned a terrified face to Christine, who had already run to her adopted mother and was holding her in her arms.

"Don't believe him, mummy, don't believe him," she repeated.

"Then tell me that you will never leave me again," implored the widow.

Christine was silent and Raoul resumed.

"That is what you must promise, Christine. It is the only thing that can reassure your mother and me. We will undertake not to ask you a single question about the past, if you promise us to remain under our protection in future."

"That is an undertaking which I have not asked of you and a promise which I refuse to make you!" said the young girl haughtily. "I am mistress of my own actions, M. de Chagny: you have no right to control them, and I will beg you to desist henceforth. As to what I have done during the last fortnight, there is only one man in the world who has the right to demand an account of me: my husband! Well, I have no husband and I never mean to marry!"

She threw out her hands to emphasize her words and Raoul turned pale, not only because of the words which he had heard, but because he had caught sight of a plain gold ring on Christine's finger.

"You have no husband and yet you wear a wedding-ring."

He tried to seize her hand, but she swiftly drew it back.

"That's a present!" she said, blushing once more and vainly striving to hide her embarrassment.

"Christine! As you have no husband, that ring can only have been given by one who hopes to make you his wife! Why deceive us further? Why torture me still more? That ring is a promise; and that promise has been accepted!"

"That's what I said!" exclaimed the old lady.

"And what did she answer, madame?"

"What I chose," said Christine, driven to exasperation. "Don't you think, monsieur, that this cross-examination has lasted long enough? As far as I am concerned . . . "

Raoul was afraid to let her finish her speech. He interrupted her:

"I beg your pardon for speaking as I did, mademoiselle. You know the good intentions that make me meddle, just now, in matters which, you no doubt think, have nothing to do with me. But allow me to tell you what I have seen—and I have seen more than you suspect, Christine—or what I thought I saw, for, to tell you the truth, I have sometimes been inclined to doubt the evidence of my eyes."

"Well, what did you see, sir, or think you saw?"

"I saw your ecstasy *at the sound of the voice,* Christine: the voice that came from the wall or the next room to yours . . . yes, *your ecstasy!* And that is what makes me alarmed on your behalf. You are under a very dangerous spell. And yet it seems that you are aware of the imposture, because you say to-day *that there is no angel of music!* In that case, Christine, why did you follow him that time? Why did you stand up, with radiant features, as though you were really hearing angels? . . . Ah, it is a very dangerous voice, Christine, for I myself, when I heard it, was so much fascinated by it that you vanished before my eyes without my seeing which way you passed! Christine, Christine, in the name of Heaven, in the name of your father who is in Heaven now and who loved you so dearly and who loved me too, Christine, tell us, tell your benefactress and me, to whom does that voice belong? If you do, we will save you in spite of yourself. Come, Christine, the name of the man! The name of the man who had the audacity to put a ring on your finger!"

"M. de Chagny," the girl declared coldly, "you shall never know!"

Thereupon, seeing the hostility with which her ward had addressed the viscount, Mamma Valerius suddenly took Christine's part.

"And, if she does love that man, Monsieur le Vicomte, even then it is no business of yours!"

"Alas, madame," Raoul humbly replied, unable to restrain his tears, "alas, I believe that Christine really does love him! . . . But it is not only that which drives me to despair; for what I am not certain of, madame, is that the man whom Christine loves is worthy of her love!"

"It is for me to be the judge of that, monsieur!" said Christine, looking Raoul angrily in the face.

"When a man," continued Raoul, "adopts such romantic methods to entice a young girl's affections. . . ."

"The man must be either a villain, or the girl a fool: is that it?"

"Christine!"

"Raoul, why do you condemn a man whom you have never seen, whom no one knows and about whom you yourself know nothing?"

"Yes, Christine . . . Yes . . . I at least know the name that you thought to keep from me for ever . . . The name of your Angel of Music, mademoiselle, is Erik!"

Christine at once betrayed herself. She turned as white as a sheet and stammered: "Who told you?"

"You yourself!"

"How do you mean?"

"By pitying him the other night, the night of the masked ball. When you went to your dressing-room, did you not say, 'Poor Erik?' Well, Christine, there was a poor Raoul who overheard you."

"This is the second time that you have listened behind the door, M. de Chagny!"

"I was not behind the door . . . I was in the dressing-room, in the inner room, mademoiselle."

"Oh, unhappy man!" moaned the girl, showing every sign of unspeakable terror. "Unhappy man! Do you want to be killed?"

"Perhaps."

Raoul uttered this "perhaps" with so much love and despair in his voice that Christine could not keep back a sob. She took his hands and looked at him with all the pure affection of which she was capable:

"Raoul," she said, "forget *the man's voice* and do not even remember its name . . . You must never try to fathom the mystery of *the man's voice*."

"Is the mystery so very terrible?"

"There is no more awful mystery on this earth. Swear to me that you will make no attempt to find out," she insisted. "Swear to me that you will never come to my dressing-room, unless I send for you."

"Then you promise to send for me sometimes, Christine?"

"I promise."

"When?"

"To-morrow."

"Then I swear to do as you ask."

He kissed her hands and went away, cursing Erik and resolving to be patient.

CHAPTER XI

ABOVE THE TRAP-DOORS

The next day, he saw her at the Opera. She was still wearing the plain gold ring. She was gentle and kind to him. She talked to him of the plans which he was forming, of his future, of his career.

He told her that the date of the Polar expedition had been put forward and that he would leave France in three weeks, or a month at latest. She suggested, almost gaily, that he must look upon the voyage with delight, as a stage toward his coming fame. And when he replied that fame without love was no attraction in his eyes, she treated him as a child whose sorrows were only short-lived.

"How can you speak so lightly of such serious things?" he asked. "Perhaps we shall never see each other again! I may die during that expedition."

"Or I," she said simply.

She no longer smiled or jested. She seemed to be thinking of some new thing that had entered her mind for the first time. Her eyes were all aglow with it.

"What are you thinking of, Christine?"

"I am thinking that we shall not see each other again . . . "

"And does that make you so radiant?"

"And that, in a month, we shall have to say good-by for ever!"

"Unless, Christine, we pledge our faith and wait for each other for ever."

She put her hand on his mouth.

"Hush, Raoul! . . . You know there is no question of that . . . And we shall never be married: that is understood!"

She seemed suddenly almost unable to contain an overpowering gaiety. She clapped her hands with childish glee. Raoul stared at her in amazement.

"But . . . but," she continued, holding out her two hands to Raoul, or rather giving them to him, as though she had suddenly resolved to make him a present of them, "but if we can not be married, we can . . . we can be engaged! Nobody will know but ourselves, Raoul. There have been plenty of secret marriages: why not a secret engagement? . . . We are engaged, dear, for a month! In a month, you will go away, and I can be happy at the thought of that month all my life long!"

She was enchanted with her inspiration. Then she became serious again.

"This," she said, "*is a happiness that will harm no one.*"

Raoul jumped at the idea. He bowed to Christine and said:

"Mademoiselle, I have the honor to ask for your hand."

"Why, you have both of them already, my dear betrothed! . . . Oh, Raoul, how happy we shall be! . . . We must play at being engaged all day long."

It was the prettiest game in the world and they enjoyed it like the children that they were. Oh, the wonderful speeches they made to each other and the eternal vows they exchanged! They played at hearts as other children might play at ball; only, as it was really their two hearts that they flung to and fro, they had to be very, very handy to catch them, each time, without hurting them.

One day, about a week after the game began, Raoul's heart was badly hurt and he stopped playing and uttered these wild words:

"I shan't go to the North Pole!"

Christine, who, in her innocence, had not dreamed of such a possibility, suddenly discovered the danger of the game and reproached herself bitterly. She did not say a word in reply to Raoul's remark and went straight home.

This happened in the afternoon, in the singer's dressing-room, where they met every day and where they amused themselves by dining on three biscuits, two glasses of port and a bunch of violets. In the evening, she did not sing; and he did not receive his usual letter, though they had arranged to write to each other daily during that month. The next morning, he ran off to Mamma Valerius, who told him that Christine had gone away for two days. She had left at five o'clock the day before.

Raoul was distracted. He hated Mamma Valerius for giving him such news as that with such stupefying calmness. He tried to sound her, but the old lady obviously knew nothing.

Christine returned on the following day. She returned in triumph. She renewed her extraordinary success of the gala performance. Since the adventure of the "toad," Carlotta had not been able to appear on the stage. The terror of a fresh "co-ack" filled her heart and deprived her of all her power of singing; and the theater that had witnessed her incomprehensible disgrace had become odious to her. She contrived to cancel her contract. Daae was offered the vacant place for the time. She received thunders of applause in the Juive.

The viscount, who, of course, was present, was the only one to suffer on hearing the thousand echoes of this fresh triumph; for Christine still wore her plain gold ring. A distant voice whispered in the young man's ear:

"She is wearing the ring again to-night; and you did not give it to her. She gave her soul again tonight and did not give it to you . . . If she will not tell you what she has been doing the past two days . . . you must go and ask Erik!"

He ran behind the scenes and placed himself in her way. She saw him for her eyes were looking for him. She said:

"Quick! Quick! . . . Come!"

And she dragged him to her dressing-room.

Raoul at once threw himself on his knees before her. He swore to her that he would go and he entreated her never again to withhold a single hour of the ideal happiness which she had promised him. She let her tears flow. They kissed like a despairing brother and sister who have been smitten with a common loss and who meet to mourn a dead parent.

Suddenly, she snatched herself from the young man's soft and timid embrace, seemed to listen to something, and, with a quick gesture, pointed to the door. When he was on the threshold, she said, in so low a voice that the viscount guessed rather than heard her words:

"To-morrow, my dear betrothed! And be happy, Raoul: I sang for you to-night!"

He returned the next day. But those two days of absence had broken the charm of their delightful make-believe. They looked at each other, in the dressing-room, with their sad eyes, without exchanging a word. Raoul had to restrain himself not to cry out:

"I am jealous! I am jealous! I am jealous!"

But she heard him all the same. Then she said:

"Come for a walk, dear. The air will do you good."

Raoul thought that she would propose a stroll in the country, far from that building which he detested as a prison whose jailer he could feel walking within the walls . . . the jailer Erik . . . But she took him to the stage and made him sit on the wooden curb of a well, in the doubtful peace and coolness of a first scene set for the evening's performance.

On another day, she wandered with him, hand in, hand, along the deserted paths of a garden whose creepers had been cut out by a decorator's skilful hands. It was as though the real sky, the real flowers, the real earth were forbidden her for all time and she condemned to breathe no other air than that of the theater. An occasional fireman passed, watching over their melancholy idyll from afar. And she would drag him up above the clouds, in the magnificent disorder of the grid, where she loved to make him giddy by running in front of him along the frail bridges, among the thousands of ropes fastened to the pulleys, the windlasses, the rollers, in the midst of a regular forest of yards and masts. If he hesitated, she said, with an adorable pout of her lips:

"You, a sailor!"

And then they returned to terra firma, that is to say, to some passage that led them to the little girls' dancing-school, where brats between six and ten were practising their steps, in the hope of becoming great dancers one day, "covered with diamonds . . . " Meanwhile, Christine gave them sweets instead.

She took him to the wardrobe and property-rooms, took him all over her empire, which was artificial, but immense, covering seventeen stories from the ground-floor to the roof and inhabited by an army of subjects. She moved among them like a popular queen, encouraging them in their labors, sitting down in the workshops, giving words of advice to the workmen whose hands hesitated to cut into the rich stuffs that were to clothe heroes. There were inhabitants of that country who practised every trade. There were cobblers, there were goldsmiths. All had learned to know her and to love her, for she always interested herself in all their troubles and all their little hobbies.

She knew unsuspected corners that were secretly occupied by little old couples. She knocked at their door and introduced Raoul to them as a Prince Charming who had asked for her hand; and the two of them, sitting on some worm-eaten "property," would listen to the legends of the Opera, even as, in their childhood, they had listened to the old Breton tales. Those old people remembered nothing outside the Opera. They had lived there for years without number. Past managements had forgotten them; palace revolutions had taken no notice of them; the history of France had run its course unknown to them; and nobody recollected their existence.

The precious days sped in this way; and Raoul and Christine, by affecting excessive interest in outside matters, strove awkwardly to hide from each other the one thought of their hearts. One fact was certain, that Christine, who until then had shown herself the stronger of the two, became suddenly inexpressibly nervous. When on their expeditions, she would start running without reason or else suddenly stop; and her hand, turning ice-cold in a moment, would hold the young man back. Sometimes her eyes seemed to pursue imaginary shadows. She cried, "This way," and "This way," and "This way," laughing a breathless laugh that often ended in tears. Then Raoul tried to speak, to question her, in spite of his promises. But, even before he had worded his question, she answered feverishly:

"Nothing . . . I swear it is nothing."

Once, when they were passing before an open trapdoor on the stage, Raoul stopped over the dark cavity.

"You have shown me over the upper part of your empire, Christine, but there are strange stories told of the lower part. Shall we go down?"

She caught him in her arms, as though she feared to see him disappear down the black hole, and, in a trembling voice, whispered:

"Never! . . . I will not have you go there! . . . Besides, it's not mine . . . EVERYTHING THAT IS UNDERGROUND BELONGS TO HIM!"

Raoul looked her in the eyes and said roughly:

"So he lives down there, does he?"

"I never said so . . . Who told you a thing like that? Come away! I sometimes wonder if you are quite sane, Raoul . . . You always take things in such an impossible way . . . Come along! Come!"

And she literally dragged him away, for he was obstinate and wanted to remain by the trap-door; that hole attracted him.

Suddenly, the trap-door was closed and so quickly that they did not even see the hand that worked it; and they remained quite dazed.

"Perhaps *he* was there," Raoul said, at last.

She shrugged her shoulders, but did not seem easy.

"No, no, it was the 'trap-door-shutters.' They must do something, you know . . . They open and shut the trap-doors without any particular reason . . . It's like the 'door-shutters:' they must spend their time somehow."

"But suppose it were *he*, Christine?"

"No, no! He has shut himself up, he is working."

"Oh, really! He's working, is he?"

"Yes, he can't open and shut the trap-doors and work at the same time." She shivered.

"What is he working at?"

"Oh, something terrible! . . . But it's all the better for us . . . When he's working at that, he sees nothing; he does not eat, drink, or breathe for days and nights at a time . . . he becomes a living dead man and has no time to amuse himself with the trap-doors." She shivered again. She was still holding him in her arms. Then she sighed and said, in her turn:

"Suppose it were *he*!"

"Are you afraid of him?"

"No, no, of course not," she said.

For all that, on the next day and the following days, Christine was careful to avoid the trap-doors. Her agitation only increased as the hours passed. At last, one afternoon, she arrived very late, with her face so desperately pale and her eyes so desperately red, that Raoul resolved to go to all lengths, including that which he foreshadowed when he blurted out that he would not go on the North Pole expedition unless she first told him the secret of the man's voice.

"Hush! Hush, in Heaven's name! Suppose *he* heard you, you unfortunate Raoul!"

And Christine's eyes stared wildly at everything around her.

"I will remove you from his power, Christine, I swear it. And you shall not think of him any more."

"Is it possible?"

She allowed herself this doubt, which was an encouragernent, while dragging the young man up to the topmost floor of the theater, far, very far from the trap-doors.

"I shall hide you in some unknown corner of the world, where *he* can not come to look for you. You will be safe; and then I shall go away . . . as you have sworn never to marry."

Christine seized Raoul's hands and squeezed them with incredible rapture. But, suddenly becoming alarmed again, she turned away her head.

"Higher!" was all she said. "Higher still!"

And she dragged him up toward the summit.

He had a difficulty in following her. They were soon under the very roof, in the maze of timber-work. They slipped through the buttresses, the rafters, the joists; they ran from beam to beam as they might have run from tree to tree in a forest.

And, despite the care which she took to look behind her at every moment, she failed to see a shadow which followed her like her own shadow, which stopped when she stopped, which started again when she did and which made no more noise than a well-conducted shadow should. As for Raoul, he saw nothing either; for, when he had Christine in front of him, nothing interested him that happened behind.

CHAPTER XII

APOLLO'S LYRE

On this way, they reached the roof. Christine tripped over it as lightly as a swallow. Their eyes swept the empty space between the three domes and the triangular pediment. She breathed freely over Paris, the whole valley of which was seen at work below. She called Raoul to come quite close to her and they walked side by side along the zinc streets, in the leaden avenues; they looked at their twin shapes in the huge tanks, full of stagnant water, where, in the hot weather, the little boys of the ballet, a score or so, learn to swim and dive.

The shadow had followed behind them clinging to their steps; and the two children little suspected its presence when they at last sat down, trustingly, under the mighty protection of Apollo, who, with a great bronze gesture, lifted his huge lyre to the heart of a crimson sky.

It was a gorgeous spring evening. Clouds, which had just received their gossamer robe of gold and purple from the setting sun, drifted slowly by; and Christine said to Raoul:

"Soon we shall go farther and faster than the clouds, to the end of the world, and then you will leave me, Raoul. But, if, when the moment comes for you to take me away, I refuse to go with you—well you must carry me off by force!"

"Are you afraid that you will change your mind, Christine?"

"I don't know," she said, shaking her head in an odd fashion. "He is a demon!" And she shivered and nestled in his arms with a moan. "I am afraid now of going back to live with him . . . in the ground!"

"What compels you to go back, Christine?"

"If I do not go back to him, terrible misfortunes may happen! . . . But I can't do it, I can't do it! . . . I know one ought to be sorry for people who live underground . . . But he is too horrible! And yet the time is at hand; I have only a day left; and, if I do not go, he will come and fetch me with his voice. And he will drag me with him, underground, and go on his knees before me, with his death's head. And he will tell me that he loves me! And he will cry! Oh, those tears, Raoul, those tears in the two black eye-sockets of the death's head! I can not see those tears flow again!"

She wrung her hands in anguish, while Raoul pressed her to his heart.

"No, no, you shall never again hear him tell you that he loves you! You shall not see his tears! Let us fly, Christine, let us fly at once!"

And he tried to drag her away, then and there. But she stopped him.

"No, no," she said, shaking her head sadly. "Not now! . . . It would be too cruel . . . let him hear me sing to-morrow evening . . . and then we will go away. You must come and fetch me in my dressing-room at midnight exactly. He will then be waiting for me in the dining-room by the lake . . . we shall be free and you shall take me away . . . You must promise me that, Raoul, even if I refuse; for I feel that, if I go back this time, I shall perhaps never return."

And she gave a sigh to which it seemed to her that another sigh, behind her, replied.

"Didn't you hear?"

Her teeth chattered.

"No," said Raoul, "I heard nothing."

"It is too terrible," she confessed, "to be always trembling like this! . . . And yet we run no danger here; we are at home, in the sky, in the open air, in the light. The sun is flaming; and night-birds can not bear to look at the sun. I have never seen him by daylight . . . it must be awful! . . . Oh, the first time I saw him! . . . I thought that he was going to die."

"Why?" asked Raoul, really frightened at the aspect which this strange confidence was taking.

"BECAUSE I HAD SEEN HIM!"

This time, Raoul and Christine turned round at the same time:

"There is some one in pain," said Raoul. "Perhaps some one has been hurt. Did you hear?"

"I can't say," Christine confessed. "Even when he is not there, my ears are full of his sighs. Still, if you heard . . . "

They stood up and looked around them. They were quite alone on the immense lead roof. They sat down again and Raoul said:

"Tell me how you saw him first."

"I had heard him for three months without seeing him. The first time I heard it, I thought, as you did, that that adorable voice was singing in another room. I went out and looked everywhere; but, as you know, Raoul, my dressing-room is very much by itself; and I could not find the voice outside my room, whereas it went on steadily inside. And it not only sang, but it spoke to me and answered my questions, like a real man's voice, with this difference, that it was as beautiful as the voice of an angel. I had never got the Angel of Music whom my poor father had promised to send me as soon as he was dead. I really think that Mamma Valerius was a little bit to blame. I told her about it; and she at once said, 'It must be the Angel; at any rate, you can do no harm by asking him.' I did so; and the man's voice replied that, yes, it was the Angel's voice, the voice which I was expecting and which my father had promised me. From that time onward, the voice and I became great friends. It asked leave to give me lessons every day. I agreed and never failed to keep the appointment which it gave me in my dressing-room. You have no idea, though you have heard the voice, of what those lessons were like."

"No, I have no idea," said Raoul. "What was your accompaniment?"

"We were accompanied by a music which I do not know: it was behind the wall and wonderfully accurate. The voice seemed to understand mine exactly, to know precisely where my father had left off teaching me. In a few weeks' time, I hardly knew myself when I sang. I was even frightened. I seemed to dread a sort of witchcraft behind it; but Mamma Valerius reassured me. She said that she knew I was much too simple a girl to give the devil a hold on me . . . My progress, by the voice's own order, was kept a secret between the voice, Mamma Valerius and myself. It was a curious thing, but, outside the dressing-room, I sang with my ordinary, every-day voice and nobody noticed anything. I did all that the voice asked. It said, 'Wait and see: we shall astonish Paris!' And I waited and lived on in a sort of ecstatic dream. It was then that I saw you for the first time one evening, in the house. I was so glad that I never thought of concealing my delight when I reached my dressing-room. Unfortunately, the voice was there before me and soon noticed, by my air, that something had happened. It asked what was the matter and I saw no reason for keeping our story secret or concealing the place which you filled in my heart. Then the voice was silent. I called to it, but it did not reply; I begged and entreated, but in vain. I was terrified lest it had gone for good. I wish to Heaven it had, dear! . . . That night, I went home in a desperate condition. I told Mamma Valerius, who said, 'Why, of course, the voice is jealous!' And that, dear, first revealed to me that I loved you."

Christine stopped and laid her head on Raoul's shoulder. They sat like that for a moment, in silence, and they did not see, did not perceive the movement, at a few steps from them, of the creeping shadow of two great black wings, a shadow that came along the roof so near, so near them that it could have stifled them by closing over them.

"The next day," Christine continued, with a sigh, "I went back to my dressing-room in a very pensive frame of mind. The voice was there, spoke to me with great sadness and told me plainly that, if I must bestow my heart on earth, there was nothing for the voice to do but to go back to Heaven. And it said this with such an accent of HUMAN sorrow that I ought then and there to have suspected and begun to believe that I was the victim of my deluded senses. But my faith in the voice, with which the memory of my father was so closely intermingled, remained undisturbed. I feared nothing so much as that I might never hear it again; I had thought about my love for you and realized all the useless danger of it; and I did not even know if you remembered me. Whatever happened, your position in society forbade me to contemplate the possibility of ever marrying you; and I swore to the voice that you were no more than a brother to me nor ever would be and that my heart was incapable of any earthly love. And that, dear, was why I refused to recognize or see you when I met you on the stage or in the passages. Meanwhile, the hours during which the voice taught me were spent in a divine frenzy, until, at last, the voice said to me, 'You can now, Christine Daae, give to men a little of the music of Heaven.' I don't know how it was that Carlotta did not come to the theater that night nor why I was called upon to sing in her stead; but I sang with a rapture I had never known before and I felt for a moment as if my soul were leaving my body!"

"Oh, Christine," said Raoul, "my heart quivered that night at every accent of your voice. I saw the tears stream down your cheeks and I wept with you. How could you sing, sing like that while crying?"

"I felt myself fainting," said Christine, "I closed my eyes. When I opened them, you were by my side. But the voice was there also, Raoul! I was afraid for your sake and again I would not recognize you and began to laugh when you reminded me that you had picked up my scarf in the sea! . . . Alas, there is no deceiving the voice! . . . The voice recognized you and the voice was jealous! . . . It said that, if I did not love you, I would not avoid you, but treat you like any other old friend. It made me scene upon scene. At last, I said to the voice, 'That will do! I am going to Perros to-morrow, to pray on my father's grave, and I shall ask M. Raoul de Chagny to go with me.' 'Do as you please,' replied the voice, 'but I shall be at Perros too, for I am wherever you are, Christine; and, if you are still worthy of me, if you have not lied to me, I will play you The Resurrection of Lazarus, on the stroke of midnight, on your father's tomb and on your father's violin.' That, dear, was how I came to write you the letter that brought you to Perros. How could I have been so beguiled? How was it, when I saw the personal, the selfish point of view of the voice, that I did not suspect some impostor? Alas, I was no longer mistress of myself: I had become his thing!"

"But, after all," cried Raoul, "you soon came to know the truth! Why did you not at once rid yourself of that abominable nightmare?"

"Know the truth, Raoul? Rid myself of that nightmare? But, my poor boy, I was not caught in the nightmare until the day when I learned the truth! . . . Pity me, Raoul, pity me! . . . You remember the terrible evening when Carlotta thought that she had been turned into a toad on the stage and when the house was suddenly plunged in darkness through the chandelier crashing to the floor? There were killed and wounded that night and the whole theater rang with terrified screams. My first thought was for you and the voice. I was at once easy, where you were concerned, for I had seen you in your brother's box and I knew that you were not in danger. But the voice had told me that it would be at the performance and I was really afraid for it, just as if it had been an ordinary person who was capable of dying. I thought to myself, 'The chandelier may have come down upon the voice.' I was then on the stage and was nearly running into the house, to look for the voice among the killed and wounded, when I thought that, if the voice was safe, it would be sure to be in my dressing-room and I rushed to my room. The voice was not there. I locked my door and, with tears in my eyes, besought it, if it were still alive, to manifest itself to me. The voice did not reply, but suddenly I heard a long, beautiful wail which I knew well. It is the plaint of Lazarus when, at the sound of the Redeemer's voice, he begins to open his eyes and see the light of day. It was the music which you and I, Raoul, heard at Perros. And then the voice began to sing the leading phrase, 'Come! And believe in me! Whoso believes in me shall live! Walk! Whoso hath believed in me shall never die! . . .' I can not tell you the effect which that music had upon me. It seemed to command me, personally, to come, to stand up and come to it. It retreated and I followed. 'Come! And believe in me!' I believed in it, I came . . . I came and—this was the extraordinary thing—my dressing-room, as I moved, seemed to lengthen out . . . to lengthen out . . . Evidently, it must have been an effect of mirrors . . . for I had the mirror in front of me . . . And, suddenly, I was outside the room without knowing how!"

"What! Without knowing how? Christine, Christine, you must really stop dreaming!"

"I was not dreaming, dear, I was outside my room without knowing how. You, who saw me disappear from my room one evening, may be able to explain it; but I can not. I can only tell you that, suddenly, there was no mirror before me and no dressing-room. I was in a dark passage, I was frightened and I cried out. It was quite dark, but for a faint red glimmer at a distant corner of the wall. I tried out. My voice was the only sound, for the singing and the violin had stopped. And, suddenly, a hand was laid on mine . . . or rather a stone-cold, bony thing that seized my wrist and did not let go. I cried out again. An arm took me round the waist and supported me.

I struggled for a little while and then gave up the attempt. I was dragged toward the little red light and then I saw that I was in the hands of a man wrapped in a large cloak and wearing a mask that hid his whole face. I made one last effort; my limbs stiffened, my mouth opened to scream, but a hand closed it, a hand which I felt on my lips, on my skin . . . a hand that smelt of death. Then I fainted away.

"When I opened my eyes, we were still surrounded by darkness. A lantern, standing on the ground, showed a bubbling well. The water splashing from the well disappeared, almost at once, under the floor on which I was lying, with my head on the knee of the man in the black cloak and the black mask. He was bathing my temples and his hands smelt of death. I tried to push them away and asked, 'Who are you? Where is the voice?' His only answer was a sigh. Suddenly, a hot breath passed over my face and I perceived a white shape, beside the man's black shape, in the darkness. The black shape lifted me on to the white shape, a glad neighing greeted my astounded ears and I murmured, 'Cesar!' The animal quivered. Raoul, I was lying half back on a saddle and I had recognized the white horse out of the PROFETA, which I had so often fed with sugar and sweets. I remembered that, one evening, there was a rumor in the theater that the horse had disappeared and that it had been stolen by the Opera ghost. I believed in the voice, but had never believed in the ghost. Now, however, I began to wonder, with a shiver, whether I was the ghost's prisoner. I called upon the voice to help me, for I should never have imagined that the voice and the ghost were one. You have heard about the Opera ghost, have you not, Raoul?"

"Yes, but tell me what happened when you were on the white horse of the Profeta?"

"I made no movement and let myself go. The black shape held me up, and I made no effort to escape. A curious feeling of peacefulness came over me and I thought that I must be under the influence of some cordial. I had the full command of my senses; and my eyes became used to the darkness, which was lit, here and there, by fitful gleams. I calculated that we were in a narrow circular gallery, probably running all round the Opera, which is immense, underground. I had once been down into those cellars, but had stopped at the third floor, though there were two lower still, large enough to hold a town. But the figures of which I caught sight had made me run away. There are demons down there, quite black, standing in front of boilers, and they wield shovels and pitchforks and poke up fires and stir up flames and, if you come too near them, they frighten you by suddenly opening the red mouths of their furnaces . . . Well, while Cesar was quietly carrying me on his back, I saw those black demons in the distance, looking quite small, in front of the red fires of their furnaces: they came into sight, disappeared and came into sight again, as we went on our winding way. At last, they disappeared altogether. The shape was still holding me up and Cesar walked on, unled and sure-footed. I could not tell you, even approximately, how long this ride lasted; I only know that we seemed to turn and turn and often went down a spiral stair into the very heart of the earth. Even then, it may be that my head was turning, but I don't think so: no, my mind was quite clear. At last, Cesar raised his nostrils, sniffed the air and quickened his pace a little. I felt a moistness in the air and Cesar stopped. The darkness had lifted. A sort of bluey light surrounded us. We were on the edge of a lake, whose leaden waters stretched into the distance, into the darkness; but the blue light lit up the bank and I saw a little boat fastened to an iron ring on the wharf!"

"A boat!"

"Yes, but I knew that all that existed and that there was nothing supernatural about that underground lake and boat. But think of the exceptional conditions in which I arrived upon that shore! I don't know whether the effects of the cordial had worn off when the man's shape lifted me into the boat, but my terror began all over again. My gruesome escort must have noticed it, for he sent Cesar back and I heard his hoofs trampling up a staircase while the man jumped into the boat, untied the rope that held it and seized the oars. He rowed with a quick, powerful stroke; and his eyes, under the mask, never left me. We slipped across the noiseless water in the bluey light which I told you of; then we were in the dark again and we touched shore. And I was once more taken up in the man's arms. I cried aloud. And then, suddenly, I was silent, dazed by the light . . . Yes, a dazzling light in the midst of which I had been put down. I sprang to my feet. I was in the middle of a drawing-room that seemed to me to be decorated, adorned and furnished with nothing but flowers, flowers both magnificent and stupid, because of the silk ribbons that tied them to baskets, like those which they sell in the shops on the boulevards. They were much too civilized flowers, like those which I used to find in my dressing-room after a first night. And, in the midst of all these flowers, stood the black shape of the man in the mask, with arms crossed, and he said, 'Don't be afraid, Christine; you are in no danger.' IT WAS THE VOICE!

"My anger equaled my amazement. I rushed at the mask and tried to snatch it away, so as to see the face of the voice. The man said, 'You are in no danger, so long as you do not touch the mask.' And, taking me gently by the wrists, he forced me into a chair and then went down on his knees before me and said nothing more! His humility gave me back some of my courage;

and the light restored me to the realties of life. However extraordinary the adventure might be, I was now surrounded by mortal, visible, tangible things. The furniture, the hangings, the candles, the vases and the very flowers in their baskets, of which I could almost have told whence they came and what they cost, were bound to confine my imagination to the limits of a drawing-room quite as commonplace as any that, at least, had the excuse of not being in the cellars of the Opera. I had, no doubt, to do with a terrible, eccentric person, who, in some mysterious fashion, had succeeded in taking up his abode there, under the Opera house, five stories below the level of the ground. And the voice, the voice which I had recognized under the mask, was on its knees before me, *was a man*! And I began to cry . . . The man, still kneeling, must have understood the cause of my tears, for he said, 'It is true, Christine! . . . I am not an Angel, nor a genius, nor a ghost . . . I am Erik!'"

Christine's narrative was again interrupted. An echo behind them seemed to repeat the word after her.

"Erik!"

What echo? . . . They both turned round and saw that night had fallen. Raoul made a movement as though to rise, but Christine kept him beside her.

"Don't go," she said. "I want you to know everything HERE!"

"But why here, Christine? I am afraid of your catching cold."

"We have nothing to fear except the trap-doors, dear, and here we are miles away from the trap-doors . . . and I am not allowed to see you outside the theater. This is not the time to annoy him. We must not arouse his suspicion."

"Christine! Christine! Something tells me that we are wrong to wait till to-morrow evening and that we ought to fly at once."

"I tell you that, if he does not hear me sing tomorrow, it will cause him infinite pain."

"It is difficult not to cause him pain and yet to escape from him for good."

"You are right in that, Raoul, for certainly he will die of my flight." And she added in a dull voice, "But then it counts both ways . . . for we risk his killing us."

"Does he love you so much?"

"He would commit murder for me."

"But one can find out where he lives. One can go in search of him. Now that we know that Erik is not a ghost, one can speak to him and force him to answer!"

Christine shook her head.

"No, no! There is nothing to be done with Erik except to run away!"

"Then why, when you were able to run away, did you go back to him?"

"Because I had to. And you will understand that when I tell you how I left him."

"Oh, I hate him!" cried Raoul. "And you, Christine, tell me, do you hate him too?"

"No," said Christine simply.

"No, of course not . . . Why, you love him! Your fear, your terror, all of that is just love and love of the most exquisite kind, the kind which people do not admit even to themselves," said Raoul bitterly. "The kind that gives you a thrill, when you think of it . . . Picture it: a man who lives in a palace underground!" And he gave a leer.

"Then you want me to go back there?" said the young girl cruelly. "Take care, Raoul; I have told you: I should never return!"

There was an appalling silence between the three of them: the two who spoke and the shadow that listened, behind them.

"Before answering that," said Raoul, at last, speaking very slowly, "I should like to know with what feeling he inspires you, since you do not hate him."

"With horror!" she said. "That is the terrible thing about it. He fills me with horror and I do not hate him. How can I hate him, Raoul? Think of Erik at my feet, in the house on the lake, underground. He accuses himself, he curses himself, he implores my forgiveness! . . . He confesses his cheat. He loves me! He lays at my feet an immense and tragic love . . . He has carried me off for love! . . . He has imprisoned me with him, underground, for love! . . . But he respects me: he crawls, he moans, he weeps! . . . And, when I stood up, Raoul, and told him that I could only despise him if he did not, then and there, give me my liberty . . . he offered it . . . he offered to show me the mysterious road . . . Only . . . only he rose too . . . and I was made to remember that, though he was not an angel, nor a ghost, nor a genius, he remained the voice . . . for he sang. And I listened . . . and stayed! . . . That night, we did not exchange another word. He sang me to sleep.

"When I woke up, I was alone, lying on a sofa in a simply furnished little bedroom, with an ordinary mahogany bedstead, lit by a lamp standing on the marble top of an old Louis-Philippe chest of drawers. I soon discovered that I was a prisoner and that the only outlet from my room led to a very comfortable bath-room. On returning to the bedroom, I saw on the chest of drawers a note, in red ink, which said, 'My dear Christine, you need have no concern as to your fate. You have no better nor more respectful friend in the world than myself. You are alone, at present, in this home which is yours. I am going out shopping to fetch you all the things that you can need.' I felt sure that I had fallen into the hands of a madman. I ran round my little apartment, looking for a way of escape which I could not find. I upbraided myself for my absurd superstition, which had caused me to fall into the trap. I felt inclined to laugh and to cry at the same time.

"This was the state of mind in which Erik found me. After giving three taps on the wall, he walked in quietly through a door which I had not noticed and which he left open. He had his arms full of boxes and parcels and arranged them on the bed, in a leisurely fashion, while I overwhelmed him with abuse and called upon him to take off his mask, if it covered the face of an honest man. He replied serenely, 'You shall never see Erik's face.' And he reproached me with not having finished dressing at that time of day: he was good enough to tell me that it was two o'clock in the afternoon. He said he would give me half an hour and, while he spoke, wound up my watch and set it for me. After which, he asked me to come to the dining-room, where a nice lunch was waiting for us.

"I was very angry, slammed the door in his face and went to the bath-room . . . When I came out again, feeling greatly refreshed, Erik said that he loved me, but that he would never tell me so except when I allowed him and that the rest of the time would be devoted to music. 'What do you mean by the rest of the time?' I asked. 'Five days,' he said, with decision. I asked him if I should then be free and he said, 'You will be free, Christine, for, when those five days are past, you will have learned not to see me; and then, from time to time, you will come to see your poor Erik!' He pointed to a chair opposite him, at a small table, and I sat down, feeling greatly perturbed. However, I ate a few prawns and the wing of a chicken and drank half a glass of tokay, which he had himself, he told me, brought from the Konigsberg cellars. Erik did not eat or drink. I asked him what his nationality was and if that name of Erik did not point to his Scandinavian origin. He said that he had no name and no country and that he had taken the name of Erik by accident.

"After lunch, he rose and gave me the tips of his fingers, saying he would like to show me over his flat; but I snatched away my hand and gave a cry. What I had touched was cold and, at the same time, bony; and I remembered that his hands smelt of death. 'Oh, forgive me!' he moaned. And he opened a door before me. 'This is my bedroom, if you care to see it. It is rather curious.' His manners, his words, his attitude gave me confidence and I went in without hesitation. I felt as if I were entering the room of a dead person. The walls were all hung with black, but, instead of the white trimmings that usually set off that funereal upholstery, there was an enormous stave of music with the notes of the *Dies Irae*, many times repeated. In the middle of the room was a canopy, from which hung curtains of red brocaded stuff, and, under the canopy, an open coffin. 'That is where I sleep,' said Erik. 'One has to get used to everything in life, even to eternity.' The sight upset me so much that I turned away my head.

"Then I saw the keyboard of an organ which filled one whole side of the walls. On the desk was a music-book covered with red notes. I asked leave to look at it and read, 'Don Juan Triumphant.' 'Yes,' he said, 'I compose sometimes.' I began that work twenty years ago. When I have finished, I shall take it away with me in that coffin and never wake up again.' 'You must work at it as seldom as you can,' I said. He replied, 'I sometimes work at it for fourteen days and nights together, during which I live on music only, and then I rest for years at a time.' 'Will you play me something out of your Don Juan Triumphant?' I asked, thinking to please him. 'You must never ask me that,' he said, in a gloomy voice. 'I will play you Mozart, if you like, which will only make you weep; but my Don Juan, Christine, burns; and yet he is not struck by fire from Heaven.' Thereupon we returned to the drawing-room. I noticed that there was no mirror in the whole apartment. I was going to remark upon this, but Erik had already sat down to the piano. He said, 'You see, Christine, there is some music that is so terrible that it consumes all those who approach it. Fortunately, you have not come to that music yet, for you would lose all your pretty coloring and nobody would know you when you returned to Paris. Let us sing something from the Opera, Christine Daae.' He spoke these last words as though he were flinging an insult at me."

"What did you do?"

"I had no time to think about the meaning he put into his words. We at once began the duet in Othello and already the catastrophe was upon us. I sang Desdemona with a despair, a terror which I had never displayed before. As for him, his voice thundered forth his revengeful soul at every note. Love, jealousy, hatred, burst out around us in harrowing cries. Erik's black mask made me think of the natural mask of the Moor of Venice. He was Othello himself. Suddenly, I felt a need to see beneath the mask. I wanted to know the FACE of the voice, and, with a movement which I was utterly unable to control, swiftly my fingers tore away the mask. Oh, horror, horror, horror!"

Christine stopped, at the thought of the vision that had scared her, while the echoes of the night, which had repeated the name of Erik, now thrice moaned the cry:

"Horror! . . . Horror! . . . Horror!"

Raoul and Christine, clasping each other closely, raised their eyes to the stars that shone in a clear and peaceful sky. Raoul said:

"Strange, Christine, that this calm, soft night should be so full of plaintive sounds. One would think that it was sorrowing with us."

"When you know the secret, Raoul, your ears, like mine, will be full of lamentations."

She took Raoul's protecting hands in hers and, with a long shiver, continued:

"Yes, if I lived to be a hundred, I should always hear the superhuman cry of grief and rage which he uttered when the terrible sight appeared before my eyes . . . Raoul, you have seen death's heads, when they have been dried and withered by the centuries, and, perhaps, if you were not the victim of a nightmare, you saw HIS death's head at Perros. And then you saw Red Death stalking about at the last masked ball. But all those death's heads were motionless and their dumb horror was not alive. But imagine, if you can, Red Death's mask suddenly coming to life in order to express, with the four black holes of its eyes, its nose, and its mouth, the extreme anger, the mighty fury of a demon; *and not a ray of light from the sockets*, for, as I learned later, you can not see his blazing eyes except in the dark.

"I fell back against the wall and he came up to me, grinding his teeth, and, as I fell upon my knees, he hissed mad, incoherent words and curses at me. Leaning over me, he cried, 'Look! You want to see! See! Feast your eyes, glut your soul on my cursed ugliness! Look at Erik's face! Now you know the face of the voice! You were not content to hear me, eh? You wanted to know what I looked like! Oh, you women are so inquisitive! Well, are you satisfied? I'm a very good-looking fellow, eh? . . . When a woman has seen me, as you have, she belongs to me. She loves me for ever. I am a kind of Don Juan, you know!' And, drawing himself up to his full height, with his hand on his hip, wagging the hideous thing that was his head on his shoulders, he roared, 'Look at me! I AM DON JUAN TRIUMPHANT!' And, when I turned away my head and begged for mercy, he drew it to him, brutally, twisting his dead fingers into my hair."

"Enough! Enough!" cried Raoul. "I will kill him. In Heaven's name, Christine, tell me where the dining-room on the lake is! I must kill him!"

"Oh, be quiet, Raoul, if you want to know!"

"Yes, I want to know how and why you went back; I must know! . . . But, in any case, I will kill him!"

"Oh, Raoul, listen, listen! . . . He dragged me by my hair and then . . . and then . . . Oh, it is too horrible!"

"Well, what? Out with it!" exclaimed Raoul fiercely. "Out with it, quick!"

"Then he hissed at me. 'Ah, I frighten you, do I? . . . I dare say! . . . Perhaps you think that I have another mask, eh, and that this . . . this . . . my head is a mask? Well,' he roared, 'tear it off as you did the other! Come! Come along! I insist! Your hands! Your hands! Give me your hands!' And he seized my hands and dug them into his awful face. He tore his flesh with my nails, tore his terrible dead flesh with my nails! . . . 'Know,' he shouted, while his throat throbbed and panted like a furnace, 'know that I am built up of death from head to foot and that it is a corpse that loves you and adores you and will never, never leave you! . . . Look, I am not laughing now, I am crying, crying for you, Christine, who have torn off my mask and who therefore can never leave me again! . . . As long as you thought me handsome, you could have come back, I know you would have come back . . . but, now that you know my hideousness, you would run away for good . . . So I shall keep you here! . . . Why did you want to see me? Oh, mad Christine, who wanted to see me! . . . When my own father never saw me and when my mother, so as not to see me, made me a present of my first mask!'

"He had let go of me at last and was dragging himself about on the floor, uttering terrible sobs. And then he crawled away like a snake, went into his room, closed the door and left me alone to my reflections. Presently I heard the sound of the organ; and then I began to understand Erik's contemptuous phrase when he spoke about Opera music. What I now heard was utterly different from what I had heard up to then. His Don Juan Triumphant (for I had not a doubt but that he had rushed to his masterpiece to forget the horror of the moment) seemed to me at first one long, awful, magnificent sob. But, little by little, it expressed every emotion, every suffering of which mankind is capable. It intoxicated me; and I opened the door that separated us. Erik rose, as I entered, *but dared not turn in my direction.* 'Erik,' I cried, 'show me your face without fear! I swear that you are the most unhappy and sublime of men; and, if ever again I shiver when I look at you, it will be because I am thinking of the splendor of your genius!' Then Erik turned round, for he believed me, and I also had faith in myself. He fell at my feet, with words of love . . . with words of love in his dead mouth . . . and the music had ceased . . . He kissed the hem of my dress and did not see that I closed my eyes.

"What more can I tell you, dear? You now know the tragedy. It went on for a fortnight—a fortnight during which I lied to him. My lies were as hideous as the monster who inspired them; but they were the price of my liberty. I burned his mask; and I managed so well that, even when he was not singing, he tried to catch my eye, like a dog sitting by its master. He was my faithful slave and paid me endless little attentions. Gradually, I gave him such confidence that he ventured to take me walking on the banks of the lake and to row me in the boat on its leaden waters; toward the end of my captivity he let me out through the gates that closed the underground passages in the Rue Scribe. Here a carriage awaited us and took us to the Bois. The night when we met you was nearly fatal to me, for he is terribly jealous of you and I had to tell him that you were soon going away . . . Then, at last, after a fortnight of that horrible captivity, during which I was filled with pity, enthusiasm, despair and horror by turns, he believed me when I said, 'I WILL COME BACK!'"

"And you went back, Christine," groaned Raoul.

"Yes, dear, and I must tell you that it was not his frightful threats when setting me free that helped me to keep my word, but the harrowing sob which he gave on the threshold of the tomb. . . . That sob attached me to the unfortunate man more than I myself suspected when saying good-by to him. Poor Erik! Poor Erik!"

"Christine," said Raoul, rising, "you tell me that you love me; but you had recovered your liberty hardly a few hours before you returned to Erik! Remember the masked ball!"

"Yes; and do you remember those hours which I passed with you, Raoul . . . to the great danger of both of us?"

"I doubted your love for me, during those hours."

"Do you doubt it still, Raoul? . . . Then know that each of my visits to Erik increased my horror of him; for each of those visits, instead of calming him, as I hoped, made him mad with love! And I am so frightened, so frightened! . . . "

"You are frightened . . . but do you love me? If Erik were good-looking, would you love me, Christine?"

She rose in her turn, put her two trembling arms round the young man's neck and said:

"Oh, my betrothed of a day, if I did not love you, I would not give you my lips! Take them, for the first time and the last."

He kissed her lips; but the night that surrounded them was rent asunder, they fled as at the approach of a storm and their eyes, filled with dread of Erik, showed them, before they disappeared, high up above them, an immense night-bird that stared at them with its blazing eyes and seemed to cling to the string of Apollo's lyre.

CHAPTER XIII

A MASTER-STROKE OF THE TRAP-DOOR LOVER

Raoul and Christine ran, eager to escape from the roof and the blazing eyes that showed only in the dark; and they did not stop before they came to the eighth floor on the way down.

There was no performance at the Opera that night and the passages were empty. Suddenly, a queer-looking form stood before them and blocked the road:

"No, not this way!"

And the form pointed to another passage by which they were to reach the wings. Raoul wanted to stop and ask for an explanation. But the form, which wore a sort of long frock-coat and a pointed cap, said:

"Quick! Go away quickly!"

Christine was already dragging Raoul, compelling him to start running again.

"But who is he? Who is that man?" he asked.

Christine replied: "It's the Persian."

"What's he doing here?"

"Nobody knows. He is always in the Opera."

"You are making me run away, for the first time in my life. If we really saw Erik, what I ought to have done was to nail him to Apollo's lyre, just as we nail the owls to the walls of our Breton farms; and there would have been no more question of him."

"My dear Raoul, you would first have had to climb up to Apollo's lyre: that is no easy matter."

"The blazing eyes were there!"

"Oh, you are getting like me now, seeing him everywhere! What I took for blazing eyes was probably a couple of stars shining through the strings of the lyre."

And Christine went down another floor, with Raoul following her.

"As you have quite made up your mind to go, Christine, I assure you it would be better to go at once. Why wait for to-morrow? He may have heard us to-night."

"No, no, he is working, I tell you, at his Don Juan Triumphant and not thinking of us."

"You're so sure of that you keep on looking behind you!"

"Come to my dressing-room."

"Hadn't we better meet outside the Opera?"

"Never, till we go away for good! It would bring us bad luck, if I did not keep my word. I promised him to see you only here."

"It's a good thing for me that he allowed you even that. Do you know," said Raoul bitterly, "that it was very plucky of you to let us play at being engaged?"

"Why, my dear, he knows all about it! He said, 'I trust you, Christine. M. de Chagny is in love with you and is going abroad. Before he goes, I want him to be as happy as I am.' Are people so unhappy when they love?"

"Yes, Christine, when they love and are not sure of being loved."

They came to Christine's dressing-room.

"Why do you think that you are safer in this room than on the stage?" asked Raoul. "You heard him through the walls here, therefore he can certainly hear us."

"No. He gave me his word not to be behind the walls of my dressing-room again and I believe Erik's word. This room and my bedroom on the lake are for me, exclusively, and not to be approached by him."

"How can you have gone from this room into that dark passage, Christine? Suppose we try to repeat your movements; shall we?"

"It is dangerous, dear, for the glass might carry me off again; and, instead of running away, I should be obliged to go to the end of the secret passage to the lake and there call Erik."

"Would he hear you?"

"Erik will hear me wherever I call him. He told me so. He is a very curious genius. You must not think, Raoul, that he is simply a man who amuses himself by living underground. He does things that no other man could do; he knows things which nobody in the world knows."

"Take care, Christine, you are making a ghost of him again!"

"No, he is not a ghost; he is a man of Heaven and earth, that is all."

"A man of Heaven and earth . . . that is all! . . . A nice way to speak of him! . . . And are you still resolved to run away from him?"

"Yes, to-morrow."

"To-morrow, you will have no resolve left!"

"Then, Raoul, you must run away with me in spite of myself; is that understood?"

"I shall be here at twelve to-morrow night; I shall keep my promise, whatever happens. You say that, after listening to the performance, he is to wait for you in the dining-room on the lake?"

"Yes."

"And how are you to reach him, if you don't know how to go out by the glass?"

"Why, by going straight to the edge of the lake."

Christine opened a box, took out an enormous key and showed it to Raoul.

"What's that?" he asked.

"The key of the gate to the underground passage in the Rue Scribe."

"I understand, Christine. It leads straight to the lake. Give it to me, Christine, will you?"

"Never!" she said. "That would be treacherous!"

Suddenly Christine changed color. A mortal pallor overspread her features.

"Oh heavens!" she cried. "Erik! Erik! Have pity on me!"

"Hold your tongue!" said Raoul. "You told me he could hear you!"

But the singer's attitude became more and more inexplicable. She wrung her fingers, repeating, with a distraught air:

"Oh, Heaven! Oh, Heaven!"

"But what is it? What is it?" Raoul implored.

"The ring . . . the gold ring he gave me."

"Oh, so Erik gave you that ring!"

"You know he did, Raoul! But what you don't know is that, when he gave it to me, he said, 'I give you back your liberty, Christine, on condition that this ring is always on your finger. As long as you keep it, you will be protected against all danger and Erik will remain your friend. But woe to you if you ever part with it, for Erik will have his revenge!' . . . My dear, my dear, the ring is gone! . . . Woe to us both!"

They both looked for the ring, but could not find it. Christine refused to be pacified.

"It was while I gave you that kiss, up above, under Apollo's lyre," she said. "The ring must have slipped from my finger and dropped into the street! We can never find it. And what misfortunes are in store for us now! Oh, to run away!"

"Let us run away at once," Raoul insisted, once more.

She hesitated. He thought that she was going to say yes . . . Then her bright pupils became dimmed and she said:

"No! To-morrow!"

And she left him hurriedly, still wringing and rubbing her fingers, as though she hoped to bring the ring back like that.

Raoul went home, greatly perturbed at all that he had heard.

"If I don't save her from the hands of that humbug," he said, aloud, as he went to bed, "she is lost. But I shall save her."

He put out his lamp and felt a need to insult Erik in the dark. Thrice over, he shouted:

"Humbug! . . . Humbug! . . . Humbug!"

But, suddenly, he raised himself on his elbow. A cold sweat poured from his temples. Two eyes, like blazing coals, had appeared at the foot of his bed. They stared at him fixedly, terribly, in the darkness of the night.

Raoul was no coward; and yet he trembled. He put out a groping, hesitating hand toward the table by his bedside. He found the matches and lit his candle. The eyes disappeared.

Still uneasy in his mind, he thought to himself:

"She told me that HIS eyes only showed in the dark. His eyes have disappeared in the light, but *he* may be there still."

And he rose, hunted about, went round the room. He looked under his bed, like a child. Then he thought himself absurd, got into bed again and blew out the candle. The eyes reappeared.

He sat up and stared back at them with all the courage he possessed. Then he cried:

"Is that you, Erik? Man, genius, or ghost, is it you?"

He reflected: "If it's he, he's on the balcony!"

Then he ran to the chest of drawers and groped for his revolver. He opened the balcony window, looked out, saw nothing and closed the window again. He went back to bed, shivering, for the night was cold, and put the revolver on the table within his reach.

The eyes were still there, at the foot of the bed. Were they between the bed and the window-pane or behind the pane, that is to say, on the balcony? That was what Raoul wanted to know. He also wanted to know if those eyes belonged to a human being . . . He wanted to know everything. Then, patiently, calmly, he seized his revolver and took aim. He aimed a little above the two eyes. Surely, if they were eyes and if above those two eyes there was a forehead and if Raoul was not too clumsy . . .

The shot made a terrible din amid the silence of the slumbering house. And, while footsteps came hurrying along the passages, Raoul sat up with outstretched arm, ready to fire again, if need be.

This time, the two eyes had disappeared.

Servants appeared, carrying lights; Count Philippe, terribly anxious:

"What is it?"

"I think I have been dreaming," replied the young man. "I fired at two stars that kept me from sleeping."

"You're raving! Are you ill? For God's sake, tell me, Raoul: what happened?"

And the count seized hold of the revolver.

"No, no, I'm not raving . . . Besides, we shall soon see . . . "

He got out of bed, put on a dressing-gown and slippers, took a light from the hands of a servant and, opening the window, stepped out on the balcony.

The count saw that the window had been pierced by a bullet at a man's height. Raoul was leaning over the balcony with his candle: "Aha!" he said. "Blood! . . . Blood! . . . Here, there, more blood! . . . That's a good thing! A ghost who bleeds is less dangerous!" he grinned.

"Raoul! Raoul! Raoul!"

The count was shaking him as though he were trying to waken a sleep-walker.

"But, my dear brother, I'm not asleep!" Raoul protested impatiently. "You can see the blood for yourself. I thought I had been dreaming and firing at two stars. It was Erik's eyes . . . and here is his blood! . . . After all, perhaps I was wrong to shoot; and Christine is quite capable of never forgiving me . . . All this would not have happened if I had drawn the curtains before going to bed."

"Raoul, have you suddenly gone mad? Wake up!"

"What, still? You would do better to help me find Erik . . . for, after all, a ghost who bleeds can always be found."

The count's valet said:

"That is so, sir; there is blood on the balcony."

The other man-servant brought a lamp, by the light of which they examined the balcony carefully. The marks of blood followed the rail till they reached a gutter-spout; then they went up the gutter-spout.

"My dear fellow," said Count Philippe, "you have fired at a cat."

"The misfortune is," said Raoul, with a grin, "that it's quite possible. With Erik, you never know. Is it Erik? Is it the cat? Is it the ghost? No, with Erik, you can't tell!"

Raoul went on making this strange sort of remarks which corresponded so intimately and logically with the preoccupation of his brain and which, at the same time, tended to persuade many people that his mind was unhinged. The count himself was seized with this idea; and, later, the examining magistrate, on receiving the report of the commissary of police, came to the same conclusion.

"Who is Erik?" asked the count, pressing his brother's hand.

"He is my rival. And, if he's not dead, it's a pity."

He dismissed the servants with a wave of the hand and the two Chagnys were left alone. But the men were not out of earshot before the count's valet heard Raoul say, distinctly and emphatically:

"I shall carry off Christine Daae to-night."

This phrase was afterward repeated to M. Faure, the examining-magistrate. But no one ever knew exactly what passed between the two brothers at this interview. The servants declared that this was not their first quarrel. Their voices penetrated the wall; and it was always an actress called Christine Daae that was in question.

At breakfast—the early morning breakfast, which the count took in his study—Philippe sent for his brother. Raoul arrived silent and gloomy. The scene was a very short one. Philippe handed his brother a copy of the Epoque and said:

"Read that!"

The viscount read:

"The latest news in the Faubourg is that there is a promise of marriage between Mlle. Christine Daae, the opera-singer, and M. le Vicomte Raoul de Chagny. If the gossips are to be credited, Count Philippe has sworn that, for the first time on record, the Chagnys shall not keep their promise. But, as love is all-powerful, at the Opera as—and even more than—elsewhere, we wonder how Count Philippe intends to prevent the viscount, his brother, from leading the new Margarita to the altar. The two brothers are said to adore each other; but the count is curiously mistaken if he imagines that brotherly love will triumph over love pure and simple."

"You see, Raoul," said the count, "you are making us ridiculous! That little girl has turned your head with her ghost-stories."

The viscount had evidently repeated Christine's narrative to his brother, during the night. All that he now said was:

"Good-by, Philippe."

"Have you quite made up your mind? You are going to-night? With her?"

No reply.

"Surely you will not do anything so foolish? I *shall* know how to prevent you!"

"Good-by, Philippe," said the viscount again and left the room.

This scene was described to the examining-magistrate by the count himself, who did not see Raoul again until that evening, at the Opera, a few minutes before Christine's disappearance.

Raoul, in fact, devoted the whole day to his preparations for the flight. The horses, the carriage, the coachman, the provisions, the luggage, the money required for the journey, the road to be taken (he had resolved not to go by train, so as to throw the ghost off the scent): all this had to be settled and provided for; and it occupied him until nine o'clock at night.

At nine o'clock, a sort of traveling-barouche with the curtains of its windows close-down, took its place in the rank on the Rotunda side. It was drawn by two powerful horses driven by a coachman whose face was almost concealed in the long folds of a muffler. In front of this traveling-carriage were three broughams, belonging respectively to Carlotta, who had suddenly returned to Paris, to Sorelli and, at the head of the rank, to Comte Philippe de Chagny. No one left the barouche. The coachman remained on his box, and the three other coachmen remained on theirs.

A shadow in a long black cloak and a soft black felt hat passed along the pavement between the Rotunda and the carriages, examined the barouche carefully, went up to the horses and the coachman and then moved away without saying a word, The magistrate afterward believed that this shadow was that of the Vicomte Raoul de Chagny; but I do not agree, seeing that that evening, as every evening, the Vicomte de Chagny was wearing a tall hat, which hat, besides, was subsequently found. I am more inclined to think that the shadow was that of the ghost, who knew all about the whole affair, as the reader will soon perceive.

They were giving FAUST, as it happened, before a splendid house. The Faubourg was magnificently represented; and the paragraph in that morning's EPOQUE had already produced its effect, for all eyes were turned to the box in which Count Philippe sat alone, apparently in a very indifferent and careless frame of mind. The feminine element in the brilliant audience seemed curiously puzzled; and the viscount's absence gave rise to any amount of whispering behind the fans. Christine Daae met with a rather cold reception. That special audience could not forgive her for aiming so high.

The singer noticed this unfavorable attitude of a portion of the house and was confused by it.

The regular frequenters of the Opera, who pretended to know the truth about the viscount's love-story, exchanged significant smiles at certain passages in Margarita's part; and they made a show of turning and looking at Philippe de Chagny's box when Christine sang:

> "I wish I could but know who was he
> That addressed me,
> If he was noble, or, at least, what his name is."

The count sat with his chin on his hand and seemed to pay no attention to these manifestations. He kept his eyes fixed on the stage; but his thoughts appeared to be far away.

Christine lost her self-assurance more and more. She trembled. She felt on the verge of a breakdown . . . Carolus Fonta wondered if she was ill, if she could keep the stage until the end of the Garden Act. In the front of the house, people remembered the catastrophe that had befallen Carlotta at the end of that act and the historic "co-ack" which had momentarily interrupted her career in Paris.

Just then, Carlotta made her entrance in a box facing the stage, a sensational entrance. Poor Christine raised her eyes upon this fresh subject of excitement. She recognized her rival. She thought she saw a sneer on her lips. That saved her. She forgot everything, in order to triumph once more.

From that moment the prima donna sang with all her heart and soul. She tried to surpass all that she had done till then; and she succeeded. In the last act when she began the invocation to the angels, she made all the members of the audience feel as though they too had wings.

In the center of the amphitheater a man stood up and remained standing, facing the singer. It was Raoul.

"Holy angel, in Heaven blessed . . . "

And Christine, her arms outstretched, her throat filled with music, the glory of her hair falling over her bare shoulders, uttered the divine cry:

"My spirit longs with thee to rest!"

It was at that moment that the stage was suddenly plunged in darkness. It happened so quickly that the spectators hardly had time to utter a sound of stupefaction, for the gas at once lit up the stage again. But Christine Daae was no longer there!

What had become of her? What was that miracle? All exchanged glances without understanding, and the excitement at once reached its height. Nor was the tension any less great on the stage itself. Men rushed from the wings to the spot where Christine had been singing that very instant. The performance was interrupted amid the greatest disorder.

Where had Christine gone? What witchcraft had snatched her, away before the eyes of thousands of enthusiastic onlookers and from the arms of Carolus Fonta himself? It was as though the angels had really carried her up "to rest."

Raoul, still standing up in the amphitheater, had uttered a cry. Count Philippe had sprung to his feet in his box. People looked at the stage, at the count, at Raoul, and wondered if this curious event was connected in any way with the paragraph in that morning's paper. But Raoul hurriedly left his seat, the count disappeared from his box and, while the curtain was lowered, the subscribers rushed to the door that led behind the scenes. The rest of the audience waited amid an indescribable hubbub. Every one spoke at once. Every one tried to suggest an explanation of the extraordinary incident.

At last, the curtain rose slowly and Carolus Fonta stepped to the conductor's desk and, in a sad and serious voice, said:

"Ladies and gentlemen, an unprecedented event has taken place and thrown us into a state of the greatest alarm. Our sister-artist, Christine Daae, has disappeared before our eyes and nobody can tell us how!"

CHAPTER XIV

THE SINGULAR ATTITUDE OF A SAFETY-PIN

Behind the curtain, there was an indescribable crowd. Artists, scene-shifters, dancers, supers, choristers, subscribers were all asking questions, shouting and hustling one another.

"What became of her?"

"She's run away."

"With the Vicomte de Chagny, of course!"

"No, with the count!"

"Ah, here's Carlotta! Carlotta did the trick!"

"No, it was the ghost!" And a few laughed, especially as a careful examination of the trap-doors and boards had put the idea of an accident out of the question.

Amid this noisy throng, three men stood talking in a low voice and with despairing gestures. They were Gabriel, the chorus-master; Mercier, the acting-manager; and Remy, the secretary. They retired to a corner of the lobby by which the stage communicates with the wide passage leading to the foyer of the ballet. Here they stood and argued behind some enormous "properties."

"I knocked at the door," said Remy. "They did not answer. Perhaps they are not in the office. In any case, it's impossible to find out, for they took the keys with them."

"They" were obviously the managers, who had given orders, during the last entr'acte, that they were not to be disturbed on any pretext whatever. They were not in to anybody.

"All the same," exclaimed Gabriel, "a singer isn't run away with, from the middle of the stage, every day!"

"Did you shout that to them?" asked Mercier, impatiently.

"I'll go back again," said Remy, and disappeared at a run.

Thereupon the stage-manager arrived.

"Well, M. Mercier, are you coming? What are you two doing here? You're wanted, Mr. Acting-Manager."

"I refuse to know or to do anything before the commissary arrives," declared Mercier. "I have sent for Mifroid. We shall see when he comes!"

"And I tell you that you ought to go down to the organ at once."

"Not before the commissary comes."

"I've been down to the organ myself already."

"Ah! And what did you see?"

"Well, I saw nobody! Do you hear—nobody!"

"What do you want me to do down there for{sic}?"

"You're right!" said the stage-manager, frantically pushing his hands through his rebellious hair. "You're right! But there might be some one at the organ who could tell us how the stage came to be suddenly darkened. Now Mauclair is nowhere to be found. Do you understand that?"

Mauclair was the gas-man, who dispensed day and night at will on the stage of the Opera.

"Mauclair is not to be found!" repeated Mercier, taken aback. "Well, what about his assistants?"

"There's no Mauclair and no assistants! No one at the lights, I tell you! You can imagine," roared the stage-manager, "that that little girl must have been carried off by somebody else: she didn't run away by herself! It was a calculated stroke and we have to find out about it . . . And what are the managers doing all this time? . . . I gave orders that no one was to go down to the lights and I posted a fireman in front of the gas-man's box beside the organ. Wasn't that right?"

"Yes, yes, quite right, quite right. And now let's wait for the commissary."

The stage-manager walked away, shrugging his shoulders, fuming, muttering insults at those milksops who remained quietly squatting in a corner while the whole theater was topsyturvy{sic}.

Gabriel and Mercier were not so quiet as all that. Only they had received an order that paralyzed them. The managers were not to be disturbed on any account. Remy had violated that order and met with no success.

At that moment he returned from his new expedition, wearing a curiously startled air.

"Well, have you seen them?" asked Mercier.

"Moncharmin opened the door at last. His eyes were starting out of his head. I thought he meant to strike me. I could not get a word in; and what do you think he shouted at me? 'Have you a safety-pin?' 'No!' 'Well, then, clear out!' I tried to tell him that an unheard-of thing had happened on the stage, but he roared, 'A safety-pin! Give me a safety-pin at once!' A boy heard him—he was bellowing like a bull—ran up with a safety-pin and gave it to him; whereupon Moncharmin slammed the door in my face, and there you are!"

"And couldn't you have said, 'Christine Daae.'"

"I should like to have seen you in my place. He was foaming at the mouth. He thought of nothing but his safety-pin. I believe, if they hadn't brought him one on the spot, he would have fallen down in a fit! . . . Oh, all this isn't natural; and our managers are going mad! . . . Besides, it can't go on like this! I'm not used to being treated in that fashion!"

Suddenly Gabriel whispered:

"It's another trick of O. G.'s."

Rimy gave a grin, Mercier a sigh and seemed about to speak . . . but, meeting Gabriel's eye, said nothing.

However, Mercier felt his responsibility increased as the minutes passed without the managers' appearing; and, at last, he could stand it no longer.

"Look here, I'll go and hunt them out myself!"

Gabriel, turning very gloomy and serious, stopped him.

"Be careful what you're doing, Mercier! If they're staying in their office, it's probably because they have to! O. G. has more than one trick in his bag!"

But Mercier shook his head.

"That's their lookout! I'm going! If people had listened to me, the police would have known everything long ago!"

And he went.

"What's everything?" asked Remy. "What was there to tell the police? Why don't you answer, Gabriel? . . . Ah, so you know something! Well, you would do better to tell me, too, if you don't want me to shout out that you are all going mad! . . . Yes, that's what you are: mad!"

Gabriel put on a stupid look and pretended not to understand the private secretary's unseemly outburst.

"What 'something' am I supposed to know?" he said. "I don't know what you mean."

Remy began to lose his temper.

"This evening, Richard and Moncharmin were behaving like lunatics, here, between the acts."

"I never noticed it," growled Gabriel, very much annoyed.

"Then you're the only one! . . . Do you think that I didn't see them? . . . And that M. Parabise, the manager of the Credit Central, noticed nothing? . . . And that M. de La Borderie, the ambassador, has no eyes to see with? . . . Why, all the subscribers were pointing at our managers!"

"But what were our managers doing?" asked Gabriel, putting on his most innocent air.

"What were they doing? You know better than any one what they were doing! . . . You were there! . . . And you were watching them, you and Mercier! . . . And you were the only two who didn't laugh."

"I don't understand!"

Gabriel raised his arms and dropped them to his sides again, which gesture was meant to convey that the question did not interest him in the least. Remy continued:

"What is the sense of this new mania of theirs? *Why won't they have any one come near them now?*"

"What? *Won't they have any one come near them?*"

"*And they won't let any one touch them!*"

"Really? Have you noticed *That they won't let any one touch them*? That is certainly odd!"

"Oh, so you admit it! And high time, too! And *then, they walk backward!*"

"BACKWARD! You have seen our managers *walk backward*? Why, I thought that only crabs walked backward!"

"Don't laugh, Gabriel; don't laugh!"

"I'm not laughing," protested Gabriel, looking as solemn as a judge.

"Perhaps you can tell me this, Gabriel, as you're an intimate friend of the management: When I went up to M. Richard, outside the foyer, during the Garden interval, with my hand out before me, why did M. Moncharmin hurriedly whisper to me, 'Go away! Go away! Whatever you do, don't touch M. le Directeur!' Am I supposed to have an infectious disease?"

"It's incredible!"

"And, a little later, when M. de La Borderie went up to M. Richard, didn't you see M. Moncharmin fling himself between them and hear him exclaim, 'M. l'Ambassadeur I entreat you not to touch M. le Directeur'?"

"It's terrible! . . . And what was Richard doing meanwhile?"

"What was he doing? Why, you saw him! He turned about, *bowed in front of him, though there was nobody in front of him, and withdrew backward.*"

"*Backward?*"

"And Moncharmin, behind Richard, also turned about; that is, he described a semicircle behind Richard and also *walked backward!* . . . And they went *like that* to the staircase leading to the managers' office: BACKWARD, BACKWARD, BACKWARD! . . . Well, if they are not mad, will you explain what it means?"

"Perhaps they were practising a figure in the ballet," suggested Gabriel, without much conviction in his voice.

The secretary was furious at this wretched joke, made at so dramatic a moment. He knit his brows and contracted his lips. Then he put his mouth to Gabriel's ear:

"Don't be so sly, Gabriel. There are things going on for which you and Mercier are partly responsible."

"What do you mean?" asked Gabriel.

"Christine Daae is not the only one who suddenly disappeared to-night."

"Oh, nonsense!"

"There's no nonsense about it. Perhaps you can tell me why, when Mother Giry came down to the foyer just now, Mercier took her by the hand and hurried her away with him?"

"Really?" said Gabriel, "I never saw it."

"You did see it, Gabriel, for you went with Mercier and Mother Giry to Mercier's office. Since then, you and Mercier have been seen, but no one has seen Mother Giry."

"Do you think we've eaten her?"

"No, but you've locked her up in the office; and any one passing the office can hear her yelling, 'Oh, the scoundrels! Oh, the scoundrels!'"

At this point of this singular conversation, Mercier arrived, all out of breath.

"There!" he said, in a gloomy voice. "It's worse than ever! . . . I shouted, 'It's a serious matter! Open the door! It's I, Mercier.' I heard footsteps. The door opened and Moncharmin appeared. He was very pale. He said, 'What do you want?' I answered, 'Some one has run away with Christine Daae.' What do you think he said? 'And a good job, too!' And he shut the door, after putting this in my hand."

Mercier opened his hand; Remy and Gabriel looked.

"The safety-pin!" cried Remy.

"Strange! Strange!" muttered Gabriel, who could not help shivering.

Suddenly a voice made them all three turn round.

"I beg your pardon, gentlemen. Could you tell me where Christine Daae is?"

In spite of the seriousness of the circumstances, the absurdity of the question would have made them roar with laughter, if they had not caught sight of a face so sorrow-stricken that they were at once seized with pity. It was the Vicomte Raoul de Chagny.

CHAPTER XV

CHRISTINE! CHRISTINE!

Raoul's first thought, after Christine Daae's fantastic disappearance, was to accuse Erik. He no longer doubted the almost supernatural powers of the Angel of Music, in this domain of the Opera in which he had set up his empire. And Raoul rushed on the stage, in a mad fit of love and despair.

"Christine! Christine!" he moaned, calling to her as he felt that she must be calling to him from the depths of that dark pit to which the monster had carried her. "Christine! Christine!"

And he seemed to hear the girl's screams through the frail boards that separated him from her. He bent forward, he listened, . . . he wandered over the stage like a madman. Ah, to descend, to descend into that pit of darkness every entrance to which was closed to him, . . . for the stairs that led below the stage were forbidden to one and all that night!

"Christine! Christine! . . . "

People pushed him aside, laughing. They made fun of him. They thought the poor lover's brain was gone!

By what mad road, through what passages of mystery and darkness known to him alone had Erik dragged that pure-souled child to the awful haunt, with the Louis-Philippe room, opening out on the lake?

"Christine! Christine! . . . Why don't you answer? . . . Are you alive? . . . "

Hideous thoughts flashed through Raoul's congested brain. Of course, Erik must have discovered their secret, must have known that Christine had played him false. What a vengeance would be his!

And Raoul thought again of the yellow stars that had come, the night before, and roamed over his balcony. Why had he not put them out for good? There were some men's eyes that dilated in the darkness and shone like stars or like cats' eyes. Certainly Albinos, who seemed to have rabbits' eyes by day, had cats' eyes at night: everybody knew that! . . . Yes, yes, he had undoubtedly fired at Erik. Why had he not killed him? The monster had fled up the gutter-spout like a cat or a convict who—everybody knew that also— would scale the very skies, with the help of a gutter-spout . . . No doubt Erik was at that time contemplating some decisive step against Raoul, but he had been wounded and had escaped to turn against poor Christine instead.

Such were the cruel thoughts that haunted Raoul as he ran to the singer's dressing-room.

"Christine! Christine!"

Bitter tears scorched the boy's eyelids as he saw scattered over the furniture the clothes which his beautiful bride was to have worn at the hour of their flight. Oh, why had she refused to leave earlier?

Why had she toyed with the threatening catastrophe? Why toyed with the monster's heart? Why, in a final access of pity, had she insisted on flinging, as a last sop to that demon's soul, her divine song:

"Holy angel, in Heaven blessed,
My spirit longs with thee to rest!"

Raoul, his throat filled with sobs, oaths and insults, fumbled awkwardly at the great mirror that had opened one night, before his eyes, to let Christine pass to the murky dwelling below. He pushed, pressed, groped about, but the glass apparently obeyed no one but Erik . . . Perhaps actions were not enough with a glass of the kind? Perhaps he was expected to utter certain words? When he was a little boy, he had heard that there were things that obeyed the spoken word!

Suddenly, Raoul remembered something about a gate opening into the Rue Scribe, an underground passage running straight to the Rue Scribe from the lake . . . Yes, Christine had told him about that . . . And, when he found that the key was no longer in the box, he nevertheless ran to the Rue Scribe. Outside, in the street, he passed his trembling hands over the huge stones, felt for outlets . . . met with iron bars . . . were those they? . . . Or these? . . . Or could it be that air-hole? . . . He plunged his useless eyes through the bars . . . How dark it was in there! . . . He listened . . . All was silence! . . . He went round the building . . . and came to bigger bars, immense gates! . . . It was the entrance to the Cour de l'Administration.

Raoul rushed into the doorkeeper's lodge.

"I beg your pardon, madame, could you tell me where to find a gate or door, made of bars, iron bars, opening into the Rue Scribe . . . and leading to the lake? . . . You know the lake I mean? . . . Yes, the underground lake . . . under the Opera."

"Yes, sir, I know there is a lake under the Opera, but I don't know which door leads to it. I have never been there!"

"And the Rue Scribe, madame, the Rue Scribe? Have you never been to the Rue Scribe?"

The woman laughed, screamed with laughter! Raoul darted away, roaring with anger, ran up-stairs, four stairs at a time, down-stairs, rushed through the whole of the business side of the opera-house, found himself once more in the light of the stage.

He stopped, with his heart thumping in his chest: suppose Christine Daae had been found? He saw a group of men and asked:

"I beg your pardon, gentlemen. Could you tell me where Christine Daae is?"

And somebody laughed.

At the same moment the stage buzzed with a new sound and, amid a crowd of men in evening-dress, all talking and gesticulating together, appeared a man who seemed very calm and displayed a pleasant face, all pink and chubby-cheeked, crowned with curly hair and lit up by a pair of wonderfully serene blue eyes. Mercier, the acting-manager, called the Vicomte de Chagny's attention to him and said:

"This is the gentleman to whom you should put your question, monsieur. Let me introduce Mifroid, the commissary of police."

"Ah, M. le Vicomte de Chagny! Delighted to meet you, monsieur," said the commissary. "Would you mind coming with me? . . . And now where are the managers? . . . Where are the managers?"

Mercier did not answer, and Remy, the secretary, volunteered the information that the managers were locked up in their office and that they knew nothing as yet of what had happened.

"You don't mean to say so! Let us go up to the office!"

And M. Mifroid, followed by an ever-increasing crowd, turned toward the business side of the building. Mercier took advantage of the confusion to slip a key into Gabriel's hand:

"This is all going very badly," he whispered. "You had better let Mother Giry out."

And Gabriel moved away.

They soon came to the managers' door. Mercier stormed in vain: the door remained closed.

"Open in the name of the law!" commanded M. Mifroid, in a loud and rather anxious voice.

At last the door was opened. All rushed in to the office, on the commissary's heels.

Raoul was the last to enter. As he was about to follow the rest into the room, a hand was laid on his shoulder and he heard these words spoken in his ear:

"Erik's secrets concern no one but himself!"

He turned around, with a stifled exclamation. The hand that was laid on his shoulder was now placed on the lips of a person with an ebony skin, with eyes of jade and with an astrakhan cap on his head: the Persian! The stranger kept up the gesture that recommended discretion and then, at the moment when the astonished viscount was about to ask the reason of his mysterious intervention, bowed and disappeared.

CHAPTER XVI

MME. GIRY'S ASTOUNDING REVELATIONS AS TO HER PERSONAL RELATIONS WITH THE OPERA GHOST

Before following the commissary into the manager's office I must describe certain extraordinary occurrences that took place in that office which Remy and Mercier had vainly tried to enter and into which MM. Richard and Moncharmin had locked themselves with an object which the reader does not yet know, but which it is my duty, as an historian, to reveal without further postponement.

I have had occasion to say that the managers' mood had undergone a disagreeable change for some time past and to convey the fact that this change was due not only to the fall of the chandelier on the famous night of the gala performance.

The reader must know that the ghost had calmly been paid his first twenty thousand francs. Oh, there had been wailing and gnashing of teeth, indeed! And yet the thing had happened as simply as could be.

One morning, the managers found on their table an envelope addressed to "Monsieur O. G. (private)" and accompanied by a note from O. G. himself:

The time has come to carry out the clause in the memorandum-book. Please put twenty notes of a thousand francs each into this envelope, seal it with your own seal and hand it to Mme. Giry, who will do what is necessary.

The managers did not hesitate; without wasting time in asking how these confounded communications came to be delivered in an office which they were careful to keep locked, they seized this opportunity of laying hands, on the mysterious blackmailer. And, after telling the whole story, under the promise of secrecy, to Gabriel and Mercier, they put the twenty thousand francs into the envelope and without asking for explanations, handed it to Mme. Giry, who had been reinstated in her functions. The box-keeper displayed no astonishment. I need hardly say that she was well watched. She went straight to the ghost's box and placed the precious envelope on the little shelf attached to the ledge. The two managers, as well as Gabriel and Mercier, were hidden in such a way that they did not lose sight of the envelope for a second during the performance and even afterward, for, as the envelope had not moved, those who watched it did not move either; and

Mme. Giry went away while the managers, Gabriel and Mercier were still there. At last, they became tired of waiting and opened the envelope, after ascertaining that the seals had not been broken.

At first sight, Richard and Moncharmin thought that the notes were still there; but soon they perceived that they were not the same. The twenty real notes were gone and had been replaced by twenty notes, of the "Bank of St. Farce"![21]

The managers' rage and fright were unmistakable. Moncharmin wanted to send for the commissary of police, but Richard objected. He no doubt had a plan, for he said:

"Don't let us make ourselves ridiculous! All Paris would laugh at us. O. G. has won the first game: we will win the second."

He was thinking of the next month's allowance.

Nevertheless, they had been so absolutely tricked that they were bound to suffer a certain dejection. And, upon my word, it was not difficult to understand. We must not forget that the managers had an idea at the back of their minds, all the time, that this strange incident might be an unpleasant practical joke on the part of their predecessors and that it would not do to divulge it prematurely. On the other hand, Moncharmin was sometimes troubled with a suspicion of Richard himself, who occasionally took fanciful whims into his head. And so they were content to await events, while keeping an eye on Mother Giry. Richard would not have her spoken to.

"If she is a confederate," he said, "the notes are gone long ago. But, in my opinion, she is merely an idiot."

"She's not the only idiot in this business," said Moncharmin pensively.

"Well, who could have thought it?" moaned Richard. "But don't be afraid ... next time, I shall have taken my precautions."

The next time fell on the same day that beheld the disappearance of Christine Daae. In the morning, a note from the ghost reminded them that the money was due. It read:

Do just as you did last time. It went very well. Put the twenty thousand in the envelope and hand it to our excellent Mme. Giry.

And the note was accompanied by the usual envelope. They had only to insert the notes.

This was done about half an hour before the curtain rose on the first act of Faust. Richard showed the envelope to Moncharmin. Then he counted

2   Flash notes drawn on the "Bank of St. Farce" in France correspond
      with those drawn on the "Bank of Engraving" in England.—
      Translator's Note.

the twenty thousand-franc notes in front of him and put the notes into the envelope, but without closing it.

"And now," he said, "let's have Mother Giry in."

The old woman was sent for. She entered with a sweeping courtesy. She still wore her black taffeta dress, the color of which was rapidly turning to rust and lilac, to say nothing of the dingy bonnet. She seemed in a good temper. She at once said:

"Good evening, gentlemen! It's for the envelope, I suppose?"

"Yes, Mme. Giry," said Richard, most amiably. "For the envelope . . . and something else besides."

"At your service, M. Richard, at your service. And what is the something else, please?"

"First of all, Mme. Giry, I have a little question to put to you."

"By all means, M. Richard: Mme. Giry is here to answer you."

"Are you still on good terms with the ghost?"

"Couldn't be better, sir; couldn't be better."

"Ah, we are delighted . . . Look here, Mme. Giry," said Richard, in the tone of making an important confidence. "We may just as well tell you, among ourselves . . . you're no fool!"

"Why, sir," exclaimed the box-keeper, stopping the pleasant nodding of the black feathers in her dingy bonnet, "I assure you no one has ever doubted that!"

"We are quite agreed and we shall soon understand one another. The story of the ghost is all humbug, isn't it? . . . Well, still between ourselves, . . . it has lasted long enough."

Mme. Giry looked at the managers as though they were talking Chinese. She walked up to Richard's table and asked, rather anxiously:

"What do you mean? I don't understand."

"Oh, you, understand quite well. In any case, you've got to understand . . . And, first of all, tell us his name."

"Whose name?"

"The name of the man whose accomplice you are, Mme. Giry!"

"I am the ghost's accomplice? I? . . . His accomplice in what, pray?"

"You do all he wants."

"Oh! He's not very troublesome, you know."

"And does he still tip you?"

"I mustn't complain."

"How much does he give you for bringing him that envelope?"

"Ten francs."

"You poor thing! That's not much, is it?

"Why?"

"I'll tell you that presently, Mme. Giry. Just now we should like to know for what extraordinary reason you have given yourself body and soul, to this ghost . . . Mme. Giry's friendship and devotion are not to be bought for five francs or ten francs."

"That's true enough . . . And I can tell you the reason, sir. There's no disgrace about it . . . on the contrary."

"We're quite sure of that, Mme. Giry!"

"Well, it's like this . . . only the ghost doesn't like me to talk about his business."

"Indeed?" sneered Richard.

"But this is a matter that concerns myself alone . . . Well, it was in Box Five one evening, I found a letter addressed to myself, a sort of note written in red ink. I needn't read the letter to you sir; I know it by heart, and I shall never forget it if I live to be a hundred!"

And Mme. Giry, drawing herself up, recited the letter with touching eloquence:

MADAM:

1825. Mlle. Menetrier, leader of the ballet, became Marquise de Cussy.

1832. Mlle. Marie Taglioni, a dancer, became Comtesse Gilbert des Voisins.

1846. La Sota, a dancer, married a brother of the King of Spain.

1847. Lola Montes, a dancer, became the morganatic wife of King Louis of Bavaria and was created Countess of Landsfeld.

1848. Mlle. Maria, a dancer, became Baronne d'Herneville.

1870. Theresa Hessier, a dancer, married Dom Fernando, brother to the King of Portugal.

Richard and Moncharmin listened to the old woman, who, as she proceeded with the enumeration of these glorious nuptials, swelled out, took courage and, at last, in a voice bursting with pride, flung out the last sentence of the prophetic letter:

1885. Meg Giry, Empress!

Exhausted by this supreme effort, the box-keeper fell into a chair, saying: "Gentlemen, the letter was signed, 'Opera Ghost.' I had heard much of the ghost, but only half believed in him. From the day when he declared that my little Meg, the flesh of my flesh, the fruit of my womb, would be empress, I believed in him altogether."

And really it was not necessary to make a long study of Mme. Giry's excited features to understand what could be got out of that fine intellect with the two words "ghost" and "empress."

But who pulled the strings of that extraordinary puppet? That was the question.

"You have never seen him; he speaks to you and you believe all he says?" asked Moncharmin.

"Yes. To begin with, I owe it to him that my little Meg was promoted to be the leader of a row. I said to the ghost, 'If she is to be empress in 1885, there is no time to lose; she must become a leader at once.' He said, 'Look upon it as done.' And he had only a word to say to M. Poligny and the thing was done."

"So you see that M. Poligny saw him!"

"No, not any more than I did; but he heard him. The ghost said a word in his ear, you know, on the evening when he left Box Five, looking so dreadfully pale."

Moncharmin heaved a sigh. "What a business!" he groaned.

"Ah!" said Mme. Giry. "I always thought there were secrets between the ghost and M. Poligny. Anything that the ghost asked M. Poligny to do M. Poligny did. M. Poligny could refuse the ghost nothing."

"You hear, Richard: Poligny could refuse the ghost nothing."

"Yes, yes, I hear!" said Richard. "M. Poligny is a friend of the ghost; and, as Mme. Giry is a friend of M. Poligny, there we are! . . . But I don't care a hang about M. Poligny," he added roughly. "The only person whose fate really interests me is Mme. Giry . . . Mme. Giry, do you know what is in this envelope?"

"Why, of course not," she said.

"Well, look."

Mine. Giry looked into the envelope with a lackluster eye, which soon recovered its brilliancy.

"Thousand-franc notes!" she cried.

"Yes, Mme. Giry, thousand-franc notes! And you knew it!"

"I, sir? I? . . . I swear . . . "

"Don't swear, Mme. Giry! . . . And now I will tell you the second reason why I sent for you. Mme. Giry, I am going to have you arrested."

The two black feathers on the dingy bonnet, which usually affected the attitude of two notes of interrogation, changed into two notes of exclamation; as for the bonnet itself, it swayed in menace on the old lady's tempestuous chignon. Surprise, indignation, protest and dismay were furthermore displayed by little Meg's mother in a sort of extravagant movement of offended virtue, half bound, half slide, that brought her right under the nose of M. Richard, who could not help pushing back his chair.

"HAVE ME ARRESTED!"

The mouth that spoke those words seemed to spit the three teeth that were left to it into Richard's face.

M. Richard behaved like a hero. He retreated no farther. His threatening forefinger seemed already to be pointing out the keeper of Box Five to the absent magistrates.

"I am going to have you arrested, Mme. Giry, as a thief!"

"Say that again!"

And Mme. Giry caught Mr. Manager Richard a mighty box on the ear, before Mr. Manager Moncharmin had time to intervene. But it was not the withered hand of the angry old beldame that fell on the managerial ear, but the envelope itself, the cause of all the trouble, the magic envelope that opened with the blow, scattering the bank-notes, which escaped in a fantastic whirl of giant butterflies.

The two managers gave a shout, and the same thought made them both go on their knees, feverishly, picking up and hurriedly examining the precious scraps of paper.

"Are they still genuine, Moncharmin?"

"Are they still genuine, Richard?"

"Yes, they are still genuine!"

Above their heads, Mme. Giry's three teeth were clashing in a noisy contest, full of hideous interjections. But all that could be clearly distinguished was this *Leit-Motif*:

"I, a thief! . . . I, a thief, I?"

She choked with rage. She shouted:

"I never heard of such a thing!"

And, suddenly, she darted up to Richard again.

"In any case," she yelped, "you, M. Richard, ought to know better than I where the twenty thousand francs went to!"

"I?" asked Richard, astounded. "And how should I know?"

Moncharmin, looking severe and dissatisfied, at once insisted that the good lady should explain herself.

"What does this mean, Mme. Giry?" he asked. "And why do you say that M. Richard ought to know better than you where the twenty-thousand francs went to?"

As for Richard, who felt himself turning red under Moncharmin's eyes, he took Mme. Giry by the wrist and shook it violently. In a voice growling and rolling like thunder, he roared:

"Why should I know better than you where the twenty-thousand francs went to? Why? Answer me!"

"Because they went into your pocket!" gasped the old woman, looking at him as if he were the devil incarnate.

Richard would have rushed upon Mme. Giry, if Moncharmin had not stayed his avenging hand and hastened to ask her, more gently:

"How can you suspect my partner, M. Richard, of putting twenty-thousand francs in his pocket?"

"I never said that," declared Mme. Giry, "seeing that it was myself who put the twenty-thousand francs into M. Richard's pocket." And she added, under her voice, "There! It's out! . . . And may the ghost forgive me!"

Richard began bellowing anew, but Moncharmin authoritatively ordered him to be silent.

"Allow me! Allow me! Let the woman explain herself. Let me question her." And he added: "It is really astonishing that you should take up such a tone! . . . We are on the verge of clearing up the whole mystery. And you're in a rage! . . . You're wrong to behave like that . . . I'm enjoying myself immensely."

Mme. Giry, like the martyr that she was, raised her head, her face beaming with faith in her own innocence.

"You tell me there were twenty-thousand francs in the envelope which I put into M. Richard's pocket; but I tell you again that I knew nothing about it . . . Nor M. Richard either, for that matter!"

"Aha!" said Richard, suddenly assuming a swaggering air which Moncharmin did not like. "I knew nothing either! You put twenty-thousand francs in my pocket and I knew nothing either! I am very glad to hear it, Mme. Giry!"

"Yes," the terrible dame agreed, "yes, it's true. We neither of us knew anything. But you, you must have ended by finding out!"

Richard would certainly have swallowed Mme. Giry alive, if Moncharmin had not been there! But Moncharmin protected her. He resumed his questions:

"What sort of envelope did you put in M. Richard's pocket? It was not the one which we gave you, the one which you took to Box Five before our eyes; and yet that was the one which contained the twenty-thousand francs."

"I beg your pardon. The envelope which M. le Directeur gave me was the one which I slipped into M. le Directeur's pocket," explained Mme. Giry. "The one which I took to the ghost's box was another envelope, just like it, which the ghost gave me beforehand and which I hid up my sleeve."

So saying, Mme. Giry took from her sleeve an envelope ready prepared and similarly addressed to that containing the twenty-thousand francs. The managers took it from her. They examined it and saw that it was fastened with seals stamped with their own managerial seal. They opened it. It contained twenty Bank of St. Farce notes like those which had so much astounded them the month before.

"How simple!" said Richard.

"How simple!" repeated Moncharmin. And he continued with his eyes fixed upon Mme. Giry, as though trying to hypnotize her.

"So it was the ghost who gave you this envelope and told you to substitute it for the one which we gave you? And it was the ghost who told you to put the other into M. Richard's pocket?"

"Yes, it was the ghost."

"Then would you mind giving us a specimen of your little talents? Here is the envelope. Act as though we knew nothing."

"As you please, gentlemen."

Mme. Giry took the envelope with the twenty notes inside it and made for the door. She was on the point of going out when the two managers rushed at her:

"Oh, no! Oh, no! We're not going to be 'done' a second time! Once bitten, twice shy!"

"I beg your pardon, gentlemen," said the old woman, in self-excuse, "you told me to act as though you knew nothing . . . Well, if you knew nothing, I should go away with your envelope!"

"And then how would you slip it into my pocket?" argued Richard, whom Moncharmin fixed with his left eye, while keeping his right on Mme. Giry: a proceeding likely to strain his sight, but Moncharmin was prepared to go to any length to discover the truth.

"I am to slip it into your pocket when you least expect it, sir. You know that I always take a little turn behind the scenes, in the course of the evening, and I often go with my daughter to the ballet-foyer, which I am entitled to do, as her mother; I bring her her shoes, when the ballet is about to begin . . . in fact, I come and go as I please . . . The subscribers come and go too . . . So do you, sir . . . There are lots of people about . . . I go behind you and slip the envelope into the tail-pocket of your dress-coat . . . There's no witchcraft about that!"

"No witchcraft!" growled Richard, rolling his eyes like Jupiter Tonans. "No witchcraft! Why, I've just caught you in a lie, you old witch!"

Mme. Giry bristled, with her three teeth sticking out of her mouth.

"And why, may I ask?"

"Because I spent that evening watching Box Five and the sham envelope which you put there. I did not go to the ballet-foyer for a second."

"No, sir, and I did not give you the envelope that evening, but at the next performance . . . on the evening when the under-secretary of state for fine arts . . ."

At these words, M. Richard suddenly interrupted Mme. Giry:

"Yes, that's true, I remember now! The under-secretary went behind the scenes. He asked for me. I went down to the ballet-foyer for a moment. I was on the foyer steps . . . The under-secretary and his chief clerk were in the foyer itself. I suddenly turned around . . . you had passed behind me, Mme. Giry . . . You seemed to push against me . . . Oh, I can see you still, I can see you still!"

"Yes, that's it, sir, that's it. I had just finished my little business. That pocket of yours, sir, is very handy!"

And Mme. Giry once more suited the action to the word, She passed behind M. Richard and, so nimbly that Moncharmin himself was impressed by it, slipped the envelope into the pocket of one of the tails of M. Richard's dress-coat.

"Of course!" exclaimed Richard, looking a little pale. "It's very clever of O. G. The problem which he had to solve was this: how to do away with any dangerous intermediary between the man who gives the twenty-thousand francs and the man who receives it. And by far the best thing he could hit upon was to come and take the money from my pocket without my noticing it, as I myself did not know that it was there. It's wonderful!"

"Oh, wonderful, no doubt!" Moncharmin agreed. "Only, you forget, Richard, that I provided ten-thousand francs of the twenty and that nobody put anything in my pocket!"

CHAPTER XVII

THE SAFETY-PIN AGAIN

Moncharmin's last phrase so dearly expressed the suspicion in which he now held his partner that it was bound to cause a stormy explanation, at the end of which it was agreed that Richard should yield to all Moncharmin's wishes, with the object of helping him to discover the miscreant who was victimizing them.

This brings us to the interval after the Garden Act, with the strange conduct observed by M. Remy and those curious lapses from the dignity that might be expected of the managers. It was arranged between Richard and Moncharmin, first, that Richard should repeat the exact movements which he had made on the night of the disappearance of the first twenty-thousand francs; and, second, that Moncharmin should not for an instant lose sight of Richard's coat-tail pocket, into which Mme. Giry was to slip the twenty-thousand francs.

M. Richard went and placed himself at the identical spot where he had stood when he bowed to the under-secretary for fine arts. M. Moncharmin took up his position a few steps behind him.

Mme. Giry passed, rubbed up against M. Richard, got rid of her twenty-thousand francs in the manager's coat-tail pocket and disappeared . . . Or rather she was conjured away. In accordance with the instructions received from Moncharmin a few minutes earlier, Mercier took the good lady to the acting-manager's office and turned the key on her, thus making it impossible for her to communicate with her ghost.

Meanwhile, M. Richard was bending and bowing and scraping and walking backward, just as if he had that high and mighty minister, the under-secretary for fine arts, before him. Only, though these marks of politeness would have created no astonishment if the under-secretary of state had really been in front of M. Richard, they caused an easily comprehensible amazement to the spectators of this very natural but quite inexplicable scene when M. Richard had no body in front of him.

M. Richard bowed . . . to nobody; bent his back . . . before nobody; and walked backward . . . before nobody . . . And, a few steps behind him, M. Moncharmin did the same thing that he was doing in addition to pushing away M. Remy and begging M. de La Borderie, the ambassador, and the manager of the Credit Central "not to touch M. le Directeur."

Moncharmin, who had his own ideas, did not want Richard to come to him presently, when the twenty-thousand francs were gone, and say:

"Perhaps it was the ambassador . . . or the manager of the Credit Central . . . or Remy."

The more so as, at the time of the first scene, as Richard himself admitted, Richard had met nobody in that part of the theater after Mme. Giry had brushed up against him . . .

Having begun by walking backward in order to bow, Richard continued to do so from prudence, until he reached the passage leading to the offices of the management. In this way, he was constantly watched by Moncharmin from behind and himself kept an eye on any one approaching from the front. Once more, this novel method of walking behind the scenes, adopted by the managers of our National Academy of Music, attracted attention; but the managers themselves thought of nothing but their twenty-thousand francs.

On reaching the half-dark passage, Richard said to Moncharmin, in a low voice:

"I am sure that nobody has touched me . . . You had now better keep at some distance from me and watch me till I come to door of the office: it is better not to arouse suspicion and we can see anything that happens."

But Moncharmin replied. "No, Richard, no! You walk ahead and I'll walk immediately behind you! I won't leave you by a step!"

"But, in that case," exclaimed Richard, "they will never steal our twenty-thousand francs!"

"I should hope not, indeed!" declared Moncharmin.

"Then what we are doing is absurd!"

"We are doing exactly what we did last time . . . Last time, I joined you as you were leaving the stage and followed close behind you down this passage."

"That's true!" sighed Richard, shaking his head and passively obeying Moncharmin.

Two minutes later, the joint managers locked themselves into their office. Moncharmin himself put the key in his pocket:

"We remained locked up like this, last time," he said, "until you left the Opera to go home."

"That's so. No one came and disturbed us, I suppose?"

"No one."

"Then," said Richard, who was trying to collect his memory, "then I must certainly have been robbed on my way home from the Opera."

"No," said Moncharmin in a drier tone than ever, "no, that's impossible.

For I dropped you in my cab. The twenty-thousand francs disappeared at your place: there's not a shadow of a doubt about that."

"It's incredible!" protested Richard. "I am sure of my servants . . . and if one of them had done it, he would have disappeared since."

Moncharmin shrugged his shoulders, as though to say that he did not wish to enter into details, and Richard began to think that Moncharmin was treating him in a very insupportable fashion.

"Moncharmin, I've had enough of this!"

"Richard, I've had too much of it!"

"Do you dare to suspect me?"

"Yes, of a silly joke."

"One doesn't joke with twenty-thousand francs."

"That's what I think," declared Moncharmin, unfolding a newspaper and ostentatiously studying its contents.

"What are you doing?" asked Richard. "Are you going to read the paper next?"

"Yes, Richard, until I take you home."

"Like last time?"

"Yes, like last time."

Richard snatched the paper from Moncharmin's hands. Moncharmin stood up, more irritated than ever, and found himself faced by an exasperated Richard, who, crossing his arms on his chest, said:

"Look here, I'm thinking of this, *I'm thinking of what I might think* if, like last time, after my spending the evening alone with you, you brought me home and if, at the moment of parting, I perceived that twenty-thousand francs had disappeared from my coat-pocket . . . like last time."

"And what might you think?" asked Moncharmin, crimson with rage.

"I might think that, as you hadn't left me by a foot's breadth and as, by your own wish, you were the only one to approach me, like last time, I might think that, if that twenty-thousand francs was no longer in my pocket, it stood a very good chance of being in yours!"

Moncharmin leaped up at the suggestion.

"Oh!" he shouted. "A safety-pin!"

"What do you want a safety-pin for?"

"To fasten you up with! . . . A safety-pin! . . . A safety-pin!"

"You want to fasten me with a safety-pin?"

"Yes, to fasten you to the twenty-thousand francs! Then, whether it's here, or on the drive from here to your place, or at your place, you will feel the hand that pulls at your pocket and you will see if it's mine! Oh, so you're suspecting me now, are you? A safety-pin!"

And that was the moment when Moncharmin opened the door on the passage and shouted:

"A safety-pin! . . . somebody give me a safety-pin!"

And we also know how, at the same moment, Remy, who had no safety-pin, was received by Moncharmin, while a boy procured the pin so eagerly longed for. And what happened was this: Moncharmin first locked the door again. Then he knelt down behind Richard's back.

"I hope," he said, "that the notes are still there?"

"So do I," said Richard.

"The real ones?" asked Moncharmin, resolved not to be "had" this time.

"Look for yourself," said Richard. "I refuse to touch them."

Moncharmin took the envelope from Richard's pocket and drew out the bank-notes with a trembling hand, for, this time, in order frequently to make sure of the presence of the notes, he had not sealed the envelope nor even fastened it. He felt reassured on finding that they were all there and quite genuine. He put them back in the tail-pocket and pinned them with great care. Then he sat down behind Richard's coat-tails and kept his eyes fixed on them, while Richard, sitting at his writing-table, did not stir.

"A little patience, Richard," said Moncharmin. "We have only a few minutes to wait . . . The clock will soon strike twelve. Last time, we left at the last stroke of twelve."

"Oh, I shall have all the patience necessary!"

The time passed, slow, heavy, mysterious, stifling. Richard tried to laugh.

"I shall end by believing in the omnipotence of the ghost," he said. "Just now, don't you find something uncomfortable, disquieting, alarming in the atmosphere of this room?"

"You're quite right," said Moncharmin, who was really impressed.

"The ghost!" continued Richard, in a low voice, as though fearing lest he should be overheard by invisible ears. "The ghost! Suppose, all the same, it were a ghost who puts the magic envelopes on the table . . . who talks in Box Five . . . who killed Joseph Buquet . . . who unhooked the chandelier . . . and who robs us! For, after all, after all, after all, there is no one here except you and me, and, if the notes disappear and neither you nor I have anything to do with it, well, we shall have to believe in the ghost . . . in the ghost."

At that moment, the clock on the mantlepiece gave its warning click and the first stroke of twelve struck.

The two managers shuddered. The perspiration streamed from their foreheads. The twelfth stroke sounded strangely in their ears.

When the clock stopped, they gave a sigh and rose from their chairs.

"I think we can go now," said Moncharmin.

"I think so," Richard a agreed.

"Before we go, do you mind if I look in your pocket?"

"But, of course, Moncharmin, *you must*! . . . Well?" he asked, as Moncharmin was feeling at the pocket.

"Well, I can feel the pin."

"Of course, as you said, we can't be robbed without noticing it."

But Moncharmin, whose hands were still fumbling, bellowed:

"I can feel the pin, but I can't feel the notes!"

"Come, no joking, Moncharmin! . . . This isn't the time for it."

"Well, feel for yourself."

Richard tore off his coat. The two managers turned the pocket inside out. *The pocket was empty.* And the curious thing was that the pin remained, stuck in the same place.

Richard and Moncharmin turned pale. There was no longer any doubt about the witchcraft.

"The ghost!" muttered Moncharmin.

But Richard suddenly sprang upon his partner.

"No one but you has touched my pocket! Give me back my twenty-thousand francs! . . . Give me back my twenty-thousand francs! . . . "

"On my soul," sighed Moncharmin, who was ready to swoon, "on my soul, I swear that I haven't got it!"

Then somebody knocked at the door. Moncharmin opened it automatically, seemed hardly to recognize Mercier, his business-manager, exchanged a few words with him, without knowing what he was saying and, with an unconscious movement, put the safety-pin, for which he had no further use, into the hands of his bewildered subordinate . . .

CHAPTER XVIII

THE COMMISSARY,
THE VISCOUNT AND THE PERSIAN

The first words of the commissary of police, on entering the managers' office, were to ask after the missing prima donna.

"Is Christine Daae here?"

"Christine Daae here?" echoed Richard. "No. Why?"

As for Moncharmin, he had not the strength left to utter a word.

Richard repeated, for the commissary and the compact crowd which had followed him into the office observed an impressive silence.

"Why do you ask if Christine Daae is here, *M. Le Commissaire*?"

"Because she has to be found," declared the commissary of police solemnly.

"What do you mean, she has to be found? Has she disappeared?"

"In the middle of the performance!"

"In the middle of the performance? This is extraordinary!"

"Isn't it? And what is quite as extraordinary is that you should first learn it from me!"

"Yes," said Richard, taking his head in his hands and muttering. "What is this new business? Oh, it's enough to make a man send in his resignation!"

And he pulled a few hairs out of his mustache without even knowing what he was doing.

"So she . . . so she disappeared in the middle of the performance?" he repeated.

"Yes, she was carried off in the Prison Act, at the moment when she was invoking the aid of the angels; but I doubt if she was carried off by an angel."

"And I am sure that she was!"

Everybody looked round. A young man, pale and trembling with excitement, repeated:

"I am sure of it!"

"Sure of what?" asked Mifroid.

"That Christine Daae was carried off by an angel, *M. Le Commissaire* and I can tell you his name."

"Aha, M. le Vicomte de Chagny! So you maintain that Christine Daae was carried off by an angel: an angel of the Opera, no doubt?"

"Yes, monsieur, by an angel of the Opera; and I will tell you where he lives . . . when we are alone."

"You are right, monsieur."

And the commissary of police, inviting Raoul to take a chair, cleared the room of all the rest, excepting the managers.

Then Raoul spoke:

"M. le Commissaire, the angel is called Erik, he lives in the Opera and he is the Angel of Music!"

"The Angel of Music! Really! That is very curious! . . . The Angel of Music!" And, turning to the managers, M. Mifroid asked, "Have you an Angel of Music on the premises, gentlemen?"

Richard and Moncharmin shook their heads, without even speaking.

"Oh," said the viscount, "those gentlemen have heard of the Opera ghost. Well, I am in a position to state that the Opera ghost and the Angel of Music are one and the same person; and his real name is Erik."

M. Mifroid rose and looked at Raoul attentively.

"I beg your pardon, monsieur but is it your intention to make fun of the law? And, if not, what is all this about the Opera ghost?"

"I say that these gentlemen have heard of him."

"Gentlemen, it appears that you know the Opera ghost?"

Richard rose, with the remaining hairs of his mustache in his hand.

"No, M. Commissary, no, we do not know him, but we wish that we did, for this very evening he has robbed us of twenty-thousand francs!"

And Richard turned a terrible look on Moncharmin, which seemed to say:

"Give me back the twenty-thousand francs, or I'll tell the whole story."

Moncharmin understood what he meant, for, with a distracted gesture, he said:

"Oh, tell everything and have done with it!"

As for Mifroid, he looked at the managers and at Raoul by turns and wondered whether he had strayed into a lunatic asylum. He passed his hand through his hair.

"A ghost," he said, "who, on the same evening, carries off an opera-singer and steals twenty-thousand francs is a ghost who must have his hands very full! If you don't mind, we will take the questions in order. The singer first, the twenty-thousand francs after. Come, M. de Chagny, let us try to talk seriously. You believe that Mlle. Christine Daae has been carried off by an individual called Erik. Do you know this person? Have you seen him?"

"Yes."

"Where?"

"In a church yard."

M. Mifroid gave a start, began to scrutinize Raoul again and said:

"Of course! . . . That's where ghosts usually hang out! . . . And what were you doing in that churchyard?"

"Monsieur," said Raoul, "I can quite understand how absurd my replies must seem to you. But I beg you to believe that I am in full possession of my faculties. The safety of the person dearest to me in the world is at stake. I should like to convince you in a few words, for time is pressing and every minute is valuable. Unfortunately, if I do not tell you the strangest story that ever was from the beginning, you will not believe me. I will tell you all I know about the Opera ghost, M. Commissary. Alas, I do not know much! . . . "

"Never mind, go on, go on!" exclaimed Richard and Moncharmin, suddenly greatly interested.

Unfortunately for their hopes of learning some detail that could put them on the track of their hoaxer, they were soon compelled to accept the fact that M. Raoul de Chagny had completely lost his head. All that story about Perros-Guirec, death's heads and enchanted violins, could only have taken birth in the disordered brain of a youth mad with love. It was evident, also, that Mr. Commissary Mifroid shared their view; and the magistrate would certainly have cut short the incoherent narrative if circumstances had not taken it upon themselves to interrupt it.

The door opened and a man entered, curiously dressed in an enormous frock-coat and a tall hat, at once shabby and shiny, that came down to his ears. He went up to the commissary and spoke to him in a whisper. It was doubtless a detective come to deliver an important communication.

During this conversation, M. Mifroid did not take his eyes off Raoul. At last, addressing him, he said:

"Monsieur, we have talked enough about the ghost. We will now talk about yourself a little, if you have no objection: you were to carry off Mlle. Christine Daae to-night?"

"Yes, M. le Commissaire."

"After the performance?"

"Yes, M. le Commissaire."

"All your arrangements were made?"

"Yes, M. le Commissaire."

"The carriage that brought you was to take you both away . . . There were fresh horses in readiness at every stage . . . "

"That is true, M. le Commissaire."

"And nevertheless your carriage is still outside the Rotunda awaiting your orders, is it not?"

"Yes, M. le Commissaire."

"Did you know that there were three other carriages there, in addition to yours?"

"I did not pay the least attention."

"They were the carriages of Mlle. Sorelli, which could not find room in the Cour de l'Administration; of Carlotta; and of your brother, M. le Comte de Chagny . . . "

"Very likely . . . "

"What is certain is that, though your carriage and Sorelli's and Carlotta's are still there, by the Rotunda pavement, M. le Comte de Chagny's carriage is gone."

"This has nothing to say to . . . "

"I beg your pardon. Was not M. le Comte opposed to your marriage with Mlle. Daae?"

"That is a matter that only concerns the family."

"You have answered my question: he was opposed to it . . . and that was why you were carrying Christine Daae out of your brother's reach . . . Well, M. de Chagny, allow me to inform you that your brother has been smarter than you! It is he who has carried off Christine Daae!"

"Oh, impossible!" moaned Raoul, pressing his hand to his heart. "Are you sure?"

"Immediately after the artist's disappearance, which was procured by means which we have still to ascertain, he flung into his carriage, which drove right across Paris at a furious pace."

"Across Paris?" asked poor Raoul, in a hoarse voice. "What do you mean by across Paris?"

"Across Paris and out of Paris . . . by the Brussels road."

"Oh," cried the young man, "I shall catch them!" And he rushed out of the office.

"And bring her back to us!" cried the commisary gaily . . . "Ah, that's a trick worth two of the Angel of Music's!"

And, turning to his audience, M. Mifroid delivered a little lecture on police methods.

"I don't know for a moment whether M. le Comte de Chagny has really carried Christine Daae off or not . . . but I want to know and I believe that, at this moment, no one is more anxious to inform us than his brother . . . And now he is flying in pursuit of him! He is my chief auxiliary! This, gentlemen, is the art of the police, which is believed to be so complicated and which, nevertheless appears so simple as soon its you see that it consists in getting your work done by people who have nothing to do with the police."

But M. le Commissaire de Police Mifroid would not have been quite so satisfied with himself if he had known that the rush of his rapid emissary was stopped at the entrance to the very first corridor. A tall figure blocked Raoul's way.

"Where are you going so fast, M. de Chagny?" asked a voice.

Raoul impatiently raised his eyes and recognized the astrakhan cap of an hour ago. He stopped:

"It's you!" he cried, in a feverish voice. "You, who know Erik's secrets and don't want me to speak of them. Who are you?"

"You know who I am! . . . I am the Persian!"

CHAPTER XIX

THE VISCOUNT AND THE PERSIAN

Raoul now remembered that his brother had once shown him that mysterious person, of whom nothing was known except that he was a Persian and that he lived in a little old-fashioned flat in the Rue de Rivoli.

The man with the ebony skin, the eyes of jade and the astrakhan cap bent over Raoul.

"I hope, M. de Chagny," he said, "that you have not betrayed Erik's secret?"

"And why should I hesitate to betray that monster, sir?" Raoul rejoined haughtily, trying to shake off the intruder. "Is he your friend, by any chance?"

"I hope that you said nothing about Erik, sir, because Erik's secret is also Christine Daae's and to talk about one is to talk about the other!"

"Oh, sir," said Raoul, becoming more and more impatient, "you seem to know about many things that interest me; and yet I have no time to listen to you!"

"Once more, M. de Chagny, where are you going so fast?"

"Can not you guess? To Christine Daae's assistance . . . "

"Then, sir, stay here, for Christine Daae is here!"

"With Erik?"

"With Erik."

"How do you know?"

"I was at the performance and no one in the world but Erik could contrive an abduction like that! . . . Oh," he said, with a deep sigh, "I recognized the monster's touch! . . . "

"You know him then?"

The Persian did not reply, but heaved a fresh sigh.

"Sir," said Raoul, "I do not know what your intentions are, but can you do anything to help me? I mean, to help Christine Daae?"

"I think so, M. de Chagny, and that is why I spoke to you."

"What can you do?"

"Try to take you to her . . . and to him."

"If you can do me that service, sir, my life is yours! . . . One word more: the commissary of police tells me that Christine Daae has been carried off by my brother, Count Philippe."

"Oh, M. de Chagny, I don't believe a word of it."

"It's not possible, is it?"

"I don't know if it is possible or not; but there are ways and ways of carrying people off; and M. le Comte Philippe has never, as far as I know, had anything to do with witchcraft."

"Your arguments are convincing, sir, and I am a fool! . . . Oh, let us make haste! I place myself entirely in your hands! . . . How should I not believe you, when you are the only one to believe me . . . when you are the only one not to smile when Erik's name is mentioned?"

And the young man impetuously seized the Persian's hands. They were ice-cold.

"Silence!" said the Persian, stopping and listening to the distant sounds of the theater. "We must not mention that name here. Let us say 'he' and 'him;' then there will be less danger of attracting his attention."

"Do you think he is near us?"

"It is quite possible, Sir, if he is not, at this moment, with his victim, *in the house on the lake*."

"Ah, so you know that house too?"

"If he is not there, he may be here, in this wall, in this floor, in this ceiling! . . . Come!"

And the Persian, asking Raoul to deaden the sound of his footsteps, led him down passages which Raoul had never seen before, even at the time when Christine used to take him for walks through that labyrinth.

"If only Darius has come!" said the Persian.

"Who is Darius?"

"Darius? My servant."

They were now in the center of a real deserted square, an immense apartment ill-lit by a small lamp. The Persian stopped Raoul and, in the softest of whispers, asked:

"What did you say to the commissary?"

"I said that Christine Daae's abductor was the Angel of Music, *alias* the Opera ghost, and that the real name was . . . "

"Hush! . . . And did he believe you?"

"No."

"He attached no importance to what you said?"

"No."

"He took you for a bit of a madman?"

"Yes."

"So much the better!" sighed the Persian.

And they continued their road. After going up and down several staircases which Raoul had never seen before, the two men found themselves in front of a door which the Persian opened with a master-key. The Persian and Raoul were both, of course, in dress-clothes; but, whereas Raoul had a tall hat, the Persian wore the astrakhan cap which I have already mentioned. It was an infringement of the rule which insists upon the tall hat behind the scenes; but in France foreigners are allowed every license: the Englishman his traveling-cap, the Persian his cap of astrakhan.

"Sir," said the Persian, "your tall hat will be in your way: you would do well to leave it in the dressing-room."

"What dressing-room?" asked Raoul.

"Christine Daae's."

And the Persian, letting Raoul through the door which he had just opened, showed him the actress' room opposite. They were at the end of the passage the whole length of which Raoul had been accustomed to traverse before knocking at Christine's door.

"How well you know the Opera, sir!"

"Not so well as 'he' does!" said the Persian modestly.

And he pushed the young man into Christine's dressing-room, which was as Raoul had left it a few minutes earlier.

Closing the door, the Persian went to a very thin partition that separated the dressing-room from a big lumber-room next to it. He listened and then coughed loudly.

There was a sound of some one stirring in the lumber-room; and, a few seconds later, a finger tapped at the door.

"Come in," said the Persian.

A man entered, also wearing an astrakhan cap and dressed in a long overcoat. He bowed and took a richly carved case from under his coat, put it on the dressing-table, bowed once again and went to the door.

"Did no one see you come in, Darius?"

"No, master."

"Let no one see you go out."

The servant glanced down the passage and swiftly disappeared.

The Persian opened the case. It contained a pair of long pistols.

"When Christine Daae was carried off, sir, I sent word to my servant to bring me these pistols. I have had them a long time and they can be relied upon."

"Do you mean to fight a duel?" asked the young man.

"It will certainly be a duel which we shall have to fight," said the other, examining the priming of his pistols. "And what a duel!" Handing one of the pistols to Raoul, he added, "In this duel, we shall be two to one; but you must be prepared for everything, for we shall be fighting the most terrible adversary that you can imagine. But you love Christine Daae, do you not?"

"I worship the ground she stands on! But you, sir, who do not love her, tell me why I find you ready to risk your life for her! You must certainly hate Erik!"

"No, sir," said the Persian sadly, "I do not hate him. If I hated him, he would long ago have ceased doing harm."

"Has he done you harm?"

"I have forgiven him the harm which he has done me."

"I do not understand you. You treat him as a monster, you speak of his crime, he has done you harm and I find in you the same inexplicable pity that drove me to despair when I saw it in Christine!"

The Persian did not reply. He fetched a stool and set it against the wall facing the great mirror that filled the whole of the wall-space opposite. Then he climbed on the stool and, with his nose to the wallpaper, seemed to be looking for something.

"Ah," he said, after a long search, "I have it!" And, raising his finger above his head, he pressed against a corner in the pattern of the paper. Then he turned round and jumped off the stool:

"In half a minute," he said, "he shall be *on his road*!" and crossing the whole of the dressing-room he felt the great mirror.

"No, it is not yielding yet," he muttered.

"Oh, are we going out by the mirror?" asked Raoul. "Like Christine Daae."

"So you knew that Christine Daae went out by that mirror?"

"She did so before my eyes, sir! I was hidden behind the curtain of the inner room and I saw her vanish not by the glass, but in the glass!"

"And what did you do?"

"I thought it was an aberration of my senses, a mad dream.

"Or some new fancy of the ghost's!" chuckled the Persian. "Ah, M. de Chagny," he continued, still with his hand on the mirror, "would that we had to do with a ghost! We could then leave our pistols in their case . . . Put down your hat, please . . . there . . . and now cover your shirt-front as much as you can with your coat . . . as I am doing . . . Bring the lapels forward . . . turn up the collar . . . We must make ourselves as invisible as possible."

Bearing against the mirror, after a short silence, he said:

"It takes some time to release the counterbalance, when you press on the spring from the inside of the room. It is different when you are behind the wall and can act directly on the counterbalance. Then the mirror turns at once and is moved with incredible rapidity."

"What counterbalance?" asked Raoul.

"Why, the counterbalance that lifts the whole of this wall on to its pivot. You surely don't expect it to move of itself, by enchantment! If you watch, you will see the mirror first rise an inch or two and then shift an inch or two from left to right. It will then be on a pivot and will swing round."

"It's not turning!" said Raoul impatiently.

"Oh, wait! You have time enough to be impatient, sir! The mechanism has obviously become rusty, or else the spring isn't working . . . Unless it is something else," added the Persian, anxiously.

"What?"

"He may simply have cut the cord of the counterbalance and blocked the whole apparatus."

"Why should he? He does not know that we are coming this way!"

"I dare say he suspects it, for he knows that I understand the system."

"It's not turning! . . . And Christine, sir, Christine?"

The Persian said coldly:

"We shall do all that it is humanly possible to do! . . . But he may stop us at the first step! . . . He commands the walls, the doors and the trapdoors. In my country, he was known by a name which means the 'trap-door lover.'"

"But why do these walls obey him alone? He did not build them!"

"Yes, sir, that is just what he did!"

Raoul looked at him in amazement; but the Persian made a sign to him to be silent and pointed to the glass . . . There was a sort of shivering reflection. Their image was troubled as in a rippling sheet of water and then all became stationary again.

"You see, sir, that it is not turning! Let us take another road!"

"To-night, there is no other!" declared the Persian, in a singularly mournful voice. "And now, look out! And be ready to fire."

He himself raised his pistol opposite the glass. Raoul imitated his movement. With his free arm, the Persian drew the young man to his chest and, suddenly, the mirror turned, in a blinding daze of cross-lights: it turned like one of those revolving doors which have lately been fixed to the entrances of most restaurants, it turned, carrying Raoul and the Persian with it and suddenly hurling them from the full light into the deepest darkness.

CHAPTER XX

IN THE CELLARS OF THE OPERA

"Your hand high, ready to fire!" repeated Raoul's companion quickly.

The wall, behind them, having completed the circle which it described upon itself, closed again; and the two men stood motionless for a moment, holding their breath.

At last, the Persian decided to make a movement; and Raoul heard him slip on his knees and feel for something in the dark with his groping hands. Suddenly, the darkness was made visible by a small dark lantern and Raoul instinctively stepped backward as though to escape the scrutiny of a secret enemy. But he soon perceived that the light belonged to the Persian, whose movements he was closely observing. The little red disk was turned in every direction and Raoul saw that the floor, the walls and the ceiling were all formed of planking. It must have been the ordinary road taken by Erik to reach Christine's dressing-room and impose upon her innocence. And Raoul, remembering the Persian's remark, thought that it had been mysteriously constructed by the ghost himself. Later, he learned that Erik had found, all prepared for him, a secret passage, long known to himself alone and contrived at the time of the Paris Commune to allow the jailers to convey their prisoners straight to the dungeons that had been constructed for them in the cellars; for the Federates had occupied the opera-house immediately after the eighteenth of March and had made a starting-place right at the top for their Mongolfier balloons, which carried their incendiary proclamations to the departments, and a state prison right at the bottom.

The Persian went on his knees and put his lantern on the ground. He seemed to be working at the floor; and suddenly he turned off his light. Then Raoul heard a faint click and saw a very pale luminous square in the floor of the passage. It was as though a window had opened on the Opera cellars, which were still lit. Raoul no longer saw the Persian, but he suddenly felt him by his side and heard him whisper:

"Follow me and do all that I do."

Raoul turned to the luminous aperture. Then he saw the Persian, who was still on his knees, hang by his hands from the rim of the opening, with his pistol between his teeth, and slide into the cellar below.

Curiously enough, the viscount had absolute confidence in the Persian, though he knew nothing about him. His emotion when speaking of the "monster" struck him as sincere; and, if the Persian had cherished any sinister designs against him, he would not have armed him with his own hands. Besides, Raoul must reach Christine at all costs. He therefore went on his knees also and hung from the trap with both hands.

"Let go!" said a voice.

And he dropped into the arms of the Persian, who told him to lie down flat, closed the trap-door above him and crouched down beside him. Raoul tried to ask a question, but the Persian's hand was on his mouth and he heard a voice which he recognized as that of the commissary of police.

Raoul and the Persian were completely hidden behind a wooden partition. Near them, a small staircase led to a little room in which the commissary appeared to be walking up and down, asking questions. The faint light was just enough to enable Raoul to distinguish the shape of things around him. And he could not restrain a dull cry: there were three corpses there.

The first lay on the narrow landing of the little staircase; the two others had rolled to the bottom of the staircase. Raoul could have touched one of the two poor wretches by passing his fingers through the partition.

"Silence!" whispered the Persian.

He too had seen the bodies and he gave one word in explanation:

"*He!*"

The commissary's voice was now heard more distinctly. He was asking for information about the system of lighting, which the stage-manager supplied. The commissary therefore must be in the "organ" or its immediate neighborhood.

Contrary to what one might think, especially in connection with an opera-house, the "organ" is not a musical instrument. At that time, electricity was employed only for a very few scenic effects and for the bells. The immense building and the stage itself were still lit by gas; hydrogen was used to regulate and modify the lighting of a scene; and this was done by means of a special apparatus which, because of the multiplicity of its pipes, was known as the "organ." A box beside the prompter's box was reserved for the chief gas-man, who from there gave his orders to his assistants and saw that they were executed. Mauclair stayed in this box during all the performances.

But now Mauclair was not in his box and his assistants not in their places.

"Mauclair! Mauclair!"

The stage-manager's voice echoed through the cellars. But Mauclair did not reply.

I have said that a door opened on a little staircase that led to the second cellar. The commissary pushed it, but it resisted.

"I say," he said to the stage-manager, "I can't open this door: is it always so difficult?"

The stage-manager forced it open with his shoulder. He saw that, at the same time, he was pushing a human body and he could not keep back an exclamation, for he recognized the body at once:

"Mauclair! Poor devil! He is dead!"

But Mr. Commissary Mifroid, whom nothing surprised, was stooping over that big body.

"No," he said, "he is dead-drunk, which is not quite the same thing."

"It's the first time, if so," said the stage-manager

"Then some one has given him a narcotic. That is quite possible."

Mifroid went down a few steps and said:

"Look!"

By the light of a little red lantern, at the foot of the stairs, they saw two other bodies. The stage-manager recognized Mauclair's assistants. Mifroid went down and listened to their breathing.

"They are sound asleep," he said. "Very curious business! Some person unknown must have interfered with the gas-man and his staff . . . and that person unknown was obviously working on behalf of the kidnapper . . . But what a funny idea to kidnap a performer on the stage! . . . Send for the doctor of the theater, please." And Mifroid repeated, "Curious, decidedly curious business!"

Then he turned to the little room, addressing the people whom Raoul and the Persian were unable to see from where they lay.

"What do you say to all this, gentlemen? You are the only ones who have not given your views. And yet you must have an opinion of some sort."

Thereupon, Raoul and the Persian saw the startled faces of the joint managers appear above the landing—and they heard Moncharmin's excited voice:

"There are things happening here, Mr. Commissary, which we are unable to explain."

And the two faces disappeared.

"Thank you for the information, gentlemen," said Mifroid, with a jeer.

But the stage-manager, holding his chin in the hollow of his right hand, which is the attitude of profound thought, said:

"It is not the first time that Mauclair has fallen asleep in the theater. I remember finding him, one evening, snoring in his little recess, with his snuff-box beside him."

"Is that long ago?" asked M. Mifroid, carefully wiping his eye-glasses.

"No, not so very long ago . . . Wait a bit! . . . It was the night . . . of course, yes . . . It was the night when Carlotta—you know, Mr. Commissary—gave her famous 'co-ack'!"

"Really? The night when Carlotta gave her famous 'co-ack'?"

And M. Mifroid, replacing his gleaming glasses on his nose, fixed the stage-manager with a contemplative stare.

"So Mauclair takes snuff, does he?" he asked carelessly.

"Yes, Mr. Commissary . . . Look, there is his snuff-box on that little shelf . . . Oh! he's a great snuff-taker!"

"So am I," said Mifroid and put the snuff-box in his pocket.

Raoul and the Persian, themselves unobserved, watched the removal of the three bodies by a number of scene-shifters, who were followed by the commissary and all the people with him. Their steps were heard for a few minutes on the stage above. When they were alone the Persian made a sign to Raoul to stand up. Raoul did so; but, as he did not lift his hand in front of his eyes, ready to fire, the Persian told him to resume that attitude and to continue it, whatever happened.

"But it tires the hand unnecessarily," whispered Raoul. "If I do fire, I shan't be sure of my aim."

"Then shift your pistol to the other hand," said the Persian.

"I can't shoot with my left hand."

Thereupon, the Persian made this queer reply, which was certainly not calculated to throw light into the young man's flurried brain:

"It's not a question of shooting with the right hand or the left; it's a question of holding one of your hands as though you were going to pull the trigger of a pistol with your arm bent. As for the pistol itself, when all is said, you can put that in your pocket!" And he added, "Let this be clearly understood, or I will answer for nothing. It is a matter of life and death. And now, silence and follow me!"

The cellars of the Opera are enormous and they are five in number. Raoul followed the Persian and wondered what he would have done without his companion in that extraordinary labyrinth. They went down to the third cellar; and their progress was still lit by some distant lamp.

The lower they went, the more precautions the Persian seemed to take. He kept on turning to Raoul to see if he was holding his arm properly, showing him how he himself carried his hand as if always ready to fire, though the pistol was in his pocket.

Suddenly, a loud voice made them stop. Some one above them shouted:

"All the door-shutters on the stage! The commissary of police wants them!"

Steps were heard and shadows glided through the darkness. The Persian drew Raoul behind a set piece. They saw passing before and above them old men bent by age and the past burden of opera-scenery. Some could hardly drag themselves along; others, from habit, with stooping bodies and outstretched hands, looked for doors to shut.

They were the door-shutters, the old, worn-out scene-shifters, on whom a charitable management had taken pity, giving them the job of shutting doors above and below the stage. They went about incessantly, from top to bottom of the building, shutting the doors; and they were also called "The draft-expellers," at least at that time, for I have little doubt that by now they are all dead. Drafts are very bad for the voice, wherever they may come from.[3]

The two men might have stumbled over them, waking them up and provoking a request for explanations. For the moment, M. Mifroid's inquiry saved them from any such unpleasant encounters.

The Persian and Raoul welcomed this incident, which relieved them of inconvenient witnesses, for some of those door-shutters, having nothing else to do or nowhere to lay their heads, stayed at the Opera, from idleness or necessity, and spent the night there.

But they were not left to enjoy their solitude for long. Other shades now came down by the same way by which the door-shutters had gone up. Each of these shades carried a little lantern and moved it about, above, below and all around, as though looking for something or somebody.

"Hang it!" muttered the Persian. "I don't know what they are looking for, but they might easily find us . . . Let us get away, quick! . . . Your hand up, sir, ready to fire! . . . Bend your arm . . . more . . . that's it! . . . Hand at the level of your eye, as though you were fighting a duel and waiting for the word to fire! Oh, leave your pistol in your pocket. Quick, come along, down-stairs. Level of your eye! Question of life or death! . . . Here, this way, these stairs!" They reached the fifth cellar. "Oh, what a duel, sir, what a duel!"

Once in the fifth cellar, the Persian drew breath. He seemed to enjoy a rather greater sense of security than he had displayed when they both stopped in the third; but he never altered the attitude of his hand. And Raoul, remembering the Persian's observation—"I know these pistols can be relied upon"—was more and more astonished, wondering why any one should be so gratified at being able to rely upon a pistol which he did not intend to use!

---

3   M. Pedro Gailhard has himself told me that he created a few
       additional posts as door-shutters for old stage-carpenters whom he
       was unwilling to dismiss from the service of the Opera.

But the Persian left him no time for reflection. Telling Raoul to stay where he was, he ran up a few steps of the staircase which they had just left and then returned.

"How stupid of us!" he whispered. "We shall soon have seen the end of those men with their lanterns. It is the firemen going their rounds."[4]

The two men waited five minutes longer. Then the Persian took Raoul up the stairs again; but suddenly he stopped him with a gesture. Something moved in the darkness before them.

"Flat on your stomach!" whispered the Persian.

The two men lay flat on the floor.

They were only just in time. A shade, this time carrying no light, just a shade in the shade, passed. It passed close to them, near enough to touch them.

They felt the warmth of its cloak upon them. For they could distinguish the shade sufficiently to see that it wore a cloak which shrouded it from head to foot. On its head it had a soft felt hat . . .

It moved away, drawing its feet against the walls and sometimes giving a kick into a corner.

"Whew!" said the Persian. "We've had a narrow escape; that shade knows me and has twice taken me to the managers' office."

"Is it some one belonging to the theater police?" asked Raoul.

"It's some one much worse than that!" replied the Persian, without giving any further explanation.[5]

4	In those days, it was still part of the firemen's duty to watch over the safety of the Opera house outside the performances; but this service has since been suppressed. I asked M. Pedro Gailhard the reason, and he replied: "It was because the management was afraid that, in their utter inexperience of the cellars of the Opera, the firemen might set fire to the building!"

5	Like the Persian, I can give no further explanation touching the apparition of this shade. Whereas, in this historic narrative, everything else will be normally explained, however abnormal the course of events may seem, I can not give the reader expressly to understand what the Persian meant by the words, "It is some one much worse than that!" The reader must try to guess for himself, for I promised M. Pedro Gailhard, the former manager of the Opera, to keep his secret regarding the extremely interesting and useful personality of the wandering, cloaked shade which, while

"It's not . . . he?"

"He? . . . If he does not come behind us, we shall always see his yellow eyes! That is more or less our safeguard to-night. But he may come from behind, stealing up; and we are dead men if we do not keep our hands as though about to fire, at the level of our eyes, in front!"

The Persian had hardly finished speaking, when a fantastic face came in sight . . . a whole fiery face, not only two yellow eyes!

Yes, a head of fire came toward them, at a man's height, but with no body attached to it. The face shed fire, looked in the darkness like a flame shaped as a man's face.

"Oh," said the Persian, between his teeth. "I have never seen this before! . . . Pampin was not mad, after all: he had seen it! . . . What can that flame be? It is not HE, but he may have sent it! . . . Take care! . . . Take care! Your hand at the level of your eyes, in Heaven's name, at the level of your eyes! . . . know most of his tricks . . . but not this one . . . Come, let us run . . . it is safer. Hand at the level of your eyes!"

And they fled down the long passage that opened before them.

After a few seconds, that seemed to them like long minutes, they stopped.

"He doesn't often come this way," said the Persian. "This side has nothing to do with him. This side does not lead to the lake nor to the house on the lake . . . But perhaps he knows that we are at his heels . . . although I promised him to leave him alone and never to meddle in his business again!"

So saying, he turned his head and Raoul also turned his head; and they again saw the head of fire behind their two heads. It had followed them. And it must have run also, and perhaps faster than they, for it seemed to be nearer to them.

At the same time, they began to perceive a certain noise of which they could not guess the nature. They simply noticed that the sound seemed to move and to approach with the fiery face. It was a noise as though thousands of nails had been scraped against a blackboard, the perfectly unendurable noise that is sometimes made by a little stone inside the chalk that grates on the blackboard.

They continued to retreat, but the fiery face came on, came on, gaining on them. They could see its features clearly now. The eyes were round and staring, the nose a little crooked and the mouth large, with a hanging lower

---

condemning itself to live in the cellars of the Opera, rendered such immense services to those who, on gala evenings, for instance, venture to stray away from the stage. I am speaking of state services; and, upon my word of honor, I can say no more.

lip, very like the eyes, nose and lip of the moon, when the moon is quite red, bright red.

How did that red moon manage to glide through the darkness, at a man's height, with nothing to support it, at least apparently? And how did it go so fast, so straight ahead, with such staring, staring eyes? And what was that scratching, scraping, grating sound which it brought with it?

The Persian and Raoul could retreat no farther and flattened themselves against the wall, not knowing what was going to happen because of that incomprehensible head of fire, and especially now, because of the more intense, swarming, living, "numerous" sound, for the sound was certainly made up of hundreds of little sounds that moved in the darkness, under the fiery face.

And the fiery face came on . . . with its noise . . . came level with them! . . .

And the two companions, flat against their wall, felt their hair stand on end with horror, for they now knew what the thousand noises meant. They came in a troop, hustled along in the shadow by innumerable little hurried waves, swifter than the waves that rush over the sands at high tide, little night-waves foaming under the moon, under the fiery head that was like a moon. And the little waves passed between their legs, climbing up their legs, irresistibly, and Raoul and the Persian could no longer restrain their cries of horror, dismay and pain. Nor could they continue to hold their hands at the level of their eyes: their hands went down to their legs to push back the waves, which were full of little legs and nails and claws and teeth.

Yes, Raoul and the Persian were ready to faint, like Pampin the fireman. But the head of fire turned round in answer to their cries, and spoke to them:

"Don't move! Don't move! . . . Whatever you do, don't come after me! . . . I am the rat-catcher! . . . Let me pass, with my rats! . . . "

And the head of fire disappeared, vanished in the darkness, while the passage in front of it lit up, as the result of the change which the rat-catcher had made in his dark lantern. Before, so as not to scare the rats in front of him, he had turned his dark lantern on himself, lighting up his own head; now, to hasten their flight, he lit the dark space in front of him. And he jumped along, dragging with him the waves of scratching rats, all the thousand sounds.

Raoul and the Persian breathed again, though still trembling.

"I ought to have remembered that Erik talked to me about the rat-catcher," said the Persian. "But he never told me that he looked like that . . . and it's funny that I should never have met him before . . . Of course, Erik never comes to this part!"

"Are we very far from the lake, sir?" asked Raoul. "When shall we get there? . . . Take me to the lake, oh, take me to the lake! . . . When we are at the lake, we will call out! . . . Christine will hear us! . . . And *he* will hear us, too! . . . And, as you know him, we shall talk to him!" "Baby!" said the Persian. "We shall never enter the house on the lake by the lake! . . . I myself have never landed on the other bank . . . the bank on which the house stands. . . . You have to cross the lake first . . . and it is well guarded! . . . I fear that more than one of those men—old scene-shifters, old door-shutters—who have never been seen again were simply tempted to cross the lake . . . It is terrible . . . I myself would have been nearly killed there . . . if the monster had not recognized me in time! . . . One piece of advice, sir; never go near the lake . . . And, above all, shut your ears if you hear the voice singing under the water, the siren's voice!"

"But then, what are we here for?" asked Raoul, in a transport of fever, impatience and rage. "If you can do nothing for Christine, at least let me die for her!" The Persian tried to calm the young man.

"We have only one means of saving Christine Daae, believe me, which is to enter the house unperceived by the monster."

"And is there any hope of that, sir?"

"Ah, if I had not that hope, I would not have come to fetch you!"

"And how can one enter the house on the lake without crossing the lake?"

"From the third cellar, from which we were so unluckily driven away. We will go back there now . . . I will tell you," said the Persian, with a sudden change in his voice, "I will tell you the exact place, sir: it is between a set piece and a discarded scene from *Roi De Lahore*, exactly at the spot where Joseph Buquet died . . . Come, sir, take courage and follow me! And hold your hand at the level of your eyes! . . . But where are we?"

The Persian lit his lamp again and flung its rays down two enormous corridors that crossed each other at right angles.

"We must be," he said, "in the part used more particularly for the waterworks. I see no fire coming from the furnaces."

He went in front of Raoul, seeking his road, stopping abruptly when he was afraid of meeting some waterman. Then they had to protect themselves against the glow of a sort of underground forge, which the men were extinguishing, and at which Raoul recognized the demons whom Christine had seen at the time of her first captivity.

In this way, they gradually arrived beneath the huge cellars below the stage. They must at this time have been at the very bottom of the "tub" and at an extremely great depth, when we remember that the earth was dug out at fifty feet below the water that lay under the whole of that part of Paris.[6]

The Persian touched a partition-wall and said:

"If I am not mistaken, this is a wall that might easily belong to the house on the lake."

He was striking a partition-wall of the "tub," and perhaps it would be as well for the reader to know how the bottom and the partition-walls of the tub were built. In order to prevent the water surrounding the building-operations from remaining in immediate contact with the walls supporting the whole of the theatrical machinery, the architect was obliged to build a double case in every direction. The work of constructing this double case took a whole year. It was the wall of the first inner case that the Persian struck when speaking to Raoul of the house on the lake. To any one understanding the architecture of the edifice, the Persian's action would seem to indicate that Erik's mysterious house had been built in the double case, formed of a thick wall constructed as an embankment or dam, then of a brick wall, a tremendous layer of cement and another wall several yards in thickness.

At the Persian's words, Raoul flung himself against the wall and listened eagerly. But he heard nothing . . . nothing . . . except distant steps sounding on the floor of the upper portions of the theater.

The Persian darkened his lantern again.

"Look out!" he said. "Keep your hand up! And silence! For we shall try another way of getting in."

And he led him to the little staircase by which they had come down lately.

They went up, stopping at each step, peering into the darkness and the silence, till they came to the third cellar. Here the Persian motioned to Raoul to go on his knees; and, in this way, crawling on both knees and one hand—for the other hand was held in the position indicated—they reached the end wall.

Against this wall stood a large discarded scene from the *Roi De Lahore*. Close to this scene was a set piece. Between the scene and the set piece there was just room for a body . . . for a body which one day was found hanging there. The body of Joseph Buquet.

The Persian, still kneeling, stopped and listened. For a moment, he seemed to hesitate and looked at Raoul; then he turned his eyes upward,

---

6   All the water had to be exhausted, in the building of the Opera. To give an idea of the amount of water that was pumped up, I can tell the reader that it represented the area of the courtyard of the Louvre and a height half as deep again as the towers of Notre Dame. And nevertheless the engineers had to leave a lake.

toward the second cellar, which sent down the faint glimmer of a lantern, through a cranny between two boards. This glimmer seemed to trouble the Persian.

At last, he tossed his head and made up his mind to act. He slipped between the set piece and the scene from the *Roi De Lahore*, with Raoul close upon his heels. With his free hand, the Persian felt the wall. Raoul saw him bear heavily upon the wall, just as he had pressed against the wall in Christine's dressing-room. Then a stone gave way, leaving a hole in the wall.

This time, the Persian took his pistol from his pocket and made a sign to Raoul to do as he did. He cocked the pistol.

And, resolutely, still on his knees, he wiggled through the hole in the wall. Raoul, who had wished to pass first, had to be content to follow him.

The hole was very narrow. The Persian stopped almost at once. Raoul heard him feeling the stones around him. Then the Persian took out his dark lantern again, stooped forward, examined something beneath him and immediately extinguished his lantern. Raoul heard him say, in a whisper:

"We shall have to drop a few yards, without making a noise; take off your boots."

The Persian handed his own shoes to Raoul.

"Put them outside the wall," he said. "We shall find them there when we leave."[7]

He crawled a little farther on his knees, then turned right round and said:

"I am going to hang by my hands from the edge of the stone and let myself drop *into his house*. You must do exactly the same. Do not be afraid. I will catch you in my arms."

Raoul soon heard a dull sound, evidently produced by the fall of the Persian, and then dropped down.

He felt himself clasped in the Persian's arms.

"Hush!" said the Persian.

And they stood motionless, listening.

The darkness was thick around them, the silence heavy and terrible.

Then the Persian began to make play with the dark lantern again, turning the rays over their heads, looking for the hole through which they had come, and failing to find it:

---

7   These two pairs of boots, which were placed, according to the Persian's papers, just between the set piece and the scene from the *Roi De Lahore*, on the spot where Joseph Buquet was found hanging, were never discovered. They must have been taken by some stage-carpenter or "door-shutter."

"Oh!" he said. "The stone has closed of itself!"

And the light of the lantern swept down the wall and over the floor.

The Persian stooped and picked up something, a sort of cord, which he examined for a second and flung away with horror.

"The Punjab lasso!" he muttered.

"What is it?" asked Raoul.

The Persian shivered. "It might very well be the rope by which the man was hanged, and which was looked for so long."

And, suddenly seized with fresh anxiety, he moved the little red disk of his lantern over the walls. In this way, he lit up a curious thing: the trunk of a tree, which seemed still quite alive, with its leaves; and the branches of that tree ran right up the walls and disappeared in the ceiling.

Because of the smallness of the luminous disk, it was difficult at first to make out the appearance of things: they saw a corner of a branch . . . and a leaf . . . and another leaf . . . and, next to it, nothing at all, nothing but the ray of light that seemed to reflect itself . . . Raoul passed his hand over that nothing, over that reflection.

"Hullo!" he said. "The wall is a looking-glass!"

"Yes, a looking-glass!" said the Persian, in a tone of deep emotion. And, passing the hand that held the pistol over his moist forehead, he added, "We have dropped into the torture-chamber!"

What the Persian knew of this torture-chamber and what there befell him and his companion shall be told in his own words, as set down in a manuscript which he left behind him, and which I copy *Verbatim*.

CHAPTER XXI

INTERESTING AND INSTRUCTIVE VICISSITUDES OF A PERSIAN IN THE CELLARS OF THE OPERA

THE PERSIAN'S NARRATIVE

It was the first time that I entered the house on the lake. I had often begged the "trap-door lover," as we used to call Erik in my country, to open its mysterious doors to me. He always refused. I made very many attempts, but in vain, to obtain admittance. Watch him as I might, after I first learned that he had taken up his permanent abode at the Opera, the darkness was always too thick to enable me to see how he worked the door in the wall on the lake. One day, when I thought myself alone, I stepped into the boat and rowed toward that part of the wall through which I had seen Erik disappear. It was then that I came into contact with the siren who guarded the approach and whose charm was very nearly fatal to me.

I had no sooner put off from the bank than the silence amid which I floated on the water was disturbed by a sort of whispered singing that hovered all around me. It was half breath, half music; it rose softly from the waters of the lake; and I was surrounded by it through I knew not what artifice. It followed me, moved with me and was so soft that it did not alarm me. On the contrary, in my longing to approach the source of that sweet and enticing harmony, I leaned out of my little boat over the water, for there was no doubt in my mind that the singing came from the water itself. By this time, I was alone in the boat in the middle of the lake; the voice—for it was now distinctly a voice—was beside me, on the water. I leaned over, leaned still farther. The lake was perfectly calm, and a moonbeam that passed through the air hole in the Rue Scribe showed me absolutely nothing on its surface, which was smooth and black as ink. I shook my ears to get rid of a possible humming; but I soon had to accept the fact that there was no humming in the ears so harmonious as the singing whisper that followed and now attracted me.

Had I been inclined to superstition, I should have certainly thought that

I had to do with some siren whose business it was to confound the traveler who should venture on the waters of the house on the lake. Fortunately, I come from a country where we are too fond of fantastic things not to know them through and through; and I had no doubt but that I was face to face with some new invention of Erik's. But this invention was so perfect that, as I leaned out of the boat, I was impelled less by a desire to discover its trick than to enjoy its charm; and I leaned out, leaned out until I almost overturned the boat.

Suddenly, two monstrous arms issued from the bosom of the waters and seized me by the neck, dragging me down to the depths with irresistible force. I should certainly have been lost, if I had not had time to give a cry by which Erik knew me. For it was he; and, instead of drowning me, as was certainly his first intention, he swam with me and laid me gently on the bank:

"How imprudent you are!" he said, as he stood before me, dripping with water. "Why try to enter my house? I never invited you! I don't want you there, nor anybody! Did you save my life only to make it unbearable to me? However great the service you rendered him, Erik may end by forgetting it; and you know that nothing can restrain Erik, not even Erik himself."

He spoke, but I had now no other wish than to know what I already called the trick of the siren. He satisfied my curiosity, for Erik, who is a real monster—I have seen him at work in Persia, alas—is also, in certain respects, a regular child, vain and self-conceited, and there is nothing he loves so much, after astonishing people, as to prove all the really miraculous ingenuity of his mind.

He laughed and showed me a long reed.

"It's the silliest trick you ever saw," he said, "but it's very useful for breathing and singing in the water. I learned it from the Tonkin pirates, who are able to remain hidden for hours in the beds of the rivers."[8]

I spoke to him severely.

"It's a trick that nearly killed me!" I said. "And it may have been fatal to others! You know what you promised me, Erik? No more murders!"

"Have I really committed murders?" he asked, putting on his most amiable air.

"Wretched man!" I cried. "Have you forgotten the rosy hours of Mazenderan?"

---

8   An official report from Tonkin, received in Paris at the end of July, 1909, relates how the famous pirate chief De Tham was tracked, together with his men, by our soldiers; and how all of them succeeded in escaping, thanks to this trick of the reeds.

"Yes," he replied, in a sadder tone, "I prefer to forget them. I used to make the little sultana laugh, though!"

"All that belongs to the past," I declared; "but there is the present . . . and you are responsible to me for the present, because, if I had wished, there would have been none at all for you. Remember that, Erik: I saved your life!"

And I took advantage of the turn of conversation to speak to him of something that had long been on my mind:

"Erik," I asked, "Erik, swear that . . . "

"What?" he retorted. "You know I never keep my oaths. Oaths are made to catch gulls with."

"Tell me . . . you can tell me, at any rate . . . "

"Well?"

"Well, the chandelier . . . the chandelier, Erik? . . . "

"What about the chandelier?"

"You know what I mean."

"Oh," he sniggered, "I don't mind telling you about the chandelier! . . . *It wasn't I!* . . . The chandelier was very old and worn."

When Erik laughed, he was more terrible than ever. He jumped into the boat, chuckling so horribly that I could not help trembling.

"Very old and worn, my dear daroga![9] Very old and worn, the chandelier! . . . It fell of itself! . . . It came down with a smash! . . . And now, daroga, take my advice and go and dry yourself, or you'll catch a cold in the head! . . . And never get into my boat again . . . And, whatever you do, don't try to enter my house: I'm not always there . . . daroga! And I should be sorry to have to dedicate my Requiem Mass to you!"

So saying, swinging to and fro, like a monkey, and still chuckling, he pushed off and soon disappeared in the darkness of the lake.

From that day, I gave up all thought of penetrating into his house by the lake. That entrance was obviously too well guarded, especially since he had learned that I knew about it. But I felt that there must be another entrance, for I had often seen Erik disappear in the third cellar, when I was watching him, though I could not imagine how.

Ever since I had discovered Erik installed in the Opera, I lived in a perpetual terror of his horrible fancies, not in so far as I was concerned, but I dreaded everything for others.[10]

---

9   DAROGA is Persian for chief of police.

10   The Persian might easily have admitted that Erik's fate also
       interested himself, for he was well aware that, if the government

And whenever some accident, some fatal event happened, I always thought to myself, "I should not be surprised if that were Erik," even as others used to say, "It's the ghost!" How often have I not heard people utter that phrase with a smile! Poor devils! If they had known that the ghost existed in the flesh, I swear they would not have laughed!

Although Erik announced to me very solemnly that he had changed and that he had become the most virtuous of men *since he was loved for himself*—a sentence that, at first, perplexed me most terribly—I could not help shuddering when I thought of the monster. His horrible, unparalleled and repulsive ugliness put him without the pale of humanity; and it often seemed to me that, for this reason, he no longer believed that he had any duty toward the human race. The way in which he spoke of his love affairs only increased my alarm, for I foresaw the cause of fresh and more hideous tragedies in this event to which he alluded so boastfully.

On the other hand, I soon discovered the curious moral traffic established between the monster and Christine Daae. Hiding in the lumber-room next to the young prima donna's dressing-room, I listened to wonderful musical displays that evidently flung Christine into marvelous ecstasy; but, all the same, I would never have thought that Erik's voice—which was loud as thunder or soft as angels' voices, at will—could have made her forget his ugliness. I understood all when I learned that Christine had not yet seen him! I had occasion to go to the dressing-room and, remembering the lessons he had once given me, I had no difficulty in discovering the trick that made the wall with the mirror swing round and I ascertained the means of hollow bricks and so on—by which he made his voice carry to Christine as though she heard it close beside her. In this way also I discovered the road that led to the well and the dungeon—the Communists' dungeon—and also the trap-door that enabled Erik to go straight to the cellars below the stage.

A few days later, what was not my amazement to learn by my own eyes and ears that Erik and Christine Daae saw each other and to catch the monster stooping over the little well, in the Communists' road and sprinkling the forehead of Christine Daae, who had fainted. A white horse, the horse out of the *Profeta*, which had disappeared from the stables under the Opera, was

---

of Teheran had learned that Erik was still alive, it would have been all up with the modest pension of the erstwhile daroga. It is only fair, however, to add that the Persian had a noble and generous heart; and I do not doubt for a moment that the catastrophes which he feared for others greatly occupied his mind. His conduct, throughout this business, proves it and is above all praise.

standing quietly beside them. I showed myself. It was terrible. I saw sparks fly from those yellow eyes and, before I had time to say a word, I received a blow on the head that stunned me.

When I came to myself, Erik, Christine and the white horse had disappeared. I felt sure that the poor girl was a prisoner in the house on the lake. Without hesitation, I resolved to return to the bank, notwithstanding the attendant danger. For twenty-four hours, I lay in wait for the monster to appear; for I felt that he must go out, driven by the need of obtaining provisions. And, in this connection, I may say, that, when he went out in the streets or ventured to show himself in public, he wore a pasteboard nose, with a mustache attached to it, instead of his own horrible hole of a nose. This did not quite take away his corpse-like air, but it made him almost, I say almost, endurable to look at.

I therefore watched on the bank of the lake and, weary of long waiting, was beginning to think that he had gone through the other door, the door in the third cellar, when I heard a slight splashing in the dark, I saw the two yellow eyes shining like candles and soon the boat touched shore. Erik jumped out and walked up to me:

"You've been here for twenty-four hours," he said, "and you're annoying me. I tell you, all this will end very badly. And you will have brought it upon yourself; for I have been extraordinarily patient with you. You think you are following me, you great booby, whereas it's I who am following you; and I know all that you know about me, here. I spared you yesterday, in *My Communists' Road*; but I warn you, seriously, don't let me catch you there again! Upon my word, you don't seem able to take a hint!"

He was so furious that I did not think, for the moment, of interrupting him. After puffing and blowing like a walrus, he put his horrible thought into words:

"Yes, you must learn, once and for all—once and for all, I say—to take a hint! I tell you that, with your recklessness—for you have already been twice arrested by the shade in the felt hat, who did not know what you were doing in the cellars and took you to the managers, who looked upon you as an eccentric Persian interested in stage mechanism and life behind the scenes: I know all about it, I was there, in the office; you know I am everywhere— well, I tell you that, with your recklessness, they will end by wondering what you are after here . . . and they will end by knowing that you are after Erik . . . and then they will be after Erik themselves and they will discover the house on the lake . . . If they do, it will be a bad lookout for you, old chap, a bad lookout! . . . I won't answer for anything."

Again he puffed and blew like a walrus.

"I won't answer for anything! . . . If Erik's secrets cease to be Erik's secrets, *it will be a bad lookout for a goodly number of the human race!* That's all I have to tell you, and unless you are a great booby, it ought to be enough for you . . . except that you don't know how to take a hint."

He had sat down on the stern of his boat and was kicking his heels against the planks, waiting to hear what I had to answer. I simply said:

"It's not Erik that I'm after here!"

"Who then?"

"You know as well as I do: it's Christine Daae," I answered.

He retorted: "I have every right to see her in my own house. I am loved for my own sake."

"That's not true," I said. "You have carried her off and are keeping her locked up."

"Listen," he said. "Will you promise never to meddle with my affairs again, if I prove to you that I am loved for my own sake?"

"Yes, I promise you," I replied, without hesitation, for I felt convinced that for such a monster the proof was impossible.

"Well, then, it's quite simple . . . Christine Daae shall leave this as she pleases and come back again! . . . Yes, come back again, because she wishes . . . come back of herself, because she loves me for myself! . . ."

"Oh, I doubt if she will come back! . . . But it is your duty to let her go."
"My duty, you great booby! . . . It is my wish . . . my wish to let her go; and she will come back again . . . for she loves me! . . . All this will end in a marriage . . . a marriage at the Madeleine, you great booby! Do you believe me now? When I tell you that my nuptial mass is written . . . wait till you hear the KYRIE . . ."

He beat time with his heels on the planks of the boat and sang:

"KYRIE! . . . KYRIE! . . . KYRIE ELEISON! . . . Wait till you hear, wait till you hear that mass."

"Look here," I said. "I shall believe you if I see Christine Daae come out of the house on the lake and go back to it of her own accord."

"And you won't meddle any more in my affairs?"

"No."

"Very well, you shall see that to-night. Come to the masked ball. Christine and I will go and have a look round. Then you can hide in the lumber-room and you shall see Christine, who will have gone to her dressing-room, delighted to come back by the Communists' road . . . And, now, be off, for I must go and do some shopping!"

To my intense astonishment, things happened as he had announced. Christine Daae left the house on the lake and returned to it several times, without, apparently, being forced to do so. It was very difficult for me to clear my mind of Erik. However, I resolved to be extremely prudent, and did not make the mistake of returning to the shore of the lake, or of going by the Communists' road. But the idea of the secret entrance in the third cellar haunted me, and I repeatedly went and waited for hours behind a scene from the Roi de Lahore, which had been left there for some reason or other. At last my patience was rewarded. One day, I saw the monster come toward me, on his knees. I was certain that he could not see me. He passed between the scene behind which I stood and a set piece, went to the wall and pressed on a spring that moved a stone and afforded him an ingress. He passed through this, and the stone closed behind him.

I waited for at least thirty minutes and then pressed the spring in my turn. Everything happened as with Erik. But I was careful not to go through the hole myself, for I knew that Erik was inside. On the other hand, the idea that I might be caught by Erik suddenly made me think of the death of Joseph Buquet. I did not wish to jeopardize the advantages of so great a discovery which might be useful to many people, "to a goodly number of the human race," in Erik's words; and I left the cellars of the Opera after carefully replacing the stone.

I continued to be greatly interested in the relations between Erik and Christine Daae, not from any morbid curiosity, but because of the terrible thought which obsessed my mind that Erik was capable of anything, if he once discovered that he was not loved for his own sake, as he imagined. I continued to wander, very cautiously, about the Opera and soon learned the truth about the monster's dreary love-affair.

He filled Christine's mind, through the terror with which he inspired her, but the dear child's heart belonged wholly to the Vicomte Raoul de Chagny. While they played about, like an innocent engaged couple, on the upper floors of the Opera, to avoid the monster, they little suspected that some one was watching over them. I was prepared to do anything: to kill the monster, if necessary, and explain to the police afterward. But Erik did not show himself; and I felt none the more comfortable for that.

I must explain my whole plan. I thought that the monster, being driven from his house by jealousy, would thus enable me to enter it, without danger, through the passage in the third cellar. It was important, for everybody's sake, that I should know exactly what was inside. One day, tired of waiting for an opportunity, I moved the stone and at once heard an astounding music: the monster was working at his Don Juan Triumphant, with every door in his house wide open. I knew that this was the work of his life. I was careful not to stir and remained prudently in my dark hole.

He stopped playing, for a moment, and began walking about his place, like a madman. And he said aloud, at the top of his voice:

"It must be finished *first*! Quite finished!"

This speech was not calculated to reassure me and, when the music recommenced, I closed the stone very softly.

On the day of the abduction of Christine Daae, I did not come to the theater until rather late in the evening, trembling lest I should hear bad news. I had spent a horrible day, for, after reading in a morning paper the announcement of a forthcoming marriage between Christine and the Vicomte de Chagny, I wondered whether, after all, I should not do better to denounce the monster. But reason returned to me, and I was persuaded that this action could only precipitate a possible catastrophe.

When, my cab set me down before the Opera, I was really almost astonished to see it still standing! But I am something of a fatalist, like all good Orientals, and I entered ready, for anything.

Christine Daae's abduction in the Prison Act, which naturally surprised everybody, found me prepared. I was quite certain that she had been juggled away by Erik, that prince of conjurers. And I thought positively that this was the end of Christine and perhaps of everybody, so much so that I thought of advising all these people who were staying on at the theater to make good their escape. I felt, however, that they would be sure to look upon me as mad and I refrained.

On the other hand, I resolved to act without further delay, as far as I was concerned. The chances were in my favor that Erik, at that moment, was thinking only of his captive. This was the moment to enter his house through the third cellar; and I resolved to take with me that poor little desperate viscount, who, at the first suggestion, accepted, with an amount of confidence in myself that touched me profoundly. I had sent my servant for my pistols. I gave one to the viscount and advised him to hold himself ready to fire, for, after all, Erik might be waiting for us behind the wall. We were to go by the Communists' road and through the trap-door.

Seeing my pistols, the little viscount asked me if we were going to fight a duel. I said:

"Yes; and what a duel!" But, of course, I had no time to explain anything to him. The little viscount is a brave fellow, but he knew hardly anything about his adversary; and it was so much the better. My great fear was that he was already somewhere near us, preparing the Punjab lasso. No one knows better than he how to throw the Punjab lasso, for he is the king of stranglers even as he is the prince of conjurors. When he had finished making the little sultana laugh, at the time of the "rosy hours of Mazenderan," she herself used to ask him to amuse her by giving her a thrill. It was then that he introduced the sport of the Punjab lasso.

He had lived in India and acquired an incredible skill in the art of strangulation. He would make them lock him into a courtyard to which they brought a warrior—usually, a man condemned to death—armed with a long pike and broadsword. Erik had only his lasso; and it was always just when the warrior thought that he was going to fell Erik with a tremendous blow that we heard the lasso whistle through the air. With a turn of the wrist, Erik tightened the noose round his adversary's neck and, in this fashion, dragged him before the little sultana and her women, who sat looking from a window and applauding. The little sultana herself learned to wield the Punjab lasso and killed several of her women and even of the friends who visited her. But I prefer to drop this terrible subject of the rosy hours of Mazenderan. I have mentioned it only to explain why, on arriving with the Vicomte de Chagny in the cellars of the Opera, I was bound to protect my companion against the ever-threatening danger of death by strangling. My pistols could serve no purpose, for Erik was not likely to show himself; but Erik could always strangle us. I had no time to explain all this to the viscount; besides, there was nothing to be gained by complicating the position. I simply told M. de Chagny to keep his hand at the level of his eyes, with the arm bent, as though waiting for the command to fire. With his victim in this attitude, it is impossible even for the most expert strangler to throw the lasso with advantage. It catches you not only round the neck, but also round the arm or hand. This enables you easily to unloose the lasso, which then becomes harmless.

After avoiding the commissary of police, a number of door-shutters and the firemen, after meeting the rat-catcher and passing the man in the felt hat unperceived, the viscount and I arrived without obstacle in the third cellar, between the set piece and the scene from the Roi de Lahore. I worked the stone, and we jumped into the house which Erik had built himself in the double case of the foundation-walls of the Opera. And this was the easiest thing in the world for him to do, because Erik was one of the chief contractors under Philippe Garnier, the architect of the Opera, and continued to work by himself when the works were officially suspended, during the war, the siege of Paris and the Commune.

I knew my Erik too well to feel at all comfortable on jumping into his house. I knew what he had made of a certain palace at Mazenderan. From being the most honest building conceivable, he soon turned it into a house of the very devil, where you could not utter a word but it was overheard or repeated by an echo. With his trap-doors the monster was responsible for endless tragedies of all kinds. He hit upon astonishing inventions. Of these, the most curious, horrible and dangerous was the so-called torture-chamber. Except in special cases, when the little sultana amused herself by inflicting suffering upon some unoffending citizen, no one was let into it but wretches condemned to death. And, even then, when these had "had enough," they were always at liberty to put an end to themselves with a Punjab lasso or bowstring, left for their use at the foot of an iron tree.

My alarm, therefore, was great when I saw that the room into which M. le Vicomte de Chagny and I had dropped was an exact copy of the torture-chamber of the rosy hours of Mazenderan. At our feet, I found the Punjab lasso which I had been dreading all the evening. I was convinced that this rope had already done duty for Joseph Buquet, who, like myself, must have caught Erik one evening working the stone in the third cellar. He probably tried it in his turn, fell into the torture-chamber and only left it hanged. I can well imagine Erik dragging the body, in order to get rid of it, to the scene from the Roi de Lahore, and hanging it there as an example, or to increase the superstitious terror that was to help him in guarding the approaches to his lair! Then, upon reflection, Erik went back to fetch the Punjab lasso, which is very curiously made out of catgut, and which might have set an examining magistrate thinking. This explains the disappearance of the rope.

And now I discovered the lasso, at our feet, in the torture-chamber! . . . I am no coward, but a cold sweat covered my forehead as I moved the little red disk of my lantern over the walls.

M. de Chagny noticed it and asked:

"What is the matter, sir?"

I made him a violent sign to be silent.

CHAPTER XXII

IN THE TORTURE CHAMBER

THE PERSIAN'S NARRATIVE CONTINUED

We were in the middle of a little six-cornered room, the sides of which were covered with mirrors from top to bottom. In the corners, we could clearly see the "joins" in the glasses, the segments intended to turn on their gear; yes, I recognized them and I recognized the iron tree in the corner, at the bottom of one of those segments . . . the iron tree, with its iron branch, for the hanged men.

I seized my companion's arm: the Vicomte de Chagny was all a-quiver, eager to shout to his betrothed that he was bringing her help. I feared that he would not be able to contain himself.

Suddenly, we heard a noise on our left. It sounded at first like a door opening and shutting in the next room; and then there was a dull moan. I clutched M. de Chagny's arm more firmly still; and then we distinctly heard these words:

"You must make your choice! The wedding mass or the requiem mass!" I recognized the voice of the monster.

There was another moan, followed by a long silence.

I was persuaded by now that the monster was unaware of our presence in his house, for otherwise he would certainly have managed not to let us hear him. He would only have had to close the little invisible window through which the torture-lovers look down into the torture-chamber. Besides, I was certain that, if he had known of our presence, the tortures would have begun at once.

The important thing was not to let him know; and I dreaded nothing so much as the impulsiveness of the Vicomte de Chagny, who wanted to rush through the walls to Christine Daae, whose moans we continued to hear at intervals.

"The requiem mass is not at all gay," Erik's voice resumed, "whereas the wedding mass—you can take my word for it—is magnificent! You must take a resolution and know your own mind! I can't go on living like this, like a mole in a burrow! Don Juan Triumphant is finished; and now I want to live like everybody else. I want to have a wife like everybody else and to take her out on Sundays. I have invented a mask that makes me look like anybody. People will not even turn round in the streets. You will be the happiest of women. And we will sing, all by ourselves, till we swoon away with delight. You are crying! You are afraid of me! And yet I am not really wicked. Love me and you shall see! All I wanted was to be loved for myself. If you loved me I should be as gentle as a lamb; and you could do anything with me that you pleased."

Soon the moans that accompanied this sort of love's litany increased and increased. I have never heard anything more despairing; and M. de Chagny and I recognized that this terrible lamentation came from Erik himself. Christine seemed to be standing dumb with horror, without the strength to cry out, while the monster was on his knees before her.

Three times over, Erik fiercely bewailed his fate:

"You don't love me! You don't love me! You don't love me!"

And then, more gently:

"Why do you cry? You know it gives me pain to see you cry!"

A silence.

Each silence gave us fresh hope. We said to ourselves:

"Perhaps he has left Christine behind the wall."

And we thought only of the possibility of warning Christine Daae of our presence, unknown to the monster. We were unable to leave the torture-chamber now, unless Christine opened the door to us; and it was only on this condition that we could hope to help her, for we did not even know where the door might be.

Suddenly, the silence in the next room was disturbed by the ringing of an electric bell. There was a bound on the other side of the wall and Erik's voice of thunder:

"Somebody ringing! Walk in, please!"

A sinister chuckle.

"Who has come bothering now? Wait for me here . . . *I am going to tell the siren to open the door.*"

Steps moved away, a door closed. I had no time to think of the fresh horror that was preparing; I forgot that the monster was only going out perhaps to perpetrate a fresh crime; I understood but one thing: Christine was alone behind the wall!

The Vicomte de Chagny was already calling to her:

"Christine! Christine!"

As we could hear what was said in the next room, there was no reason why my companion should not be heard in his turn. Nevertheless, the viscount had to repeat his cry time after time.

At last, a faint voice reached us.

"I am dreaming!" it said.

"Christine, Christine, it is I, Raoul!"

A silence.

"But answer me, Christine! . . . In Heaven's name, if you are alone, answer me!"

Then Christine's voice whispered Raoul's name.

"Yes! Yes! It is I! It is not a dream! . . . Christine, trust me! . . . We are here to save you . . . but be prudent! When you hear the monster, warn us!"

Then Christine gave way to fear. She trembled lest Erik should discover where Raoul was hidden; she told us in a few hurried words that Erik had gone quite mad with love and that he had decided *to kill everybody and himself with everybody* if she did not consent to become his wife. He had given her till eleven o'clock the next evening for reflection. It was the last respite. She must choose, as he said, between the wedding mass and the requiem.

And Erik had then uttered a phrase which Christine did not quite understand:

"Yes or no! If your answer is no, everybody will be dead *and buried*!"

But I understood the sentence perfectly, for it corresponded in a terrible manner with my own dreadful thought.

"Can you tell us where Erik is?" I asked.

She replied that he must have left the house.

"Could you make sure?"

"No. I am fastened. I can not stir a limb."

When we heard this, M. de Chagny and I gave a yell of fury. Our safety, the safety of all three of us, depended on the girl's liberty of movement.

"But where are you?" asked Christine. "There are only two doors in my room, the Louis-Philippe room of which I told you, Raoul; a door through which Erik comes and goes, and another which he has never opened before me and which he has forbidden me ever to go through, because he says it is the most dangerous of the doors, the door of the torture-chamber!"

"Christine, that is where we are!"

"You are in the torture-chamber?"

"Yes, but we can not see the door."

"Oh, if I could only drag myself so far! I would knock at the door and that would tell you where it is."

"Is it a door with a lock to it?" I asked.

"Yes, with a lock."

"Mademoiselle," I said, "it is absolutely necessary, that you should open that door to us!"

"But how?" asked the poor girl tearfully.

We heard her straining, trying to free herself from the bonds that held her.

"I know where the key is," she said, in a voice that seemed exhausted by the effort she had made. "But I am fastened so tight . . . Oh, the wretch!"

And she gave a sob.

"Where is the key?" I asked, signing to M. de Chagny not to speak and to leave the business to me, for we had not a moment to lose.

"In the next room, near the organ, with another little bronze key, which he also forbade me to touch. They are both in a little leather bag which he calls the bag of life and death . . . Raoul! Raoul! Fly! Everything is mysterious and terrible here, and Erik will soon have gone quite mad, and you are in the torture-chamber! . . . Go back by the way you came. There must be a reason why the room is called by that name!"

"Christine," said the young man. "We will go from here together or die together!"

"We must keep cool," I whispered. "Why has he fastened you, mademoiselle? You can't escape from his house; and he knows it!"

"I tried to commit suicide! The monster went out last night, after carrying me here fainting and half chloroformed. He was going *to his banker,* so he said! . . . When he returned he found me with my face covered with blood . . . I had tried to kill myself by striking my forehead against the walls."

"Christine!" groaned Raoul; and he began to sob.

"Then he bound me . . . I am not allowed to die until eleven o'clock to-morrow evening."

"Mademoiselle," I declared, "the monster bound you . . . and he shall unbind you. You have only to play the necessary part! Remember that he loves you!"

"Alas!" we heard. "Am I likely to forget it!"

"Remember it and smile to him . . . entreat him . . . tell him that your bonds hurt you."

But Christine Daae said:

"Hush! . . . I hear something in the wall on the lake! . . . It is he! . . . Go away! Go away! Go away!"

"We could not go away, even if we wanted to," I said, as impressively as I could. "We can not leave this! And we are in the torture-chamber!"

"Hush!" whispered Christine again.

Heavy steps sounded slowly behind the wall, then stopped and made the floor creak once more. Next came a tremendous sigh, followed by a cry of horror from Christine, and we heard Erik's voice:

"I beg your pardon for letting you see a face like this! What a state I am in, am I not? It's *the other one's fault*! Why did he ring? Do I ask people who pass to tell me the time? He will never ask anybody the time again! It is the siren's fault."

Another sigh, deeper, more tremendous still, came from the abysmal depths of a soul.

"Why did you cry out, Christine?"

"Because I am in pain, Erik."

"I thought I had frightened you."

"Erik, unloose my bonds . . . Am I not your prisoner?"

"You will try to kill yourself again."

"You have given me till eleven o'clock to-morrow evening, Erik."

The footsteps dragged along the floor again.

"After all, as we are to die together . . . and I am just as eager as you . . . yes, I have had enough of this life, you know . . . Wait, don't move, I will release you . . . You have only one word to say: 'NO!' And it will at once be over *with everybody*! . . . You are right, you are right; why wait till eleven o'clock to-morrow evening? True, it would have been grander, finer . . . But that is childish nonsense . . . We should only think of ourselves in this life, of our own death . . . the rest doesn't matter . . . *You're looking at me because I am all wet*? . . . Oh, my dear, it's raining cats and dogs outside! . . . Apart from that, Christine, I think I am subject to hallucinations . . . You know, the man who rang at the siren's door just now—go and look if he's ringing at the bottom of the lake-well, he was rather like . . . There, turn round . . . are you glad? You're free now . . . Oh, my poor Christine, look at your wrists: tell me, have I hurt them? . . . That alone deserves death . . . Talking of death, I MUST SING HIS REQUIEM!"

Hearing these terrible remarks, I received an awful presentiment . . . I too had once rung at the monster's door . . . and, without knowing it, must have set some warning current in motion.

And I remembered the two arms that had emerged from the inky waters . . . What poor wretch had strayed to that shore this time? Who was 'the other one,' the one whose requiem we now heard sung?

Erik sang like the god of thunder, sang a *Dies Irae* that enveloped us as in a storm. The elements seemed to rage around us. Suddenly, the organ and the voice ceased so suddenly that M. de Chagny sprang back, on the other side of the wall, with emotion.

And the voice, changed and transformed, distinctly grated out these metallic syllables: "WHAT HAVE YOU DONE WITH MY BAG?"

CHAPTER XXIII

THE TORTURES BEGIN

THE PERSIAN'S NARRATIVE CONTINUED.

The voice repeated angrily: "What have you done with my bag? So it was to take my bag that you asked me to release you!"

We heard hurried steps, Christine running back to the Louis-Philippe room, as though to seek shelter on the other side of our wall.

"What are you running away for?" asked the furious voice, which had followed her. "Give me back my bag, will you? Don't you know that it is the bag of life and death?"

"Listen to me, Erik," sighed the girl. "As it is settled that we are to live together . . . what difference can it make to you?"

"You know there are only two keys in it," said the monster. "What do you want to do?"

"I want to look at this room which I have never seen and which you have always kept from me . . . It's woman's curiosity!" she said, in a tone which she tried to render playful.

But the trick was too childish for Erik to be taken in by it.

"I don't like curious women," he retorted, "and you had better remember the story of *Blue-Beard* and be careful . . . Come, give me back my bag! . . . Give me back my bag! . . . Leave the key alone, will you, you inquisitive little thing?"

And he chuckled, while Christine gave a cry of pain. Erik had evidently recovered the bag from her.

At that moment, the viscount could not help uttering an exclamation of impotent rage.

"Why, what's that?" said the monster. "Did you hear, Christine?"

"No, no," replied the poor girl. "I heard nothing."

"I thought I heard a cry."

"A cry! Are you going mad, Erik? Whom do you expect to give a cry, in this house? . . . I cried out, because you hurt me! I heard nothing."

"I don't like the way you said that! . . . You're trembling . . . You're quite excited . . . You're lying! . . . That was a cry, there was a cry! . . . There is some one in the torture-chamber! . . . Ah, I understand now!"

"There is no one there, Erik!"

"I understand!"

"No one!"

"The man you want to marry, perhaps!"

"I don't want to marry anybody, you know I don't."

Another nasty chuckle. "Well, it won't take long to find out. Christine, my love, we need not open the door to see what is happening in the torture-chamber. Would you like to see? Would you like to see? Look here! If there is some one, if there is really some one there, you will see the invisible window light up at the top, near the ceiling. We need only draw the black curtain and put out the light in here. There, that's it . . . Let's put out the light! You're not afraid of the dark, when you're with your little husband!"

Then we heard Christine's voice of anguish:

"No! . . . I'm frightened! . . . I tell you, I'm afraid of the dark! . . . I don't care about that room now . . . You're always frightening me, like a child, with your torture-chamber! . . . And so I became inquisitive . . . But I don't care about it now . . . not a bit . . . not a bit!"

And that which I feared above all things began, *automatically.* We were suddenly flooded with light! Yes, on our side of the wall, everything seemed aglow. The Vicomte de Chagny was so much taken aback that he staggered. And the angry voice roared:

"I told you there was some one! Do you see the window now? The lighted window, right up there? The man behind the wall can't see it! But you shall go up the folding steps: that is what they are there for! . . . You have often asked me to tell you; and now you know! . . . They are there to give a peep into the torture-chamber . . . you inquisitive little thing!"

"What tortures? . . . Who is being tortured? . . . Erik, Erik, say you are only trying to frighten me! . . . Say it, if you love me, Erik! . . . There are no tortures, are there?"

"Go and look at the little window, dear!"

I do not know if the viscount heard the girl's swooning voice, for he was too much occupied by the astounding spectacle that now appeared before his distracted gaze. As for me, I had seen that sight too often, through the little window, at the time of the rosy hours of Mazenderan; and I cared only for what was being said next door, seeking for a hint how to act, what resolution to take.

"Go and peep through the little window! Tell me what he looks like!"

We heard the steps being dragged against the wall.

"Up with you! . . . No! . . . No, I will go up myself, dear!"

"Oh, very well, I will go up. Let me go!"

"Oh, my darling, my darling! . . . How sweet of you! . . . How nice of you to save me the exertion at my age! . . . Tell me what he looks like!"

At that moment, we distinctly heard these words above our heads:

"There is no one there, dear!"

"No one? . . . Are you sure there is no one?"

"Why, of course not . . . no one!"

"Well, that's all right! . . . What's the matter, Christine? You're not going to faint, are you . . . as there is no one there? . . . Here . . . come down . . . there! . . . Pull yourself together . . . as there is no one there! . . . *But how do you like the landscape?*"

"Oh, very much!"

"There, that's better! . . . You're better now, are you not? . . . That's all right, you're better! . . . No excitement! . . . And what a funny house, isn't it, with landscapes like that in it?"

"Yes, it's like the Musee Grevin . . . But, say, Erik . . . there are no tortures in there! . . . What a fright you gave me!"

"Why . . . as there is no one there?"

"Did you design that room? It's very handsome. You're a great artist, Erik."

"Yes, a great artist, in my own line."

"But tell me, Erik, why did you call that room the torture-chamber?"

"Oh, it's very simple. First of all, what did you see?"

"I saw a forest."

"And what is in a forest?"

"Trees."

"And what is in a tree?"

"Birds."

"Did you see any birds?"

"No, I did not see any birds."

"Well, what did you see? Think! You saw branches And what are the branches?" asked the terrible voice. "THERE'S A GIBBET! That is why I call my wood the torture-chamber! . . . You see, it's all a joke. I never express myself like other people. But I am very tired of it! . . . I'm sick and tired of having a forest and a torture-chamber in my house and of living like a mountebank, in a house with a false bottom! . . . I'm tired of it! I want to have a nice, quiet flat, with ordinary doors and windows and a wife inside it, like anybody else! A wife whom I could love and take out on Sundays and keep amused on week-days . . . Here, shall I show you some card-tricks? That will help us to pass a few minutes, while waiting for eleven o'clock to-morrow evening . . . My dear little Christine! . . . Are you listening to me? . . . Tell me you love me! . . . No, you don't love me . . . but no matter, you will! . . . Once, you could not look at my mask because you knew what was behind . . . And now you don't mind looking at it and you forget what is behind! . . . One can get used to everything . . . if one wishes . . . Plenty of young people who did not care for each other before marriage have adored each other since! Oh, I don't know what I am talking about! But you would have lots of fun with me. For instance, I am the greatest ventriloquist that ever lived, I am the first ventriloquist in the world! . . . You're laughing . . . Perhaps you don't believe me? Listen."

The wretch, who really was the first ventriloquist in the world, was only trying to divert the child's attention from the torture-chamber; but it was a stupid scheme, for Christine thought of nothing but us! She repeatedly besought him, in the gentlest tones which she could assume:

"Put out the light in the little window! . . . Erik, do put out the light in the little window!"

For she saw that this light, which appeared so suddenly and of which the monster had spoken in so threatening a voice, must mean something terrible. One thing must have pacified her for a moment; and that was seeing the two of us, behind the wall, in the midst of that resplendent light, alive and well. But she would certainly have felt much easier if the light had been put out.

Meantime, the other had already begun to play the ventriloquist. He said:

"Here, I raise my mask a little . . . Oh, only a little! . . . You see my lips, such lips as I have? They're not moving! . . . My mouth is closed—such mouth as I have—and yet you hear my voice . . . Where will you have it? In your left ear? In your right ear? In the table? In those little ebony boxes on the mantelpiece? . . . Listen, dear, it's in the little box on the right of the mantelpiece: what does it say? *Shall I turn the scorpion?*' . . . And now, crack! What does it say in the little box on the left? *Shall I turn the grasshopper?*' . . . And now, crack! Here it is in the little leather bag . . . What does it say? *I am the little bag of life and death!*' . . . And now, crack! It is in Carlotta's throat, in Carlotta's golden throat, in Carlotta's crystal throat, as I live! What does it say? It says, 'It's I, Mr. Toad, it's I singing! I FEEL WITHOUT ALARM—CO-ACK—WITH ITS MELODY ENWIND ME—CO-ACK!' . . . And now, crack! It is on a chair in the ghost's box and it says, *Madame Carlotta is singing to-night to bring the chandelier down!*' . . . And now, crack! Aha! Where is Erik's voice now? Listen, Christine, darling! Listen! It is behind the door of the torture-chamber! Listen! It's myself in the torture-chamber! And what do I say? I say, 'Woe to them that have a nose, a real nose, and come to look round the torture-chamber! Aha, aha, aha!'"

Oh, the ventriloquist's terrible voice! It was everywhere, everywhere. It passed through the little invisible window, through the walls. It ran around us, between us. Erik was there, speaking to us! We made a movement as though to fling ourselves upon him. But, already, swifter, more fleeting than the voice of the echo, Erik's voice had leaped back behind the wall!

Soon we heard nothing more at all, for this is what happened:

"Erik! Erik!" said Christine's voice. "You tire me with your voice. Don't go on, Erik! Isn't it very hot here?"

"Oh, yes," replied Erik's voice, "the heat is unendurable!"

"But what does this mean? . . . The wall is really getting quite hot! . . . The wall is burning!"

"I'll tell you, Christine, dear: it is because of the forest next door."

"Well, what has that to do with it? The forest?"

"*Why, didn't you see that it was an african forest?*"

And the monster laughed so loudly and hideously that we could no longer distinguish Christine's supplicating cries! The Vicomte de Chagny shouted and banged against the walls like a madman. I could not restrain him. But we heard nothing except the monster's laughter, and the monster himself can have heard nothing else. And then there was the sound of a body falling on the floor and being dragged along and a door slammed and then nothing, nothing more around us save the scorching silence of the south in the heart of a tropical forest!

CHAPTER XXIV

"BARRELS! . . . BARRELS! . . . ANY BARRELS TO SELL?"

THE PERSIAN'S NARRATIVE CONTINUED

I have said that the room in which M. le Vicomte de Chagny and I were imprisoned was a regular hexagon, lined entirely with mirrors. Plenty of these rooms have been seen since, mainly at exhibitions: they are called "palaces of illusion," or some such name. But the invention belongs entirely to Erik, who built the first room of this kind under my eyes, at the time of the rosy hours of Mazenderan. A decorative object, such as a column, for instance, was placed in one of the corners and immediately produced a hall of a thousand columns; for, thanks to the mirrors, the real room was multiplied by six hexagonal rooms, each of which, in its turn, was multiplied indefinitely. But the little sultana soon tired of this infantile illusion, whereupon Erik altered his invention into a "torture-chamber." For the architectural motive placed in one corner, he substituted an iron tree. This tree, with its painted leaves, was absolutely true to life and was made of iron so as to resist all the attacks of the "patient" who was locked into the torture-chamber. We shall see how the scene thus obtained was twice altered instantaneously into two successive other scenes, by means of the automatic rotation of the drums or rollers in the corners. These were divided into three sections, fitting into the angles of the mirrors and each supporting a decorative scheme that came into sight as the roller revolved upon its axis.

The walls of this strange room gave the patient nothing to lay hold of, because, apart from the solid decorative object, they were simply furnished with mirrors, thick enough to withstand any onslaught of the victim, who was flung into the chamber empty-handed and barefoot.

There was no furniture. The ceiling was capable of being lit up. An ingenious system of electric heating, which has since been imitated, allowed the temperature of the walls and room to be increased at will.

I am giving all these details of a perfectly natural invention, producing, with a few painted branches, the supernatural illusion of an equatorial forest blazing under the tropical sun, so that no one may doubt the present balance of my brain or feel entitled to say that I am mad or lying or that I take him for a fool.[11]

I now return to the facts where I left them. When the ceiling lit up and the forest became visible around us, the viscount's stupefaction was immense. That impenetrable forest, with its innumerable trunks and branches, threw him into a terrible state of consternation. He passed his hands over his forehead, as though to drive away a dream; his eyes blinked; and, for a moment, he forgot to listen.

I have already said that the sight of the forest did not surprise me at all; and therefore I listened for the two of us to what was happening next door. Lastly, my attention was especially attracted, not so much to the scene, as to the mirrors that produced it. These mirrors were broken in parts. Yes, they were marked and scratched; they had been "starred," in spite of their solidity; and this proved to me that the torture-chamber in which we now were *had already served a purpose.*

Yes, some wretch, whose feet were not bare like those of the victims of the rosy hours of Mazenderan, had certainly fallen into this "mortal illusion" and, mad with rage, had kicked against those mirrors which, nevertheless, continued to reflect his agony. And the branch of the tree on which he had put an end to his own sufferings was arranged in such a way that, before dying, he had seen, for his last consolation, a thousand men writhing in his company.

Yes, Joseph Buquet had undoubtedly been through all this! Were we to die as he had done? I did not think so, for I knew that we had a few hours before us and that I could employ them to better purpose than Joseph Buquet was able to do. After all, I was thoroughly acquainted with most of Erik's "tricks;" and now or never was the time to turn my knowledge to account.

To begin with, I gave up every idea of returning to the passage that had brought us to that accursed chamber. I did not trouble about the possibility of working the inside stone that closed the passage; and this for the simple reason that to do so was out of the question. We had dropped from too great a height into the torture-chamber; there was no furniture to help us reach that passage; not even the branch of the iron tree, not even each other's

---

11   It is very natural that, at the time when the Persian was writing, he
       should take so many precautions against any spirit of incredulity on
       the part of those who were likely to read his narrative. Nowadays,
       when we have all seen this sort of room, his precautions would be
       superfluous.

shoulders were of any avail.

There was only one possible outlet, that opening into the Louis-Philippe room in which Erik and Christine Daae were. But, though this outlet looked like an ordinary door on Christine's side, it was absolutely invisible to us. We must therefore try to open it without even knowing where it was.

When I was quite sure that there was no hope for us from Christine Daae's side, when I had heard the monster dragging the poor girl from the Louis-Philippe room *lest she should interfere with our tortures*, I resolved to set to work without delay.

But I had first to calm M. de Chagny, who was already walking about like a madman, uttering incoherent cries. The snatches of conversation which he had caught between Christine and the monster had contributed not a little to drive him beside himself: add to that the shock of the magic forest and the scorching heat which was beginning to make the prespiration{sic} stream down his temples and you will have no difficulty in understanding his state of mind. He shouted Christine's name, brandished his pistol, knocked his forehead against the glass in his endeavors to run down the glades of the illusive forest. In short, the torture was beginning to work its spell upon a brain unprepared for it.

I did my best to induce the poor viscount to listen to reason. I made him touch the mirrors and the iron tree and the branches and explained to him, by optical laws, all the luminous imagery by which we were surrounded and of which we need not allow ourselves to be the victims, like ordinary, ignorant people.

"We are in a room, a little room; that is what you must keep saying to yourself. And we shall leave the room as soon as we have found the door."

And I promised him that, if he let me act, without disturbing me by shouting and walking up and down, I would discover the trick of the door in less than an hour's time.

Then he lay flat on the floor, as one does in a wood, and declared that he would wait until I found the door of the forest, as there was nothing better to do! And he added that, from where he was, "the view was splendid!" The torture was working, in spite of all that I had said.

Myself, forgetting the forest, I tackled a glass panel and began to finger it in every direction, hunting for the weak point on which to press in order to turn the door in accordance with Erik's system of pivots. This weak point might be a mere speck on the glass, no larger than a pea, under which the spring lay hidden. I hunted and hunted. I felt as high as my hands could reach. Erik was about the same height as myself and I thought that he would not have placed the spring higher than suited his stature.

While groping over the successive panels with the greatest care, I endeavored not to lose a minute, for I was feeling more and more overcome with the heat and we were literally roasting in that blazing forest.

I had been working like this for half an hour and had finished three panels, when, as ill-luck would have it, I turned round on hearing a muttered exclamation from the viscount.

"I am stifling," he said. "All those mirrors are sending out an infernal heat! Do you think you will find that spring soon? If you are much longer about it, we shall be roasted alive!"

I was not sorry to hear him talk like this. He had not said a word of the forest and I hoped that my companion's reason would hold out some time longer against the torture. But he added:

"What consoles me is that the monster has given Christine until eleven to-morrow evening. If we can't get out of here and go to her assistance, at least we shall be dead before her! Then Erik's mass can serve for all of us!"

And he gulped down a breath of hot air that nearly made him faint.

As I had not the same desperate reasons as M. le Vicomte for accepting death, I returned, after giving him a word of encouragement, to my panel, but I had made the mistake of taking a few steps while speaking and, in the tangle of the illusive forest, I was no longer able to find my panel for certain! I had to begin all over again, at random, feeling, fumbling, groping.

Now the fever laid hold of me in my turn . . . for I found nothing, absolutely nothing. In the next room, all was silence. We were quite lost in the forest, without an outlet, a compass, a guide or anything. Oh, I knew what awaited us if nobody came to our aid . . . or if I did not find the spring! But, look as I might, I found nothing but branches, beautiful branches that stood straight up before me, or spread gracefully over my head. But they gave no shade. And this was natural enough, as we were in an equatorial forest, with the sun right above our heads, an African forest.

M. de Chagny and I had repeatedly taken off our coats and put them on again, finding at one time that they made us feel still hotter and at another that they protected us against the heat. I was still making a moral resistance, but M. de Chagny seemed to me quite "gone." He pretended that he had been walking in that forest for three days and nights, without stopping, looking for Christine Daae! From time to time, he thought he saw her behind the trunk of a tree, or gliding between the branches; and he called to her with words of supplication that brought the tears to my eyes. And then, at last:

"Oh, how thirsty I am!" he cried, in delirious accents.

I too was thirsty. My throat was on fire. And, yet, squatting on the floor, I went on hunting, hunting, hunting for the spring of the invisible door . . .

especially as it was dangerous to remain in the forest as evening drew nigh. Already the shades of night were beginning to surround us. It had happened very quickly: night falls quickly in tropical countries . . . suddenly, with hardly any twilight.

Now night, in the forests of the equator, is always dangerous, particularly when, like ourselves, one has not the materials for a fire to keep off the beasts of prey. I did indeed try for a moment to break off the branches, which I would have lit with my dark lantern, but I knocked myself also against the mirrors and remembered, in time, that we had only images of branches to do with.

The heat did not go with the daylight; on the contrary, it was now still hotter under the blue rays of the moon. I urged the viscount to hold our weapons ready to fire and not to stray from camp, while I went on looking for my spring.

Suddenly, we heard a lion roaring a few yards away.

"Oh," whispered the viscount, "he is quite close! . . . Don't you see him? . . . There . . . through the trees . . . in that thicket! If he roars again, I will fire! . . ."

And the roaring began again, louder than before. And the viscount fired, but I do not think that he hit the lion; only, he smashed a mirror, as I perceived the next morning, at daybreak. We must have covered a good distance during the night, for we suddenly found ourselves on the edge of the desert, an immense desert of sand, stones and rocks. It was really not worth while leaving the forest to come upon the desert. Tired out, I flung myself down beside the viscount, for I had had enough of looking for springs which I could not find.

I was quite surprised—and I said so to the viscount—that we had encountered no other dangerous animals during the night. Usually, after the lion came the leopard and sometimes the buzz of the tsetse fly. These were easily obtained effects; and I explained to M. de Chagny that Erik imitated the roar of a lion on a long tabour or timbrel, with an ass's skin at one end. Over this skin he tied a string of catgut, which was fastened at the middle to another similar string passing through the whole length of the tabour. Erik had only to rub this string with a glove smeared with resin and, according to the manner in which he rubbed it, he imitated to perfection the voice of the lion or the leopard, or even the buzzing of the tsetse fly.

The idea that Erik was probably in the room beside us, working his trick, made me suddenly resolve to enter into a parley with him, for we must obviously give up all thought of taking him by surprise. And by this time he must be quite aware who were the occupants of his torture-chamber. I called him: "Erik! Erik!"

I shouted as loudly as I could across the desert, but there was no answer to my voice. All around us lay the silence and the bare immensity of that stony desert. What was to become of us in the midst of that awful solitude?

We were beginning literally to die of heat, hunger and thirst . . . of thirst especially. At last, I saw M. de Chagny raise himself on his elbow and point to a spot on the horizon. He had discovered an oasis!

Yes, far in the distance was an oasis . . . an oasis with limpid water, which reflected the iron trees! . . . Tush, it was the scene of the mirage . . . I recognized it at once . . . the worst of the three! . . . No one had been able to fight against it . . . no one . . . I did my utmost to keep my head *and not to hope for water*, because I knew that, if a man hoped for water, the water that reflected the iron tree, and if, after hoping for water, he struck against the mirror, then there was only one thing for him to do: to hang himself on the iron tree!

So I cried to M. de Chagny:

"It's the mirage! . . . It's the mirage! . . . Don't believe in the water! . . . It's another trick of the mirrors! . . . "

Then he flatly told me to shut up, with my tricks of the mirrors, my springs, my revolving doors and my palaces of illusions! He angrily declared that I must be either blind or mad to imagine that all that water flowing over there, among those splendid, numberless trees, was not real water! . . . And the desert was real! . . . And so was the forest! . . . And it was no use trying to take him in . . . he was an old, experienced traveler . . . he had been all over the place!

And he dragged himself along, saying: "Water! Water!"

And his mouth was open, as though he were drinking.

And my mouth was open too, as though I were drinking.

For we not only saw the water, but *we heard it*! . . . We heard it flow, we heard it ripple! . . . Do you understand that word "ripple?" . . . *It is a sound which you hear with your tongue*! . . . You put your tongue out of your mouth to listen to it better!

Lastly—and this was the most pitiless torture of all—we heard the rain and it was not raining! This was an infernal invention . . . Oh, I knew well enough how Erik obtained it! He filled with little stones a very long and narrow box, broken up inside with wooden and metal projections. The stones, in falling, struck against these projections and rebounded from one to another; and the result was a series of pattering sounds that exactly imitated a rainstorm.

Ah, you should have seen us putting out our tongues and dragging ourselves toward the rippling river-bank! Our eyes and ears were full of water, but our tongues were hard and dry as horn!

When we reached the mirror, M. de Chagny licked it . . . and I also licked the glass.

It was burning hot!

Then we rolled on the floor with a hoarse cry of despair. M. de Chagny put the one pistol that was still loaded to his temple; and I stared at the Punjab lasso at the foot of the iron tree. I knew why the iron tree had returned, in this third change of scene! . . . The iron tree was waiting for me! . . .

But, as I stared at the Punjab lasso, I saw a thing that made me start so violently that M. de Chagny delayed his attempt at suicide. I took his arm. And then I caught the pistol from him . . . and then I dragged myself on my knees toward what I had seen.

I had discovered, near the Punjab lasso, in a groove in the floor, a black-headed nail of which I knew the use. At last I had discovered the spring! I felt the nail . . . I lifted a radiant face to M. de Chagny . . . The black-headed nail yielded to my pressure . . .

And then . . .

And then we saw not a door opened in the wall, but a cellar-flap released in the floor. Cool air came up to us from the black hole below. We stooped over that square of darkness as though over a limpid well. With our chins in the cool shade, we drank it in. And we bent lower and lower over the trap-door. What could there be in that cellar which opened before us? Water? Water to drink?

I thrust my arm into the darkness and came upon a stone and another stone . . . a staircase . . . a dark staircase leading into the cellar. The viscount wanted to fling himself down the hole; but I, fearing a new trick of the monster's, stopped him, turned on my dark lantern and went down first.

The staircase was a winding one and led down into pitchy darkness. But oh, how deliciously cool were the darkness and the stairs? The lake could not be far away.

We soon reached the bottom. Our eyes were beginning to accustom themselves to the dark, to distinguish shapes around us . . . circular shapes . . . on which I turned the light of my lantern.

Barrels!

We were in Erik's cellar: it was here that he must keep his wine and perhaps his drinking-water. I knew that Erik was a great lover of good wine. Ah, there was plenty to drink here!

M. de Chagny patted the round shapes and kept on saying:

"Barrels! Barrels! What a lot of barrels! . . . "

Indeed, there was quite a number of them, symmetrically arranged in two rows, one on either side of us. They were small barrels and I thought that Erik must have selected them of that size to facilitate their carriage to the house on the lake.

We examined them successively, to see if one of them had not a funnel, showing that it had been tapped at some time or another. But all the barrels were hermetically closed.

Then, after half lifting one to make sure it was full, we went on our knees and, with the blade of a small knife which I carried, I prepared to stave in the bung-hole.

At that moment, I seemed to hear, coming from very far, a sort of monotonous chant which I knew well, from often hearing it in the streets of Paris:

"Barrels! . . . Barrels! . . . Any barrels to sell?"

My hand desisted from its work. M. de Chagny had also heard. He said:

"That's funny! It sounds as if the barrel were singing!"

The song was renewed, farther away:

"Barrels! . . . Barrels! . . . Any barrels to sell? . . . "

"Oh, I swear," said the viscount, "that the tune dies away in the barrel! . . . "

We stood up and went to look behind the barrel.

"It's inside," said M. de Chagny, "it's inside!"

But we heard nothing there and were driven to accuse the bad condition of our senses. And we returned to the bung-hole. M. de Chagny put his two hands together underneath it and, with a last effort, I burst the bung.

"What's this?" cried the viscount. "This isn't water!"

The viscount put his two full hands close to my lantern . . . I stooped to look . . . and at once threw away the lantern with such violence that it broke and went out, leaving us in utter darkness.

What I had seen in M. de Chagny's hands . . . was gun-powder!

CHAPTER XXV

THE SCORPION OR THE GRASSHOPPER: WHICH?

THE PERSIAN'S NARRATIVE CONCLUDED

The discovery flung us into a state of alarm that made us forget all our past and present sufferings. We now knew all that the monster meant to convey when he said to Christine Daae:

"Yes or no! If your answer is no, everybody will be dead *and buried*!"

Yes, buried under the ruins of the Paris Grand Opera!

The monster had given her until eleven o'clock in the evening. He had chosen his time well. There would be many people, many "members of the human race," up there, in the resplendent theater. What finer retinue could be expected for his funeral? He would go down to the tomb escorted by the whitest shoulders in the world, decked with the richest jewels.

Eleven o'clock to-morrow evening!

We were all to be blown up in the middle of the performance . . . if Christine Daae said no!

Eleven o'clock to-morrow evening! . . .

And what else could Christine say but no? Would she not prefer to espouse death itself rather than that living corpse? She did not know that on her acceptance or refusal depended the awful fate of many members of the human race!

Eleven o'clock to-morrow evening!

And we dragged ourselves through the darkness, feeling our way to the stone steps, for the light in the trap-door overhead that led to the room of mirrors was now extinguished; and we repeated to ourselves:

"Eleven o'clock to-morrow evening!"

At last, I found the staircase. But, suddenly I drew myself up on the first step, for a terrible thought had come to my mind:

"What is the time?"

Ah, what was the time? . . . For, after all, eleven o'clock to-morrow evening might be now, might be this very moment! Who could tell us the time? We seemed to have been imprisoned in that hell for days and days . . . for years .

. . since the beginning of the world. Perhaps we should be blown up then and there! Ah, a sound! A crack! "Did you hear that? . . . There, in the corner . . . good heavens! . . . Like a sound of machinery! . . . Again! . . . Oh, for a light! . . . Perhaps it's the machinery that is to blow everything up! . . . I tell you, a cracking sound: are you deaf?"

M. de Chagny and I began to yell like madmen. Fear spurred us on. We rushed up the treads of the staircase, stumbling as we went, anything to escape the dark, to return to the mortal light of the room of mirrors!

We found the trap-door still open, but it was now as dark in the room of mirrors as in the cellar which we had left. We dragged ourselves along the floor of the torture-chamber, the floor that separated us from the powder-magazine. What was the time? We shouted, we called: M. de Chagny to Christine, I to Erik. I reminded him that I had saved his life. But no answer, save that of our despair, of our madness: what was the time? We argued, we tried to calculate the time which we had spent there, but we were incapable of reasoning. If only we could see the face of a watch! . . . Mine had stopped, but M. de Chagny's was still going . . . He told me that he had wound it up before dressing for the Opera . . . We had not a match upon us . . . And yet we must know . . . M. de Chagny broke the glass of his watch and felt the two hands . . . He questioned the hands of the watch with his finger-tips, going by the position of the ring of the watch . . . Judging by the space between the hands, he thought it might be just eleven o'clock!

But perhaps it was not the eleven o'clock of which we stood in dread. Perhaps we had still twelve hours before us!

Suddenly, I exclaimed: "Hush!"

I seemed to hear footsteps in the next room. Some one tapped against the wall. Christine Daae's voice said:

"Raoul! Raoul!" We were now all talking at once, on either side of the wall. Christine sobbed; she was not sure that she would find M. de Chagny alive. The monster had been terrible, it seemed, had done nothing but rave, waiting for her to give him the "yes" which she refused. And yet she had promised him that "yes," if he would take her to the torture-chamber. But he had obstinately declined, and had uttered hideous threats against all the members of the human race! At last, after hours and hours of that hell, he had that moment gone out, leaving her alone to reflect for the last time.

"Hours and hours? What is the time now? What is the time, Christine?"

"It is eleven o'clock! Eleven o'clock, all but five minutes!"

"But which eleven o'clock?"

"The eleven o'clock that is to decide life or death! . . . He told me so just before he went . . . He is terrible . . . He is quite mad: he tore off his mask and his yellow eyes shot flames! . . . He did nothing but laugh! . . . He said, 'I give you five minutes to spare your blushes! Here,' he said, taking a key from the little bag of life and death, 'here is the little bronze key that opens the two ebony caskets on the mantelpiece in the Louis-Philippe room . . . In one of the caskets, you will find a scorpion, in the other, a grasshopper, both very cleverly imitated in Japanese bronze: they will say yes or no for you. If you turn the scorpion round, that will mean to me, when I return, that you have said yes. The grasshopper will mean no.' And he laughed like a drunken demon. I did nothing but beg and entreat him to give me the key of the torture-chamber, promising to be his wife if he granted me that request . . . But he told me that there was no future need for that key and that he was going to throw it into the lake! . . . And he again laughed like a drunken demon and left me. Oh, his last words were, 'The grasshopper! Be careful of the grasshopper! A grasshopper does not only turn: it hops! It hops! And it hops jolly high!'"

The five minutes had nearly elapsed and the scorpion and the grasshopper were scratching at my brain. Nevertheless, I had sufficient lucidity left to understand that, if the grasshopper were turned, it would hop . . . and with it many members of the human race! There was no doubt but that the grasshopper controlled an electric current intended to blow up the powder-magazine!

M. de Chagny, who seemed to have recovered all his moral force from hearing Christine's voice, explained to her, in a few hurried words, the situation in which we and all the Opera were. He told her to turn the scorpion at once.

There was a pause.

"Christine," I cried, "where are you?"

"By the scorpion."

"Don't touch it!"

The idea had come to me—for I knew my Erik—that the monster had perhaps deceived the girl once more. Perhaps it was the scorpion that would blow everything up. After all, why wasn't he there? The five minutes were long past . . . and he was not back . . . Perhaps he had taken shelter and was waiting for the explosion! . . . Why had he not returned? . . . He could not really expect Christine ever to consent to become his voluntary prey! . . . Why had he not returned?

"Don't touch the scorpion!" I said.

"Here he comes!" cried Christine. "I hear him! Here he is!"

We heard his steps approaching the Louis-Philippe room. He came up to Christine, but did not speak. Then I raised my voice:

"Erik! It is I! Do you know me?"

With extraordinary calmness, he at once replied:

"So you are not dead in there? Well, then, see that you keep quiet."

I tried to speak, but he said coldly:

"Not a word, daroga, or I shall blow everything up." And he added, "The honor rests with mademoiselle . . . Mademoiselle has not touched the scorpion"—how deliberately he spoke!—"mademoiselle has not touched the grasshopper"—with that composure!—"but it is not too late to do the right thing. There, I open the caskets without a key, for I am a trap-door lover and I open and shut what I please and as I please. I open the little ebony caskets: mademoiselle, look at the little dears inside. Aren't they pretty? If you turn the grasshopper, mademoiselle, we shall all be blown up. There is enough gun-powder under our feet to blow up a whole quarter of Paris. If you turn the scorpion, mademoiselle, all that powder will be soaked and drowned. Mademoiselle, to celebrate our wedding, you shall make a very handsome present to a few hundred Parisians who are at this moment applauding a poor masterpiece of Meyerbeer's . . . you shall make them a present of their lives . . . For, with your own fair hands, you shall turn the scorpion . . . And merrily, merrily, we will be married!"

A pause; and then:

"If, in two minutes, mademoiselle, you have not turned the scorpion, I shall turn the grasshopper . . . and the grasshopper, I tell you, *hops jolly high*!"

The terrible silence began anew. The Vicomte de Chagny, realizing that there was nothing left to do but pray, went down on his knees and prayed. As for me, my blood beat so fiercely that I had to take my heart in both hands, lest it should burst. At last, we heard Erik's voice:

"The two minutes are past . . . Good-by, mademoiselle . . . Hop, grasshopper! "Erik," cried Christine, "do you swear to me, monster, do you swear to me that the scorpion is the one to turn?

"Yes, to hop at our wedding."

"Ah, you see! You said, to hop!"

"At our wedding, ingenuous child! . . . The scorpion opens the ball . . . But that will do! . . . You won't have the scorpion? Then I turn the grasshopper!"

"Erik!"

"Enough!"

I was crying out in concert with Christine. M. de Chagny was still on his knees, praying.

"Erik! I have turned the scorpion!"

Oh, the second through which we passed!

Waiting! Waiting to find ourselves in fragments, amid the roar and the ruins!

Feeling something crack beneath our feet, hearing an appalling hiss through the open trap-door, a hiss like the first sound of a rocket!

It came softly, at first, then louder, then very loud. But it was not the hiss of fire. It was more like the hiss of water. And now it became a gurgling sound: "Guggle! Guggle!"

We rushed to the trap-door. All our thirst, which vanished when the terror came, now returned with the lapping of the water.

The water rose in the cellar, above the barrels, the powder-barrels— "Barrels! . . . Barrels! Any barrels to sell?"—and we went down to it with parched throats. It rose to our chins, to our mouths. And we drank. We stood on the floor of the cellar and drank. And we went up the stairs again in the dark, step by step, went up with the water.

The water came out of the cellar with us and spread over the floor of the room. If, this went on, the whole house on the lake would be swamped. The floor of the torture-chamber had itself become a regular little lake, in which our feet splashed. Surely there was water enough now! Erik must turn off the tap!

"Erik! Erik! That is water enough for the gunpowder! Turn off the tap! Turn off the scorpion!"

But Erik did not reply. We heard nothing but the water rising: it was half-way to our waists!

"Christine!" cried M. de Chagny. "Christine! The water is up to our knees!"

But Christine did not reply . . . We heard nothing but the water rising.

No one, no one in the next room, no one to turn the tap, no one to turn the scorpion!

We were all alone, in the dark, with the dark water that seized us and clasped us and froze us!

"Erik! Erik!"

"Christine! Christine!"

By this time, we had lost our foothold and were spinning round in the water, carried away by an irresistible whirl, for the water turned with us and dashed us against the dark mirror, which thrust us back again; and our throats, raised above the whirlpool, roared aloud.

Were we to die here, drowned in the torture-chamber? I had never seen that. Erik, at the time of the rosy hours of Mazenderan, had never shown me that, through the little invisible window.

"Erik! Erik!" I cried. "I saved your life! Remember! . . . You were sentenced to death! But for me, you would be dead now! . . . Erik!"

We whirled around in the water like so much wreckage. But, suddenly, my straying hands seized the trunk of the iron tree! I called M. de Chagny, and we both hung to the branch of the iron tree.

And the water rose still higher.

"Oh! Oh! Can you remember? How much space is there between the branch of the tree and the dome-shaped ceiling? Do try to remember! . . . After all, the water may stop, it must find its level! . . . There, I think it is stopping! . . . No, no, oh, horrible! . . . Swim! Swim for your life!"

Our arms became entangled in the effort of swimming; we choked; we fought in the dark water; already we could hardly breathe the dark air above the dark water, the air which escaped, which we could hear escaping through some vent-hole or other.

"Oh, let us turn and turn and turn until we find the air hole and then glue our mouths to it!"

But I lost my strength; I tried to lay hold of the walls! Oh, how those glass walls slipped from under my groping fingers! . . . We whirled round again! . . . We began to sink! . . . One last effort! . . . A last cry: "Erik! . . . Christine! . . . "

"Guggle, guggle, guggle!" in our ears. "Guggle! Guggle!" At the bottom of the dark water, our ears went, "Guggle! Guggle!"

And, before losing consciousness entirely, I seemed to hear, between two guggles:

"Barrels! Barrels! Any barrels to sell?"

CHAPTER XXVI

THE END OF THE GHOST'S LOVE STORY

The previous chapter marks the conclusion of the written narrative which the Persian left behind him.

Notwithstanding the horrors of a situation which seemed definitely to abandon them to their deaths, M. de Chagny and his companion were saved by the sublime devotion of Christine Daae. And I had the rest of the story from the lips of the daroga himself.

When I went to see him, he was still living in his little flat in the Rue de Rivoli, opposite the Tuileries. He was very ill, and it required all my ardor as an historian pledged to the truth to persuade him to live the incredible tragedy over again for my benefit. His faithful old servant Darius showed me in to him. The daroga received me at a window overlooking the garden of the Tuileries. He still had his magnificent eyes, but his poor face looked very worn. He had shaved the whole of his head, which was usually covered with an astrakhan cap; he was dressed in a long, plain coat and amused himself by unconsciously twisting his thumbs inside the sleeves; but his mind was quite clear, and he told me his story with perfect lucidity.

It seems that, when he opened his eyes, the daroga found himself lying on a bed. M. de Chagny was on a sofa, beside the wardrobe. An angel and a devil were watching over them.

After the deceptions and illusions of the torture-chamber, the precision of the details of that quiet little middle-class room seemed to have been invented for the express purpose of puzzling the mind of the mortal rash enough to stray into that abode of living nightmare. The wooden bedstead, the waxed mahogany chairs, the chest of drawers, those brasses, the little square antimacassars carefully placed on the backs of the chairs, the clock on the mantelpiece and the harmless-looking ebony caskets at either end, lastly, the whatnot filled with shells, with red pin-cushions, with mother-of-pearl boats and an enormous ostrich-egg, the whole discreetly lighted by a shaded lamp standing on a small round table: this collection of ugly, peaceable, reasonable furniture, *at the bottom of the opera cellars,* bewildered the imagination more than all the late fantastic happenings.

And the figure of the masked man seemed all the more formidable in this old-fashioned, neat and trim little frame. It bent down over the Persian and said, in his ear:

"Are you better, daroga? . . . You are looking at my furniture? . . . It is all that I have left of my poor unhappy mother."

Christine Daae did not say a word: she moved about noiselessly, like a sister of charity, who had taken a vow of silence. She brought a cup of cordial, or of hot tea, he did not remember which. The man in the mask took it from her hands and gave it to the Persian. M. de Chagny was still sleeping.

Erik poured a drop of rum into the daroga's cup and, pointing to the viscount, said:

"He came to himself long before we knew if you were still alive, daroga. He is quite well. He is asleep. We must not wake him."

Erik left the room for a moment, and the Persian raised himself on his elbow, looked around him and saw Christine Daae sitting by the fireside. He spoke to her, called her, but he was still very weak and fell back on his pillow. Christine came to him, laid her hand on his forehead and went away again. And the Persian remembered that, as she went, she did not give a glance at M. de Chagny, who, it is true, was sleeping peacefully; and she sat down again in her chair by the chimney-corner, silent as a sister of charity who had taken a vow of silence.

Erik returned with some little bottles which he placed on the mantelpiece. And, again in a whisper, so as not to wake M. de Chagny, he said to the Persian, after sitting down and feeling his pulse:

"You are now saved, both of you. And soon I shall take you up to the surface of the earth, *to please my wife.*"

Thereupon he rose, without any further explanation, and disappeared once more.

The Persian now looked at Christine's quiet profile under the lamp. She was reading a tiny book, with gilt edges, like a religious book. There are editions of *The Imitation* that look like that. The Persian still had in his ears the natural tone in which the other had said, "to please my wife." Very gently, he called her again; but Christine was wrapped up in her book and did not hear him.

Erik returned, mixed the daroga a draft and advised him not to speak to "his wife" again nor to any one, *because it might be very dangerous to everybody's health.*

Eventually, the Persian fell asleep, like M. de Chagny, and did not wake until he was in his own room, nursed by his faithful Darius, who told him that, on the night before, he was found propped against the door of his flat, where he had been brought by a stranger, who rang the bell before going away.

As soon as the daroga recovered his strength and his wits, he sent to Count Philippe's house to inquire after the viscount's health. The answer was that the young man had not been seen and that Count Philippe was dead. His body was found on the bank of the Opera lake, on the Rue-Scribe side. The Persian remembered the requiem mass which he had heard from behind the wall of the torture-chamber, and had no doubt concerning the crime and the criminal. Knowing Erik as he did, he easily reconstructed the tragedy. Thinking that his brother had run away with Christine Daae, Philippe had dashed in pursuit of him along the Brussels Road, where he knew that everything was prepared for the elopement. Failing to find the pair, he hurried back to the Opera, remembered Raoul's strange confidence about his fantastic rival and learned that the viscount had made every effort to enter the cellars of the theater and that he had disappeared, leaving his hat in the prima donna's dressing-room beside an empty pistol-case. And the count, who no longer entertained any doubt of his brother's madness, in his turn darted into that infernal underground maze. This was enough, in the Persian's eyes, to explain the discovery of the Comte de Chagny's corpse on the shore of the lake, where the siren, Erik's siren, kept watch.

The Persian did not hesitate. He determined to inform the police. Now the case was in the hands of an examining-magistrate called Faure, an incredulous, commonplace, superficial sort of person, (I write as I think), with a mind utterly unprepared to receive a confidence of this kind. M. Faure took down the daroga's depositions and proceeded to treat him as a madman.

Despairing of ever obtaining a hearing, the Persian sat down to write. As the police did not want his evidence, perhaps the press would be glad of it; and he had just written the last line of the narrative I have quoted in the preceding chapters, when Darius announced the visit of a stranger who refused his name, who would not show his face and declared simply that he did not intend to leave the place until he had spoken to the daroga.

The Persian at once felt who his singular visitor was and ordered him to be shown in. The daroga was right. It was the ghost, it was Erik!

He looked extremely weak and leaned against the wall, as though he were afraid of falling. Taking off his hat, he revealed a forehead white as wax. The rest of the horrible face was hidden by the mask.

The Persian rose to his feet as Erik entered.

"Murderer of Count Philippe, what have you done with his brother and Christine Daae?"

Erik staggered under this direct attack, kept silent for a moment, dragged himself to a chair and heaved a deep sigh. Then, speaking in short phrases and gasping for breath between the words:

"Daroga, don't talk to me . . . about Count Philippe . . . He was dead . . . by the time . . . I left my house . . . he was dead . . . when . . . the siren sang . . . It was an . . . accident . . . a sad . . . a very sad . . . accident. He fell very awkwardly . . . but simply and naturally . . . into the lake! . . . "

"You lie!" shouted the Persian.

Erik bowed his head and said:

"I have not come here . . . to talk about Count Philippe . . . but to tell you that . . . I am going . . . to die . . . "

"Where are Raoul de Chagny and Christine Daae?"

"I am going to die."

"Raoul de Chagny and Christine Daae?"

"Of love . . . daroga . . . I am dying . . . of love . . . That is how it is . . . loved her so! . . . And I love her still . . . daroga . . . and I am dying of love for her, I . . . I tell you! . . . If you knew how beautiful she was . . . when she let me kiss her . . . alive . . . It was the first . . . time, daroga, the first . . . time I ever kissed a woman . . . Yes, alive . . . I kissed her alive . . . and she looked as beautiful as if she had been dead!"

The Persian shook Erik by the arm:

"Will you tell me if she is alive or dead."

"Why do you shake me like that?" asked Erik, making an effort to speak more connectedly. "I tell you that I am going to die . . . Yes, I kissed her alive . . . "

"And now she is dead?"

"I tell you I kissed her just like that, on her forehead . . . and she did not draw back her forehead from my lips! . . . Oh, she is a good girl! . . . As to her being dead, I don't think so; but it has nothing to do with me . . . No, no, she is not dead! And no one shall touch a hair of her head! She is a good, honest girl, and she saved your life, daroga, at a moment when I would not have given twopence for your Persian skin. As a matter of fact, nobody bothered about you. Why were you there with that little chap? You would have died as well as he! My word, how she entreated me for her little chap! But I told her that, as she had turned the scorpion, she had, through that very fact, and of her own free will, become engaged to me and that she did not need to have two men engaged to her, which was true enough.

"As for you, you did not exist, you had ceased to exist, I tell you, and you were going to die with the other! . . . Only, mark me, daroga, when you were yelling like the devil, because of the water, Christine came to me with her beautiful blue eyes wide open, and swore to me, as she hoped to be saved, that she consented to be MY LIVING WIFE! . . . Until then, in the depths of her eyes, daroga, I had always seen my dead wife; it was the first time I saw *my living wife* there. She was sincere, as she hoped to be saved. She would not kill herself. It was a bargain . . . Half a minute later, all the water was back in the lake; and I had a hard job with you, daroga, for, upon my honor, I thought you were done for! . . . However! . . . There you were! . . . It was understood that I was to take you both up to the surface of the earth. When, at last, I cleared the Louis-Philippe room of you, I came back alone . . . "

"What have you done with the Vicomte de Chagny?" asked the Persian, interrupting him.

"Ah, you see, daroga, I couldn't carry *him* up like that, at once. . . . He was a hostage . . . But I could not keep him in the house on the lake, either, because of Christine; so I locked him up comfortably, I chained him up nicely—a whiff of the Mazenderan scent had left him as limp as a rag—in the Communists' dungeon, which is in the most deserted and remote part of the Opera, below the fifth cellar, where no one ever comes, and where no one ever hears you. Then I came back to Christine, she was waiting for me."

Erik here rose solemnly. Then he continued, but, as he spoke, he was overcome by all his former emotion and began to tremble like a leaf:

"Yes, she was waiting for me . . . waiting for me erect and alive, a real, living bride . . . as she hoped to be saved . . . And, when I . . . came forward, more timid than . . . a little child, she did not run away . . . no, no . . . she stayed . . . she waited for me . . . I even believe . . . daroga . . . that she put out her forehead . . . a little . . . oh, not much . . . just a little . . . like a living bride . . . And . . . and . . . I . . . kissed her! . . . I! . . . I! . . . I! . . . And she did not die! . . . Oh, how good it is, daroga, to kiss somebody on the forehead! . . . You can't tell! . . . But I! I! . . . My mother, daroga, my poor, unhappy mother would never . . . let me kiss her . . . She used to run away . . . and throw me my mask! . . . Nor any other woman . . . ever, ever! . . . Ah, you can understand, my happiness was so great, I cried. And I fell at her feet, crying . . . and I kissed her feet . . . her little feet . . . crying. You're crying, too, daroga . . . and she cried also . . . the angel cried! . . . " Erik sobbed aloud and the Persian himself could not retain his tears in the presence of that masked man, who, with his shoulders shaking and his hands clutched at his chest, was moaning with pain and love by turns.

"Yes, daroga . . . I felt her tears flow on my forehead . . . on mine, mine! . . . They were soft . . . they were sweet! . . . They trickled under my mask . . . they mingled with my tears in my eyes . . . yes . . . they flowed between my lips . . . Listen, daroga, listen to what I did . . . I tore off my mask so as not to

lose one of her tears . . . and she did not run away! . . . And she did not die! .
. . She remained alive, weeping over me, with me. We cried together! I have
tasted all the happiness the world can offer!"

And Erik fell into a chair, choking for breath:

"Ah, I am not going to die yet . . . presently I shall . . . but let me cry! . . .
Listen, daroga . . . listen to this . . . While I was at her feet . . . I heard her say,
'Poor, unhappy Erik!' . . . AND SHE TOOK MY HAND! . . . I had become
no more, you know, than a poor dog ready to die for her . . . I mean it,
daroga! . . . I held in my hand a ring, a plain gold ring which I had given her
. . . which she had lost . . . and which I had found again . . . a wedding-ring,
you know . . . I slipped it into her little hand and said, 'There! . . . Take it! .
. . Take it for you . . . and him! . . . It shall be my wedding-present a present
from your poor, unhappy Erik . . . I know you love the boy . . . don't cry any
more! . . . She asked me, in a very soft voice, what I meant . . . Then I made
her understand that, where she was concerned, I was only a poor dog, ready
to die for her . . . but that she could marry the young man when she pleased,
because she had cried with me and mingled her tears with mine! . . . "

Erik's emotion was so great that he had to tell the Persian not to look at
him, for he was choking and must take off his mask. The daroga went to the
window and opened it. His heart was full of pity, but he took care to keep
his eyes fixed on the trees in the Tuileries gardens, lest he should see the
monster's face.

"I went and released the young man," Erik continued, "and told him to
come with me to Christine . . . They kissed before me in the Louis-Philippe
room . . . Christine had my ring . . . I made Christine swear to come back, one
night, when I was dead, crossing the lake from the Rue-Scribe side, and bury
me in the greatest secrecy with the gold ring, which she was to wear until
that moment. . . . I told her where she would find my body and what to do
with it . . . Then Christine kissed me, for the first time, herself, here, on the
forehead—don't look, daroga!—here, on the forehead . . . on my forehead,
mine—don't look, daroga!—and they went off together . . . Christine had
stopped crying . . . I alone cried . . . Daroga, daroga, if Christine keeps her
promise, she will come back soon! . . . "

The Persian asked him no questions. He was quite reassured as to the fate
of Raoul Chagny and Christine Daae; no one could have doubted the word
of the weeping Erik that night.

The monster resumed his mask and collected his strength to leave the
daroga. He told him that, when he felt his end to be very near at hand, he
would send him, in gratitude for the kindness which the Persian had once
shown him, that which he held dearest in the world: all Christine Daae's

papers, which she had written for Raoul's benefit and left with Erik, together with a few objects belonging to her, such as a pair of gloves, a shoe-buckle and two pocket-handkerchiefs. In reply to the Persian's questions, Erik told him that the two young people, at soon as they found themselves free, had resolved to go and look for a priest in some lonely spot where they could hide their happiness and that, with this object in view, they had started from "the northern railway station of the world." Lastly, Erik relied on the Persian, as soon as he received the promised relics and papers, to inform the young couple of his death and to advertise it in the *Epoque.*

That was all. The Persian saw Erik to the door of his flat, and Darius helped him down to the street. A cab was waiting for him. Erik stepped in; and the Persian, who had gone back to the window, heard him say to the driver:

"Go to the Opera."

And the cab drove off into the night.

The Persian had seen the poor, unfortunate Erik for the last time. Three weeks later, the Epoque published this advertisement:

"Erik is dead."

EPILOGUE

I have now told the singular, but veracious story of the Opera ghost. As I declared on the first page of this work, it is no longer possible to deny that Erik really lived. There are to-day so many proofs of his existence within the reach of everybody that we can follow Erik's actions logically through the whole tragedy of the Chagnys.

There is no need to repeat here how greatly the case excited the capital. The kidnapping of the artist, the death of the Comte de Chagny under such exceptional conditions, the disappearance of his brother, the drugging of the gas-man at the Opera and of his two assistants: what tragedies, what passions, what crimes had surrounded the idyll of Raoul and the sweet and charming Christine! . . . What had become of that wonderful, mysterious artist of whom the world was never, never to hear again? . . . She was represented as the victim of a rivalry between the two brothers; and nobody suspected what had really happened, nobody understood that, as Raoul and Christine had both disappeared, both had withdrawn far from the world to enjoy a happiness which they would not have cared to make public after the inexplicable death of Count Philippe . . . They took the train one day from "the northern railway station of the world." . . . Possibly, I too shall take the train at that station, one day, and go and seek around thy lakes, O Norway, O silent Scandinavia, for the perhaps still living traces of Raoul and Christine and also of Mamma Valerius, who disappeared at the same time! . . . Possibly, some day, I shall hear the lonely echoes of the North repeat the singing of her who knew the Angel of Music! . . .

Long after the case was pigeonholed by the unintelligent care of M. le Juge d'Instruction Faure, the newspapers made efforts, at intervals, to fathom the mystery. One evening paper alone, which knew all the gossip of the theaters, said:

"We recognize the touch of the Opera ghost."

And even that was written by way of irony.

The Persian alone knew the whole truth and held the main proofs, which came to him with the pious relics promised by the ghost. It fell to my lot to complete those proofs with the aid of the daroga himself. Day by day, I kept him informed of the progress of my inquiries; and he directed them.

He had not been to the Opera for years and years, but he had preserved the most accurate recollection of the building, and there was no better guide than he possible to help me discover its most secret recesses. He also told me where to gather further information, whom to ask; and he sent me to call on M. Poligny, at a moment when the poor man was nearly drawing his last breath. I had no idea that he was so very ill, and I shall never forget the effect which my questions about the ghost produced upon him. He looked at me as if I were the devil and answered only in a few incoherent sentences, which showed, however—and that was the main thing—the extent of the perturbation which O. G., in his time, had brought into that already very restless life (for M. Poligny was what people call a man of pleasure).

When I came and told the Persian of the poor result of my visit to M. Poligny, the daroga gave a faint smile and said:

"Poligny never knew how far that extraordinary blackguard of an Erik humbugged him."—The Persian, by the way, spoke of Erik sometimes as a demigod and sometimes as the lowest of the low—"Poligny was superstitious and Erik knew it. Erik knew most things about the public and private affairs of the Opera. When M. Poligny heard a mysterious voice tell him, in Box Five, of the manner in which he used to spend his time and abuse his partner's confidence, he did not wait to hear any more. Thinking at first that it was a voice from Heaven, he believed himself damned; and then, when the voice began to ask for money, he saw that he was being victimized by a shrewd blackmailer to whom Debienne himself had fallen a prey. Both of them, already tired of management for various reasons, went away without trying to investigate further into the personality of that curious O. G., who had forced such a singular memorandum-book upon them. They bequeathed the whole mystery to their successors and heaved a sigh of relief when they were rid of a business that had puzzled them without amusing them in the least."

I then spoke of the two successors and expressed my surprise that, in his Memoirs of a Manager, M. Moncharmin should describe the Opera ghost's behavior at such length in the first part of the book and hardly mention it at all in the second. In reply to this, the Persian, who knew the *Memoirs* as thoroughly as if he had written them himself, observed that I should find the explanation of the whole business if I would just recollect the few lines which Moncharmin devotes to the ghost in the second part aforesaid. I quote these lines, which are particularly interesting because they describe the very simple manner in which the famous incident of the twenty-thousand francs was closed:

"As for O. G., some of whose curious tricks I have related in the first part of my Memoirs, I will only say that he redeemed by one spontaneous fine action all the worry which he had caused my dear friend and partner and, I am bound to say, myself. He felt, no doubt, that there are limits to a joke, especially when it is so expensive and when the commissary of police has been informed, for, at the moment when we had made an appointment in our office with M. Mifroid to tell him the whole story, a few days after the disappearance of Christine Daae, we found, on Richard's table, a large envelope, inscribed, in red ink, "WITH O. G.'S COMPLIMENTS." It contained the large sum of money which he had succeeded in playfully extracting, for the time being, from the treasury. Richard was at once of the opinion that we must be content with that and drop the business. I agreed with Richard. All's well that ends well. What do you say, O. G.?"

Of course, Moncharmin, especially after the money had been restored, continued to believe that he had, for a short while, been the butt of Richard's sense of humor, whereas Richard, on his side, was convinced that Moncharmin had amused himself by inventing the whole of the affair of the Opera ghost, in order to revenge himself for a few jokes.

I asked the Persian to tell me by what trick the ghost had taken twenty-thousand francs from Richard's pocket in spite of the safety-pin. He replied that he had not gone into this little detail, but that, if I myself cared to make an investigation on the spot, I should certainly find the solution to the riddle in the managers' office by remembering that Erik had not been nicknamed the trap-door lover for nothing. I promised the Persian to do so as soon as I had time, and I may as well tell the reader at once that the results of my investigation were perfectly satisfactory; and I hardly believed that I should ever discover so many undeniable proofs of the authenticity of the feats ascribed to the ghost.

The Persian's manuscript, Christine Daae's papers, the statements made to me by the people who used to work under MM. Richard and Moncharmin, by little Meg herself (the worthy Madame Giry, I am sorry to say, is no more) and by Sorelli, who is now living in retirement at Louveciennes: all the documents relating to the existence of the ghost, which I propose to deposit in the archives of the Opera, have been checked and confirmed by a number of important discoveries of which I am justly proud. I have not been able to find the house on the lake, Erik having blocked up all the secret entrances.[12] On the other hand, I have discovered the secret passage of the

---

12   Even so, I am convinced that it would be easy to reach it by draining the lake, as I have repeatedly requested the Ministry of Fine Arts to do. I was speaking about it to M. Dujardin-Beaumetz, the under-

Communists, the planking of which is falling to pieces in parts, and also the trap-door through which Raoul and the Persian penetrated into the cellars of the opera-house. In the Communists' dungeon, I noticed numbers of initials traced on the walls by the unfortunate people confined in it; and among these were an "R" and a "C." R. C.: Raoul de Chagny. The letters are there to this day.

If the reader will visit the Opera one morning and ask leave to stroll where he pleases, without being accompanied by a stupid guide, let him go to Box Five and knock with his fist or stick on the enormous column that separates this from the stage-box. He will find that the column sounds hollow. After that, do not be astonished by the suggestion that it was occupied by the voice of the ghost: there is room inside the column for two men. If you are surprised that, when the various incidents occurred, no one turned round to look at the column, you must remember that it presented the appearance of solid marble, and that the voice contained in it seemed rather to come from the opposite side, for, as we have seen, the ghost was an expert ventriloquist.

The column was elaborately carved and decorated with the sculptor's chisel; and I do not despair of one day discovering the ornament that could be raised or lowered at will, so as to admit of the ghost's mysterious correspondence with Mme. Giry and of his generosity.

However, all these discoveries are nothing, to my mind, compared with that which I was able to make, in the presence of the acting-manager, in the managers' office, within a couple of inches from the desk-chair, and which consisted of a trap-door, the width of a board in the flooring and the length of a man's fore-arm and no longer; a trap-door that falls back like the lid of a box; a trap-door through which I can see a hand come and dexterously fumble at the pocket of a swallow-tail coat.

That is the way the forty-thousand francs went! . . . And that also is the way by which, through some trick or other, they were returned.

Speaking about this to the Persian, I said:

"So we may take it, as the forty-thousand francs were returned, that Erik was simply amusing himself with that memorandum-book of his?"

"Don't you believe it!" he replied. "Erik wanted money. Thinking himself without the pale of humanity, he was restrained by no scruples and he employed his extraordinary gifts of dexterity and imagination, which he

secretary for fine arts, only forty-eight hours before the publication of this book. Who knows but that the score of *Don Juan Triumphant* might yet be discovered in the house on the lake?

had received by way of compensation for his extraordinary uglinesss, to prey upon his fellow-men. His reason for restoring the forty-thousand francs, of his own accord, was that he no longer wanted it. He had relinquished his marriage with Christine Daae. He had relinquished everything above the surface of the earth."

According to the Persian's account, Erik was born in a small town not far from Rouen. He was the son of a master-mason. He ran away at an early age from his father's house, where his ugliness was a subject of horror and terror to his parents. For a time, he frequented the fairs, where a showman exhibited him as the "living corpse." He seems to have crossed the whole of Europe, from fair to fair, and to have completed his strange education as an artist and magician at the very fountain-head of art and magic, among the Gipsies. A period of Erik's life remained quite obscure. He was seen at the fair of Nijni-Novgorod, where he displayed himself in all his hideous glory. He already sang as nobody on this earth had ever sung before; he practised ventriloquism and gave displays of legerdemain so extraordinary that the caravans returning to Asia talked about it during the whole length of their journey. In this way, his reputation penetrated the walls of the palace at Mazenderan, where the little sultana, the favorite of the Shah-in-Shah, was boring herself to death. A dealer in furs, returning to Samarkand from Nijni-Novgorod, told of the marvels which he had seen performed in Erik's tent. The trader was summoned to the palace and the daroga of Mazenderan was told to question him. Next the daroga was instructed to go and find Erik. He brought him to Persia, where for some months Erik's will was law. He was guilty of not a few horrors, for he seemed not to know the difference between good and evil. He took part calmly in a number of political assassinations; and he turned his diabolical inventive powers against the Emir of Afghanistan, who was at war with the Persian empire. The Shah took a liking to him.

This was the time of the rosy hours of Mazenderan, of which the daroga's narrative has given us a glimpse. Erik had very original ideas on the subject of architecture and thought out a palace much as a conjuror contrives a trick-casket. The Shah ordered him to construct an edifice of this kind. Erik did so; and the building appears to have been so ingenious that His Majesty was able to move about in it unseen and to disappear without a possibility of the trick's being discovered. When the Shah-in-Shah found himself the possessor of this gem, he ordered Erik's yellow eyes to be put out. But he reflected that, even when blind, Erik would still be able to build so remarkable a house for another sovereign; and also that, as long as Erik was alive, some one would know the secret of the wonderful palace. Erik's death was decided upon, together with that of all the laborers who had worked under his orders. The execution of this abominable decree devolved upon the daroga of Mazenderan. Erik had shown him some slight services and procured him many a hearty laugh. He saved Erik by providing him with the means of escape, but nearly paid with his head for his generous indulgence.

Fortunately for the daroga, a corpse, half-eaten by the birds of prey, was found on the shore of the Caspian Sea, and was taken for Erik's body, because the daroga's friends had dressed the remains in clothing that belonged to Erik. The daroga was let off with the loss of the imperial favor, the confiscation of his property and an order of perpetual banishment. As a member of the Royal House, however, he continued to receive a monthly pension of a few hundred francs from the Persian treasury; and on this he came to live in Paris.

As for Erik, he went to Asia Minor and thence to Constantinople, where he entered the Sultan's employment. In explanation of the services which he was able to render a monarch haunted by perpetual terrors, I need only say that it was Erik who constructed all the famous trap-doors and secret chambers and mysterious strong-boxes which were found at Yildiz-Kiosk after the last Turkish revolution. He also invented those automata, dressed like the Sultan and resembling the Sultan in all respects,[13] which made people believe that the Commander of the Faithful was awake at one place, when, in reality, he was asleep elsewhere.

Of course, he had to leave the Sultan's service for the same reasons that made him fly from Persia: he knew too much. Then, tired of his adventurous, formidable and monstrous life, he longed to be some one "like everybody else." And he became a contractor, like any ordinary contractor, building ordinary houses with ordinary bricks. He tendered for part of the foundations in the Opera. His estimate was accepted. When he found himself in the cellars of the enormous playhouse, his artistic, fantastic, wizard nature resumed the upper hand. Besides, was he not as ugly as ever? He dreamed of creating for his own use a dwelling unknown to the rest of the earth, where he could hide from men's eyes for all time.

The reader knows and guesses the rest. It is all in keeping with this incredible and yet veracious story. Poor, unhappy Erik! Shall we pity him? Shall we curse him? He asked only to be "some one," like everybody else.

---

13   See the interview of the special correspondent of the *Matin*, with Mohammed-Ali Bey, on the day after the entry of the Salonika troops into Constantinople.

But he was too ugly! And he had to hide his genius *or use it to play tricks with*, when, with an ordinary face, he would have been one of the most distinguished of mankind! He had a heart that could have held the empire of the world; and, in the end, he had to content himself with a cellar. Ah, yes, we must needs pity the Opera ghost.

I have prayed over his mortal remains, that God might show him mercy notwithstanding his crimes. Yes, I am sure, quite sure that I prayed beside his body, the other day, when they took it from the spot where they were burying the phonographic records. It was his skeleton. I did not recognize it by the ugliness of the head, for all men are ugly when they have been dead as long as that, but by the plain gold ring which he wore and which Christine Daae had certainly slipped on his finger, when she came to bury him in accordance with her promise.

The skeleton was lying near the little well, in the place where the Angel of Music first held Christine Daae fainting in his trembling arms, on the night when he carried her down to the cellars of the opera-house.

And, now, what do they mean to do with that skeleton? Surely they will not bury it in the common grave! . . . I say that the place of the skeleton of the Opera ghost is in the archives of the National Academy of Music. It is no ordinary skeleton.

THE PARIS OPERA HOUSE

THE SCENE OF GASTON LEROUX'S NOVEL, "THE PHANTOM OF THE OPERA"

That Mr. Leroux has used, for the scene of his story, the Paris Opera House as it really is and has not created a building out of his imagination, is shown by this interesting description of it taken from an article which appeared in Scribner's Magazine in 1879, a short time after the building was completed:

"The new Opera House, commenced under the Empire and finished under the Republic, is the most complete building of the kind in the world and in many respects the most beautiful. No European capital possesses an opera house so comprehensive in plan and execution, and none can boast an edifice equally vast and splendid.

"The site of the Opera House was chosen in 1861. It was determined to lay the foundation exceptionally deep and strong. It was well known that water would be met with, but it was impossible to foresee at what depth or in what quantity it would be found. Exceptional depth also was necessary, as the stage arrangements were to be such as to admit a scene fifty feet high to be lowered on its frame. It was therefore necessary to lay a foundation in a soil soaked with water which should be sufficiently solid to sustain a weight of 22,000,000 pounds, and at the same time to be perfectly dry, as the cellars were intended for the storage of scenery and properties. While the work was in progress, the excavation was kept free from water by means of eight pumps, worked by steam power, and in operation, without interruption, day and night, from March second to October thirteenth. The floor of the cellar was covered with a layer of concrete, then with two coats of cement, another layer of concrete and a coat of bitumen. The wall includes an outer wall built as a coffer-dam, a brick wall, a coat of cement, and a wall proper, a little over a yard thick. After all this was done the whole was filled with water, in order that the fluid, by penetrating into the most minute interstices, might deposit a sediment which would close them more surely and perfectly than it would be possible to do by hand. Twelve years elapsed before the completion of the building, and during that time it was demonstrated that the precautions taken secured absolute impermeability and solidity.

"The events of 1870 interrupted work just as it was about to be prosecuted most vigorously, and the new Opera House was put to new and unexpected uses. During the siege, it was converted into a vast military storehouse and filled with a heterogeneous mass of goods. After the siege the building fell into the hands of the Commune and the roof was turned into a balloon station. The damage done, however, was slight.

"The fine stone employed in the construction was brought from quarries in Sweden, Scotland, Italy, Algeria, Finland, Spain, Belgium and France. While work on the exterior was in progress, the building was covered in by a wooden shell, rendered transparent by thousands of small panes of glass. In 1867 a swarm of men, supplied with hammers and axes, stripped the house of its habit, and showed in all its splendor the great structure. No picture can do justice to the rich colors of the edifice or to the harmonious tone resulting from the skilful use of many diverse materials. The effect of the frontage is completed by the cupola of the auditorium, topped with a cap of bronze sparingly adorned with gilding. Farther on, on a level with the towers of Notre-Dame, is the gable end of the roof of the stage, a 'Pegasus', by M. Lequesne, rising at either end of the roof, and a bronze group by M. Millet, representing 'Apollo lifting his golden lyre', commanding the apex. Apollo, it may here be mentioned, is useful as well as ornamental, for his lyre is tipped with a metal point which does duty as a lightning-rod, and conducts the fluid to the body and down the nether limbs of the god.

"The spectator, having climbed ten steps and left behind him a gateway, reaches a vestibule in which are statues of Lully, Rameau, Gluck, and Handel. Ten steps of green Swedish marble lead to a second vestibule for ticket-sellers. Visitors who enter by the pavilion reserved for carriages pass through a hallway where ticket offices are situated. The larger number of the audience, before entering the auditorium, traverse a large circular vestibule located exactly beneath it. The ceiling of this portion of the building is upheld by sixteen fluted columns of Jura stone, with white marble capitals, forming a portico. Here servants are to await their masters, and spectators may remain until their carriages are summoned. The third entrance, which is quite distinct from the others, is reserved for the Executive. The section of the building set aside for the use of the Emperor Napoleon was to have included an antechamber for the bodyguards; a salon for the aides-de-camp; a large salon and a smaller one for the Empress; hat and cloak rooms, etc. Moreover, there were to be in close proximity to the entrance, stables for three coaches, for the outriders' horses, and for the twenty-one horsemen acting as an escort; a station for a squad of infantry of thirty-one men and ten cent-gardes, and a stable for the horses of the latter; and, besides, a salon for fifteen or twenty domestics. Thus arrangements had to be made to accommodate in this part of the building about one hundred persons, fifty horses, and half-a-dozen carriages. The fall of the Empire suggested some changes, but ample provision still exists for emergencies.

"Its novel conception, perfect fitness, and rare splendor of material, make the grand stairway unquestionably one of the most remarkable features of the building. It presents to the spectator, who has just passed through the subscribers' pavilion, a gorgeous picture. From this point he beholds the ceiling formed by the central landing; this and the columns sustaining it, built of Echaillon stone, are honeycombed with arabesques and heavy with ornaments; the steps are of white marble, and antique red marble balusters rest on green marble sockets and support a balustrade of onyx. To the right and to the left of this landing are stairways to the floor, on a plane with the first row of boxes. On this floor stand thirty monolith columns of Sarrancolin marble, with white marble bases and capitals. Pilasters of peach-blossom and violet stone are against the corresponding walls. More than fifty blocks had to be extracted from the quarry to find thirty perfect monoliths.

"The foyer de la danse has particular interest for the habitues of the Opera. It is a place of reunion to which subscribers to three performances a week are admitted between the acts in accordance with a usage established in 1870. Three immense looking-glasses cover the back wall of the FOYER, and a chandelier with one hundred and seven burners supplies it with light. The paintings include twenty oval medallions, in which are portrayed the twenty danseuses of most celebrity since the opera has existed in France, and four panels by M. Boulanger, typifying 'The War Dance', 'The Rustic Dance', 'The Dance of Love' and 'The Bacchic Dance.' While the ladies of the ballet receive their admirers in this foyer, they can practise their steps. Velvet-cushioned bars have to this end been secured at convenient points, and the floor has been given the same slope as that of the stage, so that the labor expended may be thoroughly profitable to the performance. The singers' foyer, on the same floor, is a much less lively resort than the foyer de la danse, as vocalists rarely leave their dressing-rooms before they are summoned to the stage. Thirty panels with portraits of the artists of repute in the annals of the Opera adorn this foyer.

"Some estimate . . . may be arrived at by sitting before the concierge an hour or so before the representation commences. First appear the stage carpenters, who are always seventy, and sometimes, when L'Africaine, for example, with its ship scene, is the opera, one hundred and ten strong.

Then come stage upholsterers, whose sole duty is to lay carpets, hang curtains, etc.; gas-men, and a squad of firemen. Claqueurs, call-boys, property-men, dressers, coiffeurs, supernumeraries, and artists, follow. The supernumeraries number about one hundred; some are hired by the year, but the 'masses' are generally recruited at the last minute and are generally working-men who seek to add to their meagre earnings. There are about a hundred choristers, and about eighty musicians.

"Next we behold equeries, whose horses are hoisted on the stage by means of an elevator; electricians who manage the light-producing batteries; hydrauliciens to take charge of the water-works in ballets like La Source; artificers who prepare the conflagration in Le Profeta; florists who make ready Margarita's garden, and a host of minor employees. This personnel is provided for as follows: Eighty dressing-rooms are reserved for the artists, each including a small antechamber, the dressing-room proper, and a little closet. Besides these apartments, the Opera has a dressing-room for sixty male, and another for fifty female choristers; a third for thirty-four male dancers; four dressing-rooms for twenty female dancers of different grades; a dressing-room for one hundred and ninety supernumeraries, etc."

A few figures taken from the article will suggest the enormous capacity and the perfect convenience of the house. "There are 2,531 doors and 7,593 keys; 14 furnaces and grates heat the house; the gaspipes if connected would form a pipe almost 16 miles long; 9 reservoirs, and two tanks hold 22,222 gallons of water and distribute their contents through 22,829 2-5 feet of piping; 538 persons have places assigned wherein to change their attire. The musicians have a foyer with 100 closets for their instruments."

The author remarks of his visit to the Opera House that it "was almost as bewildering as it was agreeable. Giant stairways and colossal halls, huge frescoes and enormous mirrors, gold and marble, satin and velvet, met the eye at every turn."

In a recent letter Mr. Andre Castaigne, whose remarkable pictures illustrate the text, speaks of a river or lake under the Opera House and mentions the fact that there are now also three metropolitan railway tunnels, one on top of the other.